The Kings Falcon

Roundheads & Cavaliers - Book 3

Stella Riley

CONTENTS

PROLOGUE
September 2nd and 3rd, 1650

Scene One
Dunbar, Scotland

'We are upon an engagement very difficult. The enemy has blocked up our way … and our lying here daily consumes our men, who fall sick beyond imagination.'
Oliver Cromwell to Sir Arthur Haselrig

It was fair to say, decided Eden Maxwell, that the invasion of Scotland hadn't so far been a howling success. In the six weeks since crossing the border, they had advanced twice from Dunbar only to fall back as their supplies ran out and utterly failed to bring General Leslie to battle. Not exactly an impressive record; and not one likely to improve if the campaign was allowed to drag on into the winter.

There were mitigating factors, of course. The weather had been consistently cold and wet, causing sickness and exposure amongst the men; the Scots had removed every beast and grain of corn, thus making it impossible to live off the country; and canny David Leslie, with roughly thirty-five thousand men to their own sixteen, was using his local knowledge to take up one unassailable position after another. None of these made life easy. On the other hand, it might conceivably be argued that under commanders like John Lambert, George Monck and Old Noll himself, the finest fighting machine in Europe ought to be able to overcome such difficulties – particularly in view of the fact that the Scots' army, as well as being raw and ill-equipped, had also been purged by the Kirk of almost all the Royalists and everyone who'd supported the first Duke of Hamilton's *Engagement* with the late King.

As Eden understood it, the ministers of the Kirk were eager to drive out the English invaders but nervous of amassing an army that might become a tool in the hands of the young man who had been proclaimed

1

their King but who they didn't entirely trust. And that was somewhat ironic – because the New Model's presence north of the border was due solely to Westminster's conviction that the Scots were on the point of sweeping into England and reclaiming Charles Stuart's lost throne for him.

It was a conviction not everyone shared. Sir Thomas Fairfax had resigned rather than lead an invasion force – with the result that Cromwell had been appointed Lord-General in his place. Oliver, of course, had no such reservations. Having crushed Ireland with a savagery which Eden, grateful not to have been there, found disturbing, he had promptly led the New Model north to subdue the unruly Scots. Only, after weeks of marching hither and thither through the mud, here they were amongst the swamps and bogs outside Dunbar, in a place where you couldn't even pitch a tent, with Leslie's Scots overlooking them from Doon Hill, blocking the road to Berwick and outnumbering them two to one.

It wasn't a pleasant predicament and Eden would be glad to know how his superiors planned to resolve it. He himself had spent the morning drawing up his fellows in battle order in anticipation of an attack. Not, so far as Eden could see, that there was the slightest need for Leslie to put himself to so much trouble. All he had to do was to sit tight and wait for their next move.

Except that he didn't. One minute the Scots were perched on their impregnable hillside, looking as though they'd sit it out till Doomsday … and the next they were preparing to descend.

Eden reached for his perspective glass and took a long look. Then, laying it aside, he said softly, 'Bloody hell. Now why is he doing that?'

Major Cartwright's countenance tightened and he considered reminding the Colonel that Parliament had recently passed an Act against profanity. Instead, he said stiffly, 'I couldn't say, sir. An attack, perhaps?'

'Possibly. But *why*? Unless … but no. I know the Kirk's hanging round his neck like a stone but Leslie's too experienced to allow a pack of preachers to run his campaign for him.'

Major Cartwright stood ramrod straight and stared into the middle distance.

Eden drew a faintly exasperated breath. Isaac Cartwright was conscientious but lacked both flair and humour. Now, for example, he gloomily announced that the Lord would show them the way if they only stood firm and had faith.

'Then I wish he'd hurry up about it,' returned Eden dryly. And then, in response to a distant outburst of noise, 'Something's happening on our right. Find out what.'

By the time Major Cartwright returned with the news that their outpost on the far side of the Brox Burn had been overpowered, the afternoon was wearing on and the Scottish descent well-advanced. Removing his gaze from the position Leslie was taking up on the lower slopes, Eden said, 'And?'

'There's information to suggest that General Leslie thinks we've shipped off half of our Foot and most of the artillery. He doesn't believe we'll fight.'

Eden turned sharply. 'Doesn't he, indeed?'

'No, sir.'

Eden pocketed his perspective glass and flexed his shoulders beneath the weight of his sodden buff coat. 'Then let's hope the Lord-General has a workable plan.'

The Major's expression grew fervent. 'I shall pray for it.'

'That,' murmured Eden, 'is bound to make all the difference.'

Afternoon became evening and Eden sought what shelter could be had for his men before returning to Dunbar in search of some supper. Then, at a little after ten o'clock, Major-General Lambert walked in saying, concisely, 'The Council of War has finally decided not to make Leslie's day by shipping off the Foot and decided that the gaps in his front are wide enough to push a troop of Horse through. Consequently, we're ordered to try fording the Brox Burn near the Berwick Road and mount an attack.'

Colonel Maxwell didn't bother remarking on the obvious difficulties of this plan but said merely, 'When?'

'Two hours before dawn. I want to be across before first light.'

Eden nodded and started pulling on his coat. 'Anything else?'

'Nothing,' returned Lambert with a dry smile, 'that you won't think of yourself.'

* * *

Outside, the night was still windy and wet with clouds obscuring the moon. As silently as possible, Lambert had the Army moved closer to the screen of trees and shrubs beside the burn while the heavy artillery was drawn to the edge of the ravine. Eden and his fellow officers worked ceaselessly to organise matters and Cromwell rode back and forth, agitatedly chewing his lip.

Once the Army had been re-positioned, Lambert began the mammoth task of moving six regiments of Horse and three-and-a-half of Foot over the burn. It was four in the morning and still pitch dark. Eden, whose regiment was one of the first to cross, found the business extremely tricky. Horses slithered on steep banks made treacherous with mud; infantrymen lost their footing and collided, grunting, with each other; and every squelching boot and jingle of harness sounded uncannily loud above the whistling wind.

Incredibly, all remained quiet in the Scottish lines and the cavalry was able to make the crossing in just under an hour, apparently undetected, with the infantry trudging behind. On the other bank, detachments of Horse and Foot under Cromwell waited alongside the artillery.

Eden, awaiting Lambert's signal to attack, loosened his sword in its scabbard, checked his pistol and cast a final glance over his assembled regiment. Somewhere behind him, he could hear Major Cartwright praying.

Dawn was breaking, bleak and grey, as Lambert's cavalry made its first headlong charge up the hill towards the enemy's right wing while, taken by surprise, the Scots leapt to arms and to horse as best they could. There was an exchange of pistol-fire, followed by the roaring thud of artillery; and then two bodies of horsemen met head on in a fierce clash of steel. The world erupted into noise and confusion and the earth vibrated.

From the fringes of the mêlée, Eden bellowed staccato orders and strove to gain an over-all view of the situation. Then a troop of Scottish lancers pelted downhill at them ... and, after the first shock of impact, Eden found his regiment being driven back. Until the futility of it became plain, the English cavalry struggled to hold their ground – but finally Lambert's trumpet sounded the Recall and Eden set about withdrawing his men in order to re-form.

This was where discipline paid off and Eden was grateful that he'd inherited a regiment trained by Gabriel Brandon. Gathering his men with brisk efficiency beneath the steadily lightening sky, he exchanged a couple of sentences with Major-General Lambert and sent off a reconnaissance party to report on how General Monck was faring.

The answer was not encouraging.

'He's being pushed back,' Eden told Lambert tersely. 'Smaller numbers and lower ground.'

'Reserves,' snapped Lambert. And wheeled his horse about, shouting for a message to be sent to Cromwell.

It was never delivered. From away to their right came a huge cry of 'Lord of Hosts!' and the Lord-General's infantry started pouring across the burn and up the slopes towards Monck and the Scots. Further away still, the English artillery thundered and growled, its smoke swirling madly about on the wind.

And then the sun came up.

'Now let God arise and his enemies shall be scattered.'

Cromwell's reserve troops smashed into Leslie's Foot and engaged it at push of pike, causing the Scottish line to waver and give ground.

'Now!' shouted Lambert.

His trumpet sounded the Charge and Eden's fellows swept forward with the rest against the enemy Horse. What followed was brief and bloody. Pistols were discharged, then used as clubs; the discordant ring of steel on steel mingled with strangled screams; and the Scots cavalry foundered and then disintegrated. Men were cut down like corn-stalks to be trampled beneath the hooves of both sides. And as the retreat became a rout, Lambert swung his regiments about to support the Foot.

Soaked from the incessant rain and liberally spattered with mud, Eden did his duty by his men whilst fighting as hard as any of them. A bullet tore unnoticed through his sleeve; and though the sword-cut on his thigh was a different matter, it was not serious enough to stop him spitting the fellow who gave it to him.

In an hour, it was all over. In addition to those Scots who lay dead on the field, three thousand more were taken prisoner. By the middle of the afternoon, Lord-General Cromwell was gloating over a hoard of fifteen thousand enemy weapons and two hundred colours.

Later, whilst having his wound dressed, Eden received a brief visit from his superior officer.

'Will you still be able to dance?' asked Lambert with his customary sardonic smile.

'As well as I could before – which is to say, not very,' responded Eden, wincing as the surgeon touched a tender spot. 'Your idea, was it?'

'The attack? Yes.' A pause. 'You did well today. When Oliver recovers, I'll tell him so.'

The hazel eyes narrowed. 'He was injured?'

'No,' replied Lambert aridly. 'But, as yet, he hasn't stopped laughing.'

* * *

Scene Two
Théâtre du Marais in Paris, that same day ...
'What's in a name? That which we call a rose,
by any other name would smell as sweet.'
William Shakespeare

Two very different women sat in the deserted Green Room. The younger one, a dainty creature with long-lashed grey eyes and a torrent of dark copper curls, looked faintly sulky; the other, some ten years older and possessed of glossy brown hair and a trim waist, wore an expression of restrained exasperation.

The girl said mutinously, 'I'm ready. You know I'm ready. So why won't Froissart let me have some lines?'

'You'll be ready when I say you're ready,' came the calm reply. 'And Froissart will give you a speaking role when I tell him to.'

'When *you* tell him to?'

'Yes. Just because I no longer go on-stage myself, doesn't mean my opinion doesn't carry any weight.'

'No. I'm sorry.' The girl sighed, turning to look at the woman who was both her friend and her mentor. Until a runaway dray had left her with a scarred left cheek and a slight limp, Pauline Fleury had enjoyed a dazzling stage career of her own. Since then, however, she'd kept the theatre running on well-oiled wheels and lived again through a series of carefully chosen protégées. 'I know how lucky I am to have you helping me. And I also know that, no matter how hard I work, I'll never be as good as you. But it's been five *years*, Pauline. How much longer do I have to wait before I'm given a chance?'

'Not long. Just a few more months as a walker and then --'

'But it's so *boring!* Walk here, stand there. Smile, hide behind your fan. Exit downstage right. And so on and so on – and bloody so on. It's driving me sodding mad.'

'That's as maybe – but it's how everyone starts.' Madame Fleury looked up from the hem she was mending. 'I thought that, amongst a number of other things, I'd taught you to pass as a lady?'

The porcelain skin flushed a little. 'You did.'

'Then you'll watch your language.'

'I do. Mostly.' The girl picked restlessly at a fold of her shabby skirt. 'It just feels as though everything I've learned is being wasted.'

'My heart bleeds. However, if you feel that your potential is going unrecognised and that I'm holding you back, you can always go and audition for Floridor at the Hôtel de Bourgogne. I won't say you'll be much better off than here. But so long as you can regurgitate the right words and walk across the stage without tripping over your feet, he'll take you on for your looks alone.'

The flush deepened. 'I don't want that.'

'In which case, you'll hold your tongue and stop complaining – or find another way of earning your living.'

'I don't want to do that, either.'

And she didn't. She really didn't. Life in the theatre carried its penalties, of course; automatic excommunication at the beginning, burial in unconsecrated ground at the end ... and, in between, the widespread assumption that one was a whore. But for a girl born in a dingy back-street to a retired mercenary and a laundress, even the gift of beauty brought few choices. Marriage, perhaps, to an artisan or a tradesman who'd provide her with a roof over her head and a child a year; work as a maid, scrubbing pots and polishing floors whilst fending off the attentions of the master of the house; or selling her body at street corners in the hope of attracting a rich protector. To all of which, the stage was infinitely preferable.

Consequently, with a reluctant grin, she said, 'All right, Pauline. You've made your point – and I'll behave. It's just that I'm two weeks behind on the rent and the old witch of a landlady lies in wait every time I step through the door.'

'Perhaps if you stopped that old sot you call your father spending every last sou in the wine-shop, paying for the hovel you live in wouldn't be so much of a problem,' said Pauline tartly. Then added, 'Is *that* what all this has been about? Money?'

'Partly. I can't make ends meet on what I earn as a walker. The increase in wages I'd get for just a handful of lines would make all the difference.' She sat up again, a look of uncertainty crossing the beautiful face. 'There's Delphine and Hortense as well. They've been waiting for a role as long as me. What if Froissart picks one of them?'

Pauline gave her a look of impatient incredulity.

'Oh – for God's sake! Hortense has a voice like a shrew and Delphine's turning into a tub of lard from all the pastries she stuffs herself with. Neither one of them can hold a candle to you – not in looks nor in talent, either. The next new face will be yours. But not just yet. Timing is the important thing. If we get that right, I'm counting on you eclipsing Marie d'Amboise inside a year.'

The grey eyes flew wide and then the girl burst out laughing.

'Me? Steal parts from Madame d'Amboise? Now I *know* you're joking.'

'I'm not. She admits to being thirty-five – which means she's at least forty – and she's been leading-lady at the Marais since I made way for her.' Pauline's mouth curled in an acidulous grin. 'Time she bowed out in favour of some new blood. You.'

'Bloody hell! Sorry. You actually mean it, don't you?'

'Yes. I actually mean it. A fresh face. What are you now? Nineteen?'

'Twenty – as of yesterday. September the sodding second. Sorry, again.'

'You should have said. I'd have brought you a cake.'

'After what you just said about Delphine?'

Pauline gave a snort of laughter.

'Maybe not. But there's something you'll need to consider before you make your debut. At least, I'm assuming you won't want your real name on the playbill?'

'God, no.' She shuddered. 'Over my dead body.'

'So you'll need to come up with a stage name. Not something like Floridor or Bellerose. Something that sounds real.'

There was a long silence and finally the girl said slowly, 'Actually, I already have.'

'And?'

'Athenais de Galzain. I'd like to become Athenais de Galzain.'

ACT ONE

THE LAST CRUSADE
January to September, 1651

'The army may look well – but it won't fight.'
General Leslie to Charles the Second

ONE

On the first day of January, 1651, Francis Langley stood at the back of Scone Cathedral and watched a tall young man, five months short of his twenty-first birthday, receive – as a reward for several months of gritting his teeth – something which already rightfully belonged to him.

On the surface, the occasion looked just as it should. The young Prince, robed as befitted his station and with the royal regalia laid out before him, sat beneath a crimson velvet canopy supported by the eldest sons of six Earls. The vacant throne stood atop an impressive stage, some four feet off the ground and covered in rich carpets ... around which the flower of Scottish nobility, splendidly attired, rubbed elbows with the cream of the Kirk. But there the illusion ended. For the crowning of a king, though a serious business, ought also to contain an element of rejoicing; and this one had so far been about as cheerful as an interment.

It wasn't a surprise. After forcing Charles to take both Covenants, making him publicly repent the sins of his parents as well as his own and ordaining two fast days, the Scots were scarcely likely to allow the coronation itself to be marred by any hint of pleasure. The handful of English Royalists had been relegated to the edges; the Engagers, those gentlemen who'd fought for the late King at Preston, had been prohibited altogether; and the only persons permitted to have a hand in the ceremony itself were those whose Covenanting principles met the exacting standards of Archibald Campbell, Marquis of Argyll. Francis, of course, wasn't supposed to be there at all – which is why he was lurking as unobtrusively as possible in a dimly-lit corner.

The Moderator of the General Assembly delivered an epic sermon, liberally laced with gloom. Major Langley shifted his shoulders against the cold stone, smothered a yawn and let dire warnings about tottering crowns and sinful kings flow over him. One became immune, after a time, to austere Scottish strictures. And a formal crowning would do much to dilute such humiliations.

Charles knelt to affirm his oath to the Covenants. His voice was devout enough and his promise to establish Presbyterianism in his other dominions was made without a hint of either reluctance or cynicism.

Francis smiled, silently applauding ... and immediately found himself encompassed by the obliquely considering stare of the fellow who'd ridden in on the previous evening with a bundle of heavily-sealed letters. Francis responded with one sardonically raised brow before restoring his attention to the ceremony. Not everyone, he reflected, thought this particular game worth the candle.

Charles ascended the waiting throne. Lord Lyon, the King of Arms, announced that he was *the rightful and undoubted heir of the Crown* and those present responded with a resounding cry of *God save King Charles the Second!* – upon which His Majesty was escorted back to the chair he'd occupied during the interminable sermon for the reading of the Coronation Oath. Francis watched Charles kneel to affirm this before being invested with kingly robes and the articles of state; he set his jaw and suppressed a desire to fidget when the minister prayed that the Lord would *purge the Crown from the sins and transgressions of them that did reign before*; and he let out a breath he hadn't known he'd been holding when the Marquis of Argyll finally placed the crown on Charles's head.

The tradition of anointing the sovereign had been dispensed with as superstitious ritual but, at long last, Charles was declared King of Great Britain, France and Ireland; and, amidst more pious exhortations from the Moderator, he was led to the throne so that the nobles could touch the crown and swear fidelity.

'Argyll the kingmaker,' murmured the courier. 'And even more Friday-faced than usual. The debacle at Dunbar, do you think? Or perhaps it's merely that squint of his.'

Francis turned his head and encountered a gleaming stare.

'Both, I imagine.'

'But one more than the other,' came the bland reply. 'Contrary to present appearances, his power isn't quite what it was. One even hears rumours of the return of Hamilton.'

Wondering where someone who'd only just arrived might have picked up that particular rumour, Francis said gently, 'Does one? I wouldn't know. But it would certainly account for Argyll's expression ... even allowing for the squint.'

The other man said nothing. The Scots finished swearing fealty and King Charles the Second rose to solemnly beseech the ministers that if at any time they saw him breaking his Covenant, they would instantly tell him of it. Then, with becoming dignity and a flourish of trumpets, the royal procession passed back down the aisle … and, in due course, Francis found himself outside with the rest.

His companion from the cathedral was nowhere to be seen and, instead, his arm was taken by the Duke of Buckingham, who drawled, 'The throne's gain is clearly the theatre's loss. Such clarity of diction despite having his tongue firmly in his cheek! I'm impressed.'

'And indiscreet,' sighed Francis. 'Shall we go? It's extremely cold and the banquet awaits.'

'It's bound to be dreary. There will be speeches, God help us all … and insufficient wine to drown them out. But I'm amazed the coronation committee thought fit to invite you – if indeed they did? Come to think of it, I'm not *entirely* sure why they asked *me*.'

It wasn't true, of course. Twenty-two years old, blessed with startling good looks and frequently too clever for his own good, George Villiers, second Duke of Buckingham, was not used to being ignored.

Smiling faintly, Francis said, 'For your entertainment value, George. Why else?'

'Do you think so? I thought it had rather more to do with my having been more or less reared alongside the Lord's *un*anointed. But I daresay you know best … so I'll try to live up to everyone's expectations.'

Inside the banqueting chamber, wax candles burned bright and log fires blazed in the great hearths. Long tables gleamed with silver plate, fine glassware and monogrammed damask and, winnowing between these and the arriving guests, liveried servants handed out cups of spiced wine. No expense, it appeared, had been spared. It was just a pity, thought Francis, that the company wasn't better.

Undeterred by the fact that His Majesty was still hemmed in by Argyll and a clutch of black-clad ministers, Buckingham sauntered towards him. Francis made polite conversation with various acquaintances and then took his place, as directed, at one of the lower tables with the rest of his unwelcome compatriots.

'Well, well,' said a familiar voice cheerfully. 'You again. We are obviously perceived to be of the same lowly status. Or do I mean tarred with the same brush?'

Francis turned slowly and took his time about replying.

Of roughly his own age and height, the courier was as fair as he himself was dark and dressed in well-worn buff leather. Knowing how few Royalists had any money these days and aware that his own blue satin was decidedly shabby, Francis passed over this sartorial breach and concentrated on the intelligence evident in the fine-boned face and the gleam of humour in the dark green eyes.

Holding out his hand, he said lightly, 'Francis Langley – unemployed Major of Horse.'

His fingers were taken in a cool, firm grip.

'Ashley Peverell – jack-of-all-trades,' came the reply. And, dropping into the adjacent seat, 'Don't tell me. You were purged from the army before Dunbar?'

'Well before it. And you?'

'Oh – I was already *persona non grata*.' Bitterness mingled oddly with nonchalance. 'I fought at Preston – for all the good that did.'

An Engager, then, thought Francis. *If Argyll knew that, the door would have been slammed in your face. But it explains how you know about Hamilton.* He said merely, 'I was at Colchester.'

'Ah. Then you doubtless have better cause for resentment than I. However. At least you haven't become a glorified errand boy.'

The conversation had arrived, quicker than Francis expected, at the point which interested him. He said, 'The letters you took to the King last night?'

'The very same. Speculation rife, is it?'

'Naturally. Anything to break the monotony.'

Ashley Peverell grinned.

'A cry from the heart, if ever I heard one. But I'm afraid I'm going to disappoint you. I've merely been doing the rounds in England. You know the sort of thing. Can you offer a few guineas to help feed and clothe your King? *Alas, sir, I can barely feed and clothe my family.* Can His Majesty rely on your support in the event of another invasion? *He has my very good wishes, sir. More than that, I cannot guarantee.* And so on and so on and depressingly, unsurprisingly so on.'

Francis frowned. 'Is it really as bad as that?'

'Yes. Oh - people are sick of the so-called Commonwealth. They're tired of the Rump clinging to power while it ordains fines for swearing and penalties for adultery – and they resent the monthly assessments and the Excise. But not everyone will ally themselves with the Scots and many wish His Majesty hadn't taken the Covenant. Then again, out of the total support I *have* been promised, experience has taught me not to expect to see more than half of it when the time comes.'

'You're turning into a cynic, Ash,' remarked a voice from the far side of the table. 'It won't do, you know.'

Two pairs of eyes, one green and one deep blue, turned towards the speaker – a thin-faced young man with a shock of unruly brown hair.

'My God,' groaned Ashley. 'Somebody should have warned me.' Then, laughing and stretching out a hand, 'How are you Nick? Still looking for dragons to slay?'

'You could put it that way,' returned Sir Nicholas Austin, accepting the hand with unabashed good-humour, 'though I personally wouldn't. And I suppose you're going to tell me that there are plenty of them here.'

'Look around and judge for yourself.'

Nicholas cocked an eyebrow at Francis.

'Major Langley – I'm shocked. I thought you only had truck with respectable people.'

'One tries,' murmured Francis. 'As it happens, Mr Peverell and I have only just met.'

Nicholas blinked and opened his mouth to speak. Forestalling him, Ashley said, 'Hallelujah. The food is coming. Along, I hope, with another jug of claret.'

Taking the hint, Nicholas said, 'Hold on to that hope but don't rely on it. They'll be making sure no one gets drunk. After all, it would be a pity if we started to enjoy ourselves, wouldn't it?'

The food was good and plentiful. Capons jostled numerous varieties of fish, venison sat cheek-by-howl with partridge and woodcock, and delicately flavoured creams and custards nestled between pastries filled with beef and apricots. The wine, on the other hand, continued to arrive slowly and in niggardly quantities. Even the King, still politely listening to Argyll, was frequently seen to be nursing an empty glass.

Ashley diverted a flagon from a table to his right and Francis liberated another from the one behind him. Vociferous complaints arose. From his place beside Charles, his Grace of Buckingham watched enviously.

'It seems to me,' remarked Ashley Peverell at length, 'that our sovereign lord deserves a small celebration more in keeping with his tastes.'

'I daresay,' agreed Francis. 'But exquisite ladies of easy virtue don't exactly abound in Perth. And his reputation is widespread enough already.'

'His bastard by Lucy Walter? Quite. But he must be able to enjoy himself outside the bedchamber. Amidst friends, for example ... over a few bottles, in the private room of a tavern. It shouldn't be too difficult to arrange.'

Francis looked at him.

'Is that a suggestion?'

'Call it more of a challenge.'

Major Langley lifted one dark brow.

'A challenge? How medieval. But I think ... I really think I must accept.'

* * *

In the end, the party in the upper room of the Fish Inn to which Charles was discreetly conducted later that evening, was augmented by two persons. Buckingham – because, as the King's closest friend, he couldn't be left out; and Alexander Fraizer, because his ability to mingle medicine with intrigue meant that he'd find out anyway. Also, as Ashley pointed out, after the amount they'd all eaten and the amount they intended to drink, a doctor might come in handy.

To preserve His Majesty's incognito, bottles were fetched and carried by Ashley's servant, Jem – a burly individual whose fund of thieves' cant made Francis wonder where Mr Peverell had found him and soon had the King memorising phrases.

By the time toasts had been drunk and the coronation thoroughly dissected and joked about, everyone was pleasantly mellow. Then

Charles said, 'Try not to laugh your boots off, gentlemen – but Argyll thinks I should marry.'

'Does he?' Buckingham reached for the bottle. 'How quaint of him. And whom does he suggest as a potential bride?'

'A paragon of birth, beauty and virtue. In short, the Lady Anne Campbell.'

The room fell abruptly silent.

'His daughter?' asked Nicholas feebly. 'He wants you to marry his daughter?'

Charles nodded, his dark eyes impassive.

There was another silence. Then Ashley said, 'They must be allowing the Engagers back.'

Buckingham's brows rose.

'I thought we were discussing His Majesty's proposed marriage?'

'We are. Argyll's position has been slipping since Dunbar. The return of Hamilton and the Engagers will destroy it completely. But with the English holding Edinburgh and everything to the south of it, the Scots army needs all the help it can get – so the repeal of the Act of Classes is only a matter of time. Consequently, Argyll is trying to join his star to the King's before it vanishes completely. Simple.'

Francis eyed him thoughtfully. Whoever – or whatever – Ashley Peverell was, there was plainly nothing wrong with his intellect. The King obviously knew this already for he said, 'So tell me, Ash. How badly do I need him?'

'A lot less than you did yesterday,' came the frank reply. 'If I'm right about the Engagers, the only influence Argyll will soon have left to him is over the Kirk – and since you can't afford trouble from that direction, you'll have to go on charming him for a while longer.' Ashley grinned. 'But a marriage negotiation is a weighty matter which can take months, Sir. And you can't even contemplate it without Her Majesty, your mother's consent.'

'Which, of course, she won't give,' murmured Charles with an answering gleam.

'No. But you don't need to tell Argyll that.'

'I wouldn't think,' remarked Buckingham, 'that he'll *need* telling. However ... since you seem to have it all worked out, perhaps you'd like to evaluate His Majesty's chances of regaining his throne in the not-too-distant future.'

Alexander Fraizer said flatly, 'That's no a fair question, your Grace – and one nobody here could fairly answer.'

'Not you or I, certainly, Sandy. But I'm sure Colonel Peverell is much better informed than we are.'

Colonel Peverell? Francis looked across at Nicholas and received a rueful shrug.

'Or perhaps,' added the Duke, slanting a slyly malicious smile in the Colonel's direction, 'you prefer to be called The Falcon?'

Francis narrowly suppressed a groan.

The Falcon? *Really?* Christ. Who *was* this fellow?

'Not particularly,' said Ashley prosaically. 'We all know the general situation. Ireland has been left groaning under Henry Ireton's boot; Mazarin will offer us nothing while France remains at war with Spain; and the death of William of Orange means we can expect little of the Dutch. As for England – sporadic risings like the one in Norfolk before Christmas are crushed within hours. So for the time being, our only real hope lies in a strong, fully-united Scots Army.'

'Woven about yourself and the Engagers, no doubt,' said Buckingham sweetly. 'So you'll gladly do penance in sackcloth and ashes like poor Middleton?'

Colonel Peverell fixed him with a cool, faintly impatient stare.

'Why not? If His Majesty can swallow his pride, I'm not about to stand on mine. Francis – pass the bottle, will you? This is supposed to be a celebration. Doesn't anyone know any funny stories?'

Buckingham did and immediately embarked on an anecdote about a pair of startled lovers and a misdirected golf ball. Francis leaned towards Ashley and said softly, 'George doesn't like you, does he? Any particular reason?'

'You'd better ask him.'

'On the contrary. I think I'd better not.' Amusement stirred behind the sapphire eyes and then was gone. 'Why didn't you say you were a colonel?'

'I didn't want to put you to the trouble of saluting. Does it matter?'

'It shouldn't. But I can't help wondering why you didn't want Nick to reveal it.'

'No reason that will make you feel any better. Get ready to laugh. Buckingham's building up to his grand finale.'

Curiosity had always been Francis's besetting sin and he had no qualms about indulging it. Fortunately, one golfing tale had a way of leading to another – so it wasn't difficult to get the King and Sandy Fraizer started on the last game they had played together. Smiling, Francis turned back to the Colonel.

'I've heard this one. It takes about ten minutes. So … where were we?'

'Nowhere that I can recall. Don't you like golf?'

'Not as a topic of conversation. It ranks alongside *Generals I have known* and *How I lost my leg at Naseby*.'

Ashley laughed. 'My God. How do you pass the time?'

'I read. Poetry, mostly. And I write a little.' Francis re-filled both their glasses and sat back. 'In truth, though I trained at Angers, I expected to spend my life at Court. It was the war that made me a soldier – and not, I'm afraid, a particularly good one. By the time we got to Marston Moor, Rupert had cured my worst faults and I learned a whole lot more at Colchester. But I'm no military genius … and I still prefer books to battles.' He smiled again. 'That's my guilty secret. What's yours?'

Ashley drew a short breath and then loosed it.

'You don't give up, do you?'

'Rarely. But at least I'm asking you, not Nick.'

'It wouldn't do you an enormous amount of good if you did. But there's no need to show me the stick,' came the dust-dry response. Then, with a slight shrug, 'You wish to know if my military rank is a courtesy title? It isn't.'

'And The Falcon?'

'Does things the Colonel can't – and isn't a sobriquet I either sought or want.'

'I … see.'

'I doubt it.' Ashley grinned suddenly. 'But if you can't live without at least one incident from my murky past ... between Preston and joining Charles in late '48, I took to the High Toby.'

Francis blinked. 'I beg your pardon?'

'I was a highwayman. Jem says I was a very bad one – but that's due to a difference of opinion coupled with the fact that it was his profession long before it was mine. You must have guessed that, of course. His vocabulary is extremely ... colourful.'

'Incomprehensible, more like.'

'Not to me, fortunately.' Ashley stood up and stretched, then turned back to murmur wickedly, 'You're right about Buckingham, by the way. Asking him about me wouldn't be very tactful.'

'So I had assumed. Is there a good reason?'

'He certainly thinks so. Her name was Veronique.'

Charles and the doctor reached the end of their golfing reminiscences and the talk became general once more. By the time Jem Barker appeared with fresh supplies, the party was growing very merry and Buckingham was decidedly the worse for wear.

Dumping his cargo on the table, Mr Barker said, 'Here's some more boozing-cheats for you – though I reckon you've all got bread-and-cheese in your heads already, going by the din.' He bent a severe gaze upon the Duke and then, turning to Ashley, said, 'Better watch that'n. Looks about ready to flay the fox, to me.'

The door banged shut behind him and, amidst the laughter, Charles said unsteadily, 'F-flay the fox?'

'Throw up,' translated Colonel Peverell obligingly.

'In my presence?' demanded the King. 'He'd better not. It isn't respectful.' He paused, looking at Ashley. 'You're not drunk, are you? Why not?'

'Because someone has to see you safe home again, Sir.'

'I don't *want* to be seen home. I don't want to be discreet. And I'm sick of not being able to stir without a pack of preachers at my heels.' The dark, Stuart eyes gathered an obstinate glow. 'It's got to change, Ash.'

'It *has* changed, Your Majesty. You've been crowned.'

'Not in England. Nor, without a united army, will I ever be – and amidst all the damned squabbling, I can't see how I'm to get one.'

'A royal progress,' said Francis languidly. And then, when Charles peered owlishly at him, 'Travel about those areas not occupied by Cromwell. Draw the people to you – and make sure that the Kirk is aware of it.'

There was a short silence. Then Nicholas said hazily, 'Rose-petals and banners, cheering crowds and hosts of pretty girls ... fountains flowing with wine --'

'In *Scotland*?' murmured Ashley.

'True,' said the King. 'But it's a good idea for all that. Popularity is important.' He paused, his face creasing in a tipsy, sardonic smile. 'Not that I'm ever going to be popular with the Kirk unless I repent being born.'

'Long-nosed canting miseries,' grumbled Sandy Fraizer into his glass. 'They fair give me the marthambles.'

'Me too.' Lurching to his feet, Buckingham grabbed a bottle and collapsed back into his seat with it. 'Whole bloody country givesh me the marthambles.'

'And Cromwell,' pronounced Nicholas. 'Let's not forget Old Noll. Lucky Noll, warty Noll, Noll the nose.' And sang, '*Nose, nose, nose, nose – who gave thee that jolly red nose?*'

And with enthusiastic if imperfect unison, his companions responded, '*Cinnamon and ginger, nutmeg and cloves – that's what gave thee that jolly red nose!*'

One song led to another. Sir Nicholas climbed uncertainly on his chair and conducted the ensemble with a poker. Dr Fraizer beat time on the log-box, the King used a pair of pewter plates as cymbals and his Grace of Buckingham, slightly green about the gills, participated with a series of violent hiccups.

Then the door burst open and Jem Barker flew backwards into the room on the end of someone's fist.

Nicholas fell off his perch.

In the doorway, three men-at-arms made way for the stern-faced Moderator of the General Assembly and a pair of horrified ministers.

'Shit,' burped Buckingham. And threw up in the hearth.

Silence engulfed the room and Ashley stared rather desperately at Francis.

'Oh dear,' he said mildly. 'Sackcloth and ashes all round, I think.'

And gave way to helpless laughter.

TWO

Although it necessitated a good deal of grovelling, the affair at the Fish Inn did not become common knowledge and Charles, having written to ascertain his mother's views on a possible union with Lady Anne Campbell, wisely set off on an immediate tour of north-eastern Scotland. Unsurprisingly, Major Francis Langley and Sir Nicholas Austin were not amongst those permitted to accompany him – which meant that they had the pleasure of watching the second Duke of Hamilton's return to Court occasion Argyll's sulky withdrawal from it. And around the end of the month, Colonel Peverell disappeared again on undisclosed business.

He went to Ireland first to see if things were really as bad as people said. They were. Thousands starved on a land devastated by war; and while Irish Royalists and Irish patriots continued to exist in mutual distrust, Commissary-General Ireton extended his grip on everything outside the mountains and the bogs.

Disguised as a peat-cutter in clothes that itched, Ashley evaluated what he saw. And when both stealth and his assumed *persona* failed him, he despatched the problem in the usual unpleasant but extremely final way and put it from his mind. It wasn't the first time and it probably wouldn't be the last but it was sometimes necessary. He just preferred not to keep count.

He spent five days trying to talk sense into a clutch of O'Neils; and then, aware that he was wasting his time and wanting a bath more than he'd ever wanted anything in his life, he took ship for The Hague.

The crossing in a filthy, leaking tub was a bad one and the news at the other end no better. Ashley had known that William of Orange's stubborn, solitary opposition to the Commonwealth had died with him. What he *hadn't* known was that the Prince's death had also allowed Holland to take the lead amongst the United Provinces, with the result that negotiations were even now taking place with Westminster. In vain did the exiled Royalists try to cheer him with descriptions of how difficult they were making life for the Parliamentarian envoys. Ashley merely shrugged and remarked that making Oliver St. John go about armed to the teeth with a couple of body-guards in attendance wasn't going to solve anything. Then, leaving his compatriots muttering darkly to themselves, he left on the next leg of his Odyssey.

Arriving in Paris amidst the rain and wind of early March, he gave Sir Edward Hyde an unvarnished account of how matters stood in Scotland and received, in return, a gloomy picture of the latest obstacles being set in the way of his fellow agents in England, coupled with an alarmingly long list of recent arrests. Amongst these was a name worrying enough to set Ashley scouring Paris for the best-informed and most elusive spy he knew ... which was how, two painstaking days later, he ended up in the crowded pit of the Théâtre du Marais.

By the time he arrived, the play was already well under way. A florid, middle-aged actor was engaged in verbose seduction of a well-endowed actress somewhat taller than himself and demonstrably past her first blush. The female half of the audience appeared enthralled; the gallants in the pit brimmed with boisterous advice – of which 'Get a box to stand on!' seemed generally the most popular. Colonel Peverell sighed, shoved his playbill unread into his pocket and started looking about for One-Eyed Will.

The theatre, which had originally been a tennis-court, was smarter than he had expected owing to a fortuitous fire which had caused it to be largely rebuilt some six or seven years ago. Lit by a huge chandelier, the proscenium stage was wide and deep with a good-sized apron surrounded by footlight candles. The old spectators' galleries had been replaced by comfortable boxes – though, from most of them, it was only possible to watch the play by leaning over the parapet. Jostled on all sides, Ashley stood in the pit, systematically scanning faces until, in one of the front off-stage boxes, he recognised the distinctive black silk eye-patch and mop of wild dark hair belonging to Sir William Brierley.

Since he was in the company of two other gentlemen and a lady, Ashley hesitated briefly and then, shrugging, started elbowing his way in their direction.

With the mischievous restlessness around him fast approaching its zenith, this was not easy. On stage, the statuesque heroine swooned into the arms of her would-be seducer, knocking his wig askew. Undeterred and clasping her to his manly chest, the hero delivered another epic speech and attempted to haul her to a couch. Predictably, the wits advised him to make two trips. Casting his well-wishers a venomous glance, the actor concluded his speech and exited stage-left with a swish of his cloak to an accompanying chorus of stamping and whistles.

Purposefully but without haste, Ashley pursued his winnowing course, vaguely aware that, on the stage, a girl costumed as a maid-servant had skimmed out from the wings to fan the recumbent leading-lady with her apron. The pit, now well into its collective stride, suggested various other ways of reviving Madame d'Amboise.

'Get her corset off!' shouted one.

'Fetch a bucket of water!' yelled another.

'Send for the Vicomte de Charenton!' howled a third.

The pit roared its approval and, this time, even the boxes shook with laughter. Stuck between a fat fellow reeking of garlic and a world-weary slattern peddling oranges, Ashley reflected that he'd known quieter battle-fields and wondered how the actors stood it. Just now, for example, the girl playing the maid was still kneeling beside the leading lady. Neither showed any sign of trying to carry on with the play which, until the noise died down, was probably wise. Then, just as Ashley sucked in his breath prior to fighting his way closer to One-Eyed Will, the girl rose swiftly to her feet and stepped downstage into the blaze of candles surrounding the apron.

The effect on the audience was immediate and remarkable. The stamping stopped; the catcalls withered into uncertainty; and the laughter turned into a medley of appreciative whistles before fading into something very close to silence. Ashley took a good, long look ... and understood why.

Seen properly for the first time in the full glare of the lights, the girl was mind-blowingly beautiful. A dainty, lissom creature with a hand-span waist, a torrent of glowing, copper curls and an exquisite heart-shaped face set with huge dark eyes; a fantasy made flesh ... and guaranteed to stop any man's breath for a moment. The only thing wrong, decided Ashley clinically, was that she clearly knew it and was enjoying the effect.

As swiftly as the thought had come, he realised it was wrong. Although he couldn't read her eyes from where he stood, he could see indecision in the line of her shoulders and the way her hands were gripping her apron. A smile curled his mouth. At a guess, she had a few lines – probably pitifully few – and, since she didn't want to waste them on an audience that wouldn't shut up, she'd stormed downstage. Only now the audience *had* shut up, she'd realised that she was out of position. Ashley's smile grew as he waited to see what she'd do about it.

What she did was to draw a very deep breath. The effect this had on her body had Ashley and most of the men around him drawing one with her. The audience was absolutely silent now, waiting for her to speak. She lifted her chin, smiling a little. Then, seizing a candle from the nearest sconce, she embarked smoothly on her opening speech and swirled back to the couch to twitch an ostrich feather from Marie d'Amboise's head-dress, singe it and wave it under that lady's nose.

Madame d'Amboise coughed and regained consciousness with remarkable, if unconvincing rapidity. Ashley was startled into a choke of amusement, the gallants in the pit hooted with laughter and the acrid smell of burned feathers drifted into the front boxes. Avoiding the leading lady's furious glare, the girl played the rest of her brief scene without apparent deviation and exited to an unexpected storm of applause.

Ashley Peverell watched her go and wondered if, under the paint, she looked as good close to as she did from a distance. Then, reminding himself that he hadn't come here to watch the play, he turned his attention back to the business in hand.

By dint of a good deal of unmannerly shoving, he eventually reached his goal and immediately found himself impaled on Sir William's one and only eye.

'Well, I'm damned,' drawled that gentleman lazily. 'A face I never thought to see again ... back from the dead and come to haunt me. How are you, Colonel?'

'Bruised,' replied Ashley. And with an audacious smile at the pretty brunette, 'I don't suppose you'd care to invite me into your private haven?'

She smiled coquettishly.

'By all means, sir. Come and be welcome.'

Needing no further telling, Ashley hoisted himself over the parapet and bowed over the lady's hand. 'Madame, you are a pearl amongst women and may count me your most willing slave.'

She gave a trill of laughter.

'William – your friend is charming. Aren't you going to introduce him?'

'He's a rogue and a mountebank,' remarked Sir William calmly. Then, with a wave of his handkerchief, 'However, *mes amis* ... allow me to present Colonel Peverell, formerly of His Majesty's Horse and latterly of God alone knows where. Ashley ... meet Mistress ... er ...'

'Verney,' supplied the brunette firmly and with something resembling defiance. '*Lady* Verney.'

'Of course,' murmured Will, watching Ashley kiss the lady's hand. 'Also Sir Hugo Verney ... and Jean-Claude Minervois, Vicomte de Charenton.'

Mechanically going through the obligatory courtesies, Ashley was aware of several things. Sir Hugo looked uncomfortable; the Vicomte was not in the best of tempers; and Will's eye was brimming with wicked amusement.

Oh God, thought Ashley. *It's a* ménage à quatre. Cinq, *if you count that busty piece on the stage. How long before I can get Will away?*

As it happened, he didn't have to wait very long at all. The third act drew to a close amidst increasingly ribald comments from the pit and, after some desultory discussion on the merits of the play and whether or not Arnaud Clermont was past his professional best, Sir William said suavely, 'Celia, my angel – you'll forgive me if Ashley and I desert you? So much gossip to catch up on and, one suspects, so little time in which to do it, you know?' Then, barely giving her time to nod, 'Hugo, my dear fellow ... *such* a pleasure to see you. You must both sup with me one day soon. And Jean-Claude ... what can one say? One had no notion that your liaison with the delectable d'Amboise was so widely known. But naturally one sees that the *cachet* it gives the lady is bound to place a strain upon her discretion. So difficult for you, *mon brave*. One cannot but sympathise.'

Still smiling and with the merest hint of a pause, Sir William turned to Ashley.

'Come, my loved one. The play is about to resume and we must not interrupt it. Farewell, one and all. *Bon nuit!*' Upon which, he swept Ashley away.

'And that, as they say, was *definitely* better than the play,' he remarked, linking arms with Ashley. 'It's not Marie d'Amboise's fault that the whole of Paris knows Charenton's bedding her. It's milord himself who does the boasting. And then he gets disgruntled when the wags make a game of him. The man, my dear,' finished Will blandly, 'is an absolute prick.'

Laughing, Ashley said, 'And you're a shit-stirrer. I'm surprised he didn't hit you.'

'No, no. He'd be afraid I might hit him back.'

'Which, of course, you would.' Ashley was perfectly well-aware that Sir William's effete manner was only skin deep and that below it lay a dangerous and, when necessary, ruthless man. 'And what of the Verneys? Something not quite right there either, I fancy.'

'You *were* awake, weren't you?' came the admiring reply. 'Can't you guess? The fair Celia is Verney's mistress – but not, alas, Mistress Verney.'

'Ah.'

'Exactly. One understands that Hugo still has a wife in England, clinging tenaciously to the family estates and rearing a son ... and similarly, Celia is still married to one of Cromwell's up-and-coming officers. So what we have here is caps over the windmill and the world well lost for love. All very well in its way ... but one wonders whether having the right body in bed is sufficient compensation for social leprosy.' Will's mouth curled wryly. 'One may be a threadbare exile – but one has one's standards.'

'A lady conducts her affaires with discretion and a gentleman doesn't inflict his whore on polite company?' recited Ashley. And then, 'How nice that some people still have nothing better to think about.'

'It would be if it were true.'

'And isn't it?'

'Oh no,' came the gentle reply. 'Most of our compatriots here have lost everything except their pride – and that, they preserve at all costs. One can't really blame them. After all, you and I do it too. The only difference is that we've grown so used to banging our heads against the wall, we don't know how to stop.' He paused and gestured to a shallow flight of steps. 'My humble abode – within which lie a couple of bottles of reasonably palatable burgundy.'

Ashley paused. 'Louise?'

'Visiting her family. Fortunately. I am aware that she likes you far too well.'

Moving on up the steps and laughing a little, Ashley said, 'You should marry her, then.'

'I daresay I will when I can support her adequately. Shall we?'

Sir William's lodgings comprised three neat rooms on the first floor. While his host busied himself with the wine, Ashley dropped into a carved chair by the hearth and attempted to poke some life into the almost dormant fire. Then, when Will handed him a glass and sat down opposite him, he said bluntly, 'You'll have guessed, I daresay, that I've come from Scotland. To cut a long story short, I'm gathering information in an attempt to assess the chances of a second invasion succeeding where the first one failed.'

Sir William's brows rose.

'Excuse my asking … but do you really think there's the remotest chance of the Scots ever fielding a viable army?'

'Meaning you don't?'

'No. I don't. However. Let us put that aside for the moment. What do you want to know?'

'Hyde says Tom Coke's been arrested. I need to know how much he knows – and whether he's likely to make Cromwell's spy-master a present of it.'

'Oh dear.' Will sat back in his chair and contemplated his wine-glass. The fire was burning brighter now and its glow was dully reflected in the silk eye-patch, giving its wearer an appearance of demonic menace. Finally, in a tone of acid finality, he said, 'Thomas Coke will have spilled his guts on the first time of asking and, in all probability, has gone on babbling ever since. As for what he can reveal … I have to say that, in common with the rest of our agents, it's too damned much. That has always been our problem. If no one knew more than they needed to, we'd be a great deal more efficient than we are.' He paused briefly and looked across at Ashley. 'The unfortunate truth is that *you* are careful and *I* am careful. But the rest of the buggers treat espionage like a game of Blind Man's Buff.'

'I know.' Ashley sighed. 'I've worked with a few of them, God help me. But what about Coke? Do you have any idea what he may have been involved with? Or who?'

'Oh yes,' returned Will, wryly. And told him.

At the end of it, Ashley stared into the fire without speaking. Then he said, 'Oh bloody hell. And there's not a thing we can do about it, is there?'

'There's nothing anyone can do about it.' There was another long pause. Then Will said, 'This invasion fantasy of yours. Tell me about it.'

'It's less of a fantasy than you might think. The Scots want Cromwell out of their country so much they've crowned Charles and are letting the Engagers back. They have an army of sorts. Admittedly, it's neither huge nor well-equipped and it's far from well-trained ... but, to a degree at least, all those faults might be mended.'

'I do so admire optimism. But pray go on. Who is commanding?'

'Well, David Leslie, of course. And --'

'Ah yes. Canny, cautious old Leslie. The general who, despite knowing the ground like the back of his hand, managed to get wiped out at Dunbar. Next?'

'Edward Massey.'

'The hero of Gloucester? Well, one can't sneer at him. It's a pity, though, that his best successes occurred whilst fighting for the Parliament. A number of good English Royalists may balk at serving under a former enemy.'

Ashley eyed him with foreboding. 'Hamilton.'

'The parsons like that family less than the devil. They'll be snapping at his heels like terriers. Still ... I suppose he may be luckier than his late brother. Any more?'

'The Earl of Derby.'

Sir William laughed.

'Oh – please! That man never got anything right in his life. The only thing he's any good at is being quarrelsome – and, in the company you've described, there'll be plenty of opportunity for that.' The laughter faded and, in a different tone, he said, 'I'm sorry, Ashley. I'm desperately sorry … but I don't think you've a cat in hell's chance. And it's not just the lack of good leadership. Very few Cavaliers will fight beside the Scots – and none of the Scots will have anything to do with the Catholics. What hope can such a clutch of ill-assorted factions have against the New Model? Cromwell will chew it up and spit out the pieces.'

The time the silence yawned like a cavern. Then Ashley said ruefully, 'I hope you're wrong … though I suspect you're not. But you see, Charles is set on it, if only the Scots will agree. And what other option is there?'

'Truthfully?' Will's smile was faintly twisted. 'None.'

'None,' agreed Ashley. 'So even if failure *is* guaranteed, I can't just wash my hands of it, can I?'

'Actually, that might be the most helpful thing you *can* do. You and everyone else who has both a brain and enough field experience to recognise when the writing's on the wall.'

'It's not that simple, Will. I can't just abandon Charles. Not only because if an invasion does take place, he'll go with it – but because, if he's to make a better job of kingship than his father, he needs the right sort of men around him now. Englishmen without a religious axe to grind … and ones who don't keep their brains in their breeches. You see?'

'Only too well. You'll go with Charles and, if necessary, you'll die for him … but not for any of the excellent reasons you've just put forward.' Sir William paused and reached for the bottle. 'You'll do it because you'd never forgive yourself if you didn't. And so, having established that point, we may as well get drunk.'

* * *

While two English gentlemen were setting the world to rights over their second bottle, Athenais de Galzain was being taught the error of her ways.

Assistant-Manager Froissart lectured her on the self-discipline required by good stage-craft. An actor, he said, was supposed to stick religiously to the play as it had been rehearsed and not plunge headlong into impulsive changes. This basic rule was for the protection of all because if everyone took it into their heads to do what they liked, no one would know whether they were coming or going.

Athenais accepted this with meekly downcast eyes and was therefore unaware that Monsieur Froissart's stern tone accorded ill with the glint of amusement in his face. She just made numerous sincere apologies and promised never to do such a thing again.

The second, inevitably, was from Marie d'Amboise.

'You stupid little slut! What the hell do you think you were doing? Trying to get a laugh at my expense?'

'No. It was just that the audience wouldn't shut up and --'

'Then you wait until they do.'

'I *did* wait. If I'd waited much longer, half of them would have gone home.'

'Don't get smart with me, girl. Who the hell do you think you are?'

Your successor, I hope, thought Athenais. But had the sense not to say it. Instead, knowing that annoying the leading-lady further was only going to store up trouble for herself, she adopted a humble tone and lied. 'I'm sorry, Madame. It was a mistake.'

'Don't make it again,' snapped Marie. 'Not if you expect to get another role after this one.'

And finally, when everyone else had left the theatre, Pauline Fleury gave her a shrewdly considering stare and said, 'Presumably tonight has taught you something?'

Athenais sighed. 'God, Pauline. Not you as well.'

'Me as well. So?'

'So I've learned not to get creative in performance,' came the long-suffering reply.

'Anything else?'

'If I get myself into a hole, it's up to me to dig myself out of it?'

'Exactly. The one lesson no one else can teach you.' Pauline grinned suddenly. 'Well done.'

Athenais looked back warily. 'You're not annoyed with me?'

'Not as much as I would have been if you hadn't turned your mistake into an advantage. Using the feathers was both clever and funny. The audience liked it.'

'Monsieur Froissart didn't.'

'You'd be surprised. He was bound to issue a reprimand. But he's just seen you make the audience take notice. Unless I miss my guess, he'll be taking particular notice himself from now on.'

* * *

Colonel Peverell arose next morning with mill-wheels grinding inside his head and the aggravating knowledge that he only had himself to blame. Gritting his teeth, he washed, shaved, dressed ... and decided he was never going to drink again. Then, unable to face breakfast, he went off to reclaim his hired horse from the stables where he had lodged it.

It was only then, whilst paying his shot, that he found the crumpled playbill from the Théâtre du Marais still in his pocket ... and, by process of elimination, worked out that the stunning red-head who'd played the maid-servant rejoiced under the name of Mademoiselle de Galzain.

He was half-way back to the coast before it occurred to him to wonder why he'd wanted to know.

THREE

In Scotland, the weather remained bleak enough to stop Cromwell advancing to Fife – which was a huge relief to everyone in Perth. But after General Monck took Tantallon Castle, the persuasions which the King had addressed to ministers in Aberdeen and elsewhere finally began to bear fruit. General Middleton went on a massive recruiting drive ... and the trickle of Engagers turning up to take their turn on the stool of repentance suddenly became a flood.

The Scots Parliament assembled on March 13th. By the end of the month, a new committee had been appointed to manage the army and the King had graciously been given permission to command it. The northern clans who'd fought under Montrose – scandalously executed the previous May – were no longer prohibited from serving and the thorny question of repealing the Act of Classes was broached, if not completely resolved. All in all, remarked Francis to Nicholas Austin, it began to look as if His Majesty might get his invasion force after all.

Meanwhile, although Monck repeated the triumph of Tantallon at Blackness Castle, a combination of inhospitable spring weather and Cromwell's rumoured ill-health prevented the English from finishing what they had started and gave the Scots time to prepare. Throughout April, Major Langley and Captain Austin drilled daily with their men – and, by the beginning of May, had progressed to testing their skills in a series of surprise raids on the English lines.

It was after one such skirmish that Francis, en route for a tub of hot water and some clean clothes, walked slap into the last person he'd expected to see.

'My God,' remarked Colonel Peverell, looking him over with gentle astonishment. 'Have you been *working?*'

'Merely relieving one of Noll's outposts of its colours and a field-piece. And we can't *all* spend our time riding about paying house-calls.'

Ashley spared a thought for the two corpses he'd left rotting in a Limerick bog but said merely, 'Jealous? Don't be. It's not nearly as much fun as you might think. And I was about to offer to buy you a drink.'

'After last time,' drawled Francis, 'I'm not sure that's good idea.'

He was bluffing, of course. Even his urgent desire for a bath wasn't enough to make him pass up the chance to hear whatever information Colonel Peverell's travels might have made him privy to. So he allowed himself to be led to the nearest tavern and, when the pot-boy had served them with ale, said lightly, 'Very well. I'm listening. What have you been up to these last three months?'

'Putting my ear to the ground,' came the laconic reply. 'I also met Captain Titus on his way back with the Queen's views on the Campbell marriage. And – whilst not questioning Lady Anne's eligibility – Her Majesty feels that her son shouldn't marry at all without first consulting his loyal English subjects.'

'Very tactful. She must have changed substantially since I last met her.'

'Yes. Well, she's learned a few hard lessons in recent years. And though they won't stop her trying to do the King's breathing for him, they may remind her to hold her tongue when he refuses to let her.'

'We can but hope.' Francis was well-aware that the Queen's besetting sin was a tendency to shout her grievances from the highest roof-top. But because he was also aware that Colonel Peverell had avoided answering his original question, he said, 'You've been to Paris, then?'

'Briefly.' Ashley re-filled his cup and grinned. 'The Théâtre du Marais has a new attraction. A delectable little red-head, who – judging by the reaction of the male half of the audience – won't be playing bit-parts for long.'

'Fascinating.' Francis crossed one leg over the other and refused to be diverted. 'You're not very forthcoming, are you?'

'No.' The gold-flecked green eyes looked back austerely. 'I find that I – and others – live longer that way.'

'Ah. Cloak-and-dagger stuff again.'

'That's one way of putting it.'

'I see.' Francis decided it was time to put Colonel Peverell straight on a few things. He said, 'You're not the only one to do this kind of work, you know. In the summer of '47, I took letters from the Queen to various loyal gentlemen in the midlands and north.' He smiled reminiscently. 'I delivered them, too – though it was touch and go at one stage and I was forced to spend three extremely uncomfortable nights in a Knaresborough cellar.'

The Colonel's gaze sharpened.

'Not ... *not* underneath the Widow Jessop's shop?'

Francis sat up.

'How do you know that?'

'It was my network.'

'*Yours?*'

'Yes. I set it up and kept it functioning. The only thing I don't understand is how you passed through it without my knowledge.' He stopped and then said slowly, 'Or no. Perhaps I do. Did Venetia Clifford have a hand in it, by any chance?'

Francis's eyes widened.

'Yes. You know her?'

'I used to. She was betrothed to Ellis Brandon but married his half-brother instead.' Ashley's smile was tinged with acid. 'Aside from the fact that the other fellow was a Colonel in the New Model, it could only have been a change for the better.'

'It was certainly better for me,' agreed Francis, leaning back again and re-crossing his legs. 'I won't bore you with the details, but – if it weren't for Gabriel Brandon, I'd probably still be languishing in the Tower right now. He's a decent fellow.'

'I know. I met him once.' Colonel Peverell laughed. 'But that's another story.'

'And Ellis?'

'Ellis,' replied Ashley flatly, 'thought himself suited to what you call 'cloak-and-dagger' stuff. In reality, he was a damned liability. He and those like him are the reason I don't talk about what I do.'

'Which brings us neatly back to the beginning of this conversation,' observed Francis. And, holding up one hand, 'I'm not asking for state secrets. But giving me a general picture of how matters stand in England wouldn't be any risk to your neck, would it?'

There was a brief silence. Then, on a faint explosion of breath, Ashley said, 'Very well. That far but no further. The truth is that the government is extremely nervous and damnably efficient. A good many of our friends have recently been arrested and a ban on race-meetings is making it difficult for those still at liberty to continue to meet in any numbers. Sir Henry Hyde was executed in March for seeking help from the Sultan of Turkey. John Birkenhead – one-time editor of *Mercurius Aulicus* but now a rather useful agent – was captured and his papers seized by the Council of State. These led to the arrest of Thomas Coke – who will by now have offered every name he knows in the hope of saving his skin.' He paused, then added flatly, 'And the results of that could be cataclysmic.'

'I see.' Frowning slightly, Francis looked up from his tankard. 'It's not very encouraging, is it? And ill-timed, too, since the army here is shaping up so well. Nick and I were beginning to look forward to a small invasion.'

'Well, since this is probably the best chance Charles will ever have of mounting *any* kind of invasion, we may as well go *on* looking forward to it.'

'Thank you. Did you say we?'

'Unless my dubious talents are required elsewhere, yes. If there's the smallest chance of Charles regaining his throne, I want to be there to see it.' The mobile mouth twisted wryly. 'Then again ... for the likes of us, what else is there?'

'Delectable red-haired actresses?' asked Francis, grinning. 'Of whom you may now tell me every luscious detail.'

* * *

In the month that followed, Argyll returned but still refused to speak to Hamilton; the army established itself in a strong position at Stirling; and a good many people spent a lot of time inspecting defences and discussing strategy. Colonel Peverell was not despatched on any further missions ... and in due course, Major Langley and Captain Austin learned that he had been given command of their own regiment.

'Christ,' breathed Nicholas feebly. 'Whose idea was that?'

'Mine,' returned the Colonel. 'I thought you deserved an officer who understands you. But perhaps you dislike the idea?'

'Not at all,' sighed Francis. 'Only think what a happy family we shall be.'

'Quite,' grinned Ashley. 'Only think.'

* * *

On May 29th, the King's twenty-first birthday was celebrated with bells, bonfires and salvoes of artillery. Four days later, Charles received precisely the gift he wanted when the Act of Classes was finally repealed, allowing the Engagers to return openly ... and, within a week, it was being enthusiastically reported that *'the King's power is absolute, all factions composed and the army cheerful, accomplished and numerous'*.

It wasn't, as Ashley remarked, strictly true; but it did a lot for everyone's *joie-de-vivre*.

* * *

By the end of June, the situation was promising enough to make General Leslie agree with the King's determination to advance and the army marched to Torwood in the hills south of Sterling. The result was that Cromwell spent the next fortnight attempting to bring them to battle; and Major Langley discovered why Nicholas had turned pale at the prospect of having Ashley Peverell as their Colonel.

The problem, quite simply, was one of keeping up. He was never still, blindingly capable and had eyes in the back of his head. At the end of a week, Francis came to the conclusion that it was not unlike serving under Prince Rupert; at the end of two, he decided that it was actually much worse; and, after three, respect was becoming tarnished with the natural aggravation born of dealing with perfection on a daily basis. Then, just as Francis's temper began to fray, the business at Inverkeithing changed everything.

It began on July 17th when Cromwell shipped a couple of thousand men across the Forth at Queensferry to cut the Scots off from their supplies in Stirling. Colonel Peverell urged an immediate attack. General Leslie dismissed the notion and, instead, sent some four thousand men under Sir John Brown to stem the tide. Two days later, scouts reported that the English had been reinforced by a further two thousand men commanded by Major-General Lambert ... and this time Ashley asked Leslie for permission to personally assist Brown but was met with a flat refusal. He was still arguing when Lambert engaged Brown at Inverkeithing and wiped the floor with him. And that was when Francis saw the paragon hurl a number of accurate but unforgivable accusations at General Leslie's head and lose his temper so thoroughly that he had to be physically removed.

Shown unceremoniously back to his quarters, with orders to stay there, Colonel Peverell flung his hat across the room and himself into a chair. Then, fixing his Major with a wild, green stare he said, 'Bloody buggering hell! Has he any sodding idea what he's doing? He's supposed to be a General, for Christ's sake! Is he going to sit on his arse through the entire campaign, leaving his men to be needlessly butchered? Does the stupid bastard intend to fight at *all* – or is he just along for the ride? Because if he is …. if he *is*, I for one would sooner be court-martialled than follow his fucking orders!'

Francis waited until the tirade ground to a halt and then said reflectively, 'How fortunate we're not in England. By my calculations, that speech would have cost you more than you have in your pockets.' Then, when all he got was another smouldering glance, 'All right. By all means, let's wallow. Then you can take a deep breath and consider the fact that General Leslie is unlikely to forgive you.'

Shrugging, Ashley described tersely and in the vernacular, what General Leslie might do with himself.

'An interesting idea – but scarcely conducive to Anglo-Scottish harmony.'

'Tell that to the poor devils who died today – most of them needlessly, I might add.'

'Point taken. But will creating ill-feeling throughout the army bring them back? And are all our efforts and His Majesty's prospects to be buried with them?'

There was a long silence while the latent fury gradually faded from Ashley's face. Then, shutting his eyes and letting his head drop back against his chair, he said tonelessly, 'Hell. You'd better find me a sheet of paper.'

It was unexpected.

'Paper? Why?'

'Why do you think?' His eyes opened again, their expression bitterly ironic. 'I'll have to swallow my bile and apologise. And since Leslie won't receive me, I'm going to have to write him a damned love-letter.'

FOUR

Thanks to some tactful intervention by the King, General Leslie was eventually persuaded to accept Colonel Peverell's apology and allow him to return to duty. This was just as well for, during the week that followed, Cromwell started moving slowly and circuitously northwards, taking Inchgarvie and Burntisland. And that, as everyone in the Royalist camp was well-aware, gave them a choice between turning back to defend Perth or letting it fall while they marched south.

As far as Charles was concerned, there was only one answer to this question and, on July 30th, he finally forced General Leslie to accept it. Argyll (who couldn't accept it at all) promptly went off in a huff again – causing Hamilton to remark that all the rogues had now left them. And Charles swept into the billet shared by Ashley, Francis and Nicholas saying, 'I've done it. We march for Carlisle tomorrow.'

Nicholas's grin threatened to split his face.

'Oh well done, Sir – well done indeed! *Now* we'll show them! Just wait till I tell the men.' He paused on his way to the door. 'I can tell them, can't I?'

'By all means.' Smiling a little, the King stepped aside to let him pass. Then, looking at Colonel Peverell, 'Well, Ash? *Will* we show them?'

'I hope so, Sir. We'll certainly do our best.'

'I know,' returned Charles. 'If I didn't, we'd be heading for Perth instead. Or then again – perhaps not. This opportunity may not come again and they say that the secret of success lies in seizing the hour.' The smile returned, albeit sardonically. 'I just hope the hour I'm seizing isn't the wrong one.'

When he had gone, Francis murmured meditatively, 'So this is it, then. The day we've all been waiting for.'

'Bring on the drums and trumpets.'

'How long before Cromwell sets out after us?'

'Three or four days, perhaps. Without reinforcements, Perth will fall like a ripe plum. But it isn't only Cromwell we have to worry about,' said Ashley a trifle grimly. 'It's Lilburne and Harrison in the north and hostile local militia just about everywhere else. It's the difficulty of recruiting along the way without wasting time – and the four hundred miles lying between us and London.' He paused briefly. 'If anyone thinks this is going to be fun, they're deluding themselves.'

* * *

They crossed the border on August 6th with sixteen thousand men and reached Carlisle three days later. They were not made welcome. Meanwhile, the Duke of Buckingham (who had been sulking at not being given a senior command) was sent on ahead with General Massey to do some advance recruiting while, behind them, Cromwell took Perth and set off in apparently leisurely pursuit. Worried by the lack of haste, Colonel Peverell obtained permission to undertake some personal reconnaissance and returned with the sobering news that Lambert was already well on his way to join Harrison with between three and four thousand Horse.

Charles looked up from the map he'd been perusing with Hamilton.

'Where?' he demanded. 'Where will they try to stop us?'

'I can't be sure, Sir – but I'd hazard a guess at somewhere in the region of Preston.' Ashley's mouth curled slightly. 'There's nothing like familiar ground, after all. And they probably hope it will be as lucky for them now as it was in '48.'

He didn't add that they could do with a little luck themselves. He didn't think he needed to.

The dark Stuart eyes rested on him broodingly.

'You were there, weren't you?'

'At Preston? Yes, Sir.'

'And was it luck that gave the New Model their victory?'

Ashley hesitated for a moment, wondering how to answer in a way that was neither discouraging nor untruthful. Then, unable to think of one, he said bluntly, 'No, Sir. It was bad leadership on our side. If Lord Callander had sent even a thousand more men to Sir Marmaduke Langdale, the outcome might have been very different.'

'But he didn't.'

'No.' Ashley stopped again and then, looking the King directly in the eye, said, 'Sir, some generals have a tendency to hold back the reserves until it's too late to use them at all.'

'And Cromwell?'

'Isn't one of them.'

'I see.' Charles restored his attention to the map. 'Thank you.'

* * *

The army resumed its plodding march into England and the Scots grew grumpier with every passing mile. Charles was proclaimed King at Penrith; Kendal and Lancaster fell wearily behind them and Preston, when they got there, proved miraculously free of the enemy. Warrington, on the other hand, did not. Major-Generals Lambert and Harrison lay south of the river with roughly nine thousand Horse.

'Ah well,' said Ashley to his unservile servant. 'I was right about them choosing familiar ground. They'll probably try to hold the bridge against us. But if memory serves me correctly, they may find that difficult.'

Jem Barker spat on the Colonel's breast-plate and polished it with his sleeve.

'How come?'

'According to my information, the bulk of their force is cavalry – and cavalry need open ground. Amidst the hedges and ditches south of Warrington Bridge, there *is* no open ground. Consequently, I doubt they'll be able to hold us.'

'Less of the 'us',' Jem grunted. 'I've told you afore. I give up fighting after Marston Moor and I ain't about to take it up again now. Still ... it's good you've got it all worked out. Busy as a body-louse, ain't you?'

'You know me. No task too large, no detail too small.'

'Maybe so. But you're seeking a hare in a hen's nest this time, Captain. Noticed General Leslie's face, have you? Looks as miserable as a gib-cat, he does.'

'That's his natural expression,' murmured Ashley. 'Jem ... do you *have* to spit on my armour?'

'Being as we ain't got no polish – yes.' Mr Barker set about buckling the back and breast into position. 'I heard as Hamilton said this caper was 'grasp all or lose all'. Wouldn't dice on them odds, myself. And I can't see a fop-doodle like Buckingham bringing good, honest northern lads flocking in, neither.'

Nor could Colonel Peverell but he merely said, 'I'd like to be ready today, if possible.'

'Put your sword on, then,' retorted Jem, stepping back. 'I'm done. Fine as a lord's bastard you look, too. Major Langley'll be using you as a mirror.'

It was the morning of August 16th. Having ascertained the enemy's position, the Royalist army covered the remaining miles to Warrington with increased alertness and arrived at the bridge over the Mersey in time to see Lambert and Harrison pulling their troops back to guard the London road rather than engage over unfavourable ground.

Colonel Peverell watched appreciatively for a time and then, finding the King beside him, said blandly, 'Such a nice, orderly retreat. Do I have permission to spoil it a bit?'

Charles smiled.

'More than that, Ash. You have my express *order* to do so. And Leslie can go hang.'

Ashley grinned and, wheeling his horse, threw a series of concise orders to his Major. Fortunately, Francis had been expecting them ... and, in less than five minutes, the regiment was trotting smartly across the bridge in the wake of Lambert's rear-guard.

It was only a brief skirmish and it inflicted little damage. It did, however, clear a path for the advancing Royalists and its effect on morale was enormous. By evening, even the dourest Scots were talking about how the New Model had fled before them; and Ashley's own men – having fought their first action under his leadership – were as one in deciding that their pernickety Colonel might be a rattling good fellow after all.

* * *

It was the first and only moment of encouragement. Despite all the King's high hopes, the Lancashire Royalists did not flock to his banner as he moved on south and no Catholics appeared at all. This was a bitter blow. Charles had known that his English supporters might be reluctant to join with the Covenanters but he had counted on using his personal presence to sway them. What he *hadn't* bargained for was that the Royalist leaders who hadn't compounded for their estates were mostly in prison ... or that when General Massey left to go recruiting again, he took with him a declaration from the ministers of the Kirk, telling the Presbyterians not to associate with the Malignants. The result was that the Cavaliers stayed offendedly at home and recruits only arrived by the handful.

Leaving the volatile Earl of Derby to use his local influence to mend matters, Charles decided to march on by way of Whitchurch and the Welsh borders in the hope of finding more support there than he had in the north. Once more, he was disappointed. When he sent the Governor of Shrewsbury a cordial summons to surrender, he received a curt refusal addressed to *'The Commander-in-Chief of the Scottish Army'*. Gloom descended once more on the weary, travel-stained army; and Colonel Peverell found maintaining his customary *éclat* required a good deal of well-concealed effort.

Sometimes, when fatigue and anxiety regarding the current situation started to weigh more heavily than usual, Ashley strove to restore his mental balance by letting himself drift briefly into a memory. Anything would do so long as it was far removed from the all-too-frequent responsibility he bore for the lives of men ... both the ones he did his damnedest to save in battle and the ones he'd occasionally been required to snuff out in secret. The latter had a nasty habit of crawling wraith-like from the shadows of his mind when he tried to snatch a couple of hours sleep. And when telling himself that he'd never killed anyone he hadn't had to didn't banish them, he summoned brighter times to push them back into the dark.

It was a well-practised trick and one that generally served him well. Unfortunately – and for no good reason that he could think of – when he employed it these days the image that came to mind was always the same. The image of a slender, red-haired girl in a blue gown, illuminated by a dozen candles. In one sense, this was highly enjoyable. In another, it was bloody aggravating – because indulging in mildly erotic fantasies whilst sharing quarters with Francis and Nicholas was not just ridiculous but potentially downright embarrassing.

So he gritted his teeth, shoved Athenais de Galzain back with the other spectres ... and lay open-eyed, staring into the dark.

* * *

Lichfield and Wolverhampton fell gradually away behind them ... then Kidderminster and Hartlebury. And on Friday August 22nd, having marched three hundred miles in three weeks, they arrived at the gates of the one place they felt might actually welcome them. Worcester; the first city to declare for Charles 1 and one of the last to surrender. A jewel set between the Severn and the Teme, backed by the Malvern hills … and known, proudly, as the Loyal City.

It was a place Ashley Peverell knew very well indeed. For the truth – which not even Jem Barker knew – was that his home lay not a dozen miles distant.

He hadn't been near it since the day, shortly after Naseby, when – with their father scarcely cold upstairs – his elder brother had calmly announced that he was turning his coat to the winning side before they lost everything. There had been a monumental row and Ashley had left before the funeral. That had grieved him – but, at the time, it had seemed better than watching James lick the Parliament's boots and overturn everything their father had stood for.

Worse was to come. When he went back a few weeks later, ready to apologise for his loss of temper and to suggest that he and James could somehow manage their differences with a degree of civility, it was to discover that the girl to whom he had given his heart – and who he'd believed had given hers to him – had decided a baronet with a tidy estate would suit her better than a virtually penniless younger son. In short, she'd married his brother.

Now, however, was no time to think of that. Although people were flooding out to greet them, there were still all the usual formalities to be gone through and the matter of Parliament's small garrison to be dealt with before the army could enter the city – all of which probably amounted to a minor action, followed by yet another night under canvas. And that, when one was responsible for tired, dispirited troopers whose clothes were in ruins and some of whom lacked shoes, was all that should concern one.

Sufficient to the day, Ashley told himself firmly as he formed the freshest of his men into an advance party. But as he entered the city, he still couldn't help hoping that he didn't meet anyone who knew him.

He didn't. And, aided by droves of enthusiastic citizens, ejecting Lambert's five hundred men proved a relatively simple matter. Watching them ride hell for leather in the direction of Gloucester,

Ashley was aware that he ought to order some sort of pursuit. Unfortunately, he also knew that his fellows didn't have the energy.

On the following morning, the army finally filed into the city behind their King. The populace was out in force, cheering wildly. And though Charles's buff-coat and scarlet silk sash were no longer quite as pristine as when they had left Stirling, he still presented a brave figure, sitting straight in the saddle, smiling his lazily intimate smile and allowing his hand to be grasped and kissed. He looked, remarked Francis, every inch the romantic young Prince, come to claim his kingdom. And it was to be hoped that the impression bore fruit.

Received by Mayor Lysons and Sheriff Brydges, Charles was ceremoniously conducted to the Guildhall where he was proclaimed King of Great Britain, France and Ireland and offered the keys of his 'ancient and loyal city' of Worcester. To complete the drama, His Majesty promptly knighted the Mayor ... before asking the city officials what they could do for his poor, foot-sore soldiers.

They did what they could. They scoured the city for shoes and stockings and made public buildings available for the great number of soldiers who could not be accommodated elsewhere. By nightfall, Ashley and Francis had managed to billet their men and find stabling for the horses. It was all make-shift, of course, but it was better than another night on the road – and at least there was hot food to be had. Beyond that, it wasn't possible to look.

Before they fell asleep, Francis said, 'It must be about a hundred miles to London from here.'

'About that,' agreed Ashley.

'And Cromwell and Lambert and the rest are presumably hot on our heels by now.'

'I think you can rely on that.'

'And yet we're lingering here to rest the men.'

Ashley said nothing and there was a long silence.

'Dear me,' remarked Francis, with restrained foreboding. 'It's beginning to sound just like Colchester.'

* * *

The next day being Sunday, was partly taken up with a glowingly Royalist sermon delivered by the Reverend Crosby from the cathedral pulpit. After that, notices went out calling every man between sixteen and sixty to join His Majesty at the Pitchcroft on Tuesday; and, in the meantime, parish constables were ordered to start repairing the city's crumbling, half-demolished walls.

'Hell's teeth!' grumbled Nicholas. 'Don't tell me we're *staying?*'

Having spent the last two hours at a Council of War, Colonel Peverell was in no mood for lengthy discussion. He said crisply, 'We have to make a stand somewhere. And how much further do you think we'll get?'

'I don't know. But *here?* It would take months to make this place secure.'

'Not necessarily. Its natural defences are excellent. Or at least, they will be by the time we've blown up the bridges at Bewdley, Upton, Powick and Bransford. And we're not planning on withstanding a siege.'

'Now that,' observed Francis, '*is* good news. But if we stay long enough for Cromwell's cohorts to assemble about us, precisely how are we to avoid one?'

'We face them in the field,' replied Ashley tonelessly.

'Ah. And beat them from our path, no doubt?'

'Yes.'

Sardonic blue eyes met expressionless green ones.

Nicholas looked from one to the other of them and then, drawing a long breath, said with creditable lightness, 'Oh. Well, I suppose that's all right, then.'

FIVE

On Monday morning, engineers took parties of men out to blow up the bridges over the Severn and the Teme and work started on the city's defences. On Tuesday, the army's senior officers accompanied the King to the rendezvous at the Pitchcroft and found themselves barely outnumbered by the Worcestershire Royalists who attended it. And on Wednesday, leaving Francis to send out scouting parties and collate their various reports, Ashley Peverell put the cause he served before his natural repugnance and rode the twelve miles to Milcombe Park.

It was a neat, moderate-sized estate and the land looked well-tended. That, of course, was no surprise. While Ashley and their father had gone off to fight for the King, James had stayed behind watching over the family acres – less, Ashley had often thought, because he loved them than because they saved him risking his neck and represented his inheritance. But though James had wished the King well at first, the reverses following Marston Moor had changed his view. Consequently, for the last year of their father's life, the house – on the rare occasions when they had all been in it together – had been a battle-ground.

The house. As if on cue, it came into view through the trees … a modest, stone-built manor peering over a low curtain wall and possessed, it appeared, of an elegant new wing. Ashley paused for a moment, staring at large mullioned windows topped by the family's heraldic device of a griffin; and then, with an ironic grin, he nudged his horse into motion again.

The maid who opened the door was a stranger. Ashley melted her with a smile and managed, without giving his name, to get her to go in search of Sir James. The room she left him in was one of the new ones. Ashley looked at the collection of books growing along one wall and wondered where the money was coming from. Then the door opened and his brother walked in.

Recognition of his visitor stopped Sir James Peverell dead and temporarily deprived him of breath. For perhaps half a minute, the two men faced each other in silence; one tall and lithe, his hair bleached by the sun and his skin lightly tanned … the other, darker and slightly

48

shorter and already putting on flesh. There were only two years between them. To a casual observer, it looked more like ten.

Finally, his voice clipped and wary, James said, 'I suppose I should have expected this as soon as I heard that Charles Stuart is in Worcester. Doubtless you're still indulging in pointless heroics?'

'I'm still fighting for my King,' agreed Ashley with gentle emphasis. 'Each to his own, you know. And I haven't your passion for architecture and literature.' He glanced around at the books. 'Read them all, have you?'

James's mouth tightened. He was no great reader and his brother knew it. He said repressively, 'They are an investment. And my sons will read them one day.' He paused and then, with a hint of awkwardness, added, 'Elizabeth and I are blessed with two healthy boys.'

Ashley's eyes remained expressionless.

'My congratulations. Lizzie is well, I take it?'

'Never better.'

'And Jenny?'

James hesitated before saying curtly, 'She's well enough. About to be betrothed. Young Cotterell, you know.'

Ashley didn't know but was confident that their young sister wouldn't marry anyone she didn't want to. He said slowly, 'She never replied to my letters.'

'Her choice,' came the bald reply. Then, quickly, 'Why are you here? Not, I presume, merely to ask after everyone's health?'

'Not entirely, no.'

'Then perhaps you could get to the point.'

Ashley smothered a sigh. It wasn't going well – and coming to the point at this stage wasn't likely to make it any better. On the other hand, the longer he put it off, the more chance there was that he'd be provoked into saying something unfortunate ... not because he couldn't lie and smile with the best but because he and James had an unfailing knack of getting under each other's skin.

Shrugging slightly, he said, 'Very well. But do you think we might sit down? Or are you overwhelmingly eager to be rid of me?'

A vestige of colour touched James's face and he said stiffly, 'I don't care either way. Sit, if you wish. Would you like me to send for wine?'

'No, no.' Ashley dropped into a chair by the empty hearth. 'I wouldn't want to put you to any trouble. And it would probably take more than you have in your cellar to mend our differences.'

'If you're still bearing a grudge against me for marrying Elizabeth --'

'I don't bear grudges, James.' Ashley impaled him on a very direct stare. 'And I haven't come here to quarrel with you – about Lizzie or anything else. I said what I had to say at our last meeting – as did you. But we are left with the inescapable fact that we're poles apart. What I call a principle, you call stupidity; and where I see something worth fighting for, you see only a lost cause. You don't care for having a brother flirting with the Council of State's black-list – and I can't reconcile myself to having one who's a trimmer. In short, the only thing we have in common is a desire not to be tarred with the same brush.'

'True.' James sat down, crossing one leg tidily over the other. 'I'm glad we understand each other that well at least. So what do you want?'

'My inheritance,' said Ashley simply. And, when his brother's hands clenched on the carved arms of his chair, 'It's all right. There's no need to have an apoplexy. I'm not asking for money. I don't even want a hundred acres and a cow. But I feel fairly sure that Father's will must have made provision for me … and I want to claim some form of it now. What you might call a once-and-for-all payment.'

'So what,' asked James slowly, 'did you have in mind?'

'Father's collection of firearms.'

'*What?*'

'You heard me. He had over thirty different pieces, as I recall. I also want all the pistols and muskets you reclaimed from the troop he raised for the King, along with every bag of shot and barrel of powder that we amassed in the event of Milcombe ever being besieged.' Ashley leaned back and smiled. 'I'm sure you still have it all. You're not the man to dispose of things without turning a coin on the transaction. But the New Model has its own suppliers … and selling arms to the side you'd just deserted would have been a bit tricky, wouldn't it?'

'I was never actively Royalist,' snapped James. 'I never fought.'

'I know. But that's something best not discussed, don't you think? And it's beside the point, anyway. We were talking about arms and ammunition.'

'*You* were. I was wondering at your colossal nerve.'

'I'm sure you were.' Once again, the barb was delicately placed. 'Let's put it this way. So long as my way of life continues to be an embarrassment to you, you would prefer me to remain both distant and discreet.'

'*Discreet?* You've *never* been discreet!'

'No? Think about it. You haven't seen or heard from me in six years. Not, if you will excuse me from pointing it out, since I came back waving an olive branch and found you had married Lizzie.'

'Elizabeth was free to make her choice,' came the swift, defensive reply. 'There was no contract between the two of you.'

'No *formal* contract, perhaps.' Ashley's smile was hard-edged and controlled. 'However, it hardly signifies now. As to the matter of my discretion ... have the authorities ever been here asking about me?'

James hunched one shoulder. 'No. What of it?'

'Simply that, if I were as careless as you imply, you'd have had Thomas Scot camping on your doorstep,' returned Ashley smoothly. And then, when his brother looked blank, 'He runs the intelligence service – rather efficiently, too. I don't think you'd like him as a house-guest.'

This time the point hit home and James erupted from his chair.

'Are you threatening me?'

'Not at all. I'm merely pointing out how much worse things might be.' Ashley also rose and held the furious grey gaze with a cool one of his own. 'And now perhaps we can return to the business which brought me here?'

'Blackmailing me into supplying arms to Charles Stuart's Scotch army?'

'Granting me the only thing I've ever asked of you.'

'Don't split hairs! If I was caught assisting the invasion --'

'You won't be. Just load the things I've asked for on to a cart, cover it with canvas and let me drive it away. You have my word that no one will ever know where it came from.' Ashley paused and then added dryly, 'A miniature arsenal is no use to you, James ... but at this precise moment in time, it would mean a great deal to me. And in return for it, I'm prepared to disappear for good.'

'That's generous of you,' mocked James. 'Your precious army must be very badly equipped.'

'It could certainly be better. Are you going to let me have the things I asked for ... or shall we return to the subject of my letters to Jenny so you can admit that she never had them. For she didn't, did she?'

'I don't know what --'

'Yes, you do – just as *I* always know when you're lying.' Ashley waited and, when no reply was forthcoming, added blightingly, 'Adding spite to stupidity, James? Since you presumably read the letters, you knew that there was no reason to with-hold them other than your determination to take anything that was mine – including Jenny's affection.'

'That's not true! I never did so. And you can't--'

'I think,' said Ashley softly, 'you would be ill-advised to predict what I can and cannot do. I also think that, if you want to be rid of me as quickly as possible, you will give me what I asked for.'

The message was perfectly clear. James's hands clenched at his sides and he wished he could smash one of them into his brother's face. Ashley's expression told him that this would be a mistake. Seething, he drew a long painful breath and said curtly, 'Very well. Wait here while I see to it. I don't want you --'

'To advertise my presence unnecessarily? I think you've made that abundantly clear.' Ashley dropped back into a chair. 'In which case, I imagine I can rely on you not taking all day over it.'

James cast him a glance of acute dislike and stamped from the room, shutting the door with a distinct snap.

Ashley gazed around him at the impressive array of books, the carved panelling and the expensive furniture. His mouth curled wryly. Whatever income his father had left him was plainly going to come in very useful if James intended to continue spending at this rate. Then the door opened again, just a little way, and a pair of wide blue eyes examined him around it. Ashley's stomach tightened and he stood up.

Elizabeth slid around the door and stood, leaning against it. She said breathlessly, 'Ashley. I thought … from what the maid said, I guessed … but I had to be sure.'

'That the black-sheep had returned?' He managed something that was almost a smile. 'And now that you know, you may scurry away again.'

'Why should I do that?'

'Oh – I don't know. Perhaps because we have nothing to say to one another? After all, you successfully avoiding speaking to me at all on the occasion of my last ill-timed visit … so there can be nothing worth adding now.' He folded his arms and conducted a leisurely – and somehow faintly insulting – appraisal. The honey-brown hair was the same, as were the long-lashed eyes. But the girlish angles had been replaced with lush, womanly curves and her expression held a hint of restlessness. He said, 'That is a very … decorative … gown, Lizzie. Were you going somewhere?'

'No.' She'd changed into it specially but didn't want him to know that. Nervously fingering the profusion of trimming on her bodice, she said abruptly, 'Don't call me Lizzie. No one does that now.'

'As you wish, my lady.' He made an extravagant bow. 'So – aside from satisfying your ladyship's curiosity – did your ladyship want anything else?'

'Don't! I didn't mean that. You know I didn't.'

'I'm not sure I know you at all … or indeed that I ever did.'

He continued to contemplate her, unable to define his feelings. He hadn't expected to see her or to care whether or not he did. It had been six years, after all and the twenty-four year-old he'd been then was now a different person. The hurt he'd felt at the time had long since faded into shadow. And yet, looking at her now, he remembered how much he'd believed he loved her; remembered how sure he'd been that she felt the same; and remembered how, returning to find her married to his brother without either warning or a word of explanation, had left him feeling as though something had been ripped from his chest. It was a recollection. No more than that … but he didn't want it. He said, 'What do you want with me, Elizabeth?'

'I don't know. I just ...' She shrugged helplessly. 'I suppose I thought I should ... perhaps I should explain.'

'It's a little late for that, don't you think? And unnecessary. You chose James because, having inherited the title and the land, he was a better prospect than myself. We won't go into why he asked you. And clearly,' he gestured vaguely to the room, 'you are happy with your choice.'

Suddenly wanting to deny what he'd said but unable, under his cool, implacable gaze, to find the words, she blurted, 'Are you married?'

'No.' A pause. And then, on a note of mocking amusement, 'Oh dear. You're not thinking I've remained unwed on your account?'

'No. My goodness – of course not!'

One raised brow suggested that he didn't entirely believe her but he said merely, 'What, then?'

Elizabeth found herself at a loss again. What she thought was that he still looked exactly the same. A little harder, perhaps – his muscles more clearly defined; but still as tall and lithe and wildly attractive as he'd always been. Long tawny hair lay in careless waves on broad shoulders; dark green eyes, flecked with gold were set between ridiculously long lashes; and the chiselled planes and angles of his face were nothing short of breath-taking. She forced herself to swallow. He was sinfully beautiful and possessed of an indefinable air of danger that was as alluring as it was exciting. And she had thrown him away in favour of money and status ... and James. James who came to her bed twice every week on exactly the same days and made love to her in exactly the same tediously unimaginative way that frequently made her want to scream. She suspected that if Ashley made a woman scream, it would be for other reasons entirely.

The idea made heat rise to her cheeks and she said quickly, 'I suppose you're in Worcester with Charles Stuart?'

'I'm in Worcester with His Majesty King Charles the Second,' he corrected coolly, 'and it's time I completed my business with James and returned there.' He made an unsmiling but perfectly correct bow and said, 'It's been fun, my dear. We must do it again some time. But for now, you needn't bother to show me out. I know the way.'

Five minutes later, Ashley strode out into the courtyard, his face utterly bleak. He found his brother behind the stables, fastening down a loaded cart; and, without troubling to mention Elizabeth, he said, 'Are you done here?'

'Yes.' James arose from his task and looked back with open dislike. 'You'll find everything you asked for. But if anyone learns where it came from, I'll do my best to see you hanged.'

'You wouldn't be the first one to try.' Ashley tethered his horse to the back of the cart. 'Since it would be a waste of breath, I won't ask you to give Jenny my love – or to suggest you try to be less of a horse's arse in future.'

'Just get the hell away from here,' snapped James through clenched teeth. 'I'd prefer never to lay eyes on you again.'

'My God. A point of agreement at last.' Swinging himself up on to the driving seat, Ashley glanced down and said, 'Goodbye, brother. I won't say it's been a pleasure. But at least the time hasn't been entirely wasted.' And, setting the horse in motion, he drove through the gate and away out of sight.

* * *

Having spent the remainder of the day lurking in a copse near Milcombe, Ashley brought his booty into Worcester under cover of darkness and disposed of it in the appropriate quarter where it was gratefully received. Then he made his way back to his billet.

Francis was there, poring over a map but he looked up as the door opened and said, 'Ah. So there you are. I hope you've had an enjoyable day?'

'Not especially.' Ashley dropped into a settle by the fire. 'You?'

'Likewise.' Francis straightened and surveyed him unsmilingly. 'Cromwell has combined with Lambert, Harrison, Fleetwood and Desborough. He is now at Evesham with roughly thirty thousand men and more coming in every minute. He is also, according to the latest reports, showing signs of splitting his forces.'

Ashley shut his eyes. 'Between where?'

'The London road and the area to our west around Upton.' There was a long pause. Then, 'May I ask where the *hell* you've been all day?'

'Collecting supplies. Has my absence been a problem?'

'No – but it could have been.' For once, Francis's voice was stripped of its habitual languor. 'To put it bluntly, I've a particular aversion to vanishing commanders – for which you may thank Lord Norwich. Consequently, I would appreciate it if you could either leave the secret missions to others or at least have the decency to keep me informed of your whereabouts.'

Intense irritation informed Colonel Peverell's gaze but he said merely, 'I'll bear it in mind. Have you reported your findings to His Majesty?'

'Naturally. I left him conferring with Hamilton, Middleton and Leslie at the Commandery.'

Ashley nodded, relieved that he wouldn't have to take care of the matter himself. It had been a long day and his mind was still awash with thoughts he didn't want. He hoped a night's sleep would clear them away. He said, 'Have the bridges been blown?'

'Yes.' Francis experienced a rare flash of intuition and his brief gust of temper evaporated. Turning away in search of the ale-jug, he said, 'I gather something is on your mind.'

'Nothing of any consequence,' shrugged Ashley. And, with a grin, 'You'd better take care, you know. We may be living in one another's pockets – but we're not married.'

'God forbid.' Francis passed him a cup of ale. 'I prefer redheads.'

'I know. My meagre description of Mademoiselle de Galzain --'

'Meagre? I seem to recall you dwelling on her charms in some detail.'

'—had you salivating,' finished Ashley, undisturbed.

'Had us *both* salivating,' corrected Francis. And, with a smile, 'I take it we're changing the subject?'

'I was under the impression that you'd already done so.'

Francis raised faintly quizzical brows. Before he could speak, however, the door opened and Nicholas came in.

Ashley murmured, 'Another wanderer returns ... hopefully having ordered us some supper.'

'Supper?' echoed Nicholas absently. 'Oh – no. Sorry. I didn't think of it.'

The Major and the Colonel exchanged glances. Despite being built like a whippet, Nick's appetite was legendary.

Francis drawled, 'Dear me. You must be ailing.'

'No. I never felt better in my life.'

'In that case,' stated Ashley, 'it must be a girl.'

Nicholas flushed and said crossly, 'Well, as it happens, I *did* meet a girl. But it's not at all what you think.'

'That's a very rash assumption,' observed Francis. 'How do you know what we're thinking?'

'Because it never varies. The only things you two care about are whether or not a girl is pretty and available. Mostly the latter.'

'He's got us there,' said Ashley to Francis. And to Nicholas, 'So I take it the young lady wouldn't meet the banal but high standards so beloved of Francis and myself?'

'Probably not. But that's beside the point. Her looks have nothing to do with it.'

Francis yawned. 'I'm afraid you've lost me.'

'Naturally.'

His voice laced with laughter, Ashley said, 'You mustn't be too hard on us, you know. We're just common soldiers with the usual low tastes. Well, I am, anyway,' he added as Francis sat up again. 'So tell us, Nick. If the lady's looks have nothing to do with your interest in her ... what has?'

'Well, she – she seemed unhappy,' responded Nicholas reluctantly. 'Frightened to go home and frightened not to. And she was such a little slip of a thing – no more than seventeen, I'll swear.' He paused and, with a shrug, added, 'I don't know why ... but I got the impression that someone bullies her.'

There was a long silence. Then, 'I might have known,' breathed Ashley. 'I might have known. You feel sorry for her. With you, what else could it possibly be?'

SIX

Not far away in a half-timbered house on Friar Street, Magistrate Joshua Vincent's seventeen-year-old step-daughter pushed her food about her plate and let the family's talk flow by her. It was odd, she thought, how you could exchange a couple of sentences with a stranger over a packet of spilled embroidery silks and come away feeling that something magical had happened. It wouldn't last, of course. She didn't know the young man's name and was unlikely ever to see him again, since he was clearly what her step-father would call 'one of Charles Stuart's God-cursed Malignants'. So it really wasn't sensible to go on thinking of someone who would probably be hard-pressed to recognise her again.

'Is there summat wrong with the stew, Verity?'

Joshua's rough voice cut across her thoughts.

'N-no, Father. Nothing.'

'Then get on and eat it, girl. There's a good many as'd be glad of what's on your plate.'

'Yes, Father.' Verity bent her glossy dark head over the fricassee and hoped Joshua wouldn't embark on his favourite theme.

Typically, her step-sister made sure that he did so.

'Perhaps Verity isn't very partial to rabbit,' suggested Barbara sweetly, her bright blue gaze travelling to her step-mother. 'No doubt you're both used to better things.'

Six months of marriage to Joshua had still not taught gentle, genteel Sarah Vincent how to deal with the sudden attacks of her step-daughter. She said quickly, 'No. No, indeed. We lived very simply. Particularly after – after my husband died.'

She swallowed, wishing she hadn't mentioned Gerald. It upset her and Joshua didn't like it. The problem was that Gerald Marriott, though poor as the proverbial church mouse, had been a gentleman – whereas rich, self-made Joshua still displayed the speech and manners of the Birmingham ironworks that had been the basis of his fortune.

He had nothing to do with iron now, of course. *Now* he was making money in ways of which Sarah preferred to remain ignorant. A roof over the heads of Verity and herself, plus food on the table was what mattered.

'You say you lived simply?' He scowled her from beneath bushy brows. 'Hand-to-mouth is what *I'd* call it. You've never been as well provided-for as you are now. *And* I've taken your daughter in and treated her as my own.'

'Yes, Joshua. You're very good to us.'

'I'm glad you realise it.' Mollified, Joshua reached for the parsnips and glanced at his daughter. 'Where's Nat tonight?'

Barbara shrugged. 'I don't know. Did you want him particularly?'

'Yes. I've a job needs doing tomorrow – and I've business down at the court house.' He looked back at his wife. 'And that reminds me. It's time a few of your fine friends started inviting us to dine so as Barbara can meet some proper gentlemen. God knows, I've told you over and over again to put on your best gown and go visiting. But do you? Oh no. You just sit here as if you was still in mourning.'

Barbara leaned back in her chair and drawled, 'Perhaps Sarah is ashamed of us.'

'Ashamed?' bellowed Joshua. 'By God, you'd better not be!'

'I'm not,' Sarah protested. 'Of course I'm not.'

'Then you'd best prove it, hadn't you? As soon as the district's free of Scotch rabble – which won't be far off if what I've heard today is true – you can take Barbara and drive out to Milcombe Park and some of the other big houses hereabouts. Pay a few calls and come back with some invitations.'

Sarah nodded, struggling to hide her dismay. Out of the ranks of her former acquaintances, she could count on one hand those who might consider visiting her in Friar Street and could think of no one at all who might invite Joshua to dine.

Gathering up her courage, Verity attempted to change the subject.

'Why do you think the Royalist army will soon be gone, sir?'

'Because Cromwell's at Evesham,' grunted Joshua. And, reflectively picking his teeth, 'If the Scots stay, they'll be caught like rats in a trap – so they'll leave. And good riddance, to 'em. Because if the General's going to thrash 'em, I'd sooner he didn't do it here.'

Something shifted behind Verity's bodice and she wished she hadn't eaten the rabbit.

Barbara sat up again.

'You've gone quite pale, Verity. You can't surely be in sympathy with this stupid invasion. Or can you?'

'No,' she replied quickly. 'No. I just hope there isn't a battle here. That's all.'

But it wasn't all. The Cavalier army was no longer an amorphous body of strangers. She'd met one of them. And that night, she lay in her bed tracing his face over and over in her mind.

It was a thin face with laughing brown eyes set beneath mobile brows. Not a handsome face, perhaps ... but infinitely kind.

She didn't know who he was and never would. But she didn't want him to be thrashed or caught like a rat in a trap, so she laced her fingers together and prayed hard that God would protect him. It wasn't much; but it was better than lying in the dark, wondering if her step-brother would come home drunk again ... and, if he did, whether the bolt on her door was still strong enough to keep him out.

* * *

On the following morning, Joshua Vincent faced his son across the width of his splendid, panelled parlour and gave him his orders for the day.

Pallid and pink-eyed from the previous night's excesses, Nathaniel said unwarily, '*Oxfordshire?*' Then, more carefully, 'Oh God. Does it have to be today?'

'I've just said so, haven't I? Do you think I've got where I am by sitting on my arse and saying tomorrow'll do?'

Nathaniel eyed his bull-necked father with veiled dislike and smothered a yawn.

'Can't you go?'

'No I bloody can't. I've other fish to fry today. A bit of business down at the gaol.'

'Oh.' Nathaniel's mouth curled. There was only one sort of case that interested his father enough to warrant time spent outside the court-room. The sort that didn't arise often and usually only when people had a particular axe to grind. 'A witch?'

Joshua nodded. 'A wench from Rushwick, accused of over-looking the blacksmith's wife and causing a neighbour's cow to sicken. She makes a living with her needle – but there's some as think she's better-off than she ought to be on a bit of sewing.'

Right, thought Nathaniel cynically. Stories from distant parts spoke of witches who flew or changed shape. Here in Worcester they merely stopped hens from laying or curdled the cream. He wondered if his father really believed all this nonsense or whether he enjoyed a witch-trial for other reasons entirely. The last thought caused him to say idly, 'Is she young?'

'No more'n twenty-five. A black-haired, buxom piece with over-bold eyes.'

'Well, that should make it interesting for you. But you'd best have a care, Father.' Nathaniel's teeth gleamed in a malicious smile. 'After all, if she really *is* a witch, she may decide to over-look *you*.'

* * *

The cell in which Deborah Hart was chained stank of damp, fetid straw. She had been there a week, she thought – though it was hard to be sure. She had lost count of how many times the light had come and gone, filtering dimly down from the grating high above her head and enabling her to see the big grey rat which, next to her gaoler, was her most regular visitor. All she was sure of was that her hair was crawling with lice, the second gaoler hadn't put his hand up her skirt since she'd smashed her iron-clad wrist against his face … and the rat was gaining confidence.

To begin with, she'd tried to come up with a way of proving that this whole mess had begun when Tom Barnet, the blacksmith, had put his arm around her while his wife was watching. A small piece of carelessness which was not Deborah's fault but for which Mistress Barnet was making her pay dearly. Tom, so far as she knew, had merely received a clout on the ear with a skillet.

A charge of over-looking was easy to make but difficult to disprove. On the other hand, if that had been all she was accused of, Deborah felt she might have had a reasonable chance of talking her way out of it. Unfortunately, the first whisper of witchcraft tended to bring other accusations flooding in; and before she'd been in the gaol a day, Zachary

Paine had added his mite by swearing that she'd caused his cow to go dry and made his best sow miscarry. All that was needed now, therefore, was for someone to say they'd seen her talking to her cat. Or perhaps, thought Deborah a shade hysterically, it was enough merely to *have* a cat.

She'd been interrogated twice so far – once by the parish constable immediately after he'd arrested her and then again by the sheriff after Zack Paine had finished making his deposition. Neither occasion had resulted in anything worse than repeated questioning and being made to walk round in circles because the constable was convinced that the devil didn't like it. In one sense, this was a relief. In another, it meant that the worst was still to come. Everyone knew what they did to witches and Deborah existed in mortal dread of having those terrible, degrading things done to her. Dying, she often thought, would be preferable. But not – *not* by burning.

It was due, so the gaoler said, to the arrival of the Scottish army that her case had not yet come to court. Deborah gave silent thanks and hoped Charles Stuart stayed forever. Then, on a morning when the town outside her grating was still alive with booted feet and busy voices, the door of her cell opened to reveal a thickset, expensively-dressed man she had never seen before.

For a moment, he bent a beetle-browed stare on her. Then, curtly addressing the gaoler, he said, 'Bring her up. The stench in here'd make a dog vomit.'

Gripped by sudden panic, Deborah clung to her chains and tried to prevent the gaoler unlocking the manacles about her wrists – but to no avail. Weakened and dizzy, she was dragged upstairs to a small guard-room and thrown into the corner. A table stood in the centre of the room and the stranger sat on the edge of it, swinging his foot and trapping her with his eyes.

Joshua Vincent surveyed the woman he'd previously only seen through the grille of her cell door and was glad to see that he'd been right about her. She was young and sturdy and, beneath the grime, her skin looked very white. Worthier meat, he thought, than the two old crones who were all that had previously come his way.

Until the case of Granny Collett, Joshua hadn't known how engrossing the business of witch-finding could be. Now, however, it was one of his main interests. He took care not to examine the reasons for this too carefully. He merely reminded himself that the Bible quite clearly said *'Thou shalt not suffer a witch to live'* – which was something no one could argue with.

He let the silence drag on while he wondered if it would be unwise to dismiss the guard. Then, reluctantly deciding that it probably would, he withdrew the witch-probe from his pocket and laid it gently on the table beside him where the woman could see it.

Deborah had never seen one before but she knew what it was. Her lungs froze and she gazed at it with horrified fascination. Meanwhile, the man said abruptly, 'I'm Magistrate Vincent. Maybe you've heard of me?'

She had – and again experienced that terrifying paralysis. He was the man who'd prosecuted two other women before her. One had drowned during the ducking; the other had been hanged.

Deborah swallowed and tried to pull herself together. The other women had been old and feeble-witted. She was neither. Forcing herself to sound calmer than she was, she said, 'I've heard of you, sir. They say you consider yourself an expert.'

'More than anyone else round here. Worry you, does it?'

'Why should it? If you know something of witchcraft, you'll be able to tell the innocent from the guilty. And I am innocent.'

'I'll decide that.' Her apparent composure would have been annoying if he hadn't been able to see the fear underneath it. He removed his hat, unfastened his cloak and said, 'Start walking.'

Slowly, she obeyed. The gaoler grinned and stepped out of her path. When she had circled the room twice, Joshua said, 'Faster.'

She quickened her pace a little.

Joshua waited until she had circled the room some half-dozen times and then began his questions.

'How long have you lived at Rushwick?'

'Three years, sir. The cottage was my uncle's and I came to live in it when he died.'

'And where was you afore that?'

'All manner of places. My husband was a soldier in the New Model and I travelled with him.'

'Where is he now, then?'

'Dead.'

Joshua frowned. He hadn't bargained for her being a widow. Reminding her to continue walking, he said slyly, 'Did Mistress Barnet do summat to offend you?'

Deborah's nerves tightened but she kept her steps steady.

'Nothing. Indeed, I scarcely know her.'

'Then maybe you were jealous of her. He's a well-set fellow, the smith. And now his wife's laid low with cramps and headaches. Sure you didn't ill-wish her so you could have him?'

'Quite sure. If she's ailing, she should see a doctor. But perhaps she's pretending to be ill to support her accusation against me.'

'And the sow that miscarried? Was that pretending?'

After a week of privation, the walking and talking was making her dizzy. She said, 'I know nothing of that – nor the cow that went dry. Neither can I think why Mr Paine should suppose I'd want to do him an ill turn.'

That wasn't strictly true but she wasn't sure it was a good idea to admit having to fend off Zack Paine's attentions as well as those of Tom Barnet. The magistrate would probably say she'd bewitched both of them.

Joshua fell silent for a time, noting how flushed she was becoming and making sure that she saw his hand resting on the wicked-looking probe. Then he said, 'Repeat the Lord's Prayer.'

Deborah had been expecting this. It was the first test; the one they said no true witch could pass. All she had to do was recite the whole prayer without stumbling over the words. But the sight of his fingers straying with obscene pleasure over and around the sharp, steel implement was making her insides curdle and bringing a cold sweat to her brow. He was going to use it. He could hardly wait.

'Our Father who art in Heaven,' she began, 'hallowed be thy name ...'

Once more her orbit showed her his hand toying tenderly with the bodkin. She told herself to concentrate on the prayer – to look away – but found that she couldn't.

'Forgive us our trespasses,' she managed faintly. His eyes mirrored the intent of his hands and she began to feel sick. 'As we forgive those that trespass against us. Lead us not into temptation but ...' She could almost feel the long needle piercing her flesh and see the man's enjoyment as it did so. 'But deliver us ... deliver us from ...' Bile rose in her throat and she clamped her hands hard over her mouth, retching.

Joshua Vincent turned triumphantly to the gaoler.

'You saw that. Know what it means?'

The man nodded uneasily. It meant that for a week he'd been guarding a real witch. His fingers curled into the sign against the evil eye.

'Good,' said Joshua. 'I'll be calling you as a witness. Now strip her for the search.'

Deborah's hands slid away from her face. 'No.'

The gaoler looked scarcely more enthusiastic. 'Me, sir?'

'Yes – you,' snapped Joshua. 'If she struggles, call the other guards to help you. Now get on with it. I haven't got all day.'

The threat of an increased audience was enough to numb Deborah into passivity. Shutting her eyes, she stood like a stone while the gaoler's rough and slightly unsteady hands pulled at her clothing. Her gown slid to the floor, then her petticoats and shift. Cold air struck her skin and her cheeks burned. Automatically, she tried to cover herself with her hands; and then, frightened by the silence around her, opened her eyes.

The gaoler wore an expression part-nervous and part-lascivious. Joshua Vincent, a small disquieting smile hovering about his mouth, was conducting a deliberately slow head-to-foot appraisal that made her want to scream. Then, when she thought she could stand it no longer, he got up and walked towards her.

He was still holding the probe. She shuddered.

Joshua paced slowly round her, halting briefly behind her before moving on again. He said, 'Move your arms.' And when she made no move to uncover herself, 'Move your arms or I'll call the rest of the guards.'

The threat was plain enough. A distant, strangely indistinct pain began to hover behind her eyes. Very, very slowly, Deborah lowered her arms.

For a moment, he simply stared at her breasts. Then he reached out and began handling her. To the watching gaoler, Joshua's movements probably looked like a business-like search for the witch-mark. Deborah knew differently. She felt every loathsome, lingering touch, every sly squeeze, every disgusting but well-disguised intrusion.

The pain behind her eyes increased and a voice in her head said, *Why are you permitting this? There are ways to fight.* And then, commandingly, *Use them!*

She drew a deep, bracing breath and then another. Courage – or something very like it – began to return and, with it, a cold intense rage. Harvesting every ounce of strength, she channelled it against the magistrate. And finally, without warning, she raised her eyes.

The impact of her gaze – fathomless, dark as the pit of hell and blazing with contempt – struck Joshua like a blow. It was as though she was forcing him to look into all the worst corners of his mind. Bitterness filled his mouth and he could feel himself suffocating. His hand dropped from her flesh and he took a step backwards, tugging at his collar.

'Witch,' he gasped. *'Witch!'*

Deborah said nothing. As quickly as it had come, her strength vanished.

Joshua stared down at the probe. The bitch had cheated him. Later on, he'd work out how. Now all he wanted was to make her sorry. Drawing a rasping breath, he ordered the gaoler to summon the other guards.

Deborah stumbled towards her clothes. The magistrate kicked them away from her and then three brawny fellows appeared in the doorway, their eyes on stalks. She wrapped her arms about her body and backed away.

Snatching up his hat, Joshua Vincent said jerkily, 'I haven't time to question the slut further today – but I want you all to witness that there's a witch-mark on her neck and another on the inside of her right thigh. Once that's done, you can take her back to her cell. And watch her. If she's got a familiar, I want to know about it.' And, brushing past the guards, he was gone.

The three newcomers closed in on Deborah. One of them was the man she'd hit in the face with her fetters. The bruise still showed and he stroked it meaningfully.

'Well now, lads,' he said. 'The magistrate left us with a job to do – but he didn't say we'd to hurry about it. So I reckon we'd best shut the door. Don't you?'

Deborah opened her mouth to scream but the sound was never delivered. Her feet were knocked from beneath her and she came down hard on the stone floor. She heard the door slam shut and the bar drop into place. Then there were hands holding her down ... and a new nightmare began.

SEVEN

At dusk that same evening, Major-General Lambert and Colonel Maxwell stood on the east bank of the Severn some ten miles south of Worcester and stared down on the remains of Upton Bridge. Finally, Lambert said dispassionately, 'They've made a damned poor job of this, in my opinion.'

'Agreed.' Eden surveyed the disconnected piers which had once formed a series of arches supporting the road. 'They were probably in a hurry. But, even so, somebody ought to be court-martialled for leaving those spars across the gaps.'

Lambert nodded. 'Can we make use of it?'

'Is there a choice?' grimaced Eden.

'None that I can see. Our orders are to drive General Massey out of Upton and then hold the west bank to prevent the enemy retreating into Wales. And to do that we have to cross the river.' Lambert paused, frowning a little. 'I wonder how many men Massey has posted in those entrenchments on the Worcester road? Not many, I'll warrant. And if they think the bridge is impassable, they may concentrate their look-outs in other directions.' Another pause. Then, slowly, 'If we could just get some of our fellows across to hold the bridge-head on the other side until we can get the rest of the force up ...'

The implication, though unfinished, was obvious. Eden looked at the river, some hundred yards in width, and then at the narrow, flimsy looking spars linking the arches, high above the water. Then he said, 'Let me hand-pick some volunteers and we'll see what we can do.'

'No.' Lambert encompassed him in a direct, dark gaze. 'I can't afford to lose you.'

Eden grinned wryly.

'You can't afford to lose the only chance you've got, either. And who else is likely to offer once they've seen the problem?'

Since there was no satisfactory answer to this, the cold pre-dawn of Friday, August 29th saw Colonel Maxwell and seventeen of his best men setting out to accomplish a feat that even an acrobat would have found daunting.

The planks were no more than ten inches wide, unsecured and horribly flexible ... while below and ready to drown them if they fell, ran the deep rapidly-flowing waters of the Severn. Furthermore, if the enemy was keeping a good look-out, there was the added possibility that Eden's little band might at any moment be seen and fired upon. It was not a pleasant prospect and one which made the descent into the ravine at Dunbar look like child's-play.

Eden had ordered his fellows to set out at intervals and take their time. Unfortunately, he hadn't foreseen the dizzying effect that moving water far below had on the eye. Since he was the first to cross, he was the first one it affected. After half a dozen yards, his head began to swim and he could feel his balance becoming uncertain. He stopped and stood very still for a moment, averting his eyes from the water and breathing deeply. Then, lowering himself carefully into a sitting position astride the plank, he started levering himself forward. It was a slow business but it seemed to work. Turning, he watched the man behind gratefully following his example ... and then the man after that.

One by one, they hauled themselves across the river in a series of ungainly hops. Had it not been so tiring and dangerous, it might have been funny. As it was, Eden was just thankful when all eighteen of them made it safely to the opposite bank. His satisfaction, however, was destined to be short-lived. While he was still praising the men for their fortitude and forming them up ready to guard the bridge-head, roughly three hundred Scots poured down upon them from the Worcester road.

'Hell's teeth!' muttered Eden. And, with swift urgency, 'Into the churchyard. Take cover and fire at will. *Move!*'

They moved. They found shelter behind walls and amidst tombstones and they rained the heaviest fire possible upon the oncoming Scots for the five minutes which was all it took to prove how untenable their position was. With one trooper dead and a second shot in the shoulder, Eden ordered a further retreat into the church.

He lost another man on the way. Sixteen of them now and a fellow whose right arm was useless. Once inside, with the door barred behind them, he said crisply, 'Fire from the windows. Do what you can but don't take any risks. If we can hold them off for half an hour or so, the Major-General will send help.'

To their credit, none of them asked how Lambert was going to get a regiment across the river in time to save them. They knew he'd do his best. In the meantime, every one of them was grateful that Colonel Maxwell had chosen to lead this mission in person – for if anyone could keep them alive, he could.

The attack came hard and fast. The Scots pushed on to the church and surrounded it with a hail of shot. Then, pressing closer, they tried thrusting pikes through the windows. Inside, Eden's men fired and re-loaded at a furious pace – avoiding the murderous jabs as best they could and cheering sardonically every time one of the enemy fell. Hands and faces became blackened with powder and the air around them was filled with acrid smoke. The Scots pulled back but their assault did not weaken. One of Eden's troopers fell, shot in the head. Another took a bullet through the throat. The others continued their dogged defence.

Half an hour passed and ammunition started to run low. Eden boosted his men's morale as best he could. Then he saw something that brought his flow of banter to an abrupt stop; a rough and ready catapult, preparing to fire flaming faggots.

'Oh Christ,' he breathed.

Eden knew what he wanted to do but felt, on this occasion, that he owed the men their say. Turning, he said, 'They're going to fire the church. We're dead if we leave and dead if we stay. They might, however, accept a surrender.'

Thirteen filthy faces stared grimly back at him and for a few seconds no one spoke. Then Sergeant Trotter spat accurately through the window and spoke for them all.

'Surrender?' he said. 'Bugger that!'

Eden grinned.

'Thank you,' he said.

* * *

Since being alerted by the first shots, Lambert had been extremely busy. It was obvious that, with the Scots buzzing about like flies on a dung-hill, no one could re-cross the river and live but he wasn't going to lose eighteen men and his best senior officer if he could help it. A locally-born captain maintained that, being low-tide, the river was just about fordable a little way downstream. Not entirely convinced but

70

open to any possibility, Lambert sent a detachment of dragoons to try it and, if they succeeded in crossing, to waste no time in relieving Colonel Maxwell. Then he paced up and down the east bank in a fury of impatience, waiting.

The dragoons set off, grumbling under their breath. The horses were equally unhappy. At best, the water was breast-deep – at worst, seemingly fathomless. Sometimes wading and sometimes swimming, they floundered their way across the Severn and gained the far bank. It seemed to take an age but as soon as he was sure they'd made it, Lambert spun on his heel and despatched two regiments of Horse – one being Eden's own – in their wake.

Inside the church, matters were critical. The door was burning ferociously, bales of straw blazed outside the windows and smoke was clogging everyone's lungs. In ten minutes – or perhaps less, thought Eden – they'd all be insensible. If one was going to die, there must be better ways of doing it.

Choking, he stepped away from his window and, with difficulty, said, 'You've done sterling work, gentlemen. I'm sure the enemy are as impressed as I am. But just in case they're not … shall we break out and charge?'

This time only twelve weary faces looked back.

'Why not?' coughed the sergeant. 'Got nothing to lose, have we? And I'd as soon not fry, if it's all the same to you, sir.'

They set about uprooting benches to use as battering rams on the blazing door. Busy and struggling to breathe, they were not immediately aware of new and increased noise from outside. Finally, however, the door gave way before them … and they found themselves gazing out on a large number of Scottish backsides.

The dragoons had arrived and made an initially successful charge but were being pushed back. Eden stared, passed a hand over his eyes and stared again. The men around him managed a ragged cheer. Then, dead on cue, the cavalry came up … and for the survivors in the church, there was nothing to do but watch.

Suddenly outnumbered, the Scots shuddered under the impact and, fighting all the way, slowly began to give ground. Eden caught a glimpse of Edward Massey – one-time ally and so-called hero of Gloucester –

fighting like a man possessed despite the blood streaming down his thigh. Seconds later, he thought he saw a face that was even more familiar. Then the fight eddied chaotically out of the churchyard and turned into a full-blown retreat.

Major Cartwright appeared before the doorway and saluted.

'I thank God for your preservation, Colonel. I trust you've sustained no injury?'

'Give me your horse,' said Eden.

The Major stared at him. 'Sir?'

'Give me your horse and see these men to safety,' snapped Eden. *'Now!'*

Thirty seconds later, impelled by instinct rather than logic, he was galloping in the wake of his regiment with no very clear idea of why he was doing it.

Major-General Lambert, arriving beside him at the head of reinforcements, lifted one dark brow and said, 'I'm pleased to see you in one piece – even if you do look like a blackamoor.'

Grinning faintly, Eden gestured up the Worcester road.

'The Scots have withdrawn to their entrenchments. I presume you'd like them driven out again?'

'Naturally. I'd hate to see your efforts go to waste.'

And he ordered an immediate assault.

General Massey and his fellows defended their position hotly and for a time the New Model hurled itself against the earthworks with little result. But gradually, as more and more of Lambert's troops continued to pour up from the river, the Scots were forced back from their lines. And it was then, as they embarked on a hard-fought retreat, that Eden again saw the man he'd ridden from the churchyard to find.

Separated by a dozen yards and a handful of battling horsemen, bloodshot hazel eyes met frowning sapphire ones. For a long, dangerous moment, both men froze. Then the Cavalier found himself under attack ... and Eden started hacking his way purposefully through the mêlée towards him.

Not without difficulty, Major Langley despatched his assailant and waited till Eden was within earshot before saying, 'You were in the church?'

'Can't you tell?' Eden raised his sword and took a hard, furious swipe at his one-time friend and brother-in-law.

Francis parried the blow. The force of it jarred every bone in his body.

'All right,' he gasped. 'All right – point taken. But how was I to know?'

'And what difference would it have made if you had?' Eden's blade flashed again and steel rasped on steel. 'You and your bastards nearly roasted a dozen of my men alive.'

Francis eyed him warily and kept his mouth shut. He'd never been any match for Eden with a sword and still wasn't.

A disquieting smile curled Eden's mouth and he attacked again, saying, 'What's the matter? Cat got your tongue?'

Defending himself as best he could, Francis said breathlessly, 'What do you want me to say? Right now, an apology isn't going to mean much, is it?'

'Nothing at all.' Eden's assault continued with unabated speed and ferocity. 'But what's happened to your witty repartee? You used to talk more than anyone I know.'

'I wouldn't want to risk … boring you.' Francis's wrist ached and his shoulder was on fire. He tried to retreat but was pursued and forced to engage again. Steel ripped through his sleeve, scoring his arm. Involuntarily, he said, 'Christ, Eden. Finish it, will you?'

Almost before the words had left his lips, he found himself facing the Colonel at close quarters over their locked blades. Eden said irritably, 'Don't be a bigger fool than you can help, Francis. We both know I'm not going to kill you.'

'Do we?' Major Langley struggled to drag some air into his lungs. 'Speaking for myself, I never like to take these things for granted.'

Something that might have been humour stirred in the smoke-reddened gaze. There was an infinitesimal pause and then, with an abruptness that nearly dislocated Francis's wrist, Eden disengaged his sword.

'Liar,' he said flatly. 'You took it for granted I'd get you out of the Tower three years ago, didn't you? And if you're grateful, all I can is that you've a bloody funny way of showing it.'

'My lamentable manners,' murmured Francis, all-too-aware that the moment was fast approaching when, if Eden didn't take him prisoner, someone else would. Discreetly gathering his reins, he said, 'I rejoice to see you safe. But I really do hope we don't meet again for some time.'

'So do I,' retorted Eden. And delivered a hefty whack on the rump of Major Langley's horse at the precise moment that the Major himself applied his spurs.

The horse went off as if fired from a cannon. Francis narrowly avoided being unseated and an uncharacteristic expletive drifted back on the air.

His mouth curling slightly, Eden turned his attention back to the business in hand.

* * *

The defeat at Upton was a bitter blow to the King's army. Before it, everyone had been able to congratulate themselves on the improvements to Worcester's defences. After it, said Colonel Peverell, there seemed little point in constructing elaborate earthworks if they were only going to hand them over to Pokenose Noll.

Nevertheless – despite the desultory cannon-fire raining down from the New Model's hurriedly erected batteries – work on the fortifications proceeded at an even more frenetic pace than before. Foregate was blocked up and the other gates strengthened; ditches were dug and gun-emplacements studded the walls to the north-east; and, most impressive of all, a huge star-shaped mound known as Fort Royal grew rapidly south-east of the Sidbury Gate. To the west, of course, lay the river.

'It's not enough, Sir,' Colonel Peverell told the King bluntly on the evening after the disaster at Upton. 'Fort Royal is well enough in its way – but we haven't sufficient artillery to arm it fully and it's overlooked by the enemy guns at Red Hill and Perry Wood. Fresh regiments and levies of Militia are joining Cromwell with practically every hour that passes, so his total force now must be well in excess of thirty thousand. And the outpost he's left at Upton under General Fleetwood is so large it stretches nearly as far as Powick.'

Charles, who had spent the day touring the defences and trying to put fresh heart into the despondent Scots, leaned wearily back in his chair and closed his eyes.

'I know. But what do you suggest we do about it?'

'There's little we can do - except to keep Cromwell's batteries as busy as possible,' returned Ashley. And then, slowly, 'Of course ... the risks would be greatly reduced if Your Majesty were elsewhere.'

The dark Stuart eyes opened again.

'No.'

'Forgive me, Sir. But --'

'No,' said Charles again. 'I haven't come this far to turn back now and I've no intention of deserting all those who have given up everything for me. And even if I was prepared to leave – where could I go?'

Sighing, Ashley acknowledged the truth of this but immediately added that the King might at least move to more secure lodgings.

'Why?' His Majesty glanced around the comfortable, panelled room of the small house off the Corn Market where he had chosen to establish himself. 'If Cromwell gets this far, it will be because all is lost. Until then, I'm safer here than I would be down at the Commandery with Hamilton and the rest.' He smiled faintly and added, 'You worry too much, Ash.'

'A martyr to my nerves. Quite, Sir. I could do with a distraction.'

'So why don't you come to the point?'

A reluctant grin dawned.

'Am I so transparent?'

'As glass. Well? You're keeping me from my supper, you know.'

'My apologies, Sir.' Colonel Peverell bowed, now entirely without humour. 'I'll be brief. What I had in mind was a sortie against the artillery on Cromwell's extreme left at Bund's Hill. I've spoken to his Grace of Hamilton about it and he agrees that, in addition to spiking the guns, it would be to our advantage to try and sink the bridge of boats which Cromwell is assembling across the Severn between himself and General Fleetwood.' He paused and fixed his King with a gleaming green-gold stare. 'With your permission, Sir – and, of course that of General Leslie – I'd thought of attempting something of the sort tomorrow night.'

* * *

Having obtained the King's consent and spent a further two hours discussing the details of his idea with Hamilton, Will Legge and a handful of other commanders, Colonel Peverell eventually joined Major Langley and Captain Austin in the Cardinal's Hat on Friar Street. Noisy, cheerful and wreathed in pipe-smoke, the tap-room was packed with the usual random mixture of soldiers and locals. Ashley jammed himself into a corner, freed his elbows long enough to eat a slice of beef pie and then said softly, 'Don't make any plans for tomorrow night.'

Francis and Nicholas both looked at him with perfect comprehension but said nothing.

'I'll give you the minutiae later but our basic aims will be to disable artillery and wreck communications. Major Knox, meanwhile, will be doing the same elsewhere.' Ashley smiled blandly at Francis. 'Perhaps this will stop you brooding about Upton.'

Level brows rose over expressionless blue eyes.

'Who said that I was?'

'Me. Or has the unaccustomed reserve that's settled over you since yesterday another cause entirely?'

Francis hesitated. He'd said little about what had happened at Upton – less because he was unwilling to admit he'd met an old friend among the enemy there than because of what he might be led into saying about his old friend's wife. Celia ... who had abandoned both husband and children to become Hugo Verney's mistress and who was Francis's own sister. He also wasn't sure what to make of his encounter with Eden. Three years ago there had been enough friendship left between them for Eden to help him flee the country; yesterday it seemed as if all that remained was a memory. And that was somewhat ironic because, in the days when they had done everything together, they'd had almost nothing in common – whereas now, Francis suspected they'd become more alike than either of them would wish to admit.

Some of the ash from Nick's pipe settled on Francis's cuff and he brushed it fastidiously aside. Then, meeting Colonel Peverell's eyes, he said lightly, 'Reserve? Perish the thought. It's merely that I don't see the point in giving one's friends the chance to say *I told you so.*'

'Well, I *did* tell you so – and Ned Massey too, come to that,' retorted Ashley. 'We should have deployed more men out there if we expected to hold the position.'

'Quite. But what's done is done – so let's just hope for better fortune tomorrow,' remarked Nicholas philosophically. 'God knows, we could do with a bit of good luck – if only to cheer up the Scots. Half of 'em are prophesying doom and disaster and the rest are crying into their porridge and wishing they'd stayed at home.'

Francis and Ashley exchanged glances. Then Francis said dryly, 'We all occasionally wish that. But the Scots are more fortunate than most of us. At least they have homes to which they may legitimately return.'

* * *

The next day brought yet more bad news when the Earl of Derby arrived with only a handful of personal followers in place of the promised army. The fifteen hundred Royalists he had recruited through the north, he explained, had been decimated at Wigan six days ago by Robert Lilburne. Despondency deepened amongst the Scots and the need for some small success to revive morale became critical. Colonel Peverell resolved to do his best.

By evening, he and Major Knox had done everything in their power to ensure both the success of their respective missions and also to synchronise the attacks. Fortunately, the night was comfortingly dark and, in order to help tell friend from foe, it had been ordained that both assault parties would wear their shirts over their back-and-breast plates.

'I should prefer,' shuddered Francis, when told of this, 'not to be seen dead in such a guise.'

'And I would prefer,' retorted Ashley, 'that neither of us will be seen dead at *all*.'

Wraith-like in their white shirts, the two troops Ashley had selected assembled in the courtyard of the Commandery and listened to their Colonel's final instructions. Then, without further ado, they set off into the night.

Getting a hundred troopers over even a small distance in the dark is not easy. Doing it in silence is more difficult still. Previously, Francis had scarcely noticed the creak of leather or the metallic rasp of weapons. Tonight, it deafened him. And the number of men who stumbled, grunting, into pot-holes began to fray imperceptibly at his nerves ... until, that was, he did it himself and wrenched his ankle.

A few camp-fires glowed along the Parliamentary lines but all seemed quiet. According to Colonel Peverell's scouts, the Bund's Hill guns were guarded by no more than two hundred musketeers who, if they could be taken by surprise, should not be difficult to overpower. Ashley took his men as close as was wise before pausing to form them up for the last, mad dash. Then he gave the signal.

His little force poured across the Kempsey road, still in silence but with a turn of speed that was little short of miraculous. At the same moment, rows of heads appeared in the entrenchments in front of them and the night erupted into a murderous hail of musket-fire.

Six of Ashley's men dropped like stones. The rest threw themselves instinctively on to their stomachs and set about shooting back. Grimly and with a minimum of communication, Ashley and Francis addressed themselves to the task of losing as few men as possible – but even so, eleven more men died and seventeen others were injured before the retreat was completed. And by then, Ashley was boiling over with bitter rage.

As soon as the danger was behind them and it was possible to speak, he said unevenly, 'They knew we were coming, God damn it!' Then, half under his breath, 'Hell and the devil confound it. Can *nothing* go right?'

* * *

Major Knox's assault on Red Hill was equally unsuccessful and resulted in considerable loss of life – one of which was his own. Enquiries into the betrayal were instantly set in hand and, within hours, a tailor named Guise was hauled off to the gallows.

'One wonders how he got his information,' remarked Francis.

'The usual way. Some stupid bugger got drunk and shot his mouth off,' snapped Ashley. 'It's always happening. That's why telling no one more than they need to know – and not even *that* until the last minute – is a sodding necessity if you want to stay alive.'

* * *

By noon on September 2nd, dispositions in both armies were largely complete. Ready to repulse any advance made by Generals Fleetwood and Lambert from Upton, Pitscotty's highlanders sat north-east of the

Teme's confluence with the Severn and Colonel Keith had established outposts at Powick. The Cavaliers under the King and Lord Hamilton stood between Fort Royal and the New Model troops at Perry Wood and Red Hill … and, in solitary splendour, General Leslie's Horse occupied the Pitchcroft. Even the bridges of boats that Cromwell had been busily assembling over the Severn and the Teme lay ready and waiting; and yet, surprisingly, he made no move to attack.

'What the devil is he waiting for?' muttered Colonel Peverell, pacing restlessly back and forth between the guns of Fort Royal. 'He's cut us off from London and Wales, he outnumbers us by roughly two to one and he can cross either river whenever he chooses. So why is he still *waiting?*'

Francis opened his mouth to say he hadn't the remotest idea … and then closed it again, struck by a sudden thought. He said slowly, 'For tomorrow?'

Ashley stared at him. 'What?'

'Tomorrow. September 3rd. The anniversary of his victory at Dunbar?'

'Christ,' said Ashley. And, turning to go, added, 'I'll tell Hamilton. But don't worry. I'll see you get full credit.'

'I'm sure,' retorted Francis with asperity. 'After all, it's probably just my imagination running away with me.'

* * *

At home in Friar Street, Verity Marriott was finding the tension stifling. For four days, Joshua had been in a foul mood; Barbara was sniping even more than usual; and the intermittent roaring of the great guns at Fort Royal coupled with the thudding replies from Perry Wood and Red Hill were giving everyone a headache and causing a good many breakages in the kitchen.

By mid-afternoon, Verity could stand it no longer and, taking her cloak, slipped out through the back door. The street was busy with soldiers going about their business, few of whom spared her so much as a glance. She walked aimlessly towards the Sidbury Gate and then, when the press of troopers and horses grew thicker, turned right to the Cathedral in the hope that it might be quieter there.

It wasn't. Commanding superb views to the south and west over the Severn, it was in constant use as a look-out post. Deciding it would be foolish to go inside, she hoisted herself on to a wall and settled down to watch the comings and goings.

Twenty minutes later, Captain Sir Nicholas Austin strode out of the north door and came to an abrupt stop in front of her.

'My God,' he said blankly. 'What are you doing here?'

Stunned to see him again and paralysed by shyness, Verity flushed and muttered something about having come out for a breath of air.

'You're alone?'

'Y-yes.'

'Well, you shouldn't be. It's not safe. Haven't your family any sense?'

His frown dismayed her. She didn't know about last night's sortie or the fact that he'd spent the day flying about delivering messages and was tired, hungry and over-stretched. She only knew that he looked cross. She said haltingly, 'I didn't tell anyone I was going out. If I had, they'd have stopped me.'

Something in her voice pierced Nicholas's preoccupation. The heart-shaped face was strained and there were shadows under her eyes. She looked even more vulnerable than she'd done that day outside the Guildhall; and that, of course, was why he remembered her.

Puppies, children and fragile creatures always did well with Nicholas. Since boyhood, his strongest characteristics had been an urge to protect the helpless and a desire to right wrongs. Ashley maintained that he'd been born several centuries too late. Nick ruefully agreed that it was probably true and suspected that it would get him into trouble one day. Now, looking at the girl, an all-too-familiar concern stirred and he said, 'Something's wrong, isn't it? Do you want to tell me about it?'

The unexpected kindness made her want to cry. She swallowed and shook her head.

'Not particularly. And you're busy.'

'I can spare five minutes,' lied Nicholas, sitting on the wall beside her. 'Or even ten.'

He smiled and her breath leaked away. She said the only thing that mattered.

'I don't know your name.'

'Nicholas Austin. And yours?'

'Verity. Verity Marriott – though I'm supposed to call myself Vincent now. My mother re-married, you see.' She shook her head. 'But that doesn't matter.'

'Doesn't it?'

She looked up into warm brown eyes and was lost.

'Yes. But I can't talk about it.'

Without thinking, Nick took her hand in his.

'Try,' he said.

EIGHT

The morning of September 3rd was spent in a state of heightened tension as the Royalist army continued to await Cromwell's attack. Colonel Peverell divided the time between his regiment just below Fort Royal, the army's headquarters in the Commandery and the look-out atop the Cathedral tower. In this way he was able to at least *feel* busy during the last empty hours until it was time to fight.

At around noon, standing amidst a handful of other officers beside the King on the Cathedral tower, he saw and heard the first signs of activity; the crackle of musket-fire and puffs of smoke ascending from Colonel Keith's outpost in the village of Powick. Ashley's muscles tightened but he said nothing. The view, even through a perspective glass, was annoyingly indistinct but everyone knew that the outpost was too small to be held against a full attack. Keith's stand, when it came, would be made at Powick Bridge; the place where, nine years ago, Prince Rupert had won the first victory of the war by defeating Nathaniel Fiennes.

It was harder to watch and wait than to do. By the time it became plain that Colonel Keith had been pushed back and was now fighting desperately to hold the bridge, Ashley was in a fever of impatience. And when, away to Keith's left, the New Model started pouring across the bridge of boats at the mouth of the Teme towards Pitscotty's brigade, he said tersely, 'They're trying to turn our right wing. Doesn't anyone think it might be a good idea to stop them?'

Several pairs of eyes, their expressions varying from disapproval to agreement, turned simultaneously in his direction. Then Lord Rothes said simply, 'Quite right. If Keith is forced to give ground, Pitscotty will have to retreat or be cut off – and *vice versa*. And if both of them are driven back on Montgomery, our whole flank could be rolled right back to the city.'

A brief debate ensued until the King – as anxious as Ashley to be in the thick of things – said, 'I'll go down and assess the situation in person.'

General Middleton's brows shot up.

'I'd rather ye didn't, Sir. It's tae greet a risk.'

'This whole venture is a risk, General. And my presence may be just the encouragement the men need.' Charles glanced around him. 'Colonel Legge – Colonel Peverell. Bring up a couple of dozen of your best men and let's go.'

Will Legge saluted. 'At once, Sir.' And, discreetly, to Ashley, 'Thank God for that. I thought for a minute he was going to take Wilmot.'

'And I,' muttered Ashley, 'thought I was going to be stuck up this tower all day.'

They left the city by Bridgegate and rode fast. Activity along the banks of the Teme was now extremely fierce. Colonel Keith was still holding the bridge in the teeth of some heavy opposition from Fleetwood's troops and, also refusing to give ground, Pitscotty's highlanders were engaged in a vicious struggle with Major-General Lambert's infantry. Pikeheads pierced the smoke-laden air, bugles shrilled and steel rasped on steel. The overall impression was of sheer pandemonium.

Colonel Keith, a dogged Scots officer of some experience, had his hands full but the arrival of the King caused his face to lighten fractionally and he said, 'It isna going sae bad, Your Majesty – not that we couldna do wi' a wee bit o' support, ye understand. But I dinna doot ma laddies will fight the harder for seeing ye here.'

'They seem to be fighting like demons already,' replied Charles. 'I can ask no more of them and only wished to say how greatly their efforts – and yours, Colonel – are appreciated.' He paused briefly, surveying the fray. 'I don't need to tell you how vital it is that this bridge is held.'

'No, Sir – ye don't. And ye have ma word that we'll hold it as long as we can. Tae the last man, if needs be.'

Charles met the Colonel's eyes unsmilingly but with sincerity.

'Thank you. And whatever comes of today, you may be sure I won't forget.'

As the King turned to move on eastwards towards the Severn, Ashley said rapidly, 'Sir – with Lambert's fellows already on this side of the river, it would be madness to risk yourself visiting General Pitscotty. He seems to be holding them – just. But if something were to happen to Your Majesty ...' He stopped. Then, 'I'll go, if you wish. Meanwhile, perhaps you might put some heart into Montgomery and Dalziel.'

Charles drew a short breath, loosed it and looked at Colonel Legge who said, 'I agree, Sir. Pitscotty's position is no place for you at the moment.'

'Very well.' The King's gaze, heavy with frustration, turned back to Colonel Peverell. 'Use your charm and make my apologies for not coming in person. Ah – and Ash?'

Already turning his horse, Ashley checked. 'Sir?'

'Enjoy yourself, by all means. But don't forget to come back, will you?'

* * *

While Colonel Peverell was presenting His Majesty's compliments to General Pitscotty and begging him to stand firm, Colonel Maxwell was wiping the sweat from his eyes and trying to ease the cramp from his sword-hand whilst conferring briskly with the Major-General.

'They won't budge. We've thrown everything we've got against them and are continuing to battle over the same few yards. Pitscotty must be one hell of a General.'

'Clearly,' agreed Lambert. 'And I'm informed that Deane's fellows are faring no better at Powick. Yet one or other of us *must* push through. It doesn't matter which. If we can make Pitscotty retreat, his colleague at Powick will have to do the same. But if both of them stand, our whole strategy of driving their right wing back to the city will fail. The trouble is that neither Deane nor myself has any more men to send.'

'So what are your orders?' asked Eden, preparing to re-join his men.

'Try again? For the moment, that's all we can do. And in the meantime, I'll apprise Fleetwood of the situation.'

Colonel Maxwell gave a short, sardonic laugh. All the officers knew that Charles Fleetwood suffered from a chronic inability to make a decision and stick to it. What they *didn't* know was why Cromwell had made him second-in-command instead of Lambert.

Under his breath, Eden muttered, 'That will be a big help, I'm sure.' And rode off before the Major-General could ask him to repeat himself.

If Lieutenant-General Fleetwood came up with any good ideas, Eden never found out what they were. He spent the next half hour directing another assault against the highlanders – and was just resigning himself to yet another failure when reinforcements started pouring over the second bridge of boats which lay across the Severn. The Captain-General, it appeared, had decided to lend a hand in person and was leading three brigades against Pitscotty's left flank.

Even as he re-formed his men to support the unexpected reinforcements, Eden realised that bringing troops to support Lambert was probably the last thing Cromwell wanted to do since it might enable the Royalists to make a sally against his men on Red Hill. On the other hand, if the Scots were to be driven back and trapped in the city, there wasn't really any alternative. And even now, attacked on two sides simultaneously by vastly superior numbers, Pitscotty's fellows were still standing firm and fighting like demons. Eden found himself hoping they weren't going to hold their ground to the last man. They deserved better than that.

* * *

On the point of re-joining the King, Ashley Peverell hesitated, watching the mêlée and swearing under his breath. Then, setting spurs to his horse, he galloped off at break-neck speed to obtain the order necessary to get help.

Charles gave it in two words.

'Fetch Leslie,' he said. 'I'll send Montgomery to hold them until he gets there. Join me back at the Commandery.'

Ashley nodded curtly and set off again. Minutes later and breathing rather hard, he was at the Pitchcroft, telling David Leslie what he wanted.

The General took his time about answering. Then he said, 'His Majesty cannot have considered the matter. The ground above the Teme is too broken with hedges to be suitable for cavalry. I do not see how we could make a charge.'

'I appreciate that, sir,' said Ashley with commendable patience. 'But the situation is grave. And I'm sure your great experience will suggest some way --'

'My great experience, Colonel, tells me that my Horse is not to be wasted where it can do little good.'

'*But the highlanders are being cut to pieces!*' began Ashley. And then stopped, realising how little this would mean to the man who'd defeated Montrose. Sitting very straight and holding Leslie's eye, he said, 'General Pitscotty and his men are demonstrating loyalty and valour as great as any I've ever seen – and they're paying dearly for it. Perhaps that doesn't concern you. But the King has commanded your presence, sir. Are you refusing his order?'

'From all I've been privileged to see of you, young man,' came the irascible retort, 'I've little doubt that this notion originates less from His Majesty than from yourself. And since it is so obviously foolish --'

'You're wasting time, General. Are you going to bring your cavalry up or not?'

There was a brief, explosive silence. 'No, Colonel. I am not.'

'I see.' Ashley's gaze was like flint. 'Then I hope you can live with the consequences – and that your men are proud of you.' Upon which he jerked his horse's head about and rode fulminatingly back to Worcester.

Inside the Commandery, a Council of War was in progress. As Ashley entered, however, all eyes turned towards him and the King said, 'Well?'

'General Leslie,' announced Ashley carefully, 'considers the ground unsuitable for Horse. He won't advance.'

There was a tiny pause and then everybody started talking at once. Only the King remained silent, his expression bitter but oddly unsurprised. Then, raising his voice over the din, the Duke of Hamilton said, 'Gentlemen – please! We've time neither to damn Leslie's caution nor coerce him into action.'

Colonel Peverell threw down his hat.

'What's Pitscotty's present situation?'

'He's making a fighting retreat – and losing a great many men in the process,' answered Will Legge grimly. 'As for Colonel Keith, he's been isolated and is being forced back from the bridge. If we don't do something soon, our forces west of the Severn will be in total disarray.'

'Or worse,' said Ashley.

'Yes. Or worse.'

'The men Cromwell is leading against Pitscotty are ones he drew off from Perry Wood and Red Hill,' remarked Charles, frowning down at the large map on the table. 'Might either location be vulnerable to an assault?'

Hamilton and Legge exchanged glances. Then Hamilton said slowly, 'As vulnerable as they'll ever be.'

'So it's worth a try,' breathed Will. 'At least it may relieve the pressure on Montgomery and our other friends across the river.'

The King looked from one to the other of them and nodded.

'Very well, gentlemen. We'd better get busy.'

* * *

A short time later, Colonel Peverell descended purposefully upon his regiment's position south-east of Fort Royal and, finding Major Langley, said, 'We're going to advance against Red Hill. Are our fellows ready?'

'What do you think?' Francis hated the inevitable lull before battle and having the whole morning and half the afternoon to kill had made him irritable. 'I've had them standing to arms since before noon.'

'Good. Then you can inform the captains that the King will be leading his men out of the Sidbury Gate any minute – at which point, we join him. Hamilton, meanwhile, will ride out via St Martin's against Perry Wood.' Ashley paused, his mouth curling in something not quite a smile. 'We're hoping to catch Noll with his breeches down. So if anyone wants to pray, now would be the time.'

Francis went off without a word. But later, as the regiment swung into motion, he turned an oblique glance on Ashley and said, 'Where's Leslie?'

'Don't ask.'

There was no time to talk further. The moment came to charge and the Royalist cavalry streamed up the hill towards the New Model's lines. The Fort Royal guns gave them covering fire for as long as possible but still the ground around and amongst them exploded with answering shots from the Red Hill artillery. Even in those first few minutes, some men died or fell, horribly wounded. The rest thundered relentlessly on over the torn, vibrating earth.

The clash came with discharging pistols and savage yells. The Foot came in at push of pike ... and then the real struggle began. The terrible, bloody business of hand-to-hand combat in which there was only one basic rule; kill or die.

It was a long and bitter contest during which Ashley concentrated, minute by minute, on encouraging, steadying and re-grouping his men. He glimpsed the King, hacking and slashing with the best – apparently without thought for his personal safety; and, nearer at hand, Francis

Langley – his face set hard and his left sleeve soaked with blood. Of Nicholas, he saw no sign at all. Nor was there time to look.

Slowly but surely, Cromwell's fellows started to give ground before them, falling back from their lines and away up the hill. Cheering hoarsely, the Royalists pressed on with renewed vigour. Ashley forced his way to the King's side.

'One good push now and we could rout them,' he shouted.

Dishevelled and streaked with sweat, Charles nodded.

'I've sent for Leslie. Again. I doubt he'll come, though. I wonder if he ever meant to.'

Time passed. The ammunition ran out and men fought with the butt-end of their pistols. Exhaustion set in and the battle became a sort of stalemate. Despite their retreat, the New Model lines never quite disintegrated; and General Leslie's Horse – those desperately needed reinforcements which could have made all the difference – failed to materialise. Instead, after three hours of the hardest fighting Ashley could remember, what *did* materialise was Oliver Cromwell and the three regiments he'd led across the Severn against Pitscotty's poor, decimated highlanders.

Ashley's stomach turned ice-cold. They had come so close … so *close*. Success had been almost within their grasp. But now the scales were tipping again.

'Holy *Christ*,' he breathed. And, with feverish haste, started bellowing orders.

His men formed up fast and as best they could. They even withstood the first shock of Cromwell's offensive. But they were exhausted, disadvantaged by having to fight uphill and badly outnumbered. Retreat was inevitable – first back on their entrenchments and then beyond them. Ashley tried to keep it tight and orderly but, in the face of the waves of enemy troopers crashing down on them from the slopes above, it couldn't last. And worse was to come when Cromwell's forces over-ran Fort Royal to tear down the King's standard. Gradually Ashley's men started breaking from their units to turn and run. And the retreat became a rout.

The Royalists pelted down the hill towards the Sidbury Gate but the stone archway was too narrow to admit them easily and, within seconds, men and horses were jammed in it like a cork in a bottle as those behind pressed forward in an attempt to escape the pursuing pikes of the Ironsides.

Finding Francis beside him, Ashley yelled, 'This is suicide. They'll be massacred!'

They? thought Francis wildly. And shouted back, 'Leave it. You can't rally them. No one could. They're past listening.'

Although he knew it, Ashley couldn't help trying. He was still trying when their own guns in captured Fort Royal were turned against them. Then the Roundheads swept down like the wolf on the fold ... and all hell broke loose.

Exhilarated by triumph, the Army of Saints prosecuted the Lord's work with merciless vigour. They descended on the children of Amalek and cut them down where they stood. Suddenly the air was full of screaming and within minutes the ground beneath and around the Sidbury Gate began to resemble a charnel house. Bodies of men and horses lay in tangled, grisly heaps, their blood staining the cobbles bright red and running sluggishly into the gutters.

Francis and Ashley were amongst the few dozen who defended themselves. Ashley, indeed, would have gone on mechanically fighting had not he suddenly caught sight of the King who, with total disregard for his own life, was frantically exhorting the demoralised Scots to make one last stand.

'Hell and the devil!' swore Ashley. And, yelling for Francis to follow, started hacking a path to Charles's side at precisely the same moment that an enemy trooper swooped down from the other direction, bawling '*Belial!*'

For an instant, it seemed that the King was a dead man. Then someone dragged an abandoned ammunition cart into the oncoming trooper's path ... and somehow, His Majesty simply disappeared.

'Where the --?' began Francis.

'There,' pointed Ashley. 'That gap between the walls and the Commandery. Leave your horse and let's go.'

The passage was narrow. At the end of it, the remains of the Royalist cavalry were fleeing down Lich Street while the King, throwing himself on the nearest loose horse, beseeched them to join him. Buckingham hovered nearby and Wilmot, his plump face overflowing with distress, grasped Charles's bridle and begged him to stop.

'It's over, Your Majesty. You must see that!'

'It's not over,' snapped Charles. 'If Leslie will make one last charge --'

'Don't you mean one *first* charge?' sniped Buckingham.

'Don't be clever, George. There's no time. I must get to Leslie.'

'No, Sir,' said Ashley from behind him. 'With respect, you must *not*. If Leslie wouldn't fight before, he certainly won't do so now. And your duty is to save yourself.'

Charles stared at him in mutinous silence and Wilmot said swiftly, 'He's right, Sir. Poor Hamilton is dying. Montgomery, Pitscotty and Keith are all taken and the enemy is breaking in all around the city. You must fly – now.'

Intensely weary and awash with despairing bitterness, the King said violently, 'I'd rather you shot me than let me live to see the consequences of this day. Thousands have died. I *can't* let it be for nothing!'

'Then go, Sir,' urged Ashley. 'You can't stay here. And you'd be better employed destroying any papers you don't want ending up in Cromwell's hands.'

It was, perhaps, the only argument that could have swayed Charles. His face twisted and he said, 'Oh God. I hadn't thought of that. Letters, lists – everything! I must get to my lodging.'

'And from thence, God willing, out through St Martin's Gate,' murmured Buckingham. 'What a good idea. By all means, let us go immediately.'

Charles looked at Ashley and Francis. 'You'll come?'

'Presently. First we'll see what resistance may still be offered to cover your retreat.' Colonel Peverell smiled briefly. 'Go, Sir. And God speed you.'

The answering smile was crooked.

'Amen to that. Because the truth is that I'm better dead than taken.'

* * *

As the light began to fade, pandemonium ruled over Worcester. The citizens who, earlier in the day, had come out to watch the fight, now bolted themselves into their homes and looked down on the carnage through chinks in the shutters. Cromwell's Ironsides continued to pour into the city like avenging angels while their defeated foes ran hither and thither, hammering desperately on locked doors in a vain attempt to escape capture or death.

Only two forlorn pockets of Royalist resistance were left. Lord Rothes continued stubbornly defending the Castle Mound; and, in the High Street, the Earl of Cleveland attempted to rally the last vestiges of the King's cavalry for one final charge. Ashley and Francis caught spare horses and joined the latter ... and found themselves unexpectedly reunited with Nicholas. There was no time for more than a brief nod of acknowledgement. They had barely got their meagre troop formed up, when Fleetwood's Horse pelted down upon their rear.

The encounter was short and bloody. Caught between the devil and the deep, the Cavaliers made a fighting retreat into the side-streets and then separated to pursue the only course left to them. Flight.

Musket-fire punctuated the din of iron-shod hooves and manic voices. Reaching Friar Street and still miraculously unscathed, Ashley shouted to Nick to join himself and Francis – and had just succeeded in making himself heard when a party of Roundheads emerged behind them. Nicholas nodded and wheeled his horse to obey. Then he jerked oddly in the saddle, his mouth contorting into a surprised grimace before he toppled sideways to the ground.

Ashley started forward and then realised the hopelessness of it. He couldn't reach Nick before the enemy did. Furthermore, Francis's arm was a blood-soaked mass and his face a greyish blur which said that he wouldn't make it out of the city without help. Sick to his stomach, Ashley made the only possible choice. He grabbed Francis's bridle and hauled him down the nearest alley.

* * *

From a window overlooking the street, Verity Marriott stared down on Captain Austin's unconscious, crumpled body. Eviscerated by helplessness, she saw it semi-trampled by advancing cavalry and kicked viciously aside by a passing infantryman. She kept her eyes fixed on it until the chaos outside started to abate a little. Then she fled down the stairs and was within two steps of the door when Barbara appeared and asked where she was going. Because she couldn't tell the truth, she had to concoct a plausible lie and then suffer the torments of the damned for the best part of two hours before she could slip out of the side door unobserved.

Once clear of the house, she ran straight to the spot where Captain Austin had been lying ... only to find that she was too late.

He was no longer there.

NINE

The battle of Worcester ended later that evening when Lord Rothes finally surrendered the Castle Mound on Cromwell's terms. Out of the fifteen thousand-strong Scots army, only a couple of thousand managed to escape. Roughly three thousand lay dead at Wick or around the Sidbury Gate and, of the ten thousand or so prisoners herded into the Cathedral, more than half were wounded. For the next six days, with the stench rising vilely from the streets, Colonel Maxwell and his fellow-officers strove to deal with the multitude of corpses before turning their attention to the demolition of the city's defences.

Eden's first sight of the carnage at the Sidbury Gate made him feel ill – less at the grisly sight itself than at the unnecessary viciousness and lack of proper discipline that had created it. The shambles in front of him spoke of slaughter for slaughter's sake and, when added to Ireton's activities in Ireland – not to mention the execution of the late King – Eden was left feeling, not just disgusted, but besmirched; and for the first time, he started to truly appreciate some of Gabriel Brandon's strictures about the Lord-General. In an attempt to repair some of the damage along with his own self-disgust, he immediately ordered a detail of men to start removing those who were still alive.

Two days after the battle, Captain Sir Nicholas Austin awoke in Purgatory.

He knew it was Purgatory because of the putrid smell, the uncertain light and the terrible moaning of the other tormented souls. The only thing he didn't know was how he came to be there and how long he'd have to stay. He tried to calculate the weight of his sins ... and was still doing so when the darkness came again.

The next time he regained consciousness, the screaming agony in his arm and shoulder suggested that he might, in fact, still be alive. Since his surroundings continued to resemble the ante-chamber to hell, this possibility took some getting used to; but eventually he realised that he was lying on the stone-flagged floor of Worcester Cathedral ... and that the stench and groans arose from the countless other casualties packed in there with him. At this point, recollection returned, swiftly pursued by bitter depression; and that was when he decided that if the future held only a ride to London, followed by prison or worse, it wouldn't really matter if he didn't recover.

Sliding in and out of awareness, he didn't know how long it was before a surgeon came – or even that the man to his right had died waiting and lain there a day before being carted off for burial. Nick's head was full of heat and noise and wild, unpleasant fantasies. So when a blurred face peered beneath the reeking mess of his coat and a distant voice calmly remarked that his arm would have to come off before it killed him, he failed to take any particular notice.

Being out of his mind with fever, he mercifully knew nothing of the pain and horror which followed. Neither did he know that he'd missed being sent south with the first two batches of prisoners ... or that the surgeon who had amputated his arm didn't expect him to live until the departure of the third. And even when, against all expectation, the fever finally abated, he continued to lie motionless on the pallet to which they'd eventually moved him, staring unseeingly up at the vaulted ceiling of the cloisters above his head. With care, his mind blanked out first the pain ... and then everything else.

He was completely unaware that Verity Marriott was braving one official after another in a desperate attempt to discover what had become of him. And even if he'd known, he wouldn't have cared.

* * *

A week after the battle, Parliament offered a thousand pounds to anyone who succeeded in apprehending a man about two yards high and whose near-black hair had recently been cut short. It was a great deal of money and certainly enough to tempt somebody – even possibly a loyal somebody – into betraying the fugitive King.

Joshua Vincent, however, was intent purely on bringing the witch to court without further delay – preferably while any of the other city officers who might conceivably stand in his way were fully occupied with the devastation and chaos around them.

Using powers to which he was not strictly entitled, Joshua managed to arrange Deborah Hart's trial for the 12th – and, in so doing, wrought better than he knew because half the town was busy watching Cromwell ride away to make his report to Parliament. Even so, word concerning the witch-trial had spread and the court-room was packed. Joshua conducted the opening formalities whilst taking a good look at his audience, most of whom were men. Then he settled back in his seat and commanded that the accused be brought in.

An expectant hush fell as, bruised, filthy and bedraggled, Deborah was half-dragged to the dock. The crowd expelled a sighing breath and devoured her with its eyes. Then, still staring, it composed itself to listen.

Leaning heavily against the rail, Deborah scarcely heard the charges being read or knew anything except that her worst nightmares were about to be realised. Horrible as it had been, the evils which had befallen her in the gaol were as nothing compared to what was going to happen now. And she wasn't sure her little store of strength was equal to coping with it.

Witnesses were called. The blacksmith's wife, described in minute detail how she had suffered as a result of being over-looked ... and Zachary Paine gave evidence concerning the mysterious ills which had afflicted his livestock within hours of him repudiating the woman Hart's lewd advances. Two more of Deborah's neighbours came forward with vague but damaging accusations of *maleficium*; and the guard who'd been present at her questioning told the court of her inability to recite the Lord's Prayer without vomiting.

Finally, the proceedings arrived at the all-important question of witch-marks. Uneasy excitement rippled through the onlookers and the slight trembling in Deborah's limbs turned into violent shudders.

'Bring the woman to the floor of the court,' ordered Joshua.

Anticipation was making his palms sweat but he hid his eagerness beneath a veil of austerity while Deborah was hauled, stumbling, from her place. Then, with a careful lack of expression, he told the guards to examine her flesh for the devil's mark.

They knew where to look, of course. But they also knew that both the magistrate and the public benches would be disappointed if they completed their task too quickly ... so they started from the top and worked down.

Her gown fell to the floor, leaving her with nothing but her shift. Shaking from head to foot and being ripped apart by a silent scream, Deborah shut her eyes tight and tried to block out the touch of rough, intrusive hands and the knowledge that she was almost naked before fifty or sixty avid spectators. With the departure of Cromwell, more people arrived from outside to see the fun. They jostled each other in the doorway and thronged the corridor outside. Warming to their task, the guards played to the crowd and were rewarded with a mixture of gasps, shocked whispers and sniggers ... while, humiliated beyond endurance by the pulling up of her shift, tears slid through the dirt on Deborah's face.

Joshua waited until the mole was found before leaving his seat to examine it more closely. The courtroom fell silent, holding its breath. Then, turning and exhibiting the witch-probe to his captivated audience, he said sternly, 'If this is Satan's mark, it'll be immune to pain and it won't bleed. If it's no more than an ordinary blemish, it'll behave thus.' And, without warning, he plunged the sharp steel pin deep into the unmarked flesh of Deborah's flank.

Her eyes flew open and, unlocked by the pain, the scream she had been unable to voice tore its way from her throat to echo, high-pitched and anguished, around the room. Half of those on the public benches flinched. The rest craned their necks to see the blood.

'The reaction of innocent flesh,' observed Joshua, shifting both his own position and, with practised deftness, that of the probe in his hand. 'And now we will test the devil's mark.'

Deborah's breath was coming in raw gasps and a pulse hammered in her throat, threatening to choke her. She couldn't see what the magistrate was doing but anticipation of the pain throbbed through every nerve. She braced herself in readiness for it ... but felt only the touch of something cool and flat.

A strange murmur arose from the crowd and Joshua stepped back.

'Proof!' he thundered. 'The accused felt nothing – and there is no sign of a wound. What else can this be but the devil's work?'

A rumble of agreement flowed around the room. Many of those present made the sign against the evil eye and someone shouted, 'Burn her!'

Subduing a smile, Joshua held up his hands for silence. He didn't get it. Some sort of commotion was taking place in the doorway while, nearer the front, more voices shouted for the witch to be burned. The order of the last hour was disintegrating into confusion.

'What in Hades is going on here?' Without apparent difficulty, a crisp authoritative voice from the back made itself heard over the rising tumult and successfully quelled it. Then, 'Well? Is this a court of law or a bear-pit?'

Joshua looked down the length of the court-room into the lightly-scarred face of the Army officer who had just forced his way in, accompanied by half-a-dozen troopers. Swallowing, he replied carefully, 'It's a court. And though I don't doubt you mean well, your presence isn't needed.'

'Not needed – or not wanted?' Stripping off his gloves, Eden walked unhurriedly towards the magistrate. Then, his expression hardening as he absorbed the state of the petrified woman in the hands of the guards, 'I am Colonel Maxwell of Major-General Lambert's company ... and I repeat. What's going on here?'

'A witch trial,' snapped Joshua.

'Indeed. And you are?'

'Magistrate Vincent. And you're interrupting the due process of law.'

'Oh? From the noise, I thought it was a riot.'

'Yes – well, passions are running high,' came the grudging reply. 'The accused has just been found guilty.'

'Has she?' Revulsion stirred the hairs at the back of Eden's neck but he kept his tone perfectly level. 'I would very much like to hear how. And while you tell me, I suggest that the woman be allowed to cover herself.'

A protesting murmur arose from the crowd. Joshua hesitated and then, with a sullen jerk of his head, indicated that the guards might step back from the prisoner. Released from their grip, Deborah swayed and almost fell. Then, her expression dazed and uncomprehending, she reached for her gown and started to struggle awkwardly back into it.

Withdrawing his gaze from her, Eden strode to the corner farthest from curious ears and waited for the magistrate to follow him.

'Well?' he said.

Irritably and as unexpansively as possible, Joshua explained about the accusations and the indisputable evidence of the witch-mark. And when the Colonel remained apparently unimpressed, he added, 'This is the Lord's work. *Thou shalt not suffer a witch to live!*'

'If,' agreed Eden mildly, 'she *is* a witch. But the testimony you've described is scarcely conclusive; and for the rest ... hopefully we have learned something from the excesses of Matthew Hopkins.'

Joshua lost a little of his colour. At home in Friar Street was a well-thumbed copy of Hopkins' *Discovery of Witches*. Unfortunately, after hanging nineteen witches in a day at the Chelmsford Assizes, its author had become violently unpopular and later died under mysterious circumstances. It wasn't a fate Joshua wanted to share.

Keeping the probe carefully concealed in a fold of his robe, he said belligerently, 'If you're suggesting this trial hasn't been properly conducted – you've only to ask them as have watched it. Everything's been done openly for all to see.'

'Yes. I'm sure it has,' came the arid response. 'The unfortunate truth, however, is that people all too frequently see what they wish to see. There again ... one hears rumours of over-zealous officials and even, upon occasion, of probes being cunningly constructed in order to give the required result.' Eden waited, holding the magistrate's frozen gaze. Then, when no reply was forthcoming, he said, 'I'm sure you take my point.'

Joshua did. The implement in his hand had a small lever which caused the needle to retract. If the interfering young jackanapes in front of him insisted on examining it, his career on the bench would be finished – along with his reputation.

He said slowly, 'I don't see as this is any affair of yours. But if it'll make you feel better, I'll have the woman returned to gaol till a fresh trial can be arranged.'

Eden hesitated. He knew he was over-stepping his authority but he suddenly realised that he'd seen more blood, hatred and obscene violence in the last week than he could tolerate. And he was fairly sure that any trial the so-called witch received at the hands of this man would result in her being sent to either the gallows or the stake. Consequently, he decided to push his luck and hope that – if trouble came of it – Lambert would back him up.

'It's an idea,' he acknowledged smoothly. 'But then, so is showing me your witch-probe. On the other hand, it might be best if the accused were released into the custody of the Army while further investigations are made.' He paused and then, hiding the lie beneath a bland smile, 'It's matter in which certain of my superiors take great personal interest, you understand.'

Joshua wasn't sure he believed this but, since saying so was likely to result in him being forced to exhibit the probe, he had no choice but to remain silent. Quelling a desire to wipe out the inconvenient young officer's smug smile with the back of his hand, he shrugged and said, 'You'd better take her, then. But the good people of Worcester have a right to see justice done.'

'My point exactly,' murmured Eden. And turning, ordered his troopers to take charge of the accused.

Fortunately, they were all survivors of Upton and, though puzzled by his behaviour and uneasy about its possible outcome, they obeyed without question.

Half-relieved at the unexpected reprieve and half-frightened that the nightmare was going to begin all over again, Deborah found herself surrounded by a clutch of burly, wooden-faced individuals who – though they made no attempt to man-handle her – looked far from reassuring. Meanwhile, the whispers which had been rustling along the public benches turned into a low rumble of anger.

Ignoring it, Eden nodded to Sergeant Trotter to take the woman out. There was an out-burst of cat-calls and spitting but none of the onlookers were quite brave enough to get in the way of the Army. Eden waited until he was sure there would be no trouble. Then, according the magistrate the briefest of bows and raising his voice a little, he said, 'Your forbearance does you credit, Mr Vincent. I shall see that it's not forgotten.' Upon which Parthian shot, he stalked off in the wake of his men.

Outside in the street, Sergeant Trotter was marching Deborah Hart smartly in the direction of the Commandery and wondering what he was supposed to do with her when he got there.

Catching up with him, Eden said ruefully, 'I know, Rob – I know. But what else could I do?'

'That's as maybe, sir,' came the reproving reply. 'But what's to become of her now? We can't cope with no more prisoners – and if you send her home, her neighbours'll string her up quicker'n you can wink.'

This was something Eden had not considered. Looking at the dirty, dishevelled creature he'd rescued purely as a matter of principle, he said, 'Is that true?'

Deborah pushed back her hair with shaking hands and stammered, 'Probably. And if they d-don't, the magistrate will come for me again fast enough.' Then, drawing a long, painful breath, 'I don't understand. Why did you take me out of there? Am I not to be t-tried again?'

Frowning absently, Eden shook his head.

'Not if I can help it. Have you relatives you can go to?'

'No. My husband's dead and I – I've no one else,' she replied faintly. And, overcome with the vicissitudes of the last weeks, crumpled quietly away on to the cobbles.

* * *

While, for want of a better solution, Eden concealed Mistress Hart amidst the usual assortment of wives, mistresses and whores, Verity Marriott learned that a severely wounded officer answering Captain Austin's description had been moved, along with a number of other similarly unhopeful cases, to the cellar of the Commandery.

On the following morning, sick with fright, she followed a guard down the steps into the malodourous gloom where a dozen or so men lay struggling to retain their frail hold on life. And there amongst them, on a lumpy pallet in the corner, she found Nicholas ... his face sunken, his skin grey and his breathing scarcely perceptible beneath the thin blanket which covered him – yet still miraculously alive. Verity's nerves snarled and she froze.

Bored and eager to return to his dice-game, the guard said, 'Well?' She swallowed hard and nodded.

'Yes. It – it's my brother. Does no one ... is no one looking after him?'

The guard shrugged and, twitching back the blanket, said, 'The surgeon's already done everything he could.'

Unprepared for the mass of bandages wound awkwardly around the place where Nicholas's left arm should have been, she made a small choking sound. She knelt in the dirty straw at his and said softly, 'Nicholas? Nick? It – it's Verity.'

'You're wasting your time,' said the guard impatiently. And he tramped away.

Verity absorbed the matted brown hair, the colourless tightly-stretched skin and the empty unfocussed stare. And that was when the truth hit her. He was dying – but not of his wound, nor even of fever or infection. He was dying from lack of will to do otherwise.

Fright and misery transmuted themselves into anger. She didn't know if he was already past saving. She only knew that she had to do something. So she gritted her teeth, gave him a violent shake and said raggedly, 'Wake up. You're *not* going to die – do you hear me? *You are not going to die!*' And was about to shake him again when, from the top of the stairs came footsteps and a new, extremely disapproving voice.

'This place stinks like a bloody midden. When did you last empty the slop pails, you idle bugger?'

'Yesterday morning, Sarge.'

'That's Sergeant Trotter to you, lad. And I suppose you've been too busy with your dice-box to do it since then, have you?'

'I'm here on guard-duty, Sergeant. I ain't a flaming cleaner.'

'You're here to do as you're told. So move your arse and start getting this place fit to be seen. Colonel Maxwell's on his way to see if you've got anybody fit to send south. And if he finds the buckets full to the brim and puke all over the floor, I wouldn't like to be in your shoes - so get a move on!'

The footsteps receded and a door slammed. Verity whispered rapidly, 'Did you hear? Colonel Maxwell's coming. He's the one they say saved that woman charged with witchcraft. And if he'd put himself out for her, he might do as much for you.' She shook Nicholas again. 'Are you listening? He might be able to get you out of here. But not ... *not* if you won't wake up!' And finally, in desperation, she slapped his face.

It was nearly an hour before she met the Colonel who was her only hope and, by then, she'd managed to rouse Nicholas sufficiently to take a few sips of water but not enough to speak. Consequently, she had no idea whether he understood anything she'd been saying or not.

Colonel Maxwell, who was younger than she'd expected, frowned at her and said, 'This is no place for you. Go home.'

She stood up and pushed back her hair. 'Please. Help us.'

'To do what?' asked Eden automatically. But he already knew … just as, looking down at the fellow on the pallet, he knew that it was probably hopeless. As gently as he could, he said, 'I'm sorry … but moving him now would almost certainly kill --'

'It won't! He hasn't died yet and he won't die now. Just help me get him out of this evil place.' She spread pleading hands. 'If he was your brother or your friend, would you leave him here? *Would* you?'

'No. I wouldn't. But where do you want to take him? Back to your home?'

'I can't. My step-father would throw him into the street – and me with him.' She hesitated and then, tried a different tack. 'You met him yesterday at the courthouse. He's Magistrate Vincent.'

Eden's eyes widened slightly and he gave a short laugh. Then he stared down at Nicholas. He still thought the case was hopeless … but he had taken a strong dislike to Joshua Vincent and the conditions in the room around him were a disgrace. Finally and with reluctance, he said, 'Very well. I'll have him moved – though God knows where to. And I have nobody who can undertake the task of nursing him. So --'

'I'll do it.' Verity interrupted him without giving a second thought to what she was promising. 'I'll look after him.'

Eden wondered what on earth he was going to do with a dying man and a child and recognised that he should simply say no – just as yesterday he should have stayed out of the business of Deborah Hart. Faint ironic humour stirred and he murmured, 'I must be completely out of my mind. As for what Sergeant Trotter is going to say … I hate to think.'

* * *

Much to Eden's surprise, Nicholas Austin did not die. He made the journey from Worcester to London strapped to a pallet in one of the baggage wagons, nursed single-handedly by Verity until Sergeant Trotter – who didn't believe in witchcraft but reckoned there was no smoke without fire – enlisted the aid of Mistress Hart.

Whatever took place during the next two days was something –
judging from the expression on his sergeant's face – that Eden preferred
not to know about. But at the end of them, Deborah appeared outside
his billet one evening and said, 'The young man is better, I think – and
the girl has had some rest. She's not his sister, by the way.'

'Not?'

'No. Her name is Marriott, his is Austin. And she thinks she's in love
with him.'

'Oh my God,' groaned Eden. 'She's just a child! And I suppose she
also thinks it's mutual?'

'I hope not. As far as I can make out, she'd only met him twice before
you turned up.'

Eden closed his eyes and swore.

'Wonderful! What the hell am I supposed to do with her?'

'More to the point, what are you going to do with *him?* Put him in
prison?'

'I should. And in the end, I may not have any choice.'

'Well, at least you've saved his life. And mine.' She drew a slightly
unsteady breath. 'I don't know how to thank you for that.'

'By continuing to look after the children,' returned Eden briskly. 'And
when young Austin is fit to hold a conversation, let me know.'

* * *

By the time they reached the outskirts of London and made camp on
Hounslow Heath, Nicholas was able to sit up and even feed himself. He
had not, however, become any more communicative and only ever
spoke in response to direct questions. Informing Colonel Maxwell of
this, Deborah added, 'He's still in pain but that isn't the real problem.
He's depressed and shocked over the loss of his arm and I suspect he
thinks this journey will end in the Tower. So the only future he sees is
one he doesn't want.'

'And the girl?'

'She's starting to realise that saving a life isn't always for the best …
and it frightens her.' Deborah looked into the hazel eyes, careful to
disguise what she was beginning to feel for him. Then, with a faint
smile, 'If you've any comfort to offer, now might be a good time.'

Eden looked back at her, wishing he didn't remember what she looked like without her clothes. He also wished the night-dark eyes didn't seem to be able to see right through him. With a tolerable assumption of amusement, he said, 'What did you have in mind?'

'That's up to you, Colonel. But Nicholas won't be back on his feet for a while and Verity is seventeen years old, with no more idea of the world than a kitten. They're not going to manage on their own.'

'No. I suppose not. And what of you?'

'I'll be all right. I'll find work in a tavern or a laundry or some such. I can turn my hand to most things.' She faced him challengingly. 'Are you going to talk to Nicholas?'

Eden sighed. 'I suppose I'd better if he's well enough.'

'He's well enough. But don't be surprised if he's too apathetic to talk back.'

* * *

Verity scrambled to her feet when Colonel Maxwell appeared at the wagon and stammered, 'C-Colonel! I w-wanted to come and thank you but Sergeant Trotter said --'

'That you were to stay out of sight of the officers. Yes.' Eden's tone was pleasant but quelling. 'I'd prefer as few people as possible to know who many rules I'm breaking.' He looked into Nicholas's expressionless eyes. 'Since you're awake, I think it's time we had a talk.'

Nicholas said nothing.

Verity opened her mouth to reply for him but was forestalled by the Colonel saying firmly, 'I'd be grateful if you could leave us for a time, Mistress Marriott.' He waited for her to go and, when she had done so, sat down and came straight to the point. 'Who are you?'

'Captain Sir Nicholas Austin.'

'Which regiment?'

'Colonel Peverell's.'

'Never heard of him,' said Eden cheerfully. 'Any good, is he?'

'I thought so.' The words were ambiguous, the tone one of pure apathy.

Eden frowned slightly. 'Tell me about him.'

'What is there to say? He did his best.' A pause. 'We all did.'

'Not quite all, as I understand it. Leslie's Horse was never engaged.'

104

'Weren't they? I don't remember.'

'What's the last thing you *do* remember?'

Nicholas turned his head away. 'Seeing Ashley. Colonel Peverell. We'd got separated but I saw him again in Friar Street. He waved for me to join him only – only I was shot.'

'And he couldn't get you out?'

'Obviously not.' Nicholas's brow furrowed with effort. 'I think Francis was wounded, too. I – I remember his coat being all bloody.'

'Francis?' said Eden sharply. 'Not Francis Langley, by any chance?'

'Yes.' For the first time, Nicholas looked vaguely interested. 'Do you know him?'

Eden laughed. 'Oh yes. I've known him since I was eight. But the last time I saw him was at Upton, a couple of days before the battle. His fellows had just nearly roasted mine alive and I wanted to murder him. He thought I was going to do it, too. But it's a bit difficult to kill somebody you've been birds-nesting with, don't you find?'

'I suppose so.' Nicholas shifted restlessly and the tiny spark in his eyes faded. 'Verity says I owe you my life.'

'No. You owe Verity and Mistress Hart your life.'

'All three of you, then.' Another pause. 'What are you going to do with me?'

'Offer you a bargain,' replied Eden, having been aware for some time that it would come to this. 'Give me your word that you won't fight for Charles Stuart again and I'll --'

'With one arm?' snapped Nicholas bitterly.

'You wouldn't be the first. However. Give me your parole and I'll try to keep you out of the Tower. I can't promise – but I'll do my best.'

'Why?' A tiny flicker of hope mingled oddly with the desolation in the brown eyes. 'Why would you do that?'

Eden sighed and stood up.

'I'm not entirely sure. Let's just say I'm reluctant to have everybody's efforts on your behalf go to waste ... and leave it at that.'

'But where --?'

'Sufficient unto the day is the evil thereof. In short,' grinned Eden, 'I haven't the faintest idea. But when I find the solution, you'll be the first to know.'

ENTR'ACTE
Devizes - October 1651

At around the time Nicholas was beginning to return to the land of the living, His Majesty the King finally landed on the coast of France. His adventures in the seven weeks since the battle had included an oak tree, a priest's hole and the help of many brave and loyal souls. He'd been disguised as a groom, a scullion and an eloping lover. But he'd reached safety with his head still on his shoulders – which, under the circumstances, was a miracle.

Knowing none of this and with less help of their own to call on, Colonel Peverell and Major Langley were still lurking in a ruined barn near Devizes, wearily contemplating their next move.

They'd escaped from Worcester without too much difficulty. Jem Barker – always one step ahead of possible pursuit – had met them outside St Martin's gate, laden with as many of their combined belongings as he could carry; and because General Leslie's cavalry would naturally be fleeing north towards the border, Ashley had reasoned that their own safest course lay in the opposite direction.

They'd discarded all items of clothing which marked them as soldiers, travelled largely by night along back-roads and left the acquisition of provisions to Jem. For the first few days – despite Francis's wound refusing to completely stop bleeding and leaving him weak as a result – it had been relatively easy. By the end of a week, however, the net was beginning to tighten as Commonwealth troops arrested every suspected Cavalier in their path while they scoured the land in search of the King. And they were still many miles from the sea.

Although he was rarely out of their thoughts, they spoke of Nicholas only once. Francis said, 'He may be alive. If he is, they'll have taken him prisoner.'

And Ashley replied, 'Along with thousands of others. You've enough experience to know how these things work. Firstly, how many surgeons do you suppose they have? And by the time they've separated the living from the dead and supplied aid to those who have a chance of surviving, there'll be a fresh set of corpses.' Then, later, 'I should have gone back. I might not have been able to save him – but I should have tried.' And later still, on a furious explosion of breath, 'God damn David Leslie! If he'd engaged his Horse we could have won. God damn him to the lowest pit of hell.'

By the time they passed Devizes, Francis's arm was finally showing small signs of improvement. And that was when Ashley announced that trying to take ship for France or the Netherlands while the whole country was still on the look-out for fugitives from the battle was as quick a way as any to court capture.

'Very likely.' Unshaven and filthier than he had ever been in his life, Francis shifted his back against the rough stone wall of the barn and winced as pain lanced through his arm. 'How do you think His Majesty is faring?'

'Better than us, I hope. Wilmot was with him – and Derby and Gifford and some others. Too many, probably. The larger the party, the less likely it is to pass unnoticed. But hopefully they've managed to get Charles out of the country – or at least found him somewhere safe to hide until they can.'

'And us? How long can we go on like this? Our appearance isn't exactly calculated to go unremarked, is it?'

'No. So if we're going to wait until the chase dies down, our first task is to exchange our present clothing for something more humble.'

'Is that possible?' asked Francis, distastefully eyeing the state of his coat.

'Yes. We may be in rags – but they're *good* rags,' replied Ashley wryly. 'What we need is homespun and clouted shoes.' He thought for a moment. 'You'll have to stay out of sight until your arm is healed. Battle-wounds are likely to be a bit of a give-away. So for the time being, Jem and I will continue to forage as before. But when you're fit again, we go back into Devizes – separately, of course – and we find work.'

'I beg your pardon?'

'You heard.' Colonel Peverell smiled grimly. 'We hire ourselves out as stable-hands, potboys, gardeners, scullions – anything which doesn't require skills we haven't got. And we act. You can manage that, can't you?'

'I don't know,' said Francis truthfully. 'I really don't know. But if it's a choice between that and spending another few months in the Tower, I'll do my best. Anything, in fact, that will eventually lead us out of this nightmare and back to civilisation.'

'Predictable as ever, I see.'

'Naturally. I haven't cared to mention it ... but the thought of a bath and some decent clothes is the only thing which has been keeping me going for several miles now. That and a little fantasy of my own which I prefer to nurture in private.'

'Hold on to it,' advised Ashley. 'It may help soften the pain when Jem hacks off your lovelocks with a knife.'

ACT TWO

LA PETITE GALZAIN
Paris, May to August, 1652

'Worldly wealth he cared not for, desiring only to make both ends meet.'
Thomas Fuller

ONE

In contrast to the bright spring weather which cheered the rest of Paris, storm clouds gathered over the rue Vieille du Temple where rehearsals for the Théâtre du Marais' forthcoming revival of *Le Cid* had ground to a halt for the third time in less than an hour.

'Imbecile!' roared Clermont, storming down on Etienne Lepreux. *'Imbec-ile!* Your move is upstage. *Upstage!* Do you understand where that is? It is back there! A simple direction even a complete idiot should be able to follow. And you do not *ever*, under *any* circumstances, cross in front of *me!'*

Athenais de Galzain sat on the edge of the stage and sank her teeth into an apple. Not for the first time, she wondered whether she'd been wise to decline the tentative approach from the Illustre Théâtre. Jean-Baptiste Poquelin de Molière's clever touch with comedy was earning his troupe a sound reputation. But joining a touring company wouldn't be the quickest way of advancing her career; and at the Illustre Théâtre she would be competing for roles with Madeleine Béjart – who was as red-haired as Athenais herself and also had the advantage of being Jean-Baptiste Poquelin's mistress.

So she had remained at the Marais and generally managed to overlook its drawbacks. The first of these was that the repertoire consisted largely of old-fashioned farces. This week, for example, they were doing Rotrou's *La Bague de L'Oubli* which was forty years old and had been played so often that audiences were apt to chorus the best lines along with the actors. The second was that she was frequently required to act opposite a temperamental old fart who wasn't nearly as good as he thought he was and smelled perpetually of garlic.

Athenais spat a pip into the musician's gallery and reflected that she was heartily sick of Arnaud Clermont. He had played (as he was fond of reminding everyone) with all the Greats. What he chose to ignore – and what no one quite dared to point out – was that acting alongside Montdory and Jodelet didn't necessarily mean he shared their stature. And, as far as Athenais was concerned, the only notable things about Clermont were his dragon's breath and his sheer bloody arrogance –

both of which were likely to stop her enjoying her first chance to play Corneille.

The news that, sixteen years after having premiered it, the Marais was to present a revival of *Le Cid* had stunned the company because Corneille had been sending his plays to the Hôtel de Bourgogne for the last fifteen. Before that, the late Cardinal Richelieu had supported the Marais while the King favoured the Bourgogne – resulting in often violent rivalry between the two theatres. But when Montdory retired from the stage after suffering an apoplexy on it, Richelieu had withdrawn his patronage … resulting in the Marais' swift decline to second-rate status.

On the other hand, people came and the house was never less than two-thirds full. Athenais wondered what the *Cid* would do for the takings – and how much Manager Laroque was having to pay for the privilege of staging it. Hopefully, not too much. Corneille's last play had been a failure and the one before, not much better. Rumour had it that the Bourgogne had lost faith in his ability which, if it was true, accounted for the playwright's sudden willingness to deal with the poor relation he'd abandoned a decade and a half ago.

Behind her on the stage, Clermont's tantrum droned on.

'I cannot,' he ranted, 'tolerate working with amateurs. While lack of presence and talent may be excused in the young – an absence of any knowledge of stage-craft cannot. Perhaps Etienne should go back to doing walk-ons until he has mastered the basics of our art.'

Athenais tossed her apple-core into the pit and contemplated her ankles. Like the rest of her diminutive person, they were shapely. Indeed, it was largely her looks – coupled with the business of the feathers – which had taken her from six-line cameos to leading roles in just under a year. But it was aggravating to be regarded as just another pretty face when one also had a sound grasp of one's craft. Worse still, public taste was notoriously fickle; and though *la petite Galzain* was currently in fashion, there was no guarantee of it lasting.

The delay was lasting too long. Athenais swung her feet back on to the boards and stood up. The rest of the cast were either propping up the proscenium with expressions of profound irritation or standing about in pairs, muttering. Athenais knew how they felt. It was usually best to let Clermont run his course; but with only a week to go and the play still in shreds, they could ill-afford to waste an entire afternoon. Antoine Froissart, in charge of directing the rehearsal, obviously thought so too and was attempting, without noticeable success, to get a word in edgeways. Athenais decided that a more direct approach was called for.

Summoning her sweetest smile and ignoring Froissart's warning frown, she crossed to Clermont's side and tucked her arm through his.

'Arnaud ... naughty as it was of Etienne to cross in front of you, you shouldn't be wasting your energies in this fashion. It was a mistake and he won't do it again. Meanwhile, we've a performance tonight – and what chance has it got if our leading man is too weary to give of his best?' She paused and laid her free hand over his. 'Think how the rest of us rely on you, Arnaud. Above all, think of your *public.*'

Clermont clasped her hand and, in a voice quivering with anguish, exclaimed, 'You are right! I *do* have a duty to preserve myself. But what can one do? Selfishness is an anathema to me and the play must come first. Etienne is an imbecile!'

'I know.' Caught in a wave of foul breath, Athenais struggled not to grimace. 'I know. But you've shown him his mistake and now you must spare yourself. No – you must listen to me. If you won't have a care for yourself, the rest of us must do it for you.' She smiled again and, making the ultimate sacrifice, added, 'Would it soothe you to rehearse our love scene?'

Clermont hesitated and everybody else held their breath. Then he said, 'I'm sure it would, beloved ... and your empathy overwhelms me. Sadly, however, I am *far* too agitated to continue ... and I shudder to think what my performance may be like this evening if I don't rest. Forgive me!' He silenced Athenais with one hand and clutched his brow with the other. 'I must leave you to manage as best you may whilst I retire to my couch for the benefit of all.' And still clasping his head, he stalked from the stage and disappeared.

There was a long silence. Then, from his corner, Etienne Lepreux muttered bitterly, 'If you ask me, it would be a mercy if the old bugger retired *completely.*'

The tension disintegrated into a ripple of laughter. Athenais met Froissart's slightly desperate stare and, with a tiny shrug, said, 'Sorry, Monsieur. It went wrong.'

'It did,' agreed the assistant-manager, long-sufferingly. And then, a sudden smile breaking through, 'But it was a nice try. A trifle over-played perhaps … but beautifully scripted.'

'Mademoiselle de Galzain is a positive mine of accomplishments,' drawled a female voice from the wings. 'One is constantly amazed. In time, we shall doubtless see her picking up her pen and aping that scribbler, Molière.'

Athenais looked across at her arch-rival. Tall, dark-haired and deep-bosomed, Marie d'Amboise had been playing tragic leads for nearly a full decade before Athenais had struck the public fancy; and since she was by no means ready to retire from her position as first lady of the company, she had naturally conceived a violent dislike for her successor.

Athenais understood this and sympathised. She was even ready to admit that Marie's statuesque appearance was probably better suited to roles like Chimène than her own petite slenderness. She was not, however, prepared to be trodden on; and consequently she said gratefully, 'Thank you, Madame. I fear you flatter me … but encouragement from one of your superior age and experience is always welcome.'

An angry flush touched Marie's cheek and, seeing it, Froissart said quickly, 'Ladies and gentlemen, we've wasted enough time for one day. Arnaud's departure is unfortunate but there are still those scenes in which he doesn't appear. Mademoiselle de Galzain, Madame d'Amboise – we'll begin on page twenty-six.'

'Why?' exploded Etienne. 'I'm understudying Rodrigue – and I could play him, too. At least I'm the right age – unlike that fat old arse-worm!'

'Youth,' observed Marie d'Amboise coldly, 'isn't everything. Experience and talent still count for something.'

'I know that – and so does Clermont. Basically, he's got the experience and I've got the talent. Why else do you think he refuses to let me rehearse – if not because he's shit-scared I'll act him off the sodding stage?'

There was some truth in that, thought Athenais. Meeting Froissart's gaze, she said persuasively, 'Couldn't Etienne stand in, Monsieur? Just this once, to help the rest of us?'

'I don't see the point of rehearsing around stand-ins,' yawned Marie. 'And Clermont would be furious. He doesn't permit *anyone* to read in for him. Ever.'

'Then he ought to have stayed,' shrugged Athenais. 'He said himself that the play comes first. And if we start now, we've got time to get through the first act.'

Froissart thought about it. Part of him was eager to see what young Lepreux made of the *Cid*; another part said it might be better not to know. Lacklustre as Clermont's performances often were, he still commanded a certain following among the middle-aged matrons he'd captivated twenty years ago. Consequently, supplanting him with a newcomer of remarkable stage-presence but undistinguished appearance wasn't likely to do much for the takings – particularly in these uncertain times.

The so-called Princes' Fronde – caused by the late Cardinal Richelieu's determination to crush the power of the nobility – had boiled over the previous autumn and swiftly become a power-struggle between Louis de Bourbon, the Prince de Condé and Richelieu's successor, Cardinal Mazarin. Since then, Condé had taken Paris and forced both Court and Cardinal into exile at St. Germain. Froissart suspected that this situation was likely to be temporary. On the other hand, it was the kind of thing which could be very bad for business unless one turned it to one's advantage. And that was why he and Pierre Regnault Petit-Jean Laroque had decided to echo Condé's triumph with a piece about another great warrior.

Clermont was the devil one knew. Lepreux was a gamble and allowing him to rehearse Rodrigue would conjure up a storm – for which Manager Laroque was unlikely to thank him. Sighing, Froissart opened his mouth on a sensible refusal … and, instead, heard himself say curtly, 'Very well. Act one, scene one. Begin.'

* * *

An hour or so later when everyone else had left to snatch a brief rest before the evening performance, Athenais de Galzain – whose home lay on the far side of the Seine – sat in the Green Room with her feet up and nibbled absently on an almond cake whilst having her hair brushed.

'Etienne was good, Pauline,' she remarked meditatively, at length. '*Really* good. If Froissart had any sense, he'd ask Monsieur Laroque to give him the part.'

'And lose Clermont to the Hôtel de Bourgogne? Don't be ridiculous. Froissart knows which side his bread is buttered,' returned the wardrobe-mistress cum dresser tersely. Then, on a small explosion of breath, 'Pity the same can't be said of you.'

'Why? What have I done?'

'Opened your mouth when you should have kept it shut. You know what will happen. D'Amboise will tell Clermont it was your idea to let Etienne read in – and he'll throw a fit.'

'Let him,' sniffed Athenais. And, with a grin, 'He's always going on about his old friend Montdory. Perhaps he'll do us all a favour and go the same way – though preferably not mid-performance.' She paused and, when Pauline didn't laugh, added, 'It was a joke.'

'One you'd better not repeat.'

'I wouldn't – except to you.'

'You would. You'd say it to Clermont himself if he pushed you far enough. And unless somebody else upsets him first and worse, he's quite likely to do that tonight. So you'd better be ready to hold your tongue and deal with whatever he throws at you on stage.'

'I'm *always* ready. The daft old bugger fluffs his lines so often, I have to be.' Athenais settled back and took another bite of the cake. 'Don't worry. I can handle Clermont. And if he tries any of his little tricks, I'll have the pit on my side.'

'Don't rely on it. The pit can break you as easily as it made you.'

'So if I'm ever to get out of the Rue Benoit, I can't afford to disappoint my public,' recited Athenais obediently. 'Yes. I know.'

This remark was less flippant than it sounded. The Rue Benoit was the tiny, insalubrious alleyway between St. Severin and St. Julien-le-Pauvre where Athenais lived with her father in a three-roomed hovel … and which she was desperate to leave.

Pauline said slowly, 'Yes. Well, you know my views on that. Quite apart from it being inconvenient living so far from the theatre, the world judges by appearances. If your admirers knew how you live, they'd die laughing.'

Athenais sighed.

'There's a house on the Rue des Rosiers that would be perfect. But I can't afford it. And even if I could, I'd never talk Father into moving. Squalor doesn't bother him as long as he's got enough money to spend most of his waking hours in the tavern.'

Frowning, Pauline laid down the hair-brush and, keeping her tone perfectly neutral, said, 'Perhaps you should consider leaving him to stew in his own juice, then.'

An odd expression, half-stubborn and half-regretful, stirred in the luminous smoke-dark eyes and it was a while before Athenais said wryly, 'I consider it several times a day. But I can't do it. The drunken old sod's the only family I've got.'

* * *

Precisely as Pauline had predicted, Clermont used that night's performance of *La Bague de L'Oubli* to show Athenais the error of her ways. He threw her incorrect cues or none at all; he cut her lines, then paused where she had none before continuing with an air of subtle reproof; and he altered his moves so as to alternatively up-stage or mask her. By the end of the first act, Athenais thought she'd parried every trick in the book; after the second, she was fraught with the effort of re-arranging her speeches so they made sense and giddy from circling the stage like a blowfly; and, at some point in the third, she lost her temper.

She hid it from the audience. But as soon as the play was over she rounded on Clermont in full view of the company and, using the gutter vernacular of her childhood, told him what she thought of his acting, his professionalism and his stinking breath. Then, leaving him white with fury, she turned on her heel and stalked away.

The audience was still leaving the theatre and the street outside was thronged with carriages and chairs. Athenais found her own shabby hire-coach on the corner of the Rue de la Perle. Its driver was enjoying a leisurely pipe but as soon as she appeared, he grinned and said, 'You're early tonight. Place on fire, is it?'

'Something like that,' she agreed aridly. And then, from inside the carriage, 'Martin – I've had a downright evil evening. Can we just go?'

'Suits me,' he shrugged. And, slamming the door shut, hoisted himself on to the box and set the horses in motion.

The cobbled, tooth-rattling route took them down the Rue Vieille du Temple, then past the Hôtel de Ville and the Place de Grève to the Tour St. Jacques. From there they crossed the Pont au Change to the Ile de la Cité before leaving it again by means of the crumbling Petit Pont below the Hôtel Dieu. Athenais clung to the strap, wearily regretting her outburst at the theatre and longing for her bed. Then the coach plunged to a halt.

'*Now* what?' she muttered irritably and stuck her head out of the window.

Inexplicably, the Petit Pont was blocked with fallen scaffolding and chunks of masonry beneath which lay a cart. A handful of people were attempting to remove the debris but, since it would plainly take hours to clear the road, Martin gloomily observed that they would either have to pay the toll on the Pont au Double or go right round via the Pont Neuf.

'*Merde!*' breathed Athenais bitterly. Then, descending from the coach, 'Go home, Martin. I'll walk.'

Hefrowned. 'You can't.'

'Yes, I can. It won't take more than ten minutes – and I can take care of myself,' she replied, tying her hood firmly beneath her chin. 'Goodnight, *mon vieux*. I'll see you tomorrow.' And she walked on to the bridge and started clambering over the wreckage.

It wasn't difficult and she managed well enough until her skirt got caught – reminding her that, in her haste to leave the theatre, she hadn't bothered to get changed and was therefore still wearing her costume. This in itself was a fineable offence. If she also damaged the wretched thing, it was likely to cost her a day's wages.

She gave her skirt an experimental tug and heard an ominous tearing sound. A colourful expletive escaped her lips and she twisted round, trying to locate the source of the problem without making matters any worse. Her balance faltered.

Two capable hands grasped her about the waist and a rich, seductive voice, rippling with amusement, said, 'If you stand still for a moment, Mademoiselle, I'll disentangle you.'

Athenais found herself staring down on a tall fellow in a wide-brimmed hat and trailing black cloak. His face, no more than a pale blur in the darkness, disappeared abruptly as he bent to free her skirt from the nail-studded piece of scaffolding which had ensnared it. Then, straightening his back and holding out his arm to her, he said, 'May I help you down?'

Ignoring both arm and offer, Athenais jumped down and pulled her cloak more firmly about her. Then, uttering a frigid 'thank you', she waited for him to step aside.

He didn't do so. Instead, still on that annoying note of laughter, he said, 'Since you've been forced to abandon your conveyance, I'd be happy to escort you to your door.'

'And beyond it no doubt,' snapped Athenais witheringly. Then, 'Get out of my way. I didn't come down with the last shower – and if you want a whore, I suggest you try the Pont Neuf.'

The man stepped back and accorded a small, sardonic bow.

'Thank you for the advice. I'll bear it in mind. Just now, however, I was merely offering my protection. At this time of night, the St. Severin quarter is no place for a lady.'

Some half-dozen steps past him, Athenais halted again and turned her head.

'I know that. I live there. And fortunately, I'm no lady. So don't try your tricks on me. I've heard them all before – plus a few you haven't yet thought of.'

'I doubt that.' Laughter drifted after her across the bridge. 'And you shouldn't make so many assumptions. They'll trip you up, one day.'

Athenais continued briskly on her way.

'Bugger off,' she said.

TWO

At home in the ugly little house on the Rue Benoit, Athenais found her father snoring drunkenly over the kitchen table and, leaving him where he was, went straight to her own cramped room under the eaves. Then, throwing herself into bed, she sank into deep, dreamless slumber.

She awoke, as usual, shortly after nine and, wrapping herself in a chamber-robe which the second-hand clothes seller in St. Michel assured her had once belonged to a marquise, went down to cook herself a belated breakfast.

Her father – awake and more or less sober – was sitting by the hearth, nursing his head. Athenais's brows rose and she said blightingly, 'My God. Which has run out – Gaston's wine or your money?'

Archibald Stott, who'd fought in the German wars until the palsy had taken the use of his right arm, looked back at her blearily and, in the unlovely accents of Bridewell, said plaintively, 'Bleeding 'ell, Agnes – for Gawd's sake stop nagging, will you?'

Athenais drew an irritable breath and, sticking to French, snapped, 'I haven't started yet. And don't call me Agnes.'

'Why shouldn't I? You can use a fancy made-up 'andle at the theatre – but in this 'ouse you're plain Agnes Stott.'

It was an old argument. Usually, Athenais refused the bait. Today, with her nerves at full-stretch over the likely consequences of her attack on Clermont, she said acidly, 'Since you and *Maman* never married, that's not true, is it? But if it was, I could hardly be blamed for changing it. Agnes is bad enough, God knows. But *Stott?*'

Archie sat up rather too spryly and winced at the sudden throbbing in his head.

'I don't see what's wrong wiv it.'

'No. You wouldn't.' Snatching a pitcher from the table, Athenais turned towards the door to the yard. 'If you want breakfast, you can make a start by getting the fire going,' she remarked. And went out to the pump.

The yard stank of rotting cabbage leaves and the contents of countless *pots de chambre*. Athenais wrinkled her nose and, ignoring the jibes of the pair of slatterns gossiping by the wall, filled her pitcher and went back inside to fry slices of sausage. Archie watched her work and, in between debating ways of getting her to line his empty pockets, wondered – not for the first time – how he and Louise had managed to produce such a little beauty.

He was proud of her, in his way. Proud of her success on the stage as well as the way men looked at her. He was also sometimes uneasy about exactly how far she'd had to use the second in order to achieve the first. But he never asked any questions or told her of either emotion. He simply reminded himself that, despite her fragile appearance, his Agnes had a will of iron, the constitution of an ox and a tongue like a razor.

As for himself, he'd never meant to let her keep them both and, in the past, had tried various schemes which always seemed certain to make money but somehow never did. For a year or so after Louise had died, he'd even occasionally tried holding down a job. But when nothing worked, apathy had set in, causing him to dive deeper and deeper into the bottle. And the truth which lay inescapably at the bottom of it was that the dratted palsy had deprived him of the only thing he'd ever been any good at. Soldiering. Without that, he was left with nothing; not even self-respect.

Whereas the recent civil troubles afflicting France had failed to grasp Archie's interest, the wars in England had been a constant reminder of what he was missing. And just when he thought that the battle of Worcester had finally removed that particular thorn from his side, the Commonwealth had driven it in afresh.

As Athenais placed the platters on the table and sat down opposite him, Archie said abruptly, 'Now England's at war wiv the Dutch, I reckon the Cavaliers'll be trying their luck again.'

Athenais, whose interest in English politics registered at several points below zero, merely shrugged. Then, when her father continued staring morosely at his sausage, she relented and answered in the English he'd taught her.

'Wiv what? They got no army, no money and nobody to 'elp 'em. By all accounts, they're lucky they still got their Prince.'

Archie scowled. Everyone knew that Charles Stuart had narrowly escaped death or capture in England and only got back to Paris by the skin of his teeth, leaving his Cause in tatters behind him. Scotland was being forcibly incorporated into England; the Royalists of far-off Barbados and Virginia had submitted to the Commonwealth; and even though Henry Ireton had been dead since the previous November, Ireland still lay crushed beneath the boots of the New Model. Consequently, the Parliament had probably picked as good a time as any to go to war with the Dutch over the carrying-trade.

Through a piece of sausage, Archie said stubbornly, 'He's not a prince no more. He's King of England.'

'Noll Cromwell don't seem to fink so.'

'No. Well, he wouldn't, would he? Bloody king-killer.'

Athenais grinned faintly. She had never understood why her father was so fiercely Royalist – and suspected that he didn't either. On the other hand, she wholeheartedly agreed with his views on regicide for the simple reason that no King meant no Court – and her profession relied on patronage. Not that there had been much of that recently – what with the Fronde, His Majesty, King Louis X1V still being a few months short of his fourteenth birthday and neither his mother, the Queen-Regent nor Cardinal Mazarin having much interest in the theatre. But Marshal Turenne would eventually drive Condé from Paris so the Court could return; and, in the meantime, at least the theatres stayed open –which was more than could be said for England. But then, in a country where women's roles were played by boys, the closure of the playhouses was probably no great loss.

Here in Paris, things were very different ... and if the revival of *Le Cid* was a success, her own career would blossom with it. If, of course, she still had a job. Feeling suddenly sick, Athenais pushed her platter aside. Rightly or wrongly, Clermont was not without influence. If he set out to get her dismissed, he'd almost certainly succeed; and she'd have thrown away years of work for the fleeting satisfaction of telling an over-blown pig's bladder what she thought of him.

The possibility of being cast out of the theatre terrified her. It wasn't just the fact of not being able to act any more or of no longer being part of that warm, glittering make-believe world she escaped to every day. It was the thought of going back ... of being trapped in the sordid cage of her childhood where everyone stank of stale sweat and there wasn't always enough to eat and you saved your only pair of shoes for church on Sunday.

The real trouble, of course, was that she'd glimpsed something better ... had herself *become* something better. She'd started by sweeping the theatre floor and running errands and had ended as one of the Marais' leading actresses. But it hadn't been easy. It had taken six years of struggle and hard work. Extra tasks in return for reading lessons; hour upon hour developing proper posture and learning how to curtsy correctly – how to move, to turn, to smile, until she was graceful enough to be allowed on-stage as a walker. Then, most difficult of all, striving to eradicate every trace of the gutter from her speech before she could be trusted with a line of her own.

The result was that, along with her acting skills, Athenais had learned how to pass as a lady. The veneer might only be skin deep but it was good enough to deceive most people. The trouble was that, as long as she lived in this midden, there wasn't much point in playing the duchess every day.

'Finished wiv this, 'ave you?' Archie gestured to her half-full platter and, when she nodded, said, 'Reckon I'll finish it, then.' He eyed her obliquely. 'It ain't like you to pick at your food, Agnes. Not sick are you?'

'Yes,' said Athenais, catching his meaning and resenting it. 'I'm sick of living in this pig-sty and finding you drunk every night. I'm sick of wearing other folks' cast-offs and 'aving Marie d'Amboise sneer at me. And I'm *particularly* sick of being called bloody Agnes. But the one fing I *ain't* is sodding pregnant!'

Archie pursed his lips. 'Never fought you was.'

'Course you bloody did.'

'Didn't. A brat'd put paid to your acting, wouldn't it?'

'Yes.' She came abruptly to her feet. 'Worse still – unless you don't mind starving – it'd mean you'd 'ave to do an 'ands turn yourself once in a while. So it's just as well I've more sense than to get caught that way, ain't it?'

And she swept out without giving him time to reply.

* * *

She set off for the theatre earlier than usual but walked slower. She could only afford Martin's services for the homeward journey, so every day come rain or shine, she tramped the not inconsiderable distance between St. Severin and the Marais.

Her route took her along the Rue des Rosiers, past the house she would have sold her soul to live in. It wasn't anything spectacular; just a tall, narrow building, jammed between numerous others. But it looked as clean and neat as the road outside; and, to someone reared amid the smells and filth of the Rue Benoit, it seemed like a palace.

She arrived at the theatre to find her colleagues clustered before the stage, conversing in abnormally subdued voices. Clermont was the only one missing. All the rest fell abruptly silent as soon as she appeared.

Athenais's heart sank but, assuming an expression of mocking indulgence, she threw her cloak across a bench and said, 'Don't stop on my account. I'm sure I've missed the best bits, anyway. And doubtless Monsieur Laroque is waiting to see me.'

'In the Green Room with Froissart,' nodded Marie d'Amboise promptly. 'I'm afraid you haven't been very wise, my dear.'

'Probably not,' agreed Athenais, turning to go. 'But at least I've got some back-bone.'

She crossed the floor to the sound of her own footsteps and was just about to leave the auditorium when Etienne Lepreux called out, 'Watch your step, Athenais. They've got old pig-face with them.'

For an instant, Athenais looked back at the slender young man who – since he could out-act Clermont a hundred times over – ought to be making his debut next week as *Le Cid*. Then, with a swift smile, she thanked him and continued on her way.

Well-modulated even in rage, Clermont's voice reached her from the other side of the Green Room door.

'It is insupportable! I, Arnaud Clermont – who have worked with Montdory and Jodelet – to be insulted by a common little trollop? An arrogant ingénue who appears to think herself of such importance that she can order the company as she sees fit? It is not to be borne!'

It was as good a cue as any. Athenais opened the door and walked in saying coolly, 'Why not? The rest of us have to put up with *you* doing it all the time.'

Glaring, Clermont swung round and said, 'Bitch!' Then, once more addressing the manager, 'You see? The impertinent slut isn't even sorry!'

Petit-Jean Laroque, an ascetic-looking man in his middle fifties, who ran the Théâtre du Marais with ruthless efficiency and still occasionally played character roles, surveyed Athenais with faint irritation.

'Well, mademoiselle? Can we expect no apologies?'

'On the contrary, Monsieur – you can expect several,' replied Athenais ruefully. 'I'm sorry I've inconvenienced Monsieur Froissart and I'm sorry we're wasting good rehearsal time on a squabble. But I don't take back anything I said to Clermont last night. After the way he behaved on stage, he deserved every word.'

The actor's colour became positively apoplectic and, seeing it, Froissart said quickly, 'Doubtless there is fault on both sides. But for the sake of the play --'

'Bugger the play!' snapped Clermont. 'I want the insolent cow dismissed.'

There was a sudden, deathly hush during which Athenais stood very still, trying not to show that her heart was thudding against her ribs and her stomach a mass of painful knots. For a lot longer than she thought necessary, Manager Laroque communed silently with the ceiling. Then, expelling a long breath, he said quietly, 'I'm sorry, Arnaud. No.'

For a moment, none of his listeners could believe they had heard him correctly. Clermont's jaw dropped and Athenais groped her way feebly into the nearest chair. Finally, in something less than his usual rounded tones, Clermont said, 'What? *What* did you say?'

'I said no,' responded the manager, still calmly but with utter finality. 'I can't dismiss Mademoiselle de Galzain merely because you and she have quarrelled. Particularly when, as I understand it, she has a certain amount of right on her side.'

Athenais's breath leaked away.

Clermont, on the other hand, demanded glacially, 'What do you mean by that?'

'Simply that I don't expect a player of your stature and experience to take his personal feelings on to the stage at all – and particularly not before an audience. Consequently, I have some sympathy with

Mademoiselle's anger, if not her method of expressing it.' Laroque paused and spread expressive hands. 'As Antoine has said, there is fault on both sides. So I suggest that the two of you agree to put the episode behind you and forget that it ever happened.'

'Impossible!' declared Clermont.

Athenais re-inflated her lungs and stood up.

'Why? Come on, Arnaud. I'll kiss and make up if you will.'

'And stab me in the back later on, no doubt,' he retorted. The burning gaze encompassed Froissart. 'Antoine – I appeal to you. After what she said to me – and you heard it all – I can't possibly work with the little bitch. Nor do I intend to try.'

Froissart contemplated his finger-nails, saying nothing and there was another long, airless silence before, finally, Manager Laroque came to his feet.

'I'm truly sorry you feel that way, Arnaud – and can only hope that you'll change your mind when you've had time to consider the matter,' he said clearly. And, looking straight into the actor's florid countenance, added gently, 'It goes without saying that I would be desolate to lose you.'

This time the silence was of epic proportions. Athenais, a sudden flush mantling her cheek, kept her mouth tightly shut and left Clermont to voice her own thought.

'Do you mean to say,' he asked gratingly, 'that you are choosing this – this *doxy* in preference to myself?'

'Only if you force me to it,' replied Laroque. 'I don't deny that you are valuable, Arnaud. But I have felt for some time that your ego is stifling the company ... and I'm getting a little tired of your whims. In short, you are becoming exceedingly difficult to work with.'

Athenais folded her arms to stop herself applauding.

Clermont opened and closed his mouth rather in the manner of a cod. Then, apparently unable to think of a suitable reply, he spun on his heel and stormed out, slamming the door with an almighty crash.

Athenais and Froissart winced. Laroque sighed and said, 'God. How predictable.'

Drawing a steadying breath, Athenais said, 'Monsieur, I don't know what to say except thank you – and I promise I'll work till I drop rather than let you down.'

'You'd better, *ma fille* – because, if I'm any judge, Clermont is already on his way to offer his services to Floridor at the Bourgogne.' Laroque walked to the door and then, turning, added, 'As for your gratitude, it would be better addressed to Antoine, here. If he hadn't convinced me that your recent success isn't a mere flash-in-the-pan, I might have felt inclined to hold on to Clermont. Pain in the arse though he is.' On which note, he was gone.

Athenais curbed a faintly hysterical giggle and launched into a passionate expression of gratitude – only to realise that Froissart wasn't listening.

'*Merde!*' he muttered bitterly. 'It looks as if I'm going to have to go on myself tonight.'

* * *

Word of Laroque's stand and Froissart's part in it went round the company like wild-fire and earned the assistant-manager a resounding cheer from which only Marie d'Amboise remained aloof. A faint, sardonic smile touched Froissart's mouth and then disappeared as he instructed Etienne Lepreux to take the role of Rodrigue during the rehearsal. He said nothing, however, to suggest that the part was to be permanently re-cast and Etienne wisely asked no questions, merely setting to work with renewed zest. Everyone else eyed Athenais with perplexity verging on wary respect.

By the time the rehearsal was over and Athenais was alone with Pauline Fleury, perplexity had somehow been transformed into speculation and then into fast-moving rumour.

'What?' gasped Athenais, when Pauline told her. 'They think I'm *what?*'

'Sleeping with Froissart. After what just happened, what did you expect them to think? You know they haven't much imagination.'

Athenais gave a gurgle of laughter.

'Or too much. I never heard anything so silly. Everyone knows Froissart's never looked at another woman since he married Amalie. And if he hears anyone saying he has, he's likely to murder them.'

'So Marie d'Amboise had better watch her step,' grinned Pauline. Then, thoughtfully, 'Your stock has risen significantly today. Clermont may not come back – and Laroque can't afford to lose you as well. So now would be a good time to ask for an increase in pay.'

For a moment, Athenais was tempted. Then, shaking her head, she said, 'I can't. He's done enough for me already. I can't ask for money as well.'

Pauline stared at her acidulously.

'Then you're an idiot. How often do you suppose a chance like this comes along?'

'Not very often. But I owe Froissart --'

'You owe him your best on stage. You owe yourself some half-decent lodgings. My God, Athenais – if you don't look out for yourself in this world, no one else will.'

'I know. And I know you mean well and are probably right. But I won't do it.'

'Very noble! But you'd be better saving your principles till you can afford them.'

'It's not principle. It's more than that.' Athenais paused and added wryly, 'I expected to be thrown out on my ear today, Pauline – and all because I couldn't keep my mouth shut with a conceited old bugger who everyone knows is past it. But it's taught me a lesson. I'm never going to risk being dismissed again – not for anything. Because I know I couldn't bear it.'

THREE

Four days later, in a dingy attic overlooking a crumbling courtyard behind the Bastille, Major Langley stared across at Colonel Peverell and said gently, 'Correct me if I'm wrong ... but with scarcely a *sou* between us, the rent unpaid for three weeks, our credit utterly exhausted and nothing left worth selling – it appears that our situation is becoming the tiniest bit precarious.'

Idly casting dice, right hand against left, Ashley said absently, 'Just a touch, yes.'

'I'm so glad you agree. I wouldn't wish to be unnecessarily alarmist. It's just that my stomach is beginning to think my throat's been cut.'

'I know the feeling.'

'Quite. So unless Jem finds a rich pocket to pick --'

'He'd better not,' said Ashley.

Francis sighed. The remark had been flippant. He was perfectly well-aware that Jem's inexpert attempts at dipping had threatened to land him behind bars and caused the Colonel to threaten that Mr Barker could either desist or face a future without a certain vital piece of his anatomy.

'No,' said Francis mildly. 'I suppose he hadn't. So it appears that we're left with only one option. Who do we know who can lend us some money?'

'You tell me. No one I know has got any money.'

This, also, was all-too-depressingly true. The entire court-in-exile was living hand-to-mouth in an ever-deepening quagmire of debt. Even the King, dwelling infelicitously with his mother in the draughty, unheated rooms of the Louvre, seldom had more than a couple of *livres* in his pocket. The meagre pension granted to him by the French crown rarely amounted to much by the time Henrietta Maria had extracted the exact cost of every crumb he ate; and, since Condé's advance had caused the French royal family to retreat to St. Germain, it had ceased completely. As for his supporters, some were lucky enough to occasionally receive funds from their relatives in England. Others – like Francis, whose family had gone into exile ahead of him or Ashley, whose brother had embraced the winning side – had nothing but their wits.

Major Langley examined the threadbare cuff of his coat. Time was when he'd believed it was better to starve than be shabby … but Colchester and the six months it had taken Ashley and himself to reach Paris had changed all that.

At Colchester, he'd joked about eating turnips until the turnips were gone and the joke with them. Later, his insides heaving with revulsion, he'd watched hollow-eyed men killing dogs and cats to feed themselves and their starving families. And gradually, as day succeeded day, he had faced the ultimate horror. He'd learned that when your stomach was cleaving to your backbone, nothing existed in your head except a primitive urge to survive. And that was when Francis had looked deep inside himself for the first time and recognised something cataclysmic. All his life he'd believed that birth and privilege were an automatic passport to principle and the finer feelings generally unknown amongst the lower orders. Now he knew that, in extreme circumstances, the differences boiled down to little more than a smattering of education and the quality of one's coat.

Nothing, of course, could ever be quite that bad again. The months on the road with Ashley – taking work where they could find it, eating labourers' fare and sleeping, more often than not, in stable-lofts – had left callouses on his hands, not his soul. He already knew he was no better than the man hoeing the furrow to his right … so he had nothing left to lose.

Without looking up, he said, 'All right. If you have an alternative suggestion, I'd be happy to hear it.'

Colonel Peverell leaned back and crossed one booted leg over the other.

'We could follow the Duke of York's example and enlist under Marshal Turenne.'

'*You* could,' retorted Francis. '*I'm* likely to be shot for desertion.'

'Unlikely. It's been five years since you … discharged yourself from French service. Use a false name and no one will know you.'

'You'll excuse me if I prefer not to take the risk.'

'Oh well. If you're determined to be cautious …' shrugged Ashley. And recommenced his pointless dice-game.

Francis stared irritably through the dirty window and down into the courtyard below. Like a good many others, he'd been sold to the French army after Naseby. It had been the Parliament's way, at that time, of disposing of Royalist soldiers who would otherwise have to be fed and housed in prison. At the first opportunity and without a single qualm, Francis had deserted and returned to England. Many of the others, he was fairly sure, had chosen to stay and forge a career. So it was all very well for Ashley to say no one would know him. The way his luck had been running recently, Francis felt there was a good chance he'd be recognised before he'd got both feet through the barrack door.

This problem aside, something would have to be done – and fast. Quite apart from the daily question of how to afford a meal, he and Ashley were beginning to get on each other's nerves. Francis was quite prepared to accept that there was fault on both sides. They were, after all, very different. But in the weeks since their arrival in Paris, Ashley had changed considerably. In Scotland, at Worcester and throughout their subsequent travels, he'd been possessed of the kind of energy and ability to plan that left lesser men dizzy. Now he was gradually becoming so damned lethargic that Francis was often surprised he bothered to get out of bed. His only interest appeared to be indulging in numerous cold-blooded flirtations just to see what havoc he could wreak. And worst of all, his sense of humour was vanishing beneath a layer of moody impatience.

The culprit was inactivity. Unemployment plainly didn't suit Ashley and he was reacting badly to it. Left to his own devices, Francis was happy to cruise the book-stalls, gorging himself on plays and poetry he couldn't afford to buy or spend an hour or two trying to win the price of a meal at cards or dice. Ashley simply mouldered.

Down in the square, a shabby sedan chair carried by two brawny youths came to a halt beneath their window. Francis eyed it with vague interest. People who lived in this district couldn't afford hired conveyances and rarely had visitors who could. Then the door of the chair opened and a woman stepped out. She gave her red taffeta skirts a deft shake and glanced disparagingly up at the house.

'Oh Lord. *Now* what?' breathed Francis.

Ashley looked up. 'What is it?'

'Joy over-bounding,' came the bitter reply. 'The answer to one problem, perhaps ... but the beginning of a hundred others. In short, it's my sister.'

'Ah.' Colonel Peverell placed the dice neatly side by side and surveyed Francis thoughtfully. He had known that the Major's mother hovered on the periphery of the widowed Queen's circle, while his father dithered around Sir Edward Hyde ... and also that there was a sister somewhere ... but he'd never met any of them. He also suspected that, if the rarity with which they were mentioned was anything to go by, Francis saw precious little of them himself. Knowing what it was to be distanced from one's family, Ashley did not find this particularly odd. And because, unlike Francis, he never indulged in idle curiosity, he neither speculated on the possible causes of the estrangement nor enquired into them.

Even now, with the mysterious sister apparently on her way up the stairs to their door, he merely rose and said, 'I'll go, if you prefer it.'

Francis turned, his expression smooth and brittle as glass.

'No. Stay, by all means. She must want something or she wouldn't be here - so with any luck, she'll pay for our supper. And you never know, you may like her. I did myself, once.'

There being no obvious reply to this, Ashley sat down and maintained a discreet silence.

'Very wise,' drawled Francis. 'Life can be tricky, can't it? How much better if, like a play, there were a script for it.' He moved to the door and the sound of approaching footsteps outside it. 'Act One, Scene One. The curtain rises on a sparsely-furnished garret. Down-stage left, Colonel Discretion; up-stage right, Sir Threadbare Pride; enter Lady Wanton Coldheart.' And he threw open the door.

Taken by surprise, her hand poised to knock, Celia started violently and forgot to smile.

'For heaven's sake, Francis!' she said crossly. 'You nearly gave me an apoplexy.'

Francis's expression did not flicker by so much as a hair's breadth. Closing the door behind her, he said, 'Good afternoon, Celia. I am delighted to see you, too.'

Rising from his seat, Ashley instantly recognised the dark beauty he'd met at the Marais with One-Eyed Will and thought, *Hell's teeth. So that's it.*

Irritated but determined not to show it, Celia smiled at her brother and tilted her cheek to be kissed. Then, when he awarded her no more than a cursory bow, she twined a cajoling hand through his arm and said, 'Don't be horrid. I know you don't approve of me – but you must still love me a little bit.'

'Must I?'

'Of course. I'm your sister.'

'So you are.' Disengaging himself in one fluid movement, Francis gestured towards Ashley and said, 'You will perceive that we're not alone. Allow me to present my friend, Colonel Peverell. Ashley … my sister, Celia Maxwell.'

According Ashley the briefest of curtsies and scarcely looking at him, Celia rounded on Francis, saying, 'Don't call me that! I'm Celia Verney now.'

Dark brows rose over mocking sapphire eyes.

'Oh? He's married you, then?'

'Not yet. But he will. And sooner than you think.'

'Pardon me if I don't hold my breath.' Then, as she would have spoken, 'Celia. This bone of contention is already so well-picked as to make further exploration totally pointless, don't you think? And I'm sure Ashley has no desire to watch us quarrelling.'

'Don't mind me,' said Ashley lightly. 'Quarrel away. I'm going out.'

Celia looked at him properly for the first time, a faint frown marking her brow. She said slowly, 'We've met before, haven't we? At … at the theatre, I think?'

Damn. He'd been hoping she might not remember. Summoning a smile, he said, 'Indeed we did. Did you think I'd forgotten?'

Celia always responded well to male charm and good looks. Dimpling, she said flirtatiously, 'How would I know, sir? I'm sure you can't recall every female face you see.'

'Not all. Only the pretty ones.'

It wasn't entirely untrue, he thought. Although a little too plump for his personal taste, the glossy dark curls, long-lashed blue eyes and pouting mouth combined to make her a remarkably lovely woman. She was probably about thirty; ripe, luscious and wholly enticing. The sort few men would resist if she chose to crook her finger.

From across the room, Francis said, 'Dear me. How very intriguing. The two of you are already acquainted, then?'

'I wouldn't say that,' returned Ashley, mindful of the obvious pitfalls. 'And at the time we met, I had no idea that Mistress … Verney … was your sister.'

'No,' agreed Francis dryly. 'You wouldn't have. Do I take it that you also had the pleasure of meeting dear Hugo?'

'Yes he did,' snapped Celia. 'And there's no need to be sarcastic. Hugo loves me.'

'So,' responded Francis, 'did Eden.'

An odd expression crossed the beautiful face and, instead of answering back, Celia said, 'Actually, it was Eden I wanted to talk to you about.'

'Ah. And there I was thinking you'd come purely to enquire after my well-being.'

'That was part of my reason for coming, of course,' she replied stiffly. 'Naturally, I worry about you.'

Francis's mouth curled sardonically.

'Don't over-do it, Celia. Just tell me what you want.'

'You might ask me to sit down.'

He sighed. 'Very well. Pray be seated. The chair by the table is the more reliable of the two.'

She crossed the room in a rustle of taffeta and sat down gracefully but with some caution. Then she said, 'I'd prefer to speak to you privately.'

'Oh – for God's sake!'

'Well what's wrong with that?' She smiled coquettishly at Ashley. 'As I recall, the Colonel said he was going out.'

'On my account and yours. Not on his own.'

'Excuse me.' Ashley held up an urbane but authoritative hand. 'I believe I can speak for myself. And, having managed to get a word in edge-wise, I'd like to announce that I am, indeed, going out.' He reached for his hat and walked past Francis to the door. Then, turning, he added, 'Try not to kill each other, children – and remember that breakages have to be paid for.' Then he was gone.

'Well!' exclaimed Celia, half-affronted and half-entertained. 'He's certainly original. But I'm not sure I like being treated like one of his junior officers. Indeed, if he wasn't so extremely handsome, I'd be offended. As it is, however --'

'Come to the point, Celia.' Francis perched on the edge of the table, his face and voice imprinted with acute distaste. 'What do you want?'

She bent to re-arrange the folds of her skirt and took her time about replying. Then, still without meeting his gaze, she said rapidly, 'I want you to help me get a letter to Eden.'

'For what purpose?'

'I ... I want a divorce.'

Francis's eyes narrowed. He said, 'One presumes you've wanted a divorce for eight years. Why ask Eden now?'

This time she looked up, her expression hard with defiant determination.

'Because Hugo's wife died a month ago.'

Francis expelled a long, slow breath. Finally, he said, 'I see. You want to re-marry.'

'Well of course I do! I've always wanted it – we both have. But Hugo couldn't divorce Lucy, so --'

'Just a moment. Hugo couldn't divorce his wife – but you have no qualms about divorcing Eden?'

'Everything's different now,' she shrugged. 'Hugo's free. And I'd have thought you'd be pleased to see us married. God knows you've always despised the fact that we're not.'

'Your dubious status is only part of the problem,' he remarked. 'I am even less enamoured with the alacrity with which you abandoned your children. But let's stick to the point. Let us assume, for the sake of argument, that I manage to get a message to Eden and that, after a celebratory jig or two, he agrees to do as you ask. Just what do you expect to happen then?'

'Well ... I don't exactly know. I suppose he'll have to make a petition to somebody or other and there'll be papers to sign and so on.' She spread her hands. 'I don't know how these things work. How should I?'

'My dear simpleton, I don't know how they work either. But one thing I *do* know. Divorce can take years and is singularly unpleasant for all concerned. Remember Lord Essex? By the time he'd got rid of the trollop he married, the whole country was sniggering behind its hand and called him a cuckold. I doubt very much if Eden will want to go down that particular path. And even if he did ... with him in England and you here, the pair of you could be in your dotage before it's all over.'

Celia's expression remained stubborn.

'Then the sooner we begin, the better. And we won't know what Eden thinks unless we ask him, will we?'

'We?' asked Francis gently.

'Yes. You'll help me, won't you? You must!'

'I don't see that I must ... and I'm not sure that I will. I might, however, be persuaded to think about it.'

It took her a moment to catch his meaning. Then she said contemptuously, 'Oh. You want money, I suppose. I'm not surprised. That coat is a disgrace.'

'It is, isn't it?' A faint, disconcerting smile touched his mouth. 'However. Odd as it may seem to you, I need money in order to eat. Not just today – but also, if possible, tomorrow. And, if we are not to be evicted from this hovel, it would help if we could pay the rent.'

She hesitated, not sure whether to believe him or not. Then, deciding that the only thing which really mattered was getting him to do as she wanted, she stood up, unlaced her purse and tossed five *livres* on the table beside him.

'That's all I have. Odd as it may seem to *you*, Hugo and I aren't exactly well-off either.'

'No. But you do manage to afford one or two of life's little luxuries, don't you? Tickets for the play, for example.'

'So we occasionally take a box at the Marais,' she shrugged. 'What of it?'

'Simply that there's another trifling favour you might do me.' Francis's smile grew but somehow Celia knew it was not for her. 'I understand that the Marais is reviving *Le Cid*. There is also talk of Clermont having left to join the Hôtel de Bourgogne and being replaced with a young unknown. More alluring still, one hears of an exquisite young actress.'

'My word!' she remarked acidly. 'You *do* hear a lot, don't you? But what has all this to do with me?'

'I'd like you to invite Ashley and me to share your box for the first night of the *Cid*. I've a feeling Ashley would enjoy it – and he has so little fun, poor fellow. As for myself … well, I've always had a *penchant* for red-heads.'

'You mean you had a *penchant* for Eden's shrew of a sister. But you're welcome to share our box on Thursday – provided you can be civil to Hugo. In fact,' she concluded with an air of victory, 'I'll look forward to receiving your decision about Eden.'

She left soon after that and, when Ashley returned an hour or so later, it was to find Francis gloating over a large loaf of bread, some cheese and three meat patties.

Tossing his hat to one side, Ashley surveyed the feast and said, 'And what did you have to do to earn that? Or shouldn't I ask?'

'Ask away.' With a flourish, Francis produced a bottle of wine. 'And fear not. We can still eat tomorrow. I'm learning to shop with frugality and will make someone a wonderful wife one day. Where's Jem?'

'Downstairs with his arm round the concierge's daughter. If you don't want to squander your windfall paying the rent, a little goodwill may come in handy.' Ashley sat down and accepted the cup that Francis handed him but made no move to drink. Instead, he said slowly, 'Don't think me ungrateful – or determined to pry. But if this has cost you a price you'd sooner not have paid --'

'You mean, have I sold my soul?' Francis took the other chair and smiled. 'No. I don't think so.' And, without elaboration, he related the gist of his bargain with Celia. 'In fact, as yet, I've promised nothing. But in the end, if it enables me to squeeze another few *livres* out of her, I probably will. It can't hurt to send Eden one letter. He doesn't have to answer it, does he?'

'I suppose not.'

'And the advantages of helping Celia don't end with food on the table. They also stretch to food for the eye and the soul.' Francis paused. 'I've persuaded her to let us to share her box at the Marais for the opening night of *Le Cid*.'

For the first time in several weeks, Ashley dissolved into genuine laughter.

'Oh God. I might have known. You just want to ogle the little Galzain.'

'Of course. Don't you?'

'I wouldn't say no.' And then, returning to his original point, 'So you're going to help your sister get her divorce.'

'I'm going to help her ask for it. If Eden doesn't want to be dragged through the courts, he'll say so. On the other hand, for all I know he may want to re-marry himself by now – in which case it may suit him to be rid of Celia.'

Ashley stared down into the ruby brightness of his cup.

'Did you know him well?'

'He was my closest friend.' Francis paused and, with a shrug, added, 'But the last time I saw him, his sword was at my throat. That was at Upton.'

'Ah.' Ashley paused, registering the change in both face and voice. 'And in between?'

'In between, he married Celia. He worshipped the ground she walked on and though I suspected it wasn't completely reciprocated, I still hoped that he might be the making of her. Then the war came. My family chose one path and his, another. Celia felt stranded in the wrong camp and Eden was away a lot. Consequently, when Hugo Verney re-entered her orbit, the inevitable happened.' Francis reached for the bottle and re-filled their cups. 'On the day Eden rode home with the news that his father had been killed, he found Celia and Hugo in bed together.'

'Christ. And then?'

'Oh then Celia galloped off into the sunset with Hugo – blithely abandoning two small children. And that, of course, is the one element in this whole mess which I find totally unforgivable.'

'Understandable. And what of Eden?'

'Obviously, I've seen little of him in recent years ... but on the occasions when we do meet, he always seems to be saving my skin.

Upton was the last time. He was livid with temper but he let me go. Before that, it was the aftermath of Colchester. Now, it appears that he's risen to the rank of Colonel and is riding high in Lambert's estimation – if not old Noll's.' With a wry smile, Francis lifted his wine-cup. 'I can only wish him good fortune. He deserves it.'

FOUR

On the opening night of *Le Cid* Athenais stood like a stone beneath the ministrations of Pauline Fleury and wondered whether she was actually going to *be* sick or if it just felt like it. Of course, everyone suffered from nerves before a performance – particularly on the first night in a new role. It was normal; something you became accustomed to and knew would evaporate as soon as you walked on-stage. But tonight was somehow different. Tonight, panic was lying coiled in the pit of her stomach, numbing her limbs and paralysing her breathing. Tonight, she wasn't just nervous. She was absolutely petrified.

The reflection in the mirror showed Chimène, stiffly-robed in gold and green with unbound, jewel-strewn hair and huge, kohl-rimmed eyes. She looked, remarked a discouraging little voice at the back of her mind, like a wax doll. Beautiful but lifeless ... and not in the least like the courageous, passionate woman she was supposed to be portraying.

A shudder rippled through her and, between chattering teeth, she stammered, 'I c-can't do it. I can't g-go on.'

Pauline continued putting the finishing touches to the glowing copper hair.

'Yes, you can.'

'I can't. I've forgotten all the w-words.'

'No. They'll be there when you need them.'

'They won't. I'm going to dry. I'm going to trip over my feet and --' She clamped her hands over her mouth. 'I'm going to throw up.'

Calmly, Pauline shoved a basin in front of her.

'Use that – and mind your costume.'

Athenais cast her a glance of impotent fury and vomited neatly into the bowl. When she was done, Pauline took it away, handed her a napkin to wipe her mouth and poured her a small measure of watered wine.

'And now,' she said firmly, 'you will pull yourself together. So it's a big role; so it's been performed by great actresses before you; so the play was premiered on our own stage sixteen years ago. So what? Tonight is yours. Show Paris the *role* is now yours – and, by tomorrow, you'll be more than just the latest pretty face.'

Still shaking, the girl clutched the cup between her hands and drew a long, unsteady breath. She said, 'There must be easier ways of making a living.'

'Yes. You could do it on your back. But I thought you wanted something better than that.'

'I do.'

'Then now is your chance to prove it. You might also try remembering that Etienne has the hardest job tonight. He's got to eclipse Clermont. If he doesn't, the pit will crucify him. As yet, all they require from you is that you look stunning and get the words right. The fact that you're also going to wring their hearts out like sponges, is a bonus.'

Although her lungs still weren't functioning as they should and vipers continued to writhe behind her brocaded bodice, Athenais realised that she was beginning to feel marginally better. Managing a weak smile, she said, 'What would I do without you?'

'God knows,' came the deceptively irritable reply. And then, 'Go on. It's time you were back-stage. And mind those sleeves. If they get caught on anything, it'll cost you a week's wages.'

In the shadowy light of the wings, most of the cast already stood waiting; Marie d'Amboise as the Infanta, Etienne as Rodrigue and Froissart himself as Don Diegue. Athenais went through the usual back-stage ritual of veiled well-wishing while the noise, heat and odour of the auditorium swirled around all of them like a thick fog. Then the stage candles were lit, an expectant hush settled slowly over the theatre ... and, dead on cue, Athenais's feet carried her out before the many-headed monster that was the audience.

Her first lines came out feebly, spoken from the throat rather than the space behind her rib-cage and she heard Pauline hiss, '*Breathe, damn you!*'

Athenais forced her muscles to relax and let the air flow through her ... and, when she spoke again, her voice emerged firm, rich and flawless. Suddenly, she was free – warm and at home in the light. She was Chimène.

* * *

From his place between Celia and Ashley, Francis began by watching every nuance of her performance with a critical eye and then abandoned himself to simple enjoyment. The girl was superb – as was the young man playing Rodrigue; and the tension they created between them was as absorbing as it was remarkable. For once, even the pit was enthralled.

At some point during the second act, Francis glanced at Ashley and glimpsed an expression he could not interpret. This didn't surprise him. Despite all they'd been through together, he still knew as little about the workings of Ashley's mind as on the day they'd first met and had started to regard it as an immutable fact of life.

Although he was careful not to show it, Ashley found himself thinking less of the play than about the red-haired girl he'd last seen clambering over debris on the Petit Pont, cursing like a fish-wife. In the dark and with her face shadowed by her hood, he hadn't got a good enough look at her to discover whether the stunning looks were the result of artifice or nature, so his abiding memory of the encounter was the way she'd brushed him aside and told him she wasn't a whore. Cynically, Ashley concluded that an actress living amidst the stews of St. Severin was unlikely to be a flower of virtue either. Then, not for the first time, he asked himself why he was bothering to consider the matter.

During the second interval, he withdrew to the back of the box while Celia demanded to know whether Francis was going to help her. Sir Hugo Verney looked rather strained and had been oddly silent all evening. Ashley wondered if Francis had noticed it.

Francis had. His expression as smooth as butter, he ignored Celia's question and said, 'One feels one should say something about the death of your wife, Hugo. The difficulty is in knowing quite *what*.'

Sir Hugo's face tightened a shade more.

'You may say you're sorry Lucy's dead – and believe that I am, too.'

'Of course.' Francis inclined his head slightly. 'She can't have been more than … what? Thirty? A young woman, still. Was it very sudden?'

'A chill which went to her lungs.'

'Ah. Your son must miss her.'

A pulse started to beat at the side of Hugo's jaw. Guarding his tone as best he could, he said, 'My son is none of your business, Francis.'

'True. Unfortunately, the same can't be said of Celia. And I'm wondering whether you really wish to remain in France now – or if you'd prefer to go back to England and your son and try picking up the pieces.'

Hugo looked rather sick and, when he spoke, his voice was muffled.

'I can't go back. Lucy compounded for the estate on the understanding I wouldn't. If I return, John loses his inheritance.'

'I see,' drawled Francis. 'You can't go home … so you might as well marry Celia.'

'How dare you?' Celia erupted from her seat. 'It's not like that! Hugo – tell him!'

Francis smiled and, silencing Sir Hugo with a small languid gesture, said, 'Don't trouble yourself. I doubt if you care what I think – or Celia either, provided I do as she wants. Which, of course, I will.'

As if by magic, the wrath on Celia's face was replaced by an ecstatic smile. Hugo, by contrast, merely looked monumentally weary.

She said eagerly, 'You'll do it? You promise?'

'Yes – but in my own way,' replied Francis. 'I'll write to Eden myself. I fancy he'll respond better – and dislike it less – than receiving an egotistical, impassioned epistle from you. If and when he replies, I'll let you know. If he says yes, you may bring on the drums and trumpets. If he doesn't, you'll accept it and let the matter drop. Well?'

Celia hesitated and then shrugged her acceptance, realising it would be a mistake to argue.

'Excellent,' said Francis sardonically. 'And now, perhaps we can enjoy the rest of the play in peace.'

Silently, Ashley resumed his seat. He felt a little sorry for Sir Hugo and wondered if Francis couldn't have made his point without being quite such a bastard.

On-stage, although adamant that Rodrigue be punished for slaying her father, Chimène confessed her love for him with such poignant anguish that half the audience either reached for its handkerchief or sniffed into its sleeve. Deliberately refusing to be spellbound, Ashley folded his arms and told himself that Mademoiselle de Galzain was altogether too perfect and that it would be interesting to see her off-stage, with her face streaked with grease-paint and sweat. And as for whether or not she was as virtuous as she made out ... it really didn't matter to him one way or another.

He waited until the fourth act was over before casually suggesting to Francis that they round off the evening with a visit to the Green Room.

Francis subjected him to a long, knowing stare and said, 'Well, of course. Isn't that why we came?'

The play drew to a close and a great sigh seemed to emanate from the audience, followed by a moment of involuntary silence. Then the entire auditorium exploded into wild enthusiasm and the players took bow after bow while their public stamped and cheered and whistled. It was an ovation such as the Marais had not seen in years. And when Athenais de Galzain and Etienne Lepreux stepped forward to receive their personal acclaim, the result was little short of tumultuous.

It was some time before the audience could be persuaded to let them go. But when the din finally started to subside, Francis and Ashley thanked Celia and Hugo for their hospitality. Celia exhorted her brother to write to Eden immediately and Sir Hugo looked as though he hoped he never saw Major Langley again. Then they went their separate ways; Celia and her lover to take supper ... and Francis and his friend to pay their respects to an actress.

The passage-way behind the stage was crammed with fellows, all hell-bent on the same purpose.

'This is a mad-house,' said Ashley, squashing himself into a corner to escape the worst of the jostling. 'Let's go.'

'In a moment,' returned Francis calmly. 'For now, let's just wait and see what happens.'

A few feet away, Etienne Lepreux fought his way against the tide with a good deal of back-slapping but little attempt at detainment. The advancing hordes were intent only on swarming through the Green Room to the ladies tiring-room. Someone, however, seemed to be blocking their path.

'Will you be quiet?' demanded an irritable but well-pitched female voice. 'And you can stop pushing. It won't get you anywhere.'

The din died down a little and someone shouted, 'Let us in, Madame. We want *la petite Galzain!*'

'Want away, then,' retorted the voice, with some satisfaction. 'She's gone.'

The effect was that of a douche of cold water. There was a rumble of uncertainty. Then, with an attempt at defiance, someone shouted, 'Don't believe you!'

'Suit yourself. You can wait here all night, for all I care. But she's gone. She was tired so she slipped out the back way.'

New heart flowed through the crowd. The streets outside would be blocked with the carriages and chairs of the departing audience. It might be possible to get a glimpse of their darling yet. To a man, the admirers surged back in a concerted dash for the stage exit ... briefly jamming the doorway before spewing into the street beyond. As soon as the last of them had gone, the hitherto unseen female marched down to the door, slammed it shut and rammed the bolts home, muttering, 'Good riddance, too!' Then she stalked back to the Green Room and disappeared inside.

Unnoticed in their dark corner, Francis raised a quizzical brow at Ashley and murmured, 'I scent a ruse. Come on.'

Ashley shrugged and followed him into an unbelievably untidy room, stinking of wine-fumes and sweat. Empty bottles stood among half-eaten pies, cheese crumbs lay amidst spilled cosmetics and every chair was adrift with discarded items of clothing. Even in the army, where you were often packed in like herrings in a barrel, Ashley had never seen such a mess.

'Christ,' he said. 'What a pig-sty. Someone ought to give these people a few lessons in communal living.'

Aware of the Colonel's passion for neatness, Francis merely grinned and advanced on the tiring-room door. From the other side of it came the sound of laughter and chattering feminine voices. Francis knocked.

The laughter stopped and the same voice they'd heard earlier exclaimed, 'Hell's teeth! What now?' Then the door was wrenched open and they found themselves face to face with a woman with a scar on one cheek and a gimlet stare.

'Well?' she demanded impatiently.

Francis's bow, which swept the floor with the slightly-battered plume of his second-hand hat, would have graced a throne-room.

'Madame – I beg you to forgive our intrusion. If it is inconveniently-timed, you have only to say and we will remove ourselves directly. But we wished ... that is to say, we *hoped* that we might be permitted to pay our respects to Mademoiselle de Galzain – whose performance this evening has left us dazzled.'

Smooth-talking sod, thought Ashley.

Pauline Fleury subjected them both to a long, searching stare and finally, without giving any clue to her feelings, said, 'Wait here.'

Shutting the door again, she turned to Athenais and, lowering her voice so the rest of the women couldn't hear, said, 'Put your wrap on. You've got to see these two.'

This wasn't just unusual – it was unheard-of. Eyeing her friend with amused interest, Athenais said, 'I have?'

'You have. Judging by their clothes, they haven't two *sous* to rub together. But they're gentlemen, they're sober and they didn't ask for *la petite Galzain*.' A swift, surprisingly mischievous grin crossed lit the damaged face. 'They're also exceptionally easy on the eye.'

Athenais laughed. 'What – *both* of them?'

'Let's just say I'd be hard-pressed to choose. One's dark as night and the other all tawny-gold. Come and see. It'll only take five minutes.'

It was unknown for Pauline to spare more than a disparaging glance for the men who flocked backstage. Intrigued, Athenais rose and pulled on her robe.

'I take it you're coming with me?'

'What do you think?'

Once more assuming an expression of mild disapproval, Pauline opened the door again and indicated by means of a shooing motion that Francis and Ashley were not to be admitted to the tiring-room.

'Five minutes,' she said brusquely. 'Mademoiselle needs her rest.'

As Pauline had said, there were two men outside the door ... one dark, one fair and both equally beautiful. There were two of them ... but after the first glance, Athenais saw only one. He filled her vision and, for a handful of seconds, everything seemed to stop – as if the world around her had simply gone away. Her throat tightened, something shifted in her chest and for a moment, she forgot to breathe. Then, just as she had done earlier on the stage, she dragged air into her lungs and called upon her training.

Ashley heard Francis embarking on another epic speech and left him to get on with it while he himself took a long look at Mademoiselle de Galzain. The sudden widening of her eyes ... not brown as he'd expected, but dark grey, the colour of clouds just before a thunderstorm ... and the slight hitch in her breathing were not lost on him but he gave no sign of it. The part of him that some people called The Falcon was as adept at governing his own expression as it was at reading those of others. He wondered if her immediate reaction had been the result of recognition ... and if, behind the pretty, practised smile she now wore, she was slightly embarrassed.

Swathed in a voluminous wrapper, she remained perfectly still as she absorbed Francis's seemingly endless eloquence. Though the almond-shaped eyes were still outlined in kohl, her face was neither smothered in grease-paint nor streaked with sweat and the rich copper mane cascaded loose down her back. She looked both smaller and younger than she had on the stage, thought Ashley clinically ... but she wasn't any less beautiful. He found the fact unreasonably annoying so he reminded himself that looks weren't everything and that the girl behind the face was supremely talented in the art of pretence.

The fathomless grey gaze remained locked on Francis. And when he finally reached the end of his soliloquy, she said demurely, 'You're very kind, Monsieur. I'm glad my performance pleased you.'

'It was magnificent,' enthused Francis – for what Ashley thought was probably the third time.

'And you, Monsieur?' She flicked a polite glance in his own direction. 'Did *you* think I was magnificent?'

'I think,' responded Ashley suavely, 'that you do not need to be told. But I feel impelled to remark that Rodrigue was also superb tonight.'

Since she was clearly used to being worshipped, he'd expected her to be piqued. Instead, she said eagerly, 'He was, wasn't he? Truly brilliant, in my opinion.' Then, on a gurgle of laughter, 'I do hope somebody tells Clermont. He'll have a fit!'

Surprise stirred, bringing with it a sort of awareness that he neither expected nor wanted. He squashed it with the likelihood that this apparent generosity of spirit was probably about as genuine as the shift from gutter vernacular to smooth gentility.

Pauline gave a discreet cough. It wasn't wise, even now, to laugh at Clermont. She said, 'It's late, Athenais. If the gentlemen will excuse you, I think it's time you finished your *toilette* and went home.'

Athenais spread expressive hands.

'You see, gentlemen? I am ruled with a rod of iron. But Pauline is always right – and I *am* very tired.'

'Of course.' Taking her hand, Francis saluted it with matchless grace. 'It was extremely good of you to receive us at all. Perhaps, on some future occasion, you – and Madame, of course – might do the Colonel and myself the honour of supping with us?'

Holy hell, thought Ashley. *How does he expect us to pay for that?*

Withdrawing her hand in order to extend it carelessly to Ashley, she said pleasantly, 'That is kind of you, monsieur – but you must forgive me if I refuse. I prefer to keep my private life separate from the theatre, so I never accept such invitations.'

Thank you, God – and please don't let Francis argue, thought Ashley.

He took her fingers in his, felt them tremble a little and, like a bolt from the blue, felt a spike of pure lust. Shaken but intent on keeping it out of his eyes, he bowed over her hand but sensibly declined to kiss it and said smoothly, 'We understand perfectly, Mademoiselle ... and will strive to conquer our disappointment.'

A faint frown creased her brow and then was gone.

'Well, that's a relief,' she replied cheerfully. 'It's always a worry when gentlemen take rejection personally – so I'm delighted you're not wholly cast down.'

Francis's brows soared and Ashley narrowly suppressed a grin. Whatever else she might be, *la petite Galzain* was plainly no fool. He said, 'I'm sure Major Langley here is devastated. I, however, am a connoisseur of lost causes.'

'And don't waste your time on them?'

'Not if I can avoid it,' he replied negligently. 'On the other hand, there are sometimes worthwhile exceptions. Good night, Mademoiselle – Madame.'

Long after they had gone and Pauline was once more bustling about the tiring-room, disposing of costumes, Athenais sat before the glass mechanically brushing her hair but making no move to dress. And finally, noticing her lack of activity, Pauline said, 'All right. Which one was it?'

'What?' Pulling on her gown, the girl offered her back for lacing-up.

'Don't be coy. No one could blame you for being smitten. I've rarely seen one man as pretty as that – let alone a pair. So which took your fancy?'

'Neither, particularly – though I suppose the dark-haired one was the nicer of the two. Actually, I was wondering why the other man's voice seemed vaguely familiar – and why he didn't seem to like me very much.'

Or didn't want to, thought Pauline. But said, 'And?'

'And I've no idea,' shrugged Athenais. 'Not that it matters. They're unlikely to come back. They didn't look as though they could afford a hair-cut – let alone to be spending money on theatre tickets.'

Pauline's gaze was thoughtful.

'You're very hard to please. Unless you've got your eye on somebody else, of course.'

'Don't be ridiculous.' Athenais threw her cloak round her and headed for the door. 'You notice I haven't asked which one *you* fancied. Or perhaps you're savouring the idea of a *ménage a trois*?' And made a brisk exit.

FIVE

Paris flocked to *Le Cid*, resulting in it being held over for two weeks and then three. At the end of the first one, Froissart gave way to Pauline Fleury's constant nagging and awarded Mademoiselle de Galzain an increase in salary. By the end of the second, with Athenais fast becoming the darling of Paris, he was glad he'd done so. And at some point during the third, Pauline told Athenais that she no longer had a choice about moving from the Rue Benoit. It had become a necessity.

'What about the house on the Rue des Rosiers?' she asked. 'Is it still empty?'

'I think so,' replied Athenais, as if she didn't make a point of passing it every day to check. 'But the Widow Larousse wants twenty *livres* a month and I only earn two for every performance. So, since one still has to eat and --'

'And give your father enough money to come home sodden every night?'

Athenais sighed and said nothing.

Silent and ferocious, Pauline scowled into the middle distance. Drawing a long, resigned breath, she said, 'You could afford it if you had someone to share the rent.'

'A lodger?' Athenais gave a sudden gurgle of laughter. 'Oh yes. But how long do you think that would last with Father touching them for money once or twice a day?'

'He won't try that with me. Not after the first time, anyway.'

Athenais stared at her. '*You?*'

'If you don't like the idea, you only have to say.'

'Not *like* it?' She swallowed hard. 'Pauline – I would *love* it. But you can't possibly want to give up your rooms on the Place Royal.'

Pauline looked at the girl who was the nearest thing she had to family and whom she hoped to see become the queen of Parisian theatre. Then, in two syllables, she cast her precious independence and her tranquil, beautifully ordered existence into the void.

'Why not?' she said.

* * *

At the beginning of June, Froissart replaced *Le Cid* with a popular pot-boiler and commenced rehearsals for a lavish revival of *Cinna*. He cast Etienne Lepreux in the title role, gave Athenais the plum part of Emilie and announced that Monsieur Laroque would be making one of his rare appearances as the Emperor Augustus. Marie d'Amboise, indulging in a fit of epic sulks, became (as Etienne put it) a thoroughly livid Livia.

In the meantime, Pauline called on the Widow Larousse, offered her sixteen *livres* a month and eventually agreed upon eighteen. And Athenais spent her time at home alternately cajoling and arguing with her father – whose attitude to the proposed move was nothing if not predictable.

'Go and live in the bloody Marais? *Me?* Not sodding likely!'

'But why not?' she demanded. 'You can't like this flea-bitten 'ovel.'

'Never said I liked it, did I? But it suits me. I got friends round 'ere,' stated Archie. And, with an attempt at pathos, 'What'm I going to do in the Marais? Just tell me that. Them gentry-coves ain't going to pass the time of day with the likes of me, Agnes. And I'll wager there ain't a cheap boozing-ken for miles.'

'Good,' she snapped. 'And for Gawd's sake, don't call me Agnes – nor Stott, neither. Once we're in the Rue des Rosiers we're likely to 'ave visitors once in a while and I don't want the pit shouting for *la petite Stott* or *la Stottette* or – or little sodding Aggie!' Athenais paused and drew a calming breath. 'Pauline says --'

'That bossy cow says a sight too much! And she 'ates me. Always 'as. So if you fink I'm living in the same 'ouse as the long-nosed bitch, you got anuvver fink coming!'

She held his gaze with one of equal obstinacy.

'You ain't got no choice, you stupid old goat! I'm going to the Rue des Rosiers and Pauline's coming too because I can't afford it wivout 'er. And I'm damned if I'm going to squander money I ain't got to keep you living in this 'ole, drinking yourself into an early grave. So you're coming to the bloody Marais if I 'ave to drag you there – and that's flat!'

* * *

The opening night of *Cinna* was another triumph, with scuffles breaking out in the Rue Vieille du Temple amongst those who couldn't get in. And later, whilst taking off his make-up, Monsieur Laroque found himself honoured by a visit from the Marquis d'Auxerre – cousin, several times removed, to royalty and – more relevant still – a favoured protégée of Cardinal Mazarin.

The Marquis had returned to Paris from St. Germain, he said, especially to see the Marais Theatre's latest production and had not been disappointed. He then enquired whether the company might oblige with a private performance of Le Cid later in the year to celebrate the completion of his new house on the Isle St. Louis … and named a fee which made Laroque feel quite faint and reply that the company would be delighted. The Marquis pronounced himself overjoyed. And then, very much as an after-thought, asked if he might meet Mademoiselle de Galzain – about whom, it seemed, all Paris was talking.

Athenais, duly introduced and catching the warning gleam in Monsieur Laroque's eye, curtsied deeply and summoned her best behaviour. Monseigneur was languidly entranced. He returned the following evening bearing a posy of flowers and, three nights later, was back again with a party of friends and a box of sweetmeats. His third visit brought Athenais six lace handkerchiefs … and an invitation to supper.

Athenais accepted the gifts with maidenly reluctance but excused herself from supper – thus earning a lecture from Froissart on the necessary evils of patronage. She listened politely, then replied that the audience bought the right to see her on-stage and nothing more.

'If you believe that,' he snapped, 'you are likely to have the shortest career in the history of Parisian theatre!'

Athenais shrugged but was secretly disconcerted as much by Pauline's unaccustomed silence on the subject as by Marie d'Amboise's suddenly friendly encouragement to stand her ground. Then the Marquis returned, unoffended and ready to give chase … after which, it seemed to Athenais that she was never free of him.

* * *

It was perhaps fortunate that, before further complications could develop, Fate took a hand. The cauldron of the Prince's Fronde which had been simmering away since the previous autumn, suddenly boiled over – and the Marquis returned in haste to confer with the Cardinal.

The first indication of change came when, having accepted the thankless task of mediation, the young King of England managed to persuade the Duke of Lorraine (currently being paid by Spain to assist Condé against Mazarin) to withdraw from the fray. Infuriated by this, Condé retaliated by throwing Charles and his mother out of Paris, sending them to join the rest of the French court at St. Germain. Then, before anybody was expecting it, Marshall Turenne set about trying to reclaim the city on behalf of his royal master.

At this point, Colonel Peverell immediately enlisted on a temporary basis. He told Francis – who, for obvious reasons, refused to join him – that he was doing it for the sake of a few weeks' pay and because he wanted Charles back in Paris, away from the decadence of the French court. The truth, however, was that he had reached the limit of his endurance. The continuous inactivity of the last few months was stifling him; and if he didn't do something about it soon, he thought he'd go mad.

Fighting under Turenne to reclaim Paris was just the tonic he needed. He hadn't realised how much he missed having a sword in his hand until it was there again. He was also appalled by how out-of-condition he'd become and was glad of the chance to repair the damage before he lost his edge completely. Most of all, for the first time since he and Francis had arrived in France, he felt alive.

He had been twenty-one when the first flames of civil war had swept across England and he'd enlisted straight away under Sir John Byron. In the ten years that had followed – even during times when the fighting had temporarily stopped – he had always found other ways of serving his King; ways which made good use of his talents and energy. And then, after the disaster at Worcester, everything had come to an abrupt end. No one made plans any more. No one, indeed, seemed to know in which direction to turn. There was no army, no money and no enthusiasm. Disillusion lay over the Royalist cause like a funeral pall. And there were times now when Ashley wondered whether the struggle to which he'd devoted a decade of his life would ever – *could* ever – recover.

It was at this stage that a sensible man would decide enough was enough. At the age of thirty-one, with the reckless idealism of youth well behind him, a sensible man would stop trying to mend what couldn't be mended and look to his own life before he turned into a pathetic, ageing adventurer, sitting in taverns, boring young men to death with tales of long ago.

It was a prospect which Ashley found frightening. He had seen it happen to others; an insidious process you didn't notice until it was too late. Life, surely, must have more to offer. But what? With things as they were, there was nothing for him in England. And the only other option was to forge a career as a mercenary, taking work where he could find it. He knew that wouldn't be difficult. Marshall Turenne, for example, would be happy to have him enlist permanently. He had only to say the word and sign on the line, as it were. Unfortunately, he couldn't quite bring himself to do it because the unpalatable truth was that knowing better didn't make a jot of difference. Despite all the good advice he gave himself, he knew perfectly well that the merest hint of revival in the Royalist cause would have him taking the first ship home. In short, whether from idiocy or devotion or optimism – or just sheer, habit – he had chosen his path and, for good or ill, was unable to turn from it.

For the time being however the battle for Paris enabled him to submerge himself in action and forget his worries. His job now was to keep his men alive and his powder dry. It consumed all his energy and all of his attention. It even stopped Athenais de Galzain from sliding, uninvited, into the edges of his subconscious. And for the first time in almost a year, he came close to being happy.

* * *

Not unnaturally, as the suburbs became a battle-zone and the rattle of musket-fire was clearly audible in the heart of the city, the citizens of Paris felt rather differently. Those who could move themselves and their goods away from the guns and advancing troops, did so. Those who couldn't bolted themselves into their homes and prayed for deliverance.

Manager Laroque, meanwhile, debated closing the theatre until the worst was over and then, since they were still playing to packed houses, decided against it. For a few days more life went on with surprising normality. Then, at the end of June, Turenne drove Condé into retreat, finally trapping the Frondeurs in the Faubourg St. Antoine – their back against the closed gates of the city and their front facing the Marshal's eight thousand men. This, in Monsieur Laroque's opinion, brought the fighting too close for comfort and could not help but affect the takings. Much to the relief of everyone except Athenais, he announced that performances would be suspended until the crisis had passed.

His decision proved timely. Condé's force was no match for Turenne's. The battle of July 2nd was hard-fought and bloody and things would have gone very ill for the Frondeurs had not Anne-Marie Louise d'Orleans – otherwise popularly known as La Grande Mademoiselle – decided to support Condé instead of her cousin, the King and insisted that the gates be opened to admit the Prince's army. Then, as the Frondeurs fled to safety in the city, Mademoiselle prevented Turenne from giving chase by ordering that the guns of the Bastille be turned against him. The Marshall ended the day hopping mad at being baulked of his prey; Condé failed to persuade the Paris magistrates to shut Turenne out and prepare to withstand a siege; and La Grande Mademoiselle relinquished command of the Bastille in favour of turning her hand to mediation.

* * *

Athenais and Pauline used their unexpected holiday to take possession of the house on the Rue des Rosiers – accompanied by a surly, bitterly complaining Archie. Abandoning him to his own devices, the two women set to work with mops, buckets and quantities of elbow-grease until the house was spotless from attic to cellar. Then Pauline arranged for the removal of her own furniture from the Place Royal and, once it was installed, went off to barter with a second-hand dealer for beds, chests and all the other essentials they still lacked.

While Pauline was out, Athenais got down on her hands and knees and polished the floor of the room she had chosen as her bedchamber. It was spacious and airy and overlooked the small, rear courtyard. It also possessed a small antechamber which she vaguely supposed was probably meant to serve as a dressing-closet. The idea of Agnes Stott from the Rue Benoit having enough clothes to need a room of their own produced a fit of laughter that was half-elated, half-frightened. When all she'd ever known was a cramped, stuffy attic above a filthy, stinking yard, the thought of having two whole rooms all to herself was enough to make her dizzy. So Athenais lovingly polished the broad, well-scrubbed boards of her floor and dreamed about sheets that smelled of fresh air rather than cabbage.

* * *

During the course of the next week, Marshall Turenne took both the Bastille and then Paris. Colonel Peverell stayed on throughout the closing skirmishes until a nasty flesh-wound to his left thigh put a halt to his activities and forced him to withdraw. He returned, with a slight limp and his pay, to the quarters he shared with Major Langley to find that the vibration from the guns of the Bastille had shaken most of the plaster from the walls. He also found Francis and his sister glaring at each across the table.

When Ashley limped in, Francis's expression lightened and he rose, saying, 'My God! The hero returns – and wounded, no less. They say Condé has taken to the heather. Is it true?'

'Yes.' Ashley made Celia a slight, courteous bow and then added, 'As for La Grande Mademoiselle, one imagines that, since she took to blowing the King's army to bits, she'll no longer be deemed a suitable bride for our own sovereign lord.'

'For which he will doubtless be everlastingly grateful,' said Francis dryly.

Her mouth still set in a mulish line, Celia stood up and shook out her skirts.

'You'll tell me as soon as you hear from Eden?'

'I've already said so. Several times. I have also said he may not even have received my letter yet. It will depend on where he is. Strive for a little patience, Celia – and please stop coming here to harangue me every second or third day. It's tiresome.'

'It's no pleasure to me, either,' she snapped. 'These rooms are an absolute disgrace.'

'Then it's fortunate you don't have to live in them, isn't it?' he replied gently. 'Sadly, Ashley and I don't have any choice.' He held her gaze for a moment longer and then said, 'Was there anything else?'

'No.' She started towards the door and then turned back. 'Yes. I almost forgot. Someone told Hugo that Father is ill. Apparently Ned

Hyde thought you should be sent for but didn't know how to reach you. They're at St. Germain, of course.'

For an instant, Francis stared at her as if he couldn't believe his ears. Then, in a tone of pure disgust, he said, 'God – but you're a selfish, cold-hearted bitch. Father's ill – possibly seriously – and you *forgot?* What the hell is the *matter* with you?'

She flushed a little and fussed with her gloves but said nothing.

'When did Verney tell you this?'

'Yesterday.' She shrugged crossly. 'I came as soon as I could. And if you're so concerned, I suggest you ride to St. Germain and see for yourself.'

'Do you think I need you to tell me that? Or that I need to ask whether you've any intention of visiting him yourself?' Francis drew a long breath and tried to control his temper. 'Just go, Celia. Leave our disgraceful hovel and scuttle back to your lover. I'm beginning to think the pair of you did Eden a favour.'

SIX

Monsieur Laroque re-opened the theatre with a comedy by Paul Scarron and Athenais was glad to be working again for furnishing the house to even the most basic level had seriously depleted both her own and Pauline's resources. On the other hand, she loved every brick and didn't regret a penny. She toured the elegant rooms, listened with delight to the clack of her heels on the tiled floor of the hall and ran up and down the curving staircase for the sheer pleasure of feeling the smooth banister-rail beneath her fingers. She told herself daily that she could ask for nothing more in life … except, just possibly, to be rid of the Marquis d'Auxerre, now back from St. Germain and hell-bent on pursuing her.

Predictably, it was Pauline who brought her down to earth again.

'The house looks well enough. You, however, don't. You have only two gowns that are fit to be seen, your cloak is threadbare and your shoes are scuffed. As for your underwear – the less said the better. So we need to get you a new wardrobe.'

'We haven't got the money.'

'I'll come back to that. First you need to accept that sooner or later you're going to have to sup with the Marquis or someone similar. And you can't go looking like a parlour-maid on her Sunday off. Speaking of which – we could do with a maid of our own. Someone to do the dusting and answer the door to callers.'

'All right.' Athenais supported her chin on both palms and eyed Pauline with mingled wariness and levity. 'How do we afford it? Steal the Crown jewels? Blackmail the Queen's dressmaker? Kidnap the Marquis? Or no. He'd enjoy it too much.'

'I suggest,' came the repressive reply, 'that we rent out the attic. There are three rooms up there that we don't need – so we could probably charge four or five *livres* a month.'

'I don't wish to seem negative – but five livres a month will barely buy one gown, let alone several. It won't even cover the under-garments.'

'It'll pay a maid. I know a girl who'll work for four livres and her keep and I've told her she can come on a month's trial. As for clothes …

dressmakers are used to waiting for their money and, as Paris's newest attraction, you'll have no trouble getting credit.'

'That's nice. But if it's all the same to you, I'd as soon not go diving into debt in order to look fancy for the Marquis d'Auxerre.'

Pauline looked shrewdly back at her.

'Why? What's wrong with him?'

'Quite a lot, if the rumours are true,' responded Athenais. 'And, even if they're not, I don't see why I should hop into bed with him purely because he happens to want me to.'

'I see. And assuming he doesn't lose interest, how long do you suppose you'll be able to keep him dangling?'

'I'm not keeping him dangling! It's not my fault if he can't take no for an answer.'

'Don't be naïve, Athenais. He's used to getting what he wants and it's common knowledge that he wants you. He's rich, influential and neither old nor ill-looking. So if you make him look foolish, don't be surprised if he doesn't take it lying down.'

'I thought I was the one who was supposed to do that.'

'Very funny.'

'Isn't that what you were trying to say?'

'I was trying,' Pauline snapped back, 'to make you see things as they are. Actresses aren't renowned for their virtue. So if you carry on behaving like a virgin fresh from the convent, you'll make enemies. Worse still, you'll make yourself look ridiculous and the pit will laugh itself silly.'

Athenais stared at her hands. Put like that, it sounded unpleasantly plausible. Finally she said distantly, 'So what am I supposed to do? I don't pretend to be pure as the driven snow – but I'm not a whore and don't see why I have to become one.'

'You don't. But whether you like it or not, men like d'Auxerre make the rules. And if he chose to get you dismissed, he could do it between breakfast and dinner.'

Athenais erupted from her chair and swept to the far side of the hearth. Gripping the mantle-piece with one hand, she said unevenly, 'Are you telling me that if I want to keep everything I've earned, I've got to open my legs for any rich bastard who wants me?'

'Not *any* one. Just possibly *this* one.' Hating the conversation as much as Athenais but still needing some answers, Pauline tried to remain patient. 'You said not so long ago that you'd preserve your career at all costs. So before you tell the Marquis to go to hell, I think you should ask yourself if you meant it.'

'Of course I meant it – but I hadn't expected to have to prostitute myself! Because, whatever you say, it's not just the damned Marquis, is it? After him, there'll be another and another ... till I'm no different from the drabs on the Pont Neuf.'

Pauline frowned.

'Is there somebody else?' she asked bluntly. 'Some other fellow you want?'

'*No!*' The lie was as vehement as it was automatic and Athenais closed her mind against the face and form of the only man she'd ever seen who could stop her breath. 'No. This is about me. I don't want to be treated like something than can be bought and paid for. If I let a man into my bed, I want the choice to be mine as much as his. And, even if it's too much to expect anyone else to respect me, I'd like to go on being able to respect myself.'

'Ah.' Pauline smiled wryly. 'Sadly, the world doesn't work that way. But I wish you luck.'

'I need more than that. I need a *plan*.'

'You need a miracle,' corrected Pauline. And then, sighing, 'All right. Play for time – flirt with some of the others. Above all, don't turn yourself into a challenge and don't – *don't* try convincing the Marquis that you're preserving your chastity. He doesn't believe it and he never will. If you're lucky, he'll get bored and look elsewhere.'

'And if he doesn't ... I make my bed and lie on it?'

'If he doesn't ... you may have to.'

* * *

In the days that followed this conversation, Athenais came to the conclusion that the idea of renting out the attic wasn't a bad one – if only they could find a suitable tenant who wouldn't mind climbing three flights of stairs on a regular basis. Archie said he'd be glad of another man in the house; Pauline announced that, if a nice little widow wasn't to be found, she'd be offering the rooms to one of the new walkers at the theatre; and Archie slammed out of the house and came back, roaring drunk at two in the morning to frighten the new maid silly. Athenais kept out of the ensuing quarrel – partly because she felt it was up to Pauline and Archie to find a way of co-existing but mainly because she had other things to worry about.

Everything she'd said to Pauline was true as far as it went. It just wasn't the full story.

Having accidentally lost her virginity at the age of fourteen, Athenais had no illusions where men were concerned and knew that, to a greater or lesser degree, they were all devious bastards, out to take advantage. It was a lesson she'd learned the hard way, one evening at dusk in the grave-yard of St. Julien-le-Pauvre. She and her friend, Eugenie, had been sitting on the wall gossiping, when they were joined by Eugenie's older brother, Guillaume and one of his work-mates from the bakery, bearing bottles of cheap wine which they'd generously shared with the girls. It had been fun until Eugenie had gone off, giggling, with the other boy, leaving Athenais alone with Guillaume. Then, without warning, everything had changed.

Rough hands invaded her bodice and a hot mouth stifled her breath. Stunned by the suddenness of it and too fuddled by the wine to stop it, Athenais found herself being dragged down on to the ground. Her skirt was hauled up around her waist, a knee forced her legs apart ... and then Guillaume was plunging himself violently into her. Minutes later, it was over and he was gone, leaving her vomiting helplessly on the grass.

She'd cried for a week, too ashamed to tell anyone and petrified he'd find a way of doing it again. She grew calmer when her courses came. She grew calmer still after Guillaume tried to fondle her in the yard one night and she'd slammed her knee into his groin and left him groaning on the cobbles. Most important of all, she'd vowed never to make herself such easy prey again.

It was a vow she'd kept. In the last seven years, no man had got within arms' length of her – so the thought of sleeping with the Marquis didn't bear thinking about. But the unfortunate truth was that, if she told him to bugger off, she might have to kiss her career goodbye. And that didn't bear thinking about either.

The prospects looked pretty bleak ... but she knew that, if one wanted something badly enough, one paid the price. It was as simple as that. Or it would have been, but for the recurring image of the most diabolically beautiful man she had ever seen; the only man she'd ever wanted to reach out and touch and with whom, oddly, the thought of sharing her body was not scary at all.

So Athenais tried to put Pauline's advice into practice and found it a bit like juggling eggs. She flirted with three of her most constant admirers under the Marquis's nose and watched them lapse into jealous sniping while the Marquis himself looked on with urbane amusement and didn't appear in the least put out. By the end of a fortnight, Athenais was feeling tired and frayed. Then a moment's carelessness enabled the Marquis to get her alone.

Sliding a hand about her waist and tilting her chin with the other, he murmured, 'Play your games a little longer, *ma belle*. I can't remember when I was so entertained.'

Forcing herself to stand still, Athenais breathed in the heavy aroma of sandalwood and decided she was beginning to hate that particular perfume. Smiling, she said, 'That's nice. But who said I was playing games?'

'I did. You haven't exactly been subtle, my dear. Only don't ... *don't* make the mistake of sleeping with one of those silly boys, will you? I'm afraid that wouldn't amuse me in the slightest. Indeed, I might be tempted to do him a mischief.'

Curbing her desire to either spit in his eye or use her knee to good effect, she continued to hold his gaze as coolly as possible. Set beneath heavy black brows, the night-dark eyes held an expression she couldn't quite identify but assuredly didn't trust. She said lightly, 'Well, it's not something that need concern you, Monseigneur. At present, I don't plan to sleep with anybody at all.'

'We both know that will change.' He laughed and released her. 'You wish to be pursued. I've no objection to that. The chase is always half the fun and anticipation adds spice – particularly to a jaded palate such as mine. You probably also think I'm more likely to shower you with expensive gifts now than I will once I've ... had my wicked way. In this, you are mistaken.' He paused to remove a small fleck of fluff from his sleeve and then added, 'When you are mine, you shall have everything your heart desires. But not ... *not* before then.'

'Well, I'm glad we've cleared that up,' responded Athenais. 'But what if I *don't* become yours?'

'A hypothetical question and not worth discussing,' came the suddenly clipped reply. 'I always get what I want. And just like the rest, *ma belle* – when I want you, you'll come.'

* * *

Francis returned from St. Germain within a week, his eyes shadowed and his mouth set in a grim line. Ashley watched him drop his bag in a corner and toss his hat on top of it. Then, when Francis still didn't speak, he said carefully, 'How is your father?'

The silence persisted and became airless. Finally, Francis said baldly, 'He's dead.'

'Ah. I'm sorry to hear it.'

'He died two hours before I got there.'

This, then, was the crux of the matter and, since there was nothing he could usefully say, Ashley remained silent and waited.

'He'd been asking for me – and, thanks to Celia, I was too late.' He raked a hand through his hair and stared down at his feet. 'Just one day. That's all it needed. If she'd told me as soon as she heard ... but she didn't and I was too late. I can't ... I don't think I'll ever forgive her for that.'

Rising, Ashley poured the last of the wine into a cup and handed it to him, saying, 'What about your mother?'

'My mother,' replied Francis coldly, 'is an even bigger whore than my sister. She and my father have lived apart for years. She couldn't even be bothered to attend the funeral.'

'Christ,' muttered Ashley. By the sounds of it, Francis's family was as disastrous as his own. 'Have you ... is there anything I can do?'

'No. Thank you. I've dealt with his affairs – such as they were. Inevitably, there was little more money than was needed to pay for the burial.' Francis raised the cup and drained it in one jerky movement. 'That doesn't matter. I just wanted to be there for him. So that he had someone of his own, you know? But he's gone.' His mouth twisted in a travesty of a smile. 'He's gone. And I'm Viscount bloody Wroxton – for all the use that's likely to be.'

* * *

By the middle of August, Pauline was beginning to realise that finding a suitable tenant was easier said than done. She came up with two widows and an ageing spinster. Unfortunately, having climbed the stairs once, all three ladies promptly withdrew their interest. Next, Pauline enquired amongst the young girls employed to do walk-on parts at the theatre and again drew a blank. The trouble with mentioning the matter at the theatre, of course, was that, in no time at all, everyone knew about it. Some offered well-meaning suggestions; others made remarks about people who didn't cut their coat according to their cloth; and Marie d'Amboise suddenly became amazingly helpful.

Pauline knew why, of course. Marie was hoping Athenais would push d'Auxerre too far and come to grief, once more leaving Marie as the company's leading lady. She also apparently thought finding a lodger for the Rue des Rosiers would help bring this about and, as a consequence, was tireless in her efforts to supply a suitable candidate.

Pauline let her get on with it. A week went by in which sultry weather disintegrated into thunderstorms. Then, on an evening when Pauline was beginning to think the attic-plan doomed to failure, she was summoned to the front right off-stage box. The location told her who had sent for her ... but she couldn't for the life of her think why.

'Madame Fleury?' enquired the dark-haired Englishwoman coolly. And, when Pauline curtsied in affirmation, 'I am Lady Verney. I'm told you have rooms for rent. Is it true?'

Her French was quite good but it wasn't that which surprised Pauline. Then she thought, *Of course. D'Amboise told the Vicomte de Charenton and the Vicomte told Milady here. But why is she interested? She can't want the rooms for herself.*

Aloud, she said merely, 'Quite true, Madame.'

Celia continued languidly plying her fan.

'How many rooms?'

'Three. They're in the attic but they're reasonably large and quite well lit.'

'How much are you asking?'

'Five *livres* a month, Madame.'

Celia tilted her head thoughtfully. She'd had a very unpleasant interview with Francis during which he'd told her it would be a cold day in hell before he did anything else for her. This, since Eden had still not sent a reply, meant that she needed to mend her fences – and supplying better lodgings seemed a reasonable way of doing so. The only snag was that, when Colonel Peverell's army-pay ran out, she'd end up paying the rent herself – or rather Hugo would. So she said, 'Five *livres*? For an *attic*? Surely you're joking. Not a *sou* more than three.'

Pauline decided that things were moving too fast for her liking. She said, 'Pardon me, Madame – but before we go any further, I'd like to know who my prospective tenant might be. I assume it's not yourself?'

'Well, of course it's not me! Do I look the sort to live in a horrid attic for three *livres* a month?'

'Five,' corrected Pauline smoothly. 'No, Madame. You don't. So who is it?'

Celia drew an impatient breath and said brusquely, 'My brother and his friend. And their servant, of course.'

Pauline's heart sank. Men. Three of them.

She said carefully, 'I'm sorry, Madame. I'm not sure that will suit. I share the house with a young woman --'

'Yes, yes. I know. But I don't see why that should be a problem.' Celia raised supercilious brows and added, 'My brother is a gentleman.'

'I'm sure he is,' agreed Pauline. And thought, *But he's still a man. Worse still, he's English – and everybody knows what a barbarous lot* they *are.*

Sensing that the interview wasn't going according to plan, Celia adopted a friendlier tone and said, 'Look, my dear. My brother is a Viscount. He's acquainted with the widowed Queen and her son, King Charles. But he's hard-pressed for money just at present and his current lodgings are both damp and stupidly expensive.' She saw no need to mention the fact that, since the Colonel's pay wouldn't stretch to cover the arrears of rent, he and Francis were on the brink of eviction. Smiling into the unresponsive face, she said persuasively, 'Won't you at least consider it? Better still, let me send my brother to see you so that you may judge for yourself.'

Pauline would have liked to refuse but was aware that, if she did so, the attic might remain permanently unoccupied. With unconcealed reluctance, she said, 'Very well, Madame. I make no promises ... but you may tell your brother to call at number sixteen, Rue des Rosiers tomorrow afternoon at three o'clock.'

'Excellent.' Celia beamed at her. 'And the rent? Shall we say four *livres* a month?'

'Five,' returned Pauline stubbornly. 'Since there are three of them.'

SEVEN

Francis considered tossing Celia's note on the fire unread and then thought better of it. There was just a chance she'd decided to apologise and show some regret for their late parent – though he doubted it. The hurriedly written missive contained only the time, place and reason for his appointment that afternoon – along with instructions to put on a decent coat and at least *try* to be charming.

His mouth curled derisively. She was hoping to get around him, of course. But the lure of better lodgings for which, for a time at least, Celia could pay wasn't something to be resisted. Scanning the note again, he decided that a fragment or two of additional information might not have gone amiss. Then, because Ashley had gone off to see Marshall Turenne and taken Jem with him, he resigned himself to polishing his own boots and brushing the less shabby of his two coats in the hope of making a good impression.

At precisely three o'clock, Francis trod up the steps of number sixteen, Rue des Rosiers and plied the gleaming brass knocker. Then the door opened and he found himself face to face with the woman he'd last seen in the Green Room of the Théâtre du Marais.

The surprise was mutual. Pauline said abruptly, '*You're* Milady Verney's brother?' And absorbing the resemblance, 'But of course you are.'

Removing his hat and summoning a rueful smile, he said, 'I fear so. Francis Langley, if you recall.'

'I do, as it happens. You'd better come in.'

He bowed and stepped into the immaculate hall.

'You must think me immensely slow-witted. I had no idea, you see, whom I was to have the pleasure of meeting this afternoon. My sister even neglected to tell me your name.'

'Pauline Fleury,' came the brusque reply. 'Madame, to you. And, as for being dense, I hadn't realised you were English. You speak extremely good French – as, I seem to recall, does your friend. I understand he wants to live here, too?'

'Yes.' Something in her tone suggested to Francis that he'd better clear away any misconceptions. 'We are constrained by the emptiness of our pockets into sharing a lodging. But we're neither joined at the hip nor in love with each other – in case you were wondering.'

For the first time, the ghost of a smile appeared.

'The thought had occurred to me. Did he stay behind just to prove your point? Or did you think I might be overwhelmed by the pair of you?'

'I rather suspect,' said Francis smoothly, 'that there's very little that would overwhelm you, Madame. But no. Colonel Peverell isn't here because he went to St. Germain yesterday and hasn't yet returned.'

'Hm.' Pauline's brows rose. 'Move in lofty circles, don't you? No – don't answer that. I might not find it quite the recommendation you'd expect. On the other hand, I can see that I ought to offer you a chair so you'd better come in to the parlour.'

The room into which she led him had a sparse sort of elegance which he rather liked. In fact, if one looked beyond the white line of the scar which marred her left cheek, Madame Fleury herself was not without a certain style. She dressed well and her figure was good. The hazel eyes, too, were remarkably fine, if a trifle sharp ... and the neatly-arranged brown hair was thick and glossy. All in all, thought Francis, she was still an attractive woman and was probably no older than he was himself.

He said suddenly, 'I *am* an idiot. You're Pauline Fleury.'

'So I have said.'

'No – no. You're Pauline Fleury, the actress. I saw you play Mary in *L'Ecossaise*. It would have been early in '46, I think.'

She nodded but her expression remained unchanged. 'Did you enjoy it?'

'Yes – though I thought the play mediocre. You, on the other hand, were extremely convincing.' He smiled. 'By the end of it, I was more than half in love with you.'

'I'm flattered.' A pause. 'It was the last role I ever played.'

Taken unawares, Francis narrowly avoided the obvious pitfall. Instead, his tone as matter-of-fact as hers, he said, 'Then I'm doubly glad I saw it.'

Another faint smile dawned.

'Very good, Monsieur Langley. You have passed the test and may now sit down.' Then, when he had done so, 'The first thing I want to make clear is that I'd have preferred a female tenant. Consequently, I'm not overjoyed at the prospect of having one man stamping about over our heads – let alone three.'

'That's understandable. For my own part, however, I can only hope you'll consider giving the Colonel and me a chance to prove that we … er … don't stamp.'

'You haven't seen the rooms yet.'

'I've seen enough to know that I needn't worry about cockroaches and lice.'

If the compliment pleased her, it didn't show. She said, 'Why are you really quitting your present lodgings?'

'Because, squalid as they are, the unpleasant gentleman who owns them insists on eight *livres* a month – and we've reached the point of having to choose between paying the rent and eating.'

The lack of self-pity coupled with the fact that he hadn't tried to lie to her, roused Pauline's approval. She said, 'You don't give the impression of somebody who's spent their life scrimping and scraping. Rather the reverse. Don't you get an income from England?'

'No. My family's lands were sequestered years ago and Colonel Peverell's brother chose the winning side.' He smiled wryly. 'We're a pair of out-of-work soldiers, living on our wits – and, just at present, not making a very good job of it.'

'You're certainly not making a very good job of sounding like ideal tenants.'

'No. I *could* try telling you than I'm a Viscount and that I spent my younger days at the late King's court, writing quantities of largely indifferent poetry. But where's the use in that? Times have changed.'

There was a long silence while Pauline wrestled with her instincts. Then, giving way to them, she said, 'You'd better look at the rooms.'

Unprepared for it, Francis remained glued to his chair.

'Willingly. Does that mean that you --'

'It means I'll give you a month's trial. But if you don't pay the rent, you're out on your ear,' she warned him flatly. 'And another thing. I share this house with Mademoiselle de Galzain – and her father as well, worst luck. Him, you'd be wise to steer clear of – but that's up to you.

However, if either of you tries laying a finger on Athenais, I'll have your balls in a pie. Clear?'

'Absolutely,' agreed Francis. And thought, *Oh my God. It's going to be like staying sober in a wine-cellar.* Aloud, he added, 'You have my word that Mademoiselle will always be treated with the utmost respect.'

'She'd better be,' retorted Pauline. And then, 'Well? Are you coming? It's three flights up.'

* * *

Pauline waited until after the evening's performance before breaking the news to Athenais. Since, however, she didn't immediately reveal who the lodgers were to be, Archie slumped gloomily into his chair and muttered bitterly, 'Anuvver sodding female in the 'ouse. It's enough to make man cut 'is own throat.'

Struggling not to laugh, Athenais told him to speak French or hold his tongue. And, to Pauline, 'That's wonderful. When will she move in?'

'At the end of the week. And it's not a she.'

Athenais's brows soared. 'A man?'

'Two, actually.' With irritation, Pauline watched Archie's expression change from despondency to something akin to glee. 'And their servant. It's not what we wanted – but it's better than leaving the rooms empty.'

'It's a flaming miracle,' breathed Archie.

Athenais ignored him. His determination to speak English because Pauline couldn't was driving her demented. She said, 'Of course it's better. We needn't see much of them, after all.'

'Speak for yourself,' said Archie. 'I plans to make 'em very welcome. Very welcome *indeed*.'

His daughter impaled him on a severe gaze and, still in French, said, 'You're not to plague them. And you're not to touch them for money. Not ever. Do you hear me?'

Archie shrugged and grinned into his ale.

Fixing her eyes on a point several inches above his head, Pauline remarked that it wouldn't do him any good if he *did* try borrowing money from the tenants, since they had none to spare.

Archie looked up, frowning. Then, because he knew it was the only way to get an answer out of the old cat, he made the ultimate sacrifice and switched to French. 'What do you mean – none to spare? How do you know?'

'Because they're exiled Royalists,' came the sour reply. 'With empty pockets.'

Archie surged to his feet.

'They're English? You're saying they're bloody *English?*'

'Yes. Are you deaf as well as stupid?'

He only heard the first word. The rest was lost in a shout of delight. Pauline eyed him with acute disfavour. Then, becoming aware that Athenais was staring at her in stony silence, she said, 'What's wrong?'

'Isn't it obvious?'

'No. A minute ago you didn't care *who* lived upstairs.'

'Two – or is it three? – Englishmen are a different matter. Father's going to talk non-stop. He's going to tell them all about himself and all about me and he's going to call me Agnes. So *they'll* call me Agnes. And in no time at all, half of *Paris* will be calling me bloody Agnes – and knowing I'm a bastard and probably the colour of my garters, as well!'

Pauline reluctantly recognised the truth of this. Sober, Archie might be reasonably discreet; drunk, there was no telling what he might say.

'Then we'll have a quiet word with the lodgers. They're gentlemen and I suspect they know how to keep their mouths shut. Also, you know them.'

'I don't. The only Englishman I know is *him.*'

'Not quite,' replied Pauline. And, as briefly as possible, explained.

At some point while she was talking, the annoyance in Athenais's face was gradually replaced by an expression which Pauline couldn't interpret. Consequently, when she stopped talking and the girl still remained silent, she said, 'What's the matter? You remember them, don't you? One dark, one fair; both tall and a bit thread-bare but equally spectacular?'

To disguise the fact that a strange sensation was gripping her insides, Athenais rose and walked to the fire. Then, kneeling on the hearth, she said distantly, 'I remember. And you think they can be trusted?'

'As much as any other man,' responded Pauline cynically. 'I've already threatened dire reprisals if they bother you. And as I said, they're gentlemen. One of them is even a Viscount, for God's sake. So they follow the rules or they go. It's as simple as that.'

Athenais didn't think it was going to be simple at all. Of all the men in the world, *he* was going to be living in the same house. They might pass on the stairs or in the hall or meet in the kitchen. He might brush her hand in passing or smile at her with those extraordinary eyes. And since her insides were already tied in knots at the mere thought, she didn't know how on earth she was going to manage the reality.

Drawing a long breath, she summoned up her craft and said indifferently, 'Oh well. If you say so.' Then, half-turning and managing a flippant smile, 'And I suppose having two gallants upstairs could come in useful. At need, they might even frighten off the Marquis d'Auxerre.'

* * *

After taking formal leave of Marshall Turenne, Ashley returned to Paris and went directly to see the King – now once more inhabiting the Louvre. Charles received him in a vast, dilapidated salon where one small fire fought a losing battle with the damp and the draughts. Ashley bowed and then said bitterly, 'My God, Sir – do you *have* to live in this mausoleum?'

'Awful, isn't it?' grinned Charles. 'There's moth in the hangings, worm in the furniture and rot in the floorboards. Father would have had a fit.'

'And Her Majesty, your mother?'

'Has them constantly.' And, waving the Colonel into a chair near the pitiful fire, 'What's on your mind? I don't suppose you're here just to cheer me up.'

'As it happens, I was rather hoping to cheer us both up.'

'Ah.' Dropping into the other chair and hooking one long leg over its arm, Charles regarded his visitor with mild foreboding. 'You want to talk me into sanctioning something no one else will sanction. Yes?'

A smile touched the green eyes. 'Yes.'

'I thought so. You don't change much, do you?'

'I change more than you think, Sir. And I'm not the only one.'

'Meaning what?'

'Meaning that we've been licking our wounds for nearly a year and that if we want to salvage anything from the wreckage, we ought to be doing so before it's too late. Think about it, Sir. Ireland surrendered to Cromwell three months ago and Scotland's likely to go the same way very soon. Your friends in England have been left to try and make the best of a bad job. Given long enough, they'll succeed. As to your friends here, they're living hand-to-mouth, without either purpose or hope. Another year like the last and they'll either be so dissolute or disillusioned that they'll be useless to you.' Ashley paused. 'I know our resources are limited – but we ought at least to be *trying*. If we don't, the day will come when we won't have a man left worth counting on.'

'Including yourself?'

'Perhaps. Sir, I could name you at least three fellows who've taken to the bottle and a couple of others who spend their time picking fights. Major Langley is turning into a confirmed gamester – which, given the company he's keeping, is likely to result in someone sticking a knife in his back one dark night. I call that a damned waste.'

The dark brows rose and Charles said, 'So what are you suggesting? That I start a hare purely for the purpose of giving the out-of-work soldiery employment?'

'No, Sir.' Ashley battened down a flicker of irritation and his voice, though cool, was perfectly level. 'But I do think that – after the years of service these men have given to your father and yourself – they deserve some consideration.'

Flushing slightly, Charles left his chair and paced off across the room. Over his shoulder, he said curtly, 'Do you think I don't know that? But I'm not my own master. I'm just a piece on a chessboard. All my moves are dictated by knights and bishops and queens, in a stream of never-ending advice. God! I can't even sneeze without weighing the consequences.' He swung round to face the Colonel and added explosively, 'Do you think I'm not sick of it, too? But when you don't even own the clothes on your back, it's a bit difficult to formulate any grand plans.'

There was a long pause. Finally, Ashley said, 'So your hands are tied. But what if they weren't?'

Charles gave a bitter laugh.

'That's just the trouble. I can't field an army without foreign help and that help isn't forthcoming. The Dutch are busy fighting Cromwell at sea

– not for me, but because the Commonwealth insists on searching their cargo vessels for French goods and expects them to dip their flags every time they catch sight of the English Navy. Spain and France are still locked in a struggle the rest of Europe finally put behind it four years ago. Spain, of course, recognised the Commonwealth like a shot and though Mazarin's so far refused – and had his envoy tossed out of Whitehall as a result – I think he'll give way before the year is out rather than end up fighting on another front while he's still got Spain nipping at his backside. So who is there, do you suppose, with either the interest or the motive to help the beggar-King take back his own?'

'The beggar-King's followers,' replied Ashley quietly, 'because they've nothing to lose and everything to gain. Also, perhaps a few of your former enemies who are now dissatisfied with everything from trade to the absence of Christmas and Sunday football.'

'Dissatisfied enough to budge from their hearths?'

'As yet, probably not. But since we're not in a position to issue a call to arms, that hardly matters. What *does* matter is nourishing the support Your Majesty already has, whilst exploiting the difficulties and divisions of your enemies. Two sides of the same coin.'

Charles sighed. 'I'm sorry, Ash. It's too --' He broke off as the door opened to admit Sir William Brierley and then, with relief, said, 'Perfect timing, Will.'

'Thank you, Sir. Sadly, however, I came to inform you that the Queen, your mother, desires your presence. And I should add that she has La Grande Mademoiselle with her.'

'In which case,' responded Charles dryly, 'I won't hurry. Meanwhile, perhaps you can convince our friend here that it's too soon to start canvassing support again at home.'

'Far too soon,' agreed Sir William, advancing towards the fire. 'His Majesty's loyal subjects in England are busy keeping their heads down and their mouths shut. In short, Ashley, you can go to England, if you like – but no one is going to let you past the front door.'

'You can't be sure of that.'

'Unfortunately, I can – and have numerous letters to prove it.' He paused and then added, 'I know how you feel – really, I do. But the time for action is not yet. I'm afraid you're just going to have to be patient.'

'I've *been* patient!' snapped Ashley. And, belatedly remembering the presence of his sovereign, 'I'm sorry, Sir. I just can't --'

Charles held up one long-fingered hand.

'I know. And as soon as there's work to be done, you'll be the first to hear it. But brow-beating Ned Hyde and myself won't make it happen any quicker.'

Colonel Peverell drew a long breath and released it. 'No, Sir.'

'Upon which note,' said the King, 'I shall go and try charming Mademoiselle into buying me an army. It won't work, of course. But I draw the line at marrying the woman.'

As Charles left the room, Sir William awarded Ashley an acid-edged smile.

'You see, my dear? We all have our crosses to bear.'

'I'm well-aware of that but --'

'Do you know, Ashley ... I don't somehow think that you are. But let us not quarrel. Instead, let's remove ourselves from this depressing place and find a tavern. I suggest you spend a couple of nights at my lodging.'

'That's tempting – but what of Louise?'

'Louise,' said Will, in a tone defying either interpretation or question, 'has decamped in search of better prospects. And so, like you, I am in need of a diversion. Luckily, I know just the fellow to supply it.'

Sir William's idea of a diversion turned out to be an alarmingly clever fellow with a quick temper, a wild sense of humour and a very large nose. A man Ashley had heard much about but never previously met – and close acquaintance with whom, he later suspected, could take years off a man's life. In short, it was Cyrano de Bergerac.

Towards the end of the third bottle, this gentleman announced that they must go to the Hôtel de Bourgogne. Ashley squinted at him and remarked that, if they *had* to see a play, he'd sooner go to the Marais.

'But no, my friend,' said Cyrano firmly. 'I have business at the Bourgogne tonight. They are staging my new comedy, *Le Pédant Joué*. Last night, Montfleury mangled his role so badly that I ordered him to stay off the stage for a month while he learns his lines. Sadly, he hasn't taken me seriously. And so, we go to the Bourgogne.'

All of Paris appeared to know of Montfleury's intention to perform. The theatre was full to bursting and the atmosphere was one of gleeful anticipation which rose to a positive zenith of excitement when Cyrano strolled in half-way through the first act.

Ashley glanced at Sir William and murmured, 'Is this really necessary?'

'Yes. Apart from making up the words as he goes along, Montfleury is as stiff as our sovereign lord's cock.'

With every step Cyrano took, more and more voices fell silent until a deathly hush spread throughout the entire theatre while, on the stage, Montfleury gradually faltered to a stop, mid-sentence. Smiling, Cyrano hoisted himself on to the boards and advanced, implacably but without haste, until he was nose to nose with the quivering actor.

'I warned you,' he remarked calmly. 'You should have listened.'

And picking Montfleury up by the collar of his coat, Cyrano dropped him in the pit.

The wits howled with laughter and, within seconds, were passing the unfortunate man hand-to-hand over their heads to the door.

'Play the role yourself, Cyrano!' shouted somebody; and suddenly it became a chant. 'Go on – play it yourself!'

De Bergerac held up a hand for silence and eventually got it.

'No, no, my friends. You have already had as much entertainment as is justified in the price of your ticket.' He tilted his head and thought for a moment. 'However ... perhaps a brief ode?'

The pit roared its approval and, with a mocking bow, Cyrano embarked on a cripplingly funny extemporisation of Montfleury's shortcomings. By the time he was done, Ashley's stomach hurt.

Sailing out into the street some time later, the three of them drank some more and got into two fights. Ashley ended up with skinned knuckles and a graze on one cheek. It was not, he reflected blearily, a good long-term solution for boredom. Or not if he wanted to see his next birthday.

* * *

Returning to his lodgings two days later than expected, he walked in to find all their gear packed in a neat heap and the room once more reduced to its original dismal state. Raising an enquiring brow, he said, 'Are we going somewhere?'

'Yes,' replied Francis coldly.

'Voluntarily – or the other way?'

'Does it matter?

'I suppose not.' Ashley paused and, when Francis continued to look icily aggrieved, said, 'All right. Spit it out and let's have done with it. I'm not in the mood for --'

'Bleedin' hell,' remarked Jem Barker from the doorway. 'Been busy as a body-louse, ain't you, Major?'

'Yes,' responded Francis with asperity. And, to Ashley, 'God forbid that you should feel impelled to account for your movements. But it would occasionally be helpful if you could come back when you say you will.'

'Oh Christ,' sighed Ashley. 'Not again. You sound like somebody's wife.'

'Having had the dubious pleasure of sorting out your shirts, I *feel* like somebody's wife.'

Jem laughed. 'He's got you there, Captain.'

'And you can hold your tongue, too,' retorted Ashley. 'I also wish – if you *must* use my rank – you could get it right. We're not on the High Toby now.'

'Once a bridle-cull, always a bridle-cull,' averred Jem. And, glancing from Francis to the assembled baggage and back again, 'So where we going, then?'

'Sixteen, Rue des Rosiers.'

'Whew!' Jem rolled his eyes. 'Gawd's truth, we must be flush! We'll be strutting about like crows in a gutter afore we knows it. So have you paid the old cross-biter – or are we shooting the moon?'

There were times when Francis found Jem's vocabulary tiresome. This was one of them. He said, 'I'd be grateful if, just sometimes, you could speak the King's own English. However. The answer is yes, the rent has been paid and no, we won't have to slink away after dark. Therefore, if neither of you have any further questions, I'll go and hire a cart.'

'Don't fret your gizzard, Milord. I'll see to that,' offered Jem provocatively. 'Reckon you done enough. And you'll be happier when you've given the Captain here a good dressing-down.' Upon which note, he disappeared.

Collecting the Major's irritable gaze, Ashley said crisply, 'All right, Francis. I apologise for any inconvenience caused by my delayed return. As it happens, I spent some time trying to give His Majesty something to think about other than women – whilst also talking myself into a brief, exploratory visit to England. The first may have worked but won't last; the second may come off when everyone with a say in the matter has talked themselves to a standstill.'

The blue gaze remained largely inimical.

'I suppose,' drawled Francis, 'that it never occurs to you that it's a touch unreasonable to expect everyone to leap into action every time you speak?'

'I don't expect it. But --'

'That's not how it sounds. And as for Charles ... he may be a rakehell but he's also been cap in hand to every damned ruler he can reach, looking for an army.'

'Very well. Perhaps I expect too much.' Ashley drew a short, explosive breath. 'But if we're going to sit on our arses for another year doing sod all, I want my life back.' He stopped abruptly and, moderating his tone, said, 'So tell me. Who paid the rent and why are we removing to the Rue des Rosiers?'

'I invested the last of our money in a dice game and was lucky,' shrugged Francis. 'The rent is paid and I still have a few coins in my pocket. As for the new lodgings, Celia arranged them. After her recent failings and still with no reply from Eden, she's trying to find a way back into my good graces. Of course, as soon as Eden writes to say the only way she'll ever marry Verney is over his dead body, we'll have to shift for ourselves. But in the meantime, the rooms in the Marais are clean, lice-free and cheaper than here.' He paused and then added casually, 'They're also possessed of additional attractions.'

'Oh God,' groaned Ashley. 'I might have known. We're moving so you can bed the landlord's daughter.'

'Not quite.' His good humour restored, Francis gave a slow, seraphic smile. 'She's not the landlord's daughter – though she has both father and chaperone. And I'll wager you'll be casting as many lures as I. Possibly more. In short, she's our own very favourite red-head.'

For a long time, Ashley just stared at him. Finally, his voice curiously flat, he said, 'Is that a joke?'

'Not at all. We are going – with crumhorns and tambours – to live in the Rue des Rosiers with Athenais de Galzain.'

There was another silence.

Then, 'Bloody hell,' said Colonel Peverell.

ENTR'ACTE
London – August, 1652

At about the time Francis and Ashley were preparing to move to the Marais, Eden Maxwell was staring broodingly down upon Cheapside from the window of Luciano del Santi's parlour. Despite the fact that his Italian brother-in-law hadn't set foot in London for seven years, whereas he himself had been living there, on and off, for the last four, Eden still thought of it as Luciano's house – and probably would even when his younger brother, Toby, arrived to set up his own goldsmith's sign there.

Not that he was thinking of that now. *Now*, the only thing on his mind was the much-travelled and aggravatingly tactful letter he held crushed in his hand. In some corner of his mind, Eden recognised that Francis meant well ... that if a letter from one's brother-in-law made one want to smash something, a letter from one's bitch of a wife would probably have one climbing the walls. But until today, except in one particular which he generally managed to avoid thinking about, Eden had believed himself cured – only to discover that it wasn't completely true.

It had been eight years. Anyone who couldn't get over a woman in that time must be feeble-minded. All right; so Celia's betrayal was inextricably linked with the death of his father ... and because his daughter probably *wasn't* his daughter, he'd become a virtual stranger to his son. But his days weren't empty of purpose, nor his nights of pleasure. He had work he enjoyed and friends he valued. His life might have been changed – but it hadn't been ruined. Neither, since the day he'd found her in bed with Hugo Verney, had he ever wanted Celia back. So why in Hades did Francis's letter make him feel as if he'd been kicked in the stomach?

He half-considered reading it again and then changed his mind. He knew what it said. Celia wanted a divorce – and, being Celia, thought that to want was to have. Francis clearly knew better, understanding that Eden might be averse to becoming fodder for the news-sheets. In fact, his only miscalculation lay in the delicately-phrased suggestion that Eden might, by now, be ready to consider marrying again. He wasn't.

His life was well-ordered and the very last thing he needed was another wife. In the months since Worcester, he'd been required to do very little fighting. Instead, he'd been sitting on this committee and that while Cromwell and the rest laboured to devise a workable government. The most recent scheme, which had involved crowning the young Duke of Gloucester, had foundered like all the others before it. Despite fixing a date for its dissolution, the Rump lingered on like a bad smell, occasionally managing to put a spoke in Oliver's wheel; an Act of Union, joining Scotland to England, had been mouldering away in committee for four months without reaching resolution; and Henry Ireton had continued knocking the stuffing out of Ireland until it had succeeded in killing him the previous November – after which, despite a formal treaty of surrender at Kilkenny, the Irish continued to fight on in small pockets and recognise defeat, piecemeal.

The Dutch War had started back in May when Admiral Blake and the Dutch Admiral Tromp had clashed at the battle of Dover. A month later, Dutch ambassadors had arrived to protest about England interfering with their trading vessels all around the coast and a month after that, a state of war between the two countries had been somewhat belatedly declared in the wake of Admiral Ayscue's attack on Dutch ships off Calais. Further afield, meanwhile, Prince Rupert was picking off English merchantmen in the West Indies – thus annoying those islands which had seen the wisdom of recognising the Commonwealth.

In London, while all this was going on, Eden compiled dossiers and wrote reports and started to understand why Gabriel Brandon had predicted that one day the Army would be no place for soldiers. Fortunately, before the boredom became too much for him, chance revealed a talent he'd never previously had much use for and caused him to be seconded into the intelligence service. Years ago at Angers, Eden had fallen in love with the intricacy of ciphers. Now he spent a large part of his time breaking Dutch and Royalist codes for Thomas Scot who was still in charge of foreign intelligence and devising others for the use of the Secretary of State's growing network of domestic spies and informers. Eden wasn't especially fond of John Thurloe. He was, however, forced to admit that – judging by the last four months – the fellow was someone who specialised in getting wheels working within wheels. So much so, thought Eden, tossing the letter down on the table, that it was tempting to wonder if Thurloe wouldn't be the very person to secure one a quick and totally discreet divorce.

A door slammed below and there was a sound of feet running up the stairs. Then the parlour door opened and Nicholas Austin's head appeared round it to say, 'Sam would like to call on you later, if it's convenient – something about the *Moderate.*'

Sighing, Eden turned round. He didn't know which piece of folly was worse; inviting a Catholic Royalist to inhabit the spare bedchamber – or letting him get thick as thieves with Sam Radford. The first wouldn't do much harm provided Eden's superiors didn't get wind of it; but the second created a potentially explosive combination of Leveller and Cavalier – poles apart except on the issue of wanting to reduce the power of the Army.

'If it's convenient?' queried Eden. 'As far as I'm aware, Sam never gave a tinker's curse for anybody's convenience save his own.'

Nicholas grinned. 'I put that bit in myself. He'll be here around six.'

'I may be out. Are you going to Shoreditch?'

'Later, perhaps. Bryony gave me a message for Annis, so --'

'You really needn't make excuses to me, you know,' interrupted Eden blandly. And watched the younger man flush.

Not having felt up to taking responsibility for a seventeen-year-old girl, Eden had turned to Gabriel Brandon's foster-family. He'd persuaded the Morrells to care for Verity – in return for which she helped Annis in the house and looked after five-year-old John. The arrangement seemed to suit everyone and had also finally shaken Nicholas out of the apathy that had lasted a full month after they'd reached London.

At first, Eden had let him wallow – then irritation had set in, causing him to say abrasively, 'Are you going to mope about forever? Or are you going to pick yourself up and make the best of a bad job?' Then, when Nicholas hadn't answered, he'd added, 'You might at least spare a thought for young Verity. She burned her boats to keep you alive and now you're all she's got. So what are you going to do about her?'

Nicholas had turned an empty brown gaze on him and, in the tone of someone asking for the salt, said, 'Do you want me to marry her?'

'Don't be a bigger fool than you can help. She's not quite eighteen and seems to have become infatuated with the first fellow to show her a bit of kindness.'

'And a cripple's not a great bargain, is he?'

A dangerous gleam entered Eden's eyes.

'You're not the first man to lose a limb in battle and I doubt you'll be the last. So pull yourself together and make a courtesy call in Shoreditch. You'll find the Morrells' house easily enough – Jack's an armourer. And don't tell me you can't ride with only one arm, because you can. Unless you're a bloody daisy?'

So Nicholas had gone to Shoreditch in a mood of sullen resentment and returned subtly changed. From Jack and Annis, Eden learned that he had arrived with a face like stone and a manner only a hairsbreadth from rudeness. Then he'd come face to face with Verity – pale and forlorn, her eyes full of doubt – and stopped as if poleaxed. By the time he left, said Annis, Verity had some colour in her face and the Captain had remembered his manners.

After his second visit, Nicholas had immediately sought out Eden to say bluntly, 'You've done more for me than anyone could expect of a stranger and borne with my moods with exceptional patience – and all for no thanks that I remember making. I'd like to rectify that now, if I may.'

That had been seven months ago, since which time – in between making himself useful to Eden and forging a friendship with Samuel Radford – Nicholas had taken to visiting Shoreditch every other day. Eden hoped whatever came of it would be for the best. It would be nice to help two people live happily ever after. It was just a pity he couldn't do it for himself.

He took another cursory look at Francis's letter before shoving it away at the back of a drawer. He didn't have to think about it now. He didn't have to think about it at *all*, if he didn't want to. And as for Celia ... well, Celia could go hang.

There was a tap at the door and Eden turned, smiling, as Deborah Hart walked in. Though less buxom than she'd been before her ordeal, her skin had regained its luminosity and her eyes were serene. She said, 'I came to ask if you'd be taking your meal at home today.'

'Unfortunately, not. I'm due at Whitehall in an hour – the Officers' Council is presenting a petition for numerous reforms and the dissolution of Parliament. Oh – and it's asking for arrears of pay. Again. And if *that* doesn't take the rest of the afternoon, there's also to be some discussion about confiscating Royalist lands to fund the Navy.' He paused and added, 'I've told you before. There's no need to knock when you know I'm alone.'

She shook her head slightly. 'It's better so. More ... appropriate.'

Eden looked at her, taking in the plain blue gown and crisp white cap over neatly-arranged hair. She looked every inch the perfect housekeeper – and, indeed, she was. He'd offered her the position because doing so killed two birds with one stone. She needed work and he needed someone to run his home. Simple. What he *hadn't* anticipated was that, from being more conscious of her than was comfortable, he should progress so swiftly to wanting her ... or how, despite all his care, she had somehow *known*.

It had been on a night at the turn of the year when she'd been under his roof for almost three months that he'd gone to his room and found her waiting for him, still fully-dressed but with her hair unbound. Shock had frozen him to the threshold for several seconds before he'd had the sense to close the door. Then, walking to a point some three steps from him, she had said calmly, 'I have waited to see if there was some other woman in your life but it seems that there isn't. I am here because I want to be and because I think you do too. If that is so – and you were to ask – I could stay.'

Eden had opened his mouth on a sensible, graceful refusal and, instead, heard himself say huskily, 'Then stay.'

Smiling, she had allowed him to close the space between them. And, when he had done so and she was almost in his arms, she said, 'I know you are not in love with me. It is of no consequence so long as you never pretend. And I will be discreet.'

Eden had stopped the words with his mouth and felt the naked hunger in her response. Desire flared into a blaze and he pulled her down with him into the softness of the feather quilt, his fingers already busy with the laces of her gown. Later, he dimly remembered murmuring, 'Forgive me … and forgive my intemperance. But it's been a long time.'

And, in a voice as unsteady as his, she'd said, 'For me, also. So be as intemperate as you like, my dear … and I shall meet you half-way.'

She'd met him more than half-way – not just on that night, but on all the others that had succeeded it. She'd also kept her promise about discretion. Sometimes, Eden had difficulty equating the quietly efficient woman in the sober dress and starched cap with the wildly wanton creature who shared his bed at night. And though he was no more in love with her now than he'd been eight months ago, he was wholly addicted to the pleasures her body brought him. Sometimes he also found himself wondering if she really was a witch, after all.

Looking at her now, he said, 'You're a strange mixture, Deborah.'

She smiled and, as so often, answered his thought rather than his words.

'Don't worry. I've used no spells or charms or potions. Nor will I.'

Thinking it a joke, he said, 'Are you saying that you could?'

She shook her head and side-stepped the question.

'It wouldn't do any good. There will be someone else for you one day.'

Eden's mouth curled. He had told her about Celia. She was the only person to whom he'd ever voluntarily related the sorry tale of his marriage and it had been done to show the limits of what he had to offer. Now he said merely, 'I think we can agree that that is unlikely.'

The dark eyes continued to gaze unwaveringly into his and, with a complete absence of expression, she said again, 'There will be someone else.'

Something in her voice caused the hairs to prickle on the back of his neck.

'How do you know?' he asked unwillingly.

'Some things are clear. When you meet her, you will know.'

Following hard on the heels of Francis's letter, this was uncanny. Eden would have liked to believe that Deborah had read it – except that he knew she hadn't. He said, 'I've told you that divorce is … problematic. And Celia is still a young woman.'

'Things happen. Life is uncertain.' The odd light in her eyes faded and she shrugged slightly. 'Then again, perhaps I'm wrong. I could be. I only know that there is a woman in your future – and I am not she.'

Eden relaxed. 'Perhaps not. But I'm content with the present. Aren't you?'

'More than content.' She smiled gently. 'I love you.'

His muscles tensed again and he said rapidly, 'No. You're grateful for what I did in Worcester. That's all.'

'All? You saved my life.'

'But I don't want it as payment.'

'I know. It isn't being offered as such.' She paused and then said, 'This is not a question of payment. I love you and you know it. You've known it for a long time. You've just never let yourself acknowledge it ... and you hoped I would never say it.'

Eden turned abruptly away to the window and, with his back to her, said, 'If you know that, why *are* you saying it?'

'To point out that the pleasure we share is of my choosing and that I'm satisfied with it. To tell you that, when the time comes, I shall fade into the background without reproaches. So you need feel neither guilt nor concern for the future.'

He frowned down at his hands, wondering – as he so often had done – how it was she could identify the things he even hid from himself. He said slowly, 'You make it sound simple. But it is far more than I have the right to ask of you.'

Behind him, the dark eyes grew very bright and she dashed her hand across them. Then, summoning an untroubled smile and keeping her voice perfectly level, she said, 'My dear ... in all my life, you are the only person who has never asked *anything* of me. I sometimes wish that you would. But in the meantime, allow me the pleasure of offering.'

ACT THREE

COUP DE FOUDRE
Paris, August to November, 1652

'Who ever loved who loved not at first sight?'
Christopher Marlowe

ONE

Having left the preparation of the attic to Pauline and Archie, Athenais rose early on the day appointed in order to be out of the house when the gentlemen-lodgers arrived. She therefore left for the theatre an hour earlier than necessary, had to kick her heels until Froissart and the rest turned up – and then found herself unable to concentrate.

Matters came to a head when she bungled a speech and drifted out of position to block Marie d'Amboise's entrance at the optimum moment. The result was a short but venomous exchange, causing the remainder of the rehearsal to take place in intense *froideur*. And, at the end of it, Athenais's mood grew even blacker on discovering that the light drizzle had turned into a torrential downpour which meant that, unless she didn't mind getting soaked to the skin, she'd have to remain in the theatre.

By the time Pauline arrived, dripping, she was sitting in her wrapper, furiously brushing her hair. Without even waiting for Pauline to close the door, she said, 'Did they come?'

'Yes.' Pauline dragged off her sodden cloak and shook it, managing to shower Athenais in the process.

'So what happened?'

'Happened? Nothing. They came. Your father hung around for a while, then came downstairs with the servant. I left the pair of them sharing a bottle of wine in the kitchen. I only hope neither of them has any money or they'll be drunk as fiddler's bitches by the time we get home. Shouldn't you be getting into your costume?'

Athenais rose and shed her robe.

'What were they talking about?'

'How would I know? It was all in English.' Deftly, Pauline laced the girl into the simple blue gown she wore for the first act. 'I thought of having a word about your father but decided it might work better coming from you – preferably accompanied by a smile or two. There. That's done. Sit down and I'll do your hair.'

Athenais sat. Floating by on a cloud of patchouli, Marie d'Amboise said languidly, 'I hope we're not in for a repetition of this afternoon's fiasco, my sweet.'

'Oh sod off!' muttered Athenais.

'Now, now … is that any way to speak to me after all my efforts on your behalf?' Smiling, Marie met Athenais's eyes in the mirror. 'Isn't Lady Verney's brother to your taste?'

'I can take him or leave him. So if you want to put in a bid, don't hold back on my account.'

Marie laughed softly and sailed on.

Catching Pauline's look of enquiry, Athenais said, 'Don't ask.'

Due, perhaps, to the unceasing deluge outside, Athenais found the performance a huge effort and came off-stage feeling jaded. To discover the Marquis d'Auxerre lounging in the Green Room with several of his friends was therefore the last thing she needed.

Henri de Vauvallon, gave her his usual vapid smile and inclined his too-blonde head, while the Comte de Choiseul stared openly at her *décolletage*. She hated the pair of them.

The Marquis rose to meet her, kissed her hand and continued to hold it.

Correction. She hated all three of them.

'Good evening, *ma belle*. I'm afraid we missed the play – one of the Cardinal's interminable dinners, you know. Consequently, we're all eager for a little entertainment and have settled on the Maison Fontanelle. You'll accompany us, of course?'

The Maison Fontanelle was an establishment where gaming could be conveniently and discreetly combined with whoring. It did not, therefore, take a genius to work out where Athenais would end up if she agreed to go with them.

Allowing her hand to rest passively in his, she sighed and said, 'I'm sorry, Monseigneur --'

'Philippe. My name, if you recall, is Philippe.'

'Philippe … forgive me, but there was rehearsal all afternoon and then the performance and I'm quite exhausted.'

The heavy brows drew together as he scrutinised her face and he said reluctantly, 'You are certainly rather pale.'

'The rain makes my head ache.' The fact that he still had her hand made it easy to give a convincing shiver. 'And I think I may have caught a chill.'

'Let us hope not,' He released her and stepped back slightly. 'Froissart is working you too hard. I shall speak to him.'

'No – no, please don't,' returned Athenais quickly. 'If I don't work, I don't get paid. Worse still, I leave room for another to take my place. And what would become of me then?'

'I believe I can think of something.'

'But for how long, Mon – Philippe? You don't settle for second-best, do you?'

'Never.' The Marquis closed in again, trapping her in a corner where his body hid her from other eyes. 'But what are you saying? That you want some guarantee of permanence before coming to my bed?'

This was deeper water than Athenais had envisaged. The scent of sandalwood was overpowering and she'd have given a week's wages for the satisfaction of telling him to go to the devil. Controlling herself with an effort, she said lightly, 'Not at all. But if I did … I wouldn't be the only one making conditions, would I? I seem to recall you saying you wouldn't buy my favours. That you wanted me to come to you for yourself.'

'Ah. That rankles, does it?'

'Far from it. I respect you for it.'

'How charming.' He placed his hands on the wall either side of her shoulders and leaned a little closer. 'Let us come to the point. You want promises – but my answer is the same as before. I'll give you nothing until you come to me. And the only promise I'll make is that you'll do better by coming voluntarily than if I have to … coerce you. But make no mistake, my dear – I *will* have you. One way or another.'

Without warning Athenais's nerves snarled into a knot and she was back in the grave-yard of St. Julien-le-Pauvre. She said unevenly, 'You shouldn't count on it.'

'But I do, sweetheart. I do. And so should you.'

A predatory smile curling his mouth, he closed the gap between them and took her chin in one hand. Then, taking his time about it, he kissed her. His mouth was hard and possessive and he forced hers open so that he could take what he wanted. Managing not to shudder, Athenais shut her eyes and did not open them until he released her.

He said, 'I have to leave Paris for a few weeks, so you have time in which to decide. But don't wait too long … and choose wisely. I'd be sorry to curtail such a promising career – but I will if I have to. And as you said – what will become of you then?'

Holding her eyes with his own, he tapped her cheek with one finger and stepped back. Then, as if nothing had occurred, he led his friends urbanely from the room.

Athenais swallowed her nausea and stalked away to the tiring-room. When Pauline materialised at her side, she said abruptly, 'My skull is splitting. Unlace me and let's get out of here. I suppose there's no chance the sodding rain's stopped?'

It hadn't and they arrived home with wet feet. Pauline mulled some wine to go with their supper and came back saying, 'Stay out of the kitchen. Your father and the English servant are still there, too drunk to stand.'

With a jolt, Athenais remembered the two gentlemen in the attic. Then, brushing the thought aside, she met Pauline's eyes and said baldly, 'You were right. He says he'll have me whether I like it or not. If I resist, he'll see to it that I never act again.'

'Ah. So now we know where we stand,' came the calm reply. And when Athenais said nothing, 'You said you'd sleep with him if you had to. And it's beginning to look as if you'll have to.'

There was a long silence broken only by the cheerful crackling of the fire until, finally managing to force the words past the bile in her throat, Athenais said, 'There's your answer, then. What else is there to say?'

'A few things. To begin with, I've been assuming you're not a virgin. But I've known you since you were sixteen and, if you've had a lover during that time, you've kept it pretty dark.'

Very slowly, Athenais looked up, her expression utterly impervious.

'I'm not a virgin. The rest is of no consequence.'

'Isn't it?'

'*Christ!*' Athenais surged to her feet. 'What is this – the damned Inquisition? I've told you that, as and when it becomes necessary, I'll do what I have to. What I won't do, however is bloody well *wallow* in it. So from this point on, you can damned well do that on your own!'

* * *

Twenty-four hours went by without Athenais coming any nearer to her gentlemen-lodgers than a brisk footfall on the stairs or a light, distant voice. Their servant, on the other hand, was a different matter and was frequently to be found in the kitchen with Archie. Athenais acknowledged his presence with a cool nod and made it impossible, by her refusal to speak English, for her father to draw her into conversation. As for the man's masters, she made no attempt to put herself in their way and was naturally unaware that, while Ashley was doing his best to avoid her, Francis had so far merely been unlucky.

In the meantime, she followed her usual routine and tried, without much success, to stop thinking about both the Marquis d'Auxerre and the strangers in the attic. Then, after a night plagued with unpleasant dreams in which she failed to murder the Marquis, she arose with a raging sore throat and all the other signs of an incipient head-cold.

Pauline took one look at her and ordered her back to bed with a steaming mug of butter-ale. Eyes watering and neck swathed in red flannel, Athenais forced herself to drink the brew and then said feebly, 'It's only a chill. I'll be well enough by this evening.'

'You won't,' came the flat reply. 'No – don't argue. I'll tell Froissart that Delphine will have to go on tonight. God knows she's waited long enough for the chance.'

'What if she's better than me?' croaked Athenais.

'Don't be stupid. She's no more than moderately good at the best of times and has only today in which to prepare. And do you honestly think the pit is likely to prefer a dumpy little creature like that to yourself?'

Athenais scowled. 'There you go again – saying I'd be nothing without my looks.'

'I neither said that nor meant it. But if it were true, I'd still tell you to be grateful. If looks didn't matter, I'd still be playing leads and you and Marie d'Amboise would be scrapping over bit-parts.' Upon which Pauline walked out, shutting the door behind her with a snap.

Left alone to regret her thoughtlessness, Athenais wondered what it had cost Pauline to say something that had never been said before. For it was true. Pauline *was* a better actress than she or Marie would ever be and, but for that carelessly driven cart, she'd still be at the peak of

her career. She was only thirty-two, after all. And providing you kept
your figure, age mattered little in the theatre where clever use of paint
could take years off you. But cosmetics couldn't completely hide a scar
or disguise a limp ... with the result that Pauline knew better than
anyone just how important looks were. It must, reflected Athenais, be a
raw enough wound without a self-centred little fool, secure in her own
pretty shell, constantly rubbing salt into it.

Having resolved to apologise and be less insensitive in future, she lay
for a time, blowing her nose and feeling sorry for herself. Then
boredom began to creep in. She couldn't lie here all day with nothing to
do. Moreover, the hot brick at her feet was growing cool. Downstairs in
the parlour was a copy of a new play Froissart was considering including
in the repertoire. If she went down, she could get it ... and make a
tisane while her brick was warming in the oven. It wouldn't take above
ten minutes.

She listened for sounds elsewhere in the house. Then, detecting
none, she slid out of bed and pulled on her robe. A peep around her
door revealed the empty landing and stair-head and put an end to
hesitation. Wraith-like, Athenais padded down to the kitchen.

Mercifully, there was no sign of either Archie or his new boon-
companion. She put her brick in the side-oven and set about brewing a
concoction of herbs and honey. It was just beginning to simmer when
she heard two pairs of booted feet descending the stairs and a rich,
familiar voice saying with good-humoured impatience, 'Oh God, Jem – *I*
don't know. I imagine it would probably be all right provided you leave
everything as you find it. But you'll have to ask Madame Fleury.'

No! thought Athenais, completely horror-struck. *No, no, no! Not
him. Not now.*

'Ah. Well that's just the problem, Captain. I know I doesn't parley the
old French as good as you and his lordship but I usually got enough to
get by on.'

'You mean you speak it well enough to order a pot of ale and get your
arm round a girl's waist.'

'And what more does a man need, Captain? Answer me that. Trouble
is, the old tabby always makes out she can't understand a word I'm
saying. She looks at me like I'm something nasty stuck to her shoe and

she keeps saying pardon. Then she waves her hands about and gabs on faster'n shit off a shovel.' Jem heaved a sigh. 'Truth is, I reckon she don't like me very much.'

'If you spent less time carousing with Mr Stott, she might feel differently.'

Still frozen in mild panic behind the kitchen door, Athenais resolved never, ever to speak English to the gentlemen-lodgers until she'd improved her accent – which she realised was worse even than that of their servant.

'She might,' Jem was saying. 'Then again, she mightn't. But it don't alter the fact that I can't ask the old dragon nothing. Not and get an answer, I can't.'

'Meaning you'd like me to ask her, I suppose.'

'Yes, Captain. If you wouldn't mind.' And, hopefully, 'She's usually somewhere about at this time of day.'

There was a long pause. Then, on a note of mild exasperation, 'Jem. Just sod off, will you? Otherwise I won't be responsible for my actions.'

Athenais heard a snort of laughter, immediately followed by the sound of someone – presumably Jem – leaving the house. Then the Captain (who'd said he was a Colonel) muttered something under his breath and strode away down the hall. It struck her that he'd probably gone to the parlour in search of Pauline and that, when he didn't find her, he'd almost certainly try the kitchen. Panic spiralled out of control and sent Athenais flying across the room to snatch her pan from the heat. Then, without stopping to think, she threw herself into the pantry and shut the door.

Seconds later, she heard him coming back along the hall, his boots ringing on the tiled floor. The kitchen door swung back with a faint creak and he called, 'Madame?' Then he seemed to pause as if, realising that Pauline wasn't there, he was about to leave.

Athenais held her breath.

It would have been all right if she hadn't sneezed. It might even have been all right if she'd had any warning of it. But the sneeze came out of nowhere to arrive with malevolently disastrous timing. And it wasn't even a dainty, ladylike sneeze. It was a violent explosion that, in the confined space, set things rattling on the shelves. Athenais clamped her handkerchief over her face, unable in the pitch-black to think of anywhere to hide, while on the other side of the door, feet were heading in her direction and an aggravatingly amused voice said again, 'Madame?'

'*Merde!*' thought Athenais desperately. And promptly sneezed twice in quick succession.

Then the door opened and she was face to face with the most beautiful man she'd ever seen and whose extraordinary, gold-flecked eyes, damn him, were brimming with laughter.

Unaware that he was the one being in the entire universe she didn't want to see at this precise moment, Ashley conducted a swift appraisal and came to the inescapable conclusion that *la petite Galzain* was hiding in the larder because she looked like hell. Having previously found her perfection irritating, the discovery should have been satisfying. It ought also to have immediately bred an accusation of vanity. Due, however, to the fact that she looked about fourteen and was quite obviously ill, it produced a completely different reaction that he could have done without.

Fortunately, it was also funny. Managing not to laugh but failing to conceal the fact that he wanted to, he said, 'Mademoiselle? I'm so sorry. I hope I didn't startle you?'

Feeling every bit as foolish as she no doubt looked, Athenais could have hit him. Instead, she tried to salvage what was left of her dignity by saying freezingly, 'Not at all. I was looking for … for a lemon.'

His brows rose over an expression that said, *In the dark?* But he had the sense not to voice it. 'Ah. But you didn't find one?'

'Obviously not.' Unfortunately, as she attempted to sweep majestically past him, the words were lost in another magnificent sneeze and she half-tripped on the trailing hem of her robe.

Helpfully, the Colonel grasped her arm and, still on that annoying quiver of laughter, said, 'Allow me to assist you, Mademoiselle.'

And that was when Athenais suddenly found herself remembering clambering over fallen masonry on the Petit Pont … and wondered how on earth she hadn't recognised him before.

'You!' she croaked, accusingly. 'It was you that night on the bridge.'

'It was.' He grinned at her over folded arms. 'You told me to bugger off.'

And I'd like to do it again, she thought crossly. Furious, embarrassed and thoroughly at a disadvantage, she stalked to the fire and blew her nose again before saying abruptly, 'Did you know who I was?'

'Yes.'

She turned, frowning. 'That means you'd seen me before.'

'Once,' agreed Ashley. 'I don't recall the name of the play ... but there was some business with feathers.'

She stared at him, feeling – if possible – even more irritable. He'd seen her come perilously close to making an idiot of herself on-stage, then get out of it by means of a childish trick. He'd heard her swearing like a trooper and been spoken to with neither courtesy nor charm – which meant he knew precisely how deep the veneer of gentility went. No wonder he didn't like her. With something akin to despair, she wondered why she couldn't feel this insane attraction for his friend instead; his friend who was equally good-looking and a Viscount, to boot. But it was pointless to speculate. From the moment she'd laid eyes on him in the Green Room, the Colonel had dazzled her ... and infuriating as it was, he still did.

She opened her mouth, sneezed again and was finally able to say thickly, 'So what the devil are you doing here?'

'Here in your house – or here in the kitchen?'

'Don't be obtuse. You may have noticed that I'm not in the mood.'

'My apologies. I was looking for Madame Fleury.'

She slammed the posset pan back on the hob and blew her nose. Then, in the hope that he would go away, she said, 'Pauline's not here and won't be until late this evening. What did you want?'

Ashley wished she didn't look and sound so ill and had to crush a totally unacceptable impulse to say something comforting. Worse still was the faint but persistent undercurrent of recognition which he was at a loss to explain and from which he instinctively recoiled. It wasn't the girl's fault and he ought to be able to handle it without resorting to boorishness. On the other hand, things being what they were, he suspected that it might be best if he carried on finding fault with her.

Keeping his tone utterly neutral, he said, 'Nothing that can't wait. Forgive me for asking ... but shouldn't you be in bed?'

'Yes.' Athenais poked at the cooling, sticky mess and wondered if, once warmed up, it might still be drinkable. 'Are you going to tell me what you want or not?'

'If you wish. It was merely that Jem wondered if it would be possible to use the kitchen from time to time to cook supper. It would be cheaper than eating at the tavern and we're getting tired of pies and cold sausage.'

She turned slightly to encompass him in an oblique stare. Then, because she knew all about struggling to make ends meet and because he had stopped laughing at her, she said curtly, 'I don't see why not – so long as everything is cleared away by the time Pauline and I get home.'

'It will be. Thank you.'

His smile was courteous and impersonal but it still had a strange effect on her insides. She looked at the thick fair hair, the long-lashed green eyes and the firm jaw; she observed the lean, well-proportioned body with its graceful carriage and the strong, beautifully-boned hands. It came to her that, if it was he and not the Marquis who was hell-bent on seducing her, he wouldn't have to try very hard. She suspected that this man would never coerce a girl into his bed. He'd probably never needed to. She wondered what he would be like if he chose to exert his charm – then decided it would be better not to know. Her life was complicated enough. And something told her that, beneath his easy manner, Monsieur Peverell was nobody's plaything.

Suddenly realising that the spoon was burning her hand and deciding that the best form of defence was attack, she turned back to the pan, saying, 'I seem to recall you telling us that you are a Colonel?'

'Yes. Presently unemployed, of course – but yes.'

'And yet your man calls you Captain.'

He leaned against the wall and said in English, 'You've sharp ears, Mademoiselle.'

Cursing her own stupidity, Athenais said quickly and still in French, 'I understand enough English to know the difference between the ranks. Are you avoiding the question?'

'Not at all. Jem was once, by profession, a highwayman. For a brief time a few years ago, so was I. And in England, all highwaymen style themselves 'captain'. Simple.'

'*It* may be – but *I'm* not. Do you seriously expect me to believe that?'

'Why not? Do you think I'm too respectable? Don't. Four years of civil war and five more of pursuing a lost cause stop one being finicky and teach that the end usually justifies the means.'

She frowned, half-tempted to ask if sleeping with the right people fell into this category. Then, deciding that this wasn't something one could ask a man one barely knew, she said, 'So to what end did you become a common criminal?'

'That of financing an escape route for the melancholy man whose inability to compromise eventually cost him his head,' shrugged Ashley, his tone part-careless and part-bitter. Then, with a swift return to levity, 'And I was never common. I like to think I had *style*.'

Her brows rose. 'You sound like an actor.'

'Is that a compliment?'

'Not necessarily.' Reaching for a pewter mug, she poured the contents of the pan into it and eyed the less-than-appetising tisane dubiously.

'Yet you enjoy what you do.' It was not a question.

'You have to if you're to do it well.'

'I imagine there is a good deal of rivalry.'

'And bickering and back-stabbing – and loyalty, too, when it counts.' She paused and turning slowly back to him added, 'The worst thing is being at the mercy of the public. Put on the wrong play and we're howled off the stage. Offend our noble patrons and we're out of work. Let the pit get wind of some amusing titbit and every line brings forth a chorus of jeers.' Another pause. 'Which is why I ... I must ask a favour of you.'

Ashley's expression remained enigmatic. 'Ask away.'

'My father will talk a lot,' said Athenais uncomfortably. 'Mostly to your servant but possibly to you as well. He'll tell you things which – which I wouldn't wish to become generally known.'

'Such as what, for example?'

She drew a deep breath and said heroically, 'Such as the fact that my name isn't really Athenais de Galzain.'

Ashley had never thought it was. But because she looked as though she were confessing to murder, he had to struggle not to laugh. 'Ah.'

'It's Agnes,' she continued, determined to get the worst over with. 'Stott.'

His mouth quivered and, seeing it, she said angrily, 'It isn't funny!'

'I'm sorry. Of course it isn't,' he agreed solemnly. 'Is there more?'

'I'm also a ... I'm illegitimate.'

This, he reflected, was less amusing. He said, 'I see. If all you require is my assurance that neither Major Langley nor myself will go round gossiping to all and sundry – consider yourself duly assured.'

It was said so matter-of-factly that she did not need to wonder if he meant it. She also recognised that he could easily have bartered with her ... but that, to his credit, he hadn't even tried. A huge weight rolled off her shoulders and, with a wide, uninhibited smile, she said, 'Thank you. And for *that*, you can use the kitchen as often as you like.'

Ashley stared at her. He looked at the glowing red nose, the puffy eyelids and the length of scarlet flannel, swathing her throat. He absorbed the tangled copper hair, writhing like a nest of vipers and clashing horribly with the unflattering pink thing she was wearing. She looked perfectly dreadful. But her smile blinded him and sent desire surging through him like a rip-tide.

If he'd been capable of thinking at all, he'd have thought that was the worst that could happen. It wasn't. An unwary downward glance showed him her bare toes, peeping from beneath the hem of her wrapper ... bloodless and white with cold. He heard himself say stupidly, 'Don't you have slippers?'

'Yes. But they're too big. Also, my robe is too long and I thought I might trip on the stairs so it seemed safer to do without them.'

And that was when all his carefully erected barriers crumbled. The moment he finally admitted to himself that all his criticisms ... all his negative assumptions about Athenais de Galzain had arisen from self-preservation. He had been determined not to like her at all because he'd known there was a distinct possibility of liking her too much. And that, for any number of good reasons, couldn't be allowed to happen.

Except that it had.

He saw her clearly now, this resilient girl who'd been born with no advantages at all but had somehow managed to forge a successful career and drag herself out of the slums of St. Severin. He wondered if she'd had to use that exquisite body to achieve what she had … but suspected that she had too much steel in her spine and, possibly, too much integrity for that. Also, if she *had* done so, she'd presumably own a robe and slippers that weren't second-hand.

With some difficulty, he engaged his brain and, more sharply than he intended, said, 'Are you *completely* insane? You're ill and shouldn't be standing barefoot on this freezing floor talking to me. Go back to bed.'

'I will in a minute. I just need to get the hot brick from the oven and fetch the new --'

'God damn it!' muttered Ashley. And sweeping her up in his arms, strode to the door.

Taken completely unawares, Athenais said, 'No, Colonel – you mustn't – you don't need to – if you'll just put me down, I can --'

Colonel Peverell was already half-way across the hall and heading for the stairs.

'Which room is yours?'

'This really isn't necessary.' Her fingers curled involuntarily on his collar and she breathed in the scent of plain soap and something else she didn't recognise but which made her feel weak. 'I only wanted to --'

'Trip about for another ten minutes. Yes, I gathered. Which room?'

She sighed and gave up. He was warm and solid and his arms felt so very good.

'The second on the right.'

He pushed the door open with his shoulder, walked over to the bed and deposited her unceremoniously in the middle of it.

'Wrap yourself up and try to get warm. I'll fetch the brick for your feet and bring you a hot drink.' The severity of his expression was slightly spoiled by the almost imperceptible curl of his mouth. 'Does Milady have any other requirements?'

There was an unexpected lump in her throat but she swallowed it and said awkwardly, 'I left a play script in the parlour. If it's not too much trouble …?'

'I might possibly manage that – but only if you stay where you are. And that's an order.'

Athenais managed a feeble grin. 'Yes, Colonel.'

By the time he came back with the brick and a cup of mulled wine with honey, her feet had started to thaw but her brain was still refusing to work properly. Indeed, when he lifted the bed-covers to slide the flannel-wrapped brick in by her feet, rational thought became totally impossible.

Ashley handed her the cup, dropped the script in her lap and said, 'I'll make up the fire and then leave you in peace. If you've any sense, you'll finish the wine and go to sleep. The play will still be there tomorrow.'

She watched him deftly banking coals and raking off ash, as if it was something he did every day. She tried to make sense of him and couldn't. He might be poor but he was a gentleman – and, as such, as far out of her reach as the moon. Unfortunately.

He finished his task and stood up, dusting off his hands. Before he could speak, Athenais said shyly, 'Thank you, Colonel. I don't know why you've been so kind – but I'm very grateful.'

'Good. I'd hate to have put myself to so much trouble for nothing,' he retorted. And, with a sudden smile that turned her bones to water, 'And my name, should you wish to use it, is Ashley.'

TWO

Ashley spent the next hour cursing himself for offering her his given name and wondering what the hell had possessed him. Under the circumstances, it had been unbelievably stupid. In the space of an hour, he had progressed from dislike to desire and, finally, to something more dangerous than either. Worse still, for a fleeting second, he'd caught a look in her eyes that suggested the attraction might be mutual.

For both their sakes, there was only one thing to be done. He had to restore his barriers and try, as far as it was possible, to stay out of her way. She had built a life. It might not be totally secure or particularly lucrative ... but, in time, those things could change. And even if they didn't, she was already able to put a decent roof over her head and food on the table, all paid for by work she enjoyed and was good at. She most assuredly did *not* need a penniless would-be-lover complicating her ordered existence. And that, Ashley realised, was all he could ever be. He had nothing to offer her now and no prospects for the future. Also, she already had one millstone round her neck in the shape of her father. She couldn't afford another. So the best thing he could do for her was to leave her alone and wait for time to gently eradicate what, if anything, had happened between them in the kitchen.

The knowledge made his head hurt but he had sufficient experience to know that life was full of disappointments and impossibilities. He'd had enough of both to last him several lifetimes and had no intention of courting more. Neither for himself nor for Athenais.

* * *

Returning later that afternoon from a visit to Celia, Francis threw his hat to one side and said conversationally, 'What's the penalty for fratricide? Never mind. Whatever it is, it's probably worth it.'

Ashley looked up from the bundle of month-old English news-sheets he'd been scanning.

'What has she done now?'

'Nothing new. She wants to know why Eden hasn't replied yet – and am I *sure* he'll have received my letter – and shouldn't I write *another?* Do I not *see* how important this is? And so on and so on – and tediously, irritatingly so on.'

'Are you going to write again?'

'No. My letter may have taken its time – but it will certainly have arrived by now and I sent another note when we moved here so Eden knows where I am. If he hasn't replied, it's because he's chosen not to and writing to him again will do more harm than good. Celia, of course, can't understand that.'

Ashley leaned back and folded his arms behind his head.

'Do you think she's worried that Verney is less than eager to marry her?'

'It's possible. Not that I'd know what he thinks. He leaves the house as soon as I enter it.' Francis sat down and stared meditatively at his well-worn boots. Then, glancing up again, he said, 'On a completely different note, Celia tells me that the lovely Athenais has caught the eye of the Marquis d'Auxerre but is leading him a merry dance. Apparently people are laying bets on how long – and how much – she'll hold out for.'

A tiny frisson of something he didn't care to identify slid through Ashley's veins.

'D'Auxerre? Isn't he one of Mazarin's satellites?'

'Yes. He's also one of the biggest rakes in France and reputedly amongst the most depraved – or perverted, depending on who you listen to – which considering the competition, is no mean feat. Then again, he's indecently rich and neither decrepit nor a gargoyle ... so I don't imagine he gets too many refusals.'

'Fortunate fellow,' remarked Ashley dryly. And, unable to help himself, 'On the other hand, perhaps Mademoiselle prefers not to sell her body. Or perhaps she's heard the same rumours you have.'

'Both of those things may be true,' replied Francis cynically, 'but she and Madame are plainly in need of money. If they weren't, we wouldn't be living here. And, at the end of the day, Mistress Athenais is an actress – so I'd be amazed if she wasn't open to offers.'

Once again, something unpleasant shifted in Ashley's chest but he concealed it and said, 'You're saying she'll sleep with anyone who can afford her?'

'One would hope not.' A mischievous grin dawned. 'Shall we give d'Auxerre a run for his money? We could, you know. He may be rich and influential – but we have charm, address and a certain threadbare panache. What do you think?'

'That it's a remarkably silly idea.'

'Spoilsport. Or is it just that you don't want to play if you might not win?'

'I don't want to play at *all*. But if you think you can outclass – if not outbid - the Marquis, by all means go ahead. You'll be risking Madame Fleury removing your bollocks – but that's your problem.'

'I'll find a way round her.'

'Don't count on it.' Thoroughly irritated – as much with himself as with Francis – Ashley prowled to the window. 'This is a singularly asinine conversation. If we weren't so bloody bored, we wouldn't be having it at all.'

'Oh – I don't know,' murmured Francis provocatively. And, when no response was forthcoming, 'All right. What do you suggest we talk about?'

'Nothing. I'm sick of talking. It's all you or I – or anybody else, for that matter - does these days.' He paused, remembering the promise he'd made to Athenais. 'Speaking of which ... Mademoiselle asks that we treat her father's jug-bitten maunderings with absolute discretion. Do you think you can manage that?'

'I'll do my poor best,' retorted Francis absently. And, sitting up, 'Wait a minute. You've spoken to her?'

'This morning. She's got a --'

'You devious bastard! You've stolen a march on me – and after all that righteous indignation, too.' Francis met the Colonel's eyes and, recognising the expression in them, threw up one hand in a gesture of surrender. 'All right – all right. I take it back. So what are the revelations we're supposed to keep locked in our manly bosoms?'

'You'll know them when you hear them,' returned Ashley. And, with a mocking smile, 'Fortunately – or unfortunately, depending on your point of view – I'm not a gossip.'

* * *

Ashley wondered if Francis really would lay siege to Athenais ... and decided that, knowing Francis, he probably would but that, being a gentleman, he was unlikely to go beyond snatching a kiss if the opportunity presented itself. Even this, however, was sufficient to stir up feelings to which Ashley knew he had no right. Then again, this Marquis fellow sounded both unpleasant and dangerous; and sort who took what he wanted simply because he could. To this, Francis was infinitely preferable. And if Athenais fell victim to his charm, at least she'd be getting a Viscount.

Never one to be kept in the dark, Francis soon made sure he knew everything that Ashley knew. Then, armed with a posy of flowers and an arsenal of imaginative compliments, he embarked on his frivolous campaign of eclipsing the Marquis d'Auxerre.

It didn't go quite as he'd hoped. He found Athenais by the fire in the parlour with a book on her knee, looking more like a respectable tradesman's daughter than a siren of the stage. Jettisoning all his witty speeches, Francis bowed over her hand and laid the Michaelmas daisies in her lap, saying, 'I understand you've been ill, Mademoiselle and wished to express the hope that you're feeling better.'

'Thank you. Yes, I'm much better now. Well enough to return to the theatre.'

Since there were shadows under her eyes and her nose was still rather pink, Francis said, 'Isn't it perhaps a little soon?'

'Pauline thinks so. But it was only a chill, you know. And having been shut up for four days, I've conned my part for the next play and read two others and am now reduced to twiddling my thumbs. In short,' she sighed, 'I'm bored.'

He grinned. 'Dear me. You sound just like Ashley.'

'Do I?' Her tone expressed no more than polite interest but she waved him to a chair and said, 'The Colonel dislikes being idle?'

'Let's say he's unaccustomed to it and not adjusting well. I, on the other hand, am enjoying having time for reading and civilised conversation – and all the other pleasures one doesn't find in the army.'

'You've been fighting in the English wars since they began?'

'Give or take the odd few months here and there – yes.'

'Both of you?'

'Again, yes – but, until last year, not together. Oddly enough, prior to the King's coronation in Scotland, our paths had never previously crossed.' His mouth curled almost imperceptibly and he added, 'In actual fact, we've known each other less than two years. It just *feels* a lot longer.'

She smiled. 'Does it? Why?'

'Mostly because we've been living in each other's pockets for the last twelve months and have shared numerous unpleasant experiences.' Francis's shrug was a masterpiece of elegant self-mockery. 'After Worcester, we ditched, dug, hoed and furrowed. We chopped wood, cleaned stables, picked fruit and polished other men's boots. Worse still, we were forced to let Jem shear us in the Roundhead style ... a sacrilege from which neither of us have yet entirely recovered.' He smiled suddenly. 'But I don't repine. It has enabled me to sit here with you rather than in a dismal cell with Ashley.'

Athenais eyed him thoughtfully for a moment and then, shaking her head, 'I can't imagine either of you doing menial work.'

'Considering the state of my coat, I'm relieved to hear it.'

She laughed a little but asked curiously, 'Do neither of you want to return to England?'

'We both *want* to – but, unless we don't mind facing imprisonment, it isn't an option.'

'Imprisonment?' Her brow wrinkled in an effort of memory. 'I thought ... didn't your Parliament pass a law? A sort of pardon?'

'The Act of Oblivion,' nodded Francis. 'Yes. Sadly, amongst many other caveats, it excludes those of us who fought at Worcester last September – so it's of no help to Ashley or myself. Then again, unless things change, neither of us has anything to go back *to*.'

'Nothing at all? No home or wife?'

'Nor even a sweetheart, I'm afraid.' Aware that, thus far, the conversation had revolved as much around Colonel Peverell as it had around himself, Francis added wickedly, 'At least, *I* haven't. I can't speak for Ashley.'

Athenais continued to smile and immediately changed the subject.

Francis noticed and drew his own conclusions. He ought to have found these irritating – or at least disappointing. Instead, he was mildly amused. If the girl had conceived a fancy for Ashley – and Ashley was either not interested or not inclined to seize his advantage, the resulting situation was fraught with intriguing possibilities. Entirely without malice but with a good deal of characteristic devilment, Francis decided to exploit them.

Something else tugged at his brain. A notion he'd had before but done nothing about. Perhaps this time, he would.

* * *

It wasn't long before Pauline noticed that the man she didn't know whether to call Major Langley or Lord Wroxton was taking every opportunity to flirt with Athenais. She also noticed that Athenais wasn't doing anything to discourage him. Given his lordship's looks and easy manners, this wasn't surprising. Girls probably dropped into his lap like ripe plums. But, despite seeming to enjoy his company and happily listening to him quote poetry by the yard, Athenais showed no sign of infatuation and, as often as not, appeared to be treating him the same way she treated Etienne Lepreux. Odder still, the Viscount-Major didn't seem to mind. Pauline decided to keep a discreet eye on the situation and let matters take their course. Certainly, on present showing, it didn't look as if castration would become necessary.

* * *

Three days after Athenais's return to the theatre, Ashley sauntered through the house to the small rear courtyard which, for the past few days of fine weather, Francis had taken to occupying whilst working on some mysterious project of his own that seemed to involve a good deal of scribbling.

He wasn't there.

Instead, book in hand, Athenais was walking to and fro, muttering. It was the first time he'd seen her since her illness and he was totally unprepared for the smile of undisguised delight that illuminated her face when she caught sight of him. His heart turned over and he had to concentrate on keeping his own expression perfectly neutral ... particularly when he saw that radiant smile falter into uncertainty.

He said, 'Forgive my interruption, Mademoiselle. I thought the Major might be here.'

She shook her head, wishing he seemed just a *little* bit pleased to see her and wondering why he looked so forbidding.

'He's out, I think.' She struggled to find something else to say that might keep him there and was visited with what she recognised could either be divine inspiration or a prelude to total disaster. 'And you're not interrupting. I'm in despair with this scene.' She waved the book at him. 'Do you think ... could you possibly spare me ten minutes? Francis usually helps but ...' She shrugged helplessly.

Francis, is it? thought Ashley darkly. And, against his better judgement, let it provoke him into saying smoothly, 'I suspect you'll find me a poor substitute – but I'm at your disposal. I take it you'd like me to hear your lines?'

'Not exactly. I need you to read in.' She pushed the book into his hands and, giving him no time to demur, added, 'I'm Eloise and you're Raoul. Please begin from your first speech at the top of page twenty-seven.'

He stared at her, then glanced down at the script. And, half-way down the page saw an italicised direction for Raoul to sweep Eloise into an embrace. His brain told him this was a bad idea; his body disagreed. He said, 'I'm not sure --'

'Oh please, Colonel! Just three pages?' She knew exactly what was on them. She also, she hoped, had an inkling of what might persuade him. 'As I said, if Francis was here ...'

Her eyes were wide and innocent but Ashley was fairly certain he was being manipulated. Putting both mind and body under rigid control, he decided to do what she wanted – and see how quickly she'd regret asking.

He grinned. 'Three pages, then.'

He delivered Raoul's first two speeches. And hauled her hard against his chest as he embarked on the third one. Eloise replied with a little huff of breath and a stammered reply. Raoul gazed down at her with a lazy lift of one eyebrow and a deliberately wicked half-smile as he murmured the next words in a low, seductive tone. This was the moment when Eloise might reasonably be expected to free herself by means of a hefty shove. Instead, her body melted against his and her lips parted but no words came out ... which left Raoul wishing he didn't have the sodding book in his other hand.

It was perhaps fortunate that, at that moment, Fate – in the guise of the maidservant – intervened. The girl froze in the door way staring at

Ashley and Athenais and then, bobbing a hurried curtsy, said, 'Pardon, Mademoiselle Athenais. But Monsieur le Marquis d'Auxerre has called.'

Athenais tore herself from Ashley's grasp and said rapidly, 'I'm not here. I went out early and you don't know when I'll be back.'

'But Mademoiselle, he said --'

'I don't care what he said. Just get *rid* of him!'

'Well, I'll try,' said the girl dubiously. 'But he's settled in the parlour as if he's got all day.'

Ashley looked thoughtfully at Athenais's suddenly white face. He said, 'Stay here. I'll send him on his way – if that's what you want.'

She gripped her hands together, relief warring with doubt.

'What if he won't go?'

'He'll go,' returned Ashley calmly, moving towards the house. 'If, as I assume, he's been brought up with the rules of polite behaviour, he'll have to.'

The Marquis was lounging in a chair by the empty hearth, idly swinging one booted foot. His coat was of superbly-cut claret brocade and his lace collar, the finest Mechlin lace. The body inside this finery, observed Ashley as the Marquis frowned and stood up, was of typical French build; some three inches shorter than himself and rather stocky.

'Does Mademoiselle de Galzain permit her servants to roam the house at will and enter rooms without knocking?' his lordship demanded coldly.

Having expected something of the sort, Ashley was less offended than he chose to appear.

'I wouldn't know,' he replied unsmilingly. 'And you are under a misapprehension, sir. I am not a servant.' His bow was correct, if somewhat brusque. 'Colonel Peverell, formerly of His Majesty King Charles's forces in Scotland.'

D'Auxerre's frown became more pronounced.

'An Englishman?'

'I have that honour. And you are?'

'Philippe de Mantignon, Marquis d'Auxerre,' came the clipped response.

'Delighted,' lied Ashley. And bowed again.

The Marquis managed something that was little more than a nod.

'May I ask what you are doing in this house?'

'You may ask. One wonders, however, why it should interest you.'

There was a long, unpleasant silence during which Ashley decided that the look in the fellow's eyes spoke of knives on a dark night. Finally, the Marquis said, 'I understood that Mademoiselle de Galzain lived here.'

'She does – as do a number of other people.

'Including yourself?'

'Including myself,' agreed Ashley with a deliberately provoking smile. 'For the time being.'

'I see. How soon, then, will you be leaving?'

'Who can say? Here today and gone tomorrow, perhaps. Or then again – not.' His tone was a nice blend of urbanity and discreet mockery. 'However. If you were looking for Mademoiselle, I fear you are doomed to disappointment.'

'She's not here?'

'A fitting with her dressmaker, I believe. You could wait, of course. But for all I know, she may go directly to the theatre.'

'There is no rehearsal today,' snapped d'Auxerre abruptly.

'No? I'm afraid I don't concern myself with these things.'

'And what things *do* you concern yourself with, Colonel?'

'Those which are purely my own affair,' replied Ashley. And left the obvious implication hanging delicately in the air.

The Marquis reached for his hat, his mouth curling unpleasantly.

'If you can manage that, sir, you will save yourself a great deal of trouble.'

Recognising the threat, Colonel Peverell subdued an urge to pin the fellow to the wall and said idly, 'I daresay that may be true.'

'You can be sure of it. But I'll take up no more of your time.' He nodded again and moved to the door. 'Please tell Mademoiselle that I called.'

'Certainly.' Ashley followed, determined to see him safely off the premises. 'I'm sure she will be desolate to have missed you.'

The dark eyes swung back to him with an expression of acute dislike.

'My business and hers, Colonel. I recommend that you bear it in mind.'

The Marquis stepped over the threshold and Ashley shut the door behind him. Then, thoughtfully and without haste, he made his way back to the courtyard.

Still rigid with tension, Athenais said, 'Has he gone?'

'Yes.'

'Thank God! And thank you, too.'

'My pleasure. I didn't take to the gentleman.'

'He's *not* a gentleman,' she said acidly. 'He's a *nobleman*.'

'The two shouldn't be mutually exclusive.' He paused and then said slowly, 'I'm told the gossips are linking your name with his. I believe they're laying bets on how long you'll stay out of his bed.'

'*Merde!*' said Athenais bitterly. And sat down with a bump.

Torn between sympathy and amusement, Ashley sat beside her and said, 'Tell me about it.'

'Why? You can't help. No one can. Unless you'd like to push him down a deep well?'

'It's a thought,' he agreed. And waited.

She stared searchingly at him, guessing that he probably knew most of it anyway. Finally, drawing a deep breath, she said, 'He wants me to be his mistress and won't take no for an answer. If I don't give in, he says he'll kill my career in the theatre.'

'Can he?'

'Oh yes. He has influence and a great deal of money. He can put pressure on Monsieur Laroque to dismiss me and on Floridor at the Bourgogne not to take me on. He could hire folk to jeer and throw things every time I walk on-stage. He could threaten or bribe half of my colleagues to make me look ridiculous in performance. He could even,' she finished bitterly, 'persuade the Cardinal to close the theatre down completely for a time.'

'I see.' Ashley swallowed the nasty taste in his mouth. 'It seems an inordinate amount of trouble for a woman who doesn't want him. At least, I'm presuming you don't?'

'No. I don't. Aside from there being something about him that – that actually *repels* me, I don't want to start earning my living on my back.' She paused and spread her hands, sounding suddenly weary. 'I'm not a prude – or stupid. I know the other girls do it and that everyone thinks actresses are whores. But once you step on to that road, there's no end to it. And I don't see why I should sell my body if I don't choose to.'

Silence, punctuated only by the call of a pigeon, filled the little garden. Holding his anger in check, Ashley said tightly, 'You're right. He isn't a gentleman. If he was, he wouldn't be trying to force you – and he has absolutely no *right* to do so.'

'He doesn't need it. And, though I don't want to give in ... if it comes down to a choice between him and my career, I'll have to.'

An odd, wholly unfamiliar sensation took place in Ashley's chest. With some effort, he restrained himself from taking her hands in his and, keeping his tone light, said, 'Then we'll have to see that it doesn't come to that, won't we? Stay out of his way as much as you can and, if he becomes importunate, I presume you know how to use your knee to good effect. And if that doesn't do the trick, come to me.'

Athenais shook her head, touched that he would offer help but knowing better than to let him. She said, 'No. It's kind of you – but no. You shouldn't involve yourself. He's got too many friends and the Cardinal standing behind him. If you got in his way, there's no saying what he'd do. The man is dangerous. More so than you'd think.'

'Is he?' Colonel Peverell stood up and smiled disquietingly down on her. 'So, as it happens, am I.'

THREE

Over the next couple of days, Ashley spent some very enjoyable moments imagining bouncing the Marquis d'Auxerre off numerous hard surfaces, notably his own fists, or using his sword to put a few holes in him. The prospect of smashing something went a little way towards lifting his spirits. Sadly, the mere prospect wasn't nearly enough.

He felt as though he was in a cage. A year ago, he'd been as tolerant and well-adjusted as anyone and more so than most. Now, with impatience enveloping every nerve and sinew like bindweed, he could feel his temper becoming daily more uncertain. And, worrying as that was, the most alarming fact of all was that he couldn't see any way of changing it. A month ago, no one he spoke to seemed to think that there was either point or value in reviving the Cause. Everyone counselled caution and a further period of waiting. England as a whole, they said, was sick of upheaval and the few Royalists left there needed more time to recover from the aftermath of Worcester. Nothing, they agreed in solo and chorus, could be achieved yet. And eventually, after banging his head against a series of identical brick walls, Ashley had come to the depressing conclusion that the only man who might just manage to transform the gloomy talk into action was Prince Rupert. And Rupert, unfortunately, was somewhere in the Caribbean, playing at pirates.

And so, as day succeeded day, Ashley felt himself starting to resemble a coiled spring which had been wound too tightly. For the most part, he managed to control his tongue and create a façade of near-normality; but the pointless feelings he now cherished for Athenais, coupled with the threat hanging over her from the Marquis reduced the façade to the thinness of paper, under which violence boiled and simmered.

And then, quite by accident, he found a legitimate channel for his ill-humour.

Rising early one morning, he entered the kitchen to find Jem Barker and Archie Stott snoring over the table amidst over-turned tankards, empty bottles and pipe-ash. The room stank like a tavern at the end of a busy night. For perhaps half a minute, Colonel Peverell stood in the doorway, absorbing the scene with steadily rising anger. Then, with the suddenness of a tornado, he went into action.

Having thrown the windows wide, he advanced first on Mr Barker and, taking hold of his collar, hauled him outside into the yard. By the time the first icy douche of water hit his neck, Jem was already beginning to come round but Ashley didn't let that stop him. His hands biting like the teeth of a steel trap, he continued to hold his sodden, shivering henchman under the pump until he was satisfied that – though on the brink of drowning – Jem was fully conscious. Then, heaving him upright, he stared into the bloodshot gaze for an acutely unpleasant moment before releasing his grip long enough to deliver a single crashing blow to the jaw.

Jem went hurtling backwards, collided painfully with the log-pile and subsided on the cobbles. It took him a few seconds to recover his breath and decide, by means of cautious massage, that his jaw wasn't actually broken. Finally, in somewhat muffled accents, he said protestingly, 'Sodding hell, Captain! What --?'

'Colonel,' corrected Ashley, his voice sheathed in the iced silk of incipient danger. 'I am a Colonel. Try, if you will, to remember it. On the other hand, if you intend to become a walking sponge, you will find it more comfortable to do so out of my orbit. In short, if you're going to make this sort of thing a habit, I'm done with you. Do I make myself clear?'

'Clear enough,' muttered Jem sulkily.

'Good. Now get out of my sight and make yourself presentable,' snapped Ashley. And turning on his heel, he strode back to the kitchen to deal with Mr Stott.

Archie, being blessed with a larger capacity even than Jem, took longer to rouse and, by the time he did so, Ashley's arm was aching from operating the pump. Eventually, however, he let the older man slide to the ground in a confused, retching heap; and when the worst of the shuddering had stopped, said cuttingly, 'Someone told me you were a soldier. They lied.'

Archie looked blearily up into the cold face of his tormentor. 'Wh-what?'

'You heard. If you'd ever been a soldier, you'd have more backbone.'

Archie shook his head to clear it.

'I *was* a soldier. In the German wars.'

'Then I can only assume that either you were a damned bad one or your commanding officers weren't fussy. Speaking for myself, I prefer to leave tavern-floor sweepings where they lie.'

'You cheeky young bugger!' Archie began the laborious process of levering himself upright and promptly discovered that he wanted to be sick. Telling himself that he'd die sooner than vomit in front of this razor-tongued bastard, he said, 'Who the 'ell do you think you're talking to?'

Folding his arms, Ashley looked down on him with total contempt.

'The dregs at the bottom of a wine-vat. In the short time I've been here, you've been crapulous six nights out of seven. No wonder your daughter is ashamed of you. You're a total bloody disgrace. And if you weren't completely spineless or had any brain worth mentioning, you'd -
_'

He side-stepped as Mr Stott came hurtling down on him and casually extended one booted foot to send the other man thudding to the ground. Then, as if nothing had occurred, he continued blightingly, 'You'd realise just what a useless, slovenly old fool you've become and try to do something about it. Beginning, I would suggest, with staying sober for more than an hour at a time.'

Archie pulled himself up on one elbow and opened his mouth to retaliate. It was a mistake. Unable to control his insides any longer, he threw up.

'Oh hell,' breathed Ashley disgustedly. 'That's all it needed.' And simultaneously became aware of Pauline Fleury watching from the doorway.

For a moment, neither of them spoke. Then, carefully modifying his tone, Ashley said, 'How long have you been there?'

'Long enough.' Her tone was non-committal but the hazel eyes, had he been close enough to see, held a glimmer of approval.

'My apologies, then.' He gestured to Archie. 'I'll see to this – and to the mess in the kitchen, too, if you'll give me a minute.'

It was the first time they'd had anything approaching a proper conversation and Pauline surveyed him thoughtfully. He was still pale with temper and a pulse was hammering in his throat. She said, 'There's no need for that.'

'Since my servant is partly to blame, there is. But I think you'll find he won't make the same mistake again.'

Having passed Jem in the kitchen, drenched and clutching a swelling jaw, Pauline didn't think he would either. A rare smile dawned and she said, 'You don't mess about, do you?'

'No.' He paused, sounding suddenly tired. 'No. But I don't usually make my point with my fists.'

'I never supposed you did. But don't start regretting it. That man of yours will thank you, if he's got any sense. As for this drunken old fart – he's probably past saving. Certainly, he never listens to Athenais. But I reckon he just might pay some attention to you … if, that is, you could be bothered to take the trouble.'

There was a long silence. And then, 'Miracles,' remarked Ashley, reaching for a bucket with which to sluice down both Archie and the cobbles, 'are a little out of my line. But I'll do what I can.'

'Good. Well, in that case, you can leave the kitchen to Suzon and me. And by the time you've shaved and put on a dry shirt, there'll be some breakfast for you.' Pauline eyed him pleasantly but in a way that brooked no argument. 'Half an hour, Colonel.'

By the time he returned to the kitchen, the freshly-scrubbed table was set with bread, cheese and ale. Swathed in a spotless white apron, Pauline stood at the range, expertly frying slices of ham while the maid tripped in and out, removing the last of the debris. As Ashley hesitated in the doorway, Pauline cast him a brief glance and said, 'Sit down. This won't be long. Personally, I think meat for breakfast is a barbarous custom – but you're English, of course.'

Without moving, Ashley said, 'It's very kind of you, Madame. But --'

'It's a couple of slices of ham – not a ten-course banquet.' She transferred the meat from pan to platter and set it on the table. Then, facing him with her hands on her hips and an indulgently acidulous smile, 'If you're wondering about Athenais – she won't stir for at least another hour. So sit down and eat.'

It was unmistakably an order. Ashley sat.

For a time, she left him to eat while she moved about the kitchen setting various things to rights and turning over various possibilities in her mind. Then, when his plate was almost empty, she sat down opposite him and said, 'This can't be much of a life for you. Is there no alternative?'

His mouth twisted wryly.

'None that I can see. There's nothing for me in England – even supposing I'd go there under the present regime.'

'Aside from the fact that your King's in exile from it, what's wrong with the present regime?'

'Nearly everything. Repression, mostly … and idiotic priorities, given the state of the country after years of civil war. For example, in the last few months – rather than spend their time dealing with the things that really matter – the remnants of the so-called Parliament have passed laws against swearing, profanity and adultery.' He paused and then, because of what she'd witnessed in the yard, said, 'Not that I've any particular desire to curse, blaspheme or fornicate – but I strongly object to the principle. The playhouses are closed, the Maypoles have been burned and Christmas was cancelled some time ago. People are being told how to act and think and live. And I suspect it's going to get worse rather than better.'

'So where does that leave you personally?'

'Me? I'm thirty-one years old. I've no money, no occupation and no prospect of either. Inactivity doesn't suit me – with the result that my temper has become … unreliable. Worst of all, I don't know how to mend it.' He stood up. 'I'm sorry. You don't need to hear this. I'm only saying it because you've seen for yourself how --'

'You're saying it because I asked you. Sit down.'

Once again, he found himself obeying her. She was a remarkable woman, he thought; and quite possibly the only person with whom he could imagine having this conversation. He waited to see what she would say next. It wasn't what he expected.

'But for the war, what would your life have been?'

'I don't know. Ordinary, I suppose.' He thought. 'I'm a younger son so I'd have had to take up some profession anyway and, like as not, it would have been soldiering. I'd expected to marry … but, after my father died, my brother turned his coat to the winning side and the girl in question decided that he was the better bet.'

'That must have hurt.'

He shrugged. 'It was a long time ago. And it was probably for the best.'

'For you, maybe. But unless your brother has the edge on you in the ways that count with women, I'd be surprised if she hasn't sometimes regretted it.' Pauline surveyed him critically and then, half-smiling, said, 'You wouldn't have been easily forgettable, I imagine.'

He laughed. '*Merci*, Madame. But looks aren't everything.'

'I know that – and it's not all I meant. But looks count for a great deal. Consider Athenais, for example. She's got where she is through hard work, determination and talent. But if she'd been ugly, she'd never have got the chance. And if you want proof, you've only to look at me.'

Ashley had been looking. One side of her face was cameo-perfect … the other, sadly flawed. She had once been an extraordinarily attractive woman and the contrast her mirror showed her must be hard to bear. He said gently, 'What happened?'

'Two moments of carelessness – one mine and the other, the driver of a loaded-dray,' came the economic and dispassionate reply. 'That was six years ago. I was twenty-six and, though I shouldn't say so myself, the best actress in Paris. Now I attend to various matters at the theatre and give Froissart quantities of advice which he sometimes listens to.' She paused, as if the conversation had arrived at some predestined point. 'I take it your fighting skills don't end with your fists?'

Caught off-guard, he said, 'I'm sorry?'

She sighed. 'It's not a trick question. I'm asking if you're any good with a sword.'

A shaken laugh escaped him.

'Better than average. Why? Do you need a bodyguard?'

'That will be the day.' She eyed him reflectively and then, apparently at random, said, 'Froissart wants to stage *Mariamne*. He's getting all the mechanical devices out of storage so he can make it the most elaborate production of the season. Unfortunately, the action contains two important fight sequences. Sword fights, to be exact.'

Ashley finally began to see where this was going. 'Unfortunately?'

'Fight scenes are choreographed by our dancing-master. They're not his *forte*. To be perfectly blunt, they generally look like a couple of fellows prancing about on hot coals, trying to swat a fly. If you can do better, Froissart will pay you. Not much, I'll admit – but something. If you're interested, I'll speak to him. Well?'

He didn't know what to say so he played for time.

'Thus enabling me to pay the rent?'

'Thus giving you a reason to get up in the morning,' she retorted. 'You can suit yourself, Colonel – it's no skin off my nose. Just don't get smart with me when I'm trying to help you.'

A hint of colour touched Ashley's cheekbones and he said, 'I'm sorry. I didn't mean to sound rude or ungrateful. I was just taken by surprise. It's a knack you have.'

'I cultivate it.' A brief smile showed that he was forgiven. 'As for the play, you'll want to think it over. But don't leave it too long. Rehearsals start next week – and though we don't usually allow more than a fortnight, Froissart is scheduling three weeks for this one on account of all the gimcrackery.'

'Three weeks to teach someone to use a sword properly?' asked Ashley, aghast. 'It can't be done!'

'Three weeks to teach a precise sequence that *looks* real but won't end up with one of them maiming the other,' corrected Pauline, standing up. 'Call it a challenge. You never know. You might enjoy it.'

* * *

On the following morning, while he was still mulling over the notion of taking temporary employment at the Théâtre du Marais, Colonel Peverell received an unexpected summons to wait upon Sir Edward Hyde at the Louvre. In the passage-way outside Hyde's office, he bumped into Sir William Brierley who, when he admitted where he was bound, remarked dryly, 'Don't expect to leave with any sense of encouragement. Hyde is a gloomy devil at the best of times – and now *isn't* the best of times. In fact, I believe that things at home are getting worse rather than better. Along with Thomas Scot – with whom we're all-too-familiar – this fellow Thurloe that they've appointed Secretary of State is creating an intelligence service of frightening efficiency. Most depressing of all, they've got a new code-breaker and he's good.'

Ashley frowned. 'How do you know?'

'Because he's broken my last two cyphers. And since I'm the best cryptologist I know, the man must be well above the average. I haven't found out who he is yet – but I'm working on it.' And then, 'Enough of that. Find me when your business is done and we'll drown our sorrows together.'

* * *

Due, probably, to the heavy responsibility of being the young King's chief advisor, Sir Edward was beginning to look older than his forty-three years but he rose as soon as Ashley entered his presence and said, 'A pleasure to see you, Colonel. And I thank you for sparing the time.'

'I have a great deal of time, Sir Edward,' replied Ashley aridly. 'Take as much of it as you wish.'

'You may regret that offer when you hear my reasons for inviting you here. But please sit down and take some wine. It is of inferior quality, of course – but I daresay you are used to that. Money is in short supply all round.'

'Indeed.' Accepting both the chair and the glass, Ashley said, 'If you are at liberty to tell me, what is the latest news from England?'

'There's little you won't already have heard. Our final stronghold in Scotland, Dunottar Castle, surrendered some time ago and the royal regalia was smuggled out and hidden. I am praying there is someone who knows exactly *where*. His Majesty has appointed Sir John Middleton his Lieutenant-General for Scotland – but, since the Marquis of Argyll formally accepted the Commonwealth, the title can't be anything but an empty one.'

'Given Argyll's preference for the winning side, that was no surprise. The man is a snake – and always has been.'

'I am inclined to agree.' He paused and then said, 'For the rest, Dunkerque has surrendered to the Spanish – and the blame for *that* rests with Cromwell who appears to have signed a commercial treaty with Spain.'

'Cromwell's treating with *Catholics?*'

'Yes. Surprising, isn't it? The Commonwealth has agreed to intervene in this interminable war between France and Spain – with the result that, three days ago, Admiral Blake sank a supply convoy bound for

Dunkerque. Since the garrison surrendered the following day, one can only assume that the town was starving.' Hyde reached for his glass but merely stared down into it. 'Cromwell's decision may have had something to do with his war with the Dutch. My own view, however, is that it has more to do with Mazarin's refusal to recognise the Commonwealth.'

Ashley eyed him thoughtfully.

'Since the Cardinal offered Dunkerque to both the English and the Dutch – anything, in fact, rather than let Spain take it – I suspect he's finding its loss a bitter enough pill to make him re-think his position.'

'Sadly, I fear that may be true. All in all, we have very little to encourage us at the present time.'

'Perhaps it would help if I were to evaluate current feeling at home in person?'

'No. I have regular correspondents and all their reports are wholly depressing. And though I am aware that you would like to be more active, Colonel, His Majesty prefers you to remain within reach.' Hyde sipped his wine and then, looking up, said, 'I would also find that … useful.'

Ashley shifted restlessly. 'Why?'

'To put it bluntly, the Duke of Buckingham is luring the King into wilder and wilder excesses. Stories of their escapades get worse every day and are damaging both His Majesty's reputation and his chances of obtaining any help. Someone needs to curb his activities – and I am too old and too staid to make him listen. You, however, are not. And he has a great regard for you.'

'That may be true. I don't know. But even if His Majesty could be persuaded to distance himself from his oldest friend, Buckingham would make sure it didn't last.' He thought for a moment. 'Your best option might be to give the Duke a mission that would take him from Paris for a time.'

'I've tried that. He agrees to go – and then he finds a reason not to.'

'So what do you want of me? That I talk Charles into a proper appreciation of the things that matter? Or that I chain him to my wrist and take over his leisure activities in person?'

'A little of both, perhaps. But mainly spending time with him – riding or hawking or fencing, perhaps? Anything that doesn't involve taverns, brothels and assorted low company.' Sir Edward took a sheet of paper from the table beside him and offered it, saying, 'The matter is becoming rather urgent. And then there is this.'

Colonel Peverell's eyes travelled rapidly over the tightly-scripted page. Looking up, he said, 'Do you know where this came from?'

'No. As it happens, that was another little thing I thought you might help me with. Discreetly, of course.'

'Of course.' He frowned thoughtfully. 'Is this the original?'

'Yes.'

'It wasn't encrypted, then?'

'No.'

'Surprising.' The Colonel folded the paper and tucked into the breast of his coat for later study. 'You weren't tempted to simply buy what he's offering?'

'Five hundred *livres* for what might turn out to be nothing at all? No. I sent men to watch the designated contact point but I suspect they may have been too obvious. At any rate, no one appeared. And I've received no further communications.'

Ashley sighed and thought, *There's a surprise. You probably sent half a dozen idiots who might as well have had signs hanging round their necks.* But said only, 'Does the King know?'

'About the letter? No.' Hyde paused, his expression oddly uncomfortable. 'But this particular rumour has surfaced before and he denied it. Consequently, I felt a certain reluctance to ... question his word.' Another pause. 'I thought perhaps ...'

'That this was yet another little thing I could take care of?' finished Ashley dryly. 'You appear to have inordinate faith in both my capabilities and my standing with the King. I suppose we'd better hope that it's justified.'

FOUR

Ashley spent the usual kind of evening with Sir William and returned, slightly drunk, to the Rue des Rosiers at a little after midnight. Then, on the following morning, having risen rather later than usual with a pounding headache, he went downstairs to find Pauline Fleury. In order to minimise any jolting, he walked more carefully than usual – which was how he came to hear Athenais saying flatly, 'He's gone to England – though God knows what for. Not that I care. I just hope the ship sinks.'

There was a brief silence during which Ashley remained reprehensibly outside the kitchen door. Finally, Pauline said, 'Are you sure he was behind last night?'

'Oh for heaven's sake! Who else would it be? It was a claque, Pauline.'

'I know that. But why? Why *now* when he's not even in the country?'

'Punishment because I said no again before he left ... and a demonstration of what he can do if I don't fall into his bed when he comes back.' Athenais refrained from saying that the Marquis had also asked a number of pointed questions about Colonel Peverell and made it plain that he considered the Colonel's presence at number sixteen to be superfluous.

Pauline sighed. 'You really can't stomach him, can you?'

'No. There's something nasty about him. I don't know exactly what it is – but he scares the hell out of me.'

'If that's the case, you can't possibly give in to him.'

'Very well to say – but he's not going to give me any choice. Last night was just a warning. Think how much worse it can get.'

Deciding it was time to advertise his presence, Ashley pushed open the door saying pleasantly, 'Good morning.'

Both women swung round to face him. Pauline, as ever, controlled her expression. Clutching her chamber-robe about her and blushing a little, Athenais swiftly banished her initial, involuntary smile. Then she said bluntly, 'Did you hear any of that?'

'Are you accusing me of eavesdropping?' he asked, with a brazen grin. And when she looked at a loss, 'Yes. I heard some of it. I gather there was trouble in the theatre last night?'

'Something like that.' Realising that she didn't want to elaborate because she wasn't sure what he'd do if he had the full story, Athenais shrugged. 'It happens sometimes.'

'Tell him,' remarked Pauline quietly.

'What?'

'You could do worse. Tell him.'

Athenais looked at the Colonel, willing him not to admit what he already knew.

'No. It's over and not worth discussing.'

For the time being, at least – partly because his head hurt – Ashley decided to let her get away with it. He said smoothly, 'I've clearly interrupted something of importance and have no wish to pry. But my errand is soon discharged.' He looked at Pauline. 'My answer is yes, Madame. And if you would speak to Monsieur Froissart, I'll be grateful.'

She nodded. 'I'll see to it today.'

Athenais raised baffled brows. 'See to what?'

'The Colonel would like some employment, so I suggested that Froissart might engage him to arrange and rehearse the fight scenes in *Mariamne*,' replied Pauline. 'What do you think?'

Suddenly encompassed in a brilliant smile, Ashley had to remind himself to breathe.

'That's a wonderful idea! I don't know about Froissart – but Etienne will fall on your neck. He's already panicking at the thought of doing a couple of Dupont's so-called sword-fights.'

'I don't blame him.' Pauline looked at Ashley. 'If Froissart agrees, you'll be starting next week – every afternoon between two and five.'

'I think,' he said, reflecting that his investigations for Hyde and his efforts to keep Charles out of trouble could be dealt with around these hours, 'that I can fit that into my schedule.'

'And it would only be for three weeks.'

'I understand that.'

'Wait,' said Athenais, frowning. 'Froissart's got his heart set on a lavish production – so if he wants crowd-scenes to *look* like crowd-scenes, he'll need more walkers. Particularly men.'

Suddenly impaled on two very appraising pairs of eyes, Ashley threw up a defensive hand and said, 'No.'

'Why not?' asked Pauline. 'You can walk, can't you?'

'Well, yes.'

'And bow? And stand where and when you're told?'

'Again, yes. But --'

'There you go, then. Nothing to it.'

Ashley opened his mouth and then closed it again. He wished the iron band round his skull would relax its grip.

Athenais gave a little gurgling laugh.

'Don't look so horrified! Pauline's right – there *is* nothing to it. I'm sure you wouldn't find it beyond your capabilities, Colonel.'

'Thank you,' he replied dryly. 'But there is no way on this earth that I am strutting about in public on the stage – and that is quite final. I suggest you ask Francis – Lord Wroxton, I should say. He will probably be delighted.'

'Coward,' murmured Athenais, provocatively.

'Absolutely,' he agreed firmly. And then, 'Don't think me ungrateful. It's good of you and Madame to try to help us. And if either Francis or I can return the favour in any way, you need only ask.'

A peculiar sensation took place behind Athenais's ribs and she stood up, pulling the ancient chamber-robe more securely about her. 'Thank you. We will. And now I'd better go and dress.'

'Good,' said Pauline. 'It's a pity you can't do it when you first get up instead of coming down every morning looking like a slut.'

Athenais flushed and exited with something like a flounce.

Grinning, Ashley watched her go and, when the door closed behind her, said, 'That was a bit unkind, wasn't it?'

'No. I don't like slovenly habits and she's not in the Rue Benoit now.' Pauline smiled sourly. 'Sit down, Colonel. You look as though you've got a headache.'

He dropped to a settle. 'I have.'

'Probably serves you right, then.'

'There's no probably about it.' He broke off a piece of cheese from the platter in front of him and toyed with the idea of eating it. 'My name is Ashley – if you should feel inclined to use it.'

'I'll consider it.'

Because he didn't know what else to do with it, Ashley put the morsel in his mouth and swallowed it, shuddering. With an impatient gesture, Pauline filled a cup from a stoppered stone flagon and pushed it across the table, saying, 'Drink that. It tastes evil but it works.'

He drank it and, for one horrible moment, thought he was going to be sick. Then, miraculously, the demon inside his head put its hammer down. Setting the cup aside, he looked across at Pauline and said, 'What's a claque? And how much worse *can* it get?'

She sat down. 'So you *were* listening. Why do you want to know?'

'For fun? To pass a dull Thursday? Sheer nosiness?'

'I've told you before not to get smart with me.'

'So you have.' He surveyed her over folded arms. 'What *is* a claque?'

'People who are paid to make or break a play – or a performer. Last night, they were there to break Athenais. They didn't do it, of course – but they had a damned good try.'

'And you think they were paid by the Marquis d'Auxerre.'

She stared at him. 'How do you know that?'

'I was here when he called the other day and, since Mademoiselle didn't want to see him, I got rid of him for her. I got the impression that the gentleman is ... persistent.'

'That's one way of putting it.' Pauline leaned back, eyeing him shrewdly. 'All that before was Athenais play-acting, wasn't it? She's already told you most of it.'

'Some of it, certainly,' he conceded, carefully. 'But if I'm to be of any help, you – or she – are going to have to keep me informed. Which means you'll need to trust me.'

'Something else to consider.' Pauline stood up and, with a crooked smile, added, 'At the theatre, you'll continue to address me as Madame. Outside it ... well, outside it, I've no objection to you using my given name.'

* * *

When informed of their possible employment at the theatre, Francis's reaction was one of extravagant enthusiasm.

'We should have stage-names,' he said. 'Like Floridor and Bellerose and the rest of them. Who knows? We may become famous.'

'Unlikely,' responded Ashley. 'You are required only to pad out crowd scenes. I am confining my activities to rehearsal. *You* may want to take up acting as a profession, *I* most certainly don't.'

'Don't be such a stick-in-the-mud. Think of the advantages.'

'Other than being paid?'

'A bagatelle!' Francis snapped his fingers. 'Think of the costumes, the scenery, the applause --'

'The rotten eggs?'

'Learn to duck.' The blue eyes brimmed with laughter. 'Above all, think how utterly annoyed Celia will be when her only brother turns common actor. Really, I can't wait.'

'In that case, you'll be happy to remove your coat, find your sword and join me in the yard,' remarked Ashley blandly. 'I need to come up with a few simple but effective sequences – and I'll want you to help me demonstrate them.'

Francis glanced out of the window. 'Now? It's raining.'

'So?' Ashley threw his coat across a chair. 'You won't dissolve. And don't they say that you have to suffer for your art?'

* * *

After an hour's energetic swordplay, they re-entered the kitchen to discover that they'd been performing to an audience of one. Sober, morose and inclined to test the water, Mr Stott said, 'I fought you was supposed to be a bleeding expert.'

Pulling a couple of towels from the range and tossing one to Francis, Ashley set about drying his dripping hair and said, 'Do I take it you're not impressed?'

Archie moved to spit and then thought better of it.

'Not so as you'd notice.'

'You hear that, Francis? Mr Stott feels he could show us a thing or two.'

'Never said that, did I? Sword ain't my weapon – never was. *I*,' he finished with a sad sort of pride, 'was a *pikeman*.'

Mindful of his promise to Pauline and reflecting, with wry amusement, that in the space of three days he'd gone from being unemployed to having four jobs – only one of which involved payment – Ashley nodded. 'Which campaigns?'

'Nördlingen, Augsberg, Breda. Joined up in '21, I did. So I've seen more bloody battles than you've 'ad 'ot dinners, lad.'

'Colonel,' corrected Ashley pleasantly.

Archie stared back at him truculently.

Taking advantage of the temporary lull, Francis crossed the room saying, 'I perceive that this is my cue to exit.' And over his shoulder, 'Stage left, pursued by a bear.'

Ashley replaced the towel on the rack and started unlacing his sodden shirt. He said, 'You were never tempted to go back and fight in the wars in England?'

'I would 'ave if the sodding palsy 'adn't taken my arm. That were back in '43. And there weren't much point in going nowhere after that.'

'You could have trained the youngsters – passed on what you knew.'

Archie scowled. 'Who listens to an old soldier?'

'Young soldiers who want to live past their first battle,' came the crisp reply. 'Speaking for myself, I learned more from the sergeants than I ever did from the generals. Every sergeant I ever met knew about keeping his powder dry and not trying to be a hero.' He grinned suddenly, 'They also knew how to light a fire on a wet night and where to get a chicken.'

'Ah. Them were the days.' Archie sighed wistfully and shook his head. 'But no one's got use for a cripple.'

'I would – if there's ever an opportunity,' said Ashley. 'But only if you can stay sober five days out of seven.'

Something that might have been a grin touched the seamed face.

'Only five, Captain?'

'Six would be better – but I'll settle for what I can get. And my rank, if you wouldn't mind, is Colonel. God knows I risked my neck enough times for it.'

Archie thought about it and then nodded.

'Colonel, then.'

'Thank you. And now I'm going to get changed.' Untucking his wet shirt as he went, Ashley added, 'If you see Jem, you can tell him that it's safe to come out of hiding.'

He left the room, closing the door with one hand whilst tugging his damp shirt over his head with the other ... which was how, as he blindly turned the corner, he managed to collide with a pair of small, capable hands. He froze, knowing whose hands they were by the spear of pure fire that shot through his body. Then, struggling free of his shirt, he found himself staring into a startled dark gaze while its owner's light, intoxicating scent wove its way insidiously through his senses. His brain promptly stopped functioning.

Athenais stared at him and then stared some more. The breadth of his shoulders and the well-defined musculature of his chest and arms were spectacular; his diaphragm was flat and hard, his hips narrow; and the smooth, faintly golden skin gleamed with a faint sheen of perspiration. In every respect, he was a perfect specimen of masculinity. Her fingers itched to explore every beautiful naked inch of him and she wondered what it might be like to lick the sweat from his throat. She felt weak and strange and, in that first moment, didn't know why.

Time stopped.

He saw her looking at him and saw *how* she was looking. Moreover, her hands were still scorching the skin of his chest, depriving him of both breath and reason and sending desire raging through every nerve and sinew. His shirt dropping from his fingers, he laid his palms against the wall behind her and leaned in, his eyes brooding on her mouth. Her lips parted and her breathing quickened. He wanted her so badly he ached with it. Yet still, somehow, he managed to stop himself from touching her.

Athenais could see the burning hunger in his face and the pulse throbbing in his jaw. His heart was beating, fast and hard, beneath her palm. Molten heat surged through her blood and formed low in her belly. Her throat closed with longing. She couldn't speak, couldn't even think. She'd never wanted a man before and hadn't known it could be so fierce, so all-consuming. If he didn't put his arms around her soon, her knees were going to give way; and, if he kissed her, she thought she might burst into flames. Her mind was shouting *Please!* over and over, so loudly she was afraid she might actually say it. For the first time, her hands moved, sliding slowly around and over his skin, mapping the line and curve of his muscles … and eliciting a low purr from deep in his throat.

Ashley's sense of self-preservation was normally both strong and rapid. It was what had kept him alive and out of trouble on numerous occasions. But, since the moment Athenais had first touched him, he'd been robbed of every instinct save one. The only thing he'd managed to do so far was not to give way to it. If he touched her at all, he suspected it might end with him carrying her away to the nearest flat surface. So he drew a ragged breath and closed his eyes for a moment, searching for the reasons why this couldn't happen and sufficient self-control to stop it. Somewhere in the fog of his brain was the knowledge that there was no future in it … and that it was bound to end badly.

Time resumed a sluggish beat.

He opened his eyes. Then, with an effort greater than any he could remember, pushed himself away from her and stooped to retrieve his shirt, holding it in front of him and hoping her gaze hadn't strayed below his waist.

'My apologies.' He didn't know how he forced the words out. They felt like knives in his throat. 'I wasn't thinking – otherwise I'd have been watching where I was going and not crossing your hall half-dressed.'

She stared up at him, unable to comprehend what he was doing – or why. Her hands still tingled from contact with his skin … but hurt and disappointment flooded the rest of her until she could scarcely bear the weight of it. It wasn't fair that he could sound and look so composed when her entire body was still throbbing with something she could barely understand.

It took every scrap of strength she had to straighten her spine, lift her chin and say coolly, 'It's of no consequence, Colonel. And I've seen a man's bare chest before – quite a number of them, actually. So I'm hardly likely to be either offended or – or swooning with admiration.'

'No?' He managed to inject a thread of levity into his voice. And, as he turned to move on, 'What a shame.'

Knowing that she was probably watching, he managed to run up the stairs without either tripping or clutching at the bannister-rail. His chest hurt and his mind was in turmoil. He'd nearly – so very nearly – betrayed himself and begun something which, once started, would be almost impossible to walk away from. But holy hell ... it was so incredibly difficult. Lust was controllable. What he felt for Athenais de Galzain plainly wasn't.

Even after he had vanished from sight, Athenais remained rooted to the spot, unable to remember where she'd been going or why. Gradually, however, bewilderment turned to something she told herself was anger and she stamped into the parlour wishing she could afford to break something.

He's an imbecile or demented or just downright provoking. If he wasn't going to do anything ... if he doesn't find me attractive ... why was he looking at me like that? He knew I'd have let him. God in heaven, I as good as asked him to! Well, it's his loss. And he certainly won't get the chance to humiliate me again.

And then she sat on the sofa and tried to swallow the lump in her throat.

* * *

That evening Pauline returned with the news that Manager Laroque and Monsieur Froissart wanted to see both Colonel Peverell and Lord Wroxton at noon the following day.

Francis shook his head and said, 'Major Langley or Francis, if you please. I'm finding the title rather disconcerting at present.'

Pauline nodded. 'If you give your shirts to Suzon, she'll iron them. And be on time. Laroque hates tardiness.'

Consequently, having done the best they could with their appearance, Ashley and Francis presented themselves at the theatre ten minutes early and were left kicking their heels in the empty auditorium. Ashley, contemplating the stickiness of the floor and the assorted debris lingering in the corners, remarked that whoever cleaned the place needed a kick up the backside. Ignoring him, Francis vaulted on to the stage and executed a neat step-dance, followed by an equally neat spin – at which point the door opened and Antoine Froissart walked in.

Colouring faintly, Francis dropped back off the stage and straightened his cuffs.

Without the merest flicker of an eyelid, Froissart strode towards them saying, 'Good day, gentlemen. I am the assistant-manager. If you will be so good as to follow me, Monsieur Laroque will see you now.'

Laroque's office was a lot tidier than the rest of the theatre and, to Ashley's surprise, Pierre Regnault Petit-Jean Laroque himself looked more like a lawyer than an actor-manager. He rose when they entered and inclined his head courteously as they gave their names. Then he said, 'And which of you is to choreograph the fight scenes?'

'I am,' replied Ashley. 'But the Major will help demonstrate when necessary.'

Laroque nodded. 'We will return to that matter later, I think. First let us address Madame Fleury's suggestion that you be taken on as walkers.' He contemplated them over steepled fingers and then, glancing at Froissart, said, 'Madame has a point. Height, bearing, physical appearance – all excellent. The ladies are likely to *bouleversé*.' Then, returning briskly to the business in hand, 'Monsieur Peverell ... please walk across the room and back, finishing with a bow.'

Ashley didn't take kindly to being looked over like a piece of horse-flesh and asked if he could put foot in front of the other. It was time, moreover, to remove the Manager's misconceptions. He said, 'I'll devise and give instruction for your fights – but I have no intention of appearing on the stage in any capacity at all. Furthermore, I have no objection to being called by my given name – but, if we are to be formal, I would prefer to be addressed as Colonel.'

'I'm sure you would. But this is a theatre not the army and military titles have neither place nor meaning here. As to the rest, I will attempt to conquer my disappointment.' He looked at Francis. 'And you, Monsieur? Are you also averse to walking on my stage?'

'Not in the least,' came the cheerful reply. And, setting his left hand to his sword hilt, Francis sauntered elegantly to and fro before pausing in hesitation. 'I beg your pardon, Monsieur – but to whom am I bowing?'

Laroque and Froissart exchanged baffled glances.

Froissart said, 'To anyone. It is of no consequence.'

'Forgive me – but it is of the greatest consequence,' reproved Francis. 'Do you wish me to bow as I would to a Prince of the blood – or an elderly Marquise – or a gentleman of the lesser nobility – or a --'

Ashley's sense of humour reasserted itself. He said, 'Just do it, there's a good fellow. Bow to La Grande Mademoiselle.'

'An excellent choice!' And, sweeping the floor with the single, rather limp plume of his hat, Francis produced a perfect court obeisance.

Froissart's '*Ah!*' was one of pure appreciation.

Ashley had the feeling he'd have liked to applaud.

Laroque merely nodded and said, 'Excellent. One should have expected it. And now, gentlemen … if we return to the stage, perhaps a small demonstration of your fencing skills?'

Thank God, thought Ashley. *Once this is done, I can return to sanity.*

Tilting his head at Francis across the width of the stage, he murmured, 'Basic moves and not too fast. I wouldn't want you to strain yourself.'

'How very thoughtful,' Francis retorted, lifting his blade in the customary salute and immediately following it up with a swift, teasing and far from basic attack.

Ashley parried, side-stepped and responded with a *doublé*. Forced into an unexpected turn, Francis stumbled and had to work to regain his balance.

With a sardonic smile, Ashley dropped his sword-point and said in English, 'That was fun – though not quite the effect you were looking for. So if you've finished showing off, perhaps we can do this properly?'

'One, two, lunge, engage … three, four, reverse?' sighed Francis. 'If we must.'

'Now you're exaggerating.' Ashley looked across at Froissart and Laroque. 'Are your characters fighting in earnest or for sport?'

'One fight is in earnest – the other requires an element of comedy,' replied Froissart.

'Ah. Well, Major Langley has just ably demonstrated the second of those,' remarked Ashley. Then, 'Can the actors tumble?'

Laroque looked mildly offended. 'Pardon, Monsieur?'

'Can they tumble? Fall, roll, stand … oh never mind. Francis – engage forte to forte, push me back with a quarter-turn and for God's sake keep your blade out of the way. Now!'

Francis grinned and swung into action. Ashley went down, rolled over backwards and landed on his feet. This time Froissart *did* applaud.

'Thank you.' Ashley bowed. 'Can one of your actors do that?'

'I doubt it,' said Monsieur Laroque. And with a dry laugh, Then, 'But I'll enjoy watching them try. Wednesday at two o'clock, gentlemen. And thank you.'

FIVE

Leaving Francis to discuss the finer points of their employment (such as money) with Antoine Froissart, Colonel Peverell made his way to the Louvre. With two of his minor tasks now in train, it was time to embark on the rather more serious (unpaid) ones entrusted to him by Sir Edward Hyde.

He finally tracked the King down in a secluded corner of the gardens. Charles had an arm round a girl's waist and a hand in her bodice. Ashley sighed, turned away and waited. Charles also sighed and reluctantly released his companion with a murmured word and a kiss. The girl rose and sauntered past Ashley with a roguish glance and a swish of taffeta. The King stayed where he was and said long-sufferingly, 'Have you any idea of how long it took me to find this precise spot – and to persuade Sophie-Clarice to share it with me? Of course you haven't. So this had better be important.'

'I consider it important, Sir. But I doubt either one of us will find it enjoyable.'

'Oh God. You've been talking to Hyde, haven't you?'

'Yes. But I'm not here to deliver a lecture. I'd hoped we might simply talk – man to man.'

Charles uncoiled to his full height and stretched.

'Is that why you're wearing your sword?'

'No.' Ashley laughed wryly. 'If you really want to know, I've been engaged to devise fight sequences for a forthcoming theatrical production and to train the actors performing them. That's where I drew the line. Major Langley, however, is set on treading the boards as what they call a 'walker'.'

He'd thought Charles might find it funny. Instead, His Majesty looked sympathetic and said, 'You're both short of money?'

'We're never anything else.' Deciding it was time to change the subject, Ashley added, 'But since I *am* wearing a sword, I'm entirely at your disposal if your wrist is in need of some practice.'

'Later, perhaps - when you've said your piece. By then I might be in the mood for a little violence.' The King strolled out of the arbour, leaving the Colonel to follow him. 'Well, Ash? Shall I say it for you? You want me to be discreet, sober and, preferably, chaste. You'd like me to spend my days in sensible conversation and my evenings with an improving book. And you're going to ask me to keep away from George.'

'Not exactly, Sir. I was merely going to suggest that you allow his Grace of Buckingham to raise Cain without you from time to time. He can play merry hell with his own reputation if he likes – that's his prerogative. But those of us who want to see you regain the life you were born for would rather he didn't do it with yours.'

A bitter smile twisted the wide mouth.

'What difference does it make? You said it yourself – nothing changes.'

'Not right now. But you can't lose hope, Sir. And – if you'll permit me to be perfectly blunt – the kind of excesses you've recently been indulging in with the Duke will do you a lot of harm amongst the men whose help you've been hoping to gain. Take the Dutch, for example. On the whole, they're a fairly sedate race and --'

'Dull is the word you're looking for. Have you ever met William Frederick?'

'No, Sir. But --'

'Count yourself fortunate. The man never uses one word when ten will do.'

'Ah. I can see that might be --'

'And there's no use expecting any help from the Netherlands anyway. They've got their hands full fighting Cromwell at sea. On present showing, the war could drag on indefinitely – since neither side seems actually to be winning.'

'Sir.' Ashley stopped walking and allowed his tone to sharpen. 'This is all very well – but in many senses, it's beside the point. Tales of your doings are spinning out of control. For every girl you bed, rumour credits you with three; and for every occasion you and Buckingham engage in a little rough-and-tumble in a tavern, gossip has you picking fights right, left and centre. If you don't want Cromwell sniggering behind his hand and every ruler in Europe deciding you're too light-weight to be worth helping, you've got to employ some restraint. And if

Buckingham has trouble understanding that, I'll force the point home with him myself.'

For a long moment, Charles stared at him in silence, leaving Ashley to wonder if he'd over-stepped the mark. But finally the King said, 'You're right. I don't deny it. But at present I've nothing of any significance to fill my time. And George is always entertaining.'

'I understand the evils of inactivity only too well, Sir. And I've no wish to deny you every amusement. I'd just caution you to employ a bit more discretion and dilute my lord Buckingham's company with that of your other friends.'

'Such as yourself?'

'I'm not so presumptuous, Sir,' came the wry response. 'But, as ever, I am at your disposal.' He paused and then, not without humour, added, 'I'd also suggest Sir William Brierley – though every time I pass an evening with him I spend the following day with a sore head. Does what I'm suggesting sound so very terrible?'

'No. I suppose not.' Charles turned away and strolled on along the path. 'It's just that I'd like the illusion that some small part of my life is my own. And don't – *don't* tell me that it is and that it's called *self-control* – or I may just hit you.'

Ashley knew perfectly well that this was an empty threat. On the other hand, the fact that he'd said it, boded ill for the subject Ashley had to raise next – but he knew there was no escaping it so he said cautiously, 'If you can bear with me a little longer, Sir, there's something else.'

Charles shot him a sideways glance. 'Spit it out, then.'

'It concerns your relationship with Lucy Walter.'

Drawing a sharp breath, the King said, 'Outside the not insignificant fact that we have a son, I *have* no relationship with Lucy Walter – and haven't done since last October. When I got back here after Worcester, I sent her a pearl necklace and told her it was over. I had thought that fact and the reasons behind it were common knowledge.'

Ashley nodded. 'Her child by Viscount Taafe, to name but one? Yes. But I understand that you still pay Mistress Walter a pension?'

'I support my son. I promised Lucy a pension but have yet to find the means to pay it.' The dark Stuart eyes showed wariness oddly mingled with impatience. 'If there is a point to this, I'd appreciate hearing it.'

Ashley sighed inwardly and considered his options. There weren't many.

He said, 'Because the lady persists in calling herself your wife, there have always been rumours that you did, in fact, marry her. I need ... I'm sorry, Sir – but I have to ask if there is any truth in such talk.'

'None. How many times must I say it?'

'At least once more, I'm afraid.'

'Why?'

'Because someone is trying to turn rumour into fact.' Ashley hesitated and then said baldly, 'Someone who claims they can provide proof. And before I spend God knows how long trying to find out who it is, I'd like to know whether or not there *is* any.'

Charles was silent for so long that Ashley thought he didn't intend to answer. But finally he said wearily, 'There shouldn't be – though I wouldn't put it past Lucy to fabricate some. But if you're asking if it's possible somebody has got hold of Lucy's and my marriage lines, it isn't. *Is* that what you've heard?'

'No – or not in so many words. Just that there is written proof of a marriage. And it's hard to know what else could be meant by that.' Ashley frowned, his mind scanning the possibilities. 'Could Mistress Walter have anything else? Documents of any kind? Letters from you promising marriage or hinting that young Jemmy is legitimate? Anything at all that could account for this anonymous person's claim?'

'Not as such – and none of the things you mention.' Charles swung away a couple of steps and, still with his back to Ashley, said, 'But she does have ... papers ... which could be damaging if she chose to make them public. Papers which, in view of her recent activities, I would very much prefer to have in my own possession.'

What papers? was Ashley's immediate thought, swiftly followed by, *Christ. Is he asking me to steal them back? If so, he's going to need to be more specific.*

He said neither and, instead prompted calmly, 'What recent activities?'

237

Casting an impatient glance over his shoulder, Charles said, 'She went to London.'

Calm instantly exploded into alarm. '*What?*'

'She went to London – ostensibly to claim some inheritance or other. What she *actually* did was to get clapped in the Tower on a charge of spying for me.' Charles turned, his smile wholly sardonic. 'You don't know Lucy, do you?'

'No. I've seen her, of course, but --'

'And not looked past those stunning looks, I daresay. If you did, you'd understand how ludicrously ill-suited she is to espionage. She's self-centred, hysterical, wholly unreasonable and not at all intelligent. In short, she's the sort of spy you'd only use if you wanted them to be caught.'

'Is she still in England?'

'No. Cromwell's fellows soon recognised their mistake and hustled her aboard a ship to Flanders. She's back in Paris now – probably lodging with her latest lover. I shouldn't think you'd have too much trouble finding her if you chose to look.'

Ashley nodded, knowing that he had to start somewhere and, as yet, he had nothing else to go on. He said slowly, 'Sir ... you realise that, if there is anything you're not telling me, the time will almost certainly come when you'll have to? If enough people start to believe that you married Mistress Walter, it won't matter whether you did or not. And though I'll do my best to stop that happening, I'm unlikely to achieve much groping around in the dark.'

'You underestimate yourself, Ashley. I suspect that you can grope in the dark as well as any man – and better than most.'

* * *

On the following morning when Colonel Peverell had disappeared in pursuit of undisclosed business, Francis finally accepted that the project he'd been consumed by for the last ten days was finished. He'd written and re-written, cut, honed and polished until there was nothing more that he could logically do to it. And the knowledge made his nerves rattle.

Inevitably, he'd started it with Athenais in mind ... but a couple of things had changed that. One was the fact that, though he genuinely liked her and found her breathtakingly lovely, he had never once felt the slightest twinge of physical desire. And the other was an element which hadn't initially occurred to him but which had somehow crept into the pages and turned his mediocre little opus into something extraordinary. Or he hoped it had.

But now it was finished, he had two choices. Shove the thing out of sight and forget about it ... or show it to somebody. Now, today, before he talked himself out of it. And if he *was* going to ask someone's opinion, there was really only one possible candidate.

He found Pauline in the parlour, her feet resting on a footstool and a torrent of misty-blue satin cascading off her lap as she set stitches in a hem. Instead of its usual elegant, not-a-lock-out-of-place style, the glossy brown hair tumbled down her back, loosely caught in a ribbon; and, when she looked up at him, Francis thought he caught a gleam of surprised pleasure.

'Major Langley.' She gave him her customary half-smile and resumed her work. 'Is there something I can do for you?'

He didn't give himself time to think. He simply crossed the room and placed his cherished pages beside her on the sofa. He said, 'Yes. I'd like you to read that and let me know what you think. You needn't worry about being tactful. I'd rather have it straight from the shoulder.'

Pauline tucked her needle away and let the gown slide to the floor as she stretched out a hand for the Major's offering. She'd been aware for some days now that he was writing something and had wondered what. It seemed she was about to find out.

She said, 'And you shall have it. Now go away and walk your nerves off elsewhere. I'll call you when I'm done.'

Francis hovered for a moment and then, with a nod, left the room. Pauline smoothed the pages out on her lap and took a moment to enjoy the sound of agitated pacing in the hall before she looked down at the script. The top page merely said,

MÉNAGE
A Play in One Act
Dramatis Personae
The Husband, His Wife,
Her Lover & The Mother-in-Law

She set the pages down again and shut her eyes.

Oh dear. The most hackneyed idea in the history of theatre. What can have possessed the man?

Then, sighing, she turned the first page and started to read.

Twenty minutes later, mopping her streaming eyes and aching with laughter she'd been trying to keep silent, she opened the door and told Francis he could come back and hear the verdict.

He entered the room without speaking and, refusing the chair she indicated, stood in front of the empty hearth as if facing a firing-squad. Then he absorbed the over-bright eyes, flushed skin and the fact that Madame Fleury's hair was escaping its ribbon. She looked like a completely different person. She looked like a girl. She also looked as if she'd been laughing her head off. Francis wasn't sure how he should interpret that. He said, 'Well, Madame? What do you think?'

'I – I d-don't know where to start,' she managed. And then went off into a fresh paroxysm of helpless laughter.

Francis waited patiently for her to regain the power of speech. It occurred to him that, even if she'd hated his little play, the sight of her clutching her sides and giggling like a school-girl in some sense lessened his disappointment.

Finally, pulling herself together, Pauline said breathlessly, 'I'm sorry. There are a – a number of lines in there that tend to stick in the memory and – and I just recalled one of them.' She sat up straight again and tucked a loose strand of hair behind her ear. 'You want to know what I think? I'm ... astounded.'

'Well, that's something I suppose,' he replied.

'It is indeed.' She grinned up at him. 'Major Langley – I am not easily impressed. But your play is the sharpest, funniest, most utterly wicked thing I've read in a very long time. There's not one wasted word and the relationship between the characters is so well-observed, it cuts to the bone. The double and even sometimes *triple*-entendres are in a class of their own. And as for the character of the *belle-mére* ... that is sheer genius.' She spread her hands. 'I don't know how you did it – but I sincerely congratulate you.'

Francis was aware of an unfamiliar sensation filling his chest. His hands tingled oddly and he knew that his colour had risen. He swallowed hard and said, 'That is … I hardly know what to say, Madame.'

'Pauline.'

'Pauline,' he repeated, managing a slight bow. 'It's only an *entr'acte* or a curtain-raiser, if you will. I – obviously I hoped you might like it. But I didn't expect …' He stopped and then deciding to grasp the nettle, 'When I began it, the play had only three characters. I'm not sure when the mother-in-law arrived. But I know where she came from. You'll have noticed that she is positioned above and outside the action, in order to comment on it apparently unheard and unseen by the other protagonists?'

'I noticed she has the most evil lines – which, considering the quality of the rest, is saying something.' She stood up and held the script out to him. 'If you don't give it to Froissart, I'll take it to him myself.'

'Willingly – on one condition.'

Her brows rose. 'Conditions, Major? Really?'

'Francis,' he replied, smiling. 'And yes – really. I'll offer it to Froissart on condition that, if he decides to stage it, you agree to play the mother-in-law.'

* * *

With no more than a few judicious enquiries, Colonel Peverell traced Lucy Walter to a house near the Palais-Royal. It helped, of course, that he already knew a great deal about her.

Prior to her liaison with Charles, Lucy's lover had been Colonel Robert Sidney – and possibly that gentleman's brother as well. Her affair with the then Prince of Wales, had begun in '48 in The Hague – and had resulted, the following spring, in the birth of their son, James. The relationship had continued, on and off, until Charles left for Scotland in June, 1650 – whereupon Lucy had immediately leapt into bed with Viscount Taafe, producing a daughter less than a year later. When Charles returned to Paris after Worcester, he'd broken his links with the lady – publicly, at least. And that was when the silly female had started trying to regain his attention by means of seeing how much scandalous gossip she could cause.

All in all, Ashley wondered how Charles – who was by no means stupid – had ever put up with her in the first place. Granted, the woman was beautiful; clouds of dark hair and eyes bluer than a hot, summer sky. But her personality left a lot to be desired and she had the potential to become a bloody liability.

A coin he could ill-afford pressed into the hand of the maidservant he saw exiting the house bought him the information that Madame Walter had lodgings on the first floor. Ashley appraised the building critically and came to the conclusion that, if burglary *did* become necessary, the task wouldn't be particularly difficult. Then, he lounged in the doorway of a tavern across the street in the hope of seeing any comings and goings.

For a time, all he saw were people who were either servants or possibly tenants of other parts of the building. Then, just when he was considering giving up for the day, a gentleman emerged through the front door and, on reaching the pavement, turned to wave jauntily at the lady dimly visible at a first-floor window. Ashley's gaze remained fixed on the man, aware of a vague sense of familiarity which eventually crystalised into near-certainty. He couldn't remember the fellow's name... but what he *did* remember was Will Brierley pointing him out as the King's agent in Brussels.

Brussels? Had Lucy's journey back from England taken her by way of Brussels? It was possible, he supposed. But if that was when she'd first met Sir-whatever-his-name-was, one or both of them was a remarkably fast worker. Ashley grinned wryly, berating himself for his naiveté. Lucy had never been particularly fussy; and few men refused an offer from a beautiful woman.

Very few men, actually. It was just a damned irony that Ashley himself had to be one of them. Since the incident in the hall when he'd narrowly avoided kissing her, he had managed to see Athenais only in passing and never alone. But he'd still managed to notice that her expression was frosty when their eyes met and bewildered when she thought he wasn't looking. *Hell.*

Pushing away from the doorframe, he turned back in the direction of the Rue des Rosiers. Surveillance was a tedious business. Time to give Jem an occupation that would reduce the amount of time he had to spend with Archie and a bottle.

SIX

During the first week in October, everyone at the Théâtre du Marais rejoiced when King Louis left the palace of St. Germain and returned in state to take up residence at the Louvre. Colonel Peverell was less overjoyed and felt impelled to spend as much time as he could spare with his own sovereign, which meant that he learned the latest news from England before he might otherwise have done. This, in turn, was responsible for him having the nearest thing to a quarrel one could have with royalty when he discovered that the Highland chieftains were urging Charles to appoint leaders for a Scottish uprising – and Charles flatly refused to make him one of them.

This, however, he didn't tell Francis – merely revealing that Admiral Blake had won a resounding naval victory at the battle of Kentish Knock.

'And that,' he added, 'presumably cancels out Tromp's triumph at Plymouth. One wonders which side thinks it is winning.'

'Both, probably – since that's the normal way of things. Anything else?'

'There is – but none of it's good. Ralph Hopton died in Bruges at the end of last month. And there's a rumour – as yet unconfirmed – that Prince Maurice has been lost at sea.'

'Oh.' Francis was suddenly still. 'If it's true, Rupert must be … well, I can't imagine. They argued almost constantly – but were closer than any two brothers I ever knew.'

'Yes. So we'll have to pray it *is* just a rumour.' Ashley stood up and reached for his sword. 'Meanwhile, you and I had better take ourselves off to the theatre and attempt to earn our pay. I don't expect to make much more progress than we've done so far – but I suppose there's always hope.'

This would be their fourth rehearsal and the results so far had been negligible. Of the three actors they were required to train, only Etienne Lepreux showed the slightest potential – which was fortunate since he was required in both fights. Of the other two, Marcel thudded wildly about the stage seemingly incapable of remembering the moves and André clutched his sword like a cudgel, fell over at the least provocation and looked perpetually terrified.

Engaged in placing a sheaf of papers securely inside his coat, Francis said, 'Perhaps it's time to start praying for a miracle. With only seventeen days left, we're going to need one.'

'Don't tell me they've honoured you with a speaking role?'

'What? Oh – this.' Francis patted his chest and shrugged. 'No. It's just a little something I've been working on. Pau – Madame Fleury suggested that Froissart might like to see it.'

It had taken him until yesterday evening to charm, flatter, cajole and finally bully Pauline into agreeing to his condition. And, in the end, he'd done it by saying – with much less than his usual finesse, 'You bone-headed woman! It's your role, don't you see? I wrote the damned part for you – so the least you can do is pluck up enough courage to play it.'

Unaware of this, Ashley muttered, 'God. This theatrical nonsense is getting worse by the minute.'

'It's in my blood,' retorted Francis flippantly. 'And we can't all be philistines.'

* * *

The afternoon's rehearsal showed some slight improvement on its predecessors. Etienne had plainly practised and memorised his moves – which was good – but was now overflowing with ebullient confidence – which wasn't. André managed to fall and roll on cue but still staggered to his feet as if drunk. And Marcel still hacked and slashed like a badly-handled marionette but had at least stopped sounding like a herd of thundering elephants. At the end of two hours, when all three were sweating profusely, Ashley let them recover their breath whilst giving a twenty minute lecture on basic style and how to achieve it.

Leaving the Colonel to it, Francis ambled back to Froissart's office and rapping lightly on the door, said, 'Have you a moment, Monsieur?'

The assistant-manager looked up from the swiftly-mounting expenses of the forthcoming extravaganza. 'Only for good news. Anything else may cause me to open my veins.'

'The swordplay is a little better. If the Colonel's schedule doesn't kill them, it's beginning to look as if your actors may manage not to look utterly ludicrous.'

'Thank you. You have no idea how much better that makes me feel.'

'My pleasure.' Francis grinned and strolled across to place *Ménage* on top of Froissart's costings. 'Madame Fleury feels you should read this. I believe the word 'immediately' was mentioned somewhere.'

And he turned and left the room, closing the door behind him.

By the time Ashley joined him fifteen minutes later, a series of odd snorts and guffaws were coming from the other side of the door.

'Is he laughing or choking?' asked Ashley, leaning negligently against the wall.

'The former, I hope. He's been like this for --'

The door was suddenly hauled open and Froissart appeared clutching the script to his chest. He said, 'Where did Pauline get this? Has anyone else seen it? Does she know the writer?'

'From me. No. And yes,' drawled Francis, laughter lighting the back of his eyes.

Froissart stared at him, as if sorting out the answers. Then, incredulously, '*You* wrote it?'

'Yes. Do you like it?'

'It's unscrupulous and deadly as a well-honed razor. It's also the best piece of comedy I've seen in a long while. What do you want for it?'

'Whatever you feel it's worth,' shrugged Francis. 'There is, however, just one condition.'

'Name it.'

'The role of the mother-in-law is to be played by Madame Fleury.'

Froissart opened his mouth, then closed it again. He shook his head, regretfully.

'She won't do it.'

'Actually,' said Francis simply and with immense satisfaction, 'she will.'

* * *

While Francis was listening to Froissart's raptures and Ashley sat in a corner reading the script to see what all the fuss was about, Athenais was walking around the parlour, rehearsing her lines for *Mariamne* and enjoying the rustle of her very first brand-new gown.

It was of leaf-green taffeta, trimmed with blond lace and she thought it was the most beautiful dress in the world – and entirely deserving of the equally new and lovely corset and petticoats she wore beneath it.

The feel of it and the sighing sound it made as she walked made it hard to concentrate on her lines. More distracting still was the niggling wish that Colonel Peverell was there to see her. Perhaps if he saw her dressed like a real lady and looking her best, he might actually kiss her.

She was still wondering why he hadn't. He had wanted to. As soon as she had calmed down enough to think properly, she'd known that. For the space of a minute, everything about him had shouted that he wanted a lot more than just a kiss. And yet he hadn't taken it – despite the fact she'd made it abundantly clear that she wanted him to.

It made no sense. Men generally took what was on offer – and sometimes things that weren't. But Ashley Peverell had resumed his usual expression and stepped away from her as though nothing had happened; as though he hadn't felt that instant, overwhelming tug between their bodies ... or didn't consider it nearly as cataclysmic as she did.

She huffed an impatient breath and ordered herself to stop thinking about him. It was a waste of time and she should be concentrating on her lines. Just because the mere sound of his voice or the echo of his tread on the stairs had the ability to make her pulse stutter and her chest grow tight didn't mean he necessarily felt the same. And just because he'd shown her the sort of kindness life had taught her not to expect was no reason to turn into an emotional jelly at the merest glance from those gold-flecked green eyes.

She picked up the script and rifled through the pages, trying to remember where she'd got to. Then, just when she'd found the right place, she heard the front door open and the sound of booted feet crossing the hall.

Ashley and Francis back from the theatre? Was it that time already? She hadn't thought it so late. She tossed the script aside and flew to the small mirror over the fireplace to check that her hair was in place. If she got into the hall quickly enough, Colonel Peverell would see her in her beautiful new gown and perhaps –

The door opened and the Marquis d'Auxerre walked in.

Athenais froze, rooted to the spot in shock.

'Good afternoon, my dear.' He bowed lazily and continued to advance towards her. 'You look charming. A new gown, perhaps?'

'Yes.' Getting just that one word out was an effort. Swallowing hard, she said baldly, 'How did you get in? I didn't hear the bell.'

'I didn't ring it. You have a distressing habit of being out when I call ... and the door was unlocked.'

'You – you're saying you just walked in?' Anger started to mingle with her alarm. 'You have no right!'

He placed his hat on the table and started slowly stripping off his gloves.

'I have any right I choose to take,' came the careless reply. 'And I am here because you and I have unfinished business. Business which I intend to resolve today.'

Athenais backed away a couple of steps to put the sofa between them while she tried to think who else, other than Suzon, might be in the house. Since the day she'd become acquainted with Colonel Peverell's naked and extremely splendid chest, her father had been drinking noticeably less and started taking long walks around the city. Jem Barker, busy with some mysterious task, was rarely around during the day; Pauline had gone to visit a friend on the Rue St. Paul; and both the Colonel and the Major would be at the theatre until at least five o'clock. She wished she knew what the time was now. She wished Pauline would come home. She wished somebody had locked the front door.

Forcing herself to sound calmer than she felt, she said, 'Then perhaps you should be seated – and I will ask the maid to bring wine. If you will excuse me for a moment?'

'No. I don't believe I will.' He smiled at her. 'I am not entirely stupid, Athenais.'

'I have never thought you were.'

'No? But you hoped. And you will not stir from this room until we have reached an agreement.' He tossed his embroidered gloves down beside his hat. 'Sit down.'

'I'd rather not, if you don't mind.' She gestured to her skirts. 'The gown, you understand. It's only just arrived from the dressmaker and of course I couldn't resist trying it on – but I don't want to crush it, so it's best I remain standing.'

'Perhaps it would be best to simply remove it.'

The smile still lingered and the look in his eyes told her that he'd be happy to help. Tendrils of fear started to coil around her nerves. She lifted her chin and said primly, 'That is not the remark of a gentleman, sir.'

'No. But then, it wasn't addressed to a lady.' He moved beyond the sofa, forcing her to retreat towards the corner. 'Enough of this now. I have borne with you patiently for far longer than you deserve but the game has ceased to amuse me. Are you going to come to my bed willingly – or must I employ more ... persuasions?' Two more steps brought him close enough to stroke his fingers down her neck and along the bare skin revealed by her *décolletage*. 'I doubt you enjoyed your first experience of a claque.'

'No.' Athenais tried to side-step him and get away but his arm shot out, trapping her. 'You didn't need to do that. I knew that you could. It wasn't necessary to prove it.'

'I beg to differ. Now answer my question.'

He wasn't going to go away. Neither was he going to let her talk her way out of it this time. Even as she hesitated, he used his weight to pin her against the wall. The fingers of one hand dipped into her neckline while the other gripped her chin and he pushed his thigh between hers. Stupidly, she found herself remembering another wall and another man. A bubble of hysterical amusement floated to the surface of her mind and then was gone. That other man hadn't touched her. This one had his hands all over her and his knee in a place it had no business being. She wanted to spit in his eye but instinct was warning that she had more chance of surviving this encounter undamaged by means of conciliation rather than violence.

Then he was kissing her, forcing her mouth open and half-choking her.

A strangled sob rose in her throat as she finally realised something irrevocable. She had thought that, if it became necessary, she could do this. She'd thought she could smile and lie and let this man use her like a whore ... that she'd be able to bear it because she had to. But now, with sudden blinding clarity, she knew that she couldn't. Not because he repelled her or because she'd heard the dark things rumoured about him; not even because she now knew what it was to want a man – to crave his presence, his smile, his touch. She couldn't do it because, if she did, there would be no turning back and she'd never be clean again.

His tongue was invading her mouth and his fingers groped inside her bodice. Bile rose in her throat and, forgetting she'd intended not to fight him openly, she pushed at him with one hand and raised the other to claw at his cheek. With the speed of a snake, he released her mouth and seized her wrist in a crushing grip.

'Oh no,' he murmured as he captured her other hand and twisted both of them behind her to lock them in one of his. 'That was very foolish, my dear. Now you've annoyed me.'

Athenais wished she had a knife. Since she didn't, she met his eyes and managed to say, 'Monseigneur ... please let me go. I can't do what you want. And I'm sorry I tried to – to hit you but you're frightening me a little.'

'I'll frighten you more than a little if you continue to defy me.'

His voice was soft as silk and somehow more dangerous than if he'd shouted. With his free hand, he wrenched at the shoulder of her gown so hard she heard stitches giving way. Then, bending his head, he bit her hard on the upward slope of her breast.

Athenais yelped in pain and, now seriously frightened, struggled desperately to free herself.

Seizing a handful of her hair, he said, 'Be still. You carry my mark now. You will not refuse me.'

And then the door opened.

'What the hell--?'

Colonel Peverell froze on the threshold, momentarily transfixed by the sight of Athenais's head being dragged back by her hair and the savage red mark just above the line of her disarrayed gown. Two steps behind him, he heard Francis's startled curse.

D'Auxerre also swore and swung round to face the intrusion while, released without warning, Athenais's knees gave way and she slithered down the wall into a leaf-green puddle.

Setting one hand to his sword, the Marquis growled, 'You have no business here. Get out.'

'I don't think so.' Ashley strode forward with clenched fists. 'You're the one who'll be leaving. After I've beaten you to a bloody pulp.'

Francis's hand closed hard on his arm. 'Wait.'

Ashley shook him off. 'For what? So this piece of filth can finish what he started?'

'So you can get a hold of your temper.'

Already drawing his sword, d'Auxerre snapped, 'Don't touch me unless you've a death-wish.'

Ashley laughed coldly and continued to advance.

'With that pretty toy? Try it. Please. Just give me an excuse.'

Both the look in the Colonel's eyes and something in the tone of his voice gave the Marquis pause and, with reluctance, he rammed his sword home.

'The girl's not hurt. And you don't know what you're meddling with.'

'Neither do you.' Rage was beating through him like Thor's hammer and the desire to plough his fist into d'Auxerre face was overwhelming but somehow he found a fragment of self-control and, folding his arms, said, 'I think you had better go before you find yourself choking on your teeth. But first, Mademoiselle is owed an apology.'

'It doesn't m-matter,' stammered Athenais from the floor. 'Really. If Monseigneur would j-just go away, we need never speak of this ...'

Francis moved to stand beside Ashley, relieved that they'd avoided bloodshed. He looked the Frenchman over and, in the tone of a man who's just found a slug crawling on his boot, said, 'Monsieur d'Auxerre, I presume. I'd heard you had unfortunate preferences. I didn't realise that mauling women was one of them.'

'And who might you be?' spat the Marquis.

'Viscount Wroxton – quite definitely *not* at your service.'

The dark eyes filled with mocking spite.

'Wroxton? I know your mother. She's ... very accommodating.'

'Enough,' snapped Ashley. 'You can leave with your dignity intact or with my boot up your arse. Your choice – but make it now before my patience runs out.'

'You will regret this,' snarled d'Auxerre, walking up to him and staring him straight in the eye. 'Very, very soon.'

'The only thing I'll regret is not pasting you to the wall,' retorted Ashley, stepping aside. 'Set foot in this house again, and I'll do it. Now get out.' And, as the Marquis strode towards the door, 'Francis. Make sure he leaves.'

In the corner, Athenais had struggled to her knees. About to help her rise by taking her hands, Ashley changed his mind when he saw the state of her wrists where the d'Auxerre's fingerprints would shortly become bruises. Instead, swooping down on her, he picked her up and carried her to the sofa. Her face was paper-white, she was shaking uncontrollably and trying unsuccessfully to blink away tears.

He said gently, 'It's all right. He's gone and you're safe. Did he hurt you?'

'Not so very much.' She squinted downwards. 'He b-bit me.'

Ashley followed her gaze and swallowed a vicious oath.

'He's clearly an animal. Possibly even rabid. You'll need to clean it and apply salve.'

'Yes.' The involuntary tears were coming faster now and she brushed them away with the heel of her hand to look up at him. 'You came. Thank you. I don't know what …' She stopped and then added uncertainly, 'You're very angry.'

'Yes.' *Of course I'm bloody angry. I'm angry that this happened at all and angry that I didn't get here sooner – on top of which you're looking at me as if I was God.* 'Don't worry. I'll get over it.'

She was still cold and shaking so he put his arm round her and settled her against his chest. She curled into him, making herself as small as possible as if she'd like to crawl inside his unlaced coat. Over her head, he saw Francis standing in the doorway and responded to his look with a brief nod. Francis retreated, shutting the door behind him.

'You can cry, you know. It's nothing to be ashamed of.'

'Yes it is. It's *stupid*.'

'Is it?'

She nodded and on a distinct sob said, 'He's torn my dress.'

'Ah. So he has.' Ashley chose not to remark that, considering the things he *might* have done to her, a torn gown was a mere bagatelle. 'That's a pity.'

'It only came today.' She bent her head as if to hide from him. 'It – it's the first new dress I've ever had – *really* new, I mean. Made especially for me.'

A pain, not unlike taking a bullet, exploded in Ashley's chest. He wanted to promise her a dozen new gowns but, since he couldn't, he promised himself something he *could* accomplish. *If the bastard hurts her again, I'll kill him.*

Feeling the sudden tension in his arm, Athenais sat up and said rapidly, 'I'm sorry. This is ridiculous – snivelling over a dress. Pauline will be able to mend it for me. So I really don't know why I was crying.' It seemed vitally important that he knew she wasn't so feeble that she'd cry over anything. 'I *never* cry.'

'I'm perfectly aware that it's not just the dress – so you don't need to apologise for anything.' Laying a hand against her hair, Ashley pulled her head back against his shoulder. 'Tell me. Who let the Marquis into the house?'

'No one. He s-said the door was unlocked.'

'So he walked in on you unannounced?'

'Yes.'

'I see.' He kept his tone calm but his temper was almost at boiling point. 'And who might have left the door unlocked?'

'I don't know. Perhaps someone just forgot. Or if Suzon, ran out to buy something ...'

'Well. I think we'll take steps to make sure it doesn't happen again.' *In fact, we'll take a number of new precautions ... because I doubt very much if d'Auxerre will leave matters as they are.* He looked down at her, noticing that the colour was returning to her face. 'Do you feel a little better?'

'Yes. I'm perfectly well now. Thank you.'

He watched, as seemingly unaware of what she did, her fingers strayed to the angry bite-mark on her breast. He wanted to replace her fingers with his mouth and clean the wound with his tongue. He knew better than to do it, of course ... but his body responded automatically to the thought. She felt so *right* in his arms; warm, soft and fragile, and teasing his senses with some indefinable scent. He ought to let her go. She'd stopped shaking and was recovering her composure. She no longer needed comfort and he ought to let her go ... only he couldn't seem to make himself do it.

For a while, silence settled around them. Then Ashley said, 'I take it you refused him again?'

'Yes. I can't do it. I just can't.'

'After the way he behaved today, I'd say that's a wise decision.' He allowed a smile to enter his voice. 'But I'm a bit disappointed in you. You forgot to use your knee.'

'I couldn't. He – he pushed his leg between mine. I tried to hit him, of course … but that was when he got hold of my hands and bit me.' She sighed and, tilting her face up to his, said, 'He's not going to stop, is he?'

'I wouldn't think so, no. But look on the bright side. I imagine he's taken me in extreme dislike – even though I managed to stop myself hitting him. So he may decide to exorcise his ill-nature on me rather than you.'

Looking him straight in the eye, she said seriously, 'That is *not* a bright side. I don't want you to be hurt because of me.'

'The sentiment is appreciated – but it's not your responsibility. I'm more than capable of protecting myself against the likes of d'Auxerre.'

'Yes – if he came against you himself in the open. But he won't. He has servants to do his dirty work and if he decides to kill you, he'll use them.'

Ashley already knew that but he said, 'I doubt he'll go that far. Also, I'm fairly hard to kill – as a number of old enemies could testify.' *Most of whom are dead, as if happens.* 'And, at the moment, I'm more worried about the security in this house. We can't have *any* clown wandering off the street to whack us with his pig's bladder, now can we?'

This startled a tiny laugh out of her but her reply was unexpected enough to set alarm bells ringing. She said, 'You know … the first time we met, I thought you didn't like me.'

'Did you?' He wondered where this was going. 'And now?'

'Now … I don't know. You are very kind and – and honourable, I think. But you would be those things whether you liked me or not.' She paused, aware that his strength and warmth and the exquisite pleasure of being this close to him were making her weak and stupid but still couldn't resist saying shyly, 'That d-day in the hall, I thought perhaps you wanted to kiss me.'

He'd wanted to then and he wanted to now, God help him – which made this very dangerous ground indeed. A man with any sense at all would instantly change the subject. Ashley opened his mouth and said, 'And if I had … would you have let me?'

'Yes.' *In a heartbeat. As I would now.* 'I thought you knew that. So I wondered … why you didn't.'

This time he forced himself to lie.

'I feared what Madame Fleury might do to me. She's a formidable lady.'

'I know. She frightens me sometimes.' She hesitated again and then said almost conversationally, 'The Marquis kissed me. It was horrible.'

'If that's the case, no wonder he finds it necessary to use force.'

'Perhaps.' The pause this time was a long one while she thought, *Oh God. Why doesn't he help me? Do I have to say it straight out?* And finally, when he still didn't speak, she said baldly, 'I don't think it would be horrible with you.' And cringed inwardly before the words had left her mouth.

Somewhere amongst the tangle of his emotions was faint amusement. He said, 'That's extremely flattering. But, from what you say, you haven't experimented enough to form a proper comparison.

'No.' Athenais sat up and moved away a little so that she could look into his face. 'I never wanted to. Until now.'

His heart slammed against his ribs and he thought, *That's torn it. Damned if I do and damned if I don't, as they say.*

He sat very still, looking at her while silence lapped the edges of the room. The trouble was that he wanted to put his hands on her very, very badly; and there was a look in her eyes which suggested she wanted them there just as much. Had it just been a matter of mutual lust, he was confident of being able to stop matters going further than they should. But it wasn't just lust; certainly not on his side and not, he was beginning to suspect on hers. There was an unbelievably strong pull between them … and it wasn't solely physical. He had never felt anything like it before and, under the circumstances, it scared the hell out of him.

Summoning as easy a smile as he could manage, he made one last attempt to avert disaster.

'It was simply luck that I got here at the right time. You don't owe me anything – and you *certainly* don't have to offer payment in kind.'

She swallowed hard and held her ground.

'I'm not. That would be insulting. What I'm trying to say is that if you thought … if you'd quite like to kiss me … I wish you would.' She stopped and then added, 'After the Marquis, it might … help. But only if you want to, of course.'

If I want to? God, darling – you have no idea.

Even if he'd been capable of it, the embarrassed colour in her cheeks coupled with the wistful anxiety in her voice made refusal of any kind impossible. Telling himself the heavens weren't going to fall on account of one kiss, Ashley remained perfectly still and let his gaze drift to her mouth.

Athenais looked at the ridiculously long, gold-tipped lashes veiling his gaze and felt everything inside her start to unravel. Then, lifting one apparently lazy hand, he drew his thumb across her lower lip, raised his eyes to hers … and smiled.

Her breath snared in her throat and, without realising it, she swayed towards him. Ashley let the curved backs of his fingers slide along her jaw and down the smooth column of her throat, while his other arm curled around her waist to draw her closer. Then, lightly and without any sign of haste, his mouth brushed hers.

She gasped and her lips parted.

'You'll tell me,' he murmured, his voice low and wicked, 'if it's horrible?'

'Yes. *Oh!*' This as his tongue offered a languid caress which ended with a soft kiss at the corner of her mouth. Her hands fisted in his shirt and then, seeming to realise that there was something much more interesting beneath it, travelled wonderingly over the hard contours of his chest.

His mouth moved on, nibbling seductively along her jaw to her ear where it lingered for a while before teasing its way equally slowly back. Athenais made a tiny, inarticulate sound in the back of her throat and her fingers crept round his neck, into his hair. Ashley pulled her closer still and finally, at long last, possessed her mouth. It opened beneath his and she melted against him, soft, sweet and utterly responsive.

Any possibility of logical thought deserted him. There was nothing in the entire universe but the beautiful girl in his arms and her unconcealed longing for him; nothing but her and the raw, aching desire she sent spiralling through him. He released her mouth to feather kisses down her throat to the sensitive spot at the base of her neck and heard her sigh his name. His hands moulded her waist and rose to cup her breasts, his body hardening with every new curve he discovered. He kissed her until he was dizzy with hunger and knew that she was too.

Athenais's fingers tangled in the thick, tawny-blond hair. Flames were racing along every vein and nerve and an inferno raged deep in the core of her body. She had not known – had never realised – that it was possible to want anything as much as she wanted this man. Words hovered at the edges of her mind only to float away under the exquisite touch of his hands and evaporate as her breathing became no more than sobbing gasps.

Ironically enough, it was the Marquis d'Auxerre that Ashley had to thank for making him stop before he went a good deal further than he had intended. His fingers were already at the laces of her gown when he bent his head to kiss her breast and his jaw brushed the bite-mark, making her wince a little.

He froze, at first only aware that he had hurt her and then aghast at what he had been about to do.

'Christ Almighty,' he breathed huskily, snatching back his hands as if burned. 'God. Athenais – I'm sorry.'

'What?' She sounded dazed and her eyes were dark with arousal. 'Sorry? Why?'

He removed her arms from around his neck and created a little space between them.

'I should have … stopped … a while ago.' Still breathing rather rapidly, he lifted each of her hands to his lips in apology and then stood up. 'Trust me. A kiss is one thing. Where we were headed just now is quite another. Forgive me. I need to speak to Francis and, hopefully, your father. And the maid.'

Then, with a slightly crooked smile, he left the room before she noticed that – for the first time in his entire life – his hands were shaking.

SEVEN

The moment he walked through the door, he met Pauline.

She said tersely, 'Francis told me about d'Auxerre. How is she?'

'She's fine. I think.'

'You *think*? Is she or isn't she?'

Ashley shoved his hand through his hair and tried to engage his brain. Then, failing, he fell back on the truth.

'She's not crying or hurt or frightened, if that's what you mean. On the other hand, I suspect she wanted to get rid of the taste of the Marquis – so she asked me to kiss her.'

The fine eyes narrowed. 'And did you?'

'Yes. It may not have been – it probably wasn't a very good idea. I don't know.'

Pauline folded her arms and looked at him.

'You're saying that she liked it – which is no surprise. You're pretty and have probably had a fair bit of practice. But if she's still searching for her wits, you've only got yourself to blame. You ought to have expected it.'

'Do you think we might have this conversation later?' he asked, only too aware that he was at fault. 'Just at the moment, I'd like to throw a few obstacles in the way of any future plans the Marquis might have involving this house. With your permission, of course.'

'Do whatever you think necessary. Just don't let Athenais start imaging things that are never going to happen.'

'I'm neither a rakehell nor a complete idiot,' he snapped. And, almost but not quite beneath his breath as he walked away, 'And despite frequently being required to act like one, I'm not a bloody machine either.'

In the kitchen, he found Francis, Archie and the maid, whose name he couldn't remember.

'What have you told them?' he asked Francis.

'Only that the Marquis d'Auxerre was here, uninvited, pestering Athenais. For the rest, I've been waiting --'

'Is she all right?' demanded Archie, belligerently. 'Is my girl all right?'

'Yes. This time. But if Francis and I hadn't got back when we did, it might have been a different story.' The green-gold gaze swept round the room. 'Which is why we're going to be more careful in future. First of all, no one – and I mean *no one* – leaves this house unlocked at any time. Today, d'Auxerre simply let himself in. I don't want to know whose fault that was – but it will be a different matter if it ever happens again,' said Ashley incisively. 'We are taking precautions because I don't think we can rely on the Marquis taking today's defeat gracefully. Sooner or later, he'll be back – and the likelihood is that he'll come when he knows that Athenais is at home but Francis and I are not. So we're going to institute measures ensuring that she is never left completely alone in the house. And for that – Jem being occupied with other duties, just at present – we'll need to rely solely on you, Sergeant Stott.'

Archie, who hadn't been addressed that way in years, stood to attention.

''Onoured, Colonel. Orders of the day, sir?'

Francis had to smother a grin. Ashley, who still felt as if he'd been hit in the chest with a pike, had no such difficulty. He said, 'You know how the house works, Archie. Athenais and Pauline have fairly set routines – as, for the next couple of weeks, do the Major and myself. I need you to organise your own comings and goings so that you're on duty when everyone but Athenais is out. Do you follow?'

'I do, sir. You can rely on me.'

'I'm sure of it. If the fellow shows his face, don't let him in. And if, by any mischance, he tries to force an entry, I suggest you keep a sturdy cudgel to hand.' He paused, frowning. 'As to the rest, either the Major or I will escort Athenais to and from the theatre unless it's broad daylight and Pauline is with her. Francis; he knows who you are and won't swallow that insult so you'll need to watch your back. And you,' he looked at the maid whose name he still couldn't remember, 'will neither forget to lock the door nor admit the Marquis to this house again – even if he threatens you with the wrath of God. I trust that takes care of everything?' No one replied. 'Good. Then I'm going out for an hour.'

* * *

In the parlour, Pauline absorbed the marks on Athenais's wrists, the tooth-marks on her breast and the torn shoulder of her gown. Then she looked into the girl's face and saw something even more worrying.

Athenais was utterly radiant. Her cheeks were flushed, her eyes bright and a tiny, secret smile hovered at the corners of her lips. She looked, thought Pauline irritably, like a first-day bride. *Damn.*

'Who let d'Auxerre in?' she asked.

'Mm? Oh. No one. He said that the door was unlocked.'

Pauline began to see why Colonel Peverell was concerning himself with security.

'And then?'

'He pinned me against the wall and kissed me. Then he bit me.' She gestured to the mark as though it was of absolutely no consequence and twisted her neck to try to peer over her shoulder. 'The worst thing is that he's torn my dress. Do you think it can be mended?'

Pauline took her time examining the damage while considering a few other matters. Finally she said, 'The seam has come adrift but the actual taffeta is intact. I'll see to it.'

Athenais turned a dazzling smile on her.

'Thank you.

'You appear,' said Pauline dryly, 'to have got over being assaulted remarkably quickly.'

Some of the glow faded.

'Truthfully? I was scared witless. I thought ... I'm fairly sure that he intended to rape me.' She twisted her hands in her lap. 'I couldn't give in to him, Pauline. I've heard what some of the girls say about him – that he's not normal. And now I know it's true.'

'No. I'd have to agree that the average man doesn't generally go round biting females. We'd better put some salve on that, by the way. It looks sore.'

'Yes. Are you angry with me?'

'About turning the bastard down? No. But I think you need to recognise that he's now your enemy. And not just yours. What happened when the Colonel and Francis turned up?'

The glow was back in an instant and even more breath-taking than before.

'He – they were splendid. I wish you could have seen it. Ashley threatened to beat him to a pulp and Francis said something insulting about his personal habits. Then Ashley told him he could leave in one piece or get a boot up his arse. If I hadn't been shaking like a leaf, I'd have laughed.' She gave a tiny shrug. 'He left then, muttering something. But Ashley doesn't think he'll let it rest.'

'No. And I'll be surprised if it doesn't end in blood.'

Athenais immediately stood up. 'Where is he?'

'The Colonel? Mustering his troops, I imagine. Sit down. Nothing more is going to happen today and I want to hear the rest of it.' Pauline waited until the girl had subsided reluctantly back on the sofa. 'So d'Auxerre went off with his tail between his legs and the Colonel dried your tears?'

'Something like that.' Athenais concentrated on pleating a fold of her skirt, her colour rising a little. 'He was so kind, Pauline. You can't imagine. He didn't even laugh at me for crying over my new dress. He's … I don't know. I've never met anyone like him before.'

Pauline debated the matter for a moment and decided to grasp the nettle.

'And I imagine he kisses rather well, too.'

The storm-grey eyes flew to her face.

'How do you kn --?'

'He told me.' A wry smile dawned. 'To be fair, he looked as though he'd been knocked sideways – so I'd probably have guessed anyway.' She paused. 'What do you expect to come of it?'

'I don't know. I haven't thought about it.'

'Liar. You want him, don't you?'

Athenais took her time about answering but, in the end and because she knew better than attempt to deceive Pauline, she said simply, 'Yes.'

'Well, I can't blame you for that. He's got the manners of a gentleman and the looks of a god – so if you want to take him to bed, good luck to you. I daresay he's as skilled in that department as he seems to be in every other. But if you're hoping for more than a few pleasurable hours between the sheets, I'd advise you to think again.'

'I don't know what I was hoping for.' Athenais frowned down into her lap. 'But what you're really saying is that I shouldn't fall in love with him.'

'That,' agreed Pauline, 'is exactly what I'm saying.'

Seconds ticked by in silence before Athenais looked up again and said ruefully, 'I could be wrong ... but I think it may be a little bit late for that.'

'Oh God,' sighed Pauline. And then, 'Why am I not surprised? The two of them are as bad as each other – and you and I are equally deranged. The Colonel's saved you from a fate worse than death and got your heart in his pocket as a result. And bloody Francis has written a play and badgered me into taking the plum role. Ah.' She stopped. 'I'd better explain about that, I suppose. And if he hasn't left the only copy with Froissart, I'll get it for you to read. It ought to take your mind off the gallant Colonel for a little while.'

* * *

Ashley walked as far as the Place des Vosges and sat on a bench in the gardens. He wished there was somewhere he needed to be, somewhere that would provide a distraction – but there wasn't. He drew the letter Hyde had given him from his pocket and stared at it. Literally, just that. He'd looked at it so many times already, he knew it off by heart and had already assimilated the few clues it offered – the only useful ones being that it was written in an educated hand and in English. Now, however, he wasn't even really seeing it, let alone applying his brain. *Now* the only thought in his head was Athenais.

The moment he'd walked in and seen d'Auxerre man-handling her, he'd felt a gust of rage stronger than anything he'd ever known. In truth, it had been sheer bloodlust – and how he'd kept his hands off the bastard, he really didn't know. Everything inside him had screamed at him to rip the man limb from limb and then stamp upon the pieces. And when she'd told him about the dress, he'd wished he had.

This was bad. What he felt for her wasn't just a typical male reaction to an exceptionally beautiful woman. It wasn't simple or mild or transient ... and it certainly wasn't safe. He knew all the reasons that there couldn't be anything between them. God knew, he'd made all the arguments himself and could recite them to music. But he'd just proved, beyond all doubt, that neither his will-power nor his self-control were to be relied upon when he came within ten feet of her.

He'd been incredibly stupid. And feeble-minded. And self-indulgent. He shouldn't have kissed her. He'd known that perfectly well before he did it – and had done it anyway. He'd seen the path their conversation was taking and known what the pitfalls might be. He ought to have made his escape at the point when she asked why he hadn't kissed her that day in the hall. All he need have done was complete his exit line.

I feared what Madame Fleury might do to me. As I do again now. Goodbye.

Hindsight was a marvellous thing. It was a shame one didn't get it in advance.

But ...

Yes - exactly. *But.*

She'd melted against him and responded to his mouth as if she had waited all her life for him. She'd sighed his name and tangled her fingers in his hair and –

He hurriedly shut down that train of thought just as his body started to enjoy it. Instead, he attempted to focus on the worst aspect of the whole debacle. He was almost certain that what he felt for her, she – in part, at least – also felt for him. And even if, as yet, her feelings were confused and not quite recognised, she was still going to be hurt when he kept her at arms' length. As he clearly must.

So if she's not to become as besotted with you as you are with her, he told himself, *it would be a good idea if you stopped saving her from awkward situations and cuddling her afterwards. Unless you* want *her to know what* real *pain feels like?*

* * *

Since Francis had indeed left his one precious copy of *Ménage* with Froissart, Athenais was bereft of any distraction other than changing out of her damaged gown. Then she returned to the parlour and sat by the window, waiting for Ashley to come home. To her immense disappointment, he had still not re-appeared by the time she was due to leave for the theatre and so it was Major Langley who escorted both herself and Pauline through the streets.

262

If her mind hadn't been awash with other, more interesting images, she might have been entertained by the dialogue between her two companions.

'Having me play this part is a ridiculous idea,' grumbled Pauline.

'So you've said,' sighed Francis. 'Several times.'

'I don't know why I agreed to it.'

'But you *did* agree – as has Froissart.'

'And that's another thing. Was he drunk?'

'No. He just wants the play.'

'Of course he wants the play,' she snapped impatiently. 'But he can have it without me.'

Francis sent her a smug, glancing smile but said nothing.

Pauline stopped dead and hauled him round to face her.

'You devious *sod!* You made it a condition, didn't you? Just as you did with me. *Didn't you?*'

'Yes. And before you start ranting at me, allow me to inform you that it's a condition Froissart is extremely happy with.'

She eyed him explosively for a moment and then looked past his shoulder at Athenais.

'I don't know why *you're* laughing. This is a prime example of what I've always told you. Never trust a man. Cunning, conniving devils – every last one of them.'

'But not stupid,' grinned Athenais. And to Francis, 'Congratulations. Getting the great Fleury back on stage is quite an achievement.'

'Thank you.' He bowed slightly and started walking again.

'I'm off for most of the third act. If Froissart allows, can I read this play of yours?'

'Willingly.'

'Tell her she's not playing the wife,' said Pauline flatly.

'You're not playing the wife,' he informed Athenais obligingly. Then, to Pauline, 'Aside from the fact that Mademoiselle here is always in demand for meatier roles and my little *oeuvre* lasts about twenty minutes, why can't she play the wife?'

'Because it's perfect for Hortense Roget.'

Francis looked blank but Athenais said quickly, 'Hortense? But she's only any good at ... oh. The wife's a bitch?'

'That's one way of putting it.' Pauline slanted a glance up at Francis. 'Do you really *know* a woman like that?'

'Intimately.' The sapphire gaze hardened. 'As it happens, I have the misfortune to be related to two of them.'

Athenais opened her mouth, then closed it again.

Pauline had no such scruples. She said, 'Your sister? Lady Verney?'

'Also my mother, the Dowager Viscountess Wroxton.' He paused and then added, 'You heard what d'Auxerre said, Athenais – and it was true. My lady mother awards her favours frequently and entirely without discrimination. As for Celia ... she isn't married to Verney. She's married to a man who was once my closest friend – and who is still very much alive.' This time the pause was accompanied by a small, crooked smile. 'Every family has its skeletons, you see. And mine, you will understand, cause me to view marriage with a very jaundiced eye.'

* * *

At around the time Francis was escorting Athenais and Pauline to the theatre, Colonel Peverell paid a visit to the tavern from which Jem was watching Lucy Walter's house.

'Anything?' asked Ashley.

'Nothing new. The flash cove from Brussels was there till an hour ago – and the beau-trap with the yellow hair and the earring paid a call around noon.' Jem yawned. 'It'd help if we knew what we was looking for.'

'That is indisputably true. In the meantime, there was some trouble at our lodging earlier.'

Jem listened to a succinct version of the Marquis d'Auxerre's intrusion, then said, 'And you didn't slit his gizzard?'

'Not this time.'

Recognising what lay behind both eyes and voice, Jem nodded without any particular surprise. He knew – as he suspected Major Langley still did not – that behind the façade of Colonel Ashley Peverell lay The Falcon. And The Falcon was a different person altogether; a man extremely familiar with shadowy places and ruthless deeds. He said, 'Ah. Well, if he ends up as pie-meat, it'll be his own choice then.'

'My view exactly.' Ashley stood up. 'Do you want me to take over for the evening?'

'Nah. It's restful enough sitting here. And the serving wench has promised me supper. I reckon I'll bide a few more hours yet. And you needn't fret, Cap – Colonel. I ain't cupshot – nor likely to be. Not while I'm on watch.'

'I'm delighted to hear it.'

Jem grunted and then said, 'Don't look now – but the lady's at the open window on the left. Could be wrong, of course – but I reckon she's got her eye on you.'

'One would hope not – but let's see if you're right.' Replacing his hat, Ashley turned to leave, murmuring, 'If she turns to watch, give me a nod when I reach the corner.' And he strolled away.

At the end of the street, he paused as if deciding on his direction and glanced briefly over his shoulder. Jem nodded. He was also grinning, damn him.

Ashley turned left, out of sight of Lucy Walter's window. If she was indeed watching him watching her, either he'd been unforgivably careless or she was brighter than Charles had suggested. Whichever it was, he had no alternative but to leave all future surveillance to Jem.

The sky was growing darker now and he wasn't in any particular hurry as he zig-zagged his way through the narrow streets that led back to the Marais district. Having dragged his thoughts away from Athenais, he focussed his mind on Lucy Walter and the problem of how he was going to proceed if the next couple of days continued to produce as little useful information as the last few had done. He had no idea who he was looking for – an individual, a conspiracy or simply a thwarted lover. He also suspected that neither Charles nor Hyde had told him everything. The result was a time-consuming mess that he could well do without but which he couldn't just wash his hands of.

He was somewhere near the head of the Rue Simon when he realised that he was being followed. In one sense, this was mildly annoying. In another, it offered the possibility of working off some of his frustrations. He swung round a corner into the dim recesses of a gateway and retrieved the slim blade he kept in his boot. He was wearing his sword, of course … but, if it came to a fight, that wasn't the kind he wanted.

He stepped out again into the road and the light of someone's window. He walked on, silently now – and the footsteps followed him.

They were very light and belonged to only one person. Ashley relaxed. It was almost certainly a thief – but a very foolish one who thought to rob an armed man. D'Auxerre couldn't know where to find him now and, so far as he was aware, no one else had any reason to dog his footsteps. He mentally rifled through the various lanes and alleyways between the Rue Simon and the Rue des Rosiers and, having chosen the one that would suit both himself and a potential footpad best, he strolled on.

The point he'd selected came and went while his shadow remained just that – far enough back to keep him in sight but never close enough to be recognised.

At the foot of the steps of number sixteen, Ashley paused and waited.

At the nearest corner, the shadow also paused and watched.

So. Not a thief, he thought. Taking his time about it, he replaced the knife in his boot – sending a clear message to the shadow at the corner and causing it to melt away like smoke. *Nor an assassin, either. Something else, then. But what?*

Inside the house, he found Archie sitting just inside the kitchen from a place where he could see the hall. A hefty billet lay on the table beside him. As soon as Ashley appeared, he stood to attention and said, 'All's quiet, Colonel. And the Major's on escort duty.'

Ashley suppressed an involuntary grin. Archie was plainly taking his new status very seriously. All it needed was a salute. He said, 'Thank you, Sergeant. The ladies aren't back yet, then?'

'No, sir. Another hour it'll be.' He paused and then, a shade uncertainly, said, 'Got some mutton stew on the hob – if you should happen to fancy a bite.'

Tossing his hat and gloves down on the table, Ashley said he'd be delighted and was about to take a seat when his glance strayed to the hall and he noticed something that hadn't been there before. A folded piece of paper which had apparently been slipped under the door.

He walked over, picked it up and opened it out.

Monsieur,

I believe we may have met. If you would care to renew our acquaintance, you may call tomorrow at two in the afternoon.

Yrs.

Lucy Walter

Ashley was suddenly gripped with sardonic laughter. He'd been followed home because the woman wanted to send him an invitation. The only question was … an invitation to explain why he was watching her house or, given her reputation, to something very different indeed.

EIGHT

Any hopes Athenais had entertained about her future relationship with Colonel Peverell were soon dashed. In the days leading to the final week of rehearsal for *Mariamne*, he retreated behind a wall of impenetrable courtesy. He was perfectly pleasant and appeared utterly relaxed. He didn't openly avoid her but he made sure they were never alone. And when she tried to thank him for setting her father on the trail of long-lost sobriety, he merely replied that Archie was the one most deserving of congratulation. Within forty-eight hours, Athenais wanted to hit him.

Occasionally catching a certain gleam in her eyes, Ashley was perfectly well-aware that his love was both confused and irritated – and equally well-aware that there was nothing he could do about it. As for his *billet-doux* from Lucy Walter, he decided that it would be stupid to visit her at a time of her choosing when he didn't know what she wanted or who might be lying in wait. Consequently, he let the matter lie for three days until Jem – who was finding the potential situation a lot funnier than Ashley thought necessary – assured him that the lady was free of other callers.

'She's after your body, you lucky bugger,' grinned Jem. 'But if you ain't up for it, I'll be ready and willing to help you out.'

'Shut up,' muttered Ashley. 'I'm only doing this in case it becomes necessary to do a little house-breaking. So keep your witticisms to yourself and your eyes peeled for other visitors.'

Luckily, the maidservant who admitted him wasn't the one he'd bribed to tell him which rooms belonged to Mistress Walter. And then the lady herself was rising from her chair to greet him with a mixture of flirtation and reproof.

'Well, Monsieur. I had quite given you up,' she said in passable but not very fluent French. 'Did I not invite you some days ago?'

'A thousand pardons, Madame.' Deciding to find out whether or not she knew his nationality, Ashley answered her in the same language. 'I was desolate to disappoint you but, sadly, I was unavoidably detained on that day.' With an elegant bow, he offered the small posy he'd bought from a street-seller. 'I can only hope you'll forgive me.'

Lucy accepted the flowers with a slight inclination of her head and a coquettish smile. 'Perhaps I may do so, sir. But first you must give me your name. I am convinced that we have met before – but I am at a loss to recall when and where.'

Concluding that she wouldn't be struggling on in French if she knew he was English, Ashley switched languages and said, 'Colonel Ashley Peverell, Madame – and entirely at your service. As for a previous meeting ... I believe it was some time ago at the Louvre. And to my everlasting sorrow, we were never formally introduced.'

'Oh.' For an instant, she looked completely nonplussed. 'You're English. I – I hadn't realised. A member of the court-in-exile, I suppose?'

He shrugged. 'A mere hanger-on to the fringes, I'm afraid. Impoverished ex-soldiers are in plentiful supply and of no great use at present.'

Relief crossed her face.

'So you aren't closely-acquainted with the King?'

'Barely at all,' he lied. And, summoning the kind of smile that usually softened even the stiffest female backbone, added, 'Of course, I am aware that you have the inestimable distinction of being the mother of His Majesty's son. I hope young James is well?'

'Perfectly well – and being cared for in Rotterdam.' She took a chair by the hearth and indicated that Ashley should take the one facing it. 'You must think me very forward, Colonel. But I truly thought --'

'Please!' he said earnestly. 'I am immeasurably honoured to be here and to be meeting you in person at last. It isn't an opportunity for which I'd ever dared hope.'

Her answering smile was a masterpiece of discreet invitation.

'Then I shall ask my girl to bring wine so that we may become better acquainted.'

Rising, she opened the door and called to her maid. Ashley used the time to conduct a swift appraisal of the room. It might have been elegant had it not been for the plethora of assorted knick-knacks that littered every available surface – presumably gifts from besotted admirers. However, the only item of furniture that interested him was a small table-top writing desk with the usual lockable cavity for correspondence. One look at the key-hole was enough to tell him that opening it would be the work of less than two minutes.

Then Lucy was back and sinking gracefully into her chair. Ashley reflected that you couldn't really blame Charles. She was an exceptionally beautiful woman. It was little wonder she had fellows tripping over themselves for a taste of her favours. Long-lashed eyes of vivid blue, clouds of glossy raven hair and a mouth that would tempt a saint. If his own heart hadn't lain elsewhere, it might even have tempted him. As it was, he sincerely hoped she wasn't expecting him to do more than kiss her hand.

They drank wine and she asked him about himself – though he suspected she wasn't especially interested which made it easy to keep his replies both vague and brief. A little later, dabbing at her eyes with a lace-edged handkerchief, she revealed that she did not dare have her darling boy to live with her in Paris as she was convinced that the King would kidnap him.

'Since our ways have parted,' she finished sorrowfully, 'Charles has not been kind, you know. I truly believe that he would take our son from me if he could.'

Ashley thought that might well be true. Lucy's lovers and her habit of enacting embarrassing scenes didn't exactly make her the ideal mother. And though young James might have been born on the wrong side of the blanket, it was a *royal* blanket.

Ashley sympathised and flattered and gave every appearance of being wholly dazzled. And when he rose to leave, found himself being offered her hands, her cheek and a further invitation to take supper with her one evening. He did his duty by the first two and side-stepped the last by pleading business that would once again take him from Paris for an indeterminate length of time.

Lucy pouted a little, allowed herself to be restored to dimpled smiles and finally let him escape. Ashley left the house with a feeling of relief, shot a baleful scowl across the road at Jem and, checking that he wasn't being followed this time, strode off for the Louvre and a word or two with Sir Edward Hyde.

* * *

Four days later, he returned to the Rue des Rosiers after an hour's fencing practice with the King to find Celia Maxwell ensconced in the parlour with Pauline and Athenais. Celia was tapping an impatient foot; Athenais was turning a small cake into crumbs; and Pauline looked thunderous. None of them showed any sign of indulging in conversation.

As soon as she spied Ashley, Celia stood up and said crossly in English, 'At last. I've been waiting here for an hour. Perhaps *you* can tell me where Francis has got to?'

Like Pauline and Athenais, Ashley knew precisely where Francis had got to – and how long he was likely to stay there. But since this information had so far plainly been withheld, he said blandly, 'No. I'm afraid I can't.'

'But surely you must have *some* idea?'

'Not the sort of idea that Francis would appreciate my passing on to his sister.'

Athenais stopped torturing her cake and gave him a look that said, *My. And aren't you the clever one?* Then, because she was tired of being polite, she favoured Pauline with a low-voiced translation. Madame Fleury hastily turned a snort of laughter into a cough.

Celia scowled at them but kept her guns trained on Ashley.

'You needn't hold back on my account. I assure you, my sensibilities are not so delicate.'

'So we've 'eard,' muttered Athenais.

'I *beg* your pardon?'

'Nuffin.'

Ashley had always known her English must be execrable but it was the first time he'd heard her use it. Somehow managing to suppress a choke of laughter and stepping nobly into the breach, he said, 'As Madame and Mademoiselle have doubtless already explained, there are any number of places your brother might be.'

'I'm sure you could help me if you chose to do so.'

'No. Francis and I are not joined at the hip.' His expression became somewhat less amicable. 'Also, you must forgive me if I tell you that I dislike being called a liar.'

'I didn't do so!'

'No? I beg your pardon. I must have misunderstood.'

Celia flushed.

'I can see that I am wasting my time here. If it's not *too* much to ask, perhaps you will tell Francis that I called and that I wish him to wait on me as soon as possible – preferably today.'

'If and when I see him, I will be delighted to do so,' agreed Ashley. And then, 'Allow me to see you to the door. I'm sure the ladies will excuse you.'

It was Celia's turn to mutter. 'Ladies? *Ha!*'

By the time Ashley returned to the parlour, Athenais and Pauline were pink with laughter.

'*Ha!*' said Pauline cheerfully. 'Pot calling kettle and other similar clichés. She's perfectly awful, isn't she? And Francis, bless his heart, has put it all into his play.'

'Why didn't you tell her he's at the theatre?' asked Ashley.

'Partly,' she replied, rising to remove the plate of uneaten cakes, 'because the woman put my back up in the first two minutes; but mainly because he wouldn't want me to.'

On her way to the door, she passed Ashley who took the opportunity to filch a pastry and then, grimacing, swallowed it wholesale.

'Ugh! Almond paste. Disgusting!'

'Serves you right,' grinned Pauline. She selected a tiny lemon tart and popped it into his mouth. 'To take the taste away. What does she want with Francis?'

He took his time with the tart. Then, 'Ask him. It's not for me to say.'

'Quite right,' she approved. And left the room, humming.

Ashley suddenly realised that he was alone with Athenais for the first time since he'd kissed her. One look at her face told him that she was having exactly the same thought – and had no more idea of how to deal with it than he had himself.

In desperation, she said baldly, 'Since Francis is at the theatre, shouldn't you be there also?'

'Yes. I'm late. I was fencing with the King and lost track of the time. But this shirt – though no longer clean – is my only decent one so I didn't want to risk Etienne slashing it by mistake. His enthusiasm carries him away at times.'

She looked at him curiously and, ignoring the latter part of his speech, said, 'Do you often fight with your King?'

'Not often. Just when he requires it.'

'Is he any good?'

'Moderately so.' He paused, smiling faintly. 'I gather the Marquis hasn't visited the theatre recently?'

She shook her head. 'He's away – according to that effete friend of his, Henri de Vauvallon, on some business of the Cardinal's. That may or may not be true. One never knows.'

'No. He doesn't strike me as the type to be happy being used as an errand-boy – unless it served some purpose of his own,' came the thoughtful reply. Then, 'I'd better change my shirt and go. Francis will be tearing his hair out.'

'Of course. He can't *possibly* manage without you at his elbow, can he?' she retorted acidly. 'And it would be a shame if you and I were to exchange more than half a dozen commonplace remarks.'

Something clenched in his gut. He thought, *It would be worse if I let you drag everything into the open by putting it into words.* But he kept his expression perfectly relaxed and said politely, 'I'm sorry. Was there something you wanted to discuss?'

Yes – you stupid man. I want to know whether you only kissed me because I asked you to – or whether it meant anything to you. Closing one hand hard over the other, she said, 'You don't think we have anything to say to one another?'

'Specifically and right now? No. I don't believe so.'

'I see.' *You're going to keep on doing this, aren't you? Retreating behind a stone wall of perfect manners while you pretend you don't know what I mean. And there's nothing I can do to stop you without completely humiliating myself.* 'My mistake, then.'

He knew better to ask her what she meant which left little alternative than to say impassively, 'It would seem so. And now I really must go.'

'Then go.' She gave a slight, dismissive shrug and, though she refrained from voicing her thought, didn't bother to veil her expression.

Ashley read it without difficulty and he smiled wryly in response.

'You find me impossible? Quite.' And, as he turned to leave, 'Unfortunately, that isn't likely to change.'

* * *

During the final week before the opening of *Mariamne*, rehearsals of all kinds took place on the floor of the auditorium while the stage was readied for performance. Sets were painted and then assembled on runners or attached to a complex series of pulleys; flash-pans were cunningly inserted and fused to provide the explosive effects Froissart was demanding; clouds were suspended on wires ready to be lowered when needed and great metal sheets took up residence in the wings, waiting to provide the rumble of thunder or clamour of distant battle.

Pauline spent nearly every waking hour overseeing the seamstresses working on costumes, players walked round muttering to themselves or gathered in corners, in spare moments between full rehearsal, to work on bits of script and Ashley's swordsmen went over and over the routines he had set until their sweat could be smelled ten paces away.

Francis, outfitted as an armoured knight, was in his element.

Ashley, when he finally stopped laughing, said he looked like a lobster.

Francis agreed that he felt like one.

Athenais grew increasingly cross with herself for not being able to keep her eyes off Ashley, blade in hand and the epitome of athletic grace in his shirt-sleeves. She also found it intensely annoying that, since the start of combined rehearsals, virtually every other lady in the company was doing the same. They flirted with Francis because he flirted back. But they sighed over Ashley because, though he was invariably pleasant, his exquisite manners created a distance that rendered him unattainable – and thus increased his attraction.

Meanwhile, the days sped by like sand in a glass.

By the opening night, having sat through three dress-and-technical rehearsals, Ashley knew more about the internal workings of the theatre than he'd ever wanted to but he still elected to watch the play from the wings. He told himself that he was there to see how Etienne and the others performed under fire – and what the audience thought of a properly-constructed fight sequence. It wasn't true, of course. He wanted to watch Athenais.

Held back by a pair of jewelled combs, her hair flowed down her back in a torrent of gleaming curls that made his fingers itch; the gown of midnight-blue brocade moulded every curve of her diminutive figure and revealed an expanse of creamy skin that made his mouth water; and expert use of cosmetics rendered her eyes hypnotic and her lips seductive enough to make his body tighten. In short, merely looking at her was subtle torture.

Before her first entrance, she remained a little apart from the other players. Her thoughts appeared to be turned inward and she took long, measured breaths whilst shaking her hands loose at the wrist. In the preceding days, he'd been aware of her watching him work. Now she didn't even seem to know he was there. Every atom of concentration was focussed on what she was about to do and every distraction was firmly shut out. She looked like a soldier in the last moments before a battle. Ashley retreated into the shadows. She did not need him now.

When at last she stepped out upon the stage, the house greeted her with enthusiasm and then fell silent. Witnessing her performance at closer quarters than usual, Ashley was aware of nuances he'd never noticed before. He saw how her expression softened when she touched Etienne Lepreux's cheek ... how her breath seemed to catch when he put his arm about her ... how she all but melted into his body when they kissed. She really was an incredible actress, thought Ashley. It really looked as though she meant it.

Perhaps she does, said a nasty little demon in his head. *Then again, she was like that with you, wasn't she? If it isn't real now, it may not have been real then. Since she's so good at pretending, how could any man ever be sure that she's sincere?*

The whole thing was beginning to threaten his sanity and make him wonder what in hell was wrong with him. In his entire life, his wits had never been so scrambled over a woman. But right now the question of distinguishing truth from illusion had him clenching his fists until they ached.

The pyrotechnical effects drew gasps from the audience and then coughs and sneezes as the auditorium became wreathed in smoke. The comic fight in the second act provoked gales of laughter and good-humoured catcalls and the more violent one in Act Four finished on a storm of applause.

Exiting the stage, Etienne slapped Ashley on the shoulder and said, 'Thank you, Colonel. That felt ... it actually felt good.'

'You did well,' nodded Ashley. 'All three of you.'

Detaching himself from his corner, he passed Francis murmuring, 'Have fun. Doubtless you'll escort the ladies home?' And, leaving by the stage-door, he made his way out into the cold, night air. He'd seen the last act three times already and, knowing what was in it, had absolutely no wish to see it a fourth. His guts were churning enough as it was.

NINE

Thinking that a walk might be the best cure for his mental state, he decided to make a detour to find out if Jem had any new information. If he hadn't, Ashley reflected, there was really no point in continuing the surveillance.

A brief, specific whistle brought Jem ambling down to the corner where he waited out of sight of Mistress Walter's windows.

'A new face tonight,' grunted Jem. 'Been in there a while, an' all.'

'He's still there?'

'Aye. Tall fellow with an eye-patch.'

Ashley frowned. 'Hair?'

'Dark. Black, most likely. And lots of it.' He waited expectantly and then, when the Colonel said nothing, 'You going to wait to see him for yourself?'

'No.' The frown intensified. 'If it's who I think it is, he lives in the Rue des Minimes – near the Hôtel des Vaux. Follow him when he leaves and let me know as soon as you can. Tonight, if possible.'

'Want to give me a name, Colonel?'

'Not until I've made some further enquiries,' came the clipped reply. 'Just do as I've asked, will you?' And he walked away.

Ashley wasn't more than a street away when he realised that he was being followed. Again. Only this time, it wasn't just one pair of feet – it was at least three; and, though they were taking some care to be quiet, all of them were wearing boots. He loosened his sword in its sheath, paused briefly in the shadows of a doorway to take out his knife and then strode on in the general direction of the Rue des Rosiers.

He was making what he'd hoped would be a discreet detour between two high-walled gardens when a figure stepped out in front of him, swiftly followed by a second one. He knew immediately that they were not thieves. He also knew that they weren't there simply to hurt him. If you wanted to give someone a beating, you sent fellows with muscles and big sticks. Even in the fitful light of the courtyard, he could tell that his potential assailants were well-dressed and carrying swords. So ... a killing matter, then.

'Damn,' breathed Ashley. And then, as a third man materialised away to his left, 'Double damn.'

Dealing with two men was viable – dealing with three, less so. If all of them rushed him at once ... but they wouldn't, he thought. He hoped. One of them was in charge and would want his moment of glory. The others would only join in if Monsieur Watch-Me-Be-A-Hero's attack looked likely to fail. That meant he needed to disable the fellow very fast and very thoroughly if he was to stand any chance of getting past the other two. His gaze swept over the space around him, taking in the fact that it narrowed to half-width where the third man lounged against the wall and that, between himself and where the other two stood, a gnarled tree-branch overhung one of the walls. Finally, on the far side of the courtyard, a flight of narrow steps curled up to he knew not where – which wasn't likely to be particularly useful.

The man to his left couldn't see the knife in his right hand and was probably expecting him to draw his sword. Moreover, decided Ashley, that insolent pose spoke of over-confidence. He'd seen that kind of idiocy more times than he could count. Young fellows who'd learned their swordsmanship in the best schools and were full of bravado without ever sparing a thought about what they might be up against. This one clearly didn't know that his provocative attitude was an open invitation.

I could throw the knife. I can take him down from here.

But if he did that, the other two would be upon him before he could retrieve his blade and, for a number of reasons, he wanted it back. So keeping the knife hidden against his thigh, he strolled in seemingly idle fashion towards the would-be-hero, saying, 'Were you looking for me in particular – or would anyone be fair game?'

The man detached himself from the wall, drew his sword and took a couple of steps forward. 'I'd say that's likely to be the least of your worries.'

Mentally measuring the distance and bunching his muscles ready to spring, Ashley halted at a precisely calculated spot.

'What worries?' he asked. And threw the knife with deadly accuracy.

It took the would-be assassin straight through his Adam's apple. His face registered surprise and his knees buckled; but, before he hit the ground, Ashley was on him, wrenching the knife free with his left hand, pulling his sword screaming from its sheath and swinging round to face the other two men.

They were already bearing down on him but their pace slowed as they realised just how easily he'd despatched their comrade. One of them appeared to have half an ostrich cascading from his hat; the other's coat was adorned with the kind of elaborate floral embroidery usually favoured by women. Any professional assassin, reflected Ashley distantly, would laugh himself silly.

His own smile cold and hard, he said, 'Your choice, gentlemen. You can still walk away.'

'And you can still die,' spat Feather-head. Then, without bothering to alert his companion, he moved straight into the attack.

Ashley parried the first blow and side-stepped the second so as to put the wall behind him before the other man could join in the fray. Then the fight exploded in earnest.

Using both sword and knife along with a good deal of physical dexterity, he managed to keep his attackers at bay whilst mentally evaluating both their skill and his options. As far as the latter were concerned, he didn't have many. Running wasn't possible – and he wouldn't have done it anyway. He wanted one of these fellows either *hors de combat* or permanently out of the game – it didn't matter which – and the other on the ground facing the point of his sword so he could ask the obvious question.

These young gallants weren't here on their own account. Someone had sent them. Although he'd made various discreet enquiries regarding both Hyde's letter and Lucy Walter, none were so far likely to have occasioned a serious desire for his demise - which left only one likely choice. The Marquis bloody d'Auxerre who, Ashley suspected, would be delighted to see his head on a pike.

He twisted to avoid a vicious slash to his left hand and swept his blade in a gleaming arc to push the other man back. Steel clamoured against steel, hissing and slithering in a wild *accelerando*. It was time to get serious and to stop using his brain for any function other than keeping himself alive.

In two extremely fast and complex moves, he forced one assailant back in order to avoid a slash that would have severed his hamstring and, pivoting, delivered a single, hard kick to the other's sword-hand. It worked but not as well as he'd hoped. He succeeded in temporarily disarming Feather-head but failed to completely dodge a clumsy lunge from Monsieur Fleur. Cold steel pierced his left arm just above the elbow and, for a moment, pain took his breath. Blood started to flow down towards his hand but he kept a firm grip on the knife.

Feather-head was already sweeping around in search of his blade. Luckily, it had landed several yards away near the spiral steps. Ashley calculated that if, as he'd intended, his boot had struck the precise point on the wrist which rendered its owner's hand useless, he had about a minute of one-on-one fighting to bring the pretty fellow down. Without wasting a second of it, he launched a fierce, driving attack with both knife and sword that gave his opponent no opportunity to do more than attempt to defend himself as he retreated. His mouth set in a hard line and not taking his eyes off the man's face for an instant, Ashley completed a series of moves that gave him the opening his wanted. Deflecting the enemy blade with a savage parry, he drove his own deep into Monsieur Fleur's right shoulder at the spot that would disable his arm, whilst simultaneously hooking his feet from under him. The man howled and dropped like a stone. His hat rolled away across the cobbles, revealing bright, almost too-blond hair and the traitorous wink of a diamond in his ear.

Ashley made the connection but hadn't time to think about. The bastard wasn't going to die any time soon, so he'd question him later. Meanwhile ... he swivelled, just in time to deflect the sword-point that was about to be driven into his back.

Bloody hell, he thought, trying to recover his breath and feeling stickiness on the fingers holding the knife. *Persistent, aren't they?*

Feather-head lunged. Ashley parried, produced a clever and little known riposte and glided out of the way. Feather-head charged again, grunting. Ashley responded with a swift counter-exchange. Then, allowing the blades to tangle, he locked them together, bringing Feather-head within easy range of the knife. Feeling the sharp, slender point piercing the side of his coat just beneath the second rib, the man came to an abrupt halt, his gaze frozen like that of a rabbit in the light.

Ashley never killed by accident or if he didn't have to. Feather-head's current position was such that he couldn't do a damned thing to defend himself. Consequently, Ashley was just about to end the bout by inflicting serious but non-fatal pain when there was a tell-tale scrape of metal … and Feather-head hissed, 'Henri – *now!*'

Withdrawing the knife a fraction, Ashley smashed his knee into the fellow's groin and pivoted at the same moment – but he was a second too late. Even as Feather-head howled and went down clutching his balls, a sword was thrust deep into his own thigh and withdrawn with such excruciatingly savage clumsiness that he lost both his balance and all sense of what he was doing. His sword clattered to the ground and he dropped involuntarily on to his good knee on the cobbles. He tried to think past the blinding agony but, before he could gather himself, a boot smacked into the back of his skull, sending him down on his face. Henri, he supposed hazily, had found his blade; and, since his right arm was paralysed at the shoulder, he was using his left. Badly.

Groping for his own sword-hilt but failing to find it, Ashley rolled over just in time to see Henri poised to take another wild stab at him. There wasn't much he could do but he tried anyway, instinctively twisting to one side to avoid the blade and bringing up his knees in preparation to ram his feet into Henri's stomach. He escaped the second thrust by mere inches but the attempt to use his legs sent pain screaming through his entire body. His vision blurred, then darkened on the image of Henri coming at him again.

And, as he felt himself sliding towards oblivion, he thought, *Now? God has a sense of humour after all.*

ENTR'ACTE
London – October 1652

Colonel Maxwell contemplated the three letters lying on his desk.

The first had arrived in early September and consisted of gossip and an offer – in return for a substantial sum of money – to furnish Secretary Thurloe with proof that the young king in exile had married his mistress. The rumour was an old one and, in Eden's view, unlikely to be true. As for the gossip, most of it would already have been reported by their own agents – and this letter was clearly *not* from one of their own agents. A single glance at the code, a basic binary so simple a child could crack it and certainly not one of his, had told him that. But he'd dutifully deciphered it and asked Thomas Scot what he wanted done about it.

'For five hundred pounds? Nothing,' had been the blunt reply. 'The fellow must have windmills in his head. Offer him fifty. Or, better still, send somebody reliable to deal with it – if you take my meaning. Whatever the man's got is probably a forgery anyway.'

So Eden had sent Sergeant Trotter to a tavern in Deptford with a terse reply, two troopers and certain unorthodox orders. Three days later, the sergeant returned with a paper documenting the marriage of one Charles Stuart to Lucy Walter at St. Germain-en-Laye in September, 1649 and the information that the man from whom he'd acquired it was merely a go-between. The latter was no surprise. As for the document, despite the most careful scrutiny, neither Scot nor Eden could reach any conclusion about its authenticity. Secretary Thurloe was informed of its existence, Scot filed it away for future reference and Eden dismissed the matter from his mind.

A month later, another very different letter arrived. As soon as he saw it, Eden had the annoying feeling that there was something he ought to remember but couldn't. Inevitably, it brought him to assume that there must be a connection with the other – only to realise very quickly that there wasn't. The handwriting was completely different and this time the code was a good deal more sophisticated.

The question was, whose code was it? It wasn't one of those Eden himself devised and changed on a bi-monthly basis and neither, he was fairly sure, was it a Royalist one.

The Royalists liked inserting numbers to represent names of people and places; and Sir Edward Hyde had at least one extremely able cryptographer who'd developed another system altogether which had taken Eden the best part of two days to break and given him the most fun he'd had at work for some considerable time. He'd been tempted to send the fellow a note of congratulation but, in the end, common-sense had prevailed. He'd simply passed the translated contents – a warning to Hyde from Edward Massey that the loyalty of a supposed Royalist agent newly arrived in Paris was suspect - on to Thomas Scot. Scot, of course, knew as well as Eden did that Colonel Massey was absolutely right. Joseph Bampfield had been released from the Tower on very specific conditions at around the same time Massey himself had escaped from it.

None of which had anything to do with the second letter which Eden had chosen to withhold from both Scot and Thurloe. Though its contents suggested that it had come from one of their own agents, the business of the code suggested otherwise. There was one simple rule for watertight espionage – and this fellow was breaking it. So, since he wasn't one of Scot's spies, the writer was either a freebooter of questionable reliability or Secretary Thurloe had his own irons in the fire. The letter alluded to a possible plot which would *permanently resolve, root and branch, the causes of future civil unrest and political disturbance*. It also stated that discreet measures were already being set in place and these could be activated when the order was given.

The implications inherent in the report had worried Eden enough to hold on to it while he attempted, without success, to discover its author. He knew he ought to pass it on but the suspicion of what a so-called 'permanent resolution' might entail stayed his hand. And thus the letter had remained safely locked in his desk … until this morning when, wedged between a pair of urgent demands for naval supplies from Admiral Blake, the third one had arrived.

The latest letter was in the same hand as the previous one and used the same code. It was also explicit.

Eden's brain recoiled instinctively from a plot that was both evil and unnecessary. It also told him that he was not meant to know about it and that the letters – presumably part of a larger correspondence – had somehow arrived on his desk by mistake. In one sense, he was glad that Thurloe's system wasn't entirely error-proof as yet. In another, he wished he hadn't become privy to information which – one way or another – he couldn't just ignore.

He considered his options. He could burn the report and feign ignorance; he could give the ciphered original to either Scot or Thurloe and pretend he hadn't decoded it; or he could follow his immediate inclination and interfere. The first was cowardly, the second, risky and the last one well-nigh impossible if he didn't want to be labelled a double-agent.

It would have been helpful, he reflected, if he could have discussed his suspicions with either Major-General Lambert or Gabriel Brandon. But, having refused to fill Ireton's vacant shoes in Ireland, Lambert had temporarily retired to his estates and Gabriel hadn't set foot in London since the late King's execution. Both of them were totally out of reach in Yorkshire.

Eden read and re-read the newest despatch until its words were etched on the back of his skull. But no matter how hard he tried, he couldn't change his first conclusion for something more palatable ... and no amount of watered wine sweetened the sour taste in his mouth.

* * *

He arrived back in Cheapside to find Deborah setting the final stitches to the new shirt she had promised him. Laying her sewing aside, she rose, smiling and said, 'You're later than usual. And your face tells me that you've had a trying day.'

'Something like that.'

'Have you eaten?'

'No.' The room smelled of herbs and something else that he couldn't identify. For the first time in hours, his mind started to settle. It might have been that soothing aroma – except that he knew it wasn't. He said slowly, 'But at the moment I don't particularly want food.'

'Ah.' She took a couple of steps towards him, watching the acute tension he'd brought into the room with him turn into focus of a different sort. 'Something else, then?'

'Yes. I think ... yes.' He smiled, feeling the familiar tightening of his body as she came closer still. 'Definitely something else.'

Reaching out, Deborah trailed light fingertips along the thin, white scar on his cheek, always more prominent when he was troubled, and on down his arm until she could take his hand.

'Come, then. Nicholas is out, supper will keep ... and the cares of your day will wait for an hour.'

'An hour?' he murmured with a flicker of humour as she drew him towards the door. 'You have a flattering idea of my stamina.'

'No. I have a very precise idea of what you can offer me. And I won't settle for less.'

'Ah. Then I'd better apply myself thoroughly, hadn't I?'

She tossed a smile over her shoulder.

'Don't you always?'

Inside his room, Eden closed the door and set his arms about her, breathing in her own particular scent. Sliding her hands into his hair, Deborah pulled his face down and nipped gently at his lower lip. He gave a low rumble of approval and captured her mouth with his own while she pushed his coat aside and tugged at the collar of his shirt, seeking his skin. He broke the kiss long enough to say on a small laugh, 'Keep that up and this will be over in five minutes.'

She sighed and licked his throat.

'No. It will take longer than that for you to get my clothes off.'

'Not necessarily. But on this occasion ... perhaps.'

And, spinning her round, he grazed her neck with his teeth while his fingers sought the laces of her gown.

Slowly, enticingly, he unlaced, unhooked and untied until the floor around them was littered with her garments and Deborah wore nothing but her stockings. Eden surveyed her from head to foot, his eyes hot and intense, and said, 'God. You look so unbelievably erotic, there's probably a law against it.'

Her breathing light and rapid, she said, 'Or soon will be. My turn now.'

Eden's clothes disappeared rather more quickly in between deep, hungry kisses. And finally he was able to pull her close, flesh to flesh, his arousal hard and eager against her.

They tumbled to the bed in a tangle of limbs, their hands and mouths avid for each other. She stroked the lines and muscles of his arms, shoulders and back, sobbing his name when he teased her breasts with his tongue. This was a delight that never failed them because at the core of the conflagration was mutual generosity – purely instinctive on his part, driven by love on hers.

She was warm and willing and acutely responsive. Eden treasured every moan and gasp, every ragged breath and tremor ... all of them fuelling his own already fierce desire. He knew the extent of her pleasure now; he knew how to send her soaring and how to keep her there, helpless with passion. And when he finally joined with her, the rhythm of their loving was always perfectly, effortlessly in tune.

Some time later, lying with her head pillowed on his shoulder, he said lazily, 'You always know what I need. How is that?'

'I know when you are worried. Because of the nature of your work, I also know better than to ask you to talk about it. So I find other ways to help. Sometimes simple conversation over food, sometimes a glass or two of wine ... sometimes, this.'

She made it sound as though it was merely a matter of intuition, allied to trial-and-error. As ever, Eden suspected that there was more to it and, as ever, preferred to retain an element of doubt. He said, 'For future reference, you should know that 'this' would always be my personal choice.'

She slid her foot up his calf. 'Mine, too.'

'I noticed.' And then laughed when she bit his shoulder.

* * *

Eden arose the following morning with a possible course of action in mind but loath to implement it until he'd taken the time to thoroughly contemplate the possible ramifications. He was also busier than usual with meetings outside his normal province.

The last couple of months had seen General Fleetwood sent to Ireland in Lambert's place and eventually, the drafting of an Act of Settlement for that beleaguered country. A commercial treaty had come into force between England and – amazingly, in most people's view – Spain, under which England was to receive payment for intervening in the Franco-Spanish war; and meanwhile, as the Dutch War drifted indecisively on, Denmark had demonstrated its disapproval of the Commonwealth by throwing its support behind the other side.

Finally, on November 18th, due to Admiral Blake's frenzied insistence that he couldn't continue to prosecute the war without increased victualing and re-fitting of damaged ships, the Parliament passed a Confiscation Bill for six hundred Royalist properties in order to raise the necessary funds. Then, before the dust had settled on that, came news that Cardinal Mazarin had finally given in and formally recognised the Commonwealth.

Though he understood the need for money, Eden didn't consider the Confiscation Bill any help in uniting the country. As for Mazarin … well, words came cheap and weren't likely to amount to anything more than lip-service.

Eden reached a decision about the plot letters and embarked on the appropriate preparations. It was while he was making painstaking copies of the coded originals that a bizarre notion struck him. In order to avoid awkward questions, he waited until Thomas Scot left for a meeting with the Secretary. Then he removed the marriage lines from Lucy Walter's dossier and laid them on his own desk alongside the letters.

Well, now, he murmured to himself. *That's interesting. And odd. But not, unfortunately, madly helpful.*

* * *

Once back in Cheapside, he told Deborah he wanted an hour of complete privacy. Then he asked Nicholas Austin to join him in the parlour.

Nicholas registered the Colonel's unusually grim expression and said, 'Something's wrong?'

'I believe so.' Eden stared searchingly into the other man's face and hoped he wasn't making a huge mistake. He said flatly, 'I need your help. But I also need to be very sure that I can trust you. Can I?'

'Yes.' The answer was immediate and utterly positive. 'I owe you my life and my freedom. If there's something I can do to repay you for that, you have only to ask.'

Eden drew a long, steadying breath.

'Very well, then. I want you to take some information to Francis Langley.'

Whatever Nicholas had been expecting, it certainly wasn't that. He opened his mouth, closed it again and finally said weakly, 'Oh. I'm beginning to see what you meant about trust.'

'No. As yet, you have no idea.' He gestured to a chair. 'You'd better sit down. I've thought long and hard about this. The information you'll be carrying is highly sensitive. Consequently, it's too dangerous for you to have anything on your person that could be found if you were stopped. So I'm going to tell you what I believe is afoot and show you certain documents in my possession by way of proof of my suspicions – and you are going to remember it all, word for word. Clear, so far?'

Nicholas nodded. 'Yes. But do you know where Francis is?'

'Sixteen, Rue des Rosiers, Paris. I'm assuming that he'll trust you. But so that there will be no doubt in his mind, I'll give you a letter for him. It's one he's been expecting for some time, regarding a personal matter and I'll include – albeit in oblique terms – an instruction for him to take you seriously.' Eden paused and then added dryly, 'Not, when I explain what this is all about, that there's likely to be any problem with that. If it wasn't a bloody disgrace, I wouldn't be involving myself in it at all.'

'This all sounds somewhat ... alarming.'

'That's putting it mildly.' Eden perched on the corner of his desk and said, 'I've come across information by accident. Information I'm not supposed to have. In a nutshell, there's a plot to lure Charles Stuart and his brother James to the coast of France in order to assassinate them.'

For a long moment, Nicholas simply stared at him. Then, plainly at a loss for anything more articulate, he said feebly. 'Oh. God. You're sure?'

'As sure as I can be. It's vicious, pointless and will create more problems than it solves. Worse still, for God knows what reason, it has official backing.' Eden passed over the de-coded version of the October letter and then, when Nicholas looked up frowning, handed him the more recent one. 'As you can see, whoever this man in France is, he seems to have most of his pieces on the right squares – and, if he hasn't, he soon will have. I've done my best to discover his identity but without success – and I have no further avenues open to me. I can't prevent this atrocity from here and I haven't any valid excuse for leaving the country. I can, on the other hand, supply you with a travelling pass. You and

Francis may not be able to stop it but you can make sure that Charles is warned.'

Nicholas looked up from the letter and said thoughtfully, 'There's Ashley, too.'

'Who?'

'Colonel Peverell. I told you about him once. What I *didn't* say was that the King has a pretty high regard for him and that he ... well, from time to time, he undertakes what you might call specialist missions.'

'You mean he's an intelligence agent?'

'Of a sort,' shrugged Nicholas uncomfortably. 'If Francis is in Paris, it may be that Ashley is with him. And he'll know what to do.'

'Only if he's less inept than his fellow agents,' said Eden caustically.

'He isn't inept at all.'

'That's a relief. If the ones I know about were any good, I wouldn't be able to name them.'

Nicholas eyed him in silence for a moment and then said slowly, 'You're taking a big risk with this. If your knowledge or the use you're making of it comes to light, Cromwell will have you in the Tower and under interrogation quicker than you can spit.'

'I know. Which is why you and Francis and Colonel Peverell are going to take every precaution to keep my name out of it. My guess would be that the fellow at the head of this conspiracy has reasonable access to Charles. If that's so, you'll need to be very wary whom you trust. And if you need an example of that ... we intercepted a message from Colonel Massey, warning Ned Hyde not to rely on a former Royalist agent by the name of Bampfield. Hyde needs that information because it's true. And supplying it will help cement your credentials.' Eden paused and then added, 'You can also tell him that we have a copy of Charles's marriage lines.'

'*What?* His Majesty is married? To whom?'

'Supposedly, to his one-time mistress, Lucy Walter. Except that he probably isn't.'

'I don't understand.'

'Neither do I, entirely. Suffice it to say that I'm fairly certain the marriage certificate and those letters – which I will now have back, if you please – were written by the same person. Ergo, the certificate is a forgery.'

Nicholas blew out his cheeks, his brain reeling.

'This is beginning to seem just the tiniest bit complicated.' He stood up. 'All right. How soon do I leave?'

'Hopefully, on tomorrow's evening tide. I'll have the pass for you by then ... and my letter to Francis.'

He nodded. 'And is there anything else – anything that might help us find the assassin?'

Eden's brows rose. 'Us?'

'Well, yes. You didn't think I'd simply hand all this over to Francis and Ashley, then take the next ship back here, did you?'

'And won't you?'

'Of course not. For one thing, they're my friends. And, for another, I'll be able to feel I'm doing something useful at last.'

For the first time, Eden grinned at him.

'Well done, Nick. If you'd said anything else, I'd have been disappointed.'

ACT FOUR

MÉNAGE
Paris, November and December, 1652

'Aye – now the plot thickens very much upon us.'
George Villiers, Duke of Buckingham

ONE

In the darkness of the alley, fighting to hold on to the shreds of his consciousness when letting go of it would have been a mercy, Ashley was dimly aware of a sudden, unexpected blur of movement that made no sense. Then the blade that had been about to drive into his chest clattered from Henri's grasp and he collapsed on the cobbles and lay still.

His breath coming in ragged gasps, Ashley dropped his head on his arm and struggled to open his eyes. He was in so much screaming, burning agony that engaging his brain was a near impossibility. Dragging some air into his lungs, he gasped, 'Is he ...?'

A booted foot nudged Henri over.

'Dead? Yes.'

'Shit.' He squinted at his rescuer. Then, because he wasn't just looking at, but *up* a very large nose, he closed his eyes again. 'Don't think me ... ungrateful. But I wish ... I really wish you hadn't ... done that.'

'But why, *mon ami*? He was about to kill you. And truly,' remarked Cyrano de Bergerac dispassionately, 'Henri de Vauvallon will be no loss to anyone.'

'I needed to ... to ask ...'

'Questions? Of course. And the other fellow still lives. You, however, will *not* if you continue bleeding like a pig.' Stooping, Cyrano took hold of Ashley and prepared to get him up but, knowing what the result was likely to be, paused to say, 'Where shall I take you?'

'Sixteen ... Rue des Rosiers. But --'

Cyrano heaved him to his feet. Ashley gave a strangled grunt and finally passed out.

'*Putain!*' grunted Cyrano, shouldering what was now a dead weight. 'One day I'll learn to mind my own business.'

* * *

Summoned by the hammering of a hefty fist, Archie reached the door first with Pauline two steps behind. The sight of Cyrano de Bergerac half-carrying Colonel Peverell stopped them both in their tracks for a moment.

Then, taking in the amount of blood and the fact that Ashley was barely conscious, Archie said, 'What the buggering 'ell's 'appened?'

Pauline shoved him unceremoniously out of the way and greeted Cyrano with a brief nod.

'Monsieur de Bergerac.'

Cyrano managed a grin. 'Madame Fleury.'

'Bring him inside.' Her gaze skimmed over the blood soaking through Ashley's left sleeve and staining his hand, then on down to the leg-wound which was clearly far worse. 'We'll need to put him to bed. Would you mind --?'

'Pauline? What is it?' Athenais erupted from the parlour, horror investing her face as she clapped eyes on Ashley. 'Oh God. What happened? Is – is he --?' She swallowed. 'He's not dead, is he?'

'No. Stop talking and find Francis,' snapped Pauline, turning back to Cyrano. 'Can you get him upstairs before he bleeds all over the hall? His friend will help if --' She stopped, as Francis came running down the stairs and, stilling him with one hand, said, 'Don't ask. Just help Monsieur de Bergerac get the Colonel upstairs and try not to damage him further. Everything else can wait till we've seen how bad it is.'

'Use my room,' said Athenais, her voice not quite steady. 'The attic ... there are too many stairs. My room, Francis.'

He nodded, his mouth for once firmly closed and his expression grim.

Carefully, he and Cyrano supported the Colonel between them, balancing his weight until they could lift him clear of the floor. Ashley promptly lost his frail hold on consciousness again.

'Damn,' grunted Francis. And considered Cyrano's quiet snort decidedly misplaced.

Athenais stood like a stone in hall, twisting her hands together and watching them out of wide, frightened eyes.

'Don't just stand there,' said Pauline sharply. 'We'll need hot water, cloths and bandages. Set the kettle and some pans to boil – as many as you can. Find anything we have that can be torn into strips. Old sheets, petticoats – anything as long as it's clean. Tell your father to guard the door and have Suzon mop up this mess on the floor. *Move!*'

Then, without waiting to see if Athenais did as she'd bidden her, Pauline ran up the stairs in the wake of the gentlemen.

They had laid Ashley, still unconscious, on the bed.

Whilst trying to unlace his coat, Francis said, 'You and Ashley know each other?'

'Through a mutual friend.' Cyrano laid rolled up towels beneath the freely bleeding leg wound. 'Tonight was just chance. He was under attack – three fellows, two of them dead.'

'Do you know who?' asked Francis.

'The man I killed was Henri de Vauvallon. For the others, I can't speak. Our friend here despatched one and put the other down. He wanted to ask questions but he was bleeding too much to waste the time.' Cyrano glanced down and, shrugging slightly, added, 'Still is, for that matter.'

'What do we have?' demanded Pauline, peering over Francis's shoulder at the ruined, blood-stained shirt. 'Blade or bullet?'

'Blade,' he replied, tearing the shirt so that he could slip it from Ashley's shoulder. 'Not as bad as it looks – but still bleeding.'

'And the leg?'

'Sword thrust,' supplied Cyrano. 'Deep and clumsy. Also, a knock on the head but that is not so bad, I think.'

Pauline nodded.

'Thank you, Monsieur. We're in your debt. I'm sure Athenais will be happy to pour a glass of wine if you --'

'No, no. I'll be on my way. If you need me, send word to the *Chien Rouge*. Anyone there will know where to find me.' And with a flourishing bow and a twirl of his hat, he took his leave and went clattering down the stairs.

Pauline looked across at Francis. She said, 'Go and see how Athenais is getting on with the water and bandages, will you? And pass me the scissors from the table. I'll cut the rest of his clothes off. They're ruined, anyway.'

By the time Francis and Athenais re-appeared, bearing hot water and a stack of assorted linens, Pauline had stripped away Ashley's clothes and was trying, without much success, to staunch the flow of blood from his right thigh.

With a lifted eyebrow but none of his usual flippancy, Francis absorbed the sight of the Colonel spread out – battered, gory and totally naked – under Pauline's ministrations.

Athenais walked past him saying, 'I've brought all the towels I could find and the oldest sheets and --' Then stopped dead on a shocked gasp.

She stared and stared again, apparently transfixed. With the first faint stirring of humour, Francis suspected that she wasn't just assessing Ashley's injuries. She was enjoying the perfectly sculpted musculature of his chest and thighs, the tautness of his abdomen ... and the parts in between which, under normal circumstances, she'd never see at all. He didn't blame her from enjoying the view. He imagined any woman with breath still in her body would do the same. On the other hand, he didn't think Ashley would appreciate being surveyed in all his naked glory and was just reaching out for one of the towels Athenais was carrying when the dark gold lashes lifted a little and a slurred voice said faintly, 'Call the neighbours in, why don't you? You could sell tickets.'

Francis's mouth curled – more in relief than amusement – and he dropped the towel across Ashley's loins. Before he could speak, however, Pauline glanced across at Athenais and said, 'Stop gawking and pull yourself together. I need the water and cloths now, not tomorrow.' And, when Athenais drew a shuddering breath and crossed to her side, 'Put the water on the table and the linens here on the pillow. Francis – use some of the towels and put pressure on that leg wound. See if you can stop the bleeding – or at least, slow it down. I'm going to attend to his arm first. It's a nasty cut but compared to his leg, it's nothing. Athenais – go downstairs and fetch my sewing box from the parlour.'

Athenais lost what little colour she had left and swallowed hard.

'Sewing box? You can't mean you're going to --'

'Do you want him to die?'

'No! But surely the doctor ....'

With a visible effort, Pauline summoned a shred of patience.

'We won't get a doctor out at this time of night – and if he carries on bleeding like this, he won't last till morning. So just get the box – and the brandy from the kitchen, while you're about it.'

Athenais ran from the room but had to pause for a moment at the top of the stairs when she discovered her knees were shaking. Shock and fear were churning in her stomach and making it impossible to think clearly. She didn't know what had happened or why or how to grasp the sense of what Pauline had said. Ashley *couldn't* die. It wasn't possible. Any minute now, he'd wake up and smile that slow, bone-melting smile … and this whole nightmare would be over.

Or maybe not, said a nasty little voice at the back of her mind. She stumbled on the last step and had to grab the newel post to stop herself falling. She tried to steady her nerves, drawing one ragged breath after another. Then she fled to the kitchen for the brandy and the parlour for Pauline's sewing box and set off back upstairs. Her skirts kept getting in the way and every step was an effort. The only image in her head was that of Ashley, as she'd seen him just a few minutes ago; hurt, bleeding and barely conscious but still unbelievably beautiful. The faintly golden hue of his skin; the light and shade of perfectly formed muscle; the breadth of shoulder and length of leg; and that part of him which, even now, terrified as she was, brought a flush of heat to her belly. Then, without warning, another image intruded; that of the terrible wound on his thigh. The wound that Pauline said might kill him.

Athenais hauled her skirts higher and ran.

The scene in her bedchamber had changed very little. Pauline had cleaned the gash in Ashley's arm and was plastering it with some kind of green salve. Francis was still labouring to stem the blood-flow in the other wound with a great deal of grim-faced determination. On the floor beside the bed, a small heap of stained towels bore witness to his efforts.

As Athenais entered the room he said, 'It's lessening, I think. But if you intend to try stitching it, perhaps we should use a tourniquet.'

'Do it,' replied Pauline without turning her head. 'I'll be with you in a minute.'

Wordlessly, Athenais put the sewing box down and stood for a moment, staring down at Ashley's face. It was paper-white and, though his eyes were shut, the muscle working in his jaw suggested that he hadn't quite relapsed into insensibility. Something twisted painfully in her chest and tears she refused to shed clogged her throat.

Her movements deft but gentle, Pauline finished binding his arm and stood up. She took a second to brush a light sheen of sweat from her brow with the back of one wrist and then briskly circumnavigated the bed to where Francis was fashioning a tourniquet out of a broad strip of folded sheeting. More blood welled from the ugly wound.

Taking Pauline's place, Athenais sat down on the edge of the bed and closed both of her hands around Ashley's lax fingers. They twitched in hers and then shifted their position to grip her hard. She remained perfectly still, glad of the pain.

'Change the water, Francis,' said Pauline. 'And pour some brandy into that cup on the dresser. I'll use it to clean the needle and you can pour the rest down his throat.'

'That,' muttered Ashley between clenched teeth, 'is a splendid idea.' Then, as Pauline began the process of cleaning the wound, he gave a massive, involuntary flinch and hissed raggedly, 'Hell*fire*. Francis – just knock me out, will you? Brandy or your fist. I don't care which.' And relapsed again into white-lipped silence.

Francis glanced at Pauline and received a small nod by way of reply.

'No!' snapped Athenais. 'Pass me the brandy. You're not to hit him. He's been hurt enough!'

Wrenching her hands free, she snatched the cup from Francis and, raising Ashley's head a little, held it to his lips. A few drops trickled from the edge of his mouth but he managed to drain the cup without coughing.

'More?' she asked. And was answered with a grunt of assent.

By the time he had downed another stiff measure, Pauline had cleaned the wound as best she could considering that, despite the tourniquet, it continued to ooze. While she examined her sewing box for a suitably large needle and the thread she thought most likely to prove adequate, she said, 'You'll have to hold him for me, Francis. He's no more than half-drunk at best and this is going to hurt like seven kinds of hell.'

Francis nodded. 'Whatever you need, Duchess.'

She shot him an oblique, faintly bemused glance and then, with a tiny shake of her head, said, 'Athenais – you should go.'

'Go? No. I won't. Why should I?'

'Because this isn't going to be pretty and I doubt your stomach will be up to it.'

Athenais's mouth set in a mulish line.

'I'll manage.'

Still busy making her preparations, Pauline said, 'Maybe. But we haven't time to look after you if you don't.'

'I've told you – I'll manage.' She took a breath and wrapped Ashley's hand inside hers. 'I'm not leaving him. And that's final.'

'Don't be so bloody stubborn,' began Pauline, only to be hushed by Francis's hand on her arm.

He said quietly, 'Leave it. She's entitled to stay. She's in --'

'I know what she is – and that's why she should go.' She threaded the needle and, without looking at Athenais said, 'Suit yourself. But if you're wise, you won't watch.'

'I think,' grumbled Athenais, 'I'd worked that out for myself.'

And then the horrible process began.

At the first insertion of the needle, Ashley's fingers clamped down again on Athenais's like a vice, the breath hissed between his teeth and his whole body went rigid in an attempt to remain still. He was already in as much pain as he could bear – his damned leg a screaming, burning agony that, if he'd been able to think at all, might have alarmed him; but, the piercing drag of the thread was a torture beyond anything he could have imagined. Enduring it in dignified silence suddenly no longer seemed possible – and that *did* alarm him. A groan escaped and only sheer will-power stopped it becoming a scream. The brandy wasn't helping and he wished Francis had hit him. The needle began its second journey. His muscles ached with the effort to maintain control and his throat rebelled at his refusal to release the sound building there. He held back a flood of curses with clenched teeth and felt sweat break out all over his skin.

Athenais was distantly aware that his grip had stopped the blood supply to her hand and was possibly crushing her bones. It didn't matter. His eyes were shut tight and his brow furrowed with a mixture of pain and inflexible determination. She used her free hand to brush back a lock of damp hair and whispered uselessly, 'Stop being a hero. Yell if you want. No one will think less of you.'

He didn't answer. His mouth remained set in a tight line and his chest laboured to suck in sufficient air. Although she was careful not to look at what Pauline was doing, Athenais began to realise that, slight as they were, Ashley's reactions were filling in what her eyes couldn't see. The moment that the needle pierced his flesh, the slow pull of the thread, the needle again as it exited. The mere thought of it was nauseating and she began to feel light-headed. A ripple of cold perspiration slithered down her spine and the edges of her vision blurred, causing her to shake her head in an attempt to clear it.

On the other side of the bed and intent on her task, Pauline muttered, 'I hoped he'd pass out by now. Why the hell hasn't he?'

'Obstinacy and guts,' returned Francis. And then, 'Ah. That's unfortunate. Next time, I'll listen to you.'

Pauline glanced up just in time to see Athenais slide to the floor in a boneless heap, her hand still trapped in Ashley's. She said, 'Next time? God save us all from that. In the meantime, let's get this over with. Take a breath, Ashley. You're doing well. Just two more and we're done.'

Ashley unlocked his jaws long enough to say, 'Athenais?'

'Out cold.'

'Lucky girl.' He forced his fingers to relinquish their hold and felt her arm slip away. And braced himself for the last excruciating stitches.

* * *

Athenais came round when Francis picked her up and carried her to the shabby day-bed in the adjoining room. She said groggily, 'I'm sorry. I never fainted before. How silly.'

'We'll forgive you,' he said, setting her down. 'Sit there and put your head between your knees for a few minutes. You'll feel better.'

'No.' She started to get up. 'Ashley?'

Francis dropped one hand on her shoulder and used the other to push her head down.

'Ashley is as well as can be expected under the circumstances. Pauline is dressing the wound and cleaning him up so he can be made more comfortable. There's nothing for you to do at the moment.'

Without warning, Athenais's nerves snarled into a painful tangle. A shudder ripped through her and the tears she'd held back earlier arrived in a flood. Through chattering teeth, she said, 'I th-thought he was going to d-die.'

Francis refrained from remarking that if, on top of the blood loss, infection set in, he still might. Patting her shoulder, he murmured that Ashley was fit and healthy.

'I know.' She swallowed the stupid tears and mopped her face on her skirt. 'I know. But it was hurting him so much. I couldn't ...' She stopped, drew a deep breath and sat up. 'Do you know what happened?'

'Some of it.' He related his conversation with Cyrano de Bergerac and then added, 'Jem has just come back. He says Ashley met him somewhere near the Palais Royale before returning from the theatre. I can only assume that, since his assailants weren't ordinary thieves, he must have been followed. But we won't know the full facts until Ashley is well enough to talk.' He smiled briefly. 'And now I'm going to help Pauline tidy up – and you can look after the patient. He's likely to feel cold, by the way. Severe blood-loss does that.'

In the other room, Pauline had tossed the blood-stained linens into a corner and was pouring reddened water into a bucket. She glanced across at Athenais and said, 'Better?'

'Yes.' Athenais looked down at Ashley, silent and pale, now decently covered up to his chin with a sheet. She said, 'I'll find some blankets and put a brick in the oven and – and perhaps some warmed wine?'

'All of those,' agreed Pauline, with something that might have been a smile. 'And then you can settle in for what's left of the night. Someone needs to stay with him in case his condition changes – and in a few hours we can send for the doctor.'

Athenais nodded and, scooping up an armful of dirty towels, headed briskly for the door.

Francis watched her go and then, turning to Pauline said softly, 'She's in love with him.'

'More's the pity,' came the typical reply.

He placed his hands on her shoulders, his eyes reflecting a mixture of amusement, admiration and something that wasn't either of them. Then, when she looked back at him, he said, 'I don't think I've ever met anyone who could do what you've done tonight – and all without a single question. You're a truly amazing woman, Duchess.' And he dropped a light kiss on her lips.

She stepped back abruptly so that his hands fell away and thought, *Don't put foolish ideas in my head. And don't call me Duchess. I already like you better than I should.* But what she said was, 'I didn't notice you sitting down with your hands folded, either.'

He shrugged. 'He's my friend. So you must allow me to be grateful.'

'Willingly,' she replied with a flicker of mordant humour. 'And you can prove it by carrying the bucket downstairs.'

* * *

By the time Athenais and Suzon returned bearing blankets, a flannel-wrapped hot brick and a mug of warm claret, Ashley was flickering back and forth between unconsciousness and an uneasy doze. Athenais tucked two of the blankets around him, slid the brick in by his feet and set the claret on the hearth to keep warm. Then, having made up the fire, she wrapped the remaining coverlet around her shoulders and sat down to watch and wait.

He slept for almost an hour and then awoke, shivering.

Muttering something, he tried to curl up as if to warm himself. Inevitably, the movement jarred his wounded leg and brought him fully awake on a grunt of pain, followed by a mumbled curse.

'Lie still,' said Athenais quickly. She disentangled herself from the blanket and placed it over him. 'There. You'll be warmer now. But you mustn't move or you'll damage your leg.'

'Feels damaged enough already.' And, swallowing with apparent difficulty, 'Throat hurts.'

Athenais got the wine from the hearth, sat down on the bed beside him and helped him to sit up a little. 'Here – drink this. It will ease your throat and help to warm you.' His skin still felt icy but, aside from building up the fire again, she wasn't sure what else she could do. Searching for more blankets – and God only knew if there were any – or fetching another hot brick meant leaving him alone and she was reluctant to do that in case he tried moving again.

Ashley drank the warm wine and subsided again on the pillow with closed lids. His arm felt sore and fiery spears were stabbing his thigh, sending pain ricocheting from his toes to his groin. But the alcohol went to his head with unusual speed and, despite the severity of his discomfort, he gradually dozed off for a time.

The respite was even briefer than before and, once more, he awoke shivering. Watching him clench his jaw to stop his teeth chattering and seeing him become restless, Athenais started to worry. Francis had said he might be cold but she hadn't expected it to be as bad as this. She had to get him warm somehow ... and the only thing she could think of that might do it was to use her own body heat.

She sat beside him, being careful not to jar either of his injuries, and slid her arms about him so that his head nestled beneath her chin. He muttered something and seemed to lean closer. The shivering eased a little but didn't completely stop and he was still cold to the touch. Athenais decided that, if this approach was to be properly effective, she was going to have to intensify it.

She stood up – to a grumble of protest from Ashley – and fumbled for the laces of her gown, reasoning that the thick material was probably holding her warmth in rather than sharing it with him. As she stepped out of her voluminous petticoats, she was quite glad of two contradictory things. First, that his awareness was seriously impaired at present; and second, that she was wearing her new under-garments. Then, when she had stripped down to shift, corset and stockings, she crawled gingerly under the blankets at his side until the whole length of her body lay close against his.

Ashley muttered again. Something that sounded suspiciously like, 'Nice.'

Athenais blinked back more tears and cradled his head on her shoulder. Little by little, she felt the tremors subside and his muscles start to relax ... until finally, he fell asleep.

* * *

Between her anxiety over Ashley and the strange feelings proximity to his naked body aroused in her own, Athenais had not expected to sleep – but the next thing she knew, greyish light was creeping through the window and Pauline was standing in the doorway, holding a tray.

'Well,' remarked that lady caustically, 'I suppose that's one way to do it.'

'Do what?' In her attempt to sit up, Athenais discovered that her arm had gone numb and that the Colonel had somehow managed to pin her waist with his uninjured one. She extricated herself as gently as she could and managed to slither out of the bed. 'He was cold and Francis said to keep him warm.'

'That was handy.' A tiny smile flicked the corners of Pauline's mouth and she walked into the room to deposit the tray on the table. 'And now you'd better put some clothes on before the doctor gets here. We wouldn't want him to get the wrong idea.'

'Like you, you mean?'

'Exactly like me.' She eyed Ashley thoughtfully. 'He's starting to stir. Go and tidy yourself while I check his dressings and try to get some beef tea into him. You can use my room.'

Yawning and trying to rub the pins and needles from her arm, Athenais retrieved her gown and petticoats from the chair. She said waspishly, 'You just want to see him naked again.'

'And you don't?' retorted Pauline.

The doctor arrived half an hour later by which time Ashley was fully awake and once more in severe pain. Doctor Odelle examined Pauline's handiwork and was pleased to pronounce it exceptional. He could not, he admitted, have done better himself and was therefore loth to interfere. But he produced a different pot of salve which he said would help to reduce both the inflammation and the risk of infection and also gave Pauline a twist of paper containing opium grains – along with strict instructions on how to administer them. Then, turning to Ashley, he said, 'You're a very lucky man. This lady's prompt attentions may well have saved your leg – if not your life.'

Aside from the throbbing agony which now seemed to be invading his whole body, Ashley was getting tired of being poked and prodded and was also uncomfortably aware that he needed to relieve himself. However, he managed to find sufficient good manners to say, 'And I'm grateful. When I'm on my feet again --'

'Ah yes,' interrupted the doctor. 'As to that, you will need to remain abed for at least a week.'

'*A week?* I can't stay in bed for a week!'

'You can. And, unless you want to undo all Madame's good work, you will. The stitches will hold and the flesh will start to mend if you keep the leg elevated and still. If you don't, I won't be responsible for the consequences.' He turned, smiling at Pauline. 'I will call again in two days, Madame. But if there are signs of fever before then, you should send for me.'

Downstairs after Pauline had shown the doctor out, Athenais sniffed the new pot of salve, grimaced, and said, 'Yours smells better.'

'Thank you.' Pauline frowned thoughtfully. 'He's going to be a bad patient. You realise that, don't you? He can't be idle at the best of times, so keeping him immobile for a week will need some organisation. As soon as the pain eases – if not before – he's going to try to get up. And, if no one's there to stop him, he will.'

'A round-the-clock guard, then?'

'Yes. And don't think it will be fun. He's going to be anywhere between moody and downright furious. Remember Rosalie in *The Compliant Wife*? All sweetness and light and infuriating serenity? That's your role. So go and offer him something light to eat – but don't be surprised if he throws it at you.'

Upstairs, meanwhile, Francis lounged in the doorway and regarded Ashley cautiously.

'How do you feel?'

'Bloody awful.'

'Care to tell me what happened before that fellow de Bergerac came along?'

'No. Help me up, will you? And find a sodding chamber-pot.'

Francis couldn't quite suppress his grin but he shook his head, saying, 'No. You heard the doctor. If you want to keep your leg, you'll do as you're told. But since I sympathise with your current need, I'll send Jem up with a bottle.' And he vanished.

No sooner had Francis gone, than Athenais appeared, wearing an expression he hadn't seen before and instantly distrusted. He didn't know that, behind it, parts of her body were melting and her brain along with them. When last she'd seen him, he'd been lying flat, covered up to his neck by a sheet. Now he was sitting propped against the pillows, his torso bare but for the bandage around his left arm; and the sheer beauty of his physique made her breath catch and produced an urge to do more than just look.

Realising that Rosalie's smile had slipped, she pinned it back on and said, 'You look a little better, today. I was so worried last night.'

Ashley searched his mind and found two things. One was a hazy recollection of lying on this damned bed without a stitch on in full view, not just of Pauline, but also Francis and Athenais; the other was the bizarre notion that, at some point during the night, Athenais had been in bed with him. The first brought a hint of ridiculous colour to his cheekbones; the second he dismissed as some kind of pain-induced hallucination.

As evenly as he could, he said, 'I apologise for both the anxiety and the disruption. I also realise that this is your bedchamber and --'

'Don't worry about that. I can sleep on the couch in the dressing-closet.'

He stared at her, utterly aghast. He might be wounded but he wasn't dead. And God alone knew just how many humiliations the lack of privacy caused by her presence in the next room was likely to heap upon him. The mere thought was enough to send his muscles into spasm. He said, 'I can't possibly allow you to do that. Perhaps Francis and Jem could help me upstairs?'

'I daresay they could,' she replied dulcetly. 'But they're not going to. The doctor said you're to stay where you are for a week and that's an end of the matter.'

Ashley decided that he was extremely tired of the doctor.

'I can lie in my own bed just as easily as in yours. Not that I see the need to --'

'No. We realise that.'

'*We?*' The word cracked like a pistol shot.

'Yes. Pauline and Francis and myself. We've decided that, for the next few days, someone should be nearby to stop you disobeying orders.'

'I am not a child!' he snapped, his temper rising. 'And I most assuredly don't need a nursemaid!'

'Unfortunately, as things stand, you do.' Her smile was breathtakingly sweet and her tone, downright maddening. 'Also, no one in this house is going to help you to cripple yourself. So you may as well accept the situation and try to make the best of a bad job.'

'Finished with the platitudes, have you?'

'For the moment.' She took in the sulky set of his mouth and the baleful gleam in his eyes and said kindly, 'I know you're in pain and I understand that a week in bed sounds like a lifetime in purgatory. But when you're thinking more clearly, you'll appreciate that there really isn't any alternative. So ... do you suppose you might manage a nice coddled egg?'

Ashley's eyes narrowed still further. He had a suspicion that she was being deliberately provoking and was strongly tempted to tell her what she might do with her coddled egg. Fortunately, before he could do so, Jem Barker hove into view on the landing, clutching a stone-ware bottle. The notion that relief was at hand was great enough to banish every thought save the immediate need to be rid of her.

He said sardonically, 'That sounds delightful. And if you are good enough to prepare it, I'll certainly do my best.'

Athenais considered admitting that, if *she* cooked the egg, he'd be able to bounce it off the wall and then, with regret, decided that it wasn't at all Rosalie-like. Tilting her head slightly, she said, 'Or perhaps you'd prefer some calves-foot jelly?'

'Thank you. The egg will be fine.' It wouldn't, of course. It sounded like exactly the sort of pap he most disliked; but the jelly sounded worse and he'd agree to eat any blasted thing she liked, if only she'd just *go* before his bladder exploded.

'And later, we'll make you a custard,' she announced happily. 'Or a blancmange.'

Ashley narrowly avoided grinding his teeth. If he had a blancmange right now, he knew what he'd do with it. He said gratingly, 'By all means. But the only thing I *really* want right now is the opium – which is the one thing I haven't been offered. And, if you look behind you, you'll see that reinforcements have arrived, meaning that you may safely leave me.'

She turned her head to impale Jem with a very un-Rosalie-like scowl and, reluctantly switching to English, said, "E's not to be allowed up – no matter what 'e says.'

'No, mamzelle. No matter what.'

She nodded and stepped aside to let him pass.

Jem grinned at Ashley and brandished the bottle.

'Morning, Colonel. His lordship says you've a need for this.'

There had often been times when Ashley wanted to murder Jem. This was one of them.

Athenais stared blankly at the bottle for a second before comprehension dawned and she flushed in mortification. Forgetting Rosalie, she muttered, 'I'm so sorry. I'll go.'

Ashley shut his eyes briefly and wondered how he was going to endure a week of this. Constant pain and enforced immobility were bad enough, God knew. But this kind of embarrassment, combined with honeyed smiles and invalid slop, was already making him want to smash something.

He glared at Jem. 'Give me that.'

Mr Barker passed him the bottle. 'Need a hand, Colonel?'

This, Ashley didn't dignify with a reply. He simply snatched the receptacle and proceeded to do what he'd wanted to do for the last half-hour. It gave him nearly as much pleasure as the look on Jem's face when he handed the bottle back. Then, deciding that he might as well make the most of whatever small moments of enjoyment came his way, he said, 'Before you take that away ... tell me about the fellow last night. Where did you tail him to?'

'Same place you said,' shrugged Mr Barker. 'Who is he?'

'A friend.'

'A friend, is it? So he wouldn't have had nothing to do with what's happened to you?'

'No.'

'Going to let his lordship and me in on the details, are you?'

'Later.' Ashley tried to think, though the persistent fog in his head made it difficult. It was possible that Hyde had set Sir William Brierley on the same trail he himself had been following – though he wasn't sure why this might be so. And if Will was involved with Lucy Walter on some personal level ... well, it would be necessary to discover what that was. Finally, he said, 'I need to speak to Ned Hyde.'

'Ah. Well, you ain't going to be doing that for a week or more.'

'It appears not.'

'Can't his lordship go for you?'

It was an irritant to Ashley that, though Jem had taken years to address *him* correctly, he been happily my-lording Francis ever since he'd first learned of his inherited title.

'His lordship is too damned inquisitive for my liking – but it may come to that.'

'And me, Colonel? Do I carry on watching the skirt or start shadowing the eye-patch? Or had I ought to be watching your back instead?'

Ashley's head hurt and the agony in his leg was reaching epic proportions. He shut his eyes again and said, 'Ask me later. Just at the moment, I don't much care.'

TWO

Ashley dutifully ate his egg under Pauline's watchful gaze and was then allowed his opium. The pain gradually faded to a dull ache, his brain went fuzzy at the edges and eventually he slept. Pauline ordered Jem to remain within earshot and went downstairs to the kitchen where Athenais appeared to be trying to make a custard.

'It won't thicken,' she said, diligently stirring the mixture. 'I must have done something wrong.'

'Considering that, as we both know, you can't cook, the thing you did wrong was expecting this time to be any different,' came the caustic reply. Then, 'What are you doing down here, anyway? You're due at the theatre in an hour.'

'I'm not going.'

'I *beg* your pardon?'

'I've sent Suzon to Froissart with a note saying I've been vomiting and have stomach cramps. I may be unable to appear for several days.'

'Or even a week, perhaps?'

'I would think that very likely,' agreed Athenais demurely.

There was a short silence and then Pauline said flatly, 'No. You are *not* taking a week away from the theatre to hold Ashley Peverell's hand. You must be mad even to think of it.'

'He's ill and he needs me! And Delphine can go on in my place.'

'He's not ill – he's just got a hole in his leg which will mend well enough given time. And he doesn't need you specifically. I can take time off more easily than you, should Francis, Jem and your father prove inadequate.'

Athenais shook her head and her mouth took on a stubborn line. Abandoning the still runny custard, she said, 'That's not the point. He's been hurt because of me. Oh – he hasn't said it and he won't – but there's only one reason that I can see why he'd be set upon like that. It's bloody d'Auxerre, isn't it?'

'I'd say so. I heard Monsieur de Bergerac telling Francis that one of the assailants was Henri de Vauvallon – who, as we know, trails after the Marquis like a puppy.'

'*Vauvallon?*' echoed Athenais incredulously. 'That popinjay? I'll kill him!'

'Cyrano already has,' Pauline told her dryly. 'But let's stick to the point. None of this is a good enough reason to let Froissart down. Take today, since you've already told him – but tomorrow you should go back to work.'

'I can't. And it would be no good if I did because I can't concentrate while Ashley is ill.' She looked up, her expression tortured. 'I thought he was going to die, Pauline.'

'I understand that. But --'

'No. I don't think you do. I love him ... and last night I found out how much. I know he may not feel that way about me but it doesn't matter. If something happens to him – especially if something happens to him because of *me* – I don't know how I shall bear it.' She spread her hands in a half-helpless, half-apologetic gesture. 'So, although it may be stupid and completely illogical, I'm not leaving this house until he's better. And now I'm going upstairs with a fresh jug of water for when he wakes.'

* * *

Having sent Mr Barker to fetch one of the Colonel's shirts and then dismissed him, Athenais sat down and watched Ashley sleep. The absurdly long lashes which, but for the strong, clear lines of cheek and jaw, might have looked feminine, rested like gold-tipped shadows; the thick fair hair was rumpled and untidy, making her want to brush it from his brow; and one of his hands lay lax at his side, the fingers curved over the open palm. She ached to touch him but she didn't. His breathing was even, if a little heavy; and sleep would not only help him heal but also provide some respite from the pain.

She didn't know how long she sat there, watching and thinking. But at some point in the late afternoon, he eventually stirred and opened his eyes, blinking a little in an attempt to come fully awake.

Without speaking, Athenais filled a cup with water and handed it to him. Then, when he had drained it and she moved to replace it on the table, he said, 'What have you done to your hand?'

It was bruised from the pressure of his fingers and still rather stiff.

She shrugged and said, 'It's nothing. Just a silly accident. How do you feel?'

310

'Odd.' His brain felt muffled, as though his head was stuffed with something fluffy. His leg, unfortunately, was already wide awake and screaming. 'The opium, I suppose.' He ran a hand over his face. 'God, I need a shave.'

'You do.' She swallowed, wondering how his stubble would feel against her mouth. 'But it will wait until tomorrow, won't it?'

'Not if I'm to start feeling human again. A bath would also not go amiss.'

'A bath won't be possible but I can certainly bring water for you to wash.' She stood up. 'As to the shave – shall I call Jem?'

'No. I'd like to keep my features intact, so I'm not letting Jem near my face with a razor. And since there's nothing wrong with either my hands or my eyesight, I'm fully capable of shaving myself – if you'll be so good as to bring me the necessary gear.' He gave her a sardonic smile. 'You have my word that I won't use your absence to dance a jig.'

'I'm glad to hear it.' Placing the shirt on the bed where he could reach it, she said awkwardly, 'I assumed you'd want something to wear and Jem said you don't … you don't have a nightshirt.'

'From which you'll have deduced that I sleep in the buff.' He paused, suddenly all too aware of his nakedness beneath the covers and pierced by the memory of possibly the most embarrassing moment of his life. Keeping his tone light and even slightly bored, he said, 'Not the best idea at the moment, perhaps. Or then again, since you've already viewed the goods, maybe it doesn't matter.'

Hot colour stained her cheeks.

'It wasn't deliberate! You make it sound as if I – I …' She stopped, unable to think of how to phrase it.

He shrugged. 'Pauline said you were staring. No … gawking.'

'Pauline says a lot of things. I was *not* gawking! I was shocked. I hadn't expected …' She stopped again, catching the look in his eye and suddenly aware that he was deliberately provoking her. 'You want me to say I'm sorry? I won't. You are being utterly unreasonable and I don't think I have anything to apologise for. And now I'll get some hot water and your razor.'

Ashley watched her leave the room with her nose in the air and a martial spring in her step. He smiled to himself. Baiting her was easy, enjoyable and effective. If he hoped, during the course of the next week, to maintain the *status quo*, it was something worth remembering.

She returned with a large pot of hot water, soap, towels and his shaving gear.

Watching her haul the heavy pot, he felt suddenly annoyed and said, 'Why are you carrying that with an injured hand. Couldn't your father have helped?'

'He's taking sentry-duty seriously,' she returned coolly. 'As you instructed. Also, you may have noticed that he's lacking the use of his right arm. And living four flights up in the Rue Benoit gets one used to hauling water – so I suggest you stick to worrying about yourself.'

Ashley shut his mouth tight and said nothing more.

During the time it took him to shave, Athenais (pointedly ignoring him) removed items of apparel from the clothes-press to the dressing-closet. This indication of her determination to sleep in the adjoining room made Ashley distinctly uneasy. A glimpse of frothy cambric petticoats, a lace-trimmed corset and a pair of scarlet, beribboned garters was even more disturbing and was eventually responsible for him saying, 'I believe I've already said that I don't want you to sleep on the couch. And why aren't you at the theatre? Is there no rehearsal today?'

She carried the ancient pink wrapper through to the other room and answered him over her shoulder. 'They can manage without me.'

A new worry lodged in his gut. He finished wiping the residue of soap from his face and pulled the shirt over his head, wincing at a savage twinge from his arm. Finally, he said, 'Please tell me you're not staying at home because of me.'

Hands on hips, she swung round to face him.

'Please tell me *you're* not in this condition because of the Marquis d'Auxerre.'

There was a long silence as grey eyes met green.

Finally, his tone perfectly flat, Ashley said, 'I can't.'

'No. Neither can I.' She waited and then, when he volunteered neither information nor argument, said, 'According to Monsieur de Bergerac one of the men who attacked you was Henri de Vauvallon. Is it true?'

'Apparently. I didn't know his name until Cyrano told me – and by then he was dead.' *Very, very unfortunately. Vauvallon is connected to both d'Auxerre and Lucy Walter – and, for all I know, the two of them could be connected to each other; One-Eyed Will has now joined the cast though I've no idea why; and here I am, tied to a bloody bed.* 'But let's get one thing clear, Athenais. Whether or not the Marquis is involved, you bear no responsibility for what happened to me. None.'

'I can't see it that way.'

'Then let me spell it out for you. I am more than capable of taking care of myself. I've killed men on the battlefield – and off it, in ways you don't want to know about. I'm also involved in matters which concern neither you nor the Marquis. Last night, happened because of a small miscalculation on my part. And though I'm grateful to Cyrano, it would be helpful if he'd left Vauvallon alive. That way, I might have had some answers.'

His voice had become unusually hard and a little intimidating. He was also already beginning to look tired and strained – reminding her that, less than twenty-four hours ago, he'd lost quantities of blood. Deciding not to tax him further, Athenais took the shaving bowl from where it lay in his lap and picked up the towel. She said lightly, 'I understand what you say. But since I'd rather Henri de Vauvallon was dead than you, I'm glad Monsieur de Bergerac came upon you when he did.' And, to take any untoward inference from her words, she tossed him a grin and added, 'He is said to be quite mad, you know. Is he a friend of yours?'

Ashley leaned back against the pillows, watching her closely without appearing to do so.

'Before last night, I'd met him precisely once – so I can't say he's a friend. And I wouldn't call him mad, precisely. But he certainly has an uncanny ability to attract trouble ... fortunately coupled with an equal ability to get himself out of it.'

'Like you?'

'In one respect, perhaps. In others, not at all.' He paused. 'Go to work tomorrow, Athenais. I'm not going to die. I'll even promise to stay in bed, if that's what it takes. But I don't want this incident causing any more damage than it already has.'

* * *

Back in the kitchen with Pauline, Athenais relayed bits of this conversation to Pauline and at some point, mentioned her intention of sleeping in the dressing-closet – thus occasioning their second argument of the day.

'No,' snapped Pauline. 'Absolutely not. And this time, you'll listen to me.'

'You mean that this time, I'll do as you say. I think you sometimes forget that it isn't up to you to tell me how to behave.'

'It is when you're acting like a ninny.'

Athenais heaved an exasperated sigh.

'I'm not. And, to be honest, I don't see where the problem lies. He may need something in the night so someone ought to be nearby.'

'Somebody, yes. You, no.'

'But *why?* I'm not going to slide into bed with him again, if that's what you think. And he's hardly in any condition to pounce on me – even supposing he wanted to. As for my reputation ... God, Pauline! You can't surely be worried about *that?*'

'Difficult though it may be for you to comprehend, my objections have nothing at all to do with you. It's the Colonel I'm thinking of.'

'Are you saying I'm not?'

'No. You're not. If you were, you'd have realised a couple of things. If he needs something in the middle of the night – most probably to relieve himself – do you honestly think he's going to call you? Of course he's not. He'd sooner lie there in torment than embarrass himself that way.'

Recalling what had happened earlier in the day, Athenais flushed a little and drew patterns on a plate with her knife.

'You might also,' resumed Pauline, 'spare a thought for how hard this is for him. The pain he's enduring – bad as it undoubtedly is – is only part of it. Being trapped in bed is going to drive him mad. He's not used to needing help of any kind only now he can't do without it. And, as if that wasn't bad enough, he's supposed to rely on *you* to perform personal tasks for him? Really?'

'I – I hadn't thought of it quite like that.'

'You hadn't thought about it at *all*. You just want to hover around him like a lovesick schoolgirl, waiting for him to fall head over heels in love with you.'

'That's neither fair nor true!'

'Actually, it's both. At what point was it ever going to occur to you to allow the poor man a shred or two of dignity?' Pauline waited and, when no reply was forthcoming, said, 'Does he know this is what you were planning?'

'Yes.'

'And?'

Athenais sighed. 'And he told me not to do it.'

'There you go, then. Pity you didn't listen. But you *will* listen to me – or I'll wash my hands of you. For as long as Ashley lies in your room, you'll share mine. And Jem can sleep in the closet, ready to attend to any nocturnal requirements.'

* * *

Ashley took the opium as prescribed until the following day and then refused to take any more.

'Sure about that?' asked Pauline sceptically. She was engaged in changing the dressing on his thigh and, though the surrounding inflammation was no worse, the wound itself was still an angry red and inclined to seep a little blood. 'You're not telling me you're no longer in any pain.'

'No. But it's not as bad as it was and I'd prefer not to start relying on opiates.' He managed a faint smile and gestured to where she was gently applying the doctor's salve. 'I'd also prefer you to let me start dealing with this myself. I could, you know.'

'I daresay. But it's a bit late for maidenly modesty, wouldn't you say?'

Ashley wasn't used to being seen through so easily. He also wasn't used to lying in bed wearing nothing but his shirt with a sheet draped across his lap while a female attended to an area of his person only a few scant inches from his groin. He said evasively, 'You shouldn't have to do this.'

'I don't *have* to do it – I *choose* to. I like to see for myself that it hasn't turned green or started to suppurate – or anything else unpleasant that I can't trust you to tell me about.' She paused, reaching for clean bandages. 'And at least I've spared you the ministrations of Sister Athenais. She still won't stir from the house, of course – but at least she's not sleeping in the dressing-room.'

'For which I am eternally grateful.'

'Yes. I thought you would be.' Her head remained bent as she began applying the dressing. 'Did she say anything to you?'

He shook his head.

'I haven't spoken to her since yesterday afternoon. But since Jem doesn't seem to have come across a selection of female undergarments, I can only assume that she retrieved them while I slept.'

'Mm.' Pauline glanced up, briefly. 'How much to you remember of those minutes when I was stitching you up?'

'Was it only minutes?' He thought for a moment. 'Aside from the worst pain I've ever endured, I don't remember much at all.'

'Then you won't recall Athenais passing out.'

'No.' A frown entered his eyes. 'Did she?'

'Yes. She was sitting at your side, very carefully *not* watching what I was doing … but that didn't stop her dropping off the bed in a dead faint.'

'She has a weak stomach?' he asked, his tone deliberately careless.

'Not usually. But then, at the time, she thought you might die.'

He now knew exactly what she was telling him and it caused something in his chest to tighten – though whether from joy or dismay, he didn't know. He said, 'I'm sorry for that. It is … it's good of her to care about a mere lodger.'

Her glance said that calling himself a 'mere lodger' was definitely over-doing it.

'Yes. Isn't it? So when she apologises for not immediately understanding your needs correctly – and she will – you'll make it easy for her. And don't make the mistake of looking for hidden meanings. Athenais's artifice is all reserved for the stage.' Pauline dropped the dirty dressing into the bowl of water and stood up. 'I've been keeping visitors to a minimum but Francis has wanted to speak to you since yesterday. Shall I tell him he can come up?'

'I suppose you'd better. Jem, too, if he's here. They'll both want chapter and verse on what happened the other night – so I suppose I might as well get it over with.'

Pauline eyed him narrowly.

'Why don't you want to talk about it?'

'In most respects, because there are only three points worth mentioning,' he shrugged. 'I was attacked; I was wounded; I'm not dead. It hardly makes riveting telling, does it?'

'Don't they say that the devil is in the detail?'

'And it is. Which is why *I* generally say that, unless there's a very good reason to share them, most details are best kept to oneself.'

* * *

Francis and Jem entered the room to find Ashley shaved, wearing a clean shirt and looking rather more like Colonel Peverell than they'd expected. Unsmilingly, he told Jem to shut the door and indicated that they should both make themselves comfortable. Francis lounged on the end of the bed; Jem perched on the window-seat.

'You already have the gist of what happened,' said Ashley. 'You'll also have worked out that it was probably at the behest of d'Auxerre because one of the assailants was his creature. I don't know who the other two were but we can assume they fall into the same category. The fellow who survived may still be having difficulty walking since I did my best to relocate his balls. If you come across someone like that it might be worth asking a question or two – but we're unlikely to be that lucky.' He looked at Jem. 'Henri de Vauvallon, the man Cyrano killed, was of particular interest. Yellow hair, an earring and fancier clothes than you see on most women.'

'Ah.' Jem grunted. 'Him.' And then, 'Pity.'

'Exactly.'

Francis looked from one to the other of them and said, 'I'm obviously missing something. And though I'm aware that the two of you have your secrets --'

'This isn't personal, Francis. Ned Hyde asked me to look into something and demanded total discretion. Jem has been helping me but even he has no idea exactly what we're looking for and why. Present circumstances, however, mean that this will have to change.'

'Dear me,' drawled Francis. 'Does this mean that Jem and I are to be allowed into the secret? How delightful.'

Ashley hadn't seen that particular incarnation for some time and, just now, he found it intensely irritating.

'If we could dispense with the theatricals, I'd be grateful. The position is this. Hyde received a communication suggesting that there is proof that the King married Lucy Walter. I, personally, doubt this because I don't believe there was any marriage. But naturally, if such a document *does* exist – even if it's a forgery – Hyde wants it in his own possession rather than Cromwell's. And so, in the absence of any better ideas, Jem and I have been keeping an eye on Mistress Walter's visitors – of whom the late Monsieur de Vauvallon was one. This might have been helpful information if only the wretched fellow wasn't dead.'

'Helpful how?' asked Francis. And then, with faint impatience, 'I'm assuming you've been keeping a watch on the exquisite Lucy because you suspect she's been careless with her papers. But from what you've said so far, you've nothing significant to show for it. I think I can suggest something better than that.'

Jem snorted quietly to himself but Ashley said, 'What? The whole thing has the appearance of a wild goose chase so I'm willing to clutch at any straw – however feeble.'

Francis smiled and said simply, 'Celia.'

'Ah. I withdraw my last remark.'

'Don't be hasty. Celia is friendly with Lucy Walter. And both being fairly stupid women, all they do when they get together is gossip. I wouldn't be surprised if Celia couldn't provide us with a list of every man Lucy has … entertained … for the last year.'

'Sure about that, are you?' asked Jem sceptically. 'She ain't been visiting that I knows of.'

Ignoring this, Ashley looked at Francis, his expression thoughtful but unconvinced.

'I'd got the impression that you and Celia weren't currently on the best of terms – and that your stage debut would effectively destroy any residual goodwill.'

'And it will – when she recognises me. So far she hasn't looked under the helmet.'

This time Jem laughed outright.

Sighing, Ashley said, 'Thank you Jem. I think we can agree that that might have been better put.' And to Francis, 'She's seen *Mariamne*?'

'Twice. She came to the first night with Hugo and a couple I didn't recognise. Then again yesterday with the same couple as before and a fellow with an eye-patch.'

Silence stretched out on invisible threads as Ashley's and Jem's eyes met and locked.

'What?' asked Francis, looking from one to the other of them. 'Come on. If I've said something important, I'd quite like to be given due credit.'

'The fellow with the eye-patch is someone that I, Sir Edward Hyde and the King all know. At this point, I'm not prepared to give you a name. Suffice it to say he's one of our small but merry band-in-exile. The trouble is, Jem has recently seen him visiting Lucy Walter which – considering that His Majesty is striving to keep the lady at arms' length and also discourage her from creating further scandals – is rather hard to explain.'

'Is it? I'd have thought Mistress Lucy's proclivities make the answer obvious.'

'And it might be,' agreed Ashley. *Except that Will Brierley is probably the best agent I know and far too bright to make that kind of mistake.* 'As for Celia, I think you'd be the first to say she and discretion aren't even on nodding terms – so encourage her to gossip, by all means. But nothing I've just said is to leave this room. I hope that's abundantly clear?'

Jem moved as if to spit and then, catching the Colonel's eye, thought better of it.

'I reckon you don't need to tell me that,' he said huffily. 'Never gabbed about your affairs before, have I? If word gets into the wrong ear, it won't be *me* what puts it there.'

'It won't be me, either,' said Francis calmly. 'I've been told many times that I talk a lot but I'm not entirely stupid.'

Ashley nodded. He was starting to feel tired again and he wondered irritably how much longer this weakness was going to last. Also, without the opium, his leg was starting to hurt like a bitch. He said, 'All right.

Jem – spend what time you can keeping an eye on Mistress Walter but don't put in all the hours that God sends. It isn't worth it. Francis. Go to Hyde and tell him that I'm out of action at present and have enlisted your assistance. Then ask him if he's involved one of my colleagues in the Lucy Walter affair. He won't – or shouldn't – give you a name and you shouldn't ask for one. Yes or no will do.'

Francis nodded. 'And Celia?'

'Visit her and see what you can get. But don't arouse her suspicions.'

'Celia's mind being what it is, the only suspicion that will cross it is that I fancy the lady.' He raised a meditative brow. 'If I let her think that and she offers me an introduction, should I take it?'

'I wouldn't recommend it. Not unless you're happy to take the nice present she's likely to offer you.'

THREE

Having spent twenty-four hours whisking herself in and out of Ashley's room while he dozed, Athenais finally plucked up the courage to face him.

Standing very straight and looking him squarely in the eye, she said, 'I'm sorry. It was wrong of me to continually inconvenience you with my presence and to even *think* of sleeping in the dressing-closet. I ought to have realised that you needed some privacy – particularly from me. My only excuse is that I was worried and not thinking clearly. But I can promise that it won't happen again.'

Again, Ashley felt that little squeeze at his heart. She didn't need to say this and shouldn't feel that she had to. Although her voice was composed and there was dignity in every line of her body, he saw the hurt lying behind her eyes and wished, not for the first time, that he could say the one thing which would banish it.

Since he couldn't, he smiled at her and, with a slight shake of his head, said, 'You don't inconvenience me. How could you think it?'

'Pauline said that I – I was smothering you.'

'No. You were doing your best to look after me. And, if anyone needs to apologise, it is I. You've been toiling up and down stairs for four days without a word of thanks from me. So I'd be well-served if you left me to stew in my own ingratitude.'

'I wouldn't do that. And I haven't done it to earn your gratitude.'

'I know. But I hope you will accept it all the same.'

Athenais nodded, unsure of what to say. She was relieved that this was over and that he hadn't made it unnecessarily awkward. She'd have liked to linger and talk to him but, considering that she'd just promised to leave him in peace, that didn't seem to be an option. So she said, 'I'll go, then ... unless there's anything you need?'

'Nothing. Though I've a couple of questions, if you'll humour me?' He patted the side of the bed invitingly and, when she sat – demurely and with some hesitation – at his side, he realised it had probably been a mistake because she was close enough for him to catch the scent of her hair. 'My recollections of that first night are extremely hazy. But I think you fainted while Pauline was stitching me up, didn't you?'

Athenais groaned. 'Yes. I'd hoped you wouldn't remember.'

He didn't say that he hadn't. He merely remarked that he hadn't taken her for the sort of girl prone to swooning.

'I'm not. I've never done so before and am quite ashamed that I did it at such a moment. It was entirely stupid of me.'

'What caused it?'

'I don't know.' It was a lie but she wasn't about to tell him that seeing him suffer had been killing her. 'I wasn't watching what Pauline was doing but somehow the mere thought of it made me feel sick.' She stopped, managing a self-deprecating smile. 'The next thing I knew, Francis was carrying me into the other room and pushing my head on to my knees. I felt a complete idiot, of course – and still do. I'm sorry.'

Ashley recognised that there was something she wasn't saying but he let it go.

'If I say I'm sorry you were made to feel ill on my account, do you think we might stop apologising to each other?' he asked.

'I suppose we could try,' she responded, relaxing a little. 'What was the other thing?'

'The other thing?'

'Yes. You said you had a couple of questions. What was the other?'

He'd intended to ask her about later, when he'd felt as if he was freezing to death.

Did you really lie beside me in bed or did I dream it? Did I dream of your hair tickling my face, your arms holding me still and the warmth of your body along the length of mine?

But suddenly that didn't seem like a very good idea. Given the circumstances, it was better to think of it as an illusion than to know for a fact that it wasn't.

He said smoothly, 'I merely wondered how the theatre has managed without you these last few days and whether your absence is likely to get you into trouble.'

'They've managed well enough,' she shrugged. 'No one is indispensable, after all. Delphine has gone on in my place and Monsieur Froissart sent me the script for our next production so that I can prepare. Truth to tell, I'm not particularly sorry to miss a few performances of *Mariamne*. Etienne tries to make me laugh during the love-scenes – which is naughty of him and rather tiresome. And half of the audience only comes for the fireworks and the fighting.'

'And the other half?' He gave her an easy, deliberately charming smile. 'I think you're too modest.'

Her response was unexpected.

'Don't *do* that!' she said crossly. 'Don't smile and flatter me as if everything is all right when we both know it isn't. I realise you don't want to hear it – but I can't stomach that you've been hurt like this because of me. I could vomit every time I think of it. And the worst thing is, I don't understand why it happened. Since the day he came here, I haven't clapped eyes on d'Auxerre. He doesn't attend the theatre any more – though some say he goes to the Bourgogne instead and some, that he's spending a great deal of time at his new house on the Isle St. Louis. But whatever he's doing, he gives every appearance of having lost interest in me – in which case, what possible reason could he have for sending men to kill you? It doesn't make sense!'

This time, against his better judgement, he took her hand.

He said quietly, 'Actually, it does. He's the type of man who can't bear to lose, Athenais. He didn't take kindly to your refusal. You saw his reaction to that. Then I threw him out of the house. Not physically, as I would have liked, but that made little difference to him. And I suspect that, for a time at least, I've eclipsed you and become his primary target.' Running his thumb over and over the soft skin of her inner wrist, he held her eyes with his own. 'He may come at me again – or he may not. He may have lost interest in you – or he may not. But until we know one way or another, we'll keep all our precautions in place – and I'll give a little more attention to guarding my back.'

Athenais stared back at him, acutely conscious of his touch and wondering what he'd do if she leaned over and brushed his cheek with a kiss. Her lips parted and her breathing grew a little more rapid.

Ashley felt her pulse fluttering under his fingers and found himself sliding fathoms deep into liquid eyes the colour of smoke. She was beautiful, and passionate and, above all, *genuine*. He imagined how it would be to have her mouth under his … to slowly uncover each slender curve until every lovely inch of her lay beneath his hands … to have her helpless with hunger and gasping his name. *God.*

Inevitably, the brief fantasy produced a physical reaction which was about to make itself embarrassingly obvious. He shifted his position, raising his good knee to disguise it but something must have shown on his face for Athenais said quickly, 'You're in pain, aren't you? Is there anything I can do?'

Three things, darling – the most desirable of which I'm not capable right now, came the involuntary thought. Reprehensible, of course and also stupid since it did nothing to calm the stirring in his loins. Realising it would be wise to send her away so that his body had time to settle, he said, 'No. It's just a slight cramp. If I'm left alone for a while, I can … re-direct … my circulation.'

'Of course.' She stood up and gave him her usual dazzlingly sweet smile. 'Suzon is making a cassoulet for supper and I promised to help with the vegetables. Pauline is adamant that I shall not be idle, you see.'

She left, closing the door quietly behind her and Ashley released a breath he hadn't been aware of holding. Then he forced his mind clear and took several long, calming breaths. In one sense it was comforting to know that at least one part of his body was working correctly; in another it just added to the torments of this whole, hellish week.

* * *

After kicking his heels at the Louvre on more than one occasion and for far longer than he thought necessary, Francis returned at noon the following day with the information Ashley had asked for.

'I finally managed to see Hyde,' he said without preamble. 'It took him a while to stop pretending he didn't know what I was talking about but he was eventually persuaded to answer the question.'

'And?'

'And he hasn't involved anyone else in the matter. He seemed to feel that you were fully capable of resolving the situation without help.'

Ashley had suspected as much and wasn't particularly happy at having his suspicions confirmed. If One-Eyed Will wasn't working officially, the question of what he *was* doing became highly pertinent. Again, Ashley entertained and then dismissed the notion of an affair between Will and the King's former mistress but recognised that there was no harm in checking the matter out. And in the meantime, he needed to consider other possible alternatives – of which, just at the moment, he couldn't see any.

He said, 'Well, at least we know. It answers one question and poses a dozen others – which is hardly helpful. You'd better tell Jem to concentrate his efforts on the gentleman with the eye-patch.'

'Sir William Brierley,' said Francis, cheerfully. 'Yes.' And, with a slight shrug, 'I'm sorry. But it wasn't very difficult to establish.'

'No. I suppose not. I take it you're not personally acquainted with him?'

'Never met the fellow. But, reading between the lines, I'd guess he has certain skills ... not dissimilar to your own.'

'You're fishing,' said Ashley with a chilly smile. 'Don't.'

'All right. Have it your own way.' Francis sat down, stretched out his legs and contemplated the shabbiness of his boots. 'I've seen Celia, too – for all the good it did.'

'She wouldn't talk?'

'Oh – she talked. She talked more than I could listen.'

Ashley laughed. 'About what?'

'Nothing in the least useful. It seems that she and Lucy are not currently on speaking terms – which would explain why Jem hasn't seen her visiting. It's apparently on account of some furbelow or other. Lucy saw Celia wearing it and then went out and bought an identical one. I didn't attempt to follow all the ramifications but apparently copying another lady's fashions is an offence punishable by death or social ostracism. I was left in some doubt as to which would be worse.' He paused and, on heavy sigh, added, 'She also harangued me about Eden. She wants me to write again. And if we decide we need her help, I may actually have to do it.'

* * *

After leaving Ashley, Francis found Pauline alone in the parlour sewing something made of white cambric. She glanced up at him and said, 'I'm making a new shirt for the Colonel. The one from the night of the attack having been ruined, he's left with only the one he's wearing and another in the laundry.'

Francis was surprised to discover that, though he didn't begrudge Ashley a new shirt, he wasn't particularly thrilled to find Pauline making it with her own hands. He said, 'I'd have thought Athenais would be the one to do that.'

Pauline grinned. 'You wouldn't want to wear anything Athenais had made. She sews about as well as she cooks.' She paused to re-thread her needle. 'Did you want something?'

Yes. Some time in your company, he thought. And was again surprised by the thought.

'I wondered if Froissart has finalised the casting for *Ménage*,' he said, unable to think of anything better.

'He hasn't told you? Hortense is to play the wife, André will be the husband and Jacques gets to be the lover.' She shot him a brief but very direct glance. 'Are you sure Froissart didn't tell you? You've seen more of him this past week than I have.'

'The last time we spoke of it, he was still undecided,' replied Francis mendaciously. And then, with a flicker of his usual mischief, 'Will any of them manage to eclipse you, do you think?'

'No. But they'll do well enough.' Her needle still flying, she said, 'The Colonel is looking better.'

'And, as a result, is likely to become fractious. Yes.'

'I'm sure that, between us, we'll manage him.'

He grinned.

'Don't be coy, Duchess. You could manage him single-handed and you know it.'

'Perhaps.' She fell silent for a moment and then said, 'I asked you not to call me that.'

'No.'

She looked up sharply. 'No? What do you mean – *no*?'

'No, you haven't asked,' he replied simply.

'Oh.' A pause. Then, not quite as firmly as she'd intended, 'Well, I'm asking now. And something else on a completely different matter, if I may?'

'Of course.' He took this as an invitation to sit down. 'Anything you like.'

'You saw how Athenais feels about the Colonel.'

'At the time, it was hard to miss.'

She nodded. 'Does he know?'

'I wouldn't like to say. Ashley can hide his thoughts better than most men – or so I've found. But he's perceptive and annoyingly clever ... so I doubt we know something that he doesn't.'

'Yes. That's what I thought.' She stopped sewing to look at him. 'Since, aside from the day d'Auxerre tried to rape her, the Colonel hasn't made any move towards her, the obvious assumption is that he's not interested. But somehow, I don't think that's so.'

'No. Neither do I.' Francis grimaced slightly. 'Please tell me you're not hoping I'll ask him? He may be temporarily out of action in a physical sense but he's still got a tongue like a lash.'

'So, if your little play is anything to go by, do you.'

'Perhaps – but one needs dialogue for that. This wouldn't be. And, in truth, Ashley and I are far too old for that kind of conversation. I'm afraid you'll just have to rely on observation and intuition ... both of which are your speciality.'

* * *

By the fifth day of his confinement, Ashley had recovered most of his strength, his arm was almost healed and, though the wound in his thigh still throbbed and ached, the burning agony of the previous days had eased. And since he felt substantially better and was heartily sick of lying about like a maiden aunt with the vapours, he waited until he was fairly sure of being alone and decided to get up.

Careful as he was, two things happened immediately. The first was that his head swam sickeningly and he had to clutch at the bedpost for support; and the second was that, as soon as he tried to put his weight on it, his injured leg gave way. Ashley sat down with more haste than care and swore when pain roared through his thigh. Breathing rather hard, he stayed where he was for a few minutes and then forced himself to try again. This time it was a little easier and he managed to keep the dizziness at bay but his leg still refused to co-operate. He hung on to the bedpost, sweating and muttering a variety of curses ... and was still doing it when Athenais found him.

'What in God's name do you think you're doing?' She tossed bandages and salve on to the table in order to bear down on him like a miniature tidal wave. 'Sit down this instant!'

Ashley opened his mouth to argue and then, realising that he was standing there in nothing but his shirt, thought better of it. Subsiding cautiously on to the bed, he bestowed his miserable excuse for a leg and pulled the bed-covers over the essentials. Then, with only a modicum of restraint, he said curtly, 'I've got to start moving about at some point. If I lie here much longer, I'll ossify.'

'Another day won't hurt,' she snapped. 'Is this the first time you've tried this?'

'Obviously – or I'd be better at it.'

'And it didn't occur to you to ask one of us to help?'

'Oddly enough, it didn't.' He regarded her sarcastically over folded arms. 'Which of you was likely to say yes?'

Privately, Athenais conceded that he had a point there – though she suspected he might possibly have bullied Jem into getting him on his feet. She said accusingly, 'You *promised* me. You promised to stay in bed.'

'I said I'd stay in bed if you stopped hovering around the house in case I was about to turn up my toes,' he retorted. 'You didn't.'

'That's no excuse.'

'Yes, it is. We had an agreement. You broke it.'

'I don't care. It's still no reason to play merry hell with your – your limbs.'

A glint of something that might have been humour lurked beneath his lashes.

'Only a woman could believe that.'

'Well, I *am* a woman.'

'I think I can truthfully say that I've noticed.'

Hands on hips, she regarded him as severely as she was able over the unexpected bubble of laughter forming in her chest. 'When was the last time you did as you were told?'

'When Pauline brought me something vaguely resembling an egg custard and bade me eat it because you'd made it,' came the swift reply.

Athenais's mouth quivered.

'It *was* awful, wasn't it?'

'Dreadful.'

'I know.' On a little gurgle of laughter, she said confidingly, 'The first two were worse.'

And Ashley forgot his annoyance at being caught out of bed, his frustration with his own weakness and his boredom-induced black mood. In fact, he forgot everything except one simple truth. If he hadn't been in love with her already, he'd have lost his heart in that moment. She was utterly irresistible.

Short though it was, the silence was long enough to put a question in her eyes. He distracted her by saying, 'Look on the bright side. What you lack in culinary ability, you make up for in perseverance.'

'Yes. Pauline wishes I didn't. All those eggs, you know.' She sat at his side and began rolling the sleeve of his shirt upwards. 'She says the dressing on your arm probably isn't necessary any more. How does it feel?'

'Almost as good as new.' He waited until she'd removed the bandage and then, peering down, said, 'Yes. It will do well enough, now.'

'Just a little of the salve, then.' Athenais reached for the pot. 'Pauline thinks the scar may be very slight – unlike the one on your leg. But I suppose that, as a soldier, you don't consider scars to be any very great matter.'

Ashley listened less to the words than the light, pleasing voice and let himself drift. He absorbed the cameo-like purity of her profile; the arch of her eyebrows and the sweep of her lashes; the alabaster skin, faintly tinged with colour along her cheekbones; and finally the soft curve of her mouth ... pale and pink and infinitely tempting.

One thick lock of shining copper hair fell past her shoulder and landed on his wrist. Ashley stopped breathing for a moment. It was so close to his hand ... so very close that he couldn't resist taking hold of it and twining it round his fingers, then releasing it so that it formed a perfect glossy ringlet. Intrigued, he reached for another strand and did the same thing again.

Athenais gave a tiny laugh and said prosaically, 'It does that. The only trouble is there's so much of it that it would take hours to make the whole lot behave that way. Truthfully, it's the bane of my life – and Pauline's, too.'

'It's beautiful,' he said huskily.

She hadn't expected it. Not just the compliment, but the tone in which it was uttered. Her eyes flew to his face, searching for something that would tell her if either was to be taken seriously. He looked back at her, unwavering and darkly intent, a lock of her hair still caught between his fingers. Slowly and without releasing her gaze, he wound the curl around his hand until it began to pull her gently towards him. Athenais shivered.

Ashley had stopped thinking some time ago when it had seemed safe. Now, it was no longer safe but he couldn't remember why – or why it should matter. He drew Athenais closer and closer until he could slide his other arm about her waist. Then and only then did he release her hair to trace her cheek and jaw with almost insubstantial fingers.

The heavy-lidded gaze dropped to her mouth, causing one strong, startling beat to pulse low in her body. Her breath fluttered and nerves made her run her tongue over lips that felt suddenly dry. A faint sound echoed in the back of Ashley's throat and, leaning in, he brushed her mouth with his. Athenais gasped and, unable to wait any longer, slid her arms around his neck and pulled him closer.

'Yes,' murmured Ashley, almost inaudibly. 'Oh yes.'

And he possessed her mouth as if he had been waiting to do so for his entire life. She tasted so sweet and her response, as she melted against him, was sweeter still. He deepened the kiss and was rewarded with a tiny sound of welcome and pleasure. And he thought, *Mine. You're mine. And I am entirely, inescapably yours.*

Wildfire was spreading through Athenais's blood, creating molten heat deep in her belly. She filled her hands with his hair, trailed kisses along his throat and when his shirt stopped her exploring the unknown terrain of his chest, she gave a moan of frustration and fumbled with the fastenings. Tilting her face up for another mind-stealing kiss, Ashley tugged it free so that, at long last, she could discover the smooth warmth of his skin and the hard muscles beneath it. She sighed with pleasure.

His mouth teased its way slowly along her collar-bone while, without conscious thought yet as slowly as he had once promised himself, his fingers freed the laces of her gown until he could slide it from her shoulders. He took the time to thoroughly enjoy this new area of silky-soft skin before dealing with the impediment of her shift. But finally, it slipped away, revealing the lovely curve of her breasts ... and, for a moment, the air seemed to leave his lungs. He cupped them, marvelling at how perfectly they fitted into his palms before, lingeringly and almost reverently, he allowed himself to caress the smooth flesh. Athenais trembled and clutched at his shoulders, her breath fast and slightly ragged. He kissed her cheek, her eyelids, her jaw and set his thumbs circling the tips of her breasts until they hardened, before finally touching the sensitised flesh.

Athenais's head dropped back and she gave a sobbing moan. God, she was so incredibly, beautifully responsive. He shifted his position to pull her closer so that she might feel the state of his own arousal and know that she was not alone. His injured thigh protested but he scarcely noticed it. He wanted the rest of her clothes gone; he wanted to savour every exquisite inch with his mouth as well as his hands; he wanted to be inside her.

The door opened and Francis walked in.

For a second, he froze at the unexpected and erotic tableau in front of him. Then, recovering his presence of mind, he said, 'My apologies.' And beat a hasty retreat.

Equally shocked, Ashley and Athenais also froze.

A deep flush stained Athenais's skin – less because of what she'd been doing than because she'd been seen doing it – but she made no attempt to cover herself.

Ashley removed his hands from her and sat very, very still as the world dropped stomach-churningly back into focus.

She said unevenly, 'That was ... a little unfortunate.'

'You think so?'

His tone sounded odd, not at all what she might have expected considering what had just passed between them. She turned to look at him. His face was completely without expression, his eyes flat and opaque. Athenais didn't know whether he was embarrassed on her account or his own or whether he was just annoyed at the interruption – but she assumed it must be one of them. Stroking the tawny-fair hair back from his face, she tilted her head to kiss his jaw and murmured, 'Perhaps I should lock the door?'

There was a long silence. Then Ashley said distantly, 'Or perhaps I should help you dress.'

Her heart sank and worry started to gnaw at the edges of her mind.

'Why? It doesn't really matter that Francis knows, does it? He may say something to you, of course – but he's too much of a gentleman to speak of it to anyone else. And if I don't mind, why should you?'

He nearly said that he minded immensely that Francis had seen her half-naked but for the wild tumble of her hair but knew that it wouldn't help to admit it. So he forced his brain to function and said instead, 'What Francis knows or doesn't know is of little consequence.'

'Then what is?'

'Do you really need to ask?' He dislodged her from his lap, turning her as he did so in order to begin re-lacing her gown. 'What happened just now may have been unintentional but it was still a mistake. My fault not yours, of course.'

Athenais wriggled free and managed to swivel back to face him.

'Stop it! You can't do this again.'

'Do what?'

'Pretend there's nothing between us. Pretend you don't want me.'

Despising himself and feeling utterly sick, he summoned a faint rueful smile and did what had to be done.

'Darling – of course I want you. What man wouldn't? And I've been lying in bed for days with you popping in and out of here ministering to my every need save one – so it was inevitable that I should fantasise a little, if only to pass the time.'

She dragged herself from the bed and stood up, clutching her gown to her chest.

'Inevitable?' And when he nodded, 'You'll have to forgive me – but I'd like to be clear about this. You've been imagining removing my clothes and putting your hands on me *just to pass the time?*'

'Well, yes.' He shrugged with a nicely-judged hint of repentance. 'It's what men do – and there's little enough harm in it. But it was wrong of me to take advantage and we should be grateful that Francis brought us both to our senses before it went too far.'

Athenais wasn't grateful at all. In her opinion, it hadn't gone far enough. She was also becoming rather angry. 'I don't know whether you think I'm an idiot or merely naïve. But one thing I *do* know. Even if you *were* the kind of man to seduce a girl just to pass a dull Tuesday – which you're not – nothing that passed between us before Francis walked in had anything to do with taking advantage purely because you had the opportunity. It was more than that.'

Ashley leaned back against the pillows and began fastening his shirt with an appearance of total unconcern.

'I see. And you know this because?'

'I know it,' she said, her voice suddenly unsteady, 'because when I was fourteen, I was raped by an eighteen-year-old version of the Marquis d'Auxerre.' She watched his hands still and his face go rigid with shock. 'I know it because I know *you* – you stupid, *stupid* man! And for God knows what reason, I seem to have fallen in love with you. But until you know your own mind and are prepared either to explain why whatever this is between us can't be allowed to happen or admit that you really don't care for me, I suggest you keep your hands to yourself – because I'm not about to make this mistake again.'

And, without giving him the chance to reply, she whirled out of the room, slamming the door behind her.

FOUR

Although Francis said nothing to either Athenais or Pauline, he'd half-intended to provoke Ashley with some sly innuendo. Fortunately, before he opened his mouth, he caught sight of the Colonel's expression and recognised that saying anything at all was likely to conjure up a storm. He therefore made a swift exit, leaving Ashley lurching from window to bed to wash-stand as he hauled himself grimly around the bedchamber.

Ashley's mood was black as the deepest pit of hell. In the first moments when Athenais had slammed out of the room, he'd found himself unable to focus on anything beyond that one sentence as it rang over and over in his head.

When I was fourteen I was raped by an eighteen-year-old version of the Marquis d'Auxerre.

She'd been raped. Three words repeatedly slamming into his gut like a fist. She'd been raped. Why hadn't he guessed? Why hadn't he even considered the possibility? She'd been raped. Now he knew, the clues were all there; her aversion to d'Auxerre, her habit of keeping her admirers at a distance; her lack of sexual experience. Everything pointed to it but he, clever fellow that he was, had been too self-absorbed to look below the surface. His Athenais had been raped; worse, some bastard had raped her when she was fourteen years old, for Christ's sake. And that was when the bile had risen in his throat and sent him stumbling from the bed to vomit into the chamber-pot.

He felt marginally better after that – but not much. He'd known for some time that he couldn't touch her without becoming as eager as a schoolboy but between one breath and the next, he'd forgotten all his self-made rules and been half-way to having her. He tried to tell himself that it wouldn't have gone that far … that, even without Francis's unexpected appearance, he'd have come to his senses and stopped. The trouble was he couldn't be sure. Where Athenais was concerned, he didn't seem to have any self-control worth a damn.

Everything he'd said afterwards had been designed to annoy her into doing what he seemed incapable of doing himself – and it had worked, in that she'd told him to keep his hands off her in future. Unfortunately, she'd seen everything else he'd said for the lie it was. Worse still, she'd hurled a declaration of love in his face and revealed something about herself that made his chest feel as though a piece had been hacked out of it.

He didn't know what to do about any of it. So he harangued Jem into bringing him a pair of breeches and then set about using physical pain as a shield. He forced himself back and forth across the room until his thigh was screaming at him to stop ... and then, after a brief respite, did it all over again. It was at some point during this that Francis had stuck his head round the door, sensibly kept his mouth shut and immediately taken himself off. If he'd stayed, if he'd said one word, Ashley thought he'd probably have hit him.

By the following afternoon when Athenais had still not been near him, he realised that if matters were to be mended, she was leaving it up to him to do it. He didn't blame her for that. One way and another, he'd left her with little choice. The problem was that, if she wouldn't come to him, he was going to have to go in search of her. And if he couldn't manage the bloody bedroom, he had no chance at all of negotiating the stairs. So the second day passed like the first, heaping pain upon pain as he struggled to regain a modicum of useful mobility.

* * *

Athenais knew what he was doing. From time to time, she stood outside his door, listening to uneven footsteps and the occasional muffled curse. After six days incarceration, he had clearly reached the limit of his endurance and was determined to get back on his feet as quickly as possible. It occurred to her that he might be doing more harm than good; that someone ought to tell him to stop. But she stayed away because, if he was determined to retreat behind his invisible wall, she had no way to reach him.

She rather regretted telling him that she loved him – not because she didn't want him to know but because she suspected he was under enough self-induced pressure already. For all she knew, he was even now busy convincing himself that she expected him to go down on one knee and offer her a ring. And if he was, he'd probably continue thinking it no matter what she said. On the other hand, he must have guessed how she felt without her saying it ... unless girls usually threw themselves into his arms at the first opportunity. Athenais scowled at the notion, guessing that they probably did.

So she thought about everything except those alarmingly exquisite moments in his arms and rehearsed endless beautifully reasonable and dignified speeches. And in between, she stood outside his door and worried.

Eventually, on the second day and after two hours of spasmodic hovering, she communicated her fears to Pauline.

'What do you expect me to do about it?' came the reply. 'As of this morning, he informed me – oh-so-politely and with a smile that would make hell freeze – that he was grateful for all I'd done but would take care of his leg himself in future.'

'And you *let* him?'

'He's a big boy, Athenais. He's also alarmingly capable and far from stupid.'

'But he can't go on like this. Someone needs to make him see sense.'

'So go and try,' came the typical reply. And with a sideways glance, 'Or have the two of you had a falling-out?'

'Something like that. He's stupid and utterly pig-headed.'

'He's a man,' shrugged Pauline. 'What else did you expect?'

'Francis isn't like that.'

'Francis is *exactly* like that. Why else do you think I'm going back on-stage for the first time in nearly seven years if not because his dratted lordship thinks it's a good idea and has bullied me into it?'

Athenais allowed herself to be temporarily diverted.

'Yesterday was the first rehearsal, wasn't it? How did it go?'

'Well enough.' There was a pause and then Pauline gave the smile that totally transformed her face and that very few people ever got to see. 'Better than that, actually. Unless I'm very much mistaken, it's going to be outstanding.'

* * *

In the end, it was Francis who told Ashley that if he didn't stop punishing his leg he'd give himself a permanent limp.

'I've got to get out of this room,' snapped Ashley. 'It's driving me insane.'

'Fine. Lean on me and I'll help you downstairs.'

'And back up again? I don't think so.' He pushed his hands into his hair, then withdrew them in disgust. 'And I need a bath. But that means asking someone to haul the tub up here, along with enough water to fill it.'

'Jem and I can manage that. Anything else?'

'Yes. Don't tell Pauline or I'll have to ask permission to get the damned stitches wet.'

Francis sighed. He said, 'I recognise that you're in a lousy mood. I also recognise that you're entitled to be. But if you use that tone to Pauline, she'll take your head off – and rightly so.'

'I'm not that stupid.'

'Or that foolhardy, one would hope. Upon which note – if you'll do yourself the favour of sitting down for half an hour – I'll set about organising a bath for you. With a bit of luck, it may improve your temper. And if it doesn't, I suppose we can always drown you in it.'

* * *

Leaving Ashley soaking gratefully in a tub of hot water, Francis went downstairs to where Athenais was pacing up and down the hall. As soon as she saw him, she said, 'You've stopped him trying to maim himself?'

'For the time being.'

'And he's taking a bath?'

'He is. I left Jem up there in case he needs help. But if you wanted to scrub his back ...' He stopped and, absorbing the look on her face, drew her towards the empty parlour. 'I'm sorry. Obviously that's not funny. Do you want to tell me about it?'

She perched on the edge of the sofa.

'About what?'

'About what's troubling you and causing Ashley to look as though he's possessed by demons.' Francis sat beside her and then, when she didn't answer, said, 'I don't mean to pry and I certainly don't wish to embarrass you. But from what I glimpsed the other day, I rather had the impression that the two of you had ... come to an understanding, shall we say?'

'I thought that, too,' she replied stonily. 'But apparently not.'

'Ah.' A faint frown touched the sapphire eyes. 'Ashley's decision, presumably?'

'Yes.' Colour rose in her face as she realised that, having seen what he had, Francis could have no doubts on that score. 'He was quite adamant.'

'Did he explain why?'

'No.'

Francis's brows rose. 'He didn't say *anything?*'

'Oh yes. He said quite a lot. But none of it was true,' said Athenais bitterly. And then, sitting a little straighter, 'I'm sorry. I shouldn't be talking about this. And I wouldn't be if you hadn't … you know.'

'Yes. I'm extremely sorry about that.'

'You weren't to know.' She paused, industriously pleating a fold of her skirt. 'And I'm probably being unfair. I'm sure Ashley has his reasons.'

'Undoubtedly. But you'll forgive me for observing that, under the circumstances, you've a right to know what they are,' remarked Francis coolly. 'And I'll be quite happy to tell him that if you wish.'

'No!' She swung to face him. 'No, you mustn't do that. He wouldn't … that is, you know what he's like. And --'

She broke off, coming swiftly to her feet as the doorbell rang.

Francis also stood, saying with a grin, 'Your father will answer it. He's impatient to try out that club of his – so let us hope the visitor is a friend.'

Out in the hall, Archie stared belligerently at the stranger on the doorstep.

'Who the 'ell are you?' he demanded. And then, recollecting that the fellow probably didn't speak the King's own English, added laboriously, 'Key ett voo?'

Noting the large billet in the doorman's left hand, the visitor took a wary step back and said, 'I'm looking for Major Langley.' Then, because it seemed expected, '*Je cherche* Major Langley.'

'I got that the first time,' said Archie, scowling but relieved to be on safe linguistic ground and becoming belatedly aware that the left sleeve of the visitor's coat was empty and pinned neatly across his chest. 'What do you want wiv 'im?'

'That's my business and his. I'm told he lives here. Is that correct?'

'Might be.' Archie found himself torn. The fellow didn't *look* dangerous – but then, neither did the Marquis with his fancy ruffles and fine white hands. He said, 'I've orders not to admit any strangers.'

'Oh? Well, I'm not a stranger. Major Langley knows me very well. If he's at home, perhaps you could summon him?'

Reaching a decision, Archie said, 'Wait 'ere, then.' And promptly shut the door in the fellow's face.

Sticking his head round the parlour door, he jerked his chin at Francis, and said, 'There's a cove at the door wot says he knows you.'

'His name?'

Declining to admit that he'd forgotten to ask, Archie shrugged.

'Didn't say. All I know is 'e's English. I've left 'im on the doorstep, if you want to come and take a look.'

'Obviously a villainous-looking fellow,' murmured Francis to Athenais. 'Stay here while I see who it is.' And, out in the hall, 'For God's sake, Archie – surely it wasn't necessary to shut the door on him?'

'Can't be too careful. Colonel's orders.'

With a slight shake of his head, Francis pulled the door open ... and went rigid with disbelief. '*Nick?*'

Nicholas grinned. 'Hello, Francis. Some jealous husband out for your blood, is he?

'No. *Oh Christ.*' Recovering the use of his legs, Francis surged forward to pull his friend into a crushing embrace. 'This is – God, Nick. I can't believe it. How the *hell* --?' He stopped, realising why the hug felt awkward and changed his grip to pull Nicholas over the threshold. 'That doesn't matter. Come inside. Ignore Archie. He's here to protect the ladies – one of them, anyway. I'm sorry. I'm babbling. I'm still having trouble believing you're really here. We were so worried – you have no idea. Ashley couldn't forgive himself for not being able to get to you in time – yet here you are. How on earth did you find us?'

Finally able to get a word in edgeways, Nicholas said, 'Ash is here?'

'Yes. He's --' Francis stopped as the parlour door opened and, switching back to French, said, 'Athenais – this Captain Sir Nicholas Austin, a good friend of ours. Nick – allow me to introduce you to Mademoiselle de Galzain; the best actress in Paris bar one, if she'll forgive me for saying so.'

'I can't argue with the truth.' She smiled at Nicholas and dropped a graceful curtsy. 'I'm delighted to meet you, sir. Have you recently come from England?'

Nicholas, who was having the usual male reaction to Athenais's looks, swallowed and, in passable but rusty French, said, 'Yes. I arrived yesterday.'

'Then you should sit down and I will send Suzon in with wine.'

'You don't need to leave,' said Francis quickly.

'I do. After so long, you and Monsieur will have a great deal to talk about and I shall be very much in the way. Ah – unless you'd prefer to join Ashley upstairs?'

'Not if he's still in the bath. Perhaps you could ... or no. Then again, perhaps not.'

'Definitely not,' she agreed firmly. And left the room.

Nicholas stared after her. 'Good Lord, Francis. Is she your ... your ...?'

'No. She isn't. In fact, she isn't anybody's ... whatever the particular word was that you were looking for. She and her friend own the lease to this house and kindly allow Ashley and me to lodge here. But all that can wait. First, I want to hear about you.' He paused. 'I'm sorry about your arm. Worcester, I suppose?'

'Yes.' Nicholas kept his tone light. 'It's inconvenient at times but I'm used to it now.'

Recognising that further conversation on this point would be unwelcome, Francis said, 'So where have you been all this time? And how did you manage to find us?'

Nicholas opened his mouth to speak and then closed it again as Suzon came in carrying a tray with wine and glasses. He waited until she left and watched to make sure the door was properly shut. Then he reached into the breast of his coat and said, 'I have a letter for you.'

'A letter?' Francis took the packet, eyed the superscription and immediately recognised the handwriting. 'Eden? How is it you've brought me a letter from Eden?'

'It's a long story and most of it should probably wait until Ashley joins us. But basically, Colonel Maxwell saved both my life and my liberty after Worcester. I've been lodging with him in Cheapside for the last year. We can talk of all that later, if you wish. The important thing is that something happened recently which made him want to get a message to you – and so, here I am.' He gestured to the tray. 'You should read what he has to say. In fact, you'd probably better read it twice.'

Frowning a little, Francis did so. The letter was not written in Eden's usual economic style and described, at some length, the state of the weather, the quality of the last harvest and the fall in trade occasioned by the Dutch war. But wrapped up inside it were three pieces of salient information.

Pray tell your lady sister that her sorry situation is well-noted and that, if there is a way to rid her of this onerous burden – discreetly and without injury to either party – I will endeavour to find it.

Which, loosely translated, said, 'Tell Celia she can have her divorce if it doesn't inconvenience me.'

And a paragraph and a half later, *Your father will doubtless be interested to learn that the legal dispute regarding his country retreat has finally been resolved. A number of such cases, I believe.*

Not such good news. Eden was informing him that sequestration order on Far Flamstead had finally been enforced – presumably one of the six hundred Royalist properties confiscated to fund the Navy. Francis discovered he was quite glad he wouldn't have to tell his father that their home was irretrievably lost. Until this moment, there had always been a frail hope that one day … well, that was gone now.

Then, nearing the end, *I am sending this letter by way of a young man of good family. His loyalty and veracity are to be entirely relied upon. I believe his expertise in certain matters may be of value to you.*

In other words, 'Nicholas has important information. Listen carefully and do something about it.'

Francis drew a long breath and looked up.

'Well, at least Celia will be pleased. For the rest … what's it all about, Nick?'

'It's complicated and I'd sooner only have to go through it all once. So perhaps we could wait until Ashley comes down?'

'How long have you got?' Francis rose and picked up the wine-bottle and glasses. 'Ashley won't be coming down because he can't. So let's go and see if he's fit for company.'

'What do you mean – he can't?' Nicholas followed Francis into the hall. 'What's the matter with him?'

'A good many things, in my opinion. But the one that's keeping him upstairs is a nasty sword thrust to his thigh. It happened nearly a week ago.'

Nicholas stopped abruptly on the turn of the stair.

'Are you saying he's been incapacitated for a *week*?'

'Yes.'

'Oh God.'

'Don't worry. He won't rip up at you. He'll be too glad you're alive.' Francis stopped outside Athenais's door and knocked.

'You can come in,' said an irritable voice from within. 'I'm dry, dressed and not engaging in fleshly pleasures.'

Francis cast Nicholas a look which clearly said, *You see?* Then he opened the door saying, 'Mind your manners – or Nick and I will leave you to your own miserable devices.'

And Ashley, who had been lying on the bed with an arm flung over his eyes while he tried to decide on what, if anything, he could usefully say to Athenais, sat up with a jerk.

'What? *What* did you say?'

'You heard.' Francis stepped to one side so that Ashley could see who stood behind him. 'Nick's here.'

Colour flooded into Ashley's face and he hauled himself to his feet so fast that he had to catch at the bedpost for support. Joy, relief and sheer incredulity lit his eyes and he said unevenly, 'Oh Christ. Nick. You're alive. I'm so sorry.'

'You're sorry I'm alive?' asked Nicholas, attempting to leaven the moment. 'What kind of welcome is that?'

Knowing how Ashley must feel, Francis turned away from them to pour the wine and then, clearing his throat, he said, 'Nick has a tale to tell. And I suspect, from the way he's been behaving and the extremely peculiar letter he brought from Eden, that it's cloak-and-dagger stuff – as if we didn't have enough of that already.'

Ashley sat down on the side of the bed.

'Eden?' He looked at Francis. 'Your friend-and-brother-in-law-and-Colonel-in-the-New-Model, Eden?'

'Yes. Truthfully, how many men do you think there *are* with a name like that? And, before you ask, he's been looking after Nick for the past year.'

Ashley's eyes narrowed as they returned to Nicholas.

'He knows you're a King's man? And a Catholic?'

'Yes.'

'Yet he still helped?'

'Yes. He's a good fellow. One of the best I've ever met.' Nicholas took a large swallow of his wine. 'And he's risking his neck by sending me here to pass on information he acquired by accident and isn't supposed to have.'

Ashley shot a sharp glance at Francis before restoring his attention to Nicholas.

'Information about what?'

'A plot to assassinate the King and the Duke of York.'

Silence lapped the edges of the room.

'Go on. I won't ask if Colonel Maxwell is sure about this. I'm presuming he must be or he wouldn't have sent you – and the very nature of such a threat means that we have to take it seriously whether it exists or not,' said Ashley crisply. 'I take it he's sent us no tangible proof?'

Nicholas shook his head. 'He didn't think it wise for me to carry anything in writing in case --'

'In case you were stopped. Quite right. The Colonel plainly has more sense than most of our own agents. But he showed you something to support his suspicions?'

'Yes. I should probably mention that he's currently working for the Secretary of State as a code-breaker --'

'He *what?*' exclaimed Francis. And, with a laugh, 'God. He must *love* that. He's worse at sitting still than you are, Ashley.'

'Shut up and let Nicholas finish. Nick?'

'He deals with a lot of reports and other correspondence on a daily basis. Since he devises the codes for both Thomas Scot's and Thurloe's agents, he knows who those agents are – and, more importantly, who they *aren't*. And over the last couple of months, he's found two stray letters – probably part of some wider communication – mixed up with a pile of other stuff. Both were in the same handwriting and used the same code – but the code wasn't one of Eden's own, although it should have been.'

'Thus arousing his suspicions,' nodded Ashley. 'Yes. Who does he believe these letters were meant for?'

'Secretary Thurloe.' Nick polished off the rest of his wine and held out his glass for Francis to re-fill. 'Eden thinks he's backing the plot in secret, in case things go awry. Eden also thinks the entire concept of a double murder – after having already executed the late King – is an abomination. And he sent me to you so we can stop it.'

Another silence fell. But finally Francis said, 'You've seen these letters?'

'Yes. The first was non-specific and spoke only of permanently removing all cause of future civil and political unrest. The second was more detailed. Charles and James are to be lured to Honfleur where someone will be waiting to assassinate them. No names or dates were given and the writer seemed to be awaiting confirmation to proceed. I know it's not very much to go on, but --'

'It's enough.' Ashley stood up to ease the muscles in his injured thigh. 'Pay Hyde another visit, Francis. Tell him I have wind of a possible plot against the King's life and require to be instantly informed of any travel plans he may have – particularly in the general direction of Le Havre. Oh – and tell him on no account to mention this to His Majesty.'

Francis looked blank. 'Why not? I'd have thought His Majesty would be the *first* person you'd tell.'

'Absolutely not. I have an idea how this may be managed and I don't want Charles sticking his oar in.' He sat down again and lifted a brow at Nicholas. 'Is there anything else?'

'No. Yes. I almost forgot. Eden said to tell Hyde they've got a copy of the King's marriage lines to Lucy Walter.'

Ashley and Francis exchanged a thoughtful look.

'Bugger,' said Ashley succinctly. 'So that's where it ended up. I wonder how?'

'At least there's no further point in us looking for it.'

'*Have* you been looking for it?' asked Nicholas. 'Because if you have, there's something else Eden said to mention.'

'Which is?'

'He thinks it's a forgery. And he thinks it's a forgery because it's in the same handwriting as the two plot letters.'

For a long moment, Ashley stared at him without speaking, his expression one of sardonic irritation.

'Now why,' he invited at length, 'couldn't you have said that in the first place?'

FIVE

While the gentlemen shared their news of the last year and spoke of plots, Athenais told Pauline of the new arrival and added that they'd probably have to find another bed.

'Francis was overjoyed to see him and seemed to think that Ashley would be even more so, so I imagine they'll want him to move in here. But that will mean either shifting Jem downstairs or leaving Ashley in my room so Sir Nicholas can have the couch in the dressing-closet. What do you think?'

'I think I've had enough of sharing a bed with you tossing and turning all night long. So as soon as Ashley can manage the stairs, he can go back to the attic – and they can move the couch up there for their friend.' Her mouth curled a little and she said, '*Sir* Nicholas? Dear me. What a superior lodging-house we're running.'

Later that evening, after Pauline and Francis had left for the theatre, Ashley decided that if he put off speaking to Athenais much longer, he'd never do it at all. Consequently, he said, 'Nick … do something for me, will you?'

'Name it.'

'Find Athenais and ask her if she'd kindly spare me a few minutes of her time – at her own convenience, naturally.'

'Naturally,' agreed Nicholas with a grin. And then, 'She's a looker, isn't she?'

'Yes. She is.'

For some reason, Nicholas suspected a wealth of meaning lay behind those three short words but it was a meaning that escaped him. Then, as he turned to go, Ashley said, 'By the way, don't be surprised if she says no. And don't press it. Just say that I'd go to her if I could.'

Athenais didn't say no although Nicholas was fairly sure she was considering it. Instead, she said, 'How long have the three of you known each other?'

'On and off, about five years. But before Scotland, our acquaintance was mostly casual.' He smiled at her, the warm, frank smile that was his most attractive feature. 'The last time we were all together was at Worcester – which, in case you were wondering, is where I lost my arm.'

Athenais flushed a little. She *had* been wondering but wished he hadn't guessed it.

He said, 'It's all right, you know. No one is ever sure quite what to say, so I generally find it's best to get the thing out of the way by broaching the subject myself.'

'That's very ... brave.'

He shrugged. 'Like most things, it gets easier the more one does it.'

'Like *some* things, perhaps,' muttered Athenais. 'Others just get more difficult.'

This time Nicholas had no trouble reading the signs and said, 'If you don't want to see Ash, you've only to say. I don't mind telling him – and he's half-expecting it anyway.'

'Is he, indeed?' A martial gleam entered the storm-grey eyes. 'Why?'

'I don't know. But if you were to go upstairs, you could find out.'

Against all expectation, Athenais laughed.

'Very clever. Did *he* tell you to say that?'

'No. He told me not to press you – and that he'd have come to you if he could.'

'Oh.' She stopped laughing. 'That's worse.'

'It is, isn't it?'

* * *

Upstairs in the room he had come to hate, Ashley sat by the window staring out into the darkness and finally accepting what, deep down, he'd known all along. The thing he'd been trying to avoid had happened anyway so there was no point in continuing to prevaricate. Consequently, the only thing that would serve now was the truth – or some of it, at least. Five years of never revealing anything more than was strictly necessary had become such a deeply ingrained habit that the notion of baring his soul was more than a little alarming. He wasn't even sure it was possible.

Of course, if she didn't come he wouldn't have to say anything at all ... and he rather thought that might be worse. It occurred to him that the things he *wasn't* sure of far outstripped those he *was*. It was a worrying thought and it caused an unpleasant churning sensation in his chest.

He'd left the door open so she wouldn't have to knock. And eventually he heard the rustle of her skirts and the light tap of her shoes on the stairs. He stood up, leaning with apparently negligent grace against the window embrasure. Something inside him was wound so tightly he thought it might snap.

Athenais arrived in the doorway and stayed there, looking at him.

'Sir Nicholas says you want to see me.'

He winced. 'I hope he didn't put it like that.'

'No. He was beautifully polite. But it amounts to the same thing, doesn't it?'

'Yes. So I should thank you for coming. I'm sorry I had to ask – but the stairs are a little beyond me just yet.'

She nodded and took a couple of steps into the room, shutting the door behind her.

'Then perhaps you should sit down.'

'I can't until you do.' And, when she looked blank, 'A gentleman never sits while a lady is standing.' He smiled crookedly. 'I still have some manners, you see.'

Being unfamiliar with this type of courtesy, Athenais was unsure of her cue so she sat down and, keeping her back ramrod straight, said bluntly, 'As you're perfectly well-aware, I'm not a lady. However … do I have to invite you to sit?'

'It would be a kindness.'

'Then please do.'

'Thank you.' He sank back on to the window-seat, somehow feeling that the exchange wasn't going as well as it might. He said slowly, 'It seemed to me that we needed to talk.'

'Oh?'

It *definitely* wasn't going as well as it might.

'Yes. First and foremost, of course, I owe you an apology.'

'For what?'

'I think you know the answer to that,' he said dryly.

'No. Actually, I don't.' She decided that this was no time for maidenly modesty or sparing his feelings. She wished his eyes didn't seem to be able to see inside her head. She wished she didn't remember the taste of his mouth or the way his hands had felt on her body. She wished just looking at him didn't make her feel weak and muddled. Forcing herself not to think of those things, she said, 'Are you apologising for starting to make love to me or for suddenly stopping or for the insulting things you said afterwards?'

The blood rose under his skin.

'All three, I suppose.'

'And you think that makes everything all right?'

'No.'

'Good. Because I don't want an apology. I want the truth. I want to understand what, if anything, is happening between us. And, if you're not prepared to be honest with me, I don't see that we have anything to talk about.'

Ashley squeezed his eyes shut for a second and then, opening them, fixed her with a very direct stare. He said, 'Very well. Clearly, there is an undeniable attraction between us which I'd hoped to prevent developing into anything more. For your own sake, I'd *particularly* hoped that you wouldn't make the mistake of – of caring for me. But, from what you said yesterday, it seems I failed in that.'

'Yes,' she agreed simply. Then, 'Why is it a mistake?'

'For any number of reasons.' He was glad she'd asked that and not what he thought was the obvious question. As long as she didn't ask how he felt, there might be a chance of salvaging something. 'You know my circumstances. I'm an impoverished ex-soldier without any future prospects. Just like your father, in fact.' She would have spoken then but he held up one hand to stop her. 'Let me finish. I don't know if Pauline told you of a conversation she and I had some time ago but, if she didn't, I should add that I have nothing to go back to in England. My brother owns what used to be my home and he has made it plain that I am not welcome there. His reasons for this bring us to a part of my life that I don't normally discuss – and can't speak of now unless I'm guaranteed of your absolute discretion.'

Athenais frowned a little, not sure what to expect.

'Yes. Of course.'

'I mean it, Athenais. You are not to repeat this to anyone – not even Pauline.'

'Then I won't. Are you saying ... does Francis not know?'

'He knows some of it. Nick probably knows a little more. Neither of them knows everything.' *And nor will you if I can help it*. He said, 'As

349

you know, I hold the military rank of Colonel. But a select handful of people – one of whom is the King – know me as The Falcon.'

He'd half-expected her to laugh. Goodness only knew he'd always found the sobriquet ridiculous and could quite cheerfully have throttled the fellow who'd first come up with it.

Athenais didn't laugh. Looking into those gold-flecked green eyes, her first thought was that the name suited him … and her second, that she couldn't grasp the significance of it. She said, 'I don't understand.'

He drew a long breath and loosed it.

'I'm a Royalist agent. I've been one for five years, give or take.'

She stared at him for so long he began to think she still didn't understand. Then she said blankly, 'You're a *spy?*'

'Not exactly. When asked, I do whatever needs to be done. Much of it isn't honourable and none of it is pretty. But the political situation breeds men like me … and though I don't regret the things I've done, I'm not proud of them either.' He paused and then added, 'There's been nothing of any consequence since Francis and I arrived in Paris. But that doesn't necessarily mean there won't ever be. And I serve the King as he – or more usually Chancellor Hyde – sees fit.'

Athenais tried to come to terms with what he was telling her. He'd said something once before. Something about killing men on the battlefield and off it, in ways she didn't want to know about. It didn't fit with the man she knew … but she had no difficulty in accepting that, like her, he did what he had to and also that there was a good deal of his life about which she knew nothing.

He was waiting for her to say something – to be shocked, perhaps. He needed to know that she wasn't.

'I see. That is to say … I'm not sure why you told me. Unless you think that knowing it will make me feel differently towards you?'

He'd done it to emphasise the fact that he was sometimes required to risk his life.

'Doesn't it?'

'No.'

'Perhaps you should take time to consider – not just that but the other things I said.'

'About money and prospects and so forth? No. Those things don't matter.'

'Then they should,' he said flatly. 'You've made a life for yourself, Athenais. You've carved it out of sweat and determination and it's a hell of an achievement. I've just explained why I have nothing to offer – not just to you, but to any woman. And it's unlikely to change.'

She bent her head over her hands, pleating and re-pleating a fold of her skirt. Then she said huskily, 'As far as I'm aware, I haven't asked you for anything.'

'No. But --'

'And if I *did* ask ... it wouldn't be for anything you couldn't give, if you chose to.'

Ashley's heart constricted in a way that was becoming all-too-familiar. He didn't know what to say. He could only think, *Stop now. Please stop. Don't make me hurt you. Or myself.*

She looked up, directly into his eyes.

'I don't expect you to change your life or to offer me any promises of permanence. I only want ... well, I think you know what I want. And you said you wanted it, too. Unless that was another lie?'

In view of what she'd told him about her past this was no time to dodge the issue.

'It wasn't.' *God, darling – it really wasn't.*

'Then I don't see why ... why it's so impossible.'

Ashley could but he didn't feel up to explaining. However, before he could say anything at all, she said abruptly, 'It's not as if I'm a virgin, is it?'

His throat closed and it took a great deal of effort to say, 'No. But that is hardly your fault.'

'I know. I know it isn't. But that doesn't make it any less true.' Her colour had risen and she no longer looked nearly as composed as she'd done a little while ago. 'You should know that I haven't ... since that one time, I haven't ... there hasn't been anyone else.'

Ashley had suspected as much. It didn't make it any better. She'd been raped at fourteen, remained celibate for eight years and was sitting there offering herself to him, freely and unconditionally. It made his reservations seem suddenly very trivial. He said gently, 'Is that because you were afraid?'

'No. Yes. A little, perhaps. But mostly it was because I never met a man I wanted.'

Until you. The words hung unspoken in the air and they destroyed him.

His mind was a mass of conflictions. He was no longer sure why he was hesitating. He wondered if she knew that she could break his resolve with the smallest touch. Even when she wasn't physically present, a steady flame of wanting burned inside him. It would be so very easy to just tell the truth and stretch out his hand.

Too easy, said a distant voice in his head.

He drew a long, slightly ragged breath and said, 'I'd like you to take some time to think about this, Athenais. Will you do that?'

'What choice do I have?'

'None. But you should know that the reasons I'm holding back are on your account, not mine.' He smiled somewhat ruefully. 'And, for what it's worth, you may also wish to know that keeping my hands to myself isn't as easy as I may have led you to suppose.'

* * *

Two days slid by. Nicholas settled into the household, causing scarcely a ripple and Athenais returned to the theatre – receiving a sharp look from Monsieur Froissart and the observation that she looked remarkably well for someone who'd been throwing up for a week.

A further three days saw Ashley finally able to manage the stairs – whereupon Pauline announced that she would examine his leg whether he liked it or not to see if it was time to remove the stitches. He didn't like it but she bullied him into submission and removed her handiwork – after which he found that his thigh felt a lot easier.

And at the end of a week, Froissart at last gave Athenais and the rest of the players permission to sit in on a rehearsal for *Ménage* ... so that they could all see for themselves the genius of Pauline Fleury.

Francis had set the piece so that the husband, the wife and her lover interacted in the normal way while the mother-in-law sat on a raised platform – apparently unseen and unheard by the other characters while she delivered a pithy and wickedly funny commentary on their doings. The play was original, clever and stylishly-written. Pauline's performance raised it to the level of brilliance and the rehearsal finished in a storm of applause – in which, it was noticed, only Marie d'Amboise declined to participate.

Later, released from her lofty station and having escaped from the congratulations of her fellow actors, Pauline sought out Francis and said, 'Thank you. I thought you were mad to insist on it and that I was equally mad to agree. I was wrong. So – thank you.'

'It was my pleasure, Duchess. I knew you could do it. It was only necessary that *you* should know it, too.' He smiled at her. 'I've an idea for *Ménage Deux*. The husband, his mistress, his wife – and *her* mother. What do you think?'

I think what I feel for you is becoming dangerous.

She said, 'If it were anyone else, I'd say writing another play as good as this one is an impossibility. Since it's you, however, I'll say that I wouldn't like to put money on it.'

Francis lifted her hand and saluted it with impeccable grace.

'That is probably the nicest thing anyone has ever said to me.'

'Am I supposed to believe that?'

'Yes. Oddly enough, no one has ever rated my abilities very highly. The fact that you – who know this world so much better than I – think that I have some ... let's call it potential ... means a great deal.'

His tone was light enough but there was something behind his eyes which Pauline couldn't quite interpret. She said firmly, 'You have more than potential, Francis. You have a talent. Write *Ménage Deux* if you want – or anything else, for that matter. Froissart will snap your hand off to buy it. And if he doesn't, take it to Floridor at the Bourgogne.'

'Not the Bourgogne, no,' came the decisive reply.

'Why not? Their company is as good as ours – some would argue that it's better.'

'That's not the point.' His smile, this time, was warm and quizzical. 'Do I really have to say it?' And when she closed her lips, refusing to speak, 'I won't go to the Bourgogne – or indeed anywhere – because I need my leading-lady.'

* * *

All the way back to the Rue des Rosiers with her hand on his arm, Francis pondered on the thing he was finally beginning to recognise. He'd started writing a play just to see if he could do it ... and ended by writing it for Pauline Fleury. When he realised what he was doing, he'd told himself that it was purely because he wanted to tempt her back on-stage – but that wasn't the real reason and probably never had been. He'd done it because he'd become increasingly fascinated by her. He no longer saw the scar or noticed her slight limp. He only saw the clear, hazel eyes, the luxuriant dark brown hair and the curves of an extremely trim figure. But pleasing as those things were, her intelligence and barbed astringence attracted him more. In that sense, she reminded him a little of Kate Maxwell; the girl he had never really been in love with but fully intended to marry – though, looking back, he couldn't remember why. Certainly the feelings he detected in himself now were unlike any he'd experienced before. Feelings that had crept up on him so gradually, he'd hardly noticed they were there until he'd seen Pauline take charge on the night of Ashley's attack. And then, suddenly, he'd wondered why it had taken him so long to appreciate the full scope of Madame Pauline Fleury.

Buoyed up by the success of the rehearsal and the pleasure of having Pauline's hand on his arm, Francis's euphoric mood was swiftly banished when he entered the house to learn that his sister awaited him in the parlour.

'God,' he breathed. 'And I was in such a good mood, too.'

Pauline shook her head, grinned and promptly left him to it.

Francis sighed, straightened his cuffs and tried to summon some patience.

Celia was sitting on the sofa, her skirts spread wide enough to prohibit anyone sitting beside her.

Nicholas stood near the fire looking faintly harassed.

When Francis appeared, relief rolled off both of them in waves.

'Thank God!' snapped Celia. 'What on earth do you do with your time? I've been waiting an absolute *age* and was beginning to think you were never coming!'

'Perhaps you should make an appointment,' suggested Francis flippantly. Then, glancing at Nicholas, 'You obviously drew the short straw. Have Athenais and Ashley taken to the heather?'

'Apparently.' In the half hour he'd spent with Francis's sister, he hadn't exactly warmed to her – but neither was he prepared to be rude. According her a civil bow, he said, 'It has been a pleasure to make your acquaintance, Lady Verney – but now I'll leave you to speak to Francis privately.' And sedulously avoiding Francis's eye, he trod briskly from the room.

Francis strolled over to the hearth and leaned negligently against the mantel.

'Well, Celia? What is it this time – or do I need to ask?'

'There's no need to be so horrid. I'm utterly distraught!'

You all-too-frequently are, he thought. *I don't know how Verney stands it.*

'And what am I supposed to do about it?'

'You must write to Eden again and make him hurry.'

'For heaven's sake – it hasn't been a fortnight yet. Give the man a chance.'

'I can't. It's taken him months to say he'll do it and I can't afford to wait as long again before it's done. I need my divorce now – immediately. Otherwise, I don't know ... I'm afraid what might happen.'

Since Celia never listened to anything that didn't suit her, Francis didn't bother to point out that Eden hadn't said he *would* obtain a divorce – only that he'd look into the possibility. Sighing, he said, 'What do you mean – you're afraid what might happen? I imagine you'll go on just as you've been doing for the last eight years.'

She shook her head. 'You don't understand. It's Hugo.'

Ah. Perhaps Verney isn't standing it.

'What about him?'

'He – he's different. Now I think about it, he's been different for a while now. But I didn't really notice until I told him that Eden had agreed to the divorce and then ...' She stopped, twisting a handkerchief between her hands. 'I thought he'd be *pleased*.'

'But he wasn't?'

'No. For a long time, he didn't say anything and – and he looked at me so *coldly*, Francis. As if he no longer cared for me at all. I said I didn't understand why he wasn't happy and he – he said, *No. You wouldn't.* Then he went out.'

Francis shrugged. 'Like Eden, he's probably not thrilled at the idea of featuring in a divorce case.'

'It's not that. He's different, I tell you. He hardly escorts me anywhere anymore and spends nearly every evening with friends of his own. Sometimes he even stays away all night.' She paused, looking genuinely distressed. 'I suppose I should have noticed it sooner but it happened so gradually, you know? And there's something else.'

Francis hardly needed the something else since, from what she'd said so far, the conclusion was fairly obvious. 'Yes?'

'He used to want me all the time – but he hasn't t-touched me for weeks. Several times I've tried encouraging him to … you know …but he just makes excuses.' She looked up, seemingly baffled by it all. 'He's changed, Francis. And I don't know what to do – except that I must have the divorce quickly.'

'On the assumption that he'll still marry you?'

'Yes. He *has* to marry me. He must know that. How else am I to recover a shred of reputation? How else is he?'

Once again Francis refrained from remarking that Verney's reputation didn't suffer from living with his mistress but that Celia's good name had been destroyed the day she ran off with her lover. He said, 'I'm sorry, Celia. But if, as you must surely have guessed, he's met someone else, obtaining a divorce from Eden is unlikely to make the slightest difference. In fact, if he's thinking of leaving you --'

'He *can't* leave me!'

'He left his wife fast enough – and, like murder, I don't suppose the second time is as difficult. And if he *is* thinking of leaving, the prospect of you being free to marry will make him do it sooner rather than later.'

Her mouth set in a mulish line that Francis knew only too well.

She said, 'He won't go. I won't *let* him go. I know things he wouldn't want told. I've even *done* things – things I know I shouldn't have – because he persuaded me to.'

Francis frowned a little. 'What do you mean – you've done things? Such as what?'

'You don't need to know. Not yet, anyway.' She stood up. 'But you must write to Eden, Francis. Write to him and tell him he must *hurry*.'

'So you can blackmail Verney into marriage? If you'll excuse me saying so, that doesn't strike me as a particularly good idea – and it's hardly a suitable basis for matrimony.'

'I don't care.' She pulled on her gloves, refusing to meet her brother's eyes. 'I've been waiting years to be Lady Verney – and no one shall take it away from me now.'

SIX

Secure in the knowledge that Sir Edward Hyde would keep him informed of the King's movements and unable, as yet, to initiate further investigations, Ashley devoted the following days to regaining some semblance of physical fitness whilst staying out of Athenais's way. The first involved walking a little faster and further each day; the second was facilitated by the fact that Athenais had unexpectedly acquired a leading role in the following week's repertoire and was having to work very hard indeed in order to be ready in time.

The atmosphere at the theatre was one of unusual excitement and heightened tension as the opening night approached. Cryptic hints of the delights to come had been carefully dropped in appropriate quarters but copies of the playbill were being zealously guarded. These announced that *Ménage* – a comedy in one act by a distinguished new playwright and featuring the welcome return of Pauline Fleury – would be followed by the immensely popular *Don Japhet d'Armenie* by Paul Scarron.

On the day of the first performance, Ashley managed to limp as far as the Louvre. By the time he got there, his leg was throbbing so badly he had to grit his teeth with every step – which is why he found an unobtrusive corner in which to recover before seeking out Sir Edward Hyde. And that was how he came to see Sir Hugo Verney strolling by with his head bent intimately close to that of a well-endowed blonde, extravagantly dressed in the latest Court fashion and adorned with an indiscriminate array of gem-encrusted jewellery.

Ashley withdrew deeper into the shadows. Francis had told him about Celia's current anxieties. If the blonde was at the root of them, Ashley thought she was right to be worried. It was possible that Verney had found richer pickings than were to be had at home.

As a matter of courtesy and because he'd been unable to do so for over two weeks, he made his way to the King's apartments only to discover that His Majesty was playing tennis with Buckingham. Ashley wondered how long the Duke had been back in favour and was glad the current amusement didn't involve either women or wine. Then he retraced his steps to Hyde's sitting-room.

Sir Edward received him with raised eyebrows and the immediate offer of a chair.

'I understand you received your injury in some sort of attack?'

'Yes. Sadly, the streets are not safe these days.'

'Indeed. So it is not connected --'

'Not at all.' Whether that was true or not, he'd never know – so there was little point in giving Hyde chapter and verse on a dead man. He said, 'With regard to Lucy Walter, I have reason to believe that any marriage lines she or anyone else claims to possess will prove to be a forgery. But if you receive further communication on the subject, let me know and I'll deal with it. For the rest, my recent enquiry as to whether you'd involved a third party was because Sir William Brierley was seen to visit the lady.'

'Brierley? Why?'

'Since you didn't send him, I don't know. It will probably prove to be nothing – but I may speak to him anyway.'

'Do so, by all means.' Hyde hesitated and then said, 'Although I appreciate your current difficulties, I was concerned by your involvement of the new Lord Wroxton. I have seen little of him in recent years, of course ... but he was an extremely frivolous youth, much given to idle chatter.'

'War changes us all,' returned Ashley, accepting a glass of wine, 'and someone like Francis, more than most. I trust him – though, as ever, I don't share my every thought.'

'Certainly he seemed able to tell me very little. Scarcely more than that you wished to know of any scheme His Majesty might have to visit Le Havre.'

'I can't add much to that myself. If my information is correct, the plan is to lure the King, and his brother to Honfleur where assassins will be waiting for them. I don't know how this is to be done – or by whom – but I'm led to believe that the plot has the secret backing of Secretary Thurloe.'

'*Thurloe!*' exclaimed Hyde, sitting bolt upright. 'Are you sure?'

'As sure as I can be at this stage.'

'But that is iniquitous! A man in his position to involve himself in cold-blooded murder? I am appalled. Words fail me.'

Ashley reflected that there was a first time for everything. He opened his mouth to speak but was forestalled by Sir Edward saying more slowly, 'Although ... if the rumours are true, it would make sense.'

'What rumours?'

'That Cromwell has been holding secret talks --'

'Not so very secret if you know about them,' interposed Ashley dryly. 'However. Talks about what?'

'About the possibility of making himself King.'

For a long moment, Ashley simply stared at him. Then, in a tone of pure disgust, he said, 'Why does that somehow fail to surprise me?'

Hyde nodded. 'Of course, it may not be true – or he may have been cautioned against it. But I understand he holds state in the Banqueting House in much the same way as the late King, so the idea is not inconceivable.'

'And would make removing the rightful King and his heir a necessity?'

'Yes. Speaking of which – where did you come by your information?'

'I'm afraid I'm not at liberty to tell you that.'

'But you must. I *demand* that you do so.'

'I can't. My informant's life depends on total anonymity. And though I do not doubt your discretion, sir, I'm not willing to break my silence in any circumstances whatsoever – so you're going to have to trust me.'

Hyde recognised the note of implacability and said huffily, 'You can't expect me to be satisfied with that.'

'I don't expect it. I do, however, expect you to understand that we're incredibly lucky to have this information at all.' Ashley paused but it appeared that this time words really *had* failed the Chancellor. 'And I particularly wanted to talk to you about how we proceed.'

'I'm to be made privy to that, then?'

'Yes. With your permission, I'd like to try to apprehend the assassins. The fellow who has concocted this scheme may or may not be among them ... but if he isn't and we have his minions, he shouldn't be too difficult to trace. Also, if Thurloe *is* behind this, I'd like to find evidence of it. I imagine you'd find that useful.'

'Undoubtedly,' allowed Sir Edward. 'But since you appear to have no firm details, how do you expect to manage this?'

'We know it is to take place in Honfleur. And if the King expresses an inclination to travel to the coast, we'll know roughly *when* the trap is to be sprung. It's enough, I think.'

'You can't use His Majesty as bait. I won't --'

'I've no intention of letting His Majesty or his brother within a hundred miles of the place – which is why I specifically asked you not to breathe a word of this in his hearing. I hope you haven't done so?'

'Of course not. But if the King is not to set foot in Honfleur, the assassins aren't likely to show themselves, are they?'

'No,' said Ashley, leaning back in his chair and smiling. 'But fortunately, I have some ideas about that.'

* * *

Partly out of curiosity, partly because he'd promised and partly because he guessed the occasion might well present an opportunity for a seemingly chance meeting with One-Eyed Will, Ashley braved the pit at the Marais that evening. His guess proved to be a good one. There, in the front-right off-stage box, sat Francis's sister and Sir William. Unfortunately, the one next to it was occupied by the Marquis d'Auxerre and his usual coterie of young men.

Ashley decided that, for the time being, the anonymity of the pit was preferable – or would be if he could find a bit of wall to lean against. The place was already packed and more people were still trying to get in. Not without difficulty, he elbowed his way to a suitable spot and tried to ignore the ache in his leg.

Fortunately, he didn't have long to wait. The doors to the auditorium were slammed shut, the stage candles were lit and the curtains parted on Francis's masterpiece.

The impression was of a scene already well under-way. Amid pants and groans, a couple grappled enthusiastically on an inadequately-sized couch. The man's wig was askew and his backside pointed upwards. The woman's coiffeur was collapsing over one eye, her bodice was half-unlaced and the only thing hiding one ample bosom was the male hand clamped firmly over it.

'It seems that quantity rather than quality is the current fashion,' remarked an acidulous and slightly bored voice from above. 'But he should beware. Better men than he have been suffocated by my daughter-in-law's attributes.'

Laughter flowed through the auditorium and a surprising number of people shouted out Pauline's name. The couple on the couch continued their ungainly struggles until the audience quietened and then exchanged a few sentences which culminated in the daughter-in-law expressing the fear that her husband would find out.

'No, he won't,' said Pauline irritably. 'He inherited his brains from his father – and keeps them in the same place.'

The pit howled ... and so it went on. Ashley had thought the play funny when he read it and now he saw Pauline's tart delivery, sour glances and rare, malicious smiles heightening every nuance and inviting the audience to catch the double-entendres.

It lasted no more than half an hour and, at the end of it, the entire house was in uproar. The audience refused to let the actors leave the stage as they cheered and clapped and stamped. And then the inevitable call went up.

'Author! Author!'

Ashley's brows rose and he thought, *Interesting. Will he or won't he, I wonder?*

There was a small delay while the demands grew more and more vociferous. Then Francis walked on to the stage, doffed his hat in a typically elaborate bow and turned to applaud the cast.

Glancing automatically up at Celia, Ashley watched her face freeze and saw her fan drop from suddenly nerveless fingers. He wondered if she'd recognised herself in the character of the wife and then decided that her vanity probably wouldn't allow it.

Francis bowed again to the audience and acknowledged his cast with a wide smile and a graceful sweep of his arm. Then he crossed the boards to Pauline, took both of her hands in his own and raised each in turn to his lips, before stepping back in deference and inviting the audience to show their appreciation.

'Fleury!' came the collective cry. 'Fleury!'

Pauline smiled upon them and achieved a gracefully dignified curtsy. Then, drawing Francis with her, she stepped back into the line ... and the curtains closed.

Celia was still looking as if the ceiling had fallen on her head. Rising, Sir William said something to her and, when she nodded dumbly, turned to leave the box. Ashley abandoned his corner and set off to intercept him.

They met on the stairs and Will came to an abrupt halt.

'Ashley? How fortuitous. At last the chance of some less than asinine conversation.'

Ashley accepted the hand he was offered and grinned.

'Finding Celia Verney a trial, are you?'

'My dear, the woman's tongue runs like a fiddlestick – or at least it did until the author made his entrance. She hasn't said, of course, but he's a good-looking fellow so naturally one can't but suspect an intrigue.'

'*You* can't,' retorted Ashley. 'But you're quite mistaken. The author is her brother.'

'Her brother? Viscount Wroxton? *Is* he?'

'He is.'

'And she didn't know about his play?'

'I believe Francis thought to make it a delightful surprise.'

'She didn't *look* delighted,' remarked Will dryly. And then, 'Francis? You know him?'

Ashley nodded. 'Since Worcester. And we now share lodgings.'

'Ah. Let me guess. No love lost between him and his sister – or just a questionable sense of humour?'

'Both.'

'Intriguing. I should like to meet him some time. Just now, however, I am supposed to be fetching the fair Celia a glass of something to settle her nerves.' He sighed. 'As you may guess, events have transpired against me this evening. Armand Colbert and his lady cried off at the last minute and, as is usual these days, Verney was nowhere to be found – or at least, nowhere one would feel inclined to go looking for him.'

Ashley raised enquiring brows.

'He has another interest?'

'That is certainly one way of putting it. Angelique Latour is an exceedingly rich widow and by no means displeasing to the eye. A cynic might suspect that Celia's days may well be numbered.'

'You think Verney might marry the widow?'

'I think that, if she'll have him, he would be stupid not to. Aside from the obvious advantages, Celia can be extremely tedious.' Sir William grinned invitingly. 'I suppose you wouldn't care to share our box?'

'Not tonight, I'm afraid. The Marquis d'Auxerre is occupying the one next to yours and there is ... unfinished business ... between us that I would prefer to complete at a time and place of my own choosing.'

Will's eye narrowed.

'Take care with that, then. The fellow's a complete arse.'

'I know.' Ashley turned to go and then, as if it was a sudden after-thought, said, 'You may wish to take care yourself, by the way. There's a rumour linking your name with that of Lucy Walter.'

'Is there?' Sir William looked genuinely startled. 'Good God! Where on earth did *that* come from?'

'I've no idea. There's no truth in it, then?'

'Ashley, my dear fellow – what do you take me for? His Majesty finally acquired sufficient resources to pay the lady some small part of her promised pension and I was tasked to deliver it. I am not stupid enough to take advantage of an invitation – even if one had been offered.'

'And it wasn't?' came the deceptively mild reply. 'Poor Will. You must be slipping.'

* * *

Ashley stayed to watch the Scarron comedy purely in order to gaze his fill at Athenais in her role of Leonore. As ever, she looked breath-taking and he suspected that it was only her presence on the stage stopped the play from falling a little flat in the wake of *Ménage*. When it ended, Ashley found his way back-stage to Francis's side and murmured, 'Your piece was outstanding – as was Pauline's performance. But we'll talk later. For now, keep an eye on the Green Room. D'Auxerre's in the house tonight.'

Francis nodded and moved away. Ashley lurked in the shadows until two of the younger walkers ran him to earth and tried to lure him into mild flirtation. Then, when he was fairly sure of leaving the theatre unobserved, he slipped out through a side-door and limped home.

Archie greeted him with an odd sideways glance and handed him a sealed missive.

'A lackey from the palace brought it. Said it was from the King.'

Ashley glanced down at the seal and said, 'It is.'

'Didn't know you was acquainted with the Lord's Anointed,' remarked Archie, striving not to appear impressed. 'Know him well, do you?'

'Moderately well. But don't run away with the idea I'm his bosom friend. I'm not.' Ashley strolled towards the parlour. 'He just finds me … useful.'

His Majesty's note was brief. The King was sorry he'd missed Colonel Peverell earlier that day and would be obliged if the Colonel would wait on him the following morning.

Colonel Peverell took a moment to stare irritably at the ceiling. Another walk to the bloody Louvre. Just what he needed.

Knowing that this was no night to escape to the attic, he took a glass of wine with Nicholas in the parlour whilst providing a précis of his meeting with Hyde. At the end of it, Nicholas said, '*Do* you have a plan?'

'Yes. And I'll tell you about it in due course. But not tonight. Francis and Pauline will be back any minute and in a mood to --' He stopped, hearing sounds betokening noisy arrival. 'Celebrate. And here they come.'

Francis, Pauline and Athenais surged in, all laughing and talking at once.

Pink and endearingly giddy with excitement, Athenais looked eagerly at Ashley and said, 'Did you see it? You did, didn't you?'

'Yes. I --'

'Wasn't Pauline superb? Of course, Francis's play is marvellous – but Pauline stole every single scene. It's the best thing we've put on-stage for ages and I'm so jealous I could spit.' Turning, she pushed her hands against Francis's chest and said, 'I quite hate you. *I* could have played the wife. I'm every bit as good a bitch as Hortense.'

He grinned, caught her hands in his and kissed each in turn.

'We know, darling. And we love you anyway.' Impudent blue eyes skimmed her figure. 'But if you'll forgive me for mentioning it, you lack Hortense's … attributes.'

She dragged her hands away and tried to look offended.

'That is just rude. My attributes are perfectly adequate, thank you. And, as someone remarked this evening, quality ought to count for something.' Pivoting on her heel and without stopping to consider, she said, 'Don't you think so, Ashley?'

Caught with a mouthful of wine, Ashley narrowly avoided choking. Annoyed at being taken by surprise and even more annoyed by the expression on Francis's face, he said coolly, 'Most definitely. But I imagine you'd agree that, in other contexts, quantity isn't to be dismissed. Or so the ladies of my acquaintance have always led me to believe.'

Athenais turned scarlet and Nicholas tried, unsuccessfully, to subdue a snort of laughter.

Pauline said, 'I suspect this conversation ought to stop right there.'

'That's a shame,' muttered Francis irrepressibly. 'I hoped you might have an opinion.'

She looked at him. 'Save that sort of wit for your next script. And, in the meantime, I'm off to the kitchen for more wine. If this is to continue, I shall need a drink.'

'And I,' announced Nicholas, heading for the door, 'am off to relieve Jem for what's left of the evening.'

'Tell him he can stop tracking the eye-patch,' said Ashley. 'He'll know what that means.' And as Francis showed signs of joining the general exodus, 'With regard to that other matter, Francis ... I take it nothing transpired?'

'Nothing. He left after the second act.'

'Good. Thank you.'

Francis nodded and followed Pauline across the hall. It was the first chance he'd had to be alone with her all day. He said, 'Wine? Is that all you want? I'm disappointed.'

'Are you?' She cast him an oblique glance over her shoulder. 'Why?'

'Because I want something quite different.' And, grasping her wrist, he whirled her against him so that he could clamp his other arm about her waist. 'Something I've been thinking about for days, to be precise. This.' And he brought his mouth down on hers.

Pauline's immediate instinct was flow into his warmth and kiss him back but she fought it – and him. When he released her wrist to trail his fingers up her nape, she shoved ineffectually at his shoulders but managed to drag her mouth away to say breathlessly, 'Stop it, Francis. I know you're floating ten feet above the ground on a cloud of euphoria but --'

'Not yet, I'm not ... but soon, I hope. Kiss me.'

'No.'

'Then let me kiss you.' He nuzzled her neck and nipped gently at her earlobe. 'Please?'

That punched a fist-sized hole through her resolve but she still managed to say, 'No. Will you stop? This is ridiculous and you'll be thoroughly embarrassed in the morning.'

His hands rose to cup her face and tilt it up to his.

'I won't. Look at me, Duchess.' And when she still tried to turn away, 'Look at me.'

So, reluctantly, she looked. And then wished she hadn't.

The sapphire eyes were full of an expression she'd never seen on his or, indeed, any man's face before. A sort of bemusement, mingled with amused tenderness and the tiniest flicker of anxiety. He said, 'If you really don't want this ... if you really want me to stop, then I will. Only please don't push me away for any of the reasons you've given so far. It demeans us both.'

His gaze continued to hold hers and, for the first time in years, she realised that she had no idea what to do. For weeks now, he had been sliding deeper and deeper into her affections and, knowing it, she had constantly told herself to be careful because nothing could ever come of it. Good-looking titled gentlemen didn't belong with scarred, one-time actresses past their first blush. But right now at this moment, she sensed that if she employed her usual tone, she could hurt him. So she said carefully, 'I don't mean it that way.'

His hands dropped to her waist, holding her loosely but with a suggestion that he wasn't going to let her move away. 'What way, then?'

'It's just the play and the success of tonight. Do you think I don't know how it feels – that I'm immune to it? But it fades. And, whatever you think right now, I'm not what you want.'

'And why might that be?'

His eyes were lingering on her mouth and causing her pulse to accelerate. She shook her head, refusing to say the words he knew were in her head.

'Because of this?' Without any warning, he trailed swift kisses down her scarred cheek. Her breath caught and she shut her eyes, unable to look at him. He said, 'You know … this is so much more important to you than it is to anyone else. I can understand that. But *you* need to understand it doesn't define you. Your head, your heart and your spirit outweigh it a hundred times over. Look at me.'

She opened her eyes but kept them fixed on his throat because if she met his eyes now she suspected her will-power would collapse completely. Wishing the thing lodging in her chest would go away, she said, 'I don't know what to say to you, Francis. Except that I think you should let me go.'

'Yes. I think so, too.' And when her startled gaze flew to his, he grinned at her and said, 'That's better. And now you're going to make a bargain with me.'

'I am?'

'Yes. I'll let you go now … but next time you won't ask me to. Because next time, you'll know that I mean it.'

* * *

Behind them in the parlour, Athenais looked from Francis's retreating back to Ashley's unreadable expression and said, 'What was that about?'

'As it turns out, nothing at all.'

'Don't fob me off. *Who* left after the second act?'

Ashley sighed. 'D'Auxerre.'

All her vivacity drained away, along with most of her colour.

'Oh. He's back. I thought … it's been so long, I hoped we'd seen the last of him.' She paused, gripping her hands together. 'But why tonight? Why did he have to spoil tonight?'

'I imagine he came tonight for the same reason as the rest of Paris,' he shrugged. 'Rumours that Pauline Fleury was returning to the stage. The theatre was full to bursting and no one in the pit could talk of anything else. It was pretty much inevitable that the Marquis would put in an appearance – so I wouldn't read too much into it, if I were you.'

'No? Just as *you* weren't reading too much into it when you told Francis to watch out for him?'

'That was merely a precaution.'

She sat down on the sofa and looked up at him in silence for what seemed a very long time. Her eyes, still outlined with kohl from the evening's performance, looked huge and dark. Finally, she said, 'If he's not done with us yet ... if there's the smallest sign that it's going to start all over again ... I'll put an end to it.'

Ashley's muscles tightened and a nerve began pulsing in his jaw.

'What does that mean?'

'What do you think it means?' she retorted. And then, explosively, 'He nearly *killed* you.'

'And you think that letting him have you is going to stop him trying again?' His voice was suddenly clipped and very cold. 'Are you completely insane?'

'I'm being realistic. If he – if he gets what he wants, he'll have no reason to --'

'He doesn't *need* a reason, for Christ's sake!' Ashley reached down to grip her shoulders and haul her to her feet in front of him. 'What will it take to make you understand? He's completely amoral. He does whatever he chooses because he can and because he doesn't like to lose. If he comes at me again, it won't be on your account – it will be because I killed one of his pets. So don't imagine that spreading your legs for him will keep me safe because it won't.'

Athenais flinched at the deliberate crudeness and, in a very small voice, said, 'I'm sorry. I hadn't thought of that.'

'Obviously not.' A white shade bracketed his mouth, betokening temper barely held in check but he made himself release her. 'You are *not* going to sleep with the bloody Marquis – and that is quite final. Do you understand me?'

'Yes. But ...'

'But what? In case you hadn't noticed, I'm in no mood to argue about this.'

She looked down at her tightly-laced fingers.

'I wondered if you'd mind.'

For a moment, he stared at her bent head as if she'd spoken in some language he didn't understand. Then, dragging a hand through his hair, he snapped, 'You *are* insane. Of course I'd damned well mind.'

She tilted her head and looked into his eyes. 'Why?'

'*Why?*' Ashley suddenly felt the ground sliding away from under him. 'What kind of question is that? The man's a complete bastard.'

'Oh. Yes, of course.' She moved away from him towards the hearth and, with her back towards him, said, 'You told me to think about the things you said the other day and I have. Do you know the Vicomte de Chourval?'

The question took him completely by surprise and he frowned, wondering where it was leading. 'I've met him. Why?'

'He's offered me a house and a carriage and – oh, all the usual things. I refused, of course ... but now I'm wondering if --'

'No,' said Ashley, before he could stop himself.

'No?' She waited and, when he said nothing, 'The Vicomte is really quite kind and has the most beautiful manners, so I think I could grow to like him. And, since ... well, since you and I seem to be at an impasse, it occurred to me that perhaps now might be a good time to settle for financial security – not to mention added protection from d'Auxerre. What do you think?'

A knife twisted in his gut and he had to clamp his lips together to stop himself saying *No and no and no. Never in this life. You'll prostitute yourself over my dead body.*

He recognised that she might be trying to manipulate him ... but after what he'd told her about himself, there was a distinct possibility that she wasn't. His throat ached and something clawed at the inside of his chest. He tried telling himself that, if he was serious about not complicating her life, he ought to tell her to do as she thought fit. The problem was that he thought the words would choke him.

Athenais turned too quickly for him to guard his expression.

For a moment, stark grey eyes met tormented green ones. Then, a tiny smile quivering at the edges of her mouth, she said simply, 'I see.'

He knew that she did but still he unlocked his jaws to say, 'What do you see?'

'Everything you're refusing to say.' She walked to him and laid her palm gently against his taut cheek. 'Everything I'd sell my soul to hear.'

And that was when Ashley unravelled.

He pulled her against him, wrapping his arms about her as if he couldn't ever let go. He said desperately, 'I'm sorry. I'm so sorry. I meant it for the best – and I tried. I really did. But it's no good, is it? I can't ... I can't ... God, Athenais. I love you so much, I don't know how to tell you.'

Sliding her hands around his neck, she stood on tiptoe to kiss his jaw and, trying to contain the wild emotions that were rushing through her, said unsteadily, 'That was a very good first attempt.'

'I'll do better in time,' he murmured, shifting the position of his hands. 'Actually, I could do better now.' And he took her mouth in a lingering, sinfully tempting kiss.

Athenais gave a tiny moan and plunged her fingers into his hair. Her heart was knocking against her ribs and her senses were already alight. He was hers. He had finally stopped trying to be noble and admitted it. He was hers ... and the joy of it blazed through her like a comet.

Long minutes later, he said, 'I apologise for the way I spoke to you earlier.' He traced the line of her clavicle and beyond. 'It was just that the idea of you and d'Auxerre – or, indeed, you and any man at all – was more than I could stomach.' His tongue dipped into an unexpectedly sensitive spot beneath her ear. 'But I could have used less intemperate language.'

'Yes.' She nipped his throat and tugged at the laces of his shirt until she could find the smooth hardness of his chest. 'Intemperate. Yes.'

'Athenais.' His breath was suddenly very ragged. 'You'll need to stop doing that.'

'You don't like it?'

'I like it too much.' He trapped her exploring hand and held her away from him. 'I want ... I would like to make love to you. But --'

She batted at his hands, trying to lean close again. 'Oh yes. Please.'

'But I think you're entitled to some sort of courtship before I take you to bed. So --'

She stopped struggling and impaled him on a very direct gaze.

'Ashley, I love you. I've loved you for quite a long time. I think it began that day you carried me upstairs from the kitchen – though of course I didn't know it then. I – I also want you in a way I never thought would be possible for me. So I don't need to be courted. Although ...' A glimmer of mischief appeared. 'It would be very romantic if you carried me up to my room again.'

'Romantic.' A quiver of laughter stirred. 'Really?'

She nodded. 'But if your leg is too sore --'

Ashley swept her off her feet and into his arms.

'Bugger my leg,' he said succinctly. And, with a swift, heart-stopping grin, 'Romantic enough for you?'

SEVEN

Once in her room, Ashley pushed the door shut with his foot and set Athenais down so he could shoot the bolt. Then, imprisoning her between his body and the sturdy oak panels, he solicited her senses with another mind-stealing kiss while his fingers made short work of the laces of her gown. Then, when it dropped from her shoulders, giving him new areas to explore, he murmured, 'You have no idea how long I've fantasised about this. I imagined spending hours removing your clothes, piece by piece, and discovering every delectable inch of you.'

'Oh,' said Athenais faintly as hot pulses stirred deep inside her. 'Well ...'

'Yes.' He trailed his mouth from jaw to collar-bone and started on her corset. 'But I didn't bargain for wanting you quite this much ... so hours might be ... difficult.'

His shirt was already half unfastened. Athenais finished the job and resumed her exploration of his chest. 'Difficult?'

The corset finally yielded to his assault and he pushed both it and her gown away. Her chemise was of fine, almost transparent lawn threaded through with pale blue ribbons. For a moment, he forgot to breathe.

'Mm. I don't think ... I'm not sure I can last that long.'

He ran his hands over her arms and shoulders to cup her breasts. Athenais gasped and responded by tracing the muscles of his abdomen with her fingertips. Everything in him tightened and his arousal spiralled upwards.

It was at this point that his brain finally managed to indicate that it was fighting a losing battle with his body. He'd always known that the merest touch caused an immediate and intense physical reaction ... but he realised that now was no time to let it run away with him. This lovely girl had known only rape. It was his privilege to obliterate that memory; to make her first time with him as damned near perfect as it could possibly be ... to give her every vestige of pleasure of which he was capable. And that wasn't going to happen if he let his own desires set the pace.

He thought a shade desperately, *Even if it kills me – and it feels as though it might – I will get this right .*And then, bracingly, *So find some* *control and slow down, you randy bastard ... otherwise you don't deserve her.*

Drawing a deep, steadying breath, he said, 'That is a very inviting shift. I like the ribbons.'

God. You ass. I like the ribbons? Is that really the best you can do? You're lucky she's not doubled up, laughing herself silly.

Perhaps fortunately, Athenais ignored him.

'Your shirt,' she grumbled against his throat, 'is in the way.'

'Is it? Then I'll remove it ... presently.'

'Now, please.'

This time, doing a little better, he said, 'Presently. We have all night ... and you'll enjoy it more if we take our time.'

The ribbon had slipped out of her hair which was now straying wildly about her shoulders. Shaking it back so that she could look at him, she said not without a touch of anxiety, 'Am I doing this wrong?'

'No.' Smiling, he ran his fingers gently through the tumbled mane. 'You're doing it exactly right. But I have plans – one of which is to get as far as the bed.'

She was startled into an uncertain laugh.

'Oh. You mean ... oh. The alternative sounds rather wicked.'

'A little, perhaps. And one day we'll try it. But not tonight. Tonight you're going to let me love you properly and trust me to show you how it should be. Will you do that?'

Her breath seized and her insides turned liquid. 'Yes. Only ...'

'Only what?'

'Your shirt ... please?'

Ashley shook his head at her.

'Very well, you stubborn wench. But you'll have to let go of me for a moment.'

Reluctantly, she withdrew her hands while he tugged the shirt over his head and tossed it aside. Then on a sigh, she murmured, 'I love your chest. And your arms and your shoulders ... but, most of all your chest. It's so ... so ...'

'Stop. I'm blushing.'

Amusement fused with mild embarrassment as she stared at him in wide-eyed, wordless admiration, so he drew her back into his arms and prevented her saying anything else by sealing her lips with his own. She melted against him and he took the opportunity to untie the tapes of her petticoats. Then, as they slid from her hips, he grasped her waist, lifted her from the pool of taffeta and cambric and set her down again two steps from the bed.

'Now,' he murmured huskily, toying lazily with the drawstring of her shift. 'I'm woefully out of practice ... so tell me what these pretty ribbons do?'

Impatient, oddly anxious and already half-consumed by the wildfire in her blood, Athenais said, 'Would you like me to show you?'

His mouth went dry. If there was a fantasy more erotic than the ones he'd dreamed up himself, this was it. 'Please.'

He watched with rapt attention as her fingers slowly teased the ribbon undone, and loosening the neckline. Then, even more tantalisingly, she slid the chemise first off one white shoulder and, with only the merest suggestion of a shrug, encouraged it to slither from the other. Maddeningly provocative, the beribboned cambric came to rest just above the peak of her breasts. Ashley's body – already rock hard and ready – responded accordingly and, unable to help himself, he pushed the flimsy fabric away and closed his hand over her warm flesh.

Athenais's head fell back and she trembled. His thumb moved around, then over her nipple and a piercing spear of sensation shot down into her belly and blossomed there. She gave a shocked, involuntary moan. She hadn't known it was possible to feel like this. The thought that this was only the prelude ... that he had other pleasures in store, was both a little alarming and utterly enticing. She didn't know how her body would bear it ... but she wanted – oh God, she *really* wanted – find out.

He lifted her to sit on the bed and freed her arms so that the chemise pooled around her hips. He said, 'You are so beautiful. How is it that you're more beautiful every time I look at you?'

She shook her head so that her hair screened her body and said, 'Now *I'm* blushing.' And, when he dropped to one knee in front of her and took her foot in his hands, 'What are you doing?'

He glanced up for just long enough for her to see that the green-gold eyes were hot and dark. 'Enjoying myself.'

His hands slid up her calf and on past her knee to her garter; then, entirely without haste but shaking a little as they encountered the silken skin of her thigh, they drew both garter and stocking from her leg. He raised her bare foot to his lips and kissed her instep. Athenais's breath caught and she shut her eyes ... leaving them shut while he performed the same ritual with her other leg. When she felt him settle on the bed at her side, she opened them again and turned into him ... and was totally unprepared for the explosion of sensation as her skin met his.

Ashley pushed her down against the pillows, kissing her ever more deeply while his palms trailed over her leaving fire in their wake. Her fingers tangled in his hair and she pulled him closer, until he shifted to let his mouth follow the pattern woven by his fingers. Athenais gasped as he licked and then closed his lips around the tip of her breast, sending sparks rushing through every vein and nerve. Sensation overlaid sensation until it seemed that everything inside her was dissolving into hunger and heat.

She said helplessly, 'Ashley ... please.'

And gave a tiny sob when he rolled away and left her.

He smiled. 'A moment.' And, without moving from the side of the bed, proceeded to shed the rest of his clothing.

Breathing hard, Athenais watched out of wide, dark eyes. She had seen him naked once before and the perfection of his body had stopped her breath – but then he had been bloodied and semi-conscious. Now, standing before her whole and fully erect, his beauty brought a lump to her throat; and since there were no words for how he made her feel, she held out a hand in supplication.

Ashley lay down beside her and drew her against the length of his body. A tremor ran through her and he rejoiced. Although still acutely aware of his own desire, his focus had shifted. He found there was exquisite pleasure to be had from watching her arousal build ... from every sigh and sob and moment when she could no longer remain still. The sweetness of her response was a miraculous gift which awed and overwhelmed him. For the first time in a very long while, she made him feel that he had something to offer her after all.

Athenais's hands raced over him in their own voyage of discovery, learning the contours of hard muscle beneath slick, smooth skin. And when he progressed to the most intimate caress of all, she gave a shuddering moan and felt pulses throb in places she hadn't known existed. She twisted, writhing against him and clutched at his shoulders. Without really knowing what she was asking for, she gasped, 'I can't … oh please.'

And knowing that it was finally time, Ashley settled over her and very, very slowly joined his body with hers. Just for an instant, Athenais's eyes flew wide and then her face filled with an expression of utter bliss before her arms closed tight around him … which was when Ashley realised that, if ever anything had been worth waiting for, it was this. And when he brought her to rapturous fulfilment and was free to seek his own release, he knew that all the riches in the world were as nothing beside this one perfect moment.

* * *

When he woke, the sky outside was light and two specific aches in his body were making their presence felt. One, predictably, was in his right thigh; the other … wasn't. Both were occasioned by the fact that he had slept curved around Athenais's back. His face was lying amidst her hair, one of his arms was fastened around her waist and his loins were pressed against her firm, naked back-side. She was still fast asleep. Clearly, he wasn't.

He lay still, resisting the urge to ease one or other of his discomforts. After what seemed quite a long time, she snuffled a little in her sleep and wriggled into a slightly different position. The first made him smile. The second … didn't.

Drawing back the wild copper hair from her neck, he murmured her name. No reply. He tried again, a little louder and this time she stirred slightly, yawned and said vaguely, 'Pauline?' Before attempting to bury her head beneath the pillow.

In spite of everything, laughter rippled through him.

'No. Most assuredly *not* Pauline.'

There was a short silence, followed by a scuffle to escape the pillow and a one-word curse. Finally, a pair of sleepy, smoky-grey eyes squinted at him before recognition dawned. She twisted round and tried to heave herself up on to one elbow.

'Ashley?'

'Were you expecting somebody else?'

She yawned again and shook her head.

'I'm sorry. I'm not awake yet. What time is it?'

'Probably a little after eight.'

'*Eight?*' She flopped down again, curling into his side with her head on his shoulder, draping an arm across his chest and unwittingly endangering a number of his good intentions by sliding a knee across his thigh. 'Too early.' And snuggling a little closer, 'This is nice.'

Ashley was half-tempted to ask if it was nicer than sleeping with Pauline but she was already settling back towards sleep so he said, mildly, 'If you think eight o'clock is early – what time would you consider reasonable?'

'Mm? Oh. Ten.'

'Ten. Right.' He grinned, flipped her over on to her back and said, 'Not if you're going to sleep with me, darling.'

Her eyes opened again and she pummelled him with one half-hearted fist, before seemingly deciding that stroking his shoulder was preferable. More to see what response she could provoke than anything else, she said, 'I'm going back to sleep.'

'Are you?' He slid his thigh between hers and watched her eyes change as she realised exactly what was pressing against her hip. 'Good luck with that.'

Her pulse tripped and she came fully awake, a smile trembling into being.

'You – oh. That isn't fair.'

'No, love. It isn't.' He traced the curve of her waist with suggestive fingers. 'But if you insist on starting the day by pressing your utterly delectable arse against my outstandingly virile ...' He paused, as if selecting the right word from the list available.

'Your outstandingly virile *what?*' demanded Athenais.

'Masculine attributes,' he replied smugly. And was rewarded with a peal of laughter. 'As I was saying ... if you do that, you'll just have to abide by the consequences.'

* * *

On her way downstairs, Pauline hesitated briefly outside the door and then continued on her way, smiling wryly. If Athenais was not only awake at this hour but also laughing, there was only one likely explanation. Pauline was genuinely happy for them but couldn't help hoping, for Athenais's sake, that it wouldn't end in tears. About her own future, she preferred not to think. Francis Langley was not at all the kind of man she would ever have imagined being drawn to ... and he was *exactly* the kind of man who, even before her accident, she couldn't possibly have expected to attract. Yet it would be ridiculously easy to fall in love with him. Indeed, she told herself firmly, it was a miracle she hadn't done so already – which only went to show what a serious application of will-power could achieve under even the most challenging of circumstances.

Jem and Archie were in the kitchen, dutifully clearing away the pots from their own breakfast. Relieved that Francis wasn't also downstairs yet, Pauline gave them a nod of approval and headed for the scullery in the hope they had left some bread in the crock.

'Excuse, Madame,' said Jem in his lamentable French. 'Last night ... Colonel Peverell go out?'

'Not to my knowledge,' she replied smoothly.

Jem looked blank.

'She don't know,' muttered Archie, reluctantly helpful.

'So where the hell is he?' began Jem. And again, to Pauline, 'Last night here not sleep.'

Pauline smothered something between a laugh and a sigh of exasperation. She wasn't about to tell this pair of reprobates where the Colonel was. She *particularly* had no intention of letting Archie Stott know that Ashley was currently in his daughter's bed. So she said, 'Then I'm sure he had a good reason and will doubtless re-appear in due course. Was that all?'

Archie grinned sourly at Jem and said, 'That's her telling us to mind our own business and bugger off. Mind the door for an hour, will you? I got to take my morning constitutional.'

Pauline watched them go and then set about getting breakfast ready for herself and the other members of the household. She was just wondering whether Ashley would presently appear hand-in-hand with Athenais or beat a discreet retreat to his attic in order to materialise later, when Francis walked up behind her saying, 'Good morning, Duchess.'

The knife Pauline was holding fell from her fingers, bounced off the table-edge and embedded itself point down in the floor three inches from her foot.

She stared at it, then looked across at Francis who was also staring at it. She opened her mouth to speak but was forestalled.

'I know.' Francis held up one hand in a gesture of surrender. 'You want me to sew bells to my clothes or announce my approach with bursts of merry song.' And then, differently, 'You were very nearly hurt. I'm sorry.'

Pauline bent and retrieved the knife, weighing it absently in her fingers.

'Merry song? Can you?'

'Actually, no.' He grinned suddenly. 'In truth, I can't carry a tune to save my life.'

'Pity,' said Pauline. And, with a half-smile as she turned back to the business of making breakfast, 'Bells it is, then.'

Francis eyed her thoughtfully for a few moments and then wordlessly began putting knives, platters and mugs on the table. It occurred to him that it would be quite easy to brush against her, apparently by accident but he realised that this was more likely to damage his cause than to advance it because she'd recognise any stratagem he used for exactly what it was. He sighed, reflecting that she had more spines than a hedgehog and an uncanny knack of cutting directly to the point. In short, she was probably the most difficult woman he'd ever met and he would need to play a very clever game indeed if he hoped ever to find a way past her defences. He suddenly wondered if she thought he just wanted to lure her into bed and, if she did, how he was to combat that – since, naturally enough, he *did* want to take her to bed. It just wasn't the *only* thing he wanted.

She turned to place a basket of bread and a pat of butter on the table and said, 'There's some ham left, if you want it. Or I could fry some sausage.'

'Neither, thank you. Unlike Ashley, I've lost my taste for meat at breakfast.' He paused, 'And, speaking of Ashley … since he didn't sleep in his own bed last night and his hat and sword are still upstairs, I couldn't help wondering if ...?'

'Yes. He's with Athenais.'

'Ah.' He shot her a swift glance. 'And has he your blessing?'

She shrugged. 'Why should he want it? It's no business of mine.'

'No? You're as good as a sister to Athenais. Better, in fact. Family is about more than blood.'

'I know that. But she's twenty-two years old and entitled to make her own mistakes – if mistakes they are. She's in love with him. If it turns out that all he wants is a body, she'll find out soon enough.'

'He doesn't,' remarked a cool voice from the door.

Pauline turned slowly without any sign of discomposure.

Francis thought, *Oh damn.* And looked reluctantly round at Ashley.

His expression appeared bland enough if one discounted the chill in his eyes. He said, 'I accept that speculation must be rife and that you both mean well. However, if you have questions I'd prefer they were addressed to me directly. And, in the meantime, I promised Athenais some hot water.' Upon which, he crossed to the hob, hefted up a filled kettle and walked out.

'Ah,' said Francis. 'Yes. Well, you can't blame him for that.'

'I don't,' replied Pauline. 'I do, however, occasionally wonder what he's doing that sends Jem – and now Sir Nicholas – out at all times of the day and night ... and whether you're part of it, too.'

'You're very suspicious.'

'But not stupid.' She looked him in the eye. 'There is something, isn't there?'

'Nothing any of us are at liberty to talk about.'

'I see. Should I be worried?'

Francis hesitated slightly and then said, 'No. I don't believe so. It's totally unconnected to this house.'

'Aside from the four of you who happen to live here, you mean?'

'Well, yes. Aside from that.'

'So you'll all take care to keep it from our door, I hope.' Pauline paused and sat down at the table. 'I saw the Marquis d'Auxerre in the theatre last night. It may mean nothing – or it may not. But with a potential problem like him, I'd rather we didn't have to start contending with nefarious English issues as well. Clear?'

'Very.'

'Good. Then you'd better sit down and eat.'

Francis sat but, before he could take so much as a bite, the peace was shattered by the violent pealing of the doorbell. Immediately pushing back his stool, he looked at Pauline and said, 'It's rather early for callers, don't you think?'

'Jem is in the yard. Shall I call him?'

'If you wish – though persons with murderous intent don't generally arrive on the doorstep in broad daylight,' he replied. And walked out to answer the door.

It was Celia, her face incandescent with fury.

'You *idiot!*' she stormed, pushing past him into the hall. 'You complete and utter *imbecile!* What on earth do you think you're doing – making me a laughing-stock this way? I could positively *murder* you!'

Francis closed the door and looked back to where Pauline stood framed in the kitchen doorway.

'On the other hand,' he said with something approaching resignation, 'there's always a first time.' And to his sister, 'Good morning, Celia. Won't you come in?'

EIGHT

While Francis suffered under the lash of his sister's tongue, Athenais and Ashley made a discreet dash for the kitchen where Pauline was attempting to glean any clue from the barrage of shrill English emanating from the parlour. Ashley had his arm about Athenais's waist and she was looking up at him as though he lit the entire world.

'Poor Francis,' she murmured vaguely. 'Do you think you ought to rescue him?'

'No. Do you?'

'No.' She laid her head briefly against his shoulder and then, becoming aware of Pauline's frown, said coaxingly, 'Don't be cross, Pauline.'

'I'm not.'

'And don't worry. Just be happy for me.'

'I am,' came the terse reply. 'But at the moment I just want to know what that hell-cat is screeching about.'

Although he was fairly sure he knew the answer to this, Ashley tilted his head long enough to catch a few words of Celia's diatribe and then said, 'The play.'

'*Ménage*?' asked Pauline blankly. 'Why? Didn't she like it?'

'I imagine she liked it very much – until she found out who'd written it. Then, of course, she decided that Francis – who is, after all, a Viscount – was debasing the family name.'

'Since she doesn't *go* by the family name,' snapped Pauline, 'not to mention the fact that she's married to one man and living with another, I don't see what she's got to complain about.'

Ashley pulled out a chair for Athenais and waited for her to sit.

'You're using logic, Pauline. I don't think it's a concept Celia is familiar with. Also, I suspect she has other things on her mind at the moment.' Smiling, he took Athenais's hand and dropped a light kiss on it. 'Forgive me. The King has summoned me to the Louvre – and, if I can find Nick, I'll take him with me to pay his respects. But I promise to be back before you leave for the theatre.'

She shook her head.

'You don't have to do that. I'll be perfectly all right with Francis and Pauline.'

'I know. But I'll be here anyway.' He winced at the sound of something breaking behind the parlour door. 'God forbid that she's just smashed the mirror.'

Nicholas returned while Ashley was upstairs retrieving his hat and sword and, on being informed that he was to have the honour of calling on the King, made speedy repairs to his appearance. Ashley made his leisurely way back down the stairs, paused outside the parlour where Celia was still in full flood and, after a moment's hesitation, rapped on the door before sticking his head around it.

'Francis – forgive me for interrupting. A brief word, if you wouldn't mind.'

'Mind? I'd be delighted,' said Francis dryly. And, without so much as a glance at his sister, joined Ashley in the hall and shut the door behind him. 'You're a man who probably knows how these things are done. If I strangle her, where shall we hide the body?'

'The river is generally the most popular.' Ashley paused and then said bluntly, 'It's not any business of mine … but last night Will Brierley told me that Verney is either having an affair or possibly courting a wealthy widow by the name of Angelique Latour. Apparently the relationship has been going on for some time – and I've seen them together myself. You might want to warn Celia – or you might not. I just thought you ought to know.'

'Oh God.' Francis gazed distractedly at the ceiling. 'I don't know if I can stand more screaming. But thank you for telling me.'

Ashley nodded. 'Nick and I are waiting on the King but will be back later. In the meantime, good luck.'

Francis walked moodily back into the parlour with no idea of what to do for the best. Celia, of course, didn't wait for him to say anything at all.

'How kind of you to re-join me,' she snapped. 'Perhaps now you'll do me the honour of explaining yourself.'

'No. I don't think I will. My actions and my life have nothing whatsoever to do with you, Celia – so I reserve the right to do as I see fit. I wrote a play in which Pauline Fleury agreed to return to the stage. Personally, I'm delighted. And if you don't like it, that's your problem.'

'People will laugh themselves silly --'

'Since the play is a comedy, one would certainly hope so.'

'At *you*, you fool!'

'I doubt that. And even if they do, I don't see what difference that makes to you.'

'Oh for God's sake – how many times must I say it?' She stood up and paced to the windows, kicking furiously at her skirts. 'I don't want my friends sniggering behind their hands because my brother is no better than a common actor!'

He gave a slow, malicious smile.

'Not as good, actually. If you'd been paying attention, you might have spotted me amongst the walkers in *Mariamne*. I found the experience rather enjoyable.'

Just for a second, she stared at him as if she couldn't believe her ears. Then she spat, 'You are not – you are not *ever* to do that again. Do you hear me? Haven't you any care at *all* for our name?'

'Don't start that again. You go by Verney's name – though you've no right to it. And you tossed your reputation in the midden the day you walked out on Eden.'

She flushed. 'But I'll get it back. I'll have it back when Hugo and I are married. And if you carry on this way, I'll never speak to you again.'

'Is that a promise?' drawled Francis. And then, making his decision, 'As for *when* Verney marries you … if my information is correct, it's more a question of *if*.'

'What is that supposed to mean?'

'Last time we spoke of this, I suggested that he might have another interest.' He paused and, with a shrug, added, 'He has.'

'*What?*'

'Her name is Angelique Latour. Perhaps you know her?'

Celia dropped like a stone on to the sofa.

'The widow with the vulgar jewellery?'

'I can't speak for the jewellery – but a widow, certainly.'

For the first time since she'd arrived, Celia seemed lost for words. Then, shaking her head, she said, 'It's not true. You're lying.'

'I'm not – but suit yourself.'

'He wouldn't … Hugo wouldn't do that to me. He *wouldn't*.'

Francis managed to stop himself remarking that, if she treated Verney to the kind of scene she'd just inflicted on him, no one could blame him for wanting to walk away. He said, 'Well, doubtless you know him better than I. But if you'll take a word of advice, you'll think carefully before confronting him over this. It's likely to do more harm than good. And now, you'll have to excuse me. I have a rehearsal to attend.'

* * *

With Francis occupied in the parlour, Pauline waited until she heard the front door close behind Ashley and Sir Nicholas, then sat down at the table and watched Athenais toying absently with a piece of bread. Her skin was faintly flushed and the dark grey eyes glowed. She had never, thought Pauline, looked better.

'It appears I don't need to ask if you're happy,' she said.

Athenais shook her head, laughing a little.

'He is … I don't know. There aren't words. He's just more than anything I could ever have dreamed of. And he loves me, Pauline.' She said it with awe, as though it was the greatest miracle in creation. 'He *really* loves me. But he'd convinced himself that he shouldn't because of his – oh, his *circumstances*. He actually said he had nothing to offer me. How can he have thought that? As if it mattered!'

'Of course it matters,' replied Pauline prosaically. 'He wouldn't be the man he is if he *hadn't* thought it. His pride would have him bleed to death rather than live off a woman. And, in your case, he knows you're already supporting your father and can't afford another burden. No – I know you don't see it that way and that he'll move heaven and earth not to let it happen. But it isn't what we need to talk about right now.'

'What, then?'

'I assume you don't want to get pregnant?'

Athenais opened her mouth, then closed it again, suddenly realising how surprisingly alluring the idea of having Ashley's child actually was.

'Stop that,' said Pauline, flatly. 'You can't afford those kind of notions. What you need to be doing is taking charge of things so he doesn't have to.'

Finally Athenais said slowly, 'I don't know how.'

'That's what I thought. Time for one or two long overdue lessons, then.'

* * *

On their way up to the King's apartments in the Louvre, Nicholas said, 'Has His Majesty ever told you how he managed to get away after Worcester? I've often wondered.'

Ashley, who was finding the seemingly interminable stairs a trial, managed a short laugh.

'Yes. He's told me … and I've heard him tell the tale on numerous other occasions.'

'He likes to talk about it?'

'Actually, I don't think he does but he's asked so often, he has to. Interestingly enough, the story is never quite the same twice running.'

Nicholas looked blank. 'He lies? Why?'

'To lay false trails and litter the true one with red herrings.' Ashley paused on the landing to ease the incipient cramp in his leg. 'A lot of people helped him escape, Nick. He's just doing what he can to protect their identities.'

Charles received them immediately in his shabby rooms where the fire did little to combat the December chill. As soon as he saw who Ashley had brought with him, he strode forward holding out his hand, saying, 'Nicholas, by all that's holy! This is an unexpected pleasure. We thought you must have been taken.'

Flushing with gratification, Nicholas clasped his King's hand and said, 'I'm happy to see you safe, Sir. And yes – I *was* taken. But due to this,' he gestured to his empty left sleeve, 'and the fact that I'm no one of importance, they didn't detain me for long.'

Sincere regret informed the swarthy face.

'I'm sorry that you've suffered so grievously on my account. Be assured that it won't be forgotten.'

'Plenty of our friends went through worse,' said Nicholas. 'I count myself lucky.'

'He wants to hear of your adventures, Sir,' interposed Ashley with a grin. 'I thought the version you gave that fellow of the Cardinal's was the best so far.'

'Then that's the one I'll tell – if I can recall which it was,' retorted Charles. Then, 'But first … I'd like to speak with you privately. Nicholas, perhaps you wouldn't mind waiting in the other room for a few minutes?'

Nicholas bowed and removed himself without further ado. As soon as he had gone, Charles gestured to a chair and said, 'Some time ago, I spoke to you of certain papers in Lucy's possession.'

Ashley sat down and nodded. 'I remember.'

'I need to get them back.'

'Ah.' *Hell. If it's burglary he wants, I'm not exactly in the best physical shape for it right now.* 'How urgent is it?'

'Moderately. I'm negotiating with Denmark for some ships and talks are reaching a delicate stage. Lucy, however, is once more being difficult and making wild threats. If she goes so far as to make certain things public, the Danish envoys will walk away without a backward glance.' Charles dropped into a chair on the far side of the hearth. 'I can't afford for that to happen, Ash. Can you help me?'

'I'll do my best – though, if you want me to attend to the matter myself, it may not be possible for a few days. My leg isn't quite up to scaling walls and climbing through windows.'

'Of course. I'd forgotten. Sir Edward said you were set upon by cut-purses?'

'Yes.' Refusing to elaborate, Ashley said, 'Sir, you're going to have to be more specific with regard to these papers of yours. I'll need to know what I'm looking for.'

'Letters,' replied Charles succinctly. 'Letters I wrote to her four years ago. Most of them are perfectly harmless … but there are three or four that could be damaging if they ended up in the wrong hands. She probably keeps them all together in one bundle – so the simplest thing would be to remove them all. Also, if you come across these so-called marriage lines while you're about it, you'd better liberate them as well.' He paused and then said, 'I'm not comfortable about this, Ash. But, with things as they are, I don't have much choice.'

'Quite.' A pause; and then, 'Do you mind me asking why Mistress Walter is intent on making your life difficult?'

'Now? The usual reason. Money.'

A frown darkened Ashley's eyes. He said, 'Forgive me, Sir ... but I was under the impression that you had recently paid at least part of the lady's promised pension.'

'No. Had that been the case, she might be less ...' He sighed, shrugging. 'You know how it is, Ash. Mazarin keeps me on a damnably tight financial leash with my aunt, the Queen Dowager standing squarely behind him. Money – or rather the lack of it – is at the heart of everything these days. How are you managing?'

Ashley put aside what he'd learned for future consideration.

'I'm not. And, to put it bluntly, the situation is becoming critical. I need paid employment. But it seems I've only two options. Enlist under Turenne and quite possibly find myself posted to Spain; or offer my services to the Cardinal's guard and march up and down like a toy soldier for a man I neither trust nor respect.'

Charles sat up, looking confused.

'Do we not pay you?'

Ashley blinked. 'You, Sir?'

'The so-called Royal purse – Hyde – Secretary Nicholas in Antwerp. One of them?'

'No, Sir.' His mouth twisted wryly. 'I've served for love. And while we had an army, that was viable. Now, I'm afraid, it's not. I'll do my best to reclaim your letters, but after that --'

'Stop.' Charles looked genuinely chagrined. 'This isn't right. I've called on you over and over for years now – since before my father met his end – and you've never failed me. I assumed that, like a handful of other extremely necessary gentlemen, you were being paid. Not much, admittedly – but something. Hyde finds the money. I don't know how – but he does. And you're telling me that in what – over four years? – you've never received a penny?'

'No. But then, I never expected to.'

The King surged to his feet.

'Well, it won't do – and I wish to God you'd told me months ago. There are precious few men I rely on completely, Ashley – but you're one of them. I'm going to have this out with Hyde right now.' He stopped, apparently recalling that Nicholas was waiting in the next room. 'Apologise to Nick for me and tell him to visit me again so I can learn how he's been faring. But this can't wait. I want to hear Hyde's explanations. And I *particularly* want to hear how he's going to make it possible for you to continue in my service.' His Majesty stretched out his long arms and cracked his knuckles. 'Do you know, Ash … I'm actually quite annoyed.'

Nicholas accepted his dismissal philosophically and followed Ashley into the freezing drizzle outside. He said, 'Are you allowed to tell me what His Majesty wanted?'

'Later,' said Ashley crisply. 'For now, I want a word with Sir William Brierley.'

'Who?'

'A man I counted as both a friend and one of the best agents in the game. I want to hear him explain why he lied to me.'

NINE

Despite his best efforts, Ashley failed to find One-Eyed Will and was eventually convinced that he'd left Paris for a time – which did little to improve his own mood. He didn't like being duped; he *especially* didn't like being duped by a man he trusted. And worse than that was the lurking suspicion that, if Will had lied to him, it didn't bode well.

He tried to cheer himself with the possibility of finally being paid but he knew better than to place too much faith in it actually happening. Charles was sincere but Ashley couldn't see Hyde paying for services he'd previously had for nothing. He'd say yes to the King, then find ways to procrastinate until the matter was forgotten – secure in the knowledge that Ashley was very unlikely to ask.

Having traipsed around fruitlessly searching for Will Brierley, he and Nicholas arrived back at the house rather later than he'd anticipated but in plenty of time to escort Athenais to the theatre. As soon as he walked through the door, she came skimming down the stairs glowing with the mere pleasure of seeing him and cast herself on his chest.

Unable to remember ever being the cause of such undisguised delight and trying not to show how it moved him, he caught her, dropped a kiss on her hair and said lightly, 'What's this? Anyone would think I'd been away at the wars for months.'

She shook her head and buried her face against his throat.

Nicholas said humorously, 'You ungrateful devil. Mademoiselle Athenais can throw herself into *my* arms any time she likes.'

'I'd advise you not to hold your breath,' suggested Ashley mildly.

Athenais shot Nicholas a mischievous smile.

'Thank you, Sir Nicholas. I'll remember that for when I detect a lack of appreciation.'

'Call him Nick,' said Ashley. And, in a low, wicked murmur, 'I appreciate you. I could do it now, if you like.'

Nicholas didn't hear the words but Athenais's blush gave him the general idea. He said, 'I feel decidedly *de trop*. Shall I ask Jem to carry on searching for this Brierley fellow?'

'Yes. I doubt if he'll find him – but it's worth a try. And, if all else fails, Jem knows where he lodges so he can always watch for him there.'

Nicholas nodded and left them. Athenais said, 'Who is Monsieur Brierley?'

'Just someone I'm rather eager to speak to.' Since they were temporarily alone, he took the opportunity to kiss her. She sighed, nestled a little closer and laid her palm against his cheek. Presently, he said, 'This is a very nice welcome. I must make a habit of going out for a couple of hours on a regular basis.'

She laughed. 'Or you could just leave the room for five minutes.'

It occurred to him that being so very dear to someone might take a bit of getting used to ... and then, that he actually didn't *want* to get used to it; that he'd like to experience this unique glow every day of his life.

Twining her hair around his fingers, he said, 'I'm presuming that if Francis had murdered Celia you'd have mentioned it before now?'

'Oh!' She tensed in his arms and stared up at him in sudden alarm. 'I forgot. We've laid her out in the parlour.'

Just for a second, he almost believed her.

'Very funny.'

Athenais grinned. 'She slammed out of the house shouting something about Francis lying and ill-wishing her and never, ever believing him.'

'Ah. He told her, then.'

'Told her what?'

'That her lover is being unfaithful to her.'

'Oh dear. And is he?'

Ashley shrugged. 'He's certainly doing something – though whether it's just an affair or something more serious, I couldn't say. Has Francis spent the rest of the day talking about dropping Celia down the nearest well?'

'No – though he couldn't be blamed for wanting to. He may have said something to Pauline ... but all *I* heard him say was that he washed his hands of her and that Eden was well out of it.' She looked at him. 'Do you know him – this Eden?'

'No – though I wouldn't mind meeting him one day. He's a Roundhead, of course ... but Francis and Nick both have a high regard for him.'

'Then it's a pity he has such terrible taste in women.'

'Yes. Well, we can't all be perfect.' He grinned and kissed her again. 'I need to shave and change into a clean shirt, if I have one.'

'You have two,' she said proudly. 'I washed and ironed them myself.'

'Oh God. Tell me you iron better than you cook.'

'I can iron *beautifully*. But if you're going to be rude, you can sleep in the attic tonight.'

'And have you dragging me downstairs in the middle of the night? No. I don't think so.'

And made a swift, strategic retreat before she could retaliate.

* * *

The theatre was, if possible, even more packed than it had been on the previous evening, word of *Ménage* and Pauline Fleury's performance in it having spread like wildfire. At least half the audience had turned up for a second viewing and the other half was overflowing with anticipation. By the time the stage candles were being lit, all the boxes were packed tight and the inhabitants of the pit surged like boiling soup.

'Any sign?' asked Ashley as Francis joined him in the wings after scanning the auditorium for the Marquis d'Auxerre.

'No. I'll check again at the first interval, just in case.'

From beyond the curtain, the noise level soared to a new peak.

'Bloody hell,' murmured Ashley. 'This is unbelievable. What have you done?'

'I don't know. I certainly didn't expect it.' He shook his head. 'But it's not just the play, is it? It's Pauline. She's magnificent.'

Ashley cast him a thoughtful, sideways glance but said merely, 'Yes, she is. And, but for you, she'd still be mending costumes. So I think you're entitled to take some credit.'

'I don't need any credit,' said Francis simply. 'I just wanted to see her shine. And she does.' Then, realising he'd probably revealed more than he'd meant to, he added, 'I tailored this role to what I reasoned she would accept. But she could do much more; and I doubt Froissart will let her retire into the shadows again – even assuming she wants to.'

'She won't want to,' said Athenais, arriving in time to hear this last remark and promptly tucking herself under Ashley's arm. 'It's in her blood. For Pauline, acting is as effortless as breathing and she commands the stage. Even when she's not doing anything at all, your eyes are drawn to her. And that, gentlemen, is a rare gift. Now – hush. They're starting.'

If anything, the play's reception that evening was even more enthusiastic than it had been the night before and, once again, Francis had to join the cast on-stage for a final bow – only this time the calls were not for the author but for *'Seigneur François'*. Under cover of kissing Pauline's hands, he muttered, 'I'm not doing this tomorrow night.'

'Because Celia said so?'

'Because I feel like the freak at the fair.'

Backstage, Athenais had disappeared to ready herself for her role in *Don Japhet*. Ashley grinned at Francis and said, 'At this rate, you're going to have admirers mobbing you in the street.'

'There's a cheery thought,' came the dry retort. 'I don't suppose you'd like to make the rounds out front?'

'No. Everyone already knows you're here – and why. But if d'Auxerre makes an appearance I'd rather he remained unaware that I'm here, too. So off you go. Time to meet your public.'

Due to the number of men who wanted to shake his hand or buffet his shoulder and the ladies who leaned over the parapet of their boxes and called to him, what should have taken no more than five minutes took nearly twenty. But eventually, Francis returned – somewhat dishevelled – with the information that he'd caught sight of Cyrano de Bergerac amongst the throng but that the Marquis was still notable only by his absence.

'And I am *not*,' he finished flatly, 'running the gauntlet out there again. Pauline says there's a place back here from which it's possible to see all the centre boxes – so that will have to do.'

Ashley gave a grunt of dissatisfaction but his expression changed when Athenais appeared on-stage in a gown that glowed gold in the candlelight. Her hair was piled up in a mass of artless curls, a few of which had been allowed to escape and drift distractingly around her neck. He wondered what was holding it up and, when she passed by during the interval on her way for a change of costume, he said, 'Leave your hair like that tonight.' And saw her breathing change before she nodded.

The third act was half over when his attention sharpened and he said to Francis, 'There. Fourth box from the right. Not his usual place ... and not his usual boot-lickers, either.'

Francis sighed. 'What do you want to do?'

'Ask Pauline to stay near Athenais. If d'Auxerre runs true to form, he'll wait until the crush dies down so I'm going to lurk here until I see him move. Once he gets to the Green Room – *if* he does – I want you to keep a discreet eye on him. I'll be nearby.'

'And we are doing this because?'

'We are doing this because I'm tired of playing guessing games. This is his second consecutive appearance. If he still has designs on Athenais, I want to know so that I can deal with it once and for all. I won't tolerate her being continually frightened of the bastard.'

The cold, purposeful tone was one Francis had only heard twice before. The first time had been when he'd faced General Leslie after Inverkeithing; the second, the day they'd caught the Marquis with his hands on Athenais. Not for the first time, it occurred to Francis that The Falcon was somebody you'd rather not have as an enemy and he wondered if the Marquis had any idea what he was tangling with.

As it had been the night before, the Green Room was heaving with well-wishers. The more serious *aficionados* gathered around Pauline; besotted young men surrounded Athenais and the other young women of the company; and there were even a number of fashionable ladies, vying for Francis's attention. The room was hot, noisy and reeked of an unpleasant mixture of sweat and perfume.

Gradually, however, the crowd thinned as people started to leave. With an ease born of long practice, Pauline dispersed her admirers fairly quickly; most of the besotted gentlemen drifted away, either disconsolately alone or to await their promised supper companions; and Francis remained trapped in a corner with two ladies – each of whom seemed reluctant to leave the other in possession of the field. Pauline watched how deftly he managed to flirt with both of them at once ... and then, aware of inappropriate emotions, firmly turned her back.

Wondering where Ashley was and eager to shed the gold gown – which, lovely though it looked, was beginning to make her itch – Athenais caught Pauline's eye and indicated that she intended to withdraw to the tiring-room. Pauline nodded and tossed a seemingly expressionless glance at Francis. Then, before Athenais could take more than a step, the Marquis d'Auxerre sauntered in, trailed by a pair of over-dressed young men of languid appearance. Athenais froze; Pauline planted herself in the middle of the room; and Francis shifted his position against the wall.

'Ah,' said d'Auxerre, subtly mocking. '*Seigneur François*. Our new literary genius. Poor Corneille must be gnashing his teeth.'

'Unlikely,' returned Francis, cheerfully. 'It must be plain to the meanest intelligence that I've neither the wish nor the ability to rival masterpieces like *Le Cid*.'

A hint of colour crept along the Marquis's cheekbones at the not-quite-veiled insult. Turning away and with the merest suggestion of a bow, he said, 'Mademoiselle de Galzain ... radiant as ever, I see. And Madame Fleury.' A deeper, more correct bow for Pauline. 'I wished only to congratulate you on your very welcome return to the stage ... even in a piece so unworthy of your talents.'

'Thank you,' said Pauline, aridly. 'But I'm sorry you think so poorly of the play. Perhaps you missed some of the finer points?'

Being called stupid twice in as many minutes made d'Auxerre clench his fists.

'Or perhaps I simply have a more sophisticated palate,' he snapped. And with another brisk nod to the room in general, he stalked out.

Athenais gave a tiny, semi-hysterical giggle and sat down with a bump as relief drained the strength from her knees. She said, 'He's gone. Just like that?'

'Looks like it,' replied Pauline.

'Thank God. I've been so worried about what he might do next – and all for nothing, it seems.'

Pauline's glanced to where Francis was apparently enjoying the clinging arms and openly inviting smiles of his female admirers and wanted to slap him. Returning her attention to Athenais, she said, 'Get changed – and I'll find the Colonel. Then, if Francis can tear himself away, we can leave.'

Athenais stood up, a naughty light dancing in her eyes.

'Why, Pauline! You sound almost jealous.'

'Nauseous is what I sound. The silly widgeons have been drooling over him for the last fifteen minutes.'

'He doesn't seem to mind.'

'Of course he doesn't. That's men for you.'

She stopped as Marie d'Amboise entered the room and paused near Athenais long enough to say carelessly, 'You're wanted in Froissart's office.'

Athenais stared at her in surprise.

'Monsieur wants me? *Now?* Why?'

En route for the tiring-room, Marie shrugged and continued on her way.

'I neither know nor care.'

'How odd.' Athenais shook out her skirts and, tossing an impish grin at Pauline as she left the room, added, 'I won't be long. Meanwhile, if Francis doesn't get rid of the widgeons, you'd better do it for him.'

No more than five minutes after she had gone, Ashley walked in and, taking in the fact that Francis still had a female hanging on each arm, murmured wickedly, 'Spoilt for choice, Francis? Or contemplating decadent pleasures?'

The ladies giggled, then directed blatantly appraising glances in his own direction.

Ignoring them, he walked over to Pauline and said, 'Is Athenais getting changed?'

'No – but everything is fine. The Marquis came, made his bow and left. No more than that.'

'I know. The last I saw of him, he and his pups were passing through the auditorium towards the front door. So if she's not changing, where is she?'

'Froissart wanted to see her.'

His brows rose. 'He did? Why?'

She shrugged. 'He's probably got some new bee in his bonnet. It happens sometimes.'

A faint sense of unease prickled Ashley's mind. He said, 'How long ago was this?'

'A few minutes. If you're worried, they'll be in his office.'

'*Hell!*' Ashley spun on his heel, aware that there were two ways to approach that particular room – one of them being from the main entrance. 'Froissart's not in his office. He's out front, talking to de Bergerac. Francis – with me!'

* * *

Athenais knocked on Froissart's door, then opened it and took a step inside. A hand closed round her wrist, jerking her forward – and she found herself facing the Marquis d'Auxerre while, behind her, one of his acolytes turned the key in the lock.

For a second, shock held her immobile. Her mouth went dry and her brain refused to function. Smiling coldly, the Marquis strolled towards her saying, 'Did you think I had forgotten you, *ma petite?* You should have known better.'

Swallowing the bitterness in her throat, she concentrated on keeping her spine straight and her voice steady.

'Oddly enough, I prefer not to think of you at all.'

He halted no more than two steps away.

'Now why do I not believe that?'

'Because you don't want to?' she hazarded.

'Because the women I want don't refuse me. And I don't intend you to be the first.'

Athenais wished she could look away from his face. With that unpleasant curl still bracketing his mouth, he conducted a lingering appraisal of her body and let his gaze dwell with unconcealed intent on her *décolletage.* She told herself he wouldn't touch her – wouldn't do anything with his two friends in the room – and then wasn't so sure. Also, after last time, she couldn't stop her stomach clenching with fright.

Using every skill at her command, she managed a cool smile and said, 'Forcing me won't change the fact that I've said no, will it? And I *have* said no – repeatedly – but never with the intention of insulting you. It's simply that I ... I refuse *all* such offers.'

Please God, let him understand and back off, she prayed. *If he finds out about Ashley, there's no telling what he'll do.*

The Marquis sighed, closed the space between them and gripped her chin with hard, merciless fingers. He said, 'So many words. I am weary of them.' And pulling her against him, he took her mouth in a rough, possessive kiss.

Instinctively, Athenais twisted away but he clamped his other hand on her arm and held her fast, his tongue invading her mouth.

The door-handle rattled and was immediately followed by the deafening thud of a booted foot. The door flew in, its lock smashed, and the fellow who had been leaning against it was catapulted into the room to collide with Froissart's desk.

It happened so fast that the Marquis didn't have time to do more than turn his head.

Ashley stood in the doorway with Francis at his shoulder.

'Get your hands off her,' snapped Ashley. And held out a hand towards Athenais.

Wrenching herself from the Marquis's suddenly slack hold, she stumbled to his side. His arm closed round her and he said, 'Are you all right? The bastard hasn't hurt you?'

She shook her head. 'No. There was no time. How --?'

'Later. Francis – take her back to Pauline, would you? And you two ...' His glance skimmed d'Auxerre's apparently transfixed friends, 'Out.'

'They will stay.' D'Auxerre was plainly maintaining his *sangfroid* with an effort. 'These gentlemen don't take their orders from such as you.'

'Do they not?' Ashley turned his head, giving Athenais a little push in the direction of the door. 'Francis?'

Taking Athenais's reluctant hand, Francis said, 'Sure?'

'Perfectly.' And again to the mute pair, his expression at complete variance with his butter-soft tone, 'Don't make me say it again.'

They didn't. With muttered apologies to the Marquis, they followed Francis and Athenais from the room. The door closed behind them.

Ashley's smile was openly insulting.

'Where *do* you find them? Since they're so indistinguishable from each other, one is tempted to wonder if you don't have them specially bred. One also wonders what possible uses you have for them.'

The inference was plain and the Marquis flushed.

'Mind your mouth. You killed Henri and Jean-Claude.'

'One of them, certainly.'

'I can have you charged with murder.'

'Not unless you want to explain why you sent them to kill me. And before you put that string-and-clapper arrangement that serves you for a brain to work – allow me to inform you that I have a witness to the attack.'

'Who?'

'Does it matter?'

D'Auxerre drew a steadying breath and decided to attack the core issue.

'You will get in my way once too often.'

'I'll get in your way as often as is necessary,' retorted Ashley, strolling to within two feet of the Marquis. 'Tell me something. Just how arrogant or thick-skinned or downright stupid *are* you? The lady does not want you. Which bit of that can't you understand? Because I'm not sure how much more simply I can put it. She doesn't want you. She is not available ... and she never will be. And finally, if you ever touch her again, I won't be wasting my breath on conversation.'

There was a short, airless silence and then the Marquis said, 'You've had her.'

'What a banal mind you have.' Revulsion coiled in Ashley's stomach but he kept his expression unreadable and his voice perfectly level as he continued to press his attack. 'But I imagine the possibility hurts. The thought that I, with my shabby coat and empty pockets, might have succeeded where you, despite your title and money, have failed.' He paused to let his words sink home. Then, 'I believe I just threatened you. Didn't you notice?'

'I noticed. You can't touch me. I, on the other hand, can brush you from my path at any time I choose.'

Ashley's laugh was like splinters of ice.

'You think so? It didn't work out so well for you the last time, did it? Of course, if you were a man, you'd come for me yourself instead of sending your pets. Then again, if you were any kind of gentleman, you wouldn't be forcing yourself on an unwilling woman. But perhaps you don't mind looking ridiculous?'

'You've had her,' said d'Auxerre again, his voice thick with temper. 'If you hadn't, you'd think twice about making an enemy of me. It is the biggest mistake you've ever made.'

'No. The biggest mistake I ever made was not putting your head through the wall the day I first caught you half-way to raping a frightened girl.' He fixed the other man with an expression soul-hacking contempt. 'You just don't learn, do you?'

'From you? I've learned enough. You're a bag of wind. You daren't do more than puff words at me for fear of reprisals. As for your little whore, I'll --'

Without waiting to hear the rest and thankful that the moment had finally come, Ashley moved. He slammed his fist into the fellow's jaw hard enough to loosen a couple of teeth and knock him to the ground but not quite hard enough to render him unconscious. Then, standing over the Marquis with a look in his eye that spoke of terrible temptation to put a boot in his groin, he said, 'You were saying?'

D'Auxerre struggled to his knees and spat blood.

'You'll die for that.'

'I doubt it. Get up, why don't you? Get up and try hitting me back.' He waited for a moment and then, in a tone as insulting as he could make it, added, 'But you won't do that, will you? You won't even issue your challenge because you haven't the nerve to face up to a man. The only thing you're good at is hurting girls. You're just a stinking, pusillanimous coward.' Another pause. Then, 'Stay away from Athenais. If you touch her again, I *will* kill you. And enjoy doing it.'

* * *

Cornered immediately afterwards by an extremely anxious Athenais, Ashley merely said that he'd set the Marquis straight on a few things.

Privately, to Francis, he said disgustedly, 'The fellow's lily-livered. I insulted his intelligence, his manhood and his honour. I even knocked the bastard down. If he had an ounce of backbone, he'd have named a time and place – but he didn't. So the only thing I can hope is that I've drawn his fire from Athenais to myself ... because if I haven't, sooner or later I'm going to have to do something terminal.'

'Kill him, you mean?'

'Either that or cut off his bollocks and ram them down his throat. You're the poet. Which one do you think is more apt?'

TEN

The following day brought another visit from Celia, this time in tears.

'What's Verney done now?' asked Francis wearily.

'I don't know where he is,' sobbed Celia. 'He hasn't been home for two days. Do you think ... do you really think he's with that woman?'

'I've no idea – but it seems likely.' He looked at her, not entirely unsympathetic but feeling as though he could well do without this. 'I'm sorry, Celia. I don't know what you expect me to do about it.'

'Find him and tell him he must break with her and come back to me.'

'And you think he's going to do it because I say so? Of course he isn't.' He pinched the bridge of his nose and sat down beside her. 'I can't say I ever thought it would happen but, realistically, this was always a possibility. You're not married so you have no hold over him. If he doesn't want to be with you any more, there's nothing anyone can do about it.'

'But I gave up *everything* for him.'

Nothing that apparently mattered very much to you, thought Francis. But said dryly, 'He gave up quite a lot himself, as I recall.'

She made a dismissive gesture with one hand.

'He loves me. He's *always* loved me. And I don't understand why he's behaving this way – especially now, when there's finally a chance we could marry.' She fumbled for her handkerchief and wiped her brimming eyes. 'This can't happen. It's all wrong. We've been together for over eight years, Francis!'

'I know.'

'And I've never looked at another man in all that time.'

Having seen the way she'd eyed Ashley, Francis rather doubted that – though he was ready to believe she'd probably never done much more than look.

'Of course not.'

'So he can't just walk away from me. I won't let him.'

He sighed. 'Then talk to him. And I mean *talk*, Celia – not a barrage of tears and recrimination. But if things don't go the way you wish, there really isn't a great deal to be done.'

Her mouth compressed into a hard line and she stared down at her lap, where her fingers were systematically shredding her handkerchief. 'You said I have no hold over him – but I have. A few months ago when we were short of money, he persuaded me to do something I shouldn't have.'

'What, exactly?'

'I ... I took something.'

Francis frowned. 'You mean you stole it?'

She nodded.

'From whom?'

'That doesn't matter. Hugo said it was something this person shouldn't have anyway and, in the right quarters, it would be worth a lot of money. He made it sound like a *good* thing – as though we'd be doing the – doing a favour for someone important. Only afterwards, it started to feel ... awkward. I couldn't face my – the person in question so I had to invent a quarrel. Worse still, the man Hugo said would pay for the – for this thing I took, didn't. Or, at least, I don't think he did.' She looked up. 'But what's important is that Hugo wouldn't want people to know what he's done and how he made me help him.'

Francis was beginning to get a feeling of dire foreboding. He said, 'Celia ... please tell me you didn't steal Lucy Walter's so-called marriage lines and give them to Hugo to sell?'

Her eyes flew to meet his.

'How do you --?' She stopped abruptly.

'How do I know? You've just more or less told me.' He dropped his head in his hands and tried to think past the fact that this was getting worse and worse – and God alone knew what Ashley was going to make of it. 'Christ. I'm having trouble believing that even you could be this stupid. I'm assuming Verney expected Ned Hyde to buy it?'

She nodded. 'He said that, even if it was a forgery, Hyde would still want it so Lucy couldn't use it to cause trouble. But he didn't.'

'So what did Verney do next?'

'Next? I don't know. For all I know, he still has it.'

He doesn't, thought Francis. *Thomas Scot does. Which means Verney's loyalties are, at best, divided.* Then, knowing better than to expect Celia to concentrate on anything that didn't personally involve her, he said, 'If you think you can use this to blackmail Verney into marrying you, you're deluded. It was you who stole the letter, not him. And since you don't know what he did with it, you can't prove that he did anything at all. All you'll achieve is to brand yourself a thief.'

'But --'

He stood up.

'There aren't any buts. The whole thing is a petard waiting to blow up in your face. If you threaten Verney with this, he'll say exactly what I've just said – and then he probably *will* walk out on you. If your relationship with him is crumbling and you want to shore it up, you're going to have to keep your temper and hold an adult conversation – or, alternatively, put a smile on your face, something enticing on the rest of you and seduce him. If neither of those work, nothing will.'

* * *

'So what do you want to do about Verney?' asked Francis, when he finished relating the whole sorry tale to Ashley.

'Not a great deal. If, as Eden believes, the marriage-lines are forged, Verney hasn't exactly done much damage. But since he *could* have done, I'll make sure Hyde is aware that his allegiance is questionable – and what happens thereafter will be up to him, not me.' Ashley let his head fall back and communed silently with the ceiling for a few moments. Then he said, 'It's galling to think of the time I've wasted over Lucy Walter and Henri de Vauvallon. But in matters like this, I suppose there's always a red herring or two. And events have now moved on.' He sighed. 'His Majesty wants me to burgle Lucy's lodgings and retrieve his letters. If Celia had taken those as well, she could have saved me a great deal of trouble.'

Francis stared at him.

'You're not really going to do it, are you?'

'I said I would. I also said it would have to wait until I'm fit enough to go tripping around rooftops. But since I'm reluctant to ruin my only remaining suit of clothes, I'm going to have to ensure that the lady is otherwise engaged and hope that Jem's dalliance with the maidservant is sufficiently advanced to let me in through the front door – after which, I'll only have to pick a couple of locks.'

'*Only?*'

'Yes. It's not especially difficult.'

A prickle of suspicion made its way down Francis's neck.

'Why do I get the feeling you're telling me this for a purpose?'

Ashley grinned. 'Because I want you to reserve a box for Mistress Walter and her friends at the theatre tomorrow evening. Tell her it's by way of an apology from Celia, if you like. And then, since you don't need to watch every single performance, you can come and watch the street for me instead. All being well, we'll be back for the final curtain.'

'Watch the street for what?'

'Unexpected visitors.'

'And if I see any? No. Don't tell me. I'm supposed to hoot like an owl – or some such thing.'

'I was thinking more in terms of a piercing whistle. But if hooting is your preference, I haven't any objection.' He paused. 'So you'll do it?'

'Why not? Since larceny already runs in the family, what have I got to lose?'

* * *

Ashley told Jem that they were going house-breaking.

'Gawd!' said Mr Barker. 'Totting a crib? Are you dicked in the nob? You had enough to say when I was doing a bit of dipping!'

'That was because you were bad at it.'

'I did all right,' muttered Jem sulkily. 'And you're no ace cracksman.'

'I'm careful and I plan – which is generally sufficient. Can you get me a couple of lengths of strong wire?'

'Reckon so. What for?'

'I need to make some lock-picks.'

'Gawd!' breathed Jem again.

'And, while I'm working on that, you can continue your flirtation with that saucy piece at Mistress Walter's lodgings. Make an assignation with her for tomorrow night.'

'A what?'

'Tell her you'll be round tomorrow evening with some wine.'

Jem scratched his head and looked moderately more cheerful.

'Ah. Well, it's an ill-wind, ain't it, Colonel?'

'It certainly is.'

* * *

An hour or so later and having searched the entire house, Athenais found Ashley in the attic bending wire into small, oddly intricate shapes. She said, 'What on earth are you doing?'

He tossed the pieces aside and smiled at her.

'Nothing very important.' Reaching out, he took her hand and pulled her down beside him. 'You'll want to ask about last night.'

She nodded, colouring a little.

After the encounter with the Marquis, Ashley had accompanied her to her room, pulled the pins from her hair and kissed her with his usual languorous skill. Then he'd said, 'I'm not going to stay with you tonight. Not because I don't want to – but because that piece of vermin has left a bad taste in my mouth ... and also because there's something you and I need to talk about before taking matters any further. And so, since I can't guarantee to keep my hands off you, I'm going to sleep upstairs.'

Then he'd kissed her hands, told her that he loved her – and left.

'Yes. What did you mean?'

'About d'Auxerre? What I said. He'd made me angry and, when that happens, it sometimes takes time to dissipate.' His smile was crooked. 'One of my less attractive characteristics, I'm afraid.'

'And the thing we needed to talk about?'

'Ah. Yes.' He stared down at their clasped hands for a moment and then said bluntly, 'I don't want to get you with child.'

'Oh. No. I mean – it's all right. Pauline has already talked to me about that.'

'Has she? How very efficient of her.'

'You know what she's like,' shrugged Athenais. 'She guessed that I might not think of it and wouldn't know what to do if I did – so she's brewing a cordial I'm to drink every day. She says it's very effective.'

Ashley wasn't entirely convinced but, since he knew that the only certain way to prevent conception was abstinence and he rather suspected that might be beyond him, he said, 'And you're happy with that?'

She leaned her head against his shoulder.

'I'm happy with *you*.' She hesitated and then said, 'If I promise to remember that you need privacy sometimes, will you move downstairs with me?'

'You don't need to promise me anything except that you're sure it's what you want.'

'How could it not be?' She reached up to kiss his jaw. 'I love you.'

* * *

On the following day, learning that Nicholas was again visiting the Louvre, Ashley said, 'Tell His Majesty that I'm hoping to complete the task he set me this evening. He'll know what you mean. And you might also tell him that, if I fail to report to him tomorrow, he'd better find out why.'

'Because something will have gone wrong?'

'Yes. It shouldn't – but one never knows. And one other thing. Francis and I will escort the ladies to the theatre tonight, then disappear for a time. We should be back before the final curtain but, during our absence and just in case we're delayed, I'd like you to be on hand should the need arise. If the Marquis shows up again, Pauline will point him out to you.'

'Whereupon I don't let Athenais out of my sight?'

'Whereupon, if necessary, you chain her to your wrist.'

Nick grinned wryly. 'Only having one, that might be tricky – but I'll do my best.'

* * *

Pauline, on learning that Francis would be missing the bulk of that evening's performance, took the opportunity to appear to jump to conclusions.

'I see. One of your new lady-friends invited you to supper, has she?'

'No.' He folded his arms and grinned. 'Would you mind if she had?'

'Why should I? It's no business of mine what you do.'

'Then why did you ask?'

'Idle curiosity.'

'I see.'

She gave him a sharp glance and said, 'I don't know why you're looking so smug.'

'Yes, you do. It's because you're just a little bit jealous.'

'I most certainly am not!'

The smug expression evaporated and Francis said, 'Would it really hurt you to give me just a glimmer of encouragement?'

'As far as I can see, you don't need it.'

'Then you can't have been looking very hard.' He turned to go and the paused to say, 'Not, of course, that you're remotely interested ... but I'll be helping Ashley with something for an hour or so.'

'Wait!' Pauline took a couple of steps towards him. 'I don't want the details. But ...'

'But what?'

She drew an impatient breath. 'You'll be careful?'

The sheer, uninhibited pleasure in Francis's smile made her knees feel suddenly weak.

'I'll be careful,' he promised. 'And I thank you for asking.'

ELEVEN

Ashley and Francis remained at the theatre until *Ménage* was under way and Mistress Walter, accompanied by three gentlemen and a lady – who was *not* Celia – were ensconced in their box and looked likely to remain there. Then they slipped discreetly out of the stage door and made their way through the dark streets to find out if Jem had managed to fulfil his part of the plan.

He had. The door to the street was unlocked and no one stood guard. Ashley gestured to Francis to lurk in the deep shadows of a doorway opposite and then slid soundlessly into the house.

The picklocks being new, it took longer to open Lucy's door than Ashley had anticipated but perseverance was finally rewarded and the door swung open. Once inside the room, he waited for a few moments for his eyes to become accustomed to the dark ... then he set about taking the necessary precautions. He locked the door behind him, opened one of the street-facing windows a crack so that, if Francis signalled, he would be able to hear him and he checked that all the curtains were tightly closed. Then he took the time to locate another way out in case things went awry. A window from the dressing-closet gave on to a tiled roof some twelve feet below, from which a similar drop would take him to the yard. Sighing, Ashley loosened the window-latch and hoped he wouldn't have to use it.

He returned to the parlour, lit a single candle and set about picking the lock of the small travelling desk. Five minutes later, he had it open – only to discover that it was stuffed full of bills. Ashley flicked through them, marvelling at the staggering amount Mistress Walter owed her dressmaker. Then, finding nothing resembling the letters he was looking for, he put the bills back as he had found them and had to waste more time re-locking the desk.

He reasoned he'd now been inside the building for some fifteen minutes and he'd hoped to be in and out inside thirty but had now to conduct a thorough search. He glanced around the room. A cupboard beneath the window-seat was empty of everything except cobwebs and the books on the mantelpiece were similarly unproductive. Deciding that the bedchamber was probably the more likely place, he picked up his candle and took a look around. His heart sank. Lucy's bedroom might smell better than the Green Room at the Marais but it was certainly no tidier. Gloves, scarves, chemises and petticoats all seemed to be trying to escape confinement so that nearly every drawer and chest had something spilling out of it; on the table beneath the mirror, bracelets and jewelled combs lay amidst spilled orris powder; and when Ashley took a step towards the bed, he narrowly avoided tripping over a numerous pairs of shoes.

His first and only thought was a despairing, *This could take all night and I don't have that long*. Then, forcing himself to get a grip, he drew a deep breath and tried to approach the problem logically.

She was a woman – and not a particularly intelligent one, at that. She'd been careless enough with her marriage-lines to let Celia purloin them. If she'd discovered the loss, she'd have moved any other important papers to … where? Where did women hide things? Underneath her stays or amidst her night-rails? He really didn't want to touch those overflowing drawers and be faced with the problem of getting everything back the way it was. Stuffed under the pillow, the mattress, the bed? Worth a try, he supposed … and spent a few precious minutes fruitlessly hunting. Under the floorboards? He doubted Lucy was the type to ruin her fingernails – which was just as well since he could hardly go tramping round the room to see if anything seemed loose. Which left what?

He scanned the room again and this time noticed a large round box of the kind used for hats squashed between the top of the armoire and the ceiling. Ashley reached up, his fingers getting just enough purchase to tug it free. Being substantially shorter than himself, he reasoned that Lucy would need to stand on a stool – which meant that whatever was up there wasn't something she needed very often. Setting the box down on the bed, he lifted the lid.

It contained not one hat but three, all somewhat the worse for wear. And nestling beneath them, neatly tied up with a blue ribbon was a bundle of letters … along with a separately folded document that Ashley hadn't expected to see.

His brows rose and he murmured, 'Well now. Just how many of these things *are* there?'

He was just tucking his finds into the breast of his coat when he heard a shrill whistle and Francis's voice shouting, 'Stop! My purse, you bastard!' And then, 'Sirs – he went that way. Help me!' Followed by the sound of running feet.

Unfortunately, he also heard feminine voices in the hall below and light, slippered footsteps on the stairs.

Ashley groaned. He rammed the box back into its place, blew out the candle and shot through to the dressing-closet. The window was small and getting his shoulders through it wasn't easy. Then he lowered his body to hang by his hands from the sill and, bracing himself for the impact, let go. He dropped and rolled more or less silently but pain hissed through his injured thigh. He limped across the roof and, finding an ancient creeper, used it to access the yard without doing further damage to himself. Then he gritted his teeth and ran.

An alleyway led to the street where he could still hear Francis breathing heavily and bemoaning the theft of his purse. Ashley managed a sour grin. It was nice to know he wasn't the only one running about like an idiot. He gave it a minute and then whistled. Moments later, Francis strolled around the corner. He was actually laughing – albeit silently.

'I'm glad one of us is enjoying himself,' muttered Ashley.

'Aren't you?'

'Not especially.'

'Did you get the letters?'

'Yes. And that's not all. I also found the famous marriage-lines.'

'What?' Francis stared at him. 'But they're in London.'

'One copy may be. A second one is inside my coat. So the question arises, how many more of them are there?'

* * *

Back at the theatre, the fourth act of *Don Japhet* was well under way. While Francis joined Nicholas back-stage and established that the Marquis hadn't put in an appearance, Ashley made use of the Green Room to remove any signs of his exertions. He was just about to re-lace his coat when Pauline walked in and, taking one look at him, said, 'Stop. You'd better give that to me.'

'What?'

'Your coat. There's a split in the seam of the right sleeve. If you give it to me now, I can have it repaired before Athenais sees it and asks how it happened.'

Frowning a little, he shed his coat and handed it over, saying, 'Thank you. But why should that be undesirable?'

'Isn't it?' Pauline sat down at a table with his coat across her lap and briskly threaded a needle. 'Or perhaps you don't mind lying to her?'

He chose not to answer this, saying instead, 'How much has Francis told you?'

'About this evening? Nothing. But your coat was all right when you went out and you were favouring your leg less than you are now – which, at a guess, would suggest something involving climbing or running. Or both.' She bent her head over the sewing. 'You'll notice I don't ask you to confirm it. I know you won't.'

Ashley perched on the corner of a nearby table and eyed her thoughtfully.

'You're very observant.'

'Acting teaches you that.' She glanced up briefly. 'Is Francis all right?'

'Yes.' He smiled and decided to regain the upper hand. 'Would you mind if he wasn't?'

* * *

'Where did you go tonight?' asked Athenais later, when she and Ashley were finally alone.

'I had a small task to perform.' Very slowly and in between tantalising kisses, he started pulling the pins from her hair, watching as each heavy lock tumbled down to her shoulders.

'At *night?*'

'Yes.' Turning her around, he slid his hands through the silky, copper mass and pushed it over one shoulder.

'Oh. Something secret?'

'Yes.' He nuzzled her neck and sought the laces of her gown.

Her breath caught. 'For King Charles?'

'Mm.' His tongue found a particularly vulnerable spot beneath her ear and he felt a tremor flow through her. 'Anything else?'

'What?'

'That you'd like to know.' He eased the gown from her shoulders and let his hands stray over the curve of her breasts.

Her head fell back against his shoulder.

'No.'

'Sure?' His mouth slid along her jaw. 'If I'm wasting my time here ...'

'You're not.'

'No?' The gown slithered to the floor and he turned her back to face him in order to kiss her more thoroughly. 'Only if you'd prefer to talk some more ...'

Athenais managed a small, husky laugh and wound her arms about his neck.

'I wouldn't. I really, really wouldn't.'

'Good. Because you remember that fantasy of mine? The one where I undress you very, very slowly and worship every inch of your skin ... starting, perhaps, with your toes?'

'Oh.' The darkness in his voice sent a ripple of heat along her veins. 'That one. Yes.'

'I was rather hoping that you might humour me.'

* * *

On the following morning, leaving Athenais curled up and unutterably inviting beneath the covers, Ashley hauled himself out of bed and got ready to visit the Louvre. The water in the pitcher was cold, his only remaining suit of clothes was a disgrace and his boots needed mending. And, as if all that wasn't depressing enough, a dusting of snow lay outside the window – reminding him that Christmas was less than a week away.

He made his way to the Louvre as briskly as possible in order to keep his circulation going in the cold. Then, before seeking an audience with the King, he called in on Sir Edward Hyde and said crisply, 'You'll recall me telling you that a copy of these thrice-blasted marriage lines had made its way into the possession of Thomas Scot. I'm fairly certain that it got to London through the agency of Sir Hugo Verney – after you didn't take the bait.'

'*Verney?* How on earth --?'

'The details aren't important. I'm telling you so that you're aware Verney isn't to be trusted. You may want to have a little chat with him –

or not, as the case may be. But I'd ask that you leave my name out of any dealings with him.'

'Why?'

'My name will lead to that of Lord Wroxton. And Verney lives with his lordship's sister – who is the source of my information. I'd prefer not to be responsible for any potential rift in their household.' Without giving Hyde the chance to query this, Ashley said, 'There's more. We assumed there would only be one copy of the document I've been chasing. But last night, I came across another one.'

'Oh my God. Where?'

'Alongside some correspondence His Majesty asked me to retrieve from Mistress Walter,' came the cool reply. 'I'll give Charles the letters, of course. But it occurred to me that the marriage-lines might serve more purpose in your hands rather than his. If, like the other, the document is a forgery, you may find some way of proving it.' He handed the paper to the Chancellor. 'An error, perhaps … anything that would enable you to discredit it.'

Hyde nodded gloomily. 'How many of them do you suppose there are?'

'Copies? I've no idea. Hopefully only two – but it's impossible to be sure.' Ashley picked up his hat. 'I'll tell His Majesty --'

'Wait. You're seeing the King now?'

'Yes. He'll be impatient to know if my mission prospered.'

'Ah. Indeed. Yes.'

Hyde dithered so obviously that Ashley could have sworn he saw the wheels turning. But finally, he said abruptly, 'His Majesty has brought it to my notice that you've received no payment for your many services to the Crown. As you're doubtless aware, he wished this omission to be rectified.'

Having a fair idea where this was going, Ashley shrugged.

'He said something to that effect, certainly.'

'So I believe. Sadly, as I'm sure you'll understand, it isn't possible to reimburse you … retrospectively.' He paused again and, when Ashley declined to help him out, added long-sufferingly, 'However, we can, in some small way, recognise and reward your *current* services. Consequently, His Majesty has asked me to give you this.'

Ashley was so completely taken aback that he nearly dropped the purse Hyde handed to him. He hadn't expected it. He'd forbidden himself even to *hope* for it. He was also, as yet, far from being able to appreciate the fact that the Chancellor would have cheerfully withheld the money were it not that Ashley was bound for the King's rooms – and the King would most assuredly ask. Shuffling his thoughts into some sort of order and putting the coming month's rent and his overwhelming desire to give Athenais a Yuletide gift at the head of the list, he pocketed his pride and said smoothly, 'Thank you, Sir Edward. I'm grateful.'

'Grateful enough not to enlist under Turenne while this possible assassination plot is still unresolved, I hope,' replied Hyde testily. 'I'll ensure you receive some regular income. It may not be much – but hopefully it will serve. And now you'd better take the King his letters.'

* * *

Charles received Ashley with a look of impatient optimism.

'Well, Ash? Did you find them?'

Wordlessly, Ashley handed over the beribboned bundle and watched the King's hand close convulsively over it.

'Thank God,' Charles murmured. And, looking up, 'And thank you, too. You're the only man I could ask to do something like this and have any hope of both total discretion and a successful outcome.'

'I appreciate your confidence, Sir.'

'Sit down and stop being so formal. Did you have any problems?'

'Aside from very nearly getting caught in Mistress Walter's bedchamber? No. But I could have done without being forced to make my exit through a window. It's been a number of years since I last found that necessary.'

'That's a sad admission.'

'No, Sir. Actually, it isn't.'

The dark eyes rested on him with perfect comprehension.

'Well, about time. I was beginning to wonder whether you'd taken a vow of some sort.'

Ashley blinked. 'I'm not sure I follow.'

'No? You've met a girl, haven't you?'

There was a brief silence and then Ashley said wryly, 'Not *a* girl, Sir. *The* girl.'

'Ah. That's … different. Is she pretty?'

'She's beautiful.'

Charles leaned back in his chair and folded his arms.

'So why don't you sound happier about it? I find it hard to believe she won't have you. Not being an ugly fellow like myself, I imagine the ladies fall at your feet in droves.'

'Not that I've noticed. As for the rest, my relationship with the lady is all I could wish – but the circumstances surrounding it are not.' Ashley suspected that the next question would be one he didn't want to answer because it was likely to result in Charles turning up at the theatre to see Athenais for himself. So he got to his feet and said, 'Forgive me, Sir. I'd rather not discuss the details. I'd much rather say how grateful I am to you for speaking to Sir Edward on my behalf.'

'Don't be. Over the years, you've more than earned whatever Hyde has been able to scrape together. These alone,' he tapped the bundle of letters, 'are worth any price. So don't thank me, Ash. The gratitude is all on my side.'

* * *

During the course of that evening's performance, the thin covering of snow turned to ice – thus giving Francis the perfect excuse to put a steadying arm about Pauline's waist. She glanced sharply at him, opened her mouth as if to object and then looked away, apparently thinking better of it.

He murmured, 'That's a promising start. Do you think, if I ask very nicely, I might be granted that kiss tonight?'

It had been a week and she'd started to wonder if he'd changed his mind, insisting to herself that it would be a good thing if he had. The trouble was that, as soon as he murmured those words in her ear, every nerve in her body reacted in wild anticipation that told her how very badly she wanted to say yes. He'd told her that, when he asked again, she would know that he meant it. She hoped that might be true … but still couldn't quite let go of her instinctive caution.

She said, 'I suppose so – if it will get it out of your system. Will it?'

His arm tightened about her and laughter warmed his voice as he said, 'I think that is very unlikely. But hold on to the possibility, if it helps.'

A few steps behind them and held close at Ashley's side, Athenais tilted her face up to him and whispered, 'Do you think there is anything going on between them?'

'I suspect that Francis might like there to be.' He grinned and dropped a kiss on her hair. 'I also suspect that Pauline is not making it easy – so the outcome should be interesting.'

The four of them had barely reached the steps of number sixteen when the door was thrown open and Archie said, 'Thank Gawd! 'E's been 'ere 'alf an hour and more, pacing up and down and driving me and Jem demented. Says your lordship knows 'im but won't say what 'e wants. 'E's dicked in the nob, if you ask me.'

Drawing Athenais in out of the cold, Ashley said, 'Who is?'

''Im.' A jerk of the head indicated Sir Hugo Verney erupting into the hall from the parlour.

'Francis! At last! I have to – it's urgent that we – I need to speak to you privately.'

Francis looked coolly at his sister's lover, becoming aware that the man's face was as white as a sheet, his coat unevenly laced and his hands visibly shaking. As for the expression in his eyes, it was the look of someone standing on a cliff-edge while the ground gradually crumbled away beneath him.

He said, 'If you're here to ask me to take responsibility for Celia because you no longer --'

'No! For Christ's sake, Francis – please! It's bad. Do you think I'd be here if it wasn't?'

'You'd better hear him out,' said Ashley. 'Go into the parlour. The ladies and I will wait in the kitchen until you're done.'

'No.' Francis was beginning to find the wild desperation in Verney's face a little alarming. 'In view of everything … I want you there.'

Ashley nodded, cast a reassuring smile at Athenais and Pauline, then followed Francis and Verney into the parlour.

'Well?' asked Francis. 'What's all this about?'

'It's Celia. I've been away at St Germain for a couple of d-days. I only came back this evening and Celia … she …' He stopped, fighting for breath and shaking now in every limb. 'She s-started screaming at me about all m-manner of things. I couldn't … she wouldn't l-let me answer.

She just kept on and on, shouting accusations. That I'd been unfaithful –
that I was going to l-leave her. Other things. I don't know. She was
shouting and raging and I c-couldn't make her listen.' He stopped,
wiping sweat from his brow with his sleeve. 'Francis ... you must know
how she can be.'

'Just come to the point.'

Sir Hugo shut his eyes and, for a moment, Ashley wondered if he was
going to throw up. Then he said raggedly, 'I was half-way up the stairs
when she launched into me. I tried to get her to go back to our rooms
with me but she wouldn't. She – she was totally out of control. She
kept screaming obscenities and pummelling me with her fists.' He
stopped, his chest heaving. 'I didn't touch her, Francis – I swear I didn't.
I don't know how it happened – whether she missed her footing or got
her heel tangled in her skirts. I don't know. But she – oh God, it all
happened so fast.' He swallowed as if the words brought bile to his
throat. 'She fell.'

Ashley moved to stand beside Francis and laid a hand on his shoulder.

Francis said, 'She fell? Down the stairs? Is she hurt?'

And felt the hand on his shoulder tighten its grip as Verney said, 'No.
Francis, I'm sorry. I'm so, so sorry. She's ... dead.'

TWELVE

Silence stretched out on invisible threads while Francis simply stared at Sir Hugo, immobilised by shock. Finally he said stupidly, 'Are you sure?'

'Yes. She ...' Verney stopped again, struggling with the words. 'She hit her head on – on the stone newel. She ... I think her neck's broken.'

'Francis. Sit down.' Ashley pressed him on to the sofa. He looked across at the other man, noting that there were tears in his eyes – though whether from grief or some less acceptable emotion, he couldn't tell. He said crisply, 'You and Celia fought on the staircase and then she fell. Were there any witnesses?'

He saw fear cross Verney's face in the second it took him to shake his head.

'No. That is, I don't think so.'

'So Celia was shouting but no one came out to see what was happening?'

'N-no. N-not until ... until she fell. Then people came running.'

'Who?'

Hugo swallowed again. 'What?'

'*Who* came running?'

'Monsieur and Madame Jourdan from d-downstairs and – and their maid, I think.'

'But they weren't there when Celia fell?'

'No. I don't know. What are you saying?'

'I think,' said Ashley grimly, 'that you know exactly what I'm saying.'

Francis stood up again. 'Where is she?'

'In our rooms. We l-laid her on her bed.'

'She's alone? You left her *alone*?' Even as he said it, Francis wondered why that should matter whilst somehow knowing that it did.

'No. The maid said she'd stay until I got back. I didn't know what to do for the best. It – it seemed to me that you should know.' He looked back at Ashley, his hands hopelessly unsteady. 'I don't know how she came to fall – but it was an accident. Why are you suggesting that it – that it wasn't?'

'I'm not. I'm merely pointing out that, in the absence of any witnesses, you can't prove that it *was*.'

'But I don't need ... surely no one could think that I'd ... that I would hurt her?'

'Did you?' It was Francis who asked, his face blank of all expression but his voice ragged as a saw-blade. '*Did* she fall? Or did you push her ... or trip her ... or just move out of the way so that --'

'She fell, I tell you! I swear to God, Francis – it wasn't my fault. She was in a terrible temper and she fell. Why would I lie about it?'

'To avoid being tried for murder is a fairly convincing reason,' remarked Ashley. And then, 'Francis ... we'll come back to this later. Right now, there are other things to consider. I imagine you'll want to see Celia and perhaps send a message to your mother.'

'I'll send a message – for all the good it will do,' said Francis. 'But yes. I need to see Celia. I seem to be having trouble believing that this is real.' He stopped as if trying to think. 'I should go now. Will you tell Pauline for me?'

'Of course. And then I'm coming with you.'

For the first time, some emotion showed in the dark blue eyes.

'Thank you. I'd appreciate it.'

'Now you're being insulting,' said Ashley, calmly. 'Give me five minutes and we'll be off.'

* * *

For two long hours while the men were out, Pauline and Athenais sat in the parlour awaiting their return and indulging in desultory conversation.

'What do you think really happened?' asked Athenais.

'You mean – did she fall or did Verney push her?'

'Yes.'

Pauline shrugged. 'It could be either one. We may never know for certain – though I'll wager the Colonel is doing his damnedest to find out.'

They fell silent for a time and then Athenais said, 'This is going to be very hard for Francis. I'm glad Ashley went with him.'

'Did you think he wouldn't?'

'Not for a moment.'

'No more did I.'

Finally, at a little after one in the morning, Francis and Ashley came home.

Before the front door had closed behind them, Pauline was on her feet and out into the hall, followed more slowly by Athenais.

Ashley's expression was as grim as it had been when he'd come to tell them.

Francis looked positively drained.

Without stopping to think, Pauline crossed the tiled floor to take his cold hands in hers and said, 'Come inside. We've kept the fire going and there is brandy waiting. There's no need to talk if you'd rather not – but you should come and get warm.'

He stared down at her hands surrounding his.

'Thank you.'

She shook her head and drew him into the parlour and the seat nearest the fire. Behind them, Athenais lingered with Ashley to say, 'How bad was it?'

'It wasn't good.' He hesitated and then added, 'By the time we got there, the doctor had arrived. She has a broken neck and some serious damage to her skull. No one could have survived that.'

'And Francis?'

'Is managing well enough for the moment. In one sense, it's fortunate that they weren't close. In another, perhaps not. We'll see.' He smiled at her. 'I thought I heard mention of brandy ...?'

'Of course. Come inside. You're freezing.'

'I daresay you won't mind warming me. But first, the brandy would be very welcome.'

Francis looked up as they entered the room and said, 'I know you said it could wait until tomorrow – but I can't let it rest. I need to know what you learned from the people you questioned and what conclusions you've drawn from it. Celia may not have been a very nice person or even an especially good one ... but if there's a likelihood that Verney murdered her, I can't ignore it.'

'I wouldn't expect you to.' Ashley took the glass Athenais offered him and leaned against the mantelpiece. 'I spoke to everyone in the building that I could find. A number of them heard the quarrel. The couple downstairs even opened their door so they could listen properly without being seen. But no one actually went out into the hall until they heard Celia scream as she fell – which means that no one saw exactly what caused the fall.'

'So he could have pushed her?'

'He *could* have … but, to be honest, I can't see why he would.'

'To be rid of her so that he could marry his rich widow?' suggested Francis bitterly.

'Perhaps. But he didn't need to kill Celia in order to be rid of her,' replied Ashley. 'All he had to do was to walk out of the door.'

'You're saying you think he's innocent?'

'I'm saying that it's the most logical explanation. People don't generally commit murder without a very good reason and accidents happen. On the other hand, it's difficult to entirely acquit him of not managing to grab her when he realised she was falling – or, at least, trying to. It's an instinctive reaction, wouldn't you say?'

'For you, I daresay.'

'For anyone, Francis. Earlier this evening you saw Pauline about to slip on the ice and instantly reached out to steady her. You didn't think about it – you just did it. Perhaps Verney had no warning or was just too slow. I don't know and neither do you. But I suspect that the worst we can lay at his door is that it's possible he didn't try. And that, if you want my opinion, doesn't say anything good about him.'

Francis drained his glass and watched Pauline fill it again. He said, 'I'm not sure getting drunk is the answer.'

'It isn't,' she said calmly. 'But you've a way to go yet.'

He shut his eyes and thought for a moment. 'Eden. He'll need to be told.'

Ashley nodded. 'We'll send Nick back. I'll speak to him in the morning. Anything else?'

'No.' The blue eyes opened again, frowning a little. 'You saw her. Do you think it was quick?'

'Instantaneous.'

'Well, that's something, I suppose.' He sat up and managed a wry smile. 'It's odd. I can't honestly say I've loved her for a very long time … and yet the strangest things seem to matter. I wonder why that is?'

'Family,' said Ashley, as if it explained everything. 'Get some sleep if you can. There's nothing more to be done tonight and it will all still be there in the morning.'

'Yes. I'll go to bed in a little while. And thank you again. A brother, if I had one, could not have done more for me tonight.'

'Some wouldn't have done as much,' came the barely audible reply, as Ashley shepherded Athenais from the room. 'Goodnight.'

Francis was left looking at Pauline.

'He has a brother? I had no idea.'

'He mentioned him once,' she said, deliberately vague. 'I got the impression there wasn't much love lost between them.' And then, 'If you'd rather be alone, I'll go. Or ... I could stay, if you wish. We don't need to talk.'

'Stay, please.'

Nodding, she sat down on the arm of his chair and said nothing when he leaned his head against her arm. After a while, he said, 'I'm finding that this is one of those times when things you've said come back to haunt you. I've lost count of the times I've told Ashley that I could murder her or that I'd like to strangle her ... or some other similar thing.'

'You never meant it.'

'I don't know whether I did or not. She was so downright infuriating that, more often than not, I wanted to shake her until her teeth rattled.'

'But you didn't.'

'No. I didn't. But just now I'm wishing I'd been – if not kinder, then at least more tolerant.' He sipped the brandy and handed it to her. 'Join me, will you? Help me to remember the nice little girl she once was.'

Pauline drank and passed the glass back to him.

'Was she?'

'Yes. She was pretty, if a little plump. And she was cheerful and uncomplicated and free of artifice. That was before Eden and I went to Angers. By the time we came back, she wasn't plump any more. She'd learned to flirt and flutter her eyelashes and care about nothing but her clothes, her looks and how to make herself the centre of attention.' He paused. 'Eden didn't see that, of course. In truth, I've never been very sure *what* he saw. But he fell head over ears in love with her and would have given her anything she wanted – except the keeping of his

424

conscience. He chose the Parliament. And she wouldn't forgive him.' Another pause. 'And when she walked out on him ... when, in all these months, I never once knew her give her children even a passing thought ... I couldn't forgive *her*.'

'And now you feel you should have done?'

'No. That's just the trouble. She's dead ... but I don't feel differently about it.' Francis moved to set the glass down on the hearth and turned to face her. 'I'm sorry. None of this is what I envisioned saying to you tonight. But I thank you for having the patience to listen.'

And that was when Pauline's heart melted and her defences crumbled and she thought, *How was I ever arrogant enough to think I could resist you? If I'm what you want ... even if only for a night or the sake of a little comfort ... I'll count myself fortunate.*

Drawing his head back against her shoulder and choosing her words more carefully than usual, she said, 'You don't need to thank me. Or offer me any persuasions. I'm tired of fighting both myself and you. The kiss is yours if you want it. And, in due course, anything else.'

She felt his breath catch and it was a long time before he spoke. Then he pulled her down on to his lap, folded her close in a passive embrace and said, 'Promise me this is not because of what happened tonight.'

'It's not.'

'You're sure? Because that would really hurt.'

'I'm sure.' She met his eyes and managed a tiny laugh. 'Why would you think a woman might not want you just for yourself? You're not hard to swallow, you know.'

'You shouldn't flatter a fellow so.' Then, the hint of a smile fading into a look of acute intensity, 'You're not *any* woman, Pauline. And I'm not stupid enough to take anything about you for granted. I'd ask you to give me the same courtesy.'

'Do I not?'

'No. Not yet. But I'm hoping to change that – though not tonight. Tonight, I'll claim my long-awaited kiss. And then, if you'll permit it, I'd like to sleep with my arms round you. Just that and nothing more.' He stopped, his mouth curling wryly. 'Ah. And there it is. That moment of doubt. That second when you can't help thinking I don't *really* want you – that you're somehow unworthy.'

She sighed. 'I know what I am, Francis.'

'No. I don't think you do. And I'm not sure you know what *I* am either. So, until you do … until you stop doubting me … I'll take that one kiss and nothing more.' And tilting her chin, he lowered his mouth to hers.

Later, she would realise that she should have known what to expect. At that moment, however, the world dissolved into unimagined sweetness as, instead of taking, he offered her a gift. A slow, tender exploration that demanded nothing but promised everything. He slid his fingers into her hair, cradling her skull and very, very slowly let the kiss deepen until it spoke of untold delights. And, already melting, Pauline let him know that what he wanted – *whatever* he wanted – he could have.

* * *

Francis awoke the following morning as he'd wanted to do, with his arms around Pauline Fleury. Neither of them was naked. She was swathed in a voluminous night-rail; he was still wearing his breeches. And, when he opened his eyes, it was to find her looking at him.

Her smile reflected both uncertainty and a question.

'Good morning.'

'And to you.' He touched her scarred cheek with one light finger. 'You're awake early. Did I snore?'

The smile widened and lost its shadows.

'No. Though, since I slept through part of the night, I suppose you may have.'

'It would have been a kindness to have stopped after that first word,' observed Francis reproachfully. 'But I suppose I should know better than to expect it of you.'

'I would certainly think so.' She paused. 'If you want to escape the inevitable questions, you should go.'

'I don't care about questions. They don't have to be answered.' He removed his arm from around her and sat up. 'But you're right. I should go. I need to wash and shave and change my clothes. I need to write a letter for Nick to take to Eden. And then I need to face Verney again while a funeral is arranged.' He drew a bracing breath and swung his feet to the floor. 'If I can focus on having you to come back to, I may manage the last one with at least a semblance of civility.'

Pauline propped herself on one elbow, her hair tumbling about her shoulders.

'Do you want the truth?'

'I don't know. Do I?'

'Yes. There are times when you're too well-mannered for your own good.'

'This being one of them?'

'Yes. If trying to choke the truth out of this man Verney will make you feel any better, you should damned well do it.'

* * *

A little later, having repaired his appearance, Francis faced Ashley and Nicholas across the kitchen table. He said, 'I'm sorry to ask this, Nick – but Eden needs to be told before he does anything about a divorce and you're the only person I can ask. Leaving France shouldn't be too difficult, I imagine. Will Eden's travel passes be enough to get you back into England?'

'I hope so. At any rate, I'll soon find out.' Nicholas glanced at Ashley. 'What do I tell him about the other matter?'

'That I've alerted Hyde and have plans for dealing with it as soon as we have some indication of a date. You may also express my heartfelt appreciation both for the information he's provided and for the risk he's taken in doing it – and assure him that, aside from we three, no one is aware of his involvement. Nor will they be.'

Nicholas nodded.

'I'll tell him. I already said that you were to be trusted – but inevitably he had his doubts.'

'For which he is to be commended rather than blamed.'

'Yes.' He turned back to Francis. 'How is he likely to take the news of his wife's death?'

'I no longer know him well enough to guess,' came the reply. 'All I can say is that he loved her and she broke his heart, then trampled on it. She left not only him but also their son ... and a daughter who I suspect Eden doesn't believe is his. I don't know how – even after eight years –

any man deals with all of that. As for her death … he might be relieved. But, with Eden, I wouldn't care to count on it.'

ENTR'ACTE
London – December 1652

A large young man – brown-haired, grey-eyed and dressed in the Italian fashion – strolled along Cheapside, taking in the sights. He'd left his horse at a tavern some streets away so that he could walk the last half-mile and thus have time to absorb what was familiar and what was not. A lot of things weren't. Most noticeably, although most of the buildings were the same, the businesses inhabiting them were different. Time was when Goldsmiths' Row had been just that; the preserve of goldsmith's renting their premises from the worshipful Company. Now, the young man estimated that every other door led to a haberdasher or a bookseller or an apothecary. His expression darkened slightly. After years of war, change was to be expected and he *had* expected it. He just hadn't expected this – this *diminution*.

His footsteps slowed a little more as he came within sight of his destination. A tall, irregular building on the corner of Friday Street. A place where he'd spent what were probably four of the most formative years of his life but which he hadn't seen in a very long time. It looked the same and yet not. As was only to be expected, the sign that had once hung above the door had gone – yet, oddly, the bracket from which it had been suspended was still there. He remembered that sign in perfect detail. An ornate, convoluted knot ... exquisitely suited to its clever, convoluted owner. His own sign, when he was ready to place it there, was quite different. He'd designed it over a year ago and it had made his brother-in-law laugh.

The windows of the house gleamed and smoke issued from the chimney. He hoped that meant that someone was at home. He'd been travelling a long time and would be glad to unpack his belongings permanently. He was also missing his work.

In former days, the street door which had led to the shop would have been unlocked during business hours. Now, of course, it wasn't. He knocked and waited. Then, in due course and rather more loudly, he knocked again.

The lock rattled and the door swung open. He suddenly realised, he hadn't given any thought to who might be on the other side. Certainly he hadn't expected it to be a woman. A rather nice-looking woman, as well. Pale skin, dark hair and even darker eyes … and, beneath that simple blue gown, interestingly curved in all the right places. He smiled.

Deborah absorbed first the expensive, well-cut clothes and then the easy, open smile with its hint of a dimple in one slightly sun-tanned cheek.

Raising her brows and dropping a small curtsy, she said, 'Can I help you, sir?'

'I certainly hope so. I'm looking for Eden Maxwell and assumed I'd find him here.'

'And you are?'

The smile widened into a boyish grin.

'I'm his brother.' He swept off his hat and bowed. 'Tobias Maxwell – at your service. I assumed Eden was expecting me.'

Despite her surprise, she found herself smiling back as she held the door wide.

'He is. Your sister wrote when you left Genoa – so he's been expecting you any time this last month.'

'Yes. Well, I stopped off in a few places along the way.' Tobias paused, looking around at what had once been the shop. 'Eden's not here?'

'Not at this time of day. But come up to the parlour and get warm. I'll fetch some wine and …' She paused, eyeing his tall, broad-shouldered frame, 'I imagine you're hungry?'

'Always,' he laughed. And, as he followed her upstairs, 'Has Eden warned you about my appetite, Mistress … I'm sorry. I don't know how to address you.'

'My name is Deborah Hart and I'm your brother's housekeeper,' came the calm reply. 'Please take a seat by the fire. I'll be back in just a moment.'

The door closed behind her and Tobias was alone with his memories in a room which was the same and yet somehow different. Some of the furniture still remained from former days; the oak settle by the hearth, the large polished table and the heavy, carved desk where Luciano had worked on his designs. But the bright cushions, the array of serviceable pewter and the bowls of scented herbs were new; evidence, he supposed, of a feminine influence. He wondered idly if the luscious Mistress Hart was rather more than his brother's housekeeper and then dismissed the thought. It was no business of his, after all ... and if Eden was bedding her, good luck to him.

Deborah returned with a laden tray and set bread, cold meats and half a beef and oyster pie on the table along with a jug of wine.

'That should keep you going until supper ... but, if you need anything else, just call me.'

Engaged in pulling back a chair, Tobias paused and said, 'Do you have to go? If you're not too busy, I'd appreciate your company.'

She eyed him in a way he found mildly disconcerting though he wasn't sure why.

'You have questions.'

'Some, yes.' He helped himself to a chunk of bread, a substantial wedge of pie and, with undisguised enthusiasm, to a spoonful of Deborah's homemade pickle. 'Eden's not the most informative correspondent. Six lines is usually about it – less, if he can get away with it.'

'His work keeps him busy.'

'I daresay. But all he's told Kate and me is that he'll be employed in London for the foreseeable future. And though we know there's been no fighting since last year, we've no idea what he's been up to since then. Where is he now, for example?'

'He has an office in Whitehall.'

Tobias swallowed a mouthful of pie dipped in pickle and said, 'God – that's good. I was famished.'

Deborah laughed.

'Clearly you have a large amount of strength to keep up.'

'Dead spit of my father when he was my age, apparently.' He cut up some ham and decorated it with more pickle. 'So – an office in Whitehall? That sounds impressive. And what does he do there?'

'I suggest you ask him. He's usually home by seven.'

The light grey eyes flicked briefly to her face and then returned to his plate.

'Not for you to say?'

'No.'

'Oh. I'll wait, then.' He polished off the ham and made further inroads to the pie. 'Has he told you why I'm here?'

'Yes. You're a goldsmith and you'll be opening a shop.'

'Nearly right.' Again that disarming grin. 'I'm a *master*-goldsmith and I'll be setting up, not only a shop, but also a workshop. Speaking of which, I'm expecting two deliveries of equipment. One should turn up in the next couple of days. The other probably won't arrive before the turn of the year.'

'And these are to go where?'

'Downstairs.' Tobias stood up. 'Actually, if you don't mind, I'd like to take a look.'

'By all means,' she said. 'Unless you'd rather go up and unpack your things?'

'Later. This is a priority. And, if you don't mind, I'd really quite like to go alone.'

* * *

While Tobias was standing in the middle of Luciano del Santi's workshop and remembering the first time he'd ever seen it as a curious thirteen-year-old, his brother was sitting in an extremely long-winded Council Meeting and wishing himself elsewhere. There had been numerous such meetings in recent weeks but, in Eden's view, this was the most tediously depressing one yet.

It began, as they all had, with more complaints and chest-beating over the dismal progress of the Dutch war. Eden estimated that at least half of those present had still not got over the disaster at Dungeness on November 30th, when Admiral Tromp had thrashed Admiral Blake and then raided the English coast for cattle. The defeat was supposedly due to the failure of twenty English ships to engage – thus leaving Blake with only twenty-five vessels against Tromp's eighty-five. No one, thought Eden irritably, seemed to notice that even if Blake had been fighting with his full complement, he'd still have been heavily out-gunned so the result was unlikely to have been any different.

He listened to the usual catalogue of how many ships had been captured by the Dutch or seriously disabled and how many men, wounded or lost. Having already seen Blake's reports on all these matters and knowing everyone else had also done so, Eden slumped in his chair and let his chin sink on to his chest while the pointless words flowed on.

Thanks to the exorbitant cost of the war, money was also a major issue. Despite having confiscated the lands of six hundred Royalists, Parliament had yet to find purchasers for most of them and had therefore resorted to increasing the monthly assessment from £90,000 to £120,000. On the previous day, Eden had attended an extremely acrimonious meeting of the Council of Officers where the entire discussion had revolved around the fact that the Army's share of the assessment was being reduced by £10,000 a month to fund the Navy – thus meaning that yet more soldiers would have to be disbanded. It was, as one and all agreed, a blatant case of robbing Peter to pay Paul.

Today's meeting, of course, saw all that quite differently and Eden saw no point in stirring the pot and thus encouraging everybody to talk even more than they were already about something that wasn't going to change. He listened to general satisfaction that France had at long last formally recognised the Commonwealth and then to the not-quite-so-cheerful news that, not content with having merely cancelled Christmas, Parliament was about to issue a firm declaration that the festival was not to be observed in any form whatsoever.

Eden's backside was growing numb, causing his attention to wander. He wondered if anybody was going to mention the rumours that Cromwell was considering making himself King and, if they did, what the approval-rating was likely to be. His own view was that it was the worst idea since the removal of the late King's head ... but that it might account for Thurloe participating in a plot to assassinate the late King's eldest sons.

When he was at last released from Purgatory and able to make his way back to Cheapside he allowed himself to wonder how things were progressing in Paris. He'd told Nick on no account to write to him and not to allow Francis do to so either and hadn't therefore expected to receive any news ... so all he could do was to hope that the unknown Colonel Peverell was as efficient as Nick said he was.

* * *

He walked into the house to the enticing aroma of baking and wondered vaguely why Deborah was finding it necessary to make pastry two days running. Then he entered the parlour and saw the reason grinning at him from his favourite chair near the fire.

'Toby!' he said, striding across the room to grasp his brother's hand. 'I was beginning to think you'd got lost somewhere in the wilds of Europe.'

Accepting the hand and simultaneously managing to give Eden a hefty buffet on the shoulder, Tobias said, 'I had a few side-trips to make. But I've arrived in time for Yule – which was always the plan. You're looking well.'

'As are you. Please tell me you've stopped growing.'

'Just about. An inch over six feet, if you really want to know.'

At four inches less than that and having always wanted to be taller, Eden merely sighed and, reaching for the ale jug, said, 'And still eating for ten, I gather.'

'I prefer to say that I have a healthy appetite.' Tobias grinned and, with a lift of one brow added, 'I like your Mistress Hart, by the way.'

'Of course you do. She fed you my pie, didn't she?'

'It was a very good pie. And I assumed that, not having clapped eyes on me in four years, you wouldn't be niggardly about it.'

The last time they'd met had been in September, '48 on the occasion of their sister's wedding. Recalling this and handing his brother a cup of ale, Eden said neutrally, 'Was one of your stops at Thorne Ash?'

'Yes.'

'Is everyone well?'

'Yes.' His eyes were no longer laughing. 'Something you'd know yourself if you paid more than a two-day duty visit once a year.'

Eden's expression grew shuttered.

'I go when I can.'

You mean you go as little *as you can*, thought Tobias but saw the wisdom of changing the subject. 'So what are you doing now there isn't a war to fight?'

'I work with a fellow named Scot in the Secretary of State's office.'

'That sounds very grand. Doing what, exactly?'

'Cryptography.' And when Tobias simply stared at him, 'I make and break codes.'

'Thank you. I know what cryptography is. I just didn't know *you* could do it.'

'I like numbers and puzzles and patterns,' shrugged Eden. 'I got involved in it more or less by accident when someone discovered I had a certain aptitude.'

Tobias was still absorbing the ramifications. He said slowly, 'So being employed by the intelligence service means that your work is … confidential?'

'Most of it, yes.'

'Oh. Well that explains why you've never written anything about it to Kate … and why neither Mother nor Tabitha could tell me very much. *God.*' A sudden grin. 'My brother, the spy.'

'Now you're exaggerating.'

'Only a bit. And it must be quite exciting.'

'It has its moments – though not as often as you might think.' Eden re-filled their cups and pointedly changed the subject. 'How is Kate?'

'Much the same as ever and still ecstatically happy. Young Alessandro is turning into a rare handful and little Mariella is a delight. Kate hasn't said but I suspect there might be another one due in the summer.'

'And Luciano?'

'Busy as ever and still razor-sharp – but the most ludicrously doting husband and father you could ever wish to meet.' Tobias paused and then said, 'My apprenticeship finished around the time of Tabitha's wedding but I stayed on until Sir was prepared to admit that there was nothing more he could teach me. Now he has and I'm ready to set up my sign. Is that going to be all right with you?'

'It's better than all right, you ass! I'm surprised you needed to ask,' replied Eden. 'The only reason Luciano held on to these premises was for you.'

'I know. But you live here too and --'

'And I'll be glad of the company and eager to see you succeed – as you will.'

'Thank you.' Pleasure at his brother's vote of confidence brought a hint of colour to Tobias's cheek. He said, 'Sir left a basic stock of equipment at Thorne Ash and I've arranged for it to be delivered here two days from now. I've also ordered a further consignment from suppliers in Rotterdam which will take a little longer. I'll be setting up the workshop where it always was.'

'Ah. You know we had a fire down there? Obviously, I've had it cleared up but --'

'I've seen it. The workbench and the wall-racking will need replacing but, aside from that, it's fine.' Tobias held out his cup for more ale. 'There's a story behind that fire, isn't there?'

'There is. You met Gabriel Brandon at Tabitha's wedding, didn't you?'

'Your commanding officer? Yes.'

'Well, somebody tried to roast him alive. But perhaps I'd better start at the beginning?'

* * *

Later that night, his arms full of a sleepy and thoroughly sated Deborah, Eden said, 'What do you think of my little brother?'

'Little? He's hardly that.'

'You don't need to remind me.'

She laughed and kissed his shoulder.

'He's easy and open and charming. The young girls will be falling over themselves.' She hesitated and then said, 'Are you going to tell him I'm your mistress?'

'Probably – assuming he doesn't figure it out for himself.'

'Will he mind?'

'Why should he? And I don't care whether he does or not.' He cuddled her closer. 'Let him find his own pie-maker.'

* * *

On the following day, Eden arrived home earlier than usual and found Deborah in the parlour refreshing her bowls of scented herbs. She said, 'Why didn't you tell me that your brother is quite mad?'

'I didn't know he was. Why? What's he doing?'

'He's in the cellar beneath the cellar. A place I didn't know existed before today. And he's digging up the floor.'

'He's *what?*'

'Digging. He's been at it most of the afternoon.'

Eden shook his head.

'I didn't know there was a lower cellar, either. I'd better take a look.'

Taking a candle, Eden walked downstairs and looked around. He spotted the open trapdoor, wondered why he'd never noticed it before and then realised that it had previously lain beneath the work-bench. Peering into the dimly-lit hole, he called, 'Toby? What the hell are you doing down there?'

'Following Sir's orders,' came the echoing reply. 'And it's taken longer than expected. But I think I have it all now.'

'Have all of what?'

Eden set his feet to the narrow-runged ladder and descended with some difficulty on account of the candle.

'Luciano's Hoard.'

Reaching the bottom, Eden walked over the parts of the beaten-earth floor that Tobias didn't appear to have attacked with a spade.

'I have no idea what you're talking about.'

'No. You wouldn't have.' Tobias was sitting on the ground, covered in dirt and surrounded by numerous irregular-shaped packages. 'Back in '45, Sir had to leave a goodly amount of stock behind when he left London to catch up with Cyrus Winter – so he buried it down here.'

'And it's still there?'

'Yes.' Tobias grinned up at his brother and gestured to the one bundle he'd unwrapped.

Eden squatted beside him and looked.

Laid out on Tobias's handkerchief were some dozen exquisite pieces. A tiny parrot carved out of emerald; an amethyst intaglio depicting an eagle with a snake in its beak; and a small enamelled scent-bottle, overlaid with diamonds and rubies.

Eden stared and stared again. Then he said, 'This has been down here all the time?'

'Yes.'

'And Luciano asked you to dig it up? Why?'

'A couple of reasons. First, he's suggested that I remove all the loose stones for my own use. And second, at the time he originally buried it, he was in a hurry so I'm to re-pack it properly in waxed paper and hessian.'

'And then?'

'He left that to my discretion. But it's been safe enough down here for the last seven years, hasn't it?'

'You're going to put it *back?*' asked Eden incredulously. 'Why, for God's sake?'

'Because he doesn't need it and neither do I. Also, because he says we don't know what the future may bring and sufficient money can usually overcome any eventuality.'

'Such as what?'

'A shift in government. Father sat in the Parliament and you've fought for it. If the King should ever be restored, what do you think will happen to Thorne Ash? To Mother and Tabitha ... to your children?' Tobias stood up and started passing packages to Eden. 'Luciano's worth a bloody fortune these days ... and he wants to ensure that the family has something to fall back on, should the need arise. So you won't mind giving me a hand, will you?'

* * *

Working non-stop, it took Tobias two full days to unpack, sort and then re-package what he persisted in calling Luciano's Hoard. Seeing it spread out in all its glory on the floor of an empty bedchamber, Eden was stunned by both the sheer quantity but also the quality of what Luciano del Santi had left buried. And when Tobias insisted he choose something to give to Deborah, he selected an enamelled gold chain, set with seed pearls and rubies and looked forward to seeing it against her naked skin.

They replaced the caskets in the lower cellar on the morning of Christmas Eve and then, having washed off the signs of their endeavours, they repaired to the parlour for a well-earned glass of wine and a platter of freshly-made fruit pies. They were just embarking on the second glass when they heard the pealing of the doorbell, followed by Deborah's voice raised in welcome.

Eden set his glass to one side and stood up, unsure who his visitor might be. Then the door opened and he said blankly, *'Nick?* How in God's name did you get here?'

'With difficulty,' replied Nicholas succinctly. 'The crossing was a nightmare. I thought I'd be spending Yule at the bottom of the channel.'

He shook Eden's hand, gave Tobias a polite nod and added, 'If there's any wine left, I'd be glad of it. I'm half-soaked and freezing.'

'Take your coat off and sit by the fire,' said Eden, pouring wine. 'This is my brother, Tobias. Toby – meet Sir Nicholas Austin. He's been on a mission for me.' He handed Nicholas the glass and added, 'Nothing untoward, I hope?'

'No.'

'Good. Then you can fill me in later, when you've thawed out.'

Nicholas subsided into a chair and took a large swallow of wine. Then he said, 'I'm here because Francis asked me to come. Something's happened. It's nothing to do with the – the business that took me to France. It's something else.' He paused briefly. 'Eden, I'm sorry. I don't know how to say this except straight out.'

'So say it.'

'It's Francis's sister … your wife. She's dead.'

The words were greeted with stunned silence. Finally, Tobias said, '*Celia?*'

Nicholas nodded, keeping his eyes on Eden as he waited for him to speak. And eventually, Eden said, 'When? And how?'

'It was a week ago. She fell down the stairs and broke her neck.'

'Hallelujah,' muttered Tobias. 'Pity she didn't do it years ago.'

'Don't, Toby.' Eden drew a long, steadying breath. 'I'm not going to pretend I'm sorry she's dead. But neither am I about to burst into wild celebration.' He turned back to Nicholas. 'How's Francis?'

'Shocked, of course. But Ash is with him. And Pauline. So he'll be all right.'

'Pauline?'

Nicholas nodded and, for the first time, smiled a little.

'Yes. If you want my opinion, I think he's in love with her.'

ACT FIVE

DÉNOUEMENT
Paris, December 1652 to March 1653

'Judge not the play before the play is done; her plot hath many changes.
Every day speaks a new scene; the last act crowns the play.'
Francis Quarles

ONE

They buried Celia two days before Christmas in the churchyard of St Germain-des-Près. It was bitterly cold and, aside from Francis, Ashley and Sir Hugo Verney, only four other people deigned to attend. None of them was Celia's mother.

Back in the Rue des Rosiers, Francis put his arms around Pauline, leaned his cheek against her hair and said, 'Thank God that's over.'

She hugged him back, albeit hesitantly. 'Was it bad?'

'It could have been worse, I suppose. Though between Verney shedding tears I am quite sure meant nothing and the fact that my bitch of a mother couldn't be bothered to put in an appearance, it's hard to know how.' He released her and stepped away. 'Thank you for allowing me that crumb of comfort. I needed it.'

Pauline tried to think which of the many things she might say would be most helpful. In the end, she answered directly as she always did.

'You don't need to thank me. I thought I'd made that plain.'

'You did. You offered me something I want very much indeed ... but you offered it when I was at a particularly low ebb and I'd like us both to be sure it wasn't out of kindness. This,' he said, touching her cheek with light, almost insubstantial fingers, 'is new to me. It feels important. So I'm not about to risk it by rushing.'

A lump formed in her throat and she swallowed it.

'You speak as if you've never wanted a woman before.'

'I've wanted lots of them. And,' he smiled suddenly, 'I've had quite a few. That isn't what this is about ... and waiting seems the best way to convince you of it. But once you've accepted and got used to the idea ... well, then I'll be more than willing to take you to bed.'

'But not before?'

'No. Sadly, not before.'

She made a helpless gesture with her hands.

'I don't know what to say to you. You baffle me.'

'I know. Truth to tell, Duchess, I baffle myself as well.'

* * *

Monsieur Laroque having announced that the theatre would close for three days from Christmas Eve, Pauline and Suzon spent the day baking while Athenais decorated the house with the armfuls of greenery brought in by Ashley and Francis. Then, in the evening, everyone sat around the kitchen table enjoying a simple meal washed down with a good deal of cheap wine.

It was late when Ashley and Athenais were finally alone in her room. As it always did, passion flared at the first touch. Sometimes urgent and demanding; sometimes, like tonight, slow and languorous and incredibly sweet. But afterwards, when she was curled up against him with her fingers straying lazily over his chest, Ashley felt the familiar anxiety start to gnaw at the back of his mind.

Mostly, he managed to avoid thinking of the future by concentrating on the exquisite pleasure of the present. But sometimes, on nights like this, after they had made love he found himself unable to entirely shut out grim reality. A reality which said that this couldn't last; that the time would come when he'd have held her for the last time ... kissed her for the last time ... loved her for the last time. And when that time *did* come, he wasn't sure how he would deal with it, since the mere thought made him feel as if his guts had been wrenched out.

In the meantime, however, he'd bought a gift for her. It lay in a little velvet pouch in the pocket of his coat, waiting for the morning. It wasn't much, really. It was so much less than he'd have *liked* to give her, yet still more than he could sensibly afford. He hoped she liked it; he thought she would ... but was afraid she might not. The truth was that she'd never asked him for anything yet still invariably looked at him as if he'd torn the stars from the sky for her. And he wished he could.

He hadn't expected to sleep but the next thing he knew, dingy light was creeping through the window and Athenais was skimming her instep up and down his calf.

As soon as he opened his eyes, she said, 'Happy Christmas. It's snowing again.'

She was as flushed and excited as a child so he couldn't resist teasing her.

'Then perhaps we should stay in the warm for a little while longer.'

'No, no. We have this whole day. I want to walk in the snow and listen to the church bells and – and I want you to kiss me until I'm dizzy.'

'I can do that right here,' he said. And did so.

By the time he released her mouth, she was gasping. Ashley slid his hands tantalisingly over her and murmured, 'Do you still want bells and snow?'

'No. I want you. Just you.'

'By an odd coincidence, that's exactly what I had in mind.'

Later, when he had donned his own clothes and finished lacing Athenais into the leaf-green gown, he pulled the little pouch from his pocket and said, 'Close your eyes and stand still.'

She did it but said laughingly, 'I'm dressed. You can't be wicked now.'

He moved behind her and, setting his mouth close to her ear, breathed, 'Oh I think you'll find that I can.'

Then, withdrawing the contents of the pouch, he fastened his gift around her neck.

Her breath stopped, her eyes flew open and her fingers flew to the cool thing touching her skin.

'What--? *Oh!* Ashley? You didn't – you shouldn't – oh, let me see!'

He smiled and held the mirror out to her.

Athenais looked and looked again and was suddenly very still. A dainty silver chain, alternately studded with moonstones and amethysts, lay around the base of her throat. Slowly, almost hesitantly, she traced it with one fingertip. Her colour rose and the smoky eyes grew suspiciously bright. She said huskily, 'It's beautiful. But you shouldn't ... I know there's no money. You shouldn't have spent what little you have on this.'

The expression of dazzled awe on her face as she continued to stare into the mirror was more than sufficient reward, Ashley thought. He said gently, 'If you like it, nothing else matters in the least.'

She turned to him then and cast the mirror aside to throw her arms about his neck.

'I love it. Of course, I love it. How could I not? I never expected ... I've never had any jewellery ever before. But you need a new coat and boots. You need them so *badly* ... and yet you've done this. You break my heart ... and I've nothing to give you.'

'You've already given me something beyond price, Athenais. The best gift in the world.' He held her close until he thought the tears had stopped. 'Now let's go down and join the others. But you'll have to dry your eyes or Pauline will hit me with a skillet.'

* * *

With what, to Ashley at least, was touching delight, Athenais showed off his gift to Pauline, Francis and Archie. The results were variable.

Archie, who had yet to come to terms with the fact that his daughter was sleeping with the Colonel, said gruffly, 'No more'n he should do – unless 'e's taking you for granted.'

Pauline pulled Athenais to one side and said, 'Just so you know – he was given some money by the English Chancellor. And what isn't hanging round your neck, he gave to me for food and rent – even though I told him there was no need. So I thought you might want it to buy him a decent second-hand coat.'

And Francis merely lifted one eyebrow at Ashley and said, 'It's lovely, Athenais. And it suits you perfectly.'

The day passed swiftly and in an atmosphere of increasing good cheer. They ate Suzon's stuffed goose with roast parsnips and cabbage, before moving on to Pauline's fruit-and-nut tarts. Then, when everyone had lent a hand to clear the table, they all trooped into the parlour where Jem and Archie immediately launched into a lively rendering of *Which Nobody Can Deny*. Francis recited some verses by Suckling and Davenant, mixed in with a few of his own; Ashley was eventually persuaded to sing the parts he remembered of *To Drive The Cold Winter Away* in a light, tuneful baritone that succeeded in making Athenais cry again; and Pauline delivered a tragic monologue from Corneille's *Polyeucte* that made *everyone* cry – Jem and Archie mostly because they scarcely understood a word of it.

'Outstanding as that was, Duchess,' said Francis at length, 'we're in danger of becoming maudlin. Also, Athenais has yet to contribute to the entertainment.'

Having drunk more wine than she was accustomed to, Athenais was curled up beside Ashley. She said, 'I can't. I shall make an idiot of myself.'

'Excellent. That's just what we want.' He reached down and pulled her to her feet, grinning when she lurched a little. 'You wanted to play the wife? Now's your chance.'

She shook her head. 'I need a script.'

'No, you don't. God knows, you've watched *Ménage* enough times – and I've seen you miming the words backstage.'

'It still won't work. You need another man.'

'And we have one,' announced Francis, grinning at Ashley. 'Pauline is herself; I shall play the husband, also prompting where necessary ... and you, *mon Colonel*, can be the lover. I call that perfect casting.' He swept round, lifted Pauline on to the table and said, 'Jem – move your carcass. We need the sofa. And now ... positions, please!'

Entering into the spirit of the thing, Ashley sat down and pulled Athenais on to his lap. He said, 'I hope you all realise that I have no idea what I'm doing.'

'That's not true,' murmured Athenais naughtily. 'Unless you've forgotten since this morning?'

Archie scowled and said, 'Don't reckon anybody needed to know that.'

Waving an airy hand, Francis said, 'Begin. You'll recall, I hope, that it starts with a passionate clinch?'

Ashley bent Athenais back over his arm and leaned towards her, his eyes alight with laughter. Pitching his voice low and dark, he said, 'Well, madam. Alone at last!'

Athenais started to giggle and Francis said, 'Don't extemporise. Just kiss the girl ... and fondle her assets.'

'Bugger that,' said Archie. 'You leave her assets be.'

'I think I'll have to,' replied Ashley, regretfully, 'since I can't actually fi --' He stopped abruptly as Athenais kicked his shin with the back of her heel. 'Is that not the line?'

'No,' said Francis. 'It isn't. And you are ruining my masterpiece. Is a bit of groping and grunting beyond you?'

'Any time you like. But I thought you wanted me to do it with Athenais?'

From her perch on the table-top, Pauline started to laugh and said, 'Oh dear. Now *there's* a permutation you haven't yet thought of, Francis.'

He sent her a pained glance. 'You've just ruined the surprise. I was saving it for *Ménage Quatre.*'

'*Quatre?*' she asked. 'What happened to *Trois?*'

'The husband, the wife, the mother-in-law and *her* lover,' replied Francis, calmly. And then, 'Time to bring you down to the level of the rest of us, Duchess.'

* * *

The remainder of their brief holiday was equally carefree and was spent walking in the snow or in casual conversation by the fireside. Then the theatre re-opened and everyone went back to their normal day-to-day concerns.

Francis settled down to complete *Ménage Deux* which he'd promised to Froissart for the middle of January but was, as yet, only half-written.

Ashley paid a courtesy call on the King and established from Sir Edward Hyde that there had so far been no suggestion that His Majesty might journey to Honfleur – which, in the Chancellor's opinion, raised doubts about the validity of Colonel Peverell's information.

And Athenais and Pauline returned to the stage ... Pauline still appearing in *Ménage* which had been retained by popular demand and Athenais, in a revival of Larivey's comedy, *Les Espirits*.

At the first opportunity, Athenais visited the best of the second-hand clothes dealers in Saint-Michel and returned with a good-quality coat of dark green broadcloth which she sincerely hoped would fit Ashley. Then she hid it in Pauline's room until the first day of January, in order to give it to him as a gift for the New Year.

When the time came and she held it out, shyly smiling, Ashley simply stared but made no move to take it from her. Finally, he said, 'How did you afford this?'

'Does it matter?'

'I think so, yes. I'm aware how limited your resources are – and equally aware how little I'm able to contribute. So I'll ask again. How did you afford it?'

She had already decided that telling him it had been bought out of the rent money he'd pressed on Pauline wouldn't be a good idea so she fought back.

'You don't like it, do you?' she asked mournfully.

'That isn't the point. I --'

'To me, it is. I've had it hidden away for days, even though I could scarcely wait to give it to you. And you don't like it.' On-stage, she could sometimes summon up tears when she needed them. In real life, it didn't seem to be working. 'What's wrong with it?'

'There's nothing wrong with it,' he said impatiently. 'It's a very nice coat. But I thought we had an understanding. Come hell or high water, I will pay my way. What I will *not* do is become a charge on your purse. Ever.'

Athenais dropped dispiritedly down on the window-seat, the coat folded in her lap.

'There's no need to sound so cross. It's just a coat, for heaven's sake. In case you hadn't noticed, it isn't even new – so it was hardly expensive.'

Frowning, Ashley drew an exasperated breath and said, 'You're being deliberately obtuse. You know perfectly well how serious I am about this. How important it is to me. So you must also have known that I'm not about to start accepting gifts from you.'

Annoyance stirred and, tossing the disputed coat to one side, she stalked across to the dresser and picked up the moonstone necklace. Then, letting it dangle from one finger, she said, 'That sounds like the kind of understanding that ought to work both ways. What do you think?'

'That you've moved on to manipulation.' He stared at her over folded arms. 'It won't work. I gave you a gift because I love you and doing so gave me pleasure. It's also a matter of pride. What seems to be escaping you, is that I neither expected nor wanted anything in return.'

'Oh – stop being so stubborn! I'm not reciprocating. I bought you a coat because you needed it and because I *could*. And if you stopped harping on about pride and the rest of it, you might realise that you're not the only one to find pleasure in giving. I'd hoped to do it myself – and might have done if you weren't so utterly, infuriatingly stiff-necked.'

'I'm not being stiff-necked, Athenais. I'm asking you to accept that only things I'm left with these days are my principles.' He stopped and then, with suppressed violence, added, 'I want to provide for you, damn it. And I ought to be able to – but I can't. If you think that doesn't eat at me every day ... that it doesn't make me feel wholly inadequate, you can't know me at all. I've invaded your life with scarcely a --'

'You didn't invade my life at all. I *dragged* you into it, kicking and screaming.'

He shook his head, refusing to smile.

'I don't recall being quite that reluctant. But be that as it may, I will *not* live off your earnings. I will *not* let myself sink to the level of a kept man. And I most assuredly will *not* turn into your father.'

'My father,' she snapped back, 'is a better man than he's been in years, thanks to you. If, in your view, everything between us has to be neatly entered into the ledger, perhaps that should be written there, too.'

'That is not at all what I meant.'

'It certainly *sounded* as if it was. And what about d'Auxerre? But for you, he'd have had me twice by now. If our relationship is all about checks and balances, there are another couple of entries for your column.'

'Will you stop? That isn't at all the same thing.'

'It seems to me as though you've made up all the rules to suit yourself. It's true that we don't have much – but what we *do* have, we share. I know you want to look after me. I understand that it hurts that you can't. But life is what it is. And I won't let you spoil what we have – this wonderful, incredible thing that we have – with self-recrimination.' She paused and took a steadying breath. 'Ashley ... I've been blind to every other man since the night you and Francis stood outside the door of the Green Room; so I'd sooner lie in a ditch with you than in the lap of luxury with anyone else. And if you don't know that by now, then you can't know *me* at all.'

The wrenching pain in his chest that always came when he thought of the future silenced him for a moment. Then he said baldly, 'I know you. You are the only thing in this entire world that I want. But I don't know what's to become of us. I can't see ... God help me, I can't see that this will end well. Oh, we can go on as we are for a while – but not indefinitely. England holds nothing for me and even less for you. The playhouses are closed; and even if they weren't, women aren't permitted on the English stage. As for --'

'Not to mention the fact that I speak worse English than Jem Barker,' interposed Athenais with something not quite a smile.

'*No* one speaks worse English than Jem. Most of the time, he speaks a language all of his own. And you've a quick ear. We could correct your pronunciation any time you wanted.' Ashley struggled to return to the point at issue. 'But that's not the answer and neither is the current situation. As things stand, I only possess one saleable ability – but, in order to use it, I'm going to have to leave you here for possibly months at a time while I serve abroad. And the only other alternative is to go on as we are, hoping that Hyde will continue to pay me a pittance. It isn't good enough for me. And it *certainly* isn't good enough for you.'

'That's your opinion. Have you heard me complain?'

'No. But --'

'Good. So – leaving money out of it for a moment – what *would* be?'

'What would be what?' Ashley was beginning to feel himself turning into a gibbering wreck.

'What would be good enough for me? I assume you've got something in mind.'

He had. The trouble was that he couldn't say it. He wanted, more than he had ever wanted anything, to offer her the dignity and protection of his name ... except, with things as they were, it wouldn't provide either one. So he couldn't simply say, *Marry me* ... because, if he did, he was fairly certain she'd say, *Yes, please. How soon?*

Swallowing the bitterness in his throat, he said, 'Nothing of the least use. Why are we quarrelling?'

'Because you are a man and therefore, at times, wholly unreasonable.'

This time he did laugh and pulled her into his arms.

'An inarguable statement. I'm sorry.'

'I forgive you.' Her arms slid around him and she held him very tightly. 'And now you will try on your nice new coat. Because, if you don't, you needn't worry about Pauline. I'll hit you with a skillet myself.'

TWO

Francis finished *Ménage Deux* with four days to spare and laid it before Pauline. This time, however, he sat down across the table from her and watched her face while she read it. The first snort of laughter came quickly and others soon followed it. Relaxing slightly, he leaned back against the settle and waited for her to finish.

When she finally looked up, he said, 'Well? Is it as good as the other?'

'Yes. Perhaps even better.' She grinned. 'You really *do* have an evil mind, don't you?'

'It would appear so.' He smiled back, slowly and with intent. 'Just at the moment, for example, it's suggesting all manner of decadent things I think we might both enjoy.'

She felt the inevitable tug of response low in her body and knew her colour had risen a little but managed to say coolly, 'Oh? Such as what?'

'Such as taking the pins from your hair and ...'

He stopped, his eyes lingering on her mouth.

This time her breath fluttered.

'And what? That doesn't sound very decadent to me.'

'The rest of it is. Trust me. But a gentleman doesn't make those sort of suggestions to a lady across the kitchen table in broad daylight.'

'No?'

'No. He makes them by candlelight and in a more ... conducive ... location. Preferably between long, enticing kisses. Such things shouldn't be hurried.'

It had been a long time since Pauline had experienced physical desire for a man and she found it both exhilarating and a little alarming that Francis could produce such a reaction without even touching her.

She said, 'You're very good at this.'

'Thank you.'

And there it was. That talent he had for mingling words and glances that heated her blood with something calculated to make her laugh.

She shook her head at him. 'Don't you want to ask at what?'

'No. I'm just happy that you think I'm good at *something*.' The sapphire gaze rested on her invitingly. 'But I imagine you meant ... elegant courtship.'

'I meant seduction. You've obviously had a fair amount of practice.'

'Some – though I believe I'm still learning.' He took her hand and placed a warm kiss in her palm. 'How am I doing?'

'Well enough.' *Well enough to make me wish for candlelight and a conducive location.* Aware that he his thumb was tracing lazy circles on her wrist, causing her pulse to accelerate, she pulled her hand away and, clearing her throat, said, 'I should go. Will you give the play to Froissart today?'

Francis stood up. 'If you think it's ready.'

'It's ready.' *And so, God help me, am I.*

* * *

On the following afternoon, Jem laconically informed Colonel Peverell that the gent with the eye-patch was back in his lodgings.

'And about time,' muttered Ashley. 'Is he at home now?'

'Was when I come away.'

'Good. Then let's see if I can catch him.'

Arriving in the Rue des Minimes, Ashley trod briskly up the stairs to Sir William Brierley's room and rapped on the door. Then he was face to face with his quarry.

'Ashley? Dear me. This is a surprise,' said Will, holding the door wide in invitation. 'I've been staying with friends near Rouen for a few weeks and only returned last night. Travel in this country is so very fatiguing, don't you think?'

Ashley tossed his hat down on a table and said, 'I wouldn't know. I rarely stir from Paris.'

'You're fortunate. I find the countryside palls very quickly.'

'Then why go?'

A flicker of awareness stirred in the dark eye and then was gone.

'I was invited, my dear. Why else? Do sit down. You'll take a glass of wine, no doubt … and hopefully make me privy to all the latest gossip.'

Ashley sat, his expression unreadable. He said, 'I'm not privy to it myself. But you might be interested to know that Celia Maxwell is dead.'

Sir William froze, bottle in hand.

'Dead? How did that happen? It must have been very sudden.'

'It was. A fall and a broken neck – just a few days before Christmas.' He accepted the glass he was offered but set it to one side. 'If speculation interests you, there's a possibility that Verney pushed her – though I personally doubt he did so. I think she tripped and he just … failed to catch her.'

'Convenient for him.'

'Very.'

Sir William sat down on the other side of the hearth.

'You didn't come here to tell me that, did you?'

'No.' Ashley impaled him on a steady gaze. 'I came to ask why you lied to me.'

'Lied to you? Did I? About what?'

'Don't play the innocent, Will. You know perfectly well about what. Lucy Walter. You said you visited her to take money from the King. You didn't.'

'And you know this how?'

'How do you think? I know it because His Majesty told me,' came the impatient reply. 'Can we please stop skirting the issue? We've known each other a number of years and I've always respected your ability. I had thought that respect was mutual – but it seems not.'

'You're making assumptions.'

'Am I? In what particular?'

'You're assuming that my reason for visiting Mistress Walter must somehow be incriminating.'

'If it's not, why lie about it?'

There was a long silence while Sir William sipped his wine and stared pensively into the fire. Finally, he said, 'Two reasons, really. Firstly, I was keeping to what we both agree is the cardinal rule. Tell no one anything they don't absolutely need to know.' He looked up. 'And there was no real reason for you to know what I wanted with Lucy Walter.'

Ashley's brows rose.

'You could have said that. I would have accepted it.'

'We were in a public place, Ashley.'

'You're saying you lied for the benefit of whoever might be listening?'

'Something plausible is always preferable to a hint of mystery, don't you think?'

What Ashley thought was that it sounded overly plausible *now* but he merely said, 'And the second reason?'

'The game we play has many strands.'

They might *call* it a game, reflected Ashley, but Will knew as well as he did that those who treated it like one were likely to wind up decorating the end of a rope.

'I'm aware of that. So?'

'So not all of them are ... clearly defined.'

'I'm aware of that, too. What are you saying exactly?'

'I'm saying that your parameters and mine are rather different.' Sir William's mouth curled slightly. 'Just at present, I suspect you wouldn't approve of mine.'

Ashley eyed him narrowly.

'Why? What are you up to?'

Sir William shook his head and tutted reprovingly.

'You know better than to ask that.'

'All right. How much risk are you running?'

'A little more than normal, perhaps ... but, if all goes as I hope, the results should be worth it. And that, I'm afraid is all I intend to say on the subject.' He sipped his wine and crossed one long leg over the other. 'My turn, I think. There has been no gossip about myself and Mistress Walter because there has been nothing to occasion it. In the last six months, I have visited her only once ... yet you knew of it, didn't you?'

'Yes.'

'Who were you watching? The lady – or myself?'

Ashley didn't like anything about the way this conversation had been going but there was no doubt that it was refreshing not to have to spell everything out.

'The lady. There wouldn't have been any reason to watch you, would there?'

'No. And I'd have noticed if you had been.' Will paused. 'Let me guess. Charles wants the lady kept under the watchful eye of someone he trusts? Yes. But that's not all, is it? She has been calling herself his wife and hinting that she can prove it.' Laughter stirred. 'Don't – *don't* tell me he's had you hunting for these fabled marriage-lines?'

'You know about them?'

'I know they're a forgery, if that's what you mean.'

'How?'

'For anyone who takes the trouble to look properly, there's a verifiable mistake. The document says the marriage took place at St Germain-en-Laye on September 4th, 1649. But Charles wasn't *in* St Germain then. He was landing on Jersey. Both Hyde and Secretary Nicholas will have a record of it somewhere.'

Ashley decided he'd better pay Hyde another visit. He also thought he'd give a great deal to lay the copy in Hyde's possession next to the one Colonel Maxwell had in London. He said, 'You've plainly had the chance to scrutinise it.'

'In detail.'

'And it didn't occur to you to purloin the damned thing?'

'Steal a forgery? To what end? It seemed much more interesting to see what she did with it. You know the old saying about giving someone enough rope … and I thought Lucy might well be stupid enough to hang herself. Figuratively speaking, of course.'

'Of course,' said Ashley dryly. And thought, *Christ, Will. Why can't you ever do the obvious thing and save everybody else a lot of trouble.* 'It hasn't worked so far though, has it?'

'No. But there's always hope.'

'Is there?' Ashley swallowed his wine in one gulp and stood up. 'And you find the thought comforting?'

'Why not? It's better than nothing.'

'No. Actually it's a whole lot worse.'

* * *

Ashley went directly to see Sir Edward Hyde and, coming straight to the point, said, 'Have you had a good look at the so-called marriage lines?'

'Yes. But there doesn't seem to be anything untoward about them.'

'Look again. Look, in particular, at the when and where. And then check them against the King's whereabouts at that time.'

'You've acquired new information?'

'It would seem so. I've just been informed by Sir William Brierley that the facts don't fit.'

'How does he know?'

'That's a good question and one he's so far managed to avoid answering. But that's not the main point, is it? What really matters is whether or not he's right.'

* * *

He arrived home to find the house empty but for Archie, newly-returned from sweeping the snow from both the front steps and the yard. Catching a certain glint in the older man's eye, Ashley realised that this was the first time there had been any chance of a completely private conversation since he and Athenais had ... well, just *since*. Removing his hat and taking a moment to shake the snow from it, he said carefully, 'I imagine there are things you'd like to say to me, Sergeant.'

'One or two.'

'Very well. I'm listening.'

Archie nodded but took his time about answering. Finally, he said somewhat belligerently, 'My girl ain't no lightskirt.'

'I know she isn't – and have never for a moment thought it.'

'All very well and fine, Colonel. But what are your intentions towards 'er?'

Ashley was distantly aware that, in other circumstances, this might have been funny. As it was, it merely made his stomach clench.

'Truthfully?'

'Don't see no point in lying.'

'No. It's just ... Archie, you can't repeat what I'm about to say to Athenais. It wouldn't be helpful.'

'Between us, then. Man to man.'

'Thank you.' Ashley looked him in the eye and said bluntly, 'I love her and I wish more than anything that I could marry her – but I can't.'

'Why? Not leg-shackled already, are you?'

'No. But you know how I'm placed. My future is, at best, uncertain. So marrying Athenais wouldn't be doing her any favours. And she deserves better than to be tied to someone like me.'

'But, in the meantime, you don't mind 'aving your fun wiv 'er.'

Ashley flushed.

'It's not like that! I never intended things to work out as they have. I tried …' He stopped, aware that there was no point in saying it. Then, '*Christ*, Archie – if you think this situation is fun for me, you have no bloody idea. I'd cut off my right hand rather than hurt her. But sooner or later, it's going to be unavoidable.'

Archie nodded. 'I know.'

'You *know?* Then why the hell --'

''Cos I wanted to see if *you* did.' Archie dropped a hand on his shoulder and said, 'You make 'er 'appy, lad. 'Appier than I've ever seen 'er. So keep on doing it for as long as you can and let tomorrow take care of itself. It 'as an 'abit of doing that, you know.'

* * *

Ashley was still trying to decide if this conversation had left him feeling better or worse when Francis, Pauline and Athenais returned from the afternoon's rehearsal. Francis looked as though he'd been laughing himself silly; Pauline looked more than usually enigmatic; and Athenais looked sulky.

'God alone knows why it's taken so long,' announced Francis, 'but the King has heard about *Ménage*.'

'Which King?' asked Ashley, immediately understanding Athenais's pout.

'Ours. And he's asked for a private performance in his apartments at the Louvre.'

'When?'

'On Sunday evening,' said Athenais. 'The only night the theatre is closed. So, while I'm sitting here like an orphan, *you'll* all be at the palace.' She thumped Ashley's chest. 'Don't laugh.'

'I didn't,' he protested.

'You wanted to and that's just as bad.'

'The reason she's spitting feathers,' offered Pauline, 'is because Froissart says only the actors needed for the play are to go. As you might expect, everyone is in a fever of excitement at the notion of a command performance – so it was necessary to stop the entire company turning up.'

Ashley took Athenais's hand and dropped a light kiss on it.

'I'm sorry you're disappointed. But look on the bright side. You and I can have a whole evening to ourselves.'

'We can't,' she said gloomily.

'Why not? I don't have to go.'

'You do,' said Francis. 'Aside from the formal request to Monsieur Laroque, Charles sent a personal note addressed to you and me. Naturally, I'm invited as the author of the piece. I'm not quite sure why he wants you as well – but it seems that he does.'

'And that,' grumbled Athenais, 'is why it isn't fair and why I'm wildly jealous.' She smiled suddenly, 'But at least you now have a respectable coat to wear.'

'And at least,' replied Ashley wryly, 'I don't have to worry about getting killed in the rush when the King, the Duke of Buckingham and doubtless half-a-dozen other similarly smitten gentlemen take one look at you and trip over themselves to win a smile.'

THREE

By Saturday evening, word of the Théâtre du Marais's forthcoming royal performance had tripped blithely off the stage and was stampeding through the auditorium. The pit amused itself by thinking up new and pithy comments to shout out and one performance of *Ménage* had to be halted completely when Pauline, in her role as the *belle-mère*, retorted with a line so cuttingly funny that it reduced the entire audience to near-hysteria.

Athenais spent most of Sunday afternoon fussing over Ashley's clothes – which he found endearing and exasperating in equal parts. She ironed his best shirt, brushed the green coat and would even have polished his boots had not Archie waved her away, saying that he could do it better. Then she sat on the bed, watching him shave and giving Ashley the uneasy feeling that she was going to insist on brushing his hair and making sure that he had a clean handkerchief.

Dabbing the residual bits of soap from his face and catching her eye in the mirror, he said, 'What now? Do you want to check that I haven't missed a bit?'

'No.' She walked across to stand behind him. 'I want to kiss your back.' And, sliding her arms about his waist, she did so. 'There will be lovely women in beautiful gowns this evening, won't there?'

'Yes.' He managed to inject a subtle note of pleased anticipation into his tone. 'I imagine that there will be.'

She laid her cheek against his shoulder.

'And they will want to flirt with you.'

'You think so?'

'Yes.' Her hands tightened around him. 'You are not to notice them.'

'Well, I'll try,' he said doubtfully. 'But you'll understand that it might be difficult.'

'I won't understand at all.'

Ashley broke from her hold and turned to read her expression. The uncertainty in it all but undid him. He said gently, 'I was teasing, Athenais. With or without their beautiful gowns, there won't be a woman there who could hold a candle to you. Surely you know that?'

'Perhaps. But they'll be ladies. *Real* ladies, I mean – not --'

'Stop right there.' He grasped her shoulders and gave her a little shake. 'They may have birth and some of them may even have breeding ... but not one of them is in any way better than you. Not one. And I won't have you think it. Now stop worrying and give me a kiss. If Charles has asked me to be there, it's probably because he wants to hand me some task I'd rather not be bothered with. So there'll be no flirting – or not until I'm home again with you.'

Visibly comforted, she kissed him and then said, 'You don't mind that I'm a little bit jealous?'

'No. But I'd mind very much if I thought you didn't trust me,' he said firmly. 'Now ... it's Suzon's night off – but Jem and your father will both be here and --'

She kissed him again. 'I'll be fine. Don't worry.'

'And I'll be back as soon as I can. So you can sit by the fire and learn your next role ... or, alternatively, you can decide what forfeit you'd like me to pay to atone for my absence.' He grinned. 'I rather like that idea – so use your imagination.'

* * *

Athenais rather liked the idea, too and spent some time enjoying a couple of fairly erotic fantasies. Then, sternly telling herself that Ashley was unlikely to be home for some time and that she should therefore occupy herself more profitably, she picked up next week's script and attempted to concentrate on it.

She had barely got through the first half-dozen pages when there was an almighty crash that sounded as if it came from the kitchen, followed by curse-ridden shouts and a series of thuds and grunts. Alarmed, she tossed the play-script aside and stood up.

It's just Father and Jem – drunk and having a falling-out, she told herself.

But deep down, she knew it wasn't. Someone ... and from the noise, more than *one* someone ... had broken into the house from the yard.

Thieves, then? But instinct told her it wasn't that either. And she was suddenly ice-cold with fear.

It had only been seconds. The fight in the kitchen was still going on and she could hear items bouncing off shelves and furniture being knocked over. She could run. She *should* run. But to where? Both the stairs and the front door involved crossing the hall – which meant she might be seen. Furthermore, the door to the street would be locked, thus taking precious minutes to open; and, even assuming she made it to the upper floors, she couldn't think of anywhere she could hide where she wouldn't be found. Which left staying where she was and attempting to defend herself. Her frightened gaze skimmed the room, searching for a weapon and then, heart racing and with hands that were already starting to shake, she grabbed the poker.

It was cast iron and the sort that had a small, curved hook near the end but the length and weight of it meant that she needed both hands to hold it steady. Athenais gripped it until her knuckles glowed white.

The kitchen had gone ominously quiet. She heard the door open and a rough voice saying, 'These won't give you no trouble now, milord.'

Oh God, oh God. What's happened to Father and Jem?

There was a chink of coins, as if a purse had been tossed from one hand to another. Then she heard a different voice; low, cultured and only too familiar.

'Good. Leave now, the way you came. And not a word of this to anyone – or it will be the worse for you. Go.'

A moan rose in Athenais's throat and she took a couple of steps back from the door, holding the poker before her like a club. She'd known it must be him. If he was alone, she might just have a chance. It he wasn't … if he wasn't, she didn't dare think what might happen.

Calm, unhurried footsteps crossed the tiled floor of the hall. Then the door swung open and the Marquis d'Auxerre was smiling at her in a way that made her blood curdle. He gestured to the poker and said negligently, 'Well, my dear. What *do* you think you're going to do with that? Hit me?'

'If I must. What have you d-done with my f-father and the other man?'

'I?' He strolled towards her. 'I haven't done anything, *ma belle*. I merely had a couple of hirelings clear the way for me but they are gone now.' He halted some four paces away. 'Put the poker down.'

Athenais raised it threateningly and stepped back, shaking her head.

'Go away. You shouldn't be here. Ashley – C-Colonel Peverell will be back any minute and he --'

D'Auxerre laughed in a way that wasn't either pleasant or comforting.

'He won't. He's at the Louvre with the rest of them.' He advanced on her again. 'Did you honestly think I wouldn't hear of this special performance for the beggar-king? Why else do you think I chose tonight?'

The weight of the poker was making her arms ache and there was cramp in her hands from gripping it so tightly. Lowering it slightly, she flexed her fingers ... and disaster struck as, seizing the small shift in her concentration, the Marquis wrenched it from her grasp and flung it down.

Athenais's breath hissed through her teeth as the rough metal scored her palms and she watched her only hope slide across the floor to arrive half-way under the sofa. She said breathlessly, 'Please, Monseigneur ... please just go.'

'After all the trouble you've put me to? I don't think so.'

'Trouble? I haven't – I n-never meant --' He was moving towards her again with the lazy steps of a predator who knows the prey is caught. She backed away in the general direction of the sofa, hoping for a chance to retrieve the poker. 'I don't understand! Why are you doing this?'

'I told you some months ago that I intended to have you – willing or not – and that is still true. I also warned you not to anger me by lying with anyone else. But you did, didn't you? It's all over the theatre. You're sleeping with that filthy cur of an Englishman. *Aren't you?*'

The sudden venom in his tone made her jump.

'Yes. He – I – we l-love each other.'

'Do you? Do you indeed? Well, that will make this all the sweeter.' He was so close now he was almost touching her. 'Two birds with one stone, in fact. *If* he loves you, knowing that I've had you will hurt more than carving him up with a blade, won't it? And I *want* to hurt him, Athenais. Not only has he a nasty habit of getting in my way – he has offered me gross insults and dared to lay his hands on me. So I'll take my pleasure with you ... and then, if and when I feel so inclined, I'll hurt him a little more. Physically.'

Athenais felt sick. 'He'll kill you.'

'No. I don't think so. The Cardinal would have his head.' Gripping her chin in hard fingers, he said, 'I think we've talked enough, don't you? Are you going to remove this gown or would you like me to do it for you?' Then, with another smile, 'What a silly question. I can't imagine why I asked it.'

And, taking hold of the neckline of her gown, he ripped it savagely from her shoulders. The lacing held but the fabric surrendered to his assault and came apart in his hands. Athenais staggered and tried to grab the torn edges but he chopped her hand away with the edge of his palm, making her gasp with pain. She rammed her fists against his chest, twisting away from him. And this time he hit her across the face, so hard that she stumbled against the wall.

'Carry on fighting me if you will – but you won't win. You'll only make it harder for yourself.' He grasped another handful of her gown and tore it still further so that the seams came completely adrift and it slithered down past her waist to rest on her petticoats. 'Of course, there's no need to bother with your clothes. But I might as well see what I'm getting.'

He spun her round, forcing her against the wall with one hand whilst using the other to snap the tapes of her petticoats and yank her stay-laces free. Athenais's face was half-numb where he'd hit her. Tears trickled helplessly down her cheeks and her breath was coming in short, agonising gasps. Corset and petticoats fell away, leaving her in only her shift and she thought, *This is going to happen. I can't stop him. It's going to happen. Oh God … please God, let somebody come.*

Taking one of her arms in a bruising grip, d'Auxerre dragged her away from both the wall and the remains of her clothes. He looked her over with insulting thoroughness and then, releasing her in order to use both hands, he tore her chemise from neck to hem. Athenais used her second of freedom to lurch away from him. He halted her by seizing a handful of her hair, then used one foot to sweep her legs from under her. She landed on the floor like a sack of meal, the breath knocked from her body.

He stared down at her and lifted one faintly amused brow.

'I suppose this is where you ask me to let you go, isn't it?'

She couldn't make her throat work. It was closed tight with horror. She hadn't thought anything could ever be worse than what had happened with Guillaume in the churchyard but she'd been wrong. That had been degrading and painful ... but nothing like this. Guillaume had merely hoisted up her skirts and taken her because he felt like it and the opportunity was there. The Marquis was intent on punishing her. He didn't just want to rape her. He wanted to hurt her – and, through her, Ashley; so he was cold-bloodedly inflicting as much pain and humiliation as he could along the way. Now, for example, it seemed that he wanted her to beg ... and for a moment, she almost did so, even though she knew it would make no difference. He hadn't taken things this far to stop now and she wasn't physically strong enough to make him. She had no control here except in one tiny thing. She wouldn't plead with him only to have him laugh in her face.

Swallowing hard and clutching the torn shift about her as best she could, she said raggedly, 'Go to hell.'

So swiftly she had no time to anticipate his intention, he kicked her legs apart and dropped on one knee between them to gather both of her wrists in a bone-crushing grip. Pinioning them behind her head, he placed his other hand about her throat and applied a subtle pressure. He said, 'Oh no, my dear. I think it is you who will do that.'

His grasp on her throat was just enough to restrict the air-flow. Panic rushed through her and she struggled to free her hands. Part of her brain was afraid he was going to kill her. The other part almost wished he would so that the nightmare would be over.

Just when her hold on consciousness started to waver, he removed his hand and watched her dragging air into her lungs, his expression totally unconcerned and even a little clinical. Brushing the torn chemise out of the way so that virtually every inch of her was exposed, he conducted a leisurely appraisal. Athenais shut her eyes and felt tears sliding down into her hair. The scent of sandalwood enveloped her, making her gorge rise. A voice in her head was crying, *Don't do this. Please don't.* And she clamped her teeth together to stop it escaping.

As if he could hear it anyway, he trailed a seemingly idle hand over her breast and said, 'If you're wise, you'll stop fighting me. You would be surprised how much more unpleasant I can make this if I try. Or perhaps you enjoy pain? Is that it? Shall we find out?' And he twisted her nipple in hard, cruel fingers.

Athenais cried out.

'Was that pain?' laughed d'Auxerre. 'Or pleasure?' And he dragged the back of his hand from her clavicle to her waist so that his ornate ring scored the soft flesh.

Everything inside her started to crumble. There was no hope of escape, no point in resistance and not a vestige of dignity. There was nothing except a dark abyss of terror and despair. Harsh, ugly sobs crowded her throat and the fight went out of her. She felt his hands, carelessly intrusive, branding her whole body ... and felt like the whore he would make of her.

He slapped her face and her eyes flew open.

'That's better. No shutting out of reality and escaping into some sickly fantasy. I want you to know who's on top of you. I want you to remember this next time the bastard Englishman tries to bed you. If I let him live long enough to do it, of course.' He paused, as if giving the matter consideration. 'What do you think, *ma belle*? Shall I grant him a few more weeks? I might be persuaded to do that ... if you're a very good girl.'

With immense difficulty, Athenais mumbled, 'Why don't you just get on with it?'

Maliciously amused eyes bored into hers.

'Say please.'

'What?'

'If you're so eager ... say please. And spread your legs.'

Bile rose in her throat. 'No.'

His grip on her wrists tightened and he dug his fingernails deep into her other breast.

'Do it ... or I'll be forced to get inventive. And that may take some time.'

Revulsion and shock and fear rolled through her in shuddering waves until she was engulfed in emotions she barely recognised, each one as black as the pit of hell. She wanted to scream and carry on screaming. There was no longer anything she wouldn't do in the hope that he'd go.

On a despairing sob, she whispered, 'Please.' And let her knees fall apart.

'There.' He shifted, unfastening his breeches. 'That wasn't so hard, was it? Unlike myself, of course.'

And he plunged into her with such wild ferocity that only his grip on her hands and his weight on top of her held her in place. Only the tiniest sound of pain escaped her. She kept the howl tightly locked inside her chest and shut her mind to what he was doing. Sanity started to slip away and it became more and more difficult to hold on to any coherent thought. Turning her head, she stared sightlessly away from him towards the sofa as his body slammed into hers again and again ... until finally it was over and he slumped on top of her, his chest heaving.

Athenais lay perfectly motionless, her gaze fixed and unblinking, as she waited for him to move. Eventually, he did so – hauling himself to his feet and starting to re-arrange his clothes. He said something but she didn't hear what it was. There were only two things in her head – one of which was that, just for a moment or two, he had his back to her.

She coiled her legs into herself, rolled on to her knees and stood up. Two swift, silent strides took her to the sofa and the place where the poker lay. Swooping down, she grabbed it. And in the second he began to turn back to her, swung the thing at his head with every ounce of strength she possessed.

She missed his head but was still more successful than she knew. The curved hook on the end of the iron took him in the neck, at a point behind the jaw and just below his ear. He yelled and blood sprayed like a scarlet fountain. Leaving the poker impaled in his neck, Athenais let go of it and backed away. He wrenched it out and more blood spurted. He dropped to his knees, his hands clasped to the wound and covered in gore. He tried to say something. Athenais continued backing away until the corner of the room closed around her. The Marquis d'Auxerre slithered to the floor in a pool of his own blood. There was a gurgling noise and some twitching. And then silence.

FOUR

The private performance at the Louvre went off without a hitch and the twenty or so persons Charles had invited enjoyed it immensely. At the end, His Majesty put a small purse into the hands of its author and said, 'I don't know how you did it, Francis. But with your lines and that lady's talent,' he paused to incline his head at Pauline, 'you're destined to take the Paris stage by storm. And if I ever regain my throne, I hope you'll come and give English theatre something to live up to. God knows, after years of closure and with boys still playing the girls' parts, it could do with a good shake up.'

The three of them arrived back in the Rue des Rosiers a little after eleven. Francis was still euphoric, Pauline looked oddly flushed and Ashley was just glad to have seen the last of his Grace of Buckingham – who was as fond of barbed innuendoes as he'd always been. They entered the house and, leaving Francis to bolt the door, Ashley headed straight for the parlour to see if Athenais was still up.

The sight that met his eyes froze him on the threshold for a second. There was blood everywhere and the Marquis d'Auxerre lay in the middle of the room in a pool of it. In the far corner, Athenais was huddled on the floor clutching a bundle of gore-spattered petticoats and staring across at him out of wide, blank eyes.

'Holy hell,' breathed Ashley. Then, over his shoulder, 'Francis – keep Pauline out of here and check the kitchen.'

'What?' asked Francis blankly.

'Just do it!'

He heard Pauline asking what was wrong and called curtly, 'Stay in the hall. You don't want to see this.' And, avoiding the blood as best he could, he crossed the room towards Athenais, saying softly, 'It's all right, love. You're safe now.'

There were marks all over her and she appeared to be wearing nothing but a torn shift. Swallowing the sickness in his throat, he crouched down and held out his hand to her but wasn't surprised when she shrank back.

'Don't. You mustn't touch me.' She barely looked at him, her gaze still fixed on the mess in the middle of the floor. 'Is he dead?'

'Yes. Don't worry about it. I'll take care of everything. Just let me get you out of here.'

She looked at him then, the smoky-grey eyes suddenly no longer blank but filled with unutterable anguish. She said, 'I'm sorry. I'm sorry, I'm sorry, I'm sorry. I couldn't ... couldn't ...'

'Hush, darling.' Ashley offered his hand again and again she shrank away from him. 'I won't hurt you, Athenais. I only want to take you away from ... from *that*.'

'I'll do it.' Pauline spoke from behind him. 'She'll let me. And Francis needs you.'

Ashley turned his head and stood up, careful not to make any sudden movements. He said, 'It's bad?'

She nodded, her glance flicking meaningfully to Athenais and then back to his face.

'Go and see. It's clear enough what's happened here ... so, for the time being, the best thing you can do is leave her to me.'

Reluctant but recognising the sense of it, he stepped back and let Pauline kneel down in his place. She said, 'Athenais? I want you to come with me.'

Athenais shook her head, looking confused.

'You can't stay here. Let me help you stand up ... and we'll go upstairs. You'll feel better then.'

'I w-won't.'

'You will. Trust me.' Pauline flicked a minatory look over her shoulder at Ashley. 'Go away. You can't help her yet. And there's too much else for you to do.'

With the merest inclination of his head, Ashley walked past the corpse and took his first proper look. Then, resisting an impulse to spit on it, he crossed the hall to the kitchen.

The room was a shambles of over-turned furniture and scattered pans and platters. In the midst of it, Francis had untied Jem, pulled the filthy gag from his mouth and was busy trying to staunch blood from a blow to the head.

Archie lay on the floor in front of the hearth. His body was at an odd angle and he wasn't moving.

Ashley dropped on one knee beside him. 'Archie?'

'He's dead,' said Francis tersely. 'Somebody bashed his skull in.'

'Oh God.' He leaned his brow against his arm and shut his eyes for a moment. Then he looked down on the man who had reclaimed his life, only to lose it again so soon and thought, *I'm sorry, Archie. You didn't deserve this. And how am I going to tell your girl?*

As if reading his mind, Francis said, 'How's Athenais?'

'In shock. Pauline's with her.' Ashley cleared his throat and stood up. 'She ... I think d'Auxerre may have ... I think he assaulted her ... and she killed him.'

Francis stopped what he was doing and looked sharply across at him. 'How?'

'With the poker. He's in there.' He jerked his head in the direction of the parlour. 'It looks like a charnel-house. And we have to get rid of the body.'

Jem groaned as he started to come round. Francis held him steady with one hand and pressed a cloth to the gash in his temple with the other. He said, 'Easy, Jem. Don't try to move.' And, to Ashley, 'Clearly d'Auxerre didn't come here alone. If you're hoping to cover this up, we need to find out who else was with him.'

'I know. But right now, there's Archie to be taken care of ... and Athenais.' He stopped, trying to focus on the matter in hand. 'And, before any of that, we've got to remove every sign of what happened in the parlour before the maid comes back in the morning. I'm not having Athenais dragged into this at *all* – never mind being charged with murder.' He threw off his coat, seized a bucket and said, 'I'm going to get some water. When Jem's fit enough to talk, ask the questions.'

* * *

Pauline eventually succeeded in coaxing Athenais up the stairs to her bedchamber. Once there, she prised the girl's stiff fingers away from the bloodied petticoats and peeled her out of the ruined shift. Although she said nothing, Pauline's expression hardened when she took in the darkening bruises on Athenais's throat and wrists; and the scratch marks and smears of blood she found elsewhere caused her to fold her lips very tightly together. Then she used a soft, damp cloth to gently clean away as much as she could of Athenais's ordeal ... knowing all the time that no amount of washing would ever get rid of the stains that really mattered.

When she was done, she wrapped Athenais in a chamber-robe and tucked her underneath a quilt, saying, 'You won't rest easy until you've had a bath – so I'll see about that now. Will you be all right alone, for a few minutes? Or would you like Ashley to sit with you?'

'No.' Athenais sat up and stared at her, wild-eyed. 'I can't. I don't know ... not yet.'

'Then lie down and try to get warm. I won't be long.'

Athenais curled herself into a tight little ball, held the quilt up to her chin and stared at the wall. Every part of her was sore and aching ... one place hurting more than all the rest. But she shut her mind to it because, if she didn't, she thought she might lose her last frail shred of sanity. As it was, she didn't dare close her eyes. She knew that, if she did, she'd see him looming over her, laughing ... while he systematically inflicted pain and humiliation. While he threatened Ashley.

Ashley. Something started to fracture inside her chest. She'd told him about Guillaume and he hadn't seemed to mind. But this ... this was different. He couldn't help but mind this. No man could. Most women never got raped at all. She'd been raped twice. She couldn't quite work out what that meant ... except that it suggested the fault lay within herself. How could he bear to touch her after this? How, knowing herself utterly defiled, could she ever *let* him? The terrible clawing sensation inside her grew so bad she felt as if she was being torn apart. And, at the core of it, was guilt at what she had done.

Say please, he'd said. And she had.

* * *

Below stairs, while Ashley brought in buckets of water and Francis set them to heat up, Jem had recovered sufficiently to tell them what had happened.

'Bully-boys,' he croaked. 'Two of 'em. The sort who'll do anything for a couple of coins. Broke in from the yard and kicked the door down. Archie and me – we did what we could but they was big buggers, with cudgels. Archie went down – just knocked out, I thought. Then the pair of 'em set about me and tied me up. That's when the poncey lord come in, paid 'em and told 'em to sod off and keep their mouths shut. One of 'em smashed me round the head – and that's the last I knew.' He looked sadly at Archie. 'Didn't need to do that to him, did they? Poor old codger.'

Ashley and Francis exchanged glances. Ashley said crisply, 'We'll never find them, so it's a waste of time trying. And I doubt we need to worry about them anyway since he's unlikely to have given them his real name or told anyone else what he was about. So let's just concentrate on clearing up the mess.'

Francis nodded and started stripping off his coat and shirt, in preparation.

'What are we going to do with d'Auxerre?'

'Let the fish have him.'

'Easier said than done from here.'

'We'll manage.' As Francis had done, Ashley pulled his shirt over his head and dropped it on top of his coat. 'We'll have to.'

The door opened and Pauline came in. Her eyes widened slightly at the sight of two half-naked men but she continued on her way, saying, 'Athenais needs a bath.'

'Wait.' Ashley halted her with a hand on her arm. 'How is she? Did he ...?'

'Yes. And she's as you'd expect.' She marched into the scullery and came out hauling the hip-bath. 'I'll want some of that hot water.'

Francis said, 'I'll bring it.'

She shook her head. 'You've got your work cut out down here.'

Jem came somewhat shakily to his feet.

'Madame wants that upstairs, Colonel? I can take it.'

'You're not fit. And we'll need you later.'

'I'm all right,' insisted Jem, taking the bath from Pauline and glancing back at Ashley. 'I can help. I *want* to. Least I can do.'

Leaving Jem to fetch and carry for Pauline, Francis and Ashley assembled buckets, mops and all the cleaning-rags they could find and returned to the parlour.

'Christ Almighty!' said Francis, seeing the extent of the problem for the first time.

'Quite.' Ashley paused and then, in a tone of icy contempt, said, 'We'll have to get rid of the carcass first. We can hardly work round it and I want it gone from here before daylight. There's a rug in the hall which might do as wrapping. But first we'll have to strip it. A naked corpse will be less recognisable if it washes up somewhere.'

Later, Francis thought that he'd remember this hellish night for the rest of his life. They removed the Marquis's clothes and rolled his body in the hall rug, ready for disposal in the Seine later in the night, when the streets were at their darkest and emptiest. Then they set about cleaning up the sticky, congealing blood which seemed to have got just about everywhere. Within an hour, both of them were splattered in gore and drenched in sweat. From time to time, Francis looked at Ashley and wondered what he was thinking ... but neither of them said more than was strictly necessary to deal with the task in hand.

In fact, Ashley was trying very hard not to think of anything. He couldn't escape the picture in his head of Athenais sitting huddled in a corner when he'd first entered the room. But if, on top of the sickly smell of d'Auxerre's blood, he let himself contemplate what the evil son of a whore had done to her, he was fairly sure he'd throw up.

In due course, Jem – now with a neat dressing around his head – joined them and asked what he should do next.

'Find a cart or a barrow,' said Ashley. 'Steal it, if you have to. We've got to get to the river without being seen carrying a body-shaped bundle. And start burning the clothes.'

Jem nodded and vanished.

Without pausing in his labours, Francis said, 'Do you expect to get away with this?'

'Yes. In case you haven't yet realised, it won't be the first time.'

* * *

Pauline, meanwhile, settled Athenais in a hot bath but refrained from asking any questions. For a time, the girl just scrubbed and scrubbed and scrubbed at her skin until it was nearly raw. Eventually however she let her hands fall loose into the water and, as if the thought was a surprise, said, 'Oh. I killed him, didn't I?'

'Yes.'

'Will I ... will they hang me for it?'

'No. Don't worry. You did what you had to – and he got what he deserved.'

471

'But there was ...' She stopped, frowning perplexedly. 'I remember blood. Lots of it.'

'Ashley and Francis are taking care of it.'

'And ... and the b-body?'

'That, too.' In order to change the subject before she was asked about Archie, Pauline reached for a brush and began disentangling the thick, coppery curls over the back of the tub. 'We'll wash your hair tomorrow but for now, you need to sleep. I've put your night-rail to warm by the fire and the towels are just here. Tell me when you're ready to get out of the bath.'

A shudder rippled through the slight frame.

'Not yet.' Athenais reached for the wash-cloth again. 'I'm not clean yet.'

'A little while longer, then.' Pauline's tone remained perfectly level but her face, had Athenais been able to see it, was contorted with grief and rage and terrible understanding. 'Just a few minutes more, until the water cools.'

As she had expected, getting Athenais out of the bath and into a nightgown and bed took time, patience and a great deal of persuasion. But when she was finally tucked against the pillows, Pauline sat down beside her and said, 'I'll stay, if you wish.'

'Yes. Please.'

And suddenly, without any warning whatsoever, the howl she'd been trying to lock inside her broke loose. Hot tears scalded her cheeks and she dissolved into harsh, tearing sobs. She cried as if her heart would break ... as if she was drowning in all the sorrows of the world. She cried until her eyes were reduced to puffy slits and she could barely breathe. The deluge lasted for a long time and Pauline held her tightly throughout. But finally it lessened and then stopped – as if there were no more tears left or she lacked the energy to shed them.

And Pauline thought, *It's as well the Colonel didn't see this. Or – since you can't kill a man twice – we'd have had him cutting out the bastard's black heart and frying it.*

* * *

By the time they'd dropped d'Auxerre's weighted corpse in the river well beyond the Pont Marie, cleaned up every speck of blood they could find and laid Archie out in the cold and hitherto unused cellar with coins on his eyes, it was nearly six in the morning and every muscle in Ashley's body felt as though it had been savagely beaten. He could almost have slept where he stood – but he didn't. Instead, he went back out to the yard and washed away the night's toil under the freezing water of the pump. Then, with dread in his heart, he climbed the stairs to Athenais's room.

He opened the door softly and, by the light of a solitary candle, saw Pauline indicate that he wasn't to speak. A couple of steps brought him close enough to see that Athenais was asleep, curled up against Pauline like a child and with tearstains still on her cheeks.

Ashley wondered, after whatever she'd been through tonight, how long it would be before she turned to him for comfort. Bitterly and with an immense sense of loss, he suspected it might be a long time. He'd wanted to protect her. He'd promised to keep her safe. But, in the end, he'd failed. He hadn't been there when she needed him most … and though he knew she would never say it, it would be stupid of him to think she might ever have such whole-hearted faith in him again.

He'd thought he could sleep where he stood but he suddenly realised that there was no way he could sleep at all. With a nod for Pauline, he left the room as quietly as he'd entered it and went back down to where Francis and Jem were slumped at the table.

Francis said, 'How is she?'

'Sleeping. Pauline's with her.' He thought, *It ought to be me … but she doesn't want me now.* 'We'll see how she is in the morning.'

'So you haven't asked her anything about it?'

He shook his head. 'No. And I won't. If she wants to talk about it, she will. If she doesn't … that's her privilege.'

'Talking may help,' suggested Francis mildly.

'And then again, it may not,' came the distinctly edgy reply. 'Look … she's just gone through one of the worst experiences a woman can have – on top of which she's killed the misbegotten piece of shit who hurt her and been left sitting with his corpse for God knows how long. I don't know how that feels or how best to help her deal with it and neither do you. But I'm sure as hell not going to ask her to tell me anything she doesn't want to.' He stopped and drew a short, explosive breath. 'And now will one of you please get me a drink?'

Francis shoved the wine-bottle and a cup in his direction, then said abruptly, 'It was no accident. Last night. He knew we wouldn't be here.'

'I've gathered that much.' Ashley sloshed wine into the cup and drained it in one swallow. 'But that makes no difference now. And tomorrow, God help me, I've got to tell her about Archie.'

FIVE

As it turned out, Ashley didn't have the chance to tell Athenais anything at all because she refused to see anyone but Pauline and became distraught at the mere suggestion of receiving other visitors.

'It's not you personally,' Pauline told him, awkwardly. 'As you'd expect, she's shocked and confused.' *And convinced she's still not clean.* 'I've sent a message to Froissart saying she's sprained her ankle so he won't expect to see her for a couple of days. As for the rest ... you'll have to be patient.'

'It's not a question of patience,' replied Ashley wearily. 'It's Archie. He can't stay in the cellar indefinitely. We've told the maid that he got drunk and fell down the steps and I've had probably the worst doctor in Paris confirm that it was an accident. But we need to bury him – and we can't do that until Athenais knows.'

'No. Very well. If, by tonight, she still won't see you, I'll tell her myself.'

'You shouldn't have to. It ought to be me.'

'Why? Because you're determined to take responsibility for every leaf that falls?' She shook her head at him. 'You're not alone in this. So stop trying to bear everything on your own shoulders and let the rest of us help.'

'I'll try,' he said wryly, 'but it's not easy.' Then, 'Has she spoken to you about what happened?'

'No. And I haven't asked.'

He nodded and, after a small hesitation, 'She does know that I ... well, that I'd like to be with her?'

'I've told her. I'm just not sure how much is getting through. And now I'd better get back.' She met his eyes, her own decidedly grim. 'She's insisting on another bath.'

While, without a word of complaint, Jem – by now sporting a variety of bruises and a noticeably stiff shoulder – spent the day fetching and carrying water for Athenais, Ashley kicked his heels below stairs, waiting for a summons that he was beginning to fear wouldn't come.

At one point, catching Jem between trips, he said, '*Again?*'

'Aye. She wants to wash her hair.'

Ashley felt the first small seeds of desperation stirring in his chest. He said, 'It's the third time. This can't go on.'

'Dunno about that.' Jem shrugged uncomfortably. 'But I ain't about to say no – not after what's happened. I'll carry water all day and all night, if that's what she wants.' He straightened and looked Ashley in the eye. 'I let you down, Colonel – and I'm sorrier'n I can say.' Then he trudged off to get the next bucket.

Ashley went back to pacing the hall. He'd been at it for nearly an hour when Francis came downstairs and said, 'Go and get some sleep. After last night, you're dead on your feet. And this isn't helping Athenais.'

'I know.' Ashley shoved a hand through his hair. 'I know. But I need to see her – even if only for a moment – and she won't let me. I want to be sure she knows I'm here, waiting until she'd ready.'

'Pauline will have told her that.'

'It's not the same.' He stared at the floor. 'Last night, she told me not to touch her. She actually shrank away from me.'

Francis eyed him thoughtfully for a moment and then said, 'I can see how that would hurt. But, given the circumstances, it's not that surprising, is it?'

'No. And last night, I understood. Today, however, I'm finding it a bit more difficult.' He looked up. 'Jem thinks all this is his fault. I ought to tell him it isn't.'

* * *

Pauline let things slide until Athenais had taken her third bath and washed her hair for the second time. Then she said quietly, 'Enough, now. You're perfectly clean.'

'But I – I still *smell* him!'

'No. You only think you can. And scrubbing the skin from your body isn't going to change that. He's gone, Athenais. He can't hurt you ever again. It's over.'

'It isn't. It won't ever be over. Not now.'

Pauline looked at her for a long moment, trying to find the best thing to say.

'Do you want to tell me about it?'

Athenais shook her head.

'All right. But, if you change your mind, you've only to say.' Another pause; and then, as lightly as she was able, 'The Colonel is wearing out the hall floor. Are you ready to see him yet?'

The storm-cloud eyes showed the same signs of alarm they'd shown the last time Pauline had suggested it.

'No. I can't.'

'Why not?'

'I – I don't know. I just can't face him.'

'Well, the longer you put it off, the more difficult it will get.'

Athenais stared miserably down at her hands.

'It can't get more difficult.'

'Oh it can. Trust me. Don't you *want* to see him?'

This time her eyes filled with tears.

'Yes. Of course I want to! I m-miss him. But he'll ask me ... he'll ask ...'

'He won't. All he wants is to see how you are.' Pauline sighed and then, deciding to take the bull by the horns, 'Neither he nor Francis went to bed last night. They got rid of the Marquis's body, then they mopped and scrubbed until there wasn't any sign of what happened. Francis got some sleep earlier today but Ashley has spent the time pacing up and down, worrying himself sick about you. Also, there's something he needs to tell you.'

Athenais looked up, alarm edging into panic. 'What?'

Pauline sat down beside her and took her hands in a firm grip.

'You haven't asked ... and last night I was glad of that. But we can't go on keeping it from you. It's about your father.'

'Father? I don't ...' She stopped. 'Oh. He was in the kitchen with Jem when the men broke in. How could I have forgotten that? Was he hurt?'

'Worse than that. I'm sorry, Athenais. He's dead.'

'Dead? Father?' She looked bewildered and then shook her head. 'No. That can't be right. He'll be dead drunk. It's happened before enough times. And Jem's not hurt, so --'

'Jem was beaten and knocked out. But he's younger and quicker than Archie.' Pauline shook her a little. 'You have to listen to me, Athenais. It isn't a mistake. I wish it was. And I'm sorry I had to tell you of it now. But you need to know so we can make the appropriate arrangements.'

Athenais frowned. The ability to reason seemed a long way off and nothing Pauline was saying seemed to make any sense. 'Where is he?'

'In the cellar. It's the --'

'The *cellar*?' She stood up. 'What's he doing down there?'

'It's the coldest place and we couldn't think of anywhere else.' She stopped abruptly as Athenais headed for the door. 'Where are you going?'

'To wake him up. He'll catch his death down there.'

'Oh God,' muttered Pauline, by now thoroughly worried. Then, catching the girl's arm, 'Don't go now. We'll go in the morning.'

'Tomorrow?'

'Yes.'

'But --'

'You'll be feeling better by then.' *And maybe you'll have stopped believing he's just sleeping it off.* 'Don't worry. The Colonel's taking care of everything – just as he always does.'

Athenais drew a long, bracing breath and nodded.

'I should see him, shouldn't I?'

'Yes.'

Another nod. 'Later, then. After I've got dressed.'

'You don't need to bother about that.'

'I do,' came the obstinate reply. 'If I'm dressed, the marks won't show.'

* * *

Pauline related the gist of this conversation to Ashley and, at the end of it, said, 'So you can go up in half-an-hour or so, when she's made herself presentable. But you'll need to be careful. First off, her father's death hasn't even begun to sink in. She simply refuses to believe it. And, secondly, she's nervous about facing you.'

'Nervous?' he echoed blankly. 'Why?'

'I've no idea. To be honest, apart from the obvious shock and revulsion, I've no idea what she's thinking about anything – or even *if* she is, since it's clear she doesn't know what she wants. She makes sense one minute and none at all the next.'

'She still hasn't told you anything?'

'No. And, if I were you, I wouldn't ask.' She smiled wryly and before he could speak, added, 'Don't tell me. You weren't going to.'

* * *

Dressed in an old gown of dark blue wool, her hair tied back in a ribbon, Athenais sat on the window-seat, twisting her hands in her lap as she waited to hear Ashley's step outside her door. Anxiety gnawed at her. What would he say? What was he thinking? How would he look at her? Would she still be unable to let him touch her? Would he even *want* to? Her mind veered this way and that like a mouse in a cage. She wanted to see him so badly it hurt … and, at the same time, she wished she'd never agreed to do so.

Pauline had said something about Father; something that couldn't possibly be right. Part of her refused to think of it; another part urged her to go and see for herself. Everything seemed blurred … shrouded in a fog so thick she couldn't fight her way through it. This time yesterday, her world had been happy, optimistic and full of light. Today, there was only despair and shadows and the sense of something irretrievably lost. It felt as though she had somehow fallen into a deep, dark hole from which there was no way out.

The light tap at the door startled her, making her heart race. She tried to answer, but her mouth was tinder-dry and nothing came out. The door opened a few inches and Ashley looked across at her. He said, 'May I come in?'

She licked her lips and swallowed. 'Yes.'

He shut the door behind him and turned to look at her. The first thing that struck him was that she was looking anywhere but at him. The second was her extreme pallor and the bruises forming on her left cheek and around her throat … and a glance at her wrists showed him that they were worse. His gut clenched as he recalled the other marks, now hidden by her gown. She still hadn't looked at him, so he said carefully, 'I'll go, if that's what you want.'

Did she? She didn't know. But because he had repeatedly asked to see her … because Pauline said he'd been worried, she shook her head and managed to say, 'No.'

'Thank you.' He sat down and waited for her to speak. Then, when she didn't, he said, 'I'm so very sorry about Archie. Not only because you already have enough to bear – but that he's gone. I'll miss him.'

There it was again. The thing that Pauline had said and that couldn't possibly be true. She said uncertainly, 'He – he's in the cellar. Drunk.'

Ashley's heart ached for her.

'He's in the cellar. But he's not drunk. I wish he was.'

She frowned down at her hands. 'They ... they *killed* him?'

'Yes.'

'Why?'

'I don't know. They may not have meant to – but that doesn't change anything.' He paused. Then, 'Perhaps you'll allow me to come with you tomorrow to pay my respects.'

This time with an obvious effort and in a voice that shook just a little, she said, 'Respects? Oh. Yes.' *He's saying it's true. I ought to think about it - but I can't. I can't think about – about* that *and about Ashley at the same time.* 'If you wish.'

Silence fell and lingered. Ashley was so afraid of saying the wrong thing, he didn't know where to start. If it hadn't been for the haunted expression in her eyes and the way her hands wouldn't stay still, he might have thought her perfectly composed. As it was, he felt as if he was groping his way through a quagmire in the dark.

'Athenais ... why won't you look at me?'

A small but visible tremor passed through her.

'I will. I have.'

'No, darling. You haven't. Do you think you might try?'

She closed one hand hard over the other and very slowly forced her eyes up to his face. There was so much dread in them, Ashley felt suddenly sick. Rising, he said, 'I shouldn't have come, should I? I wanted to help – instead of which I seem to be making it worse. But when you think ...' He stopped just in time. The hurt had taken him unawares and he'd nearly said, *When you think you can bear the sight of me, let me know.* Instead, he made himself say, 'When you're ready to see me, you can tell Pauline.'

'No.' Athenais had seen the hurt – a hurt she hadn't meant to inflict. She'd also seen that he didn't look cold or distant or disgusted; all the things she'd feared he might. He just looked strained and concerned and very tired. But then, he was kind. He'd always been kind; and if he *did* feel disgust, his ingrained courtesy would never let him show it. She said breathlessly, 'It isn't you. I didn't know how ... that is, I thought you might ...' She stopped.

'You thought I might what?'

She shook her head and murmured despairingly. 'Nothing.'

Ashley sat down again, a little closer this time.

'You thought I might insist on hearing every ugly detail?'

'Perhaps.' The truth was that it didn't matter whether he did or not. She could never tell him the worst of it.

'I won't. Not ever – unless you choose to tell me. You also thought I might feel differently about you? I don't. It wasn't your fault and wouldn't have happened at all if I'd been here.'

She scarcely heard the last sentence. All she could think was that he *would* feel differently if he knew. Guilt lay like a stone on her conscience and a poison in her heart. She ought to tell him and be prepared to see his eyes condemn her before he walked away. *Say please, say please, say please.* The words rang in her head over and over, along with her own response. The single word that, more even than the rape itself, had left her defiled and unfit.

She wanted to vomit. Instead, she blurted, 'I'm sorry. Ashley ... I'm so sorry.'

'For what, love?'

He reached out to take her hand but before he could touch it, she was off in a flurry of skirts to the other side of the room.

She said, 'No. You mustn't. I c-can't bear it.'

The words were like a punch in the face but he kept both his expression and his tone perfectly level. 'You can't bear me to hold your hand?'

'No.' She folded her arms tight across her middle and bent her head so that he couldn't see her face. 'I can't ... I don't want ...'

'To be touched?'

'No.'

At all? he thought. *Or just by me?* But he didn't say it because he was afraid what her answer might be. He could comprehend some of the possible reasons she might feel like this and he'd known since he walked into the house last night that it would be a very long time before she'd be ready for intimacy. But he'd never expected her to refuse the comfort of his arms. He had thought she'd burrow into him as she had once before and let him hold her safe. The fact that she wasn't going to ... that she was deliberately shutting him out, cut straight through to the bone.

Naturally, he didn't say so. Instead, he stood up and said simply, 'I'm sorry you feel that way. But, if it's what you want, then of course I'll keep my distance.'

The pain inside her was clawing its way out again. She thought, *It's not what I want. It's what I deserve.* But said tonelessly, 'Thank you.'

Ashley inclined his head and crossed to the wash-stand.

'I'd better move my gear back upstairs.'

Athenais lifted her head, her eyes wide with misery and shock. Stupidly, she hadn't considered this. And suddenly, despite everything, she couldn't bear the thought of him being in a place that suddenly seemed very far away; a place where she couldn't see or hear him. Without stopping to think, she said, 'No. Don't.'

And that was when Ashley realised the full extent of her disorientation ... and that realisation made him forget his own hurt. He said gently, 'I can't stay here, love. You can see that, can't you?'

She could but she didn't want to. The very idea of his leaving sent panic rushing through every nerve.

'Couldn't you ... sleep in the other room? Just for a little while, until ...'

He almost said, *Until what?* But he was beginning to suspect that there was a lot more going on under the surface than he might ever know and that, as yet, putting her under even the slightest pressure was harmful.

'I'll do whatever will suit you best and for as long as you wish. You have only to say.'

She closed her eyes against the tears she refused to shed, unaware that he could see her throat working to contain them. Then, opening them again, 'I'm sorry.'

'Don't say that. You have nothing to apologise for – and certainly not to me.'

The tears came then, in a silent involuntary cataract.

'I do. I just don't know how.'

Watching her, with pure rebellion seething in his heart, Ashley did one of the most difficult things he'd ever done. He put his hands in his pockets and kept his promise.

* * *

He spent a largely sleepless night on the couch that they'd restored to its proper place after Nick had left. The thing was too short for him and therefore by no means comfortable but he'd slept in worse places so it wasn't that that kept him awake. What *did* was wondering if Athenais slept and, if she did, whether she would be plagued by nightmares; and then the question of what, if she was, he could do about it.

He stayed out of her way while she washed and dressed, hearing her familiar movements about the room and wondering if a night's rest had wrought any significant improvement. Since he had to show her Archie's body, he didn't think it very likely. The day, he suspected grimly, was only likely to get worse.

By the time he followed her downstairs, she was sitting at the kitchen table being bullied by Pauline into eating something.

Athenais said, 'I'm not hungry.'

'You said that yesterday. Eat your egg.'

'I don't want it.'

'I didn't ask if you *wanted* it.' Anxiety overlaid by impatience, marked both Pauline's voice and expression. 'I asked you to *eat* the damned thing.' She stopped, seeing Ashley lurking in the doorway. 'And you're as bad. To my knowledge, the only thing that passed *your* lips yesterday was half a bottle of wine. So sit down and have some bread and cheese.'

He took the seat opposite Athenais and, with a lop-sided smile, reached over and sliced the offending egg neatly into quarters before cutting himself a piece of cheese which he most assuredly didn't want.

'Four bites, love. That's all. And if I can do it, so can you.'

She sighed and stared down at her plate. Then, slowly but with determination, she ate.

* * *

The cellar was lit with as many candles as they'd been able to spare and Sergeant Stott lay on a raised board in a circle of them. Followed silently by Pauline and Francis and keeping Athenais behind him to block her view until they were on flat ground, Ashley led the way down the stairs. He didn't know exactly what to expect – but he had a strong feeling that it wouldn't be good.

He was right. The instant Athenais clapped eyes on her father's body, she stopped dead and gave a strange, almost unearthly howl, then immediately stopped it with her fingers. She stared and stared out of huge, dark eyes, her breathing fast and ragged.

She swayed and Ashley had to stop himself reaching for her and let Pauline support her in his stead.

At length, Athenais whispered, 'It's true. I didn't believe that it could be … but it is.' And then, taking a few more steps towards the still body, she said in English, 'Oh sodding 'ell – you daft old bugger. What've you gone and done? You wasn't supposed to go like this. You was supposed to be around plaguing me for years yet. And now, 'ere I am telling you I love you when you can't 'ear me no more. Ain't that just like you?'

Pauline, understanding the tone rather than the words, swallowed hard and Francis stared fixedly at the floor.

Ashley, forcing himself to remain perfectly still when all he wanted to do was hold her, said, still in English, 'He can hear you, love.'

Without turning her head, she said, 'Maybe. But I oughta told him afore now.'

'I think he knew.' He paused and then added wryly, 'And if there's any consolation to be had here – and God knows, there isn't much – at least he went the way he'd have wanted. In a good, honest fight … and fulfilling his promise.'

SIX

Two days later, under a lowering sky, they buried Archie in the churchyard of St Julien and on the following afternoon, Athenais returned to work. Thanks to Pauline listening to all the gossip in the Green Room and Francis paying apparently random visits to anyone he knew in the boxes, it soon became clear that, although there was some speculation about the Marquis d'Auxerre's current whereabouts, nobody seemed particularly worried. As yet, his body didn't appear to have washed up anywhere – leading Ashley to hope that, by the time it did, it would be unrecognisable. And no one was linking his name with Athenais.

'So far, so good,' observed Francis to Pauline.

And, 'Long may it last,' came the typical reply.

For Athenais, the first week was an unending struggle and the second one, scarcely less so. Off-stage, she had to force herself to do all the usual day-to-day things that no longer had any meaning; but life on-stage was somehow a little easier, though she knew her performances were no better than adequate. And at night she drew comfort from Ashley's quiet, undemanding presence on the other side of the door.

She didn't know what that quiet, undemanding presence was costing him. She didn't know that his every sense was attuned to her smallest sign of progress, or the lack of it. Nor did she know of the lengths he went to in order to avoid any awkwardness arising from his occupancy of the dressing-closet. He simply existed in a sort of limbo composed of watching and waiting. And hoping.

Ménage Deux was scheduled to go into rehearsal during the last week in January and, with the exception of Pauline, was due to be completely re-cast. Having already been taken to one side by Froissart and asked, bluntly, what the hell was the matter with Athenais, Pauline went to Francis and said, 'Given what she's been through, it's amazing she's able to go on-stage at all. But the usual flair is missing and by Act Five, she's exhausted. So I wondered how you'd feel --'

'About her playing either the wife or the mistress? Of course. Which would be best?'

'The mistress. The role is lively and flirtatious with just the right under-current of avarice and spite.' Pauline looked at him searchingly. 'Are you sure? If she doesn't recover her form, it will harm your play.'

'She'll be fine. And even if she isn't, it's a small price to pay,' he shrugged. 'Getting over what happened is bound to take time. We all know that – and Ashley more than any of us. Beneath the relaxed veneer, I suspect it's crucifying him – so anything we can do to help has got to be worth it. And then again,' he added with a grin, 'you must know that your slightest wish is my command.'

Accustomed by now to his habit of masking sincerity with a flippant manner, Pauline looked up at him and sighed. Then she did what she'd wanted to do for a very long time. She pulled his face down to hers and kissed him.

Francis, who had been waiting even longer, took full advantage, holding her hard against him and letting his hunger show. When they finally broke apart, Pauline let out a little huffing breath and said, in what was meant to be her usual tone but came out sounding confused, 'Well.'

'Well, indeed,' murmured Francis. His chest was rising and falling rather more rapidly than usual and his eyes lingered on her mouth. 'Very much so, in fact. You'll need to tell me what I did to deserve it.'

Unbelievably, she felt her cheeks grow hot. She didn't think she'd blushed properly for more than ten years. Struggling for some semblance of composure, she said, 'You offered to sacrifice something that means a great deal to you for the sake of our friends.'

'Oh – that.' He stepped back from her, his expression changing. 'I owe Ashley a debt. Not just for his help when Celia died but also for the fact that, if he hadn't got me away after Worcester, I'd probably still be rotting in an English prison. As for Athenais, it was my play that gave d'Auxerre his opportunity – so I think I owe her something, too.' He grinned suddenly. 'But if it earns me more rewards like this one, I'll happily sacrifice anything you like.'

* * *

The news that she was to be cast in *Ménage Deux* brought the first glimmer of a smile to Athenais's face in two seemingly interminable weeks. And when Pauline and Francis insisted on making her work on the role at home as well as at the theatre, she was left with little time in which to think and brood and worry.

Her courses came and, just like the first time, she shed tears of relief in private. Then, without quite realising it, she took the first tentative steps on the road to recovery. The first sign of this was when she awoke one morning to a thought which ought not to have been surprising but somehow was. It occurred to her that she'd survived rape once before … survived it, moreover, when she'd been much younger and had had no one to turn to. Logic said that, if she could do it once, she could do it again. A few days later came the realisation that, if she couldn't fight her way out of the thicket of thorns that currently surrounded her, she was giving the Marquis more power from beyond the grave than he'd ever had in life. Worse, he'd wanted to hurt Ashley and here she was, busily doing it for him. Somehow, she had to stop. She had to find a way of stiffening her spine … and shutting the Marquis away in some hidden corner of her mind until she could think of him without wanting to curl up in a dark hole and stay there.

During the last days of rehearsal, when she'd got her performance up to a level that both Francis and Pauline deemed acceptable, she was beginning – superficially at least – to manage better. Grief for her father still lay over her spirit like a pall; indeed, his loss seemed to affect the whole house in one way or another. But the stain on her conscience troubled her more. At times, she wasn't sure why that one small thing felt worse than the physical violation. Over and over again, she told herself that it shouldn't … yet, no matter how many times she repeated it, the fact remained that it did. In one single syllable, she'd betrayed Ashley in a way she considered unforgiveable. And she didn't know if she'd ever find the courage to admit it … or even if she should. Salving her own conscience at the price of his peace of mind was, at best, selfish and, at worst, cruel.

She was aware that he rarely sought her out these days and she understood why. In telling him not to touch her, she'd refused his comfort and he was finding that difficult. Sometimes she caught a look in his eyes that hinted that it was much worse than that. A look that suggested he was suffering beyond endurance – though it always vanished before she could be sure. He was unfailingly considerate and courteous and apparently possessed of an unending supply of patience. But she knew he'd retreated behind the invisible shield she remembered so well from their earliest days and that, unless she did something about it soon, he'd stay there where she couldn't reach him.

She missed him so much it was like slow starvation and wondered if he knew it and whether, if he didn't, she had any right to tell him. She missed the light in his extraordinary eyes when she smiled at him and the way laughter could gather there even though his mouth looked perfectly grave. She missed his teasing, his quick mind and his warmth at night. She missed the luxury of merely watching him shave.

There were times when she woke at night and paced her room. Twice she stopped to lean her cheek against the door that divided them, wanting nothing but to hear him breathe. The second time she almost set her hand to the latch. But guilt prevailed and she didn't.

* * *

Ashley found as many reasons as he could to stay out of the house. He spent time with Ned Hyde, discussing the situation in England and the King's chances of getting foreign aid. He also learned that William Brierley had been right about the marriage lines; that, on the date given, both Hyde's and Secretary Nicholas's records showed, independently of each other, that Charles couldn't possibly have been in St Germain-en-Laye.

At other times, Ashley fenced, played tennis and occasionally rode outside the city with Charles. It was nearly eight weeks since Nicholas had arrived with Colonel Maxwell's warning and there was still no mention of Honfleur, causing Ashley to wonder if Hyde was right and the whole plot had fallen through. This possibility coupled with the removal of the Marquis d'Auxerre suggested that a small amount of relaxation might be in permissible – with the result that he spent a couple of evenings in the *Chien Rouge* with Cyrano de Bergerac from which he returned less than sober but not quite drunk enough to step outside the mould he'd created for himself.

The constraints regarding Athenais were legion. *Don't say this … don't do that … remember to keep your hands to yourself. Don't let her see how hurt and helpless you feel. And don't ever let her see you less than fully dressed.* The litany went on and on. Sometimes he wondered how much longer he could stand it. And then, gritting his teeth, he told himself that he'd stand it as long as was necessary.

Sometimes at night he heard her moving around her room as if, like him, she was sleeping badly. Once he had an overwhelming sense that she was standing just outside his door. He lay utterly still in the darkness and held his breath … waiting, hoping, praying he might hear the click of the latch. But he didn't.

* * *

Ménage Deux opened to the same enthusiastic reception as its predecessor and Athenais received almost as great an ovation as Pauline. It was the first time Ashley had attended a performance since d'Auxerre's assault and, but for some strong words from Pauline, he probably wouldn't have attended this one either. He managed, however, to make the appropriately appreciative comments to both Athenais and Pauline and to congratulate Francis on a second masterpiece. Then he did what he'd been doing for the last month. He poured a large glass of wine and withdrew to the dressing-closet in order to be out of the way before Athenais came up to ready herself for bed. As happened quite frequently these days, he felt like smashing something. As ever, he controlled the impulse.

Not very much later and still with no trace of her usual exhilaration, Athenais also excused herself. Francis looked wryly at Pauline and said, 'Not exactly the reaction we'd been hoping for – and no sign of anything mending, either. Are you disappointed?'

'No. We were overly optimistic.' She handed him a glass of wine. 'Enough of that. It's a good play, Francis. Better than good, actually. Unless I'm much mistaken, you should prepare yourself for an approach from Floridor at the Bourgogne.'

'You think so?'

'Yes. You have a future and Josias isn't one to miss an opportunity.'

'Josias?'

'Josias de Soûlas. It's Floridor's real name. Surely you knew that?'

'Yes. I just didn't know that you were on first-name terms with him.'

'I'm not any more.'

'But?'

She sighed. 'Years ago – before my accident – he and I were lovers. Our relationship made working together difficult so I left the Bourgogne and joined the Marais. As it turned out, working for rival companies made our *relationship* difficult – so it ended.' She paused and, perhaps more sharply than she intended, added, 'I'm thirty-two years old, Francis – so you can't have thought me still a virgin. But, if you really want to know and it makes any difference whatsoever, he was the last man I ever slept with.'

'I wanted to know because you never say very much about yourself,' he replied mildly. 'As for making a difference – it doesn't, of course, because nothing can. And, if *I* have anything to do with it, the last man you sleep with will be me. Starting, perhaps, tonight?'

Pauline opened her mouth and then closed it again, unable to decide between three smart answers. In the end she chose none of them and said instead, 'The last man *ever?* That sounds very … permanent.'

'It's meant to. You see, I have a plan.'

'You do?'

'Yes. First, I'd like to take you to bed and make sure you enjoy it. And then, tomorrow – when you know exactly what you'll be getting and hopefully feel you might be able to love me, even just a little – I thought I'd ask you to marry me.' Tilting his head and bathing her in his peculiarly charming smile, he said, 'What do you think?'

This time, he had the satisfaction – not only of rendering her temporarily speechless but also of seeing her eyes become suspiciously bright. Finally, her usually crisp voice noticeably husky, she said, 'I like the first part. And I think I could love you rather more than a little. But the second part will need a lot of consideration.'

'Persuasion,' said Francis, 'is my speciality.' Taking her hands, he pulled her to her feet and into his arms. 'And if the only woman I've ever truly wanted to share the rest of my life feels she can love me more than a little, she can be assured I won't be taking no for an answer.'

* * *

While Francis was using his mouth and his voice and his hands to Pauline's immense satisfaction, Athenais was prowling around her room, completely unable to sleep. The play had gone well and, for the first time since what she now thought of as That Night, she'd actually enjoyed the performance. What she *hadn't* enjoyed was the look on Ashley's face when he thought she wasn't watching ... nor the fact that, sensing the rift between them, the other young ladies of the company had decided that he was once again fair game.

She climbed into bed, thumped the pillow and lay down with a bump. She shut her eyes and tried to calm the churning feeling behind her ribs. Half an hour later, she was still trying.

Ashley hadn't expected to sleep any better than he had the night before and the night before that. The single glass of wine which was all he'd had to drink was no help – and neither was the fact that he could hear Athenais padding around the room, prior to attacking her pillow. Yet somehow, exhaustion finally managed to catch up with him and he fell into the first really deep slumber he'd known in a while.

He awoke suddenly, groggy and disorientated, with every instinct warning him that there was someone else in the room. It was still dark but not completely so. Grey, shadowy light flowed in from the open doorway. He pushed himself up on one elbow and caught the scent of citrus and flowers. Then he saw her, sitting hunched on the floor near his feet, her arms wrapped around her upraised knees.

Aware of his movement and without turning her head, Athenais said, 'I know I shouldn't be here but I had to come.'

Ashley pulled his brain into some sort of working order but the first thought it came up with wasn't especially helpful. 'How long have you been sitting there?'

'A while. There's something I need to tell you.'

'All right.' He sat up and raked his hands through his hair. 'Go back and light a couple of candles and I'll be with you as soon as I've put some clothes on.'

'No. I can't do it like that.'

And I can't do it stark naked under a blanket, thought Ashley irritably. He said, 'The floor's like ice and you must be freezing. Go back to bed and we'll talk there, if that's what you want.'

'No.' Still she didn't turn to look at him. 'I need the dark. If I see your face or know that you can see mine, I'll lose my nerve.'

He didn't like the sound of that one bit but it had the effect of banishing his momentary irritation.

'There isn't anything you can't say to me, Athenais. I thought you knew that.'

'Yes. But this is different.' She drew a faintly unsteady breath and said, 'It will be best if you could listen without saying anything.'

God. More rules. 'I think I can manage that.'

'Thank you.' She bent her head over her knees briefly and then, raising it again, said, 'He wanted to hurt both of us. Not just me but you as well. It wasn't about possession any more. It was about revenge because I'd chosen you instead of him and because you ... you'd added injury to insult. So t-taking me was a means to both ends.' She stopped, as if groping for the words and then forced herself to continue. 'The details don't matter. It's enough to say that he – he enjoyed taking his time. If he'd just r-raped me, I might have stood it better. But he didn't.' She pressed the heels of her hands over her eyes and let them drop. 'When he had me pinned to the floor, I knew that no one would come and I c-couldn't fight him off. And I thought that, when he'd done what he came for, he'd go. So I asked him to just get on with it.' Another shuddering breath. 'And he said, *'Spread your legs and say please.'*

The nausea that had been rolling around Ashley's stomach threatened to choke him.

The bastard. The utter bastard. Of course it would never be enough for him merely to violate her body. He'd have to force her to humiliate herself as well.

He swallowed the surge of anger and waited for her to continue.

'So I did.'

For a moment, even if she hadn't asked him not to interrupt, the self-disgust in her tone would have rendered him incapable of it.

Athenais brushed the sleeve of her robe over her face and stood up.

'I'm sorry,' she said. 'So sorry. But I needed to tell you. And now I'll go.'

'Wait,' he said. But she didn't – leaving him to damn the fact that he hadn't a stitch on.

As he hurriedly dragged on his clothes he tried to understand why, if it was upsetting her so much, it had taken her all this time to tell him. And then all the pieces began to fall sickeningly into place. Anger turned to sheer, white-hot rage.

She was curled up near the pillows, still wrapped in the hideous pink chamber-robe. Without bothering to ask permission, Ashley sat on the foot of the bed and looked at her. Her fingers were busily knotting and unknotting the belt of her robe and her eyes were full of mingled misery and apprehension. He thought, *I'd like to hold you but you're still so damaged that you can't even bear to have me take your hand. And I don't dare hold mine out to you because I can't bear to watch you back away*

He tried to keep his voice neutral but the overwhelming fury inside him made working up to this gradually and with tact totally impossible. He said, 'Athenais ... have you been worrying about this because you thought it somehow made what happened your fault?'

She nodded but said nothing.

'And you thought I might see it the same way?'

Another nod. Then, in a very low, voice, 'Don't you?'

'No. I don't. And neither should you. Did you invite him into the house?'

'No.'

'Ever give him the least encouragement?'

'No.'

'Welcome his attentions, even for a moment?'

She shivered. 'You know I didn't.'

'Quite. I know you didn't.' He paused, still fighting for control. 'And what did you do as soon as the opportunity presented itself?'

This was plainly unexpected. She blinked and said, 'I hit him with the poker.'

'Yes, my brave, clever girl. You did.' He smiled at her, albeit grimly. 'So based on all this ... how do you deduce that any part of it was your fault?'

'I don't *know!*' The words seemed to burst from her. 'It's just how I feel. As if – as if I've betrayed you. And I wish I hadn't said it.'

'Well, I'm glad you did. Firstly, you didn't betray me and it's nonsense to think you did. And secondly, I'd sooner you betrayed me a hundred times over than endure a moment's pain. No.' This as she would have spoken. 'I'm not finished yet. You killed d'Auxerre – more by accident than anything else, I imagine. But look on it as having done him a favour. Because if you hadn't despatched him, I would have done. The only difference is that I'd have made it last longer and hurt more.' He stood up. 'And now we've both confessed, I suggest you get some sleep.'

Not at all sure how things stood between them, Athenais said awkwardly, 'You, too.'

'No. I'm going to walk off my temper in the rain. I'll be back later and, if you wish it, we'll talk more then. In the meantime, however, I'm not fit company for anyone. Forgive me.' On which note, he left the room.

* * *

He walked for hours without noticing where he went. He'd already known what d'Auxerre had done to her. He'd seen the marks when he'd walked in to find her huddled on the floor. But hearing her speak of it in that tired, flat little voice … listening to her apologise for what she called a betrayal but which he saw as the ultimate, vile humiliation inflicted by a sick mind … aware that he hadn't been there when she needed him … Ashley didn't know whether he wanted to vomit or smash his fist through a wall or cry. None of which self-indulgences were the least use since what had happened couldn't be mended.

Gradually, his temper cooled and he regained some of his customary self-possession. And that was when he thought of what *could* be mended.

She'd told him something that had been eating away at her for weeks; something which had plainly been incredibly hard for her to speak of. And what had he said? *You thought it would make me feel differently about you? It doesn't.*

He grimaced sardonically and thought, *Oh, well done, Ashley. What more reassurance could she possibly need? You fired questions at her like a bloody lawyer and then walked out – when what you* should *have done was to tell her that you love her. That you'll always love her. And that it's* because *you love her that you're behaving like a prize ass.*

By the time he finally returned to the house, wet and half-frozen, Athenais had already left for the theatre. In a sense, he was glad. It might give him time to get his thoughts in order before he went to her on his knees.

He'd no sooner entered the hall and was struggling out of his sodden coat when Jem erupted from the kitchen, brandishing a letter with an all-too-familiar seal.

'Been here two hours and more,' said Jem. 'The cove what brought it said it was urgent.'

Ashley broke the seal and scanned the brief message. It was urgent, all right.

Honfleur possibly imminent.

Wait on me immediately.

E. Hyde

SEVEN

Tired, cold and soaked to the skin, Ashley uttered a stream of French curses and then followed them up with a volley of English ones.

Jem grinned. 'Bugger me! I ain't heard some of them words in a good long while.'

'I'm glad you're impressed,' came the clipped reply. 'Get your coat.'

The grin dwindled into uncertainty. 'What?'

'Hyde wants to see me but I'm damned if I'm going out again tonight. I'll visit him first thing in the morning. And you're going to the Louvre to tell him so.'

'Me?' asked Mr Barker, aghast.

'That's what I said. What's the matter? Afraid to get your feet wet?'

'I'd as soon not – but it ain't that. They'll never let me in, Colonel.'

'They will because you'll be in possession of a letter bearing Hyde's seal.' He brandished the letter he'd half-crumpled in his fist. 'This one – on which I'll add a note. So pull your boots on and get your coat and don't come back until you're sure Hyde's got the message.'

When Jem had set off, grumbling, Ashley went in search of dry clothes and tried to make sense of the jumble inside his head. He needed to clarify his ideas about the Honfleur situation and how he intended to deal with it so that he could brief Hyde as concisely as possible the following morning. Unfortunately, he was bone-weary and wound as tight as a coiled spring which made thinking uncommonly difficult. He was also finding that, despite his best endeavours, his mind kept veering back to Athenais and the mess he'd made of their last conversation. He didn't know whether to wait for her to come home so he could attempt to put things right – or whether to go and hide in the attic rather than chance making everything worse. After half an hour of pacing up and down but no nearer making a decision, he started to wonder if this was what insanity felt like.

In the end, he came to the conclusion that hiding was not only cowardly but also pointless since it would only postpone the inevitable. The most sensible course was to stay downstairs on the pretext of speaking to Francis and hope Athenais's expression offered some reliable clue as to how best to proceed. If she wanted to avoid him, he'd know. And if not … well, if not he'd cross that bridge when he came to it.

He sat in the parlour and closed his eyes for a few minutes. The next thing he knew was the sound of the front door closing and wet cloaks being removed and shaken. Ashley dragged his hands over his face, hauled himself to his feet and tried to reassemble his wits. He hadn't meant to fall asleep and, since the effect of his brief doze was to make him feel worse than he had before, he wished he hadn't. Then the door opened and Athenais walked in, closely followed by Francis and Pauline.

In some distant corner of his brain, Ashley registered the fact that Francis had his arm about Pauline's waist but he didn't bother to wonder about that. Instead, he watched Athenais's eyes widen with something that might have been pleasure and saw her take a sudden, impulsive step towards him before checking herself.

He kept both his smile and his words neutral and let them encompass Francis and Pauline as well. 'Did the play go well tonight? Not that I need ask – since it always does.'

'The house wasn't full,' remarked Pauline, stepping away from Francis with slightly heightened colour. 'This incessant downpour, I suppose. I think we'll all be better for some hot spiced wine and a bite of supper.'

'I'll help you,' said Athenais quickly before Francis could volunteer. She'd spent most of the day thinking that she wanted to talk to Ashley … but now the moment was upon her, she realised that she didn't know what to say. More to the point, she didn't know what *he* might say and wasn't prepared to risk having a potentially awkward conversation where they could be interrupted at any minute. 'I'll cut some bread and cheese.' And promptly left the room.

Pauline looked first at Francis and then at Ashley before spreading her hands in a gesture of defeat. 'Jumpy as a cat,' she said. And followed in the girl's wake.

Closing the door behind her, Francis said, 'Any progress worth mentioning?'

'Some.' Although he didn't pretend to misunderstand, Ashley had no intention of discussing it so he lifted one enquiring brow and said, 'Less, it would seem, than you.'

Francis grinned and said simply, 'I'm going to marry her.'

Ashley stared at him for a moment, completely taken aback.

'Pauline? Seriously?'

'Seriously. Oh – she hasn't said yes yet. But she will. Mainly because I won't give up until she does.' He hesitated and then added, 'I never expected to feel this way about anyone. It ... it's beyond my comprehension. Unfortunately, just at present, it's slightly beyond hers as well. But I intend to change that.'

'In which case,' said Ashley, extending his hand, 'I wish you all the luck in the world. She's an exceptional woman.'

'More so than I probably deserve,' agreed Francis, gripping the outstretched fingers. 'But I'm not about to let that stand in my way. I'm sure you know the feeling.'

'Not exactly.' Ashley stepped away and said, 'I've no wish to dampen your spirits but I've had word from Ned Hyde. It seems that the Honfleur plot is still active and likely to happen quite soon. I don't have any details but I'm seeing him tomorrow and will know more then. I'd appreciate you being here when I get back so we can discuss our options.'

Francis nodded, all traces of levity and euphoria wiped from his face. 'You've a plan?'

'The outline of one. It will require some refining – and an extra player. But I've some thoughts on that as well.' His mouth curled wryly. 'Your opinion will be interesting.'

* * *

In the kitchen, Athenais sawed laboriously through a loaf and cast a brief, sideways glance at Pauline. It was the first chance for a private conversation they'd had all day and there was a question she was burning to ask. Finally, laying aside one hopelessly uneven hunk of bread and starting to cut the next, she said, 'Pauline ... are you and Francis ... I mean, are the two of you ...'

'Yes.' Crossing to her side and surveying the damage, Pauline said, 'Give me that knife before you cut your fingers off.'

Athenais leaned over to kiss her cheek.

'That's wonderful!'

'Don't get too carried away.' Two beautifully symmetrical slices joined Athenais's sorry effort. 'It's not as though it's likely to last.'

'Not last? Why wouldn't it?'

'Do I really need to spell it out? Look at me – then look at him. On top of which, he's a bloody Viscount.'

Athenais leaned against the table and folded her arms.

'Do you love him?'

'What do you think?'

'Has he said that he loves you?'

'Mind your own business.' Pauline laid the bread to one side and started slicing cheese. 'Are you and the Colonel speaking to each other yet?'

The brief light faded from Athenais's face.

'We were never *not* speaking to each other.'

'Good morning and pass the salt? Hardly what I'd call communication.'

There was a long silence. Then, hesitantly, 'I talked to him last night. I ... I told him a bit about what happened.'

Pauline abandoned the cheese and eyed her shrewdly. 'And?'

'I don't know. The thing I was most ashamed of and thought I'd never be brave enough to tell him, he ... he didn't seem to think important at all. But something else made him so angry he walked out.' She pause and then added, 'All day I've been trying to make myself believe that, given time, everything may still be all right. Only I can't yet. Not quite.'

'Do you *want* everything to be all right?'

'Of course! Yes. Of course I do.' The grey eyes were suddenly suspiciously bright. 'I just feel as if a huge gulf has opened up between us and I don't know how to cross it.'

'You could start by not pushing him away,' said Pauline bluntly. And, picking up the tray, 'Think about it. The remedy's in your hands.'

* * *

Ashley turned as the door opened on Pauline and Athenais bearing trays of sustenance and said, 'I don't suppose Jem is back yet?'

'Not that I've seen,' replied Pauline. 'What took him out in this weather?'

'An unexpected errand.' Ashley accepted a cup of mulled wine and retreated to the hearth again. Then, looking at Athenais, 'I don't know how late he'll be but I need to speak with him when he comes in so perhaps I should sleep upstairs tonight, rather than disturb you.' He saw the dismay and self-doubt in her eyes before her lashes veiled them and, feeling a faint quiver of hope, added, 'Or not. If that would be all right?'

She nodded and huddled over her wine-cup. 'Yes.'

Pauline shot Francis a meaningful glance and he picked up his cue without missing a beat.

'I'll wait for Jem,' he said firmly. 'What was it you wanted to know?'

'Just that he delivered his message to the appropriate quarter.' Put into words, Ashley realised how lame it sounded. 'It was to Hyde – so there's a chance he was denied entry.'

'Jem is a slippery fellow who rarely takes no for an answer. But I'll enquire when he comes in, just the same. Meanwhile, I suggest you go to bed. You look like a day-old corpse.' He refilled the Colonel's half-empty cup and said, 'Go – and take that with you. As you once pointed out to me, everything else will wait until tomorrow.'

'Yes. Thank you.' Ashley hesitated briefly, looking down on Athenais's bent head. 'Goodnight, then.'

The door closed behind him and silence fell. Finally, Pauline said, 'If you want to start building a bridge, Athenais, now would be the time.'

She looked up. 'I do. But I don't know how.'

'Of course you do. It's been well over a month. Time to stop putting yourself first and start remembering that Ashley is a man, not a machine and that he's hurting every bit as much as you. So go and do something about it.'

When Athenais had left the room, Francis said mildly, 'Given everything that's happened to her, wasn't that a bit harsh?'

'No. She can't wallow forever and the thing that will help her most now is helping him. In my opinion, he's waited long enough.'

* * *

Ashley sat down on the edge of the couch and tried to summon the energy to remove his clothes. She hadn't seemed to want him to retire to the attic – but she hadn't given any indication of wanting to be near him either. There were things he needed to say and he knew what they were. He just wasn't sure he was up to saying them now without making a mess of it.

He dragged off his coat and dropped his head in his hands, breathing deeply. When he looked up, Athenais stood in the doorway.

She said haltingly, 'I know you're tired so I won't keep you from your bed. I just wanted to ask ...'

'Yes?'

'What I told you this morning ... the thing you said didn't matter ... did you mean it?'

He impaled her on a very level stare

'Do you think I'd have said it if I didn't? That I'd lie to you about such a thing and at such a time?'

'No. But I felt so badly about it that it was hard to accept that you wouldn't blame me. And then, afterwards ... you were so angry that I wondered ... I wondered ...'

Ashley didn't know if it was a good thing or not that she was fixating on something d'Auxerre had made her say rather than his vicious violation of her body. He said quietly, 'I wasn't angry with you. I thought I'd said that. I was furious with d'Auxerre for just about everything. And I was even more furious with myself for not being there when you needed me.'

She shook her head, frowning.

'You couldn't have known.'

'Perhaps not. But that doesn't absolve me.' He smiled faintly. 'You see? Guilt can surface whether we deserve it or not. And while we're on the subject, I owe you an apology for this morning.'

'You don't. The things you said helped.'

'Did they?' He let his hands lie loose between his knees. 'I can't think why. I fired a lot of questions and facts at you, then walked out when what I *should* have said is that I love you. That I'll always love you and that I'll wait as long as you like if, in the end, you'll let me at least *try* to make it better.' He stopped and then added bitterly, 'No. That's nonsense. There's no way I can make it better, is there? No way even to break through this wall that's built up between us when you can't stand the thought of me touching you.'

Athenais stared him, appalled.

'No! It wasn't ... oh God. Is that what you thought?'

'What else was I to think? I've seen you on-stage and rehearsing with Francis. The same embargo doesn't apply there, does it?'

A lump formed in her throat and she tried to swallow it.

She said, 'Because they don't matter! You – it's different with you. I felt so *dirty*. All the time. I didn't want you smeared with that. And I thought ... I couldn't imagine how you would ever want to touch me again. How you could bear it.'

'Then you're as wrong as you could possibly be. What I can't bear is *not* being able to touch you. I'm not talking about sex – though I'd rather you didn't run away with the idea I'll never want to make love to you again. I'm talking about holding you when you cry and being there to catch you when you think you'll fall. Just a basic level of comfort that I need as much as I believe you do. The fact that, as yet, you can't accept it is ... difficult.' He stood up and managed a weary smile. 'Don't look so tragic. That's my problem, not yours. I've said I'll wait – and I will. But I'd be grateful if, in the meantime, you could try not to shut me out completely.'

Suddenly, the tears she'd been trying not to shed were sparkling on her lashes. Blinking them away, she crossed the room to lay her hands and her brow against his chest.

'I don't want to shut you out at all.'

The shock of unexpectedly receiving what he'd given up hoping for stopped his breath for a moment and caution kept his hands well away from her.

'You don't?'

'No. No and no and no. Not ever. I don't know how you can still see me the same way and not mind what happened. But --'

'I mind,' he said, with grim understatement. 'But for you. Not for myself.'

Her fingers tightened on his shirt and she leaned a little closer.

'I love you so much. And I'm sorry. I never meant to hurt you like this.'

'I know that.'

'Then ... do you think,' she said, looking up into his eyes, 'do you think you could hold me for a little while?'

Ashley's arms closed about her on something suspiciously like a groan.

'For as long as you like, love. And as often as you want.' *But, for the foreseeable future, I'll continue sleeping on the couch.*

* * *

On the following morning, Ashley walked in on Sir Edward Hyde before he'd finished breakfast. Swallowing a mouthful of ham and pushing back his chair, the Chancellor said irritably, 'I expected to see you last night.'

'Life is full of disappointments. But I doubt the last twelve hours brought any significant developments and I'm here now. What is the situation?'

Both the tone and the chilly expression in Colonel Peverell's eyes spoke of impatience barely held in check. Hyde said, 'Yesterday, the King received a letter. It hinted at the possibility of some kind of deal ... an arrangement with the right people, if you like ... that might lead to His Majesty's restoration.'

'Oh God.' Ashley dropped uninvited into a chair and tossed his hat on the floor beside him. 'Don't tell me. Charles swallowed it wholesale.'

'Naturally. In his position, wouldn't you?'

'Given the strength of Cromwell's grip – no, I wouldn't. Do you have this letter?'

Hyde shook his head. 'I've read it, of course. But the King is holding tight to it.'

Ashley shut his eyes for a moment and then, opening them again, said, 'All right. You'd better start at the beginning. How did it arrive?'

'It went directly to His Majesty.'

'That, in itself, doesn't bode well. Approaches of that kind would normally be made through yourself. Was it brought by messenger or did it come alongside other correspondence?'

'I don't know. Does it matter?'

'Yes. I'm trying to establish whether it got here through legitimate channels or whether we have someone inside this building with their own agenda.' He thought for a moment. 'I'll get back to that. For now, tell me what was said.'

'It intimated that a meeting could be arranged somewhere on the coast, at a time and location to be mutually agreed, between the King, the Duke of York ... and, amongst others, Major-General Lambert.'

Ashley's brows soared.

'Lambert? That's a nice touch. He's probably the least objectionable of Cromwell's generals and, from what one can gather, deep as a well. He also refused Ireland – ostensibly over the title he was offered but more likely because he didn't want to inherit Ireton's mess. Yes. I can see how it might be assumed we'd believe that.'

'But you don't.'

'No. But then, it's my function to be continuously suspicious. Also, it's too soon. Lambert – or anyone else, for that matter – would have to be assured of having a goodly proportion of the army behind him before making this kind of offer. He'd also have to be so far in opposition to Cromwell that he feared for his own liberty. If that's true of Lambert, nothing we know supports it.' He paused again. 'Put in a nutshell, what we have here is this. We've been warned of a possible plot to lure Charles and James to Honfleur where assassins await them. And now we've been handed the carrot that's going to get them there.'

'I suppose,' remarked Sir Edward judiciously, 'that we have to look at it that way.'

'If you can think of another way to look at it without putting His Majesty at risk, I'd be glad to hear it,' returned Ashley acidly. Then, when Hyde merely looked nettled, he said, 'We'll need to play along. Respond with cautious interest and wait for another letter, naming time and place. If it's Honfleur, we'll be fairly sure what we're dealing with. The unfortunate part is that we can't now keep the King in the dark. That is – I'm assuming you haven't already said anything?'

'No. It was the main reason I wanted to see you last night.'

'Of course. So do you want to talk to him – or shall I?'

The Chancellor drew a long, faintly irritated breath.

'Since you appear to have it all nicely worked out, I suggest that you do it.'

'Not to mention that this is precisely the kind of scenario Charles keeps me around to deal with.' Ashley retrieved his hat and stood up. 'Very well. I'll do it now. But a word of caution, Sir Edward. Don't weaken my hand by letting him talk you round; and don't give him any encouragement to run counter to my advice. If he starts making moves without my knowledge, I can't protect him. And, with all due respect, neither can you.'

* * *

He had to kick his heels in the King's apartments for over half-an-hour before His Majesty returned from calling upon his mother and younger sister in a far-flung part of the palace.

'Ashley?' said Charles with surprise tinged with wariness. 'My apologies. I didn't know you were here. Have you been waiting long?'

'Nothing to signify, Sir. I probably should have sent word – but since I was already here, I hoped we might speak privately.'

The dark Stuart eyes rested on him with sardonic resignation.

'You've been talking to Hyde. Again.'

'Yes. Under the circumstances, you must have expected him to send for me.'

'I suppose so. You're here to preach caution.'

Ashley grinned. 'That would make a pleasant change for me, wouldn't it? But no. Actually, there's a little more to it than that.'

'You'd better sit down, then. But before we talk, you'll doubtless be interested to hear that my Cousin Rupert has sailed to the mouth of the Loire and should arrive in Paris very soon.'

'That's good news, Sir. No doubt you're looking forward to having him at your side.'

'Yes. At least, I think so.' Charles hesitated and then apparently decided against explaining himself. Directing another, more searching glance, at Ashley, he said, 'You don't look well. Is the leg wound still bothering you?'

'Not particularly – though the muscle still stiffens if I sit for any length of time,' he replied briskly. 'Sir, Chancellor Hyde has told me of this letter you've received and I can fully understand your desire to take it at face value but --'

'But you don't think I should.'

'Sadly, no. I don't.'

'Why not?'

'For a number of fairly compelling reasons which, with your permission, we'll come to in a minute. But first I'd like to see the letter – and hear how it came to you.'

Crossing the room, Charles unlocked a drawer and withdrew a sheet of paper. As he handed it over, he said, 'It must have been delivered some time yesterday afternoon – probably by a messenger, I imagine. I found it waiting on my desk.'

'Not mixed with other correspondence?'

'No. But letters come in all the time. I'm deluged with the damned things.'

Ashley scanned the page in front of him. Its contents were pretty much as Hyde had described them – the only addition being that His Majesty could indicate his interest in exploring this opportunity by strolling in the gardens of the Tuileries Palace wearing a red plume in his hat. It was signed *A Loyal Subject.* Ashley groaned. There were times when he couldn't believe the depths of stupidity that some fellows sank to.

He said bluntly, 'If whoever wrote this did so in good faith, he wouldn't be so dead set on anonymity. However, let him think you're interested, by all means. In fact, I'd like you to. But don't pin your hopes on it leading to a meeting with Major-General Lambert because it won't.'

'You can't be sure of that.'

'Yes, Sir. I think I can.' And in concise terms, he recited the arguments he'd already laid before Hyde. At the end, he said, 'Lambert won't come – and even if he did, he's not in a position to help you. Truthfully, I doubt he knows anything at all about this. Someone is taking his name in vain.'

Charles stirred restlessly in his chair. 'To what end?'

'If my information is correct – and I suspect that it is – to a very undesirable end, Sir.' Ashley paused, still wishing he didn't have to do this but seeing no alternative. 'I believe this is the opening move in a plot to assassinate both yourself and your brother.'

The dark eyes flew suddenly wide.

'*What* information?'

'It isn't particularly detailed. Only that there might be a plan afoot to lure the two of you to the coast so you could be ... disposed of.'

'How long have you known this?'

'Some weeks. I passed what I knew to Sir Edward and --'

'But neither of you thought fit to inform me?'

'We've been waiting to see if anything came of it. Now, seemingly, it has.' He met the King's angry expression calmly and said, 'My job is to find out exactly what the situation is and check all the details before deciding how to deal with it. And I never tell anyone more than is strictly necessary.'

'Even me?'

'Not even you, Sir.' He paused. 'There's a possibility that this scheme is being discreetly driven from Secretary Thurloe's office – but I have no proof of that. Yet. At the moment, I'm still waiting to find out if this really is a serious attempt on your life and, for that, I need you to encourage this fellow to write to you again and to alert me as soon as he does so.'

'And then?'

Ashley stood up and eased the stiffness in his thigh.

'Then I'll instigate whatever measures seem most appropriate. My priority, obviously, will be keeping yourself and the Duke of York alive.'

Charles also rose, the ghost of a smile curling his mouth.

'For which we both thank you.'

'Thank me when it's over, Sir. Because the game will be played by my rules – and you may not like them.'

EIGHT

'So there it is,' finished Ashley, having relayed the gist of both meetings to Francis. 'The idiotic business of the red feather means we may be dealing with bungling amateurs but we can't assume that when His Majesty's life is at stake.'

Francis nodded. 'So we wait for a second letter?'

'Yes. And in the meantime, we start preparing the ground. It's possible we'll need a little help from Pauline. Do you think she'd be averse to that?'

'I imagine that would depend on what you were asking her to do.'

'Nothing either dangerous or difficult. But I don't want Athenais knowing anything about it. She's beginning to recover and I'm not going to allow any new worries to interfere with that.'

'Pauline will agree with you on that score, I'm sure. So what do you need her to do?'

'We'll require appropriate clothing. And I'm hoping that she can provide it from the theatre's wardrobe.'

Laughter gleamed in the sapphire eyes.

'You mean we're going to dress up? How delightful.'

'It's not likely to be nearly as much fun as you think. You are going to impersonate the Duke of York – and will therefore have to avoid being killed by mistake.'

'Ah. Right.' Francis leaned back in his chair, absorbing this. Then, 'Since, like yourself, James is fair-haired, while the King, like myself, is not – how come the roles are not reversed?'

'Because I'll be playing the part of the trusty coachman, with Jem up behind dressed as a groom. I imagine Hyde can supply us both with the necessary livery.'

'Wouldn't the King be more likely to go on horseback rather than by coach?'

'Perhaps. But then he'd be accompanied by a party of gentlemen and the quiet assassination in some back-alley would become a pitched battle. I'm guessing they won't want that.'

'I suppose not. So who's going to --?'

'I'll come back to that. For now, let's start at the beginning. If there is a second letter and it names Honfleur as the rendezvous point, I think we can assume that it's the plot Eden warned us about – and therefore put our own plans into action. Originally, I'd hoped to keep Charles completely out of the picture but that's no longer possible. Since it's almost certain that someone will be keeping track of his movements, he and James have to be seen setting out for the coast. If they don't think he's taken the bait, they'll abort the whole plan.'

'Wouldn't that be for the best?' asked Francis.

'No. We've had advance notice of this one. If they're forced to cancel it, there's a distinct possibility they'll come up with something else – and next time, we may not be so lucky.'

'Even supposing we foil this one, they could do that anyway.'

'They *could*,' agreed Ashley, 'but if things go as I hope, I don't think they will. If we can find the merest scrap of proof that Thurloe has sanctioned a scheme to murder the man who many people still regard as the rightful King, Hyde will make it public. And that ought to be enough to stop them trying again and also give Cromwell a headache.'

'Now there's a winsome thought.'

'Isn't it?' Ashley poured himself some ale and pushed the jug across the table. 'But to resume. Charles and James will appear to leave for Honfleur, accompanied by Jem and myself. So far, so good. The next part is trickier and will require some organisation. We'll need a second coach and a reliable driver for you and the man I hope will masquerade as Charles. At a suitable, pre-arranged spot, both coaches meet and we effect the exchange. Charles and James drive back in the direction of Paris, spending the night at some out-of-the way inn; and the four of us journey on to Honfleur.' He paused, frowning a little. 'That's the part that I'm most worried about. I'd be happier if the King and his brother were being taken to safety by a couple of well-trained fellows with muskets. There's a small chance that I can get help with that. If not … well, we'll cross that bridge when we come to it.'

'What about Sir Will Brierley?' suggested Francis.

'No. He's involved in some nefarious scheme of his own that I'm probably better off not knowing about.' *And I'm not as sure of him as I once was.* But he kept that thought to himself and said instead, 'The one part of all this that we can't plan for is what is actually going to happen at Honfleur. We don't know who the assassins are or how many of them there will be.'

'Or whether they'll simply shoot us in the back as soon as we break cover,' remarked Francis wryly. 'And there's another jolly thought.'

'Pistols are noisy. I'm putting my faith in them not wanting to attract undue attention.'

'Oh. Knives, then. As one of the primary targets, that makes me feel *so* much better. Speaking of which ... who do you think you can persuade to take the leading role?'

Ashley grinned and took his time about answering. Then, 'How much do you know about Cyrano de Bergerac?'

For a moment, Francis's expression was one of utter disbelief. Finally, he said, 'Discounting the gossip and aside from the celebrated occasion when he saved your life? Virtually nothing. You surely don't mean that as a serious suggestion.'

'You have a better one?'

'I've no ideas on the matter at all. But ... God, Ashley! De Bergerac? *Really?*'

'Yes, really.'

'Then you'd better not tell Hyde. He'll have a fit.'

'Several, probably.' Ashley paused and then, not without a hint of amusement, said, 'I've a fair idea of why you doubt my sanity but --'

'It's de Bergerac's sanity that worries me.'

'I've gathered that. But – loose cannon though he may be – he's not the completely wild barbarian of popular rumour. He's neither stupid nor lacking in moral fibre. And the fact that he's fought countless duels and is still alive says a great deal about his fighting skills. If he agrees to help us, there are worse men to have at your back.'

Francis sighed. 'Not to mention that we don't have much choice?'

'That too. Have I your agreement to approach him?'

'Do you need it?'

'Since you'll be risking your neck in this venture, it seems only fair.'

'Thank you for reminding me. But yes. By all means go and talk to the fellow. If he's lunatic enough to throw in his lot with us, it merely makes him no madder than you or I.'

* * *

While Ashley was off trying to track down Cyrano de Bergerac, Francis towed Pauline into her bedroom and shot the bolt. She tilted her head and looked at him.

'Don't think I don't appreciate the thought or admire your stamina – but it's the middle of the day and I'd as soon not have Athenais and the Colonel looking at us sideways.'

'Ashley is out. And I don't mind Athenais imagining that I've been overcome with lust,' he grinned, sliding hand around her waist. 'Sadly, however, that's not the reason we're here – much though I'd like it to be.'

'Oh? Then you'd better stop that, hadn't you?' she said as he nipped his way down her neck.

'Must I?' His mouth found its way to hers. 'When are you going to say you'll marry me?'

'Not today.' She twisted away from him and, holding him at arms' length, said a shade breathlessly, 'Why are we here?'

'I've forgotten. You distract me.'

'Obviously, it doesn't take much.'

'With you, darling? Nothing at all.' He gave her a deliberately lascivious glance and watched her skin warm even as her mouth quivered on the edge of laughter. It was a particular pleasure of his to tease her into shedding her usual acerbic demeanour. He wondered how many people ever saw her like this … flushed, ruffled and smiling. Then, with reluctance, he recognised that he'd better come to the point before he really did forget what it was. He said, 'However. If you sit there and I sit as far away as possible, I may manage to concentrate.'

Pauline took the window-seat and watched him subside on the edge of the bed.

'Well?'

'It's complicated,' sighed Francis. 'And highly confidential. And, at all costs, to be kept from Athenais.'

The laughter vanished abruptly and her mouth tightened.

'Which is your way of telling me that you and Ashley are involved in something dangerous, I suppose?'

'Yes.'

'So why *are* you telling me? You never have before.'

'We never needed your help before.'

'Oh God.' She drew a long, bracing breath and then said, 'Get it over with, then.'

So he did.

Frowning a little, Pauline listened without interruption and, at the end, said flatly, 'You're going to pose as the King's brother and hope not to be assassinated in his place. Is that what you're telling me?'

'More or less.'

'And inviting Cyrano de Bergerac to join in the fun?'

'Yes.'

She stood up, put her hands on her hips and fixed him with a furious glare.

'Has the Colonel *completely* lost his mind?'

Francis winced.

'I hope not – though I'll admit that the thought had occurred to me.' He waited for some sign that she was relenting and, when none came, said hesitantly, 'Will you help?'

'Help you get yourself killed, you mean?'

'It shouldn't come to that.'

'Shouldn't and won't are two different things,' she snapped. 'If I say no, will it stop you?'

'No. It will just make things a bit more difficult. But, if you want to refuse, don't let that stand in your way. I'll respect your decision.'

'Respect my request to stay out of it.'

'I'm sorry,' he said slowly. 'I can't.'

Pauline sat down again with a bump, her hands clenched in her lap. She said explosively, 'I don't want you to die.'

'I'm not wild about the idea myself. But --'

'Don't! Don't you *dare* joke about it! It isn't remotely funny.'

Actually, there was a tiny part of Francis that thought, if not exactly funny, it was at least mildly ironic. That he – the lightweight dilettante who, for years, no-one had never taken seriously – was about to risk getting his throat slit on behalf of the Duke of York. But the look on Pauline's face told him that he hadn't better say that, so he murmured, 'No. Of course not. I'm sorry.'

'Liar.' Her voice had grown distinctly husky and the hazel eyes were over-bright. 'If you were sorry you wouldn't do it.'

Not entirely sure that she wouldn't hit him, Francis sat down beside her and took her hands in his. 'I *am* sorry, Pauline. But if I let Ashley down ... and something happened to either him or the King as a result ... what sort of a man would that make me?'

'A live one. And you don't have to be a hero for me. I love you as you are.'

It was the first time she had said it in so many words. Joy exploded inside him and went fizzing through his veins. There were probably a dozen things he might have said ... but he uttered the first one that came to mind. 'Thank you.'

'Oh – you ridiculous, stubborn man!' Pauline snatched her hands from his and put her arms around him, pulling him close. 'You say these things and make me want to weep.'

'I don't mean to.'

'I know. That's the devil of it.' She laid her cheek against his and drew a long breath. 'All right. I'll get you the clothes you need and I won't tell Athenais. But you can rest assured that I'll be giving Ashley a piece of my mind that he won't forget in a hurry.'

'Excellent,' said Francis. 'I'll look forward to it.'

* * *

Ashley returned to inform Francis that Monsieur de Bergerac would be gracing them with his presence that evening once the ladies were occupied at the theatre. Francis responded by saying that Pauline would like a word with him – and then sat down to enjoy the spectacle of his love stripping away the Colonel's skin, layer by layer. Fortunately, Ashley had the good sense to let her and merely stood, mute and humble, beneath the lash of her tongue. And when she was done and had swept militantly from the room, he looked helplessly at Francis and said, 'Christ. Why couldn't she simply cut off my balls and have done with it?'

'I think she just did,' replied Francis cheerfully. 'Splendid, isn't she?'

* * *

Athenais was still struggling with the laces of her gown when she heard Ashley's footsteps on the stairs. Her stomach dipped with a mixture of shyness, pleasure and anticipation. Last night she'd finally overcome what had seemed an insurmountable hurdle and had been surprised by how very easy it had been. He'd held her in warm, passionless arms until she was ready to sleep and she'd felt safe for the first time in weeks. Then he'd kissed her hands, given her a slow, beautiful smile ... and left her alone. When she'd woken up this morning, he'd already gone out and she'd spent a good deal of time lurking in the parlour, hoping to see him only to find that, in the one brief hour she'd been required at the theatre for rehearsal, he'd come in, spoken to Francis and gone out again. Had Francis not said that Ashley was running tedious errands for the King, the shadow of uncertainty that still lingered inside her might have tempted her to wonder if he was avoiding her. As it was, she chose to ignore it and believe Francis.

Ashley tapped at the door and waited her for her to answer before he entered.

She said awkwardly, 'You don't need to do that.'

'Yes, love. I do. You took a huge step last night ... so let's just be content with that for a while, shall we? There's no hurry.'

Forgetting that her gown was only half-laced, Athenais turned to the mirror and started pinning up her hair. 'You've been very busy today.'

'Yes. Chancellor Hyde, His Majesty ... all manner of trivia and more still to come.' He took a step towards her and met her eyes in the glass, his expression carefully veiled. Then, deciding to test the solidity of the ground beneath that giant step, 'Shall I finish this for you?'

'What?' For a moment, she couldn't think what he meant.

'Your laces. There appears to be a knot.'

He sounded so natural ... except that only a few weeks ago he wouldn't have had to ask.

Flushing a little, she said, 'Oh. Yes, please. I couldn't seem to reach.'

Ashley closed the space between them and set about deftly freeing the tangle, whilst making sure his knuckles didn't brush the creamy skin of her back. He glanced briefly at her face in the mirror and said quietly, 'Don't look so worried. We just have new rules today.'

'We do?'

'Yes.' His mouth curled in a half-smile and he started drawing the laces tight. 'I set the pace ... until you tell me differently. I won't be taking anything for granted and will always ask permission. If you want more from me, you need only say so. How does that sound?'

'More than fair to me ... less than fair to you.'

'My choice.' He finished his task and immediately stepped back. 'Unfortunately, I have another meeting this evening but I could walk to the theatre with you if you'd like me to.'

Athenais turned, her face lit with shy pleasure.

'Yes. I'd like that very much.'

Her smile made his heart lose its customary rhythm. He'd feared he might never see it again. He said, 'Then I'll wait downstairs while you finish your toilette.'

'You needn't go.'

I do if I'm to pull myself together, he thought. But said lightly, 'I know. But I want a word with Jem before we go out. Assuming he hasn't disappeared again.'

Athenais watched the door close behind him. His manners, as ever, were impeccable. But she missed the teasing and the laughter ... and wondered, with a sigh, how long it might be before she saw it again.

* * *

Slouching in his chair, Cyrano de Bergerac listened in silence while Ashley outlined both the problem and his plans for dealing with it. Francis, who had already heard it, was content to keep his mouth shut; Jem, who hadn't, muttered the occasional muffled curse.

Finally, Ashley poured the Frenchman a third cup of wine and said, 'I realise I have no right to ask you to help us. I also realise that I'm already in debt to you for saving my life and that, asking you to risk yours, isn't adequate repayment. But I hope *you'll* realise that, in telling you what I have, I've just trusted you to a level far outside my normal practice.'

Cyrano's expression remained enigmatic.

'What made you take the risk?'

'Instinct coupled with lack of viable alternatives.'

Laughter stirred. 'I'm generally wary of gut-feeling but I know all about last resorts. Assuming that this King of yours lives long enough to get his crown back ... is he likely to do a better job than the last one?'

'I hope so,' said Ashley. 'What you're asking is if he and his brother are worth saving.'

'And are they?'

'More so than myself.'

'Saving you cost me nothing. Saving Charles Stuart is another matter. Fortunately for you, there's an element to all this that attracts me.'

'Death?' queried Francis brightly.

'Hazard,' came the reply. 'A touch of theatre, followed by a good fight. Something to make a man's blood flow faster. The last month has been damned dull.'

Ashley eyed him thoughtfully. 'You're saying you'll do it for fun?'

'It's as good a reason as any,' Cyrano shrugged. 'But don't let that worry you. The only way this will work is if we all stick to the plan. So maybe we should address the holes in it – starting with the place where the four of us meet up to make the switch, perhaps?'

NINE

By the time Cyrano took his leave and Francis set off to escort Athenais and Pauline home from the theatre, most of Ashley's concerns had been laid to rest. The rendezvous point had been fixed for a village just outside Louviers where de Bergerac knew the innkeeper and he'd also engaged to supply a pair of retired musketeers who owed him a favour and knew how to keep their mouths shut. These would take Cyrano and Francis from Paris and then see Charles and James safely back by a circuitous route. This, since Pauline had reluctantly agreed to provide appropriate clothing, left Ashley with little more to do than see to the hiring of a coach, acquaint Hyde with his other needs and await for the arrival of the second letter. Once that came, he could look forward to a difficult and probably acrimonious interview with Charles ... after which events were likely to overtake them.

Using his own cypher – which he was pleased to find came as easily to him as it had done two years ago – he listed everything that had been agreed, followed by a list of the minor details still to be addressed. Then he sat back and contemplated the fruit of his efforts, searching for any possible loop-holes. It *looked* water-tight enough. He hoped to God that it was.

Hearing the front door open, he folded his notes and slid them inside his coat. He stood up, automatically giving his right thigh the usual stretch and strolled into the hall, hoping to see Athenais smile.

She didn't. Her face was white and tense and she stared at him helplessly for a moment before crossing to his side and staring up at him. Ashley put an arm around her and looked past her at Francis and Pauline – both of whose expressions were a peculiar mixture of interest and smugness.

Ignoring them, Ashley looked down at Athenais and said, 'What's wrong?'

'They found a body,' she muttered, into his coat. 'In the river.'

'In private, I think,' suggested Francis, opening the parlour door.

Once inside the room, with the door shut behind them, Ashley said, 'Francis?'

'A body has been pulled from the Seine and they think it's d'Auxerre's. Something to do with a scar on his shoulder.'

Frowning, Ashley shook his head.

'That's not possible. By now, there won't be enough left of him to identify.'

'*We* know that. They obviously don't. And from what I heard tonight, this fellow can't have been in the water more than three or four days.'

'The wrong body? Good.'

'Since no one's seen the man in more than five weeks, I imagine they'll eventually work that out,' remarked Pauline. 'Meanwhile, the Cardinal has ordered an investigation.'

'So?' Feeling Athenais's fingers flex convulsively, Ashley looked reassuringly down at her and said, 'It's all right. There isn't anything to connect the Marquis to this house and nothing here for anyone to find. Francis and I were very thorough.'

She looked up at him. 'Are you sure?'

'Perfectly.' He shot an irritable glance at Francis. 'You know as well as I do that there's nothing to worry about. Why didn't you tell her?'

'He tried,' said Pauline. 'For some reason, she wanted to hear it from you.'

Suspicion stirred in Ashley's mind but he put it to one side. He said, 'Athenais, listen to me. D'Auxerre's body is never going to surface now and the fact that someone has mistakenly identified a fresh corpse will muddy the waters even further. No one is ever going to know what happened to him and you are completely safe. I guarantee it.'

She sighed and let her hands relax. 'Thank you. Everyone at the theatre was talking about it and all I could think was that I killed him and I – I ought to be sorry. But I'm not.'

'I'm not sorry either,' said Ashley. 'In fact, if you want the unvarnished truth, I'm proud of you.'

* * *

Upstairs in her room whilst taking the pins from her hair, Athenais said thoughtfully, 'Proud of me, Ashley? For killing a man?'

'No. Proud of you for taking control back and not letting the bastard get away with hurting you. And you didn't kill a man, darling. You exterminated vermin.'

She stopped what she was doing and stood for a moment, turning the hairpins over and over in her hands. 'Do you ever dream about the war? About battles?'

'Sometimes.'

'And the men you've killed?'

'Yes.' *But not those in battle.* 'It will get easier, love. But, until it does, if you have nightmares, call me. I'll always come.'

'I know. I know you will.' She summoned a smile and finished letting her hair down. 'Are you going to be busy again tomorrow?'

'Probably. And for some days after that, I suspect.' He reached for her hairbrush. 'Sit down and let me do this tonight. Time to put aside unpleasant thoughts.'

She did as he asked and felt him section off her hair, then drawn the brush though it in long, slow strokes. For a time, neither of them spoke but, after a while, she said, 'I wish ... I wish I could tell you that I ...' She stopped helplessly.

'I know. I wish it, too.' His brain had a firm grasp of what was possible between them but sometimes his body disagreed and, when that happened, he had to make sure she never saw any sign of it. 'But you'll tell me when you're ready. And we have plenty of time.'

And, like his water-tight plan, he hoped to God that it was true.

* * *

During the course of the following morning, a message arrived from Cyrano de Bergerac confirming the assistance of the ex-musketeers and offering to deal with the hire of the second coach. Pauline and Francis examined the theatre wardrobe and set selected coats, cloaks and hats together so they could be easily retrieved when the time came. And Ashley considered, then decided against, visiting Hyde to ask for servants' liveries and coin for expenses. He was averse to revealing his plans any sooner than he must and was fairly confident that, if and when another letter came, there would be at least a day's grace in which to finalise the arrangements. Unfortunately, he found that waiting made him edgy and had to work hard at not letting it show.

He spent time helping Athenais learn a new role. Froissart wanted to re-cast her role in *Ménage Deux* so she'd be free to take the lead in the next full-length play. Having initially agreed to the change, Athenais had started fretting over it and received a stern lecture from Pauline as a result. When she told Ashley about this he grinned and said, 'Pauline has her back to the wall and is taking it out on the rest of us.'

'What do you mean?'

'Francis says he's going to marry her.'

Athenais's eyes widened and her jaw dropped.

'Really? She didn't tell me *that*. She more or less admitted that she's in love with him but wouldn't say whether he loved her. And all the time, she knew *that* … and never said a word. I could murder her.'

'I gather she hasn't said yes yet – which means that Francis is probably plaguing her.'

'Good.' Athenais made a little sound half way between annoyance and laughter. 'She *deserves* to be plagued. Goodness knows, she's forever sticking her nose into my affairs. Do you think Francis might appreciate a little help?'

'I'm sure he'd be delighted,' grinned Ashley. And then, 'I take it that you think she ought to accept?'

'Yes. Don't you? I mean, I know she's an actress and he's a Viscount, but --'

'That's of no importance whatsoever.'

'Isn't it?' she asked, not without a tiny hint of wistfulness.

'No.' Something inside his chest curled up tight. 'What matters is whether Pauline is as utterly besotted as Francis. If she's not, their relationship is unlikely to last.'

'You're very gloomy,' observed Athenais. 'Why shouldn't she be besotted?'

'Why isn't she saying yes?' countered Ashley.

'Because he's handsome and charming and talented and a Viscount, of course. And she doesn't believe she's good enough for him.'

'It's that simple?'

'Yes.' *I know exactly how she feels. Particularly now.* 'She doesn't want … she wouldn't ever want to be less than he deserves.'

The thing in Ashley's chest turned into a cold, hard lump. He said, 'I suspect we're no longer talking about Pauline and Francis. And if that's so, I have only one thing to say.'

'What?'

'I'm neither talented nor titled – or even particularly charming. And you are the light of my life and the only thing that gives it true meaning. So don't ever think yourself unworthy. You're not. I'm the one who is undeservedly fortunate.'

* * *

The day dragged by with immeasurable slowness. Although he didn't think there would be any new developments, Ashley recognised the wisdom of not stirring from the house in case he was mistaken. Francis escorted Athenais and Pauline to the theatre and stayed there. Jem wandered off on some pursuit of his own. Ashley paced the hall and grew increasingly restless.

He found himself envying Francis. Envying the confidence with which he'd offered Pauline his name and his certainty that the future would take care of itself in exactly the way he wanted. From time to time since Archie's death, Ashley had contemplated asking Athenais to marry him. He had no more to offer her now than he'd ever had but he knew she would say yes without a second's hesitation. And that was why he didn't do it. He knew that she could and should do better; and the knowledge held him back.

He would be indescribably glad when this Honfleur business was over. Aside from the fact that the waiting was killing him, he found himself going over and over the details – even though he knew there was no point to it since he could already recite them to music. Even more pointless were his attempts to second-guess the enemy's plans. Once he had the final piece of information, he might make better progress with that; but, for the time being, all he could count on was the fact that there wouldn't be less than four assassins – and could be six or even eight. Four shouldn't be difficult ; six might require a little extra effort; eight would be a challenge.

Francis walked into the parlour alone, saying quietly, 'Anything?'

'No. Tomorrow, hopefully – before I start climbing the walls. Where are the girls?'

'In the kitchen – arguing. You told Athenais I intend to marry Pauline.'

'Ah. Has that created a problem?'

'Not for me. Or not yet, anyway. She's too busy fending off Athenais to drop rocks on my head for telling you in the first place. Doubtless she'll get round to that later.'

Ashley shook his head. 'I don't know what there is in that to look so pleased about. After yesterday, she scares the hell out of me.'

'And rightly so,' agreed Francis blithely. 'But you don't have the fun of talking her round and the intense pleasure of making up afterwards.'

'True. All I have is a sense of self-preservation that's warning me to make a strategic retreat before I get caught in the cross-fire. If Athenais asks, I'll be upstairs.' And he went.

Five minutes later, Athenais walked in three steps ahead of Pauline saying wickedly, 'I can't imagine why you want to marry her, Francis. She'll nag you to death inside a month. And considering that there are at least three girls at the theatre who'd take you in a heart-beat if you were to ask, I don't see what she's dithering about.'

'You're a comfort, darling – and I'll bear the thought in mind.'

'She's not a comfort – she's an interfering busybody!' snapped Pauline.

'Goodness! If that's not pot calling kettle,' retorted Athenais, enjoying herself. 'I've lost count of the number of times you've tried to do my breathing for me. All I'm doing now is returning the favour.' She smiled at Francis. 'She's a hopeless case, Francis and you have my most profound sympathy. If it were me, you wouldn't have to ask twice.'

'If it were you,' replied Francis with an answering smile, 'Ashley would have my head. He's upstairs, by the way – instead of standing shoulder to shoulder with me and taking his punishment like a man.'

'Do you blame him?' she asked, heading for the door. And, to Pauline, 'Stop being so bloody-minded. The man wrote you a play, for God's sake.'

She paused outside long enough to hear Pauline say irritably, 'What else have you told Ashley? And who else have you confided in?'

'Nothing – and no one. Credit me with a little pride. Ashley knows you well enough not to be surprised if you turn me down. Anyone else will just assume I'm useless in bed.'

Suppressing a laugh, Athenais ran lightly up the stairs.

With the exception of his coat, Ashley was still fully dressed. It occurred to her that, since That Night, he always had been. He'd even put a washing-bowl in the dressing-closet so that he could shave without removing his shirt in front of her. The degree of his care ... the lengths he seemed to consider necessary for her peace of mind made her throat ache. He never touched her unless she indicated that it would be welcome; no word of blame ever escaped his lips – only ones of undemanding affection and encouragement; and if he suffered the pangs of frustrated desire, he made sure she never knew it. She couldn't imagine what all this was costing him. But she decided it was time she at least tried to make it easier.

She closed the door, leaned against it and shook her head dolefully. 'Francis thinks you're a coward.'

'I won't argue with that. What have you been saying to Pauline?'

'This and that. It's more what I said to Francis while she was listening. I told him that other girls would show a bit more appreciation and that if he proposed to me, he wouldn't have to ask twice.'

Ashley surveyed her over folded arms. 'And did he?'

'Propose? No. He said you'd have his head – which makes him as much of a coward as you.' She hoisted herself on to the window-seat and swung her crossed ankles. 'Froissart's given my role in *Ménage* to Jacqueline. And I've got five full acts of an Alexandre Hardy tragi-comedy to learn.'

'Life is hard,' he said, laughter brimming unexpectedly in his eyes. 'I can only applaud your fortitude.'

Her mouth quivered in response.

'And so you should. I'll learn all those words ... and by the end of Act Three half the audience will be on the verge of walking out. It's very dispiriting.'

'It must be. All those young fellows sighing when you take a deep breath and never daring to take their eyes from the stage in case they miss a glimpse of ankle? Torture.'

'You have no idea. If you had, you wouldn't think it was funny.'

Ashley grinned and sat down beside her.

'Did I say it was?'

'You thought it – and that is quite enough.' She leaned her head against his shoulder. 'Is English theatre really as awful as they say?'

'I haven't much experience of it. Between leaving university and the start of the war, I spent my time in the country so the only plays I ever saw were ones performed by travelling troupes. The acting wasn't generally up to much but some of the plays were better than the ones I've seen here.'

'Shakespeare? Francis told me about him. He said there are some wonderful female roles if only the law allowed females to play them.' She yawned. 'What did you do at university?'

'All the usual things. Latin, a little Greek ... and a lot of raising merry hell.'

'Wicked man. And at your home in country?'

'I did whatever my father asked – if I wasn't quick enough to absent myself before he asked it. Took care of the horses, helped bring in the harvest, listened to the tenants.'

'And then the war came and you went to fight.'

'Yes. And once the fighting stopped, I came here and met you.' He dropped a fleeting kiss on her hair. 'So there you have it. My entire life story.'

'No,' Athenais said seriously. 'Only a part of it. As you said, the fighting has stopped ... and the Marquis is at the bottom of the river instead of trying to kill you.' She tucked her hand into his and gave a tiny, unexpected gurgle of laughter. 'Only think – there are years yet for us to plague each other.'

'Very true,' replied Ashley, shutting his mind against the inevitable thought. 'Only think.'

TEN

On the following morning after a fitful night's sleep, Ashley entered the kitchen to find Pauline staring fixedly into the steam rising from a pan of water. He said, 'If you get any reliable visions, I'd be happy to hear them.'

'What?' She blinked and turned to face him. 'Where's Athenais?'

'Still asleep.'

Pauline straightened her shoulders and crossed to the bread-crock to begin her morning routine. She said, 'I suppose I owe you an apology, don't I?'

'No. The situation *is* my fault – given that I could have avoided it altogether. And naturally you're worried. It would be amazing if you weren't.'

'Which is why we're keeping it from Athenais.'

'Yes.'

'That can't be easy for you.'

'It isn't. Sooner or later, I'm going to have to lie to her ... and that's not something I relish. But if knowing the truth has you – the strongest woman I've ever met – scared silly over what may happen --'

'Athenais, as she is just now, won't cope with it at all,' she interposed flatly. 'I know.'

He watched her for a moment, concern mingling with caution.

'Have you healed your differences with Francis?'

Head bent over slices of sausage, Pauline gave a snort of despairing laughter.

'It's impossible to be angry with Francis for more than ten minutes at a time. I don't know how he does it but he always manages to say something either ludicrous or heart-wrenching. And then he just smiles and I can't ... I can't seem to assemble a logical argument or even remember why I was angry in the first place. It's like fighting a curtain.'

Ashley smiled. 'That, in itself, must be maddening. But you know, Pauline ... if you love him that much, you really ought to put him out of his misery and marry him.'

She shot him a sharp glance and continued slicing sausage.

'Francis isn't miserable. He's damned well enjoying himself.'

'I'm sure that's what he wants you to think.'

'And you must know as well as I do that the idea of him marrying a disfigured, aging actress is totally ridiculous.'

'Don't put words in my mouth. It's not ridiculous at all. Calling your scar disfigurement is an exaggeration. And aging? By my calculation, you're roughly the same age as me and two years younger than Francis.'

'What's that got to do with it? You're both men.'

Ashley sat down and folded his arms.

'Now you're just making excuses. What is it you're frightened of?'

'Nothing!'

'Liar,' he said calmly.

Pauline slammed down the knife and turned to face him.

'All right. I think he'll regret it. Not immediately, perhaps – but in time. And I don't want to be the cause of that … or to have to witness it.'

Although Ashley understood this well enough and even sympathised with it, he chose not to say so. Instead, with a slightly taunting lift of one brow, he said, 'Life doesn't come with guarantees. Sometimes one has to take a risk. For example, I'll do my level best to return Francis to you in one piece – but I can't promise it.'

'Stop that right now!' she snapped. 'I won't be blackmailed into giving him a promise just so he'll go away happy.'

'I was thinking more in terms of an incentive,' replied Ashley, rising from the table at the sound of Francis's footsteps on the stairs. 'But I daresay you know best. And, in the meantime, if you can keep Athenais occupied today, I'd appreciate it.'

'I'll drag her off to the dressmaker. It's time she ordered a new gown.'

'That should do it. Thank you.'

* * *

With the ladies safely out of the way, Francis kept Ashley company while they waited. Once again, the hours seemed to drag by until Ashley began to wonder if anything was ever going to happen. Then, at a little after two in the afternoon, a messenger arrived from the Louvre.

Ashley broke the seal, scanned it and then looked across at Francis.

'It's come.'

'Hallelujah. You'll go to the Louvre now?'

'Yes – or rather, *we* will. I want to see Charles and Hyde at the same time so it's one meeting instead of two and, if you're present, I won't have to waste time filling you in afterwards. Also, since you're going to be risking your neck alongside mine, it would be nice if Hyde recognised the fact.' He gave a small, hard smile. 'Come on. Let's go.'

This time there was no delay in being admitted to the King's apartments. His Majesty's brows rose slightly when Francis entered in Ashley's wake but he said merely, 'Thank you for coming so promptly, gentlemen.' And held out the letter to Ashley. 'This was delivered just over an hour ago.'

Ashley took the paper but made no move to read it. He said, 'Has Sir Edward seen it?'

'Not yet. I wanted your opinions first.'

'And you shall have them, Sir. But Chancellor Hyde should be here. Not only as a matter of form but also because there are things I need him to do. Perhaps you could send for him?'

'If he knows you've arrived, he's probably sitting outside the door,' remarked Charles dryly. And, instead of calling for a servant, went to find out.

Ashley used the time to read the letter and then pass it to Francis.

It was in the same hand as the previous one and, in many respects, quite similar.

It stated that a meeting had been arranged between His Majesty the King and James, Duke of York and Major-General Lambert *'along with others of similar convictions'* in three days' time. It suggested that, as a courtesy to the Major-General whose position might otherwise become untenable, His Majesty should continue to keep his own counsel until the matter had been settled to the satisfaction of both parties. The suggested location of the meeting was the upper room of *Les Deux Pigeons*, just off the quayside at Honfleur. And finally, if His Majesty found these arrangements acceptable, he should immediately signify his assent in the same way as before.

The gazes of Ashley and Francis met and locked.

'Well,' said Francis at length. 'Now we know.'

'Quite.' And as the door opened on Charles and Sir Edward, 'Be prepared for this to get quite heated and leave most of the talking to me.'

The Chancellor greeted them with a curt nod and the King invited everyone to sit. When they had done so, Charles said, 'What do you make of this, Ash?'

'Except in one vital respect, the same as when we spoke before, Sir. Only then I merely *suspected* the offer of a meeting with Lambert was a ruse to draw you to a convenient spot where you could be quietly murdered – and now I *know* that it is.'

'How?'

'They want you to go to Honfleur – which, as Sir Edward knows, is precisely what my original information said they'd do. That isn't a coincidence. It's the plot I was warned of.' Ashley paused, aware that his next words were not going to be well-received. 'Lambert won't be there. And although, in a short while from now, you're going to stroll through the Tuileries gardens with a red feather in your hat ... neither will you.'

There was a mildly explosive pause.

'That,' said Charles coldly, 'is not your decision to make.'

'Yes, Sir. It is.'

The King left his chair, rising to his full and extremely impressive height.

'I appreciate your help, your loyalty and your expertise, Ashley. But it is not your prerogative to dictate my actions.'

Ashley also rose and faced his sovereign with an implacable stare.

'In the normal course of events, no. But in this, it is *absolutely* my prerogative. And you will set foot in Honfleur over my dead body.'

His words seemed to echo on in the frigidly furious silence which followed them.

Realising he'd stopped breathing, Francis dragged in a lungful of air. Still glued to his seat, Chancellor Hyde said tentatively, 'Your Majesty ... perhaps if Colonel Peverell were to explain his intentions ...?'

For a moment, no-one moved. Then, dropping abruptly back into his chair, Charles growled, 'Well? I'm listening.'

'Thank you.' Ashley inclined his head politely but remained on his feet. 'I want to stop this plot in a way that will send a clear message to London. If at all possible, I also want to capture at least one of the potential assassins so he can be questioned. And most of all, if there's any proof that this scenario originated in Thurloe's office, I want to find it – so that you and Sir Edward can use it as you see fit.'

The King's dark eyes became a degree or two less frosty.

'That's all very laudable. But if you're wrong and Lambert *is* there --'

'I'm not – and he won't be.' Interrupting royalty was verging on *lése majesté* but Ashley had the bit between his teeth. Ignoring Hyde's appalled stare, he said, 'I know you'd like to believe it, Sir. So would I. But it isn't going to happen and I can't let you risk your person finding that out for yourself.'

'You're wagering a great deal on this information you speak of.'

Ashley exchanged a brief glance with Francis.

'It came from an impeccable source. Someone who hazarded a great deal to send it to me.'

Charles sighed and then seemed to capitulate.

'Oh for God's sake, sit down, Ash. I take your point. But I don't see how you're going to draw the assassins out without involving me.'

'I can't,' admitted Ashley, subsiding into his chair. 'Not entirely.'

Some of the humour returned to the King's eyes.

'But naturally you have a plan. And I assume from Francis's presence that he is privy to it?'

'Not just privy – but instrumental. Which reminds me. If the Duke of York is still serving with Marshal Turenne, you'll need to recall him.'

'I've already done so. I sent a messenger to Turenne at the same time I sent one to you.' Charles leaned back and regarded Ashley. 'I assumed that he and I were going to Honfleur. Since you want James here, I presume we are still going somewhere.'

'Yes. If you and Sir Edward will bear with me, I'll explain the arrangements I've made and how I expect them to work.'

'Do. Sir Edward and I are agog with anticipation.'

And so, drawing a fortifying breath, Ashley started at the beginning, choosing his words carefully and hoping to divert attention from the imponderables. He got as far as the point where the King and his brother were to change places with Francis and another gentleman when Hyde said suddenly, 'Who?'

'A reliable fellow of the appropriate build and who is also a trained soldier,' replied Ashley a shade repressively. 'His Majesty and the Duke of York will then --'

'Who is it, Ash?' Charles leaned forward, elbows on his knees and a lazy smile playing about his mouth.

'Does it matter?'

'Only in so much as you clearly don't want to tell us. And I'd quite like to know who is impersonating me. So who is he?'

This was one of the things Ashley had hoped to avoid revealing. But seeing no help for it, he said blandly, 'Monsieur de Bergerac.'

Sir Edward nearly fell off his seat and Charles gave a bark of laughter.

'Reliable? Cyrano de Bergerac? That's not what I've heard.'

'Have you ever met him, Sir?'

'No. But the man's a legend in his own lifetime.'

'He's a good many things,' agreed Ashley. 'One of them takes the form of a willingness to risk his neck on your behalf. That Francis and I are doing so is one thing. That a Frenchman is prepared to do so, is quite another.'

'What does he want?' asked Hyde suspiciously. 'There must be something.'

'Difficult as it may be for you to believe, there isn't.' Ashley didn't bother to hide his distaste. 'I asked him to help and he agreed. He's even providing protection for His Majesty and the Duke on their journey back here.'

Although Sir Edward didn't say anything, the expression on his face was that of a man sucking a lemon. Charles hid a smile and turned back to Ashley.

'Go on. James and I return discreetly to Paris while the four of you drive on to Honfleur and take on an indeterminate number of hired killers. Is that it?'

'More or less. There are a number of other details that --'

'I'm sure there are. But you know, Ashley ... although your reasons for doing this and the methods you've devised are all good, you've no idea what odds you'll be facing. And if the end result is that you and

Francis are both killed – along with your servant and Monsieur de Bergerac – it isn't worth it. I'd sooner forgo the whole thing.'

'That's good of you, Sir, and we appreciate the thought. But, in my view, the attempt has to be made to lessen the likelihood of a similar thing happening again. This time we know what to expect. I doubt we can rely on that next time. And since I have a plan which, as Cyrano has pointed out, will work so long as everyone involved sticks to it – and three good men to execute it with me, I urge you to let us try.'

There was another long silence. Hyde opened his mouth, then shut it again and Francis contemplated his fingernails. Finally Charles said, 'Let me send half a dozen men to wait in Honfleur and assist you, should the need arise.'

'I'd rather you didn't, Sir. I prefer to rely on the men I know personally. It's usually safer in the long run.'

'God – you're a stubborn fellow! Very well. Have it your way. Now let's hear these other details you mentioned.'

Ashley listed them. A plain coach and pair, along with the uniforms he and Jem would need as coachman and groom; money for travelling expenses; departure from the Louvre under as many eyes as possible at around noon, the day after tomorrow; and any kind of jewel or insignia Charles could find that would pass muster in the dark when pinned to Cyrano's cloak.

'Why leave at midday?' objected Hyde. 'With an early start, the journey could be completed in a day. The later departure will necessitate a stop on the road.'

'Which we will need so the switch can be made after dark without anyone being the wiser.'

'And what about suitable clothes for Lord Wroxton and Monsieur de Bergerac?'

'They are being ... loaned to us ... from the wardrobe of the Théâtre du Marais.' A small but wicked smile curled Ashley's mouth. 'Lord Wroxton is a particular favourite of the lady who has charge of it.'

Hyde sniffed.

Charles, catching the faintly desperate expression on Francis's face, quirked an eyebrow, hesitated for a moment and then grinned.

'Don't worry, Francis. I won't ask – much as I would like to.'

'Thank you, Sir,' murmured Francis. 'Your restraint is appreciated.'

'I thought it might be.' And to Ashley, 'Is that everything?'

'I believe so, Sir. You'll put your brother in the picture when he arrives and I'll make sure all our other preparations are in order. If you have any questions, send for me. If not, I'll see you the day after tomorrow. When Jem and I arrive, have us brought in the back way to a place where the uniforms can be left waiting. Since we can ill-afford to lose our own clothes, I'd appreciate them being placed somewhere from which we can retrieve them when this is all over.' He stood up, waited for Francis to follow suit and then added sardonically, 'Time to take the red feather for a walk, Sir. After which you may pray, as I shall, that the assassins are no better at their work than the go-between is at his.'

* * *

'Well, that,' remarked Ashley as he and Francis made their way out of the Louvre, 'went a lot better than I expected.'

'Really?' Francis eyed him with faint incredulity. 'You cut across the King mid-sentence and told him he'd do as you said whether he liked it or not. And you think it might have been worse?'

'I thought he'd argue more and refuse to see sense.'

Francis shuddered inwardly at the thought of how things might have gone if that had happened. He said, 'Just how well do you know Charles?'

'Better than he'd like and well enough to know what I can get away with,' shrugged Ashley. 'He knows I respect him. He also knows that when I forget my company manners there's always a good reason.' He paused, grinning. 'Your own performance was impressive.'

'I didn't say anything.'

'That's what I mean. Only seven words in nearly an hour. If that didn't revise Hyde's opinion of you, nothing will.'

'He likes Cyrano even less.'

'No surprise there. And speaking of Cyrano, I suggest we run him to earth now so that he has all of tomorrow in which to prepare. And, when we've done that, you can go home and make another attempt to convert Pauline to the notion of marriage. God alone knows why ... but the woman's so much in love with you she's beginning to lose her reason.'

Grasping his arm, Francis pulled him to a halt.

'She *said* that?'

'I deduced it. As for, from *what*,' replied Ashley provocatively, 'you can't really expect me to breach a lady's confidence, now can you?'

ELEVEN

They found Cyrano de Bergerac in his usual tavern and persuaded him to leave it long enough to take a walk away from interested ears. Cyrano appeared pleased that the chase was on, promised to have everything in readiness for the time appointed and told Francis to bring their assumed clothing to his lodgings as soon as he'd acquired it. Then he went back to his interrupted dice-game.

'Are you sure he'll be all right?' muttered Francis. 'From what I've seen, he's quite likely to turn up drunk.'

'In which case you'll have the long drive to Louviers in which to sober him up.'

'You're really not worried?'

'Not about Cyrano,' came the far from reassuring reply. Then, 'How long is it since you used your sword in earnest?'

'You know the answer to that. Worcester.'

'Then we'll spend this afternoon mending that.'

Francis groaned and said nothing.

Back in the Rue des Rosiers, Francis was glad to find that Pauline and Athenais were still out. If Ashley was going to push him round and round the yard till his lungs were bursting, he really didn't want an audience.

Though still chilly, the day was bright and sunny with a promise of spring in the air. The two of them shed their coats and went outside.

'I hope,' said Francis, 'that you're going to make some allowances.'

'No. But unless you do something really stupid, I'll promise not to hurt you.'

After ten minutes, Francis thought the word 'much' should have been added to that sentence. After twenty, his wrist was on fire, his arm felt like lead and his shoulder was beginning to ache like a bitch. Stepping back out of range and holding up his left hand, he said, 'Give me a minute, will you?'

'By all means. You're hopelessly out of condition, you know.'

Francis gave him a dirty look. 'And you've got a full arsenal of nasty little tricks.'

'Thank you. They work better than the other kind – and if you survive this bout, I'll teach you a couple of them tomorrow.' He paused. 'Don't look now, but the ladies are back and standing at the window so you might want to stop leaning on your sword and puffing like an old man.'

Francis said something extremely rude but had the sense to do it quietly. Then, straightening his back and raising his sword-arm, he said, 'You realise that, just at this moment, I'd like to subject you to some serious damage?'

Ashley grinned companionably.

'Try,' he said.

Francis launched a swift attack, expecting to be made to look even more inept than he had before. Instead, Ashley gave him both space and opportunity and even allowed him to complete a couple of showy moves followed by a fairly spectacular disarm.

'Bastard,' said Francis without heat. 'You let me do that.'

'I thought you'd be more appreciative.' Ashley bent to retrieve his sword. 'But if you'd rather work for it ...'

And he engaged Francis's blade with sudden, disconcerting force. With no time to think or do anything except defend himself, Francis found himself driven relentlessly back across the yard. On the two occasions when he failed to parry in time, he was dimly aware that Ashley pulled back just enough to stop his own blade touching him. And when his back finally hit the wall and he let his sword-arm drop, Ashley's point remained motionless a scant two inches from his throat.

His lungs heaving and his heart thundering in his chest, Francis gasped, 'I'm so glad you're on my side.'

Inside the kitchen, Athenais and Pauline looked at each other.

'Well,' said Pauline, at length. 'That was fun. But now I suppose we'd better set some water to heat.'

'So they can both take a bath?'

'So Francis can soak his shoulder before it's so stiff he can't move it,' came the arid reply. And then, in a furious undertone, '*Men!* No damned sense whatsoever. Why didn't they start this a week ago?'

'Start what?' asked Athenais, her eyes once more on Ashley as he sheathed his sword and went to pick up his coat.

'Nothing.' Pauline handed her a pair of buckets and said, 'Go and tell the Colonel to fill these. Since he's feeling so spry, he might as well be useful.'

A little later, while Pauline ministered to Francis's aches and pains and Ashley had disappeared to wash and change his shirt, Athenais hovered aimlessly in the parlour for a few minutes and then, without really thinking about it, wandered upstairs to her bedchamber.

Ashley stood at the wash-stand, naked to the waist. Something hot and unexpected curled in Athenais's stomach and she froze, staring at the play of muscles in his back as he rubbed a damp cloth over his arms. Then, seeming to sense that she was there, he dropped the cloth in the basin with one hand whilst reaching for his shirt with the other.

She said huskily, 'I could wash your back.'

He half-turned, slanting an arrested, sideways glance. 'Could you?'

She nodded. 'Yes. If you like.'

Ashley decided he'd like it very much. Too much, probably – which suggested that he probably ought to refuse. But she looked … she looked as if she *wanted* to; and that was the kind of progress he'd neither expected nor even permitted himself to hope for as yet. So he smiled and said, 'I would. Thank you.'

Athenais wrung out the cloth and reached up to lift his hair away from his shoulders. It felt heavy and soft in her fingers. Her throat tightened and her mouth felt dry. She began to wash his back, aware that his muscles were tense and he was standing absolutely motionless, his head slightly downcast. Her hands started to tremble and she didn't know why any more than she understood the sensations that seemed to be waking inside her. It wasn't desire that she felt, not quite. But it was something not so very far distant.

Ashley concentrated on keeping his breathing even and his body under control. This was the nearest they had come to intimacy since that fateful night. He could feel the slight tremor in her fingers and wondered if she was perhaps less ready for it than she had thought. He told himself not to read more into it than there was and not to start looking for further, similar developments. Unfortunately, he couldn't prevent a tiny seed of hope taking root and refusing to be stamped out.

Athenais reached for the towel and, very much more slowly than was necessary, dried him off. She would have liked to slide her hands round his waist and lean her cheek against his shoulder-blades for a moment but she knew that she mustn't do it. Ashley wouldn't touch her unless she indicated that she was willing – so it would be unfair to do anything that might be construed as an invitation until she was sure she was ready. Until she was sure she could lie in his arms without hearing d'Auxerre's voice in her head.

I want you to remember this next time the bastard Englishman tries to bed you.

She shoved the thought away, started folding the towel and searched for something to say to break the silence. Finally, 'Why have you and Francis suddenly decided to practice your sword-play?'

Ashley cast a glance over his shoulder, saw the sudden darkness in her eyes and immediately pulled on his shirt.

'Francis thinks Pauline will like him better with muscles.'

The darkness faded and she responded to the smile in his voice.

'He already has muscles. And she likes him well enough as he is.'

'True. But his personal confidence is at a very low ebb, poor fellow,' replied Ashley, perjuring Francis without a second thought. Then, 'Pardon my asking – but what do *you* know about his musculature?'

'Enough.' The smile widened and became decidedly naughty. 'But a lot less than I know about yours.'

'I'm glad to hear it. Francis has begged me to favour him with another bout tomorrow. It would be a shame if I felt the need to punish him a little.'

'From what I saw, you did enough of that today,' she replied frankly. 'Pauline's cross. With both of you, I think … but mostly with you.'

'I'm getting used to that. And if Francis is clever, he'll make it work to his advantage.'

* * *

Sitting in a tub of hot water while Pauline massaged his aching shoulder, Francis was attempting to do just that. He said, 'God, that feels good.'

'Enjoy it while it lasts.'

'I am, darling. I truly am.'

'I suppose this sudden surge of activity was the Colonel's idea?'

'Yes. And it was the right one.'

'Maybe. It's just a pity he didn't think of it sooner.' She kneaded the muscles at the base of his neck, still thinking with a sick sense of dread of what he'd told her. 'You're not going to be much use the day after tomorrow if you can't raise your damned arm.'

Francis grinned up at her.

'Other parts of me are rising easily enough.'

She rotated his arm, just hard enough to make it hurt.

'Behave yourself. There are more important things to think of.'

'And all afternoon in which to think of them.' His left arm surfaced and snaked swiftly round her waist. 'Do you think we could both fit in here together?'

'Not a chance. And stop that – you're making me all wet.'

'That's a wicked thing to say to a fellow.'

'Only if the fellow in question hasn't a thought above his navel.'

'Well, be fair.' He pulled her face down for a kiss. 'I'm sitting naked in the bath ...and you're here, bending over me and affording me the most delectable view. You can't expect me to be sensible under those circumstances.'

Between his arm and the rim of the tub, Pauline found herself trapped. She said tartly, 'I rarely expect you to be sensible at all. Now let go of me and I'll get a towel.'

He let her go but only in order to stand up, sending water sloshing over the side to soak her skirts. Pauline barely had time to say more than his name when he stepped out of the bath and pulled her firmly against his streaming body. Then, in a low, enticing voice he said, 'Dear me. What can I have been thinking? You really need to get out of those wet clothes.' His fingers were already making short work of her laces and, the second her gown fell loose, he turned her so that her back was against his chest and slid his hands over and around her breasts. 'Let me help you.'

* * *

Ashley gave Jem the gist of his meeting with the King, along with a few very precise additional instructions. Part of his mind was locked on what lay ahead at Honfleur. The other part was still grappling with the fact that Athenais had seemingly sought an opportunity to put her hands on his body – which the look he glimpsed in her eyes afterwards made less encouraging than it might otherwise have been. He wondered what had caused that and whether if, instead of joking he'd asked what she was thinking, she might have told him. The trouble was that, tomorrow, he'd have to tell her that he was going away for God knew how many days and that he'd have to lie about the reason for it. As a consequence, now didn't seem the best time for inviting potentially painful confidences.

He escorted her to the theatre, keeping the conversation light and impersonal and then left Francis to bring both her and Pauline home again. And it was then that he realised he had no idea what to do with himself for the rest of the evening. He contemplated and then, for no particular reason, dismissed the idea of seeking out Sir William Brierley. He stopped part-way home at a tavern and sat in front of a pot of ale that he didn't want. Then he went back to the Rue des Rosiers and spent an hour sharpening and polishing both his sword and the knife that habitually lived in his boot. And finally, suspecting that tomorrow's difficulties could only be compounded by anything that took place between them tonight, he decided to avoid Athenais and go to bed.

* * *

The following morning dawned grey and surly. Up and dressed long before Athenais was awake, Ashley was able to slip through her room and make his way downstairs undetected. It was so early, he'd expected the rest of the house to be sleeping but realised, when he entered the kitchen, that he should have known better.

Pauline sat at the table, staring into a cup of steaming, bitter-smelling liquid that appeared to have bits of weed floating in it. Ashley eyed it uneasily and wondered if it was the same brew that Athenais had been drinking to avoid conception ... and whether she was still taking it. He didn't realise that Pauline was looking at him until she said, 'Yes it is. And since her courses came, no she isn't.'

Ashley's heart slammed in his chest.

Oh God. Why didn't I think of that? She must have been terrified. But she'd have told me if there was any chance of a child. Wouldn't she?

He said, 'You're razor-sharp for so early in the morning.'

'You think I can sleep with this hanging over us?'

'Perhaps not. Is Francis similarly afflicted?'

'God, no. I imagine you could bang pots together over his head this morning and he wouldn't stir.' She eyed him acidulously. 'But you'll be glad to know that his shoulder doesn't seem to be giving him any trouble so you'll be able to knock seven bells out of him again later. Not that it will do much good. He's not going to be up to your standard inside twenty-four hours no matter how much torture you inflict.'

Ashley drew a steadying breath and held on to his temper.

'I'm aware of that – which is why I sent Jem to the Louvre to ask Hyde to arrange for some firearms. To the best of my recollection, Francis is a reasonable shot. Does that make you feel any better?'

Pauline came abruptly to her feet.

'*Nothing* about this is going to make me feel any better until it's over and all three of you are back here, safe and sound. Odd as it seem, it's not just Francis I'm worried about. I'm also far from ecstatic at possibly having to tell Athenais why you aren't coming home.'

And, snatching up her cup, she stalked out.

It was nearly an hour before Francis materialised, yawning and looking annoyingly relaxed.

'Christ,' muttered Ashley. 'It's clear enough how you spent the night.'

'A fair proportion of it,' agreed Francis lazily. 'But one doesn't like to brag.'

'Presumably, one also doesn't like what Pauline would do to one if she caught one speaking of things one shouldn't,' came the sarcastic retort. Then, 'Come on. Let's try and get an hour in before Athenais gets up and commiserates with you for worrying about your failing physique. I had to explain yesterday's exercise somehow so I told her you were suffering from low self-esteem – but one look at your face this morning will give the lie to that.'

The sword-play went better than on the previous afternoon. Francis had never been a master-swordsman and wasn't going to become one now; but his speed and flexibility improved as the hour wore on and Ashley taught him two highly unconventional moves that combined defence with attack and could usually be counted on to drive back, if not disarm, one's adversary.

Towards the end of it, Ashley suddenly dropped his arm and said, 'Oh God. I nearly forgot. How could I have been so stupid?'

'Forgot what?'

'This.' He gestured to his blade. 'As coachman and groom, neither Jem nor I can be seen carrying a sword, can we? You'll have to take them in the coach with Cyrano.'

Francis frowned. 'I will, of course. But that will leave you unarmed.'

'Not entirely. There'll be a musket in the coach.' He reached into his boot. 'And then there's this.'

Staring at what was in his hand, Francis said blankly, 'You carry a knife in your boot.'

'No fooling you, is there?'

'Why do you carry a knife in your boot?'

'Old habits. Jem does the same.' Ashley shrugged and grinned. 'Don't worry about it. Just take the damned swords to Cyrano.'

* * *

Later, while Pauline and Francis slipped out of the house to collect their selected haul from the theatre and deliver it to Cyrano's lodgings, Ashley distracted Athenais by offering to help with her lines for the forthcoming play. She grimaced but settled down willingly enough and was soon engrossed. Ashley wished that he was. Between watching the myriad of expressions drifting across her face and listening for the sound of the front door, the play was the last thing on his mind.

When Francis finally sauntered in, Ashley lifted one brow and received an almost imperceptible nod in response. A little later, Jem stuck his head round the door and said, 'Pardon, Mamzelle. Colonel – this note come for you. The King again, I reckon.'

Ashley took the sealed missive and walked over to the window, waving Jem away.

The note was brief and merely gave directions to the room in a virtually disused part of the Louvre where 'all required items' would be waiting on the morrow. A postscript in the King's own hand confirmed that the Duke of York had returned to Paris.

Thank God, thought Ashley. *If Cyrano has done as he said, everything should be securely in place ... so there's only one thing left for me to do.*

And since I'm standing here with a letter ostensibly from Charles in my hand, now would be a sensible time.

He looked across to find Athenais's gaze fixed expectantly on his face. Summoning a rueful smile, he tapped the letter against his palm and said, 'This is something I could well do without.'

'What is?'

'A gentleman is arriving from England with a budget of correspondence and information – all of which is apparently highly confidential and would be extremely detrimental should it fall into the wrong hands. Inevitably, the result is that His Majesty wants me to go to the coast and bring both it and the courier safely to Paris.'

'Oh. When?'

'Tomorrow. For obvious reasons, he hasn't given me the full details here – just asked me to report to him in the morning. Damn.' Ashley crumpled the letter in his hand and tossed it into the fire. Then he leaned against the mantelpiece watching it burn and apparently deep in thought. 'I can only hope some of the snags that are occurring to me are also occurring to him.'

Athenais didn't like the sound of that. Still less did she like the idea of him going away. She said, 'What sort of snags?'

He looked up, his expression a perfect blend of mild annoyance and resignation.

'Organisational ones. Firstly, if these papers are so important, I'd be insane to ride off to Le Havre on my own. My horse could go lame or lose a shoe and there are hedge-thieves everywhere. Secondly, there's no guarantee that this fellow will arrive precisely when Charles thinks he will. If the weather is bad, he could be delayed for days – leaving me kicking my heels in Le Havre.' He stopped and drew an exasperated breath. 'But that isn't really what's bothering me.'

'Then what?'

'I'm going to need to take Francis and Jem with me. Francis for back-up and Jem in case messages need to be sent. And I don't like the idea of leaving you and Pauline alone here – not even for the three days that is all this should take provided everything goes smoothly.'

Athenais sat up a little straighter and shook her head.

'Pauline and I will be fine. It's not like ... before ... so you don't need to worry about us. And I'd much rather Francis and Jem were with you. You *need* them. And I – I don't want to think of you possibly facing danger on your own.'

'It wouldn't be the first time I've done so,' he murmured, smiling a little. 'But I thank you for your concern.'

'*Don't!*' She stood up in a flurry of skirts. 'Don't be so damned polite! I know things between us have been ... difficult lately. But that doesn't mean I don't care as much as I always did. You *know* it doesn't. So don't insult me by saying 'thank you' in that chilly, well-mannered way of yours. It – it makes me want to *hit* you.'

'Ah.' Quite without haste, he strolled over to face her. 'There you are.'

Athenais planted her hands on her hips and glared at him.

'I've no idea what you mean.'

'My beautiful little volcano,' he explained with a grin. 'The one that always erupts when I least expect it. But it's been a while ... and I thought I'd lost her.'

* * *

Ashley found a private moment to acquaint Francis with the story he'd given Athenais and told him to pass it on to Pauline when the opportunity arose. Later, the four of them walked to the theatre and Ashley chose to stay through the performance in order to snatch a few words with Etienne Lepreux.

Once back at home, the atmosphere was inevitably a little strained. Everyone took a glass of wine but conversation grew increasingly desultory. In the end and for different reasons, both Athenais and Pauline chose to retire, leaving Ashley and Francis facing each other across the hearth.

Ashley said, 'As far as I'm aware, we're as ready as we'll ever be. Once we leave here tomorrow, I won't see you again till the inn near Louviers – so if you've any doubts or questions, now would be the time to raise them.'

'Aside from being shut in a carriage with Cyrano de Bergerac for God knows how long, nothing springs to mind,' replied Francis lightly.

'Then I suggest we both go and face the music with our respective ladies – since that's doubtless what's in store for us tonight.' He paused and then added, 'By the way, I've arranged for Etienne Lepreux to escort them home each evening while we're away. He was happy to do it anyway but has asked for more fencing lessons by way of a reward.'

'God,' said Francis, heading for the door. 'Some people are gluttons for punishment. Speaking for myself, I hope never to face you over a sword again.'

* * *

Francis found Pauline still fully-dressed and sitting by the window, staring out into the dark. When he entered the room, she turned her head and said baldly, 'I don't mean to make this difficult for you. But I find I just can't accept the possibility that, after tomorrow, I might never see you again.'

He sat beside her and wrapped his arm around her.

'I know that. And the fact that you care that much means more to me than you can possibly imagine. As for the rest … I've faced worse, you know. Worcester was an abomination. But Ashley got me out of there and I've every faith he'll get me out of Honfleur, too – should my own skills prove insufficient.' He leaned his cheek on her hair. 'Your role is equally difficult … and hiding your concern from Athenais will require all your formidable talent.'

She nodded and disengaged herself so that she could stand up and offer him her hand. 'Come, then. Take me to bed and hold me. Just that and no more.'

'If that's what you want.'

'I want the comfort of having you close … and I want you to sleep.' She paused and drew a long, fortifying breath. 'And if you promise you'll come back to me, I'll give you another promise in return.'

Francis captured her gaze and held it. 'Yes?'

'If you come back safe … and if you're still of the same mind … I'll marry you.'

* * *

Ashley, meanwhile, walked in on something very different. Athenais had shed her clothes and was sitting cross-legged on the bed, clad in her night-rail and the hideous pink wrapper, both of which were sliding off one shoulder. The mass of curling copper curls were fastened haphazardly on top of her head, with odd strands falling about her ears and her bare toes peeked out from beneath the hem of her robe. For a second, Ashley stopped dead on the threshold, trying to recover his breathing whilst simultaneously fighting the wave of hot, wild hunger that immediately washed through him.

Oh God, he thought. *Not now. I can't do this now.*

Aware of his hesitation if unaware of its cause, Athenais smiled uncertainly and said, 'There's something I want to tell you. Something I should have said ages ago, really.'

This wasn't good. On any other night, he'd have made some excuse. On this particular night, knowing what lay ahead, he couldn't – which meant his only hope lay in keeping it as brief as possible.

'Yes?'

Her uncertainty grew. 'Won't you take off your coat and sit down for a moment?'

He didn't want to do either one. Retaining his coat was a necessity. And the position that offered the best chance of hiding the state of his body was the one that offered the least comfort. Choosing the lesser of two evils, he gritted his teeth and sat on the bed, as far away from her as possible.

He said, 'What is it you wanted to say?'

'It's ... difficult.' She looked down and started fussing with her sash. 'It's about why I haven't been able ... the reason it's taking me so long to ...' She stopped, swallowed hard and began again. 'It's what's stopping me going to bed with you.'

Holy hell. As if things weren't bad enough, it was going to be that *kind of conversation.*

'You don't need to explain. I think I understand it well enough.'

'Perhaps. Perhaps not. It isn't anything physical. I'm perfectly well. And it isn't you or that I'm afraid or that I f-find the prospect of lying with you unbearable.'

'That's comforting.' *Get to the point, darling. I'm aware that this important but I'm in serious trouble here.* 'So what is it?'

Athenais looked up, her eyes wide and apologetic.

'He said things while he was ...' Another pause. 'He did it deliberately because he wanted me to remember it if – when I lay with you again. And though I've tried to put it from my mind, I haven't quite been able to. So I'm scared it will come back at the worst possible time and ruin things between us. Do you see?'

For Ashley, mention of the Marquis had the effect of a douche of freezing water and his body reacted accordingly. Physically, the relief was indescribable. Mentally, he had the usual urge to ram his fist into something. Moving a little closer to her, he reached out and took her hand, saying quietly, 'Yes. Of course I see. And I don't want you to worry or feel obliged to do anything before you're ready. As for ruining what's between us ... he can't, love. I won't allow it.'

Her fingers twined with his and clung.

'This probably wasn't the best time to tell you,' she said, 'I don't know why it suddenly seemed so important, except that you're going away and I didn't want you to do that thinking that I don't want you any more or that I wouldn't give anything in the world for things to be as they were before.'

So would I, thought Ashley grimly. *And once bloody Honfleur is behind me, we'll have to see what can be done about that.* But he merely smiled and said, 'At the risk of having you hit me, I thank you for that – and for explaining how you feel. You should do it more often.'

'I know.' She continued to look at him as if unsure of what to say next. Then, 'Will you wake me to say goodbye in the morning?'

'I don't think so. I'll be leaving very early and you look charming when you're asleep.'

'Oh. Then would you ... do you think you could kiss me goodbye now?'

This was a good deal more than he'd either expected or hoped for.

'You're sure?'

'Yes. Please.'

'Now who's being overly-polite?' he teased, tucking an errant strand of hair behind her ear and closing the rest of the space between them. 'Do you remember what I told you to do the very first time I kissed you?'

It took her a moment to realise what he meant. Then, with a tiny laugh, she said, 'Yes. I'm to tell you if it's horrible.'

'The slightest push will do.'

He put his arms around her, being careful to hold her loosely, and slowly, lightly brushed her mouth with his own. She sighed and her eyes fluttered shut. Encouraged, Ashley slid his tongue along her lower lip and felt her lean a little closer. He kissed the corner of her mouth and then drew back, waiting.

Athenais's hands travelled from his chest up to his shoulders and she made a small sound which sounded very much like disappointment. He laid one palm firmly against her back and allowed the other to slide up into her hair. Then he laid a trail of butterfly kisses along her cheek and jaw. By the time he returned to her mouth, her lips were parted, waiting for him.

Since she seemed to be enjoying it, he cautiously allowed the kiss to deepen just a little. Then, while she still seemed ready for more, he ended it and released her.

She opened her eyes and stared into his with an expression that actually made him want to laugh. He said gravely, 'No. That's *not* the best I can do. But it's the best you're going to get for now.'

Her smile was sudden and blinding. 'No rushing?'

'No, darling. No rushing.' He let his fingers brush her cheek and then stood up. 'I'll be gone as short a time as possible. Meanwhile, I forbid you to fret.'

'I'll try not to,' said Athenais huskily. 'But know that I'll miss you.'

TWELVE

Early on the following morning, Ashley and Jem made their way to the Louvre via different routes but managed to arrive within minutes of each other. Ashley led the way to the room designated by Chancellor Hyde and discovered that it was locked. He frowned a little, then frowned rather more when he located the key on top of the lintel.

'Idiot,' he muttered. 'If you're going to leave the key for any jackass to find, why bother locking it?'

Deciding that the Colonel wasn't in the best of moods, Jem wisely kept his mouth shut and followed him inside.

Amongst a plethora of rubbish, everything he had asked for lay in readiness. Instructing Jem to change into the footman's livery, Ashley set about checking the firing-mechanism of the pistols and the bags of powder and shot that accompanied them. That done, he counted the money and was surprised by Hyde's generosity. And finally, like Jem, he shed his own clothes in favour of the coachman's dark coat and enveloping cloak. Fortunately, the outfit included a wide-brimmed hat which concealed most of his hair and gave him the sort of nondescript appearance that usually went unnoticed.

Dropping the pistols into the pockets of his heavy driving-coat, he passed the powder and shot to Jem and said, 'The coach will be in the stable-yard. But I'm not sure how long we can hang around there without inviting questions, so I think we'd better make ourselves comfortable here for an hour or so.'

'Suits me,' remarked Jem. And subsided on a heap of moth-eaten rugs.

For Ashley, the hour felt like two. He went through every step of his plans twice, praying that Francis and Cyrano had set off as planned. He tried and failed not to dwell on Athenais's invitation to kiss her. And finally he took to pacing the floor.

When he heard a clock chiming eleven, he drew a breath of pure relief and said, 'Right, then. Come on, Jem – move your sorry carcass. Time to set the game in play.'

'A game, is it?' Mr Barker heaved himself to his feet and brushed down his borrowed livery. 'Not like no game I ever played, it ain't.'

Ashley ran a critical stare over him and said briskly, 'We'll have to take your own coat with us for tomorrow night. That tunic is too damned eye-catching.'

It was dark blue, trimmed with bright yellow braid and Jem rather liked it. But he picked up his discarded coat without argument and started calculating what his chances were of keeping his new finery afterwards.

The stable-yard was busy but Ashley was relieved to see a plain black travelling coach waiting near the steps to that part of the palace where the King's apartments lay. With a curt, business-like gesture for Jem to follow him, he strode across to it and dismissed the youth who was dithering around the horses. A jerk of his head told Jem to take the lad's place while Ashley himself strutted around the coach, examining the wheels and axle. He exuded an air of one who didn't suffer fools gladly which effectively kept the other servants at bay. Then the double-doors opened and Charles and his brother sauntered down towards them.

Under cover of cuffing Jem round the head, Ashley muttered, 'You're a groom. Do your bloody job.'

And, with a bit of slightly overdone cringing, Jem shot round to open the carriage door and let down the steps.

There were numerous people in the yard, not all of them busy. Charles caught Ashley's eye for a moment and then said, 'Your name, coachman?'

'Vauban, milord. Your Majesty, I should say.' Ashley bowed low and clumsily. 'Where might I have the honour of driving Your Majesty this day?'

'Honfleur,' said Charles clearly.

'Honfleur is it?' He pursed his lips. 'Not before dark, I'm thinking.'

'By easy stages,' came the lazy reply. 'My brother and I have no wish to endure unnecessary jolting.'

'Always a smooth ride with Vauban at the reins, Your Majesty,' boasted Ashley earnestly.

Laughter stirred in the King's eyes. 'Indeed?'

'Guaranteed! So if Your Majesty and His Highness would be pleased to take your seats ... Honfleur it is.'

'Excellent,' murmured Charles as he and James climbed aboard the coach. 'Do you think three times is sufficient?'

'If it's not, they're either deaf or stupid,' breathed Ashley. And, gesturing for Jem to take up the steps and shut the door, he climbed on to the box and took up the reins.

Never having driven a team before, Ashley found negotiating the coach out of the stable-yard and through the city's busy streets a trial. The strain on his shoulders and arms surprised him and he looked forward to reaching more open road. He also looked forward to finding out if anyone was following them.

* * *

To Francis's immense relief, Cyrano de Bergerac was neither drunk nor in a mood of particular ebullience. As for the two ex-soldiers sitting on the box of the dilapidated hired coach, they were as taciturn a pair as he'd ever met and merely grunted an acknowledgement before relapsing once more into silence.

He and Cyrano loaded weapons and the costumes they would wear as the King and the Duke of York and then climbed aboard themselves. The interior of the coach smelled of sweat and onions. Francis couldn't decide which was worse.

For a time, as they rattled over the cobbles, neither he nor the Frenchman spoke. But finally Francis said curiously, 'Tell me ... are you really doing this to pass a dull Tuesday?'

'You don't think one can do something just for fun?' returned Cyrano. And then, 'Why did you write your play?'

Acknowledging the hit with a slight gesture of one hand, Francis said, 'You saw it?'

'I did. It is unusual and it made me laugh. Best of all, it got Pauline Fleury back on the boards.' Cyrano folded his arms and leaned back against the squabs. 'How did you manage that?'

'Truthfully? I bullied her into it.'

'Did you indeed? A novel experience in that lady's life, I would imagine.'

Francis refrained from comment and silence fell again. But presently Cyrano said, 'Colonel Peverell seems to know what he's doing. I hope it's not just on the surface.'

'It isn't. He is experienced in a variety of ways. And, if you really want to know, engaging in swordplay with him is like fighting two men at once,' said Francis. And added ruefully. 'Or so it seemed to me.'

Cyrano merely nodded. 'And his man ... Jem, is it?'

'An out-and-out rogue. But loyal – and reliable, when it counts.' Francis thought it was time to pose a question of his own. 'Isn't it a little late to be asking all this?'

'Not at all. Knowledge is always useful. It just doesn't make any difference now.' And tipping his hat over his eyes, Cyrano leaned back and decided to take a nap.

* * *

As soon as the city was behind them, Ashley drew up briefly to allow Jem to join him on the box. An hour later, with little other traffic on the road, he said, 'There's a horseman behind us. He's been with us since just outside Paris. Unless he's riding a slug, there's no reason he couldn't have overtaken us by now.'

'Seen him,' agreed Jem laconically. 'What do you want to do?'

'Nothing yet. We'll be pulling up for a change of horses in about an hour. He'll either pass us then, or he won't. Let's find out which.'

They rolled on to Mantes-la-Jolie and pulled up for the change. Ashley haggled with the ostler and then left Jem to oversee the setting of new horses inside the traces while he opened the carriage door and asked his passengers if they wished to stretch their legs. The Duke of York hopped down with every sign of relief. Charles followed more slowly and, noting Ashley's expression, said, 'What is it?'

'I think we're being followed, Sir. I'll know for certain if the fellow is still behind us when we leave here.'

'And if he is?'

'We leave him alone for the time being. After that ... well, we'll see.

'I don't suppose you'd like to tell me what you have in mind?'

Ashley met the King's gaze with a very direct one of his own.

'No, Sir. I wouldn't.'

They resumed their journey. And some twenty minutes later, the solitary horseman duly reappeared round a bed in the road behind them.

'Bugger,' said Jem.

'Not necessarily,' came the thoughtful reply.

* * *

Having left Paris much earlier in order to take a more meandering route, Francis and Cyrano arrived in Louviers well before the royal party and pulled up behind a cheerful-looking inn rejoicing under the name of the Fleur-de-Lys.

Cyrano jumped out, offered the inn-keeper a brief handshake and said tersely, 'Get the coach out of sight, Pierre. Are the rooms ready?'

'Of course, Monsieur.'

'Good. We'll see to the luggage and leave the rest to you. If anyone asks, we're not here.'

Upstairs in a pleasant bed-chamber, Francis said idly, 'You seem to know an inordinate number of very helpful gentlemen.'

'People don't cross me,' said Cyrano simply. 'I may not be quite as black as I'm painted – but a fearsome reputation has its uses.'

Francis laughed. 'I'll take your word for it. Ask anyone about me and they'll say I'm a frivolous fellow who talks too much.'

'And are you?'

'Not any longer.'

'Then that has its uses, as well.' He pulled a silver-laced coat of sapphire broadcloth from his portmanteau, followed by another of gold-laced crimson. 'My word ... won't we look pretty?'

'One of us will,' said Francis gently. And smiled.

Understanding his guests need to remain out of sight, the inn-keeper sent up a tray of bread and cheese, along with pots of ale. While they ate, the two of them debated the merits of the Théâtre du Marais versus the Hôtel de Bourgogne and the players of both companies. Cyrano reduced Francis to gales of laughter with an account of his last encounter with Montfleury and Francis responded with a description of his and Ashley's attempts to teach Etienne Lepreux and his colleagues to fence. They were just about to send down for more ale when sounds from outside drew them to the window.

Colonel Peverell had arrived.

Some minutes later there were sounds of movement and muted conversation from the room next door. Then, a little while later, Ashley walked in and, on glancing around the room, said, 'I'm glad you've made yourselves so comfortable.'

'No you're not,' said Francis, passing him what was left of his own mug of ale. 'You're tired, hungry and your throat's full of dust. Where's Jem?'

'Busy.' Ashley downed the ale in one swallow, reached for the last remaining piece of cheese and subsided on the edge of the bed. 'We were followed all the way from Paris. The fellow's here somewhere, lying in wait. Jem's gone to find him.'

'And then?' It was Cyrano who asked.

'I thought you and I might have a little chat with him.'

'Ah. I take it we've no intention of letting him follow us on to Honfleur?'

'What do you think?'

'Excellent.' Cyrano rose, stretched and cracked his knuckles. 'And in the meantime, while we wait for your man to return ... am I going to meet this King I'm to impersonate?'

'Yes. I don't know if it's from gratitude or curiosity ... but he's already asked for you.'

* * *

Jem came back a couple of hours later.

'The cove's stabled his mare in a deserted barn at the far end of the village. There's a flea-pit of a tavern down there and he went in for a bite. But I reckon he's planning on bedding down with his horse. Means he don't have to talk to nobody and it's as good a place as any for seeing what passes on the road out of here.'

'Well done,' said Ashley. 'Find some food and get some rest. Monsieur de Bergerac's men are watching the doors downstairs so there's nothing else for you to do tonight.'

'And the tail?' asked Jem.

'I'll deal with him. One way or another.'

Having armed themselves, Ashley and Cyrano made their way through the dark to the barn Jem had described. They spoke only once.

Cyrano said, 'If this man doesn't appear in Honfleur, can we be sure anyone else will?'

'No – but there are ways round that. And I don't want to pass up the chance of any useful information. Also, there'll be one less for us to face at the other end.'

Hanging drunkenly from its sole remaining hinge, the door to the barn was unlocked and illuminated within by the dismal light from a lantern hooked to a beam. In the far corner, their quarry lay asleep on a pile of straw with his saddle-bags under his head. Cyrano's teeth gleamed in a grin. Ashley pulled the knife from his boot and strolled noiselessly across the floor.

The first thing the sleeping man knew was the sensation of an ice-cold blade lying gently against his cheek. His eyes flew open in a wild stare and he made an involuntary choking sound.

'I'd advise you against shouting or making any sudden movements,' said Ashley, withdrawing the knife just a little. 'We'll begin with your name.'

The man swallowed hard and said, 'Who the hell are you?'

He spoke French but Ashley and Cyrano exchanged a swift glance, aware that it wasn't his native tongue.

As much to avoid revealing his own nationality as to allow Cyrano to follow the conversation, Ashley chose not to switch to English. He said, 'Who I am is of no consequence. I want to know who *you* are.'

With more nerve than good sense, considering his current situation, the fellow told Ashley to perform a feat that was anatomically impossible.

Sighing, Ashley rose and stepped back. Then, gesturing to Cyrano, 'Get him on his feet, will you?'

Cyrano did so and bounced him into the wall for good measure.

Handling the blade with casual expertise, Ashley moved in and said softly, 'You should know that I've no scruples about hurting you if it gets me what I want and that I can damage you quite a lot without impairing your ability to talk. It should also be clear to you that you're not going anywhere until my friend and I let you. So, for the third time of asking – and the last one on which I'll be polite – tell me your name.'

The look in the man's eyes suggested that he'd finally realised just how much trouble he was in. He said gruffly, 'Jack Cardale.'

'Good. Well now, Jack … you've been following my coach all day. We'll come to *why* later. First, I'd like to know what your orders were and who gave them to you.'

'I don't know what you're talking about. I've just been riding the same road as you. There's no law against that, is there?'

'None. But we both know that's not all you were doing. And, since I don't want this to take all night, I suggest you stop wasting my time.' Held in apparently playful fingers, the knife edged a little closer. 'Who are you supposed to report to when you reach Honfleur?'

'Nobody. And report what? I'm not doing anything. If you think I am, you've got the wrong man.'

'I'm certainly getting the wrong answers.' This time Ashley brought the razor-sharp tip of his blade to a point against the man's right shoulder and exerted just enough pressure to prick the skin through his coat. 'Try again. And bear in mind that I can spot a lie at twenty paces.'

Jack dragged in several ragged breaths of air. Finally, he said sullenly, 'Somebody named Guillaume at the *Coq d'Or*.'

'Guillaume who?'

He moved as if to shrug and then thought better of it.

'Don't know. I've never met him.'

'Really? Then how are the two of you to recognise each other?'

Jack clamped his jaws together and said nothing.

'How?' Ashley leaned very slightly on the blade so that it pierced flesh, causing the breath to hiss between Jack's teeth. 'If I press this knife home, your right arm will be paralysed – so don't be an idiot. How will you know each other?'

'Red feather,' mumbled Jack reluctantly.

'Oh God,' groaned Ashley. 'I might have known. How stupid *are* you people?' Then, without waiting for an answer, 'All right. Let's move on. I know you're involved in a plot to assassinate His Majesty, the King and His Grace, the Duke of York. I also know that the plan was hatched in London. I intend to make sure it fails and you're going to give me the information that will help me do it. Now. I'm presuming you've been following us in order to inform Guillaume that Charles and James have arrived as planned. Correct?'

Jack had no more colour to lose. 'More or less.'

'Elucidate.'

'What?'

'Tell me what I'm missing.' Again, Jack didn't reply. Ashley prompted him by increasing his pressure so the knife slid in another half-inch. 'Quickly.'

Past a grunt of pain, Jack said unevenly, 'I'm checking up on him.'

'Ah.' The knife remained steady, neither advancing nor retreating. 'London doesn't trust him?'

'I suppose not,' muttered Jack. 'All I was told is that he's new and they wanted to be sure he'd done what he said.'

Ashley looked across at Cyrano.

'Using an untried tool for a task of this magnitude? What does that suggest?'

'That Guillaume can do something their usual fellows can't,' came the calm reply. 'Would you like me to shake this bastard up a bit and see what falls out?'

'Not just yet.' Ashley returned his attention to Jack, now looking increasingly alarmed. 'My friend is getting bored. For myself, I've always made it a principle not to kill anyone I didn't have to ... but for a potential regicide, I'm prepared to make an exception. So why don't you just save yourself some pain and tell us everything you know.'

'Why should you care?' asked Jack, bitterly. 'You two are bloody French.'

'We have a peculiar aversion to cold-blooded murder,' returned Ashley, pleasantly contemptuous. Then, 'I assume that, like you, your fellow plotters are English. How many of them are there? I'm losing patience – so think carefully before you answer. How many?'

'I've told you. I don't --' The knife twisted slightly as it bit further into his shoulder and he yelped. 'Five, I think. Five others, sailing from Dover.'

Leaving the knife buried an inch deep in Jack's flesh, Ashley flicked a glance at Cyrano and said, 'Six. Five without this one – unless Guillaume joins the party.'

The Frenchman nodded and, using all of his considerable weight, pinned Jack to the wall by his throat. He said, 'They're not already here, then?'

'No.'

'So they're due to arrive tomorrow.'

'The next day.' Blood was soaking Jack's coat and Cyrano's hand was almost but not quite cutting off his air supply. 'Didn't … didn't want to be in France longer than necessary.'

Cyrano relaxed his grip and his eyes locked with Ashley's as they both thought, *Somebody's got the wrong day. Us – or them?*

'And the place and time of the attack?'

'Just – just off the harbour-front. After dark. Late.' And when the knife moved again, he cried, 'Don't! I don't *know*. If I knew I'd say.'

'Do we believe him?' murmured Ashley.

'Probably,' replied Cyrano. And dragging a moan of fear from Jack, 'If we don't, there's always tomorrow. But in the meantime, what do you want to do with him?'

Ashley withdrew the knife and stepped back.

'You want some fun? Knock him out.'

So with one massive punch and no warning whatsoever, the Frenchman did. Jack slithered down the wall and lay still. Cyrano grinned, flexed his fist and said, 'So now I suppose we truss him, load him on to his horse and take him with us.'

Ashley nodded. 'We can hide him overnight in the carriage you came in and leave your fellows on guard. But first we'll find his damned red feather.'

'Red feather?'

'Don't ask. Suffice it to say, we need it.' Ashley dropped on one knee and began searching Jack's pockets. 'As for this inept fellow … we'll send him back to Paris for Hyde to play with.' He located the feather and held it up in triumph. Then, with a grin, he said, 'Charles wanted a role in all of this. So I'm sure he and James won't mind a rather cramped journey home.'

THIRTEEN

With his usual good-humour, the King accepted the addition of a bound and gagged English spy to the floor of his carriage. The Duke of York was less happy with the arrangement but relapsed into silent sulkiness when he found his objections carried no weight.

At first light on the following morning, therefore, two coaches left the Fleur de Lys, travelling in different directions. The shabby hired one took a road that would eventually lead to Paris … while the more elegant of the two, with Jack Cardale's roan tied to the back of it, set off for Honfleur. Inside it, Cyrano and Francis congratulated themselves on having made a change for the better and wondered how Charles and James were enjoying the smell of stale sweat.

Since, if Mr Cardale's information was to be trusted, they were now destined to arrive at their destination a day early, Ashley kept to a steady pace and used the time to give Jem his instructions.

Mr Barker listened incredulously and then said, 'I can't do that. I ain't bloody French.'

'Neither is the fellow we intercepted.'

'But he parlays the old Fronsay. I don't.'

'I think we can assume that Guillaume understands English. In fact, for all we know, he may actually *be* English.'

'That don't make it any better,' grumbled Jem. 'He'll smell a rat. Bound to.'

'No. He won't. As yet, he doesn't know anyone was checking up on him – though if he's got half a brain he won't be surprised. You know his name and where to find him and you'll be sporting their idiotic feather so he'll have no reason to question your identity. All you have to do is let him know Charles has arrived and find out if this thing is happening tonight or tomorrow. Claim that you've replaced someone else and your orders weren't clear. Then come back and let me know what he says.'

'If I ain't walked into a knife, you mean.'

'Oh for God's sake!' Ashley drew an impatient breath. 'If it's scaring you into a jelly, I'll do it myself.'

'I ain't scared!'

'That's not how it sounds. Your nerves must be shot.'

'They're as good as yours,' snapped Jem, cut to the quick. Then, 'Oh bugger it. I'll go. And if I wind up dead, on your head be it.'

'If you wind up dead,' replied Ashley grimly, 'you can be fairly sure you won't be the only one. Now stop complaining and let me think.'

* * *

They pulled into Honfleur in the late afternoon and headed for an inn as far as possible from the pungent smell of salted fish that seeped up from the harbour. As soon as they were settled in, Ashley despatched Jem to the *Coq d'Or*. Then, while Francis and Cyrano settled down to a game of dice, he waited.

Jem returned just over an hour later – alive and unharmed but looking decidedly unsettled.

'What?' said Ashley tersely.

Jem huffed and shook his head.

'You ain't going to like it.'

'*What?*'

'Guillaume. He ain't French.'

'So?'

'So he's the bloody eye-patch,' said Jem bitterly.

There was a sudden abrupt silence, broken only by the sound of the dice Francis had been about to roll hitting the floor. Then Cyrano said disbelievingly, 'William Brierley?'

For a seemingly endless moment, his mouth set in a hard line and his eyes locked with Jem's, Ashley didn't speak. Then, in a voice like splintering ice, he said, 'He didn't recognise you?'

'No.'

'What did he say?'

'He said it's set for tonight, at the Two Pigeons by the harbour, an hour after midnight.'

'Something's not right about that,' remarked Francis, frowning.

'Clearly,' snapped Ashley, reaching for his sword. 'Not to put too fine a point on it, the whole thing stinks.'

'Perhaps the fellow we caught had it wrong?' suggested Cyrano.

'And perhaps he didn't.' Ashley snatched up his hat and headed for the door only to be stopped by Francis's hand on his arm. He said, 'Get out of my way. I've neither the time nor the inclination to discuss this now.'

'So I see,' replied Francis, tightening his grip. 'But you should at least *think*.'

'*You* think.' Ashley dislodged the restraining hand with a swift, savage chop to the wrist. '*I'm* going to get some get some answers.' And, wrenching open the door, he went clattering down the stairs.

'Hell,' breathed Francis, nursing his throbbing arm. 'Shouldn't somebody go after him. You? Me? All three of us?'

Cyrano leaned back in his chair and shook his head.

'No. He won't appreciate it. And, from what I saw last night, he's more than capable of dealing with this on his own.' He paused. 'Why didn't you mention that there's a cold-blooded bastard lurking behind that pretty face?'

* * *

By the time he arrived outside the *Coq d'Or*, Ashley had his temper under some sort of control. He was still mind-blowingly furious but he knew better than to let that rule him. He wanted the truth. And, one way or another, he intended to get it.

A coin in the right palm gained him the location of Monsieur Guillaume's room, to which a tray of food had just been delivered. Another coin assured him that there would be no interruptions. He climbed the stairs, found the door he wanted and walked in without bothering to knock.

Caught with a mouthful of chicken, Sir William Brierley shot to his feet, choked and spat. Then, still coughing, he managed to say, '*Ashley? What in God's name --?*'

'Am I doing here?' Ashley dropped the bolt of the door and leaned against it. 'Take a wild guess. I'm sure you'll figure it out.'

'Ah. Yes.' He paused for a moment, as if trying to think. Then, 'How did you find out?'

'What difference does that make?'

'None, I suppose. I just hadn't expected it.'

'Is that all you can say?' Ashley tried and failed to steady his breathing. 'What the bloody hell do you think you're doing?'

Will looked back warily. He noted the pulse hammering in the tight jaw and fact that the look in the green eyes spoke of violence, barely held in check. These signs, coupled with Ashley's mere presence were sufficient to answer most of his questions so he said wearily, 'It's not how it appears.'

'Isn't it? You're saying you *haven't* turned your coat and involved yourself in a plot to murder the King and his brother?'

'In the sense you mean it – no. I haven't.'

'What other sense is there?' Ashley gave a sharp, insulting laugh. 'Not that I'm likely to believe a word you say.'

'We've known each other a long time, Ashley. Perhaps you should hear me out first.'

'Oh – I'm sure you'll manage to make it sound convincing. You're an even better liar than I am. But unless you can provide me with proof that you're not working for Cromwell, you aren't going to leave this room in any condition to prosecute your damned plot.'

'I suspect,' sighed Sir William, 'that my damned plot is already redundant. Are Charles and James really here in Honfleur?'

'What do you think?'

'That they're not. In one sense, I suppose that's probably for the best. In another, it's going to make things a trifle … awkward.'

'Awkward?' Ashley detached himself from the door, strode forward and, with one hard shove to the chest, deposited Will back into his chair. 'You're up to your neck in Christ knows what … you're putting the King's life on the line … and you call that *awkward*? What the hell is the *matter* with you?'

Sir William ran his hands over his face, dislodging his eye-patch and then re-adjusting it. He said, 'That fellow who was here earlier. Yours, I presume?' And when he received no reply, 'Of course he is. I won't ask what you've done with the fellow he replaced. I'm sure it was something creative. Since you've saved me a job, I suppose I should be grateful. And, back at your inn I suppose are a couple of men you've brought along to pass as Charles and James. Yes?'

Folding his arms so his hands wouldn't stray to his former friend's throat, Ashley said gratingly, 'I know what I've done. What I want to know is what the fuck *you've* done.'

Will sighed and pinched the bridge of his nose.

'I've just sent four men to secure both the King and his brother.'

Ashley's eyes narrowed. 'To what end?'

'I'll come to that in a moment. Who --'

'No. We'll come to it now. Secure Charles and James for what purpose?'

'To keep them out of the way. What else? Who are my fellows *really* going to find at your inn?'

The hard mouth curled in a disquieting smile.

'Viscount Wroxton and Cyrano de Bergerac.'

Sir William's head fell back against his chair.

'*Merde*. Cyrano will massacre them.'

'Good,' snapped Ashley. Then, 'Enough of this. Have you or have you not sold your services to the Commonwealth?'

'They think I have.'

'What's that supposed to mean?'

'That I've *let* them think it. They approached me. I saw a way of obtaining information that wouldn't otherwise come our way, so I let them think I was amenable ... and that my services were for sale.' Will sat up again. 'Obviously, it took time. But then this came up. They needed someone with access to Charles and I fitted the bill. I knew it was also their way of putting me to the test but the risks seemed worth it because it offered an opportunity to tie Cromwell and Thurloe to something very few people would find acceptable. The attempted murder of the young King.'

Ashley didn't bother to remark that he was hoping to do the same thing. He said, 'Except, from what I can see, it wouldn't merely have been attempted.'

'Yes. It would. The team from London won't arrive until tomorrow and I --'

'The team?' cut in Ashley sarcastically. 'Don't you mean the enticing meeting with Major-General Lambert aimed at the King's restoration?'

'Non-existent, as you well know. Do you think I might finish?'

'Why not? I'm still waiting for the interesting part.'

Sir William ignored this and said patiently, 'I knew they'd have somebody watching – if not me, then Charles. They'd want to know he'd taken the bait. I'm assuming you made it look as though he had?'

'You mean, did I have Charles leave the Louvre in full view of twenty or so people? Yes. And now, God willing, he's more than half-way back to Paris. How exactly did *you* plan to get him out of the way?'

'I got him here a day early so the plan would go ahead but I'd have time to persuade him to leave.'

'Oh for God's sake! As if *that* was likely to work. Don't you know Charles at all? Once he was here, he'd have insisted on staying on the off-chance that Lambert actually showed up. And how did you expect to protect him then? With the fellows Cyrano has probably just finished carving into small pieces?' He paused and then said flatly, 'You are not stupid, Will – and neither am I. But everything you've told me so far is totally bloody asinine and has more holes in it than a sieve. What, for example, were you going to do tomorrow night when five would-be assassins turned up to find that neither Charles nor James is here?'

'I wasn't going to wait for that. I was planning to take them down as soon as they came ashore.' Sir William watched Ashley's expression and then drew a long breath. 'You don't believe me, do you?'

'If you were in my position, would you?'

'Probably not.'

'I take it you can't prove anything you've told me?'

'Right now? No. Of course, by now Hyde ought to have guessed that I've been flirting with the enemy – since the information he's been receiving from me recently couldn't have been obtained any other way. But he's not here so you can't ask him.'

'That's convenient for you.'

'No. Actually, it isn't.'

'Really? Any minute now you'll be telling me that Hyde heard all about the assassination plot from you – which I know damned well he didn't.'

'No,' agreed Will. 'So the question is – what are you going to do now?'

As yet, Ashley had no idea. One part of him said, *Give him a chance to prove he's honest* … while another said, *No way in hell.* He could try getting to the truth with his fists but what he knew of Will made him doubt how well that would work. The only thing he knew for certain was that he wasn't letting him loose for a single minute until this thing was over.

At length, he said curtly, 'I wish I could trust you but I can't. So you're coming with me and staying where one of us can see you until your colleagues from Dover have been dealt with – which is an added complication I could have well done without.'

'And afterwards?'

'Afterwards, you can explain yourself to Hyde and Charles and anyone else who wants to listen. So long as you don't get in my way, I don't give a tinker's damn.' With a flick of his arm, he produced the knife he'd been carrying up his sleeve. 'And don't think to give me the slip. You know what I can do with this.'

* * *

The first thing that happened when Ashley ushered Sir William ahead of him into the inn was that the landlord started haranguing him about noise and breakages. Shaking him off, Ashley assured him that everything would be taken care of and continued nudging Will up the stairs. When he arrived outside room where he'd left his three friends, he took the precaution of knocking in case one of them was waiting to bash any further intruders over the head. The door swung open on Francis, brandishing a pistol. His knuckles were skinned and a bruise was starting to darken his jaw.

'Oh,' he said, lowering his aim. 'In an absence of volunteers, we were just drawing lots to decide which of us ought to go and see if you needed rescuing. Clearly, you don't.'

Ashley pushed Will into the room without speaking, shut the door behind him and looked around. Four men, bound, gagged and somewhat the worse for wear, sat in a row on the floor beneath the window with Jem close by, rhythmically tapping what appeared to be a chair-leg against his open palm. A further glance revealed where the chair-leg had come from, along with other assorted debris.

Ashley sighed. 'Has the inn-keeper asked us to leave?'

'Not yet.' Cyrano, who had been reclining at his ease on the bed, swung his feet to the floor and fixed Sir William with a cold stare. 'These others say they're yours. Is that true?'

'Yes.' Will looked at them irritably. 'They weren't supposed to come in fighting.'

'We didn't give them a lot of choice over that. But whatever you're paying them is probably too much. I've known girls who could fight better.'

Ashley nudged Will towards the room's only remaining usable chair. He said, 'Sir William would like us to believe him innocent of any evil intent towards the King and that these battered gentlemen were sent here to secure His Majesty's person.'

'They attempted to say something of the sort,' offered Francis. 'The fact that they came in holding pistols made us disinclined to take their word for it.'

'Likely to be any more of these buggers turning up?' asked Jem. 'Only if there are, we're gonna need another room. Unless you got a better idea?'

'At the moment,' said Ashley, raking a hand through his hair, 'I have no ideas at all. Tomorrow night, five men are going to come ashore looking for the King and his brother – which means we can proceed with our original plan, just a day later than expected. As for Sir William and his friends … we can't let them loose and we've nowhere else to put them. Basically, they're just going to be a bloody nuisance.'

'You could let my so-called friends go,' said Sir William. 'They weren't doing this for love, you know. Or you could let us help.'

'Help who?' asked Francis dryly.

Will looked at Ashley.

'As I remarked earlier, we've known each other for some years. Do you honestly believe I'd sell the King or turn my sword on you?'

'Honestly?' Ashley shook his head. 'I'm no longer sure what you'd do. You lied to me about your dealings with Lucy Walter and I still don't know what the truth of *that* is.'

'It was nothing to do with this. If you really want to know, I forged the thrice-blasted marriage lines myself.'

'You *what?*'

'I included, as you very well know, a verifiable mistake. I reasoned that, if *I* didn't do it, someone else would and possibly make a fool-proof job of it. I also wanted to see what Lucy would do next. As I believe I said once before, there was a chance she'd make such an ass of herself that nobody would ever take her seriously again. Of course what she *actually* did was to lose the damned thing and demand a replacement.'

'Which you provided.'

'Yes.' He paused, taking in Ashley's expression. 'Don't tell me. You know where both copies are.'

'As it happens, I do.' Ashley looked first at Jem and then at Francis. Finally, dropping his head in his hands, he said weakly, 'Oh my God. This just gets better and better, doesn't it?'

FOURTEEN

Everyone passed a very uncomfortable night. Ashley pacified the landlord with money he'd have preferred not to part with; Cyrano placed Sir William's chair beside his fallen comrades and tied him to it; and Jem and Francis went down to the kitchen in search of supper. Then, the four of them divided the hours of darkness into shifts so that two could sleep while the other pair guarded their unwanted prisoners.

Ashley watched the dawn come up over the hot-potch of gables and uneven rooftops he could see through the window. He might have thought the town pretty if he hadn't been tired, irritable and anxious. *Les quatre fleurs*, as Cyrano had christened Will's so-called protection squad, snored fitfully from the floor. William himself also slept … but the eye-patch had come adrift in the night and, though the good eye was closed, the unseeing one glared balefully at nothing. Trying not to look and hoping Will would wake and deal with it, Ashley slit the bonds on his hands with a flick of his knife.

Behind him, Jem stretched and, peering past him, said, 'Looks like a fine day.'

'Does it?' Ashley turned away, running his hands over his face. Then, for the first time ever, said, 'I don't know whether to let the hirelings go or leave them and Will tied up here tonight. Either one would be a case of hoping for the best. And since nothing else has gone smoothly, I don't trust our luck to change now.'

Unused, even obliquely, to having his opinion sought, Jem scratched his head and said, 'I suppose we could drug 'em. There's an apothecary down the street. Want me to pay him a visit?'

'Yes. Later, perhaps. It's as good an idea as any other but I suppose we owe Francis and Cyrano their say.' He grinned wryly. 'You know … I sometimes wonder why you stay with me. This can't be the life you hoped for.'

'No – but at least it ain't dull.' Jem coloured slightly and scuffed the floor with his boot. 'And, for all we've had our ups and downs, you're the nearest thing I've had to family in a good many years. Much though I hate to say it.'

Taken by surprise and rather touched, Ashley didn't how to respond.

'Then again,' Jem went on grudgingly, 'the King ain't such a bad fellow. So if you want to gut these murdering buggers, I'm with you.'

Sir William woke up with a start and groped for his eye-patch. Then, looking blearily around the room, he said, 'How disappointing. I'd hoped it was a nightmare.'

* * *

Jem fetched food and everyone broke their fast. Between bites, *les quatre fleurs* tried to convince their captors that, if released, they'd leave town by the fastest route, saying nothing to anybody. Cyrano grunted and scowled at them. They promptly dropped their eyes and stopped bleating.

Leaving Jem on sentry-duty armed with a pistol, Ashley, Francis and Cyrano decamped to the other room, taking Sir William with them.

Ashley said, 'Call this a Council of War. We have to make a decision and I want it to be one on which we're all agreed. Will ... do those four next door have political or personal allegiance of any kind?'

'No. They're unemployed mercenaries. They are also, as you may have noticed, French.' He fished in his pocket and threw a purse across the table. 'Give them that and either get rid of them or engage them for tonight. Your choice.'

Ashley looked across the room. 'Cyrano?'

'Get rid of them. They're about as much use as a stale custard.'

'Francis?'

Shrugging, Francis said, 'I agree. We can hardly keep them here, after all.'

Ashley drew a long breath and then pushed the purse towards Cyrano.

'Send them on their way, then. Frighten them a bit first, though. Or even a lot.'

'I can do that,' grinned the Frenchman. And sauntered out.

Will flexed his shoulders and said, 'And what about myself?'

'Make your case,' replied Ashley. 'We're listening.'

'What more is there that hasn't already been said? I told you once that my parameters differed from your own. That doesn't mean my motives are any less pure – merely that, in certain respects, my methods are more flexible. *You* don't mind getting your hands dirty when something unpleasant needs to be done. *I've* no objection to letting the opposition think I can be bought and paid for like a sixpenny whore.' He paused. 'My only mistake was not informing Hyde and, if you think about it, you'll understand why I didn't. For the rest, weigh up everything you know about me and decide whether you want me at your side tonight or sitting here tied to a chair – because I've finished justifying myself.'

Finding Ashley's eyes on him, Francis said, 'It's no use asking me. Unlike yourself and Cyrano, I met Sir William for the first time yesterday. He could be Attila the Hun, for all I know.'

Cyrano returned, followed by Jem. Both of them were laughing.

'They're gone?' asked Ashley.

'Couldn't get out quick enough,' grinned Jem. 'Tripping over their own feet, they was.' And, as Cyrano tossed the purse back on the table, 'Silly devils didn't even want paying.'

'Well, that's one problem solved. The next question is whether or not we accept Will's offer of help this evening. His presence would even up the odds ... but what matters is whether we all trust him. Cyrano?'

'I've less cause to doubt him than you – and he's useful in a fight.' He smiled at Sir William. 'On the other hand, if I see the slightest sign of duplicity, I'll stick a knife in your back. *D'accord*?'

'*D'accord*,' agreed Will. 'Ashley?'

Ashley stood up and glanced round at his assembled troops.

'I think Cyrano speaks for us all,' he said. 'And now ... let's tighten a few details and look for anything we might have missed. Then Jem can collect Will's belongings from the *Coq D'Or* while the rest of us reconnoitre the ground. From what I've seen so far, it's maze of narrow alleys, running between tall houses and St Catherine's Quay – so anyone could be hiding anywhere. But fortunately, that works both ways.'

* * *

By the time all of them were satisfied that they'd done everything they could and that nothing had been overlooked, darkness had fallen. They passed the final hours over a light supper, then Francis and Cyrano changed into their royal finery and Jem, having been forbidden his smart livery, took a long look at them both.

'Damn me,' he said, grinning at Francis. 'Proper little dandy-trap, you look.'

'Thank you. I think.' Francis tugged at the fair, luxuriantly-curling wig that he was fairly sure looked ridiculous. 'This itches. And it's hot. And my hat isn't going to fit.'

'Suits you, though,' murmured Jem, wickedly. 'Pity the ladies ain't going to see you.'

'Oh – sod off, Jem. Go and torment Cyrano, why don't you?'

Mr Barker opened his mouth but, before he could deliver any further witticisms, the door opened on Ashley and Sir William. Both were booted, cloaked and armed. In addition, presumably in an attempt to render himself a little less easily identifiable, Will had removed his eye-patch. Finding himself apparently impaled on that milky blind eye, Francis repressed a shudder.

'Time for Jem, Will and myself to get into position,' said Ashley, passing pistols and shot to both Francis and Cyrano. They'd discussed the question of firearms earlier and, though concluding they weren't likely to be of much use, decided they'd be no use at all if left behind at the inn. His glance skimmed three of the faces in front of him but lingered briefly on Francis. Then he said, 'Everything strictly according to the plan, gentlemen – right up to the moment of engagement. And then we guard each other's backs. Clear?' All four nodded tersely. 'Excellent. Then good luck – and good hunting.'

It was a few minutes short of midnight and the streets were dark, most households having extinguished their lanterns. The moon was in its first quarter and largely obscured by clouds but, from time to time, a fitful light gleamed on the damp cobbles. Leaving the inn behind them, Ashley and his companions made their way to the end of the street and then silently went their separate ways.

The smell of fish became overpowering as Ashley neared the harbour. Despite the hint of patchy mist, there was more light here, many of the boats floating cheek-by-jowl with each other still having lamps hanging from their masts. Ashley slipped wraith-like along in the shadows until he reached the turning that would take him to *Les Deux Pigeons*. Just as he approached the corner, light and voices spilled into the street, causing him to pull back into the nearest doorway. He heard a pair of slurred voices raised in objection, followed by the inn-keeper's caustic tones, telling them to go home and sleep it off. Then darkness fell again as the door slammed shut and a bolt was rammed home. Ashley stayed where he was while the disappointed customers stumbled into view, apparently holding each other up, and reeled drunkenly away along the quayside.

Ashley took a moment to reflect on the fact that, since the tavern was now shut for the night, there was definitely *not* going to be any secret meeting in an upstairs room. In truth, he'd never thought there would be ... but it was helpful to have his suspicious verified.

The voices of the two inebriates faded into the distance. Ashley decided that his current position was as good as any and remained perfectly motionless, listening to and identifying every sound. Water sloshed, timbers creaked and the occasional voice drifted out from one of the vessels in the harbour. So far, there was nothing at all untoward ... but Ashley knew that somewhere not too far away, five assassins would soon be lying in wait. If, that was, they weren't there already.

Walking from the inn to the quayside, Francis and Cyrano's route would bring them out at a carefully calculated point between himself and Will, with Jem keeping pace in between them. Ashley prayed that nothing would happen before they got there and that he hadn't made a mistake trusting One-Eyed Will. Then he wondered how Francis's nerves were holding up. Strolling along in the open, knowing you were a target was no easy thing. Partly to give him something else to think about and partly because Cyrano's small fund of English was overlaid by a strong French accent which would instantly give the game away, he'd told Francis to reinforce the illusion with the occasional fragment of conversation. Francis had responded to this by remarking that he was delighted his strengths were finally being recognised – thus making everyone smile. Ashley hoped they were all still smiling a few hours from now.

He stood motionless for what seemed an age until the bell-tower of St Catherine sent his nerves into spasm by announcing that it was one o'clock. Ashley steadied his breathing and kept his eyes on the empty stretch of the quay. Presently, from somewhere away to his right came the sound of booted feet on the cobbles and he froze, trying to determine how many. Then came the drift of Francis's lazy tones complaining of the all-pervading stink. Ashley loosened his sword in its scabbard and pulled the knife from his boot.

Not long now.

Though still some distance away, Cyrano and Francis came into view. Francis seemed to be saying something about a girl which, judging by his rumble of laughter, Cyrano had understood.

Christ, thought Ashley grimly. *This is no time for bawdy jokes. Concentrate, damn you.* Then, his eyes still raking the quay for any sign of the expected attackers, *Where the hell are they?*

And that was when he saw it.

Two dark shapes cresting the low harbour wall and dropping silently some dozen yards behind Francis and Cyrano. Drawing his sword and starting to edge along the buildings at his back, Ashley checked his instinctive shout of warning when he saw the sharp turn of Cyrano's head.

He'd heard. *Thank God.*

But Francis's attention was fixed in the other direction and, following it, Ashley saw two more bodies slithering into view some way further back from where he stood. The resulting gap offered him a chance of getting to Francis and Cyrano before this second pair could close in – but only if he acted now. He could see neither Will nor Jem which, though it was as it should be, wasn't an especially comforting thought just at present. Both Cyrano and Francis were drawing their swords, preparing to fight on two fronts. Ashley pushed away from the wall and broke into a run.

Out of the corner of his eye, he saw Jem doing the same but couldn't see Will. He wondered briefly where the fifth assassin was and hoped he was wasting his time looking for Jack Cardale. Then he was skidding to a halt a couple of yards from Francis and immediately pivoted to parry an oncoming blade.

Earlier in the day, he had stressed that this would be no time for finesse. They needed to incapacitate at least one of their opponents as fast as possible if they were to stand a chance of capturing any of the others. Consequently, he met the attack with savage force and followed through with disconcerting rapidity. Taken by surprise, the fellow retreated a few steps and then tried to stand his ground. Not wanting to drift too far from the centre of the fight, Ashley let him.

On his left, Francis seemed to be holding his own against a tall fellow with an abnormally long reach while, beyond him, Cyrano was battling with the other two and apparently giving both of them a hard time. Then Jem stormed up to join him. There was still no sign of Will and Ashley hadn't the time to look.

For perhaps three minutes, the fight eddied and flowed to neither side's advantage until, becoming aware that Francis was being driven gradually back, Ashley re-doubled his own efforts. He took a slash to the forearm but ignored it. Seeking a particular opening, he delivered a swift flurry of moves until he found he wanted. Then he drove his knife through the fellow's heart and swivelled to assist Francis. Unfortunately, before he could reach him, another man dropped over the harbour wall and rushed down on him.

Where the hell is Will? thought Ashley, as he leapt to meet the unexpected attack. And, managing to turn his new opponent with a lightning riposte, found the answer. Some two dozen yards away, Sir William was occupied with a fierce engagement of his own.

Meanwhile, left facing a single swordsman, Cyrano was able to drive the fellow back until his thighs hit the low wall. A deep thrust to the shoulder was sufficient to send him plummeting backwards over it. Cyrano grinned and glanced around. Jem's inexpert hacking and slashing was working well enough and he'd seemingly managed to inflict a couple of flesh-wounds with his knife; so like Ashley before him, Cyrano swung round to help Francis ... and, again like Ashley, found himself facing yet another new enemy.

Aware of it but busy contending with a stronger and more cautious fighter than the previous one, only two thoughts got past Ashley's concentration. The first was that, presumably hampered by having only partial vision, Will was apparently making little progress; and the second was, *Christ. Seven, so far. Have they sent a bloody regiment?*

Faces appeared at windows overlooking the harbour and then promptly withdrew again. Lanterns on many of the boats were being extinguished, as the men on board disappeared below deck.

Unsurprisingly, no one wanted anything to do with what was happening on the quay.

Spinning on his heel, Ashley narrowly avoided a thrust to the shoulder. Blood was starting to drip down his hand but wasn't yet impairing his grip. He parried and followed through with an immediate riposte. His adversary jumped back and circled.

Damn.

He tried to evaluate the situation. Two down; one definitely dead – and five still standing. For the moment, at least, the odds were even. But Francis was tiring; Jem, an inexpert swordsman, was still trying to disarm his opponent so he could close in with his knife; and Will, now much closer and limping badly, was gradually driving his attacker back towards the rest of them. Cyrano was still fighting like a demon and had inflicted some damage but, like himself, had so far failed to bring his current foe down. As far as Ashley could tell, all five of them were now bleeding – some more seriously than others. So if they were all to get out of this alive, it was going to be up to either himself or Cyrano to adjust the numbers in their favour.

Francis, meanwhile, had given up thinking at all. There was cramp in his hand and his shoulder was on fire. In desperation, he tried one of the deceptive moves that Ashley had taught him and knew, even as he launched into it, that he'd mistimed it. His reward was a savage thrust to his right bicep – which would have been quite bad enough even it if *hadn't* been in precisely the same spot as the wound he'd received at Worcester. His blade clattered to the cobbles and, swearing, he dropped to one knee, a hand clamped hard over his arm.

His attacker grunted with satisfaction and booted him in the chest.

Francis went sprawling. His hat rolled away, taking the blond wig with it.

The tall fellow stared for a second and then, apparently without thinking, blurted, 'That's not York!'

Into the tiny hiatus that followed, Ashley snapped breathlessly, 'It's not the King, either. I'm surprised you haven't noticed.'

For a split second, all five assassins froze – which proved to be the undoing of two of them. Cyrano sent his adversary's sword flying from his hand and kicked him in the groin. Ashley locked blades with his own opponent, forced a disarm and knocked the fellow out with a blow to the jaw using his sword-hilt. Then he swung round and, positioning himself in between Francis and the man who'd wounded him, said, 'We can finish this or you can accept your failure and withdraw. Either one is fine by me.'

For an instant, the tall man seemed completely nonplussed. He looked around at the bodies on the ground and those of his comrades still being threatened by Jem and Will. Finally, he said warily, 'If the King isn't here – why are you? It makes no sense.'

'That depends on your point of view,' replied Ashley. 'Well? Do we battle on?'

'To what end?' The fellow drew a long breath. 'A truce, then – while my colleagues and I collect our fallen friends?'

'You can take most of them,' came the cool reply. 'But these two ...' He gestured to the man writhing at Cyrano's feet and the one still out cold at his own, '... go with us.'

'I can't agree to that!'

'You prefer the rest of your men to die? Because they *are* your men, aren't they?' Shooting a brief, meaningful glance at Cyrano, Ashley swept the point of his sword downwards to rest on the throat of the fellow on the ground. 'As I said, it's all one to me.'

The tall man started forward and then stopped abruptly when he felt an icy blade feathering his neck. Forcing the words through clenched teeth, he indicated the man Ashley was threatening and said, 'That is my brother.'

'Is it? Then I imagine you don't want to see his throat cut. But since, like you, he came here to commit regicide ... and since I only need one of you alive, you'll appreciate that I really couldn't care less whose brother he is.'

'You cold-blooded bastard!'

Francis was still sitting on the ground, breathing raggedly and watching blood seep through his fingers, but the words spoken only two nights ago by Cyrano made him look up. He couldn't see Ashley's face – but he didn't need to. That light, negligent tone and allied with the unwavering sword-point was chilling enough. Since the night they'd disposed of d'Auxerre's body, Francis had been aware of the streak of icy ruthlessness that would let Ashley do whatever he thought necessary. He also suddenly recognised that he was less dangerous when he let his temper loose than when, as now, he kept it under rigid control. Francis had glimpsed The Falcon before but never quite as clearly as at this particular moment ... and it sent an unpleasant little shiver down his spine.

'Indeed. But what does that make you?' said Ashley. He let the inevitable pause linger for a moment and then said dispassionately, 'I can kill your brother now ... or I can take him back to be hanged. Or I might consider letting both him and the other fellow go ... if you volunteer to take their place.'

The tall fellow's eyes widened. He said abruptly, 'Who the hell *are* you?'

'Someone you'd be wise to take seriously. And you?'

'Major Deane.' There was an unpleasant silence while the Major waited in vain for Ashley to speak. Finally, he said slowly, 'And if I agree – you'll leave the rest of my men alone?'

'Provided the two still on their feet don't do anything stupid – yes.'

'I have your word on that?'

'You have my word.'

The man shut his eyes, then opened them again.

'Very well. I agree.'

'Excellent,' said Ashley with something that sounded cordial but wasn't. 'And now you may order your men to stand down ... and surrender your sword to the gentleman behind you.'

FIFTEEN

Pauline maintained her usual manner through the first two nights of Francis's absence. By the third one, however, she could feel the cracks beginning to show. She did her best to plaster over them for the sake of keeping Athenais in the dark, but managing to appear cheerful as well was more than she could manage. Consequently, it was no surprise when – after hearing her snap at both Etienne and Froissart – Athenais said laughingly, 'God, Pauline. The sooner Francis comes home, the better. And don't think I won't tell him how much you've missed him – because I will.'

Pauline looked at her sourly. The glow which had been missing for so many weeks had returned to the lovely face and Athenais's spirits no longer seemed weighed down by things one could only guess at. These were good signs and would have been welcome if Pauline wasn't living with the constant fear that the reason for this improvement might never come back from Honfleur.

She said reflexively, 'And I suppose you're not missing the Colonel?'

'All the time,' came the simple reply. 'But perhaps that was what I needed.'

Pauline pressed her lips together and said nothing.

A further twenty-four hours went by, turning worry into serious alarm. They'd been gone four nights now and, by Pauline's calculations, should have been back. Nightmares prevented her sleeping and, when she tried to eat, the food seemed to stick in her throat. How she'd managed to keep it from Athenais for this long, she had no idea.

And then Athenais found her retching in the scullery and everything came to a head.

'What's wrong?' asked Athenais flatly.

'Nothing.' Pauline wiped her mouth and reached for the water-jug. 'I think the fish might have been off.'

'It wasn't – and you scarcely touched it anyway.'

'Something else then.' She shrugged and declined to turn around. 'I'm not pregnant, if that's what you were thinking.'

'I hadn't got that far, actually.' Athenais paused, thinking. 'Clearly you're worried about Francis. Why?'

'I'm not worried. Why should I be?'

'You tell me. I know they've been away a bit longer than they hoped – but Ashley said that might happen. The man with the letters was sailing from England and could be delayed by the weather – in which case, they'd have no choice but to wait for him. That must be what's happened. They're just kicking their heels and probably getting fairly annoyed about it.'

'Of course.' Pauline swallowed hard and kept her voice even. 'It's as you said yesterday. I just miss him.'

Immediately and without a shadow of a doubt, Athenais recognised the lie. In all the years they'd known each other, she'd never once heard Pauline willingly admit a weakness.

She said, 'You do, of course. But this is more than that, isn't it?' Without warning, she reached out and pulled Pauline round to face her. 'You're frightened. Why?'

Pauline shut her eyes and said nothing.

Now thoroughly alarmed, Athenais gave her a little shake. '*Why? Whatever Francis is doing, Ashley is doing it with him.* So tell me what it is. Clearly, they haven't merely ridden to the coast to collect some correspondence, have they? *Have they?*'

Opening her eyes and expelling a long breath, Pauline said, 'No.'

'What, then? What *are* they doing?'

'I can't ... Ashley made me promise not to tell you.'

'Bugger what Ashley said,' snapped Athenais. 'If he and Francis are off somewhere risking their lives, I've a right to know about it. *Is* that what they're doing?'

'Yes.' Pauline watched the grey eyes fill with the same fear that was fermenting inside her own gut. She said rebelliously, 'God damn it. I should never have promised. You'd better sit down.'

Athenais sat and listened without a word as Pauline described the whole scenario from the beginning. And even when Pauline stopped speaking, she still said nothing for a very long time. Then, finally, 'Have I got this right? They've gone to catch some assassins who can't assassinate the King because he's not there. Francis is pretending to be the Duke of York. Ashley's doing God knows what. And they've invited Cyrano de Bergerac to join the party. Am I missing anything?'

'No.'

'Have they *completely* lost their wits?'

'The Colonel apparently has,' said Pauline bitterly. 'I can't speak for the rest of them – except to say they wouldn't be doing this if he hadn't talked them into it.'

Athenais let this pass.

'And they should have been home yesterday?'

'Yes. Today, at the very latest.'

'So ... so it's possible something has gone wrong.' Her voice quivered a bit and some of the colour faded from her face. 'I wish you'd told me before.'

'To what end?'

Athenais rose and put her arms around her friend's shoulders.

'So you wouldn't have been bearing it alone,' she said.

* * *

Neither of them went to bed that night. Instead, they stayed in the parlour, dozing fitfully and hoping the prodigals might yet return. They didn't. Dawn heralded the start of yet another day and the hours continued to crawl by. At around noon, Athenais said, 'If we went to the Louvre, do you think King Charles would receive us?'

'I doubt it,' said Pauline wearily. 'But if he did?'

'He might know something. More than we do, at any rate.'

'Not much if they stuck to the original plan. And even if he did, do you think he'd share it with us?'

Athenais slumped in her chair.

'No. I suppose not.'

'Speaking about this to anyone except the King wouldn't be safe – and since he presumably doesn't know that Francis and Ashley are living here with us like a bloody *ménage à quatre*, he's got no reason to trust us.'

'I know. I'd just feel better if we could do something.'

'There's nothing *to* do but wait. And hope. And, if you think it'll do any good, pray.'

* * *

Despite everybody wanting nothing more than to go home, Ashley had decreed a day of rest and a further night's stay in Honfleur. On top of a sleepless and physically demanding night, all of them had injuries of one sort or another. His own and those of Cyrano and Jem were largely superficial but Sir William's thigh-wound had continued to bleed for longer than it should have done and Francis's arm was giving Ashley severe cause for concern. So the five of them patched each other up as best they could, got some rest in between taking turns to guard Major Deane ... and planned to start their journey back to Paris early the following morning.

Since Francis and William needed to be made as comfortable as possible and their prisoner had to be kept secure, it was agreed that Jem would drive the coach while Cyrano joined the others inside it. Ashley mounted Mr Cardale's roan and rode alongside.

By the time they got as far as Louviers, Will was improving but Francis showed signs of incipient fever. This, as far as Ashley was concerned, dictated another night's rest while they found an apothecary who could supply them with some Peruvian bark and also treat Francis's wound more efficiently than they'd been able to do themselves.

Francis, inevitably, argued.

'I'll live,' he insisted. 'And, if we press on, we can be back in Paris by tonight.'

'Another day won't make any difference,' said Ashley. 'And having made Pauline a promise, I intend to do my best to keep it.'

And so they lingered in Louviers for a further night; the fifth that they'd been away. Cyrano and Jem played dice and Sir William watched Colonel Peverell meticulously avoiding any contact with the captive Major.

By dawn on the following day, Francis's condition had improved and they took to the road again in high hopes of seeing Paris by mid-afternoon. While they stopped to change horses, Ashley issued his final instructions.

'When we're nearing the city, I'll ride ahead and warn Hyde that we're bringing the chief assassin in for questioning. Jem ... take Francis home before you follow me to the Louvre. With luck, Pauline will be there to take care of him and he'll be able to tell her that you and I will be back as soon as possible. Cyrano ... blindfold the Major as soon as we enter Paris. I don't want him knowing where we live.' Finally, he looked at Sir William. 'How you explain your involvement in all this to Hyde and the King is up to you. Unless it's unavoidable, none of us will contradict you.'

'Oh – I'll make a clean breast of it,' came the resigned reply. 'In truth, there's little alternative if I'm to continue working in the shadows.' He paused and then added, 'I don't suppose I can persuade you to join me there? You would be so very good at it.'

'Thank you. I already dislike myself quite enough without that. But I wish you luck. I imagine you'll need it.'

* * *

In the Rue des Rosiers, Sunday – the sixth day of Francis and Ashley's absence – dragged by on leaden feet. With neither rehearsal nor a performance to distract them, Pauline and Athenais wandered the house like lost souls, nerves churning with an anxiety that they were beyond discussing.

It was Pauline who saw the mud-spattered carriage draw to a halt outside the house. For a moment, she hardly dared hope ... then Jem jumped down from the box and she knew.

Shouting, 'Athenais! They're here. Oh God, they're finally here!' she flew into the hall and threw open the door to the street. Then, virtually tumbling down the steps, she looked into Francis's face and gave an involuntary sob of relief.

He smiled at her and stepped from the coach to catch her in his good arm.

'Do you know,' he murmured, 'that I'm indescribably happy to see you, too?'

Athenais arrived on the scene, scanned the occupants of the carriage and then, ignoring even the stranger with a blindfold round his eyes, said urgently, 'Francis – where's Ashley?'

'He went directly to the Louvre and will be home later, once Jem has joined him and delivered our ... guest.' He turned to Cyrano and said, 'It may not have been undiluted pleasure – but it's certainly been a privilege. Visit us when you have the time.'

'I'll do that.' The Frenchman glanced briefly at Pauline, now clutching Francis's coat as if she'd never let go and, with a grin, added, 'But for now, you shouldn't keep your lady waiting.'

As the coach rolled away, leaving Athenais staring after it, Pauline drew Francis into the house, saying tersely, 'You're hurt and you look terrible.'

'I daresay. But it's nothing that won't mend.'

'The Colonel said he'd send you home in one piece,' she complained, steering him to the kitchen in order to determine what needed to be done.

'And he has,' said Francis, sitting down with a sigh of relief and trying to unlace his coat with one hand. 'We took another nights' rest because he didn't consider me fit to travel. More to the point, he put his own body between me and that fellow you saw in the carriage. So --'

'He did what?' Athenais stood in the doorway, her face pale and set.

'He's all right,' said Francis quickly. 'A few cuts and bruises ... and, like me, in dire need of a bath. But he's perfectly fine and will be back soon so you can see for yourself.' He didn't add that, since that night on the quayside, a blanket of reserve had settled over Ashley or that he himself hadn't tried to penetrate it. If Ashley came home still not comfortable in his own skin, Athenais would see it fast enough. So, abandoning his attempt to unfasten his coat, he turned to Pauline and said, 'Give me a hand with this, will you? I caught a blade in the same place as at Worcester and it aches like the devil.'

Wordlessly, Pauline finished the task for him and helped him out of his coat. She didn't know whether she wanted to pour vitriol over his head or smother him with kisses; but, because practicality was called for, she did neither. She merely moved on to his shirt and calmly set about removing it.

Finally realising that she was *de trop*, Athenais stopped hovering in the doorway and went back to watching the street from the parlour window. Something didn't feel right. But until Ashley walked through the door, she wouldn't know what it was.

Meanwhile, in the kitchen, Pauline unwrapped Francis's arm and took stock of the damage. Then, keeping her tone perfectly matter-of-fact, she said, 'This isn't good.'

'I know.'

'There may be some injury to the muscle. And the scar's going to be a lot worse than it was before.'

'I know that too.' Reaching up, he brushed away a tear he knew she was unaware of having shed. 'Will you mind?'

'What?' She stared at him. Then, 'Don't be ridiculous. Of course I won't ...' She stopped, recognising the trap. 'Oh. Very clever.'

'Not particularly.' He smiled and drew her down beside him in order to kiss her, slowly and thoroughly. 'I've come back safe ... and I'm more or less in one piece ... so I account my promise fulfilled. How do we stand with regard to yours?'

Pauline drew an unsteady breath and laid her cheek against his so that she wouldn't have to meet his eyes. 'As I recall, there was some stipulation about you being of the same mind?'

'There was – and I am. If anything, even more so than before.' Francis slid away from her to drop on one knee at her feet. Taking both of her hands in his, he said softly, 'Look at me.' And when, with reluctance, she had done so, 'I love you. And I believe that you love me.'

'You know I do.'

'Yes. I do know it. And so you'll marry me.' His smile gathered a hint of teasing laughter. 'You'll notice that I'm not asking this time. I think we've gone beyond that. You made me a promise ... and I'm calling it in. But, if it's not too much trouble, I'd very much like to hear you say the words.'

She shook her head helplessly. She couldn't resist him in this mood and he knew she couldn't. So, as evenly as she was able, she said, 'Then yes, Francis. I'll marry you.'

He bent to place a kiss in each of her palms and then rose to sweep her back into the curve of his good arm. 'Thank you. I'll do my damnedest to make sure you never regret it.'

* * *

The rest of the afternoon wore by still with no sign of Ashley or Jem. Since carrying water upstairs wasn't feasible, Francis took a bath in the kitchen and, when he was finished, Athenais set more water to heat so that Ashley could do the same when he came home. *If* he came home. She was beginning to wonder whether the English King had found him some other labour to perform. In the end and purely for something to do, she retreated to her bedchamber and changed into the new gown which had been delivered the previous day and at which she hadn't so far even bothered to look.

It was of silver-grey brocade and it left her shoulders virtually bare. At any other time, she'd have enjoyed the feel of it against her skin and spent time admiring herself in the mirror. Now, she merely pinned up her hair, decided that the dress looked well enough and thought only of returning to her vantage point in the parlour.

She was half-way down the stairs when the front door opened and Ashley walked in, closely followed by Jem. Joy, relief and sheer love washed through her, flooding her heart and stopping her breath for a moment. Then, just as she was about to go skimming down the stairs and into his arms, something stopped her. The set of his shoulders spoke of weariness; the way he threw his hat at the table, of something else entirely. She froze, her fingers tightening hard on the bannister and waited. Jem said something she couldn't hear and received a short, hard negative. She frowned a little, feeling suddenly uncertain and aware that, thanks to her grey gown blending into the shadows, he hadn't yet seen her. Then, forcing herself not to hurry, she continued down the stairs.

Ashley turned and looked at her. She watched him straighten his back and summon a smile. A smile she felt fairly sure meant absolutely nothing. Then he said, 'I don't know whether to begin by apologising for my tardiness or by telling you how beautiful you look.'

Taking the final step into the hall, she heard herself say, 'Or then again, you could begin by explaining why you found it necessary to lie to me?'

His jaw tightened. 'I thought it was for the best.'

'And of course you always know what that is?'

'No. But it was well-intentioned.' He swung round to face Jem. 'Can you --?'

Mr Barker flung up one hand.

'Don't mind me,' he said, half-way between caution and amusement. 'I'm off to the *Chien Rouge*. That blasted Frenchman owes me a mug or two of ale and a fresh pair of dice.'

He disappeared back the way he had come, leaving Ashley and Athenais staring wordlessly at one another. Finally, Ashley said distantly, 'I'm sorry I deceived you. But if you've anything further to say on the subject, do you think it might wait until I've bathed and changed?'

Athenais advanced to within two steps of him, thinking, *It can wait forever, if you like. I don't know why I said it at all when the only thing I really want to do is hold you very tight and tell you how glad I am you're safe.* But, sensing the invisible wall about him, she said, 'The bath is in the kitchen. I've put water to heat and left towels and a clean shirt out for you. It's Suzon's day off, so you can be assured of privacy.'

'Thank you.' There was a moment of uncharacteristic hesitation before he said, 'I'm sorry. I realise you must have been worried but I need … I just need a few minutes. If that would be acceptable?'

'Perfectly.' She gritted her teeth against both the pain in her chest and the urge to splinter his infernal courtesy so that he'd tell her what was wrong. 'I'm happy to see you safe – so nothing else matters very much. But later, if you feel like talking, I'll be in the parlour.'

And she walked away from him before he could reply.

SIXTEEN

Ashley reclined in a welcome tub of hot water and attempted to dispel the fury that was still raging inside him. He couldn't believe what Hyde had asked him to do. Worse still, he couldn't believe that the man had tried to force the issue, arguing with him until he'd finally lost his temper. At some point during the outburst that had followed, the King had walked into the room and asked what was going on. Briefly and without much attempt at civility, Ashley had told him. And then, with a sinking feeling in the pit of his stomach, realised that – although, unlike Hyde, Charles was prepared to take no for an answer – His Majesty clearly seemed to think he was the right man for the job. At which point, he'd walked out before he said something completely unforgivable.

Well, he'd refused and would go on refusing – though they'd be stupid if they asked again. *Or would they?* Perhaps what seemed so incredible to him was less so to other people. Francis, for example, had looked at him differently since Honfleur ... because, just for a moment, Francis had thought him capable of killing an unconscious man. Well, in a sense, that had been the point, hadn't it? Convincing the unconscious man's brother he'd do it without a single qualm? He'd just never thought that Francis would swallow it too. And the fact that he *had* said that Ashley had come further down this road than he realised; that he'd become the kind of man Hyde would ask to – no. He shut the thought down. The matter was closed so there was no reason to think of it again. And he needed to let it go before he made an even bigger mess of his homecoming than he had so far.

He washed his hair, tipped jug after jug of water over his head and started to feel marginally better. Then he set about scrubbing away several days' worth of sweat and dirt. By the time he had finished, the water had cooled and his temper along with it. He hauled himself from the bath, dried himself off and got dressed. He emptied the water away in the yard and replaced the bath on its hook in the scullery. Then, before he thought about food or drink, he went in search of Athenais.

She was sitting in the parlour, her back ramrod straight, studying a script but she looked up as he entered the room, her eyes wide and searching. Belatedly discovering that he had no idea what to say, Ashley made a small, indeterminate gesture with one hand and waited for her to speak first.

Athenais didn't know what to say either. She only knew that he looked tense and uncertain; as if he thought anything he said might be wrong. And it was more than she could bear. Tossing the script away, she flew across the room to throw herself against his chest. His arms wrapped tight about her, he pulled her close and buried his face in her hair. For a moment or two, they held each other in silence, wanting nothing but the reality of being together. But eventually, Ashley said unevenly, 'For the last two days I've thought about little except the prospect of coming back to you. Of seeing your smile and being able to put my arms around you, if only for a moment. I wanted it so *badly* … yet was still stupid enough to let other matters get in the way when the time came. I'm sorry.'

'Don't be.' Lifting her head to look up at him, Athenais stemmed the flow of words with a finger placed lightly against his lips. 'You're here now and may hold me for as long as you wish. You could even kiss me – though it's dispiriting that I always have to ask.'

'You don't. I just didn't want to … presume.' And he possessed her mouth slowly and sweetly but with a hunger he couldn't quite hide.

Athenais gave a long sigh and slid her fingers up into his still-damp hair. She melted into him, offering everything she had and rejoicing when he allowed the kiss to deepen into something hot and gloriously seductive. His hands stroked her back and anticipation stirred in her body. Then, with a tiny groan, he pulled back and said, 'God, I've missed you.'

'Good.' She waited and when he showed no sign of continuing where he'd left off, drew him to sit beside her on the sofa. 'Pauline told me the truth. Eventually. Was it very bad?'

'Honfleur? No.' He kept his arms around her and rested his chin on her hair. 'It didn't quite go as expected … but no. It wasn't bad.' *None of us died*. 'Francis got the worst of it.'

'He'll be fine in a week or two. And Pauline has said she'll marry him.'

'Has she? It's an ill-wind, then.'

'Yes.' Athenais turned her head so that she could look at him. 'So if it's not what happened at Honfleur … what is it?'

He moved then but she didn't let him pull away.

'What is it, Ashley? What's wrong? I know there's something. I knew it as soon as I saw you. So tell me.'

He shook his head in instinctive denial. 'I can't.'

'Can't – or won't? You've invited, encouraged and sometimes pushed me into confiding in you … so take your own advice and trust me.' She smiled again and stroked the hair back from his face. 'Something happened at the Louvre, didn't it? What?'

Ashley could feel himself drowning in those beautiful storm-grey eyes and tried to pull back. He didn't want to tell her. He really didn't. On the other hand, perhaps she had a right to know to what depths other men thought he had sunk. He said abruptly, 'We sent a Commonwealth agent back from Louviers and brought the chief assassin with us from Honfleur. Hyde has them both under lock and key, pending interrogation. He's learned precious little from the first man and is determined to do better with the second. So he wants me to conduct the … interrogation.'

For a moment Athenais looked faintly baffled. Then, her gaze widened and she said, 'He wants … you're saying he asked you to *torture* them?'

'Oh – only if absolutely necessary,' returned Ashley aridly. 'He was very clear on that point. Unfortunately, he was equally clear about 'making them talk by any means available'.' He paused and looked away from her, as disgust welled up afresh. 'He thinks because I've sometimes had to kill people – men who were always in a position to fight back – that I'm bloody Torquemada.'

'I imagine you'll have told him that you're not.'

'I tried. I said no. Several times and rather forcefully. But --'

'But what? He can't *make* you do it, can he?'

'No.'

She could still see trouble clouding his eyes and said, 'So what else is worrying you?'

Ashley sighed. 'The fact that he asked at all – and his utter incredulity when I refused. He behaved as if he expected me to say, "That sounds fun. Just show me the thumbscrews and rack and I'll have it done before supper." I don't know what he thinks I am ... but it scares the hell out of me in case he's not alone in thinking it. Or worse ... that he's right.'

Athenais closed her fingers around his arm and gave him a slight shake.

'He's not. No one who knows you could *possibly* think so.'

It was a long time before he replied but finally he said reluctantly, 'Something happened in Honfleur. The details don't matter save that Francis was already wounded and I saw a way of ending it before anyone else was. It was a bluff – admittedly, not a very nice one – but I had to make it work. And I did. Too well, perhaps.'

She could hear the hurt beneath his even tone and realised how rarely he allowed it to show. Her heart contracted and she said, 'Francis. You think Francis believed it?'

'Yes. We haven't talked very much since. But I suspect he may have done.'

'I doubt it,' she replied firmly. Then, as he would have spoken, 'No. Just listen. When Francis got home, Pauline made some remark about you not having taken proper care of him. And without a second's hesitation, he told her that you'd put your own body between him and the man who'd hurt him. His words, not mine.'

Ashley shrugged uncomfortably.

'Under the circumstances, anyone would have done that.'

'No. They wouldn't. Francis knows that. And if he doesn't ... if he doesn't know better than to think ill of you ... I'll have something to say to him. Quite a *few* somethings, in fact.'

He rewarded her with a small laugh.

'You're very fierce.'

'You have no idea.' She reached up to place a kiss beneath his jaw and let her tongue slide over his skin, making his pulse jump. 'Now we've cleared that up, do you think you might relax a little?'

'I could try.' He cupped her chin with light, insubstantial fingers so that he could read her face. 'No doubt you think I've still got some making-up to do?'

'Quite a lot of it, actually.' She looked up at him between her lashes in a way he remembered only too well and her voice grew slightly husky. 'Don't you?'

And that was when he finally realised something he should have known the instant he'd kissed her. He'd drawn back because he thought he should, not because she'd wanted him to. And along the way, he'd somehow managed to miss the fact that the girl in his arms now wasn't the pale, fragile shadow he'd left behind six days ago; she was once again the warm, confident, loving creature she'd been before. And she seemed to be issuing a shyly teasing invitation. His breath stopped for a moment as he contemplated it. Then, because he had to be sure that wishful thinking wasn't confusing the signs, he said, 'More than I can possibly complete in one lifetime, love. Indeed, I've no idea where to start.'

'Really? That's disappointing.' Colour bloomed in her cheeks but she didn't look away. 'But if you need a suggestion ...?'

'Please.'

'I thought you might perhaps take me to bed.'

The words came out in a rush and this time, everything inside him seemed to disintegrate. He said, raggedly, 'Oh God, Athenais. If you're sure ... if you're quite sure ... I'd willingly go down on my knees and beg you to let me.'

She slid from his arms and stood up, extending her hand to him.

'I'm sure.'

Taking her fingers, he continued to hold them as he came to his feet. Then, because it seemed important, he said baldly, 'I promised to wait. I still can.'

'I know,' said Athenais. 'I know you can. But I can't.'

* * *

Upstairs in her room, with the door bolted behind them, Ashley began by slowly pulling the pins from her hair and letting them fall where they would while he watched her eyes darken and her breathing quicken. Then he took her in his arms again and kissed her with a tantalising lack of haste that sent desire raging through both of them. When he released her mouth to feather a trail along her cheekbones and jaw, Athenais pushed his coat from his shoulders and tugged at his shirt until she could slide her hands beneath it. A sound almost like a growl rumbled low in Ashley's throat and he reached for the laces of her gown. Then, when he had them unfastened and was about to slide the dress away, he suddenly paused and said, 'If you change your mind ... if you feel the tiniest shred of hesitation ... tell me. And I'll stop. I promise. The moment you ask me – I'll stop.'

'I know. You'll stop if I ask.' She abandoned the struggle to rid him of his shirt in favour of shrugging the gown from her shoulders. 'But you have – and I haven't.'

Laughter flared in his eyes but he said, 'My rules. Remember?'

Athenais mumbled something that sounded very like, 'Bugger your rules,' and resumed her assault on his shirt.

This time, Ashley laughed out loud and, batting her hands away, finished the job for her.

'Better?' he teased.

'Yes. Oh. Yes.' Her hands slid around his waist to his back and she laid her mouth against his shoulder. In between kisses, she said rapidly, 'Stop worrying. It's all right. I know who you are. I know *exactly* who you are – and I know what you're *not*.' Then, with scarcely a pause, as she found the dressing on his arm, 'What's this? You're hurt.'

His throat tightened and he held her very close for a moment.

'It's nothing. Little more than a scratch.'

'It doesn't *look* like a --'

He silenced her with a kiss. Then, caressing her arms as he slid the gown away, he unlaced her stays and tugged the ties of her petticoats free. Piece by piece, her clothing floated to the floor. And when she was left with nothing but her stockings and shift, he turned her so that her back was pressed close against his chest and his hands were free to cup her breasts. Athenais gave a sobbing gasp and her head fell back against his shoulder. Ashley promptly took advantage of that small, exquisitely sensitive spot that lived beneath her ear ... and the gasp became a moan.

He had always known that if and when she was ready for intimacy again, it would be not unlike their very first time together; that he would need to exert every ounce of control he could summon in order to feed her desire whilst keeping his own in check. But it was more than that, he now realised. He wanted her body to rediscover forgotten responses and to remember what was possible between them. At this precise moment, for example, he knew she was aware of his own arousal pressing against her back; knew that it excited rather than alarmed her. And though her involuntary movements were a sort of torture, he was glad of them.

Athenais felt every part of her body coming to sizzling life. She felt like the girl in the story who'd slept for a century and been woken by a kiss. Every pore and nerve and pulse was alive and singing, responding to even the lightest touch and craving more. Every inch of her skin tingled and burned. Sparks rushed through her veins and gathered into a liquid inferno deep in her belly. She'd forgotten how the crescendo could soar so swiftly into desperate and unstoppable need. *How could she have forgotten that?*

Ashley caressed her breasts through the fine lawn of her shift and then slid it aside to find her skin. She shuddered as the sharp darts of pleasure shot through her and then, pushing his hands aside, turned back to face him, pushing her fingers into his hair and dragging his mouth down to hers. He kissed her back … and then lifted her up and carried her to the bed.

For a moment, while he discarded the rest of his clothes, she sat perfectly still watching him. Then, with a slow, sinuous movement she pulled the shift over her head, tossed it aside – and smiled at him, as if in triumph at her own daring. Ashley took one look at her, clad in nothing but her stockings and that wild mane of tangled red hair and felt the air drain from his lungs as a single, heavy pulse throbbed through his body.

'Holy hell,' he managed to say. 'Are you trying to kill me?'

'No.' She frowned, as if trying to puzzle it out. And then, with interest, 'Could I?'

'Yes. Oh God. Don't do that.'

This as she lay back against the pillows and stretched her arms above her head so that her back arched and her hair tumbled away, partially unveiling her breasts.

And that was when she realised something that had always existed between them but that she'd never previously noticed. She had power over him; power to tease and torment – even make him beg, if she chose. Just for a moment, the idea was exhilarating ... until she realised that it wasn't a power she wanted. The fact that it was there and that Ashley surrendered it to her freely was enough.

Smiling, she sat up, held out her hand and said wickedly, 'Come and stop me, then.'

The gold-flecked green eyes lingered on her, dark and intent. Then, repaying her in kind, Ashley lifted one brow and said, 'Now?'

'Yes.' As always, the beauty of his body stopped her breath and sent fresh waves surging through her. 'Please.'

He settled beside her, every inch of him hot and hard, and slid one muscled thigh between hers. Athenais gave a sobbing moan and pressed closer. Then his hands were on her again, leaving trails of flame in their wake; trails that his mouth turned into a wild conflagration. She writhed against him uttering incoherent little sounds. He could feel the tension building and knew exactly how close she was to completion. He also knew she was fighting it. Knew it even before she said gasped, 'Ashley ... please. I can't ... can't ...'

'Then don't try, darling. Just let me. Let me give you this.'

And with his mouth at her breast and his fingers stroking knowingly elsewhere, he sent her hurtling over the edge.

Minutes later, when the tremors in her body subsided a little and her breathing started to settle, he smiled deep into her eyes and, with seeming laziness, resumed his caresses. His own body was screaming with need but he blocked it out, concentrating on Athenais's response. And when he was once more sure she was ready, he finally allowed himself the almost painful delight of driving, inch by exquisite inch, into the hot, sweet bliss she offered him.

Much later, sated, drowsy and still entwined with each other, they talked a little. And the last thought Ashley knew before sleep overcame him was that, now she was finally his again, there was nothing in the world that he wouldn't do in order to keep her.

* * *

It was late on the following day when they joined Francis and Pauline downstairs. Inevitably, the newly betrothed couple were in the midst of something that might have been an argument if Francis had been playing his part. Grinning down at Athenais, Ashley paused just outside and door and took a minute to eavesdrop.

'I can't do it,' Pauline was saying flatly. 'I'm an actress. I can't be a Viscountess.'

'I know.'

'And I don't want to be Lady Wroxton, either. Everybody would laugh themselves silly.' She stopped. 'What do you mean – you know?'

'I mean, I know,' came the patient reply. 'In case you haven't noticed, I don't particularly want the title myself. So I thought we might try a half-measure.'

'How is that possible?'

'Quite easily. As far as the theatre goes, you'll still be Pauline Fleury. But in private life, I wondered … I hoped you might perhaps agree to become Pauline Wroxton. No title, you see … just plain Madame.'

'And I suppose you'll be just plain Monsieur Wroxton?'

'Well, yes. That was the general idea.'

There was a long silence. Finally Pauline said bluntly, 'Are you sure you won't mind?'

'Not in the least. Now … are there any other obstacles you'd like to raise?'

'No. That is – I'm not raising obstacles.'

'Yes you are. You said you'd marry me and now you've got cold feet,' replied Francis sounding surprisingly cheerful. 'Just so long as you know you've only the rest of today to cavil because tomorrow I'm going to see the priest and arrange a wedding.'

Pauline pounced. 'You're not Catholic.'

'No. But the priest doesn't have to know that. And, having been brought up in the high church of Archbishop Laud, fortunately I'm the next best thing. Anything else?'

'No.' There was a pause. Then, on a note of laughter, she said, 'God – you're annoying.'

'I know. Fortunately my charm compensates for it.'

Leaning against the wall with his arm around Athenais, Ashley was shaking with laughter. He whispered, 'They're better than a play, aren't they?'

'Yes. But, unlikely as it seems, they're perfect for each other.' And she put her hand to the door.

Francis and Pauline drew apart without any signs of haste.

Ashley grinned and said, 'I believe congratulations are in order. When is the happy day?'

'As soon as possible – before I'm forced into desperate measures,' replied Francis, looking far from desperate. 'Just a small affair, we thought. Yourselves, of course and Jem; Cyrano, too, if he'll come. And a handful of folk from the theatre ... just those the Duchess here chooses to honour.'

'Ask Marie d'Amboise,' begged Athenais on a gurgle of laughter. 'She won't come – but the look on her face will be beyond price.'

'Maybe.' Pauline looked at Francis. 'What about your mother?'

'Hell will freeze first,' he replied in a tone that suddenly could have cut bread. The razor-edge disappeared as swiftly as it had come and he said, 'Ashley ... I'd hoped you might agree to stand up for me.'

'I'd be delighted. If you're sure?'

'Sure?' Francis looked nonplussed. 'Of course I'm sure. Why wouldn't I be?'

Before Ashley could open his mouth, Athenais said bluntly, 'Thanks to whatever happened at Honfleur, he thinks you doubt both his honour and his integrity.'

'Athenais.' Ashley's voice was very soft but there was a warning in his eyes. 'Leave it.'

'No, Athenais. Don't.' Francis stood up and faced Ashley squarely. 'I know what she means. We both do. And if you really want the truth --'

'I don't, particularly.'

'Then you should. The truth is that I didn't doubt anything about you – either then or now. How could I? You're my brother in everything but blood. But the man with me that night was The Falcon; hard, cold and efficient as a blade. And what worried me ... what *still* worries me is how much they've made you do and how much more they'll demand of you. And how long you can go on doing it before you either break or become the thing you're already struggling not to be.'

The silence that followed this unexpected declaration lingered on, lapping the edges of the room. Then Athenais broke it by walking over to Francis, putting her hands on his shoulders and reaching up to kiss his cheek.

'That was exceptionally well-said. Thank you.' And, turning to Ashley, 'At some point, you should tell Francis what you told me yesterday. But not now. *Now*,' she said, sitting down next to Pauline, 'we have a wedding to plan. Starting, I suggest, with what the bride is going to wear?'

Glad of the change of subject and even more grateful to Francis for letting the previous one drop, Ashley listened to the ladies talking about gowns and flowers and who to invite to the ceremony. It quickly became apparent that Athenais was demonstrably more excited about the event than Pauline seemed to be. She bubbled about which church they would use and whether Pauline's best amber shot-silk needed to be re-trimmed with new lace. She looked flushed and happy. And, try as he might, Ashley couldn't detect even a hint of envy or wistfulness on her own account. As far as he could tell, it hadn't seemed to occur to her that he could have offered her the same future Francis was giving Pauline but that he hadn't.

Something in his chest tightened to the point of pain but he hid it behind a smile. The possibility that Athenais was doing the same made him feel sick.

Francis was just starting to note the names of those he, Pauline and Athenais agreed should be invited from the theatre when their discussions were interrupted by the pealing of the doorbell. Relieved at the chance to escape, Ashley immediately stood up and volunteered to answer it.

For a moment, when he saw who was on the other side of the door, he wished he hadn't. It was the usual messenger from the Louvre, with a letter in one hand and a purse in the other.

Oh Christ, he thought wearily as he accepted both and sent the fellow on his way. *What now?*

Alone in the kitchen, he dropped the purse on the table and broke the seal on the letter. He'd assumed it would be from Hyde. It wasn't.

Colonel Peverell, it read.

We had no right to ask such a thing of you and you have my sincere regrets that I allowed it. I hope you will accept the purse as much in token of this, as in payment of your recent service.

I have come, belatedly perhaps, to recognise something important. Valuable as your unswerving loyalty and assistance has always been, you have offered freely something worth more. Something I find I am most reluctant to lose.

Your friendship.

Yrs.

Charles R.

A letter in the King's own hand? That was unusual enough. But an apology? Ashley read the thing again, wondering what to make of it and feeling as though a fog had invaded his head.

The purse contained a substantial amount of money. More than he'd seen for a very long time. He weighed it in his hand, frowning a little. Then a sardonic smile curled his mouth at the realisation that Sir Edward Hyde was probably spitting nails. And finally, as the fog cleared, he realised something else.

He took several moments to consider two disparate ideas. And when he'd made up his mind, he strolled back to the others and dropped the letter in Athenais's lap.

'If His Majesty ever regains his throne,' he remarked, 'that will be worth something. But in the meantime, there's always this.' And he dangled the purse before her eyes.

Athenais glanced up briefly, then returned to the letter. She said, 'He's *sorry?*'

'It would appear so.'

'Good. So he should be.'

'Don't be too hard on him. Apologies don't come easily to royalty.' Ashley grinned at Francis. 'I'll tell you all about it later. First, it occurred to me that if I'm to stand up with you at your wedding, I should probably stand beside you while you lie to the priest about your religion. What do you think?'

SEVENTEEN

The morning of the wedding dawned dry and sunny. Leaving Ashley to make sure Francis was properly turned-out, Athenais devoted herself to looking after Pauline. This, she soon realised, was easier said than done.

'Will you stop fussing?' said Pauline, sounding more anxious and impatient than Athenais thought reasonable. 'The gown is fine, my hair is fine and the flowers are beautiful. Now will you please go away and get ready yourself or we'll be late.'

'You're allowed to be late. It's the bride's prerogative. Or do you think Francis will come to his senses and make a run for it if you keep him waiting?'

'What I think is that I'd like some peace and quiet in which to compose myself ... and that I'd prefer you to follow me to church without your hair falling down your back.'

'I can be ready in minutes.'

'No, Athenais. You can't. You'll bundle your hair up, stick a few pins in it and think that will do. It won't. Also, you're not wearing that gown.'

Athenais looked down at the second-hand blue taffeta that had resumed its place as her best dress since the Marquis had destroyed the beautiful leaf-green one. She said, 'Why not? There's nothing wrong with it. And this is *your* day. No one's going to be looking at me.'

'*I* am. And since he's barely taken his eyes off you in the last four days, so is the Colonel. So go and fetch your new gown and bring it here so I can lace you into it. Then I'll do something with your hair.'

'But --'

'No buts,' said Pauline firmly. 'As you just pointed out, this is my day and I demand to be humoured. Now fetch the damned gown – and no tripping off to find Ashley. There'll be time enough for that later.'

'Mother of God,' grumbled Athenais, heading for the door. 'If this is what you're like, goodness only knows what state Francis is in.'

* * *

Upstairs in the attic, Francis was fully-dressed with the exception of his coat and lounging easily in the room's only chair while Ashley stopped shaving for possibly the fourth time to say, 'It's insane, isn't it?'

'Very possibly.'

'Is that all you can say?'

'Since I don't know which of the various schemes you've hatched is the one currently under discussion – yes.'

'I was thinking of the cellar.' He hadn't been but the topic was as good as any. 'It won't work, will it? There'll never be sufficient light.'

'We won't know until we try. Do you think you might finish shaving? Aside from the fact that the water's probably cold by now, the wedding's in an hour.'

Ashley turned back to the mirror, the razor poised in his hand. 'Also --'

'Stop,' said Francis, with unusual firmness. 'Unless you don't mind ending up covered in nicks and scrapes, you can't shave and talk at the same time. So finish what you're doing and leave the talking to me.' He contemplated, with regret, the state of his boots which, though well-polished, were still sadly scuffed. 'In essence, the idea's a good one. If you can teach someone like Etienne Lepreux to handle a sword without tripping over it, you can teach anyone. And finding pupils won't be very difficult if we put the word out at the theatre. Froissart might even agree to put something on the playbill. As for the cellar ... it's only meant to be a temporary measure until you can afford to rent somewhere more suitable. So no, it's not insane. In fact, it's surprising you didn't think of it months ago.'

Ashley finished shaving and wiped the last traces of soap from his face before reaching for his shirt. Whilst engaged in pulling it over his head, he said in somewhat muffled tones, 'And the other thing?'

Francis grinned and waited for the tawny-gold head to reappear.

'Oh that's *definitely* insane. And I, for one, can't wait to see how you expect to manage it. As for the matter of Charles ... well, that will be interesting.'

'Or not. As the case may be.'

'Quite.' Francis came unhurriedly to his feet and picked up his coat. 'For the moment, however, it might be as well if you concentrated on the task in hand. Such as putting on your boots, perhaps?'

* * *

On the floor below, Athenais stood patiently under Pauline's ministrations but couldn't help saying, 'This is all wrong, you know. You shouldn't be dressing me on your wedding-day.'

'Why not? I've been doing it for years, after all – and it gives me something to think about.'

'Do you *need* something to think about? I'd have thought Francis was enough.'

'He is. But I never expected to actually marry him. And if you really want to know, the whole thing scares me silly.'

'Then it shouldn't. Don't you know how incredibly lucky you are?'

'Yes. That's *why* it scares me silly.'

Pauline stepped back and took a look at her protégée. The amethyst and moonstone chain circled the slender white throat while the silver-grey brocade reflected the colour of Athenais's eyes and was a perfect foil for the dark red curls – now tamed into becoming submission. Pauline nodded thoughtfully and said, 'Not bad. It just needs a finishing touch.'

'No. It doesn't. Anyone would think I was about to go on-stage. Though God only knows what role --' She stopped abruptly as Pauline picked up two white silk roses and said, '*Now* what are you doing?'

'Completing the picture,' replied Pauline absently as she expertly positioned the flowers just above Athenais's left ear. And then, 'Yes. That will do, I think.'

Athenais spread her hands in a gesture of helplessness.

'I give up.' And then, returning Pauline's regard, she said, 'You look lovely, you know.'

'I look as well as can be expected,' came the typical retort. 'As to why all the fuss ... there's a reason for it – beyond the not inconsiderable fact of getting married, that is.' She paused and then said tersely, 'You know the Colonel went to make his peace with the King and that fellow Hyde?'

'Yes.'

'Well, from something Francis let slip, I don't think that's *all* he did.'

Athenais stared at her, not sure whether to be horrified or give way to laughter.

'You think he invited King Charles to your wedding? Seriously?'

'I suspect he may have done. And if His Majesty turns up with half the court-in-exile – your interfering Colonel can look forward to hearing my view on the subject later.' Pauline smiled grimly. 'Not that he's likely to enjoy it.'

* * *

The ceremony was to take place in the convent church of Sainte-Croix de la Bretonnerie which lay only a short walk away. Consequently, when Pauline and Athenais made their way downstairs, they found Francis and Ashley waiting in the hall to escort them. Smiling, Francis bowed flamboyantly over Pauline's hands before raising them to his lips and whispering something in her ear that brought a tinge of colour to her cheeks. Ashley's bow was more restrained and he said nothing at all; but the look in his eyes when they rested on Athenais was eloquent enough.

'Jem?' he called. 'Are you joining us or not?'

'Coming, Colonel. Just been helping Suzon out with a few things for after.' And he sauntered out of the kitchen.

Ashley took one look at him and said, 'Oh my God. You can't wear that.'

'I don't see as I can't.' Jem smoothed the sleeve of his beloved blue and yellow livery. 'Looks right smart, I reckon.'

'That's not the point. You were supposed to return it.'

'Well, clearly he didn't,' said Pauline, taking Francis's arm and heading towards the door. 'And if we wait for him to change, we'll be late – so he'd better come as he is. And if it causes any problems, you can blame yourself for them.'

Just for a second, Ashley communed silently with the ceiling. Then, looking ruefully at Athenais, he said, 'Has she been like that all morning?'

'Most of it.' She smiled up at him. 'You're in her black books, you know.'

'I gathered that. Fortunately, I'm becoming immune to it.'

The porch of the small church was crammed with their witnesses, all of them seemingly talking at once. Petit-Jean Laroque was there, and Antoine Froissart with his wife, Amalie; Etienne Lepreux had Athenais's understudy, Delphine, on his arm and the pair were flanked by André and Marcel, Ashley's former pupils; further away and leaning negligently against the wall, Cyrano bathed all of them in his usual wolfish smile. There was, however, no sign of royalty – for which Athenais assumed Pauline was duly grateful.

After both ladies had kissed Pauline's cheek and the men had either shaken Francis's hand or slapped him on the shoulder, everyone trooped inside. Candlelight flickered in the dim interior and the air was redolent with incense from an earlier service. Francis led Pauline down the aisle towards the place where Père Henri, the priest of Sainte-Croix, stood awaiting them. Ashley and Athenais followed just a few steps behind and their assembled guests found places in the front pews. The stage was set.

The priest, a small, plump fellow with rosy cheeks, smiled happily at Francis and then looked around enquiringly. He said, 'Monsieur Wroxton ... I was expecting to marry two couples today. Is this no longer the case?'

His words produced a sudden silence as Delphine and Amalie stopped fussing with their skirts and something André was whispering to Etienne died mid-sentence. Everyone glanced at each other before turning their heads to see if anyone else had entered the church.

'No, Father. It is still very much the case,' said Francis smoothly. And, looking round at Ashley, 'Your cue, I believe.'

Athenais stared at Francis in complete bewilderment. Then, as a possible interpretation of his words slid around the edges of her mind, she turned very, very slowly to Ashley and said, 'I don't understand. What is happening?'

His kept his eyes fixed on hers so that he wouldn't have to see the dozen people watching him embark on what suddenly didn't seem such a good idea after all and could well turn out to be a terrible mistake. Taking her hands in what he hoped was a comforting clasp, he said, 'I have a question. And I thought that, if I asked it in front of our friends, you might be – either sufficiently impressed or sufficiently sorry for me – to say yes.'

'Oh.' Athenais discovered that she felt slightly faint and knew her hands were shaking. If the ceiling had fallen on her head, she couldn't have been more shocked than she was by what she suspected he was going to say next. 'And – and the question?'

'I think you know.' He dropped to one knee in front of her to the accompaniment of sentimental sighs from Delphine and Amalie. 'I will love you to the end of my life and honour you with every breath in my body. And that being so, I am laying my heart, my hand and my name at your feet in the hope that you'll accept them. In short, I'm asking if you will overlook the fact that I'm not much of a catch and consent to be my wife.'

Without warning, Athenais's eyes filled with tears. She tugged unavailingly at his hands and said unsteadily, 'Get up. You shouldn't be kneeling to me. And you don't need to do this. I never expected it of you.'

Ashley stayed where he was.

'I know you didn't. And, until very recently, it seemed an impossibility I didn't dare contemplate. As for what I need to do … this is it.' He smiled up at her. 'I want to marry you, Athenais. I always have.'

As custom demanded, the door of the church had been left open and the little congregation were so wrapped up in the drama taking place before them that no one except the priest realised that a latecomer had, for some time, been standing silently at the back. Then a deep, resonant voice said, 'My sincerest apologies for interrupting, Ash. But I have to observe that, if the lady hasn't said yes yet, you must be making a shocking poor job of it.'

Those who recognised the exiled King of England immediately shot to their feet and made the correct obeisance. The rest, startled and confused, took a little longer. In the meantime, Charles strolled down the aisle nodding to Laroque and Froissart before pausing to say, 'Ah. Monsieur de Bergerac. No longer indulging in role-play, I see.'

Cyrano bowed. 'A good actor always knows when to quit the stage, Your Majesty.'

'Just so.'

Charles arrived at the front of the church and came to rest between Francis and Ashley, not troubling to hide his amusement.

Ashley said, 'You'll have to forgive me for not rising, Sir – but I'm sure you appreciate my difficulty.'

'Completely.' The lazy smile encompassed Athenais. 'I don't doubt that you could do much better for yourself, Mademoiselle ... but he's not such a bad fellow, you know. So if you could put him out of his misery, I'm sure he'd be eternally grateful. He can't get off his knees until you do, you see.'

Athenais looked up into the dark, Stuart eyes, then down into Ashley's green ones ... and discovered that the latter were filled with laughter. The shock of the King's arrival, hard on the heels of his proposal had scattered her wits to the point where, had Ashley released her hands just then, she might have hit him. And all around were watching eyes and a silence so acute it seemed that everyone was holding their breath.

Inevitably, it was Pauline who broke the spell.

She said caustically, 'For God's sake, Athenais. Say yes and have done with it.'

'Forget Ashley's misery and think of mine,' added Francis with mock-anxiety. 'I'd like to marry Pauline today, if possible – as a delay may give her the chance to change her mind.'

Athenais drew a long, steadying breath and looked back at Ashley. The laughter was still there but now it was mixed with something that tore at her heart. She shook her head and managed to say raggedly, 'Yes. Of course I'll marry you. I will do anything you ask except leave you. But later on, I'll probably *murder* you.'

There was a ripple of laughter. Ashley ignored it. Light flared in his eyes and, rising, he pulled Athenais into his arms and kissed her, long and hard. The laughter around them became an appreciative round of applause.

By the time he let her go, her skin was flushed and her hair, coming unravelled but she turned to Charles Stuart, dropped a deep curtsy and said a trifle breathlessly, 'I hope Your Majesty will make allowances. From everything that's happened so far, it's clear that Colonel Peverell's mind has become slightly unhinged.'

'And if it has,' retorted Charles, taking a long, appreciative look at her, 'who shall we blame for that?' Then, seeing her look of confusion, he turned to the priest and said, 'Perhaps we can now proceed, Father? And unless either of these lovely brides has any objection, I would like to stand in *loco parentis* to both of them.'

And so Père Henri was finally able to begin the marriage service which was as remarkable in its way as anything that had gone before. By the time it was over, Delphine and Amalie were mopping their eyes and more than one of the gentlemen present was finding the dusty air a trial.

Charles kissed both brides with more enthusiasm than either groom thought necessary and then made a tactful exit. The rest of the party surged back to the Rue des Rosiers for cakes and wine and then lingered until Cyrano de Bergerac announced that it was time for everyone to leave the bridal party in peace.

'Thank you,' said Ashley, shaking his hand. 'I'm in your debt. Again.'

'And one of these days, I'll come seeking payment,' replied Cyrano. And looking at Athenais, 'You realise that half the young men in Paris are going to want to kill you?'

'Then they can come here and pay for the privilege of trying,' shrugged Ashley. And briefly explained his idea for a modest fencing school in the cellar.

A few feet away, Monsieur Laroque had been ensuring that both Athenais and Pauline would be back on-stage the following evening but all three of them stopped talking in order to hear what Ashley was saying.

When he had finished, Athenais said, 'That's a wonderful idea. But exactly when were you planning on telling me about it?'

He slipped an arm around her waist.

'I rather thought you'd had enough shocks for one day.'

'The cellar?' asked Pauline. 'Isn't it too dark?'

'It's not ideal. But it will do until I can afford something better.'

'It is possible,' murmured Monsieur Laroque thoughtfully, 'that I may be able to help you with that. There is an outbuilding off the rear courtyard at the theatre. It's been unused for years, so I imagine it will require some work – but it's probably better suited to your purposes than a cellar.' He paused and gave Ashley a dry smile. 'Come and see it. If you want it, I'm sure we can reach some mutually agreeable arrangement. And now, I'll bid you all goodnight.'

And with a slight bow in the direction of Athenais and Pauline, he strolled out, leaving Ashley staring incredulously after him.

Cyrano clapped him on the back.

'There, my friend. Maybe I'll come and test your skill myself some time.'

'As often as you like,' returned Ashley. 'I suspect I'll be glad of the challenge.'

When all the guests had gone and Jem had retired to the kitchen with Suzon, Pauline collapsed on the sofa beside Francis, while Athenais curled up on Ashley's lap.

'That,' remarked Francis, idly taking down his wife's hair, 'was definitely a wedding to remember.'

Pauline smiled. 'That unfortunate priest will certainly have a hard time forgetting it.'

'Indeed,' agreed Ashley. Then, to Athenais, 'Are you happy?'

She nestled a little closer, one hand stealing inside his shirt to settle against his bare shoulder. It was a gesture Ashley was beginning to become familiar with and which seemed to make his brain go soft.

'More than happy. Actually, there isn't a word for how I feel at the moment.'

'Homicidal?' he teased. 'I thought you wanted to murder me?'

'I did. And I should. But it might have to wait until tomorrow.'

For a long time, the silence was broken only by the crackling of the fire. Then, looking dreamily into her new husband's eyes, Athenais said, 'What are you thinking about?'

Ashley tilted her chin to gaze at her with an expression that made her heart turn over.

'Tomorrow,' he said.

* * *

In later years, Pere Henri would talk of that marriage service. He'd explain that it wasn't the rarity of the double wedding that made it memorable ... or the fact that one of the grooms had proposed to his bride right there in church ... or even the unexpected presence of a King.

It was the way the eyes of the brides and grooms never strayed from each other and the depth of emotion redolent in their responses. And something else. A thing he'd never seen before. A moment of pure spirituality as a beam of golden light fought its way past the high, dirty windows to illuminate the altar plate … which in turn, reflected that light back on the faces of the four young people kneeling before him.

Throughout the rest of his long career, Père Henri looked out for that stray beam at every marriage service he conducted, hoping that one day he'd see it again.

He never did.

EPILOGUE
London - April 1653

'Go! Get you out! Take away that shining bauble there and lock up the doors!'
Oliver Cromwell to the Rump Parliament

Colonel Maxwell heard nothing further about the assassination conspiracy until the beginning of April when Thomas Scot walked in and tossed a report on his desk.

'Decode that, would you? It's from one of our agents in Paris and may be of interest.' He paused, on his way to the door. 'God knows why whoever sorts the correspondence can't deliver it to the right place. I waste half my time looking at stuff that's either meant for you or should have gone to Thurloe's office – and it's intensely irritating.'

Eden waved the paper at Scot's retreating back and settled down to his task. Since the code was one of his own, it didn't take long. The agent had picked up two possibly related rumours. First, that a certain Major Deane, along with another so far unnamed gentleman, had been taken by Chancellor Hyde's fellows and were currently under interrogation; and secondly, that the corpses of two troopers known to have served under Deane had been found on the quayside at Honfleur. The agent asked, with some asperity, what – if anything – had been going on and why he had not been informed of it. A hastily added postscript said that Prince Rupert was expected to join his cousin in Paris in the next few days.

Guarding his expression, Eden took the transposed letter next door to Scot and suggested that he read it. Scot did, then looked up frowning.

'I know nothing about any of this. Why *is* that, do you think?'

'Presumably, because orders for whatever it was didn't come from this office.'

'Exactly.' Scot stood up, half-crumpling Eden's transcript in his hand. 'Thurloe, again. Must he have his fingers in everything?' And he stormed out.

Eden watched him go, hoping that the report meant what he thought it did; that Francis and the unknown Colonel Peverell had succeeded in their mission. Like everyone these days, he could do with some cheering news.

London was a cauldron of discontent, most of which was aimed at the Rump. The Dutch War was disrupting trade to an unacceptable degree and the price of coal had tripled because the ships carrying it from Newcastle rarely made the journey unmolested. Then there was the expense of prosecuting the war itself and the number of men being pressed into service for the Navy. Inevitably, the populace was sick of the whole thing and wanted to see an end. But though Cromwell had been calling for peace negotiations for the best part of a month, Parliament had so far refused to do anything about it. And the result was that people in the streets were saying that even a Cavalier Parliament would have more integrity than the one currently sitting at Westminster.

And that wasn't the worst of it. More than half of the seats in Westminster Hall had been empty for years, making the Rump a national joke ... but the manner of how to fill them was a matter of heated dispute. Determined to retain their own seats, Harry Vane and his supporters were pushing a Bill to recruit men of their own choosing to occupy the vacancies. The Army wanted Parliament completely dissolved followed by an immediate general election. The result was deadlock and a mass of ill-feeling.

At home in Cheapside, Deborah grumbled about rising prices and Tobias, when he could be prised out of his workshop, merely said what Eden knew already. That, if the Rump had its way, there might never be a full election ever again. So it was good to see the smile on Nicholas's face when he heard that the conspiracy against the King's life seemed to have been successfully foiled.

'I knew Ash could do it,' he said simply. 'I just hope he and Francis came through it alive.'

'Since they've landed two of the assassins in prison and left another two dead at the scene, I imagine they're all right. But if you wanted to write to them now, there shouldn't be any harm in it so long as you're careful what you say.'

'Really?'

'Yes.' Eden smiled. 'You said you thought Francis was in love – which isn't something I can easily imagine even without what you've told me of the lady in question. So I'm curious to hear of any developments.'

By the fifteenth of the month, the Rump was still doggedly pursuing its Bill for selecting new Members *'of known integrity, fearing God and not scandalous in their conversation'*. And four days later, having spoken in favour of a new Parliament and been ignored, Cromwell called a conference between the Army Officers and the existing Members at his apartments in Whitehall.

Eden sat at the back amongst some of his fellow Colonels and resigned himself to a long day and a numb backside. Oliver, it appeared, had a Plan which he'd already discussed with senior officers such as Lambert, Harrison and Desborough. *They* might have liked it; Harry Vane and his fellow Members didn't – and neither did the lawyers. Eden wasn't surprised. Basically, Cromwell was suggesting temporarily replacing the entire Parliamentary system with a limited body of Godly men – purely, he said, until the country was used to the new order and Parliamentary government could be restored. The resulting debate on the advantages, disadvantages and legalities or otherwise of this raged on all afternoon, right through the evening and late into the night – by which time Eden had a pain between his shoulder-blades and a nagging headache. But finally the MP's grudgingly agreed to halt progress on their Bill to recruit new Members and to meet with Cromwell and the Officers again on the following afternoon for further discussion.

Eden walked out of Whitehall thinking irritably, *Further discussion? Really? Is there anything left that they haven't already said three or four times already? God. Am I being punished for something?*

Not bothering with the cold supper Deborah had left ready for him, he collapsed into bed beside her, gathered her into his arms and immediately fell asleep. Then, next morning, he rose well before she woke and prepared to attempt to cram a day's work into the few hours he had before being doomed to another wasted afternoon.

It didn't happen. At shortly before midday, he was alerted to the fact that all hell was breaking out at Westminster Hall. It seemed that Vane and the rest had reneged on their promise of the previous night – and that Cromwell, on being informed of it, had gone down to the House to see for himself. Except, as it turned out, that wasn't *all* he had done. He'd also taken forty or so musketeers with him ... and, after telling the House exactly what he thought of it, had summarily dissolved Parliament by force.

Throughout the next couple of hours, Eden heard most of the details and, by the time he walked down to Westminster, it was all over. The Hall was deserted, the entrances all padlocked ... and some witty fellow had wasted no time in pinning a note to the doors.

THIS HOUSE IS TO LET:
NOW UNFURNISHED

* * *

Eden walked home, deep in thought and then sought out his brother in the workshop. He said, 'Have you heard what happened today?'

'Mm?' Tobias was hunched over something that sparked blue.

Eden sighed. 'Toby. Could you stop work for just a few moments please?'

Reluctantly, Tobias turned his head and let his gaze focus on his brother.

'What?'

'Cromwell has dissolved the Rump.'

This finally engaged Tobias's full attention.

'Has he? Well, good for him!'

'No. I'm not sure that it's good at all. Look – I'd like to talk to you, if only to clear my head. And I really need a drink. Do you think we might go upstairs?'

Recognising the trouble in Eden's eyes, Tobias laid down his work and said, 'Lead on. Wine sounds good. And I wouldn't mind a slice of pie, if there's any going.'

Once settled in the parlour with food and drink, Eden said, 'Last night, Vane agreed to hold fire on the Bill to fill the empty seats with specially chosen members. This morning he tried to rush it through without Cromwell's knowledge. Cutting a long story short, Oliver called the existing Members every name under the sun. He called them mercenary wretches, thieves and prostitutes. He accused them of immoral practices and told them they had no more religion than his horse. He --'

Tobias gave a snort of laughter.

'Yes. I know. But what he did next isn't so funny. He called in a company of musketeers under Lieutenant-Colonel Worsley and had them drive out the Members by force – on peril of their lives, he said. Apparently, Harrison personally hauled Lenthall from the Speaker's chair and Cromwell had the mace removed ... that shining bauble, I believe he called it ... and the doors locked and barred.' Eden paused, frowning. 'As of noon today, England has no legal government at all.'

'A lot of people would say we're unlikely to notice the difference.'

'I daresay. And a lot of other people will remember what happened in January of 1642 when the late King went into the House to arrest five of its members. Parliament called that a breach of privilege – and it was. It was also the straw that tipped the country into civil war. And the only difference between *that* and what Oliver did today will be what happens next.' Staring moodily at the slice of pie he was pushing round his platter, Eden said, 'Four years ago, Cromwell took the late King's head. These days, he holds audiences in the Banqueting House, just as Charles used to do and now he's dispensed with Parliament. Perhaps I'm reading too much into it ... but it seems to me that he's creating a king-sized space for himself. And, if that's to be the case, I don't know what I – or indeed any of us – fought for.'

Tobias helped himself to the contents of his brother's plate and took a bite. Finally, he said thoughtfully, 'No. I would suppose not. So what will you do?'

'That's just it. I don't know.'

'Can you get leave of absence while you think about it?'

Eden blinked. 'Yes ... I imagine Lambert would give me permission.'

'Then why don't you do it? Take yourself out of London for a time and consider your options. You haven't been to Thorne Ash since you wrote and told them about Celia – so spend a few days with the family.' Another bite of Eden's pie followed the first. 'After that, you must have friends you can talk to. Colonel Brandon, for example.'

The thought of being able to sit down and thrash everything out with Gabriel was suddenly overwhelmingly appealing. His expression lightening, Eden said slowly, 'That is such a good idea, I wish I'd thought of it myself.' And, with a grin, 'It's almost – and I do mean *almost* – enough to make me forgive you for stealing my pie. Again.'

Author's Note

Even though it is seen through the eyes of three fictional characters, I have – as always – made the details of the Worcester campaign as accurate as possible.

The same is true with regard to French theatre of the period. Petit-Jean Laroque was the manager of the Théâtre du Marais where Corneille's *Le Cid* was revived in 1652, sixteen years after having originally been premiered there; and Floridor was the actor-manager of the Marais's rival company at the Hôtel de Bourgogne, where Cyrano de Bergerac forcibly removed Montfleury from the stage.

Cyrano – duellist, playwright and amateur scientist – was not quite the lovelorn fellow with the immense nose of Edmond Rostand's play. He would have been about the same age as Francis and Ashley, had retired from the military by the time this story is set and was to die in 1655, aged 36.

Though details are sketchy, there are references to a plot formulated by Thurloe in which Charles and the Duke of York were to be lured to the coast of France and assassinated. At a time when Cromwell was talking to Bulstrode Whitlock about making himself King, such a plot is by no means inconceivable. However, in the absence of concrete information and because Calais was in Spanish hands at the time, I have chosen to set this Honfleur.

The matter of whether or not Charles the Second married Lucy Walter was to raise its head many times after the Restoration – most notably when it became clear that Charles was never going to have a legitimate son and that his heir would be his Catholic brother, the Duke of York. The Duke of Monmouth, Charles' son by Lucy, was Protestant and therefore the preferred choice of many. A good deal of pressure was put upon the King to declare him legitimate … but he never did, always maintaining that his brother was his rightful heir.

Stella Riley